CLIMAX SPECIES

by

William Mark Riley

To Emma and Trevor —

Happy Travels !

Wm Riley

First edition, 2017
Copyright 2017 by William Mark Riley
ISBN: 978-1984306487
All rights reserved.

Copy editor: Kirsten Colton (www.TheFriendlyRedPen.com)
Cover design: Jessica Chandler (www.SeattleBookDesign.com)
Cover photo: Tony Karumba/Getty Images

To our ancient ancestors.
We owe them our lives.

With, without.
And who'll deny it's what
the fighting's all about?

Pink Floyd, "Us and Them," 1972

.

PROLOGUE

If you were to stand on the bright side of the moon, say somewhere near the Man in the Moon's left dimple, you'd have a splendid view of planet Earth. It's always there, more or less in the center of the moon's orbit, spinning and hurtling in tandem with the moon around the sun, our star. And if you happened to gaze down at Earth, the only planet we know of that teems with life, you might notice, somewhere near the middle, a fairly large gash. It's called the Great Rift Valley, in what we call East Africa.

The Great Rift Valley wasn't carved by rushing water like a normal valley. It was created instead by tectonic forces that have stretched and pulled at earth's delicate skin for millions of years, forming an exceptionally long, deep valley, or "graben" as geologists call them. Graben is a German word for grave. Such immense tectonic forces are constantly at work on our adolescent planet. There are, in fact, hundreds of such rift valleys scattered around the globe, concentrated in spreading centers where earth's crust can't quite decide which way to move.

But the Great Rift Valley of East Africa is unique. It is so huge that, unlike other rift valleys, it can be seen from the moon with the naked eye. And more importantly, perhaps, it was this huge gash in the side of the earth that produced the seeds of humankind. And since that time, as everyone knows, life on earth hasn't been quite the same.

Chapter 1

She stared at the tall white man, her large brown eyes wide and attentive, while two young children cried to her from beyond the tent. She ignored them, focusing instead on the man with the light blue eyes and curly red hair as he smiled at her and told her, in her native tongue, that this would not take long. His features were all quite unfamiliar to her, but the freckles, like galaxies of tiny stars, drew her attention so completely that she barely flinched as his hands moved down from her neck to feel her breasts. Then he removed her *shuka*, a simple orange cloth wrapped around her waist. His right hand shifted down farther until she felt his fingers groping inside her. Only then did she look away.

"*A-sioki,*" he said. Almost done. He leaned forward and soon she felt something hard and blunt penetrating deep inside her, pressing against her cervix. Then a twinge, a tiny pinch, and the instrument was sliding out of her.

"*A-muta,*" he said. All done. "*A-yeng'iyeng.*" But she did not want to rest. Her two young children were still crying for her. She stood up and nodded in his direction.

"*Ashe,*" she said as she turned away and threw back the flap in the tent that led outside, out to the brutal heat of the afternoon, where several other Maasai women were gathered, their shaved heads glistening with beads of sweat that reflected the fierce equatorial sun. Many small children scampered among them, and off to one side a few tall and rather lanky *moran*, young Maasai warriors, were leaning on their spears in the shade of the thorn trees, each with one leg crossed over the other. They were wrapped in orange-and-red-plaid togas, and their hair hung down to their shoulders in ochre-plastered braids like clay mop strings. They kept looking at the women, talking among themselves and occasionally laughing.

The tall white man with the red hair and beard, dressed in a white coat and faded blue jeans, whose name tag read Dr. Maxwell Taylor, motioned for one of the women to enter the tent. She put down her child but hesitated as the sound of a small plane overhead diverted everyone's attention, even the morans'. They all looked to the sky. A single-engine plane was making its approach to the landing strip a few miles south near Lake Magadi.

"Must be Oscar," said the good doctor.

And indeed it was. Professor Oscar Newman, Director of Gynecological Research at the University of Glasgow School of Medicine, and otherwise known as the "King of Contraception," was headed his way, slightly ahead of schedule. This was the man who had not only invented the world's number-one-selling contraceptive device but now, through his Newman Foundation for a Sustainable Future, freely distributed it to women in developing countries all around the world. He was flying in for the first quarterly inspection of Maasai Clinic Number One, a prototype designed to move with the seminomadic Maasai as they migrated along with their herds to the latest patches of fresh grass. As Oscar observed from his overflight, such patches were becoming more and more scarce. Many of the Maasai settlements, along with their cattle *kraals* and ceremonial *manyattas*, were all baked to a dung-dry gray. Where were they headed next? And where to move the clinic? These were important questions to Oscar, but not nearly as important as getting in touch with Elizabeth. He needed to speak with her right away.

As soon as the plane landed, he stuffed his data sheets and aerial photos into his bag, squeezed his enormous bulk through the narrow doorway of the plane, and jumped down onto the dusty landing strip. His wavy dark hair, tinged with gray as it trailed down into a thick salt-and-pepper beard, blew all about as the plane's propeller continued to spin.

Once the engine died down and Oscar had distanced himself from the grassy runway, he reached into his briefcase for his satellite phone. The battery was low after all this traveling through the wilds of East Africa but surely there was enough juice remaining for one last call home.

"Please be there," he said as he waited for the ringing tones on the other end, far away in Scotland. They rang but alas, no answer. He left a detailed message, cutting it short as the beeping of his phone signaled his time was up.

Dr. Taylor, meanwhile, tended to the needs of a few more young Maasai women before closing shop to rearrange his affairs. It would be his first inspection. Hard to believe three months had already flown by. He filed the papers strewn about his small desk and wiped it down with a damp cloth, pausing to gaze at a picture of a pretty young girl, no more than three or four, with dimples and curly blond hair. He smiled halfheartedly as he dusted the frame and put it back in its accustomed place. Then he hung his lab coat on a rack and reached for a clipboard that he used to keep track of supplies.

He had already compiled an inventory: the supplies he had started with, what he had used, what Nairobi had sent him. He had statistics and names of all the women he had seen, number and ages of children already born. All the fields on his quarterly report were filled in. He just needed to write a one-page narrative describing his three-month experience administering birth control to the Maasai. Where to begin?

It didn't matter. For at that very moment a Safari Taxi Service van came to an abrupt and rather dusty halt twenty yards from the small circle of tents. Dr. Maxwell Taylor, physician in residence, stepped outside the clinic's main examination tent to greet his employer.

"Good evening, Dr. Taylor," Oscar boomed as he descended from the vehicle. He wore a colorful Hawaiian shirt and dark, baggy shorts and immediately strode toward the small circle of tents, his broad face smiling in all directions.

"Just call me Max. It's great to see you, Dr. Newman. Nairobi radioed and said you wouldn't be here until morning."

"Slight change of plans," said Oscar as the two embraced. "How are things here at Maasai Clinic Number One?"

"Uh, very good, I suppose. I compiled all the charts and information and—"

"Yes," said Oscar, "I'm sure you have."

"Fecundity reduction targets are within reach, assuming—"

"Yes. I look forward to hearing all about it. But not now. What have you got to drink?"

Moments later Oscar Newman and Maxwell Taylor sat down to a freshly opened, well-aged bottle of single malt Scotch whisky.

"Cheers," said Max.

"Yes," said Oscar, "cheers. Cheers indeed." He leaned back in his chair but his eyes seemed to focus miles away.

"What's wrong, Oscar? You look like you've just seen a ghost."

Oscar turned his large head and looked Max squarely in the eyes. "You're right. I have. Max, I have traveled all over this world, to some very remote and very beautiful places, but there is no place in the world like this. This immense valley, the undeniable cradle of humankind. It's where it all began—where the fuse was lit that's led to this explosion of humanity, the very one you and I are trying to contain. I just needed to get away, steal a moment to reflect on all this—this great cathedral, this cathedral of, well, life itself. I only wish I had a bit more time."

3

He looked down at his glass.

"And a bit more Scotch. I was scheduled to dine with Mr. Mboto, Kenya's minister of health, an excellent chap, and a few of the local elders, but I made excuses that I needed to tend to business here at the clinic. He'll be coming by in the morning to have a look around."

"I see," said Max as he refilled Oscar's glass. "Sounds like you wanted to be sure the rookie doctor got the e-mail about the big inspection."

"Not at all. I've heard nothing but good reports about you. And we're working on getting you another assistant. Too bad about your last one."

"Well, people need to tend to aging parents."

"Yes, we do. I was planning to return to Scotland after a quick visit here. I haven't seen my poor mother in many weeks. But that's all changed as well. I'm flying to Paris instead."

"Really? Why Paris?"

Oscar turned his head once more, his puffed-up eyes, set beneath thick, dark eyebrows, fixing on Max. "Personal matters."

"Right," said Max. "How about some dinner?"

Dinner, though quite modest, was followed by more Scotch and a late night of stargazing and conversation. Max was therefore not at all prepared the following morning for the much-too-early arrival of a dull-green Jeep bearing a complete stranger. It was not Mr. Mboto, minister of health, upon whose arrival Max was to awaken a weary Oscar Newman. Whoever he was, he was wearing khaki shorts, an old denim shirt that had seen better days, and a large-brimmed straw hat. His face was thin, like his mustache, and very tan. He walked with a lanky yet vigorous stride. Max threw on a pair of pants, grabbed a shirt, and slipped into his sandals.

"Hello," he shouted as he threw back the flap of his tent.

"Hello to you, my friend." The stranger extended a hand in greeting. "My name is Francis Dermenjian. I teach botany at the University of Nairobi and was just out gathering specimens. But as is my custom whenever I cross Lake Magadi, I stop to look at the logbook at the airstrip. It is fascinating to see who visits such a remote area as this. Well, when I saw that Oscar Newman had just arrived, I decided to finally pay a visit to your clinic. I've heard all about it from my Maasai friends."

"I can just imagine," said Max, scratching his head. "Look, uh, I'm usually at work by now, but with Oscar here we're just waiting for the minister of health to arrive. They're doing a little inspection later on. But give me a few minutes and I'll get some coffee brewing."

Max cleaned off the picnic table that sat beneath a lone thorn tree just beyond the small circle of tents. Shaded in the morning, it afforded the best views of the Rift Valley, looking westward across vast plains dotted here and there with patches of levelheaded thorn trees. The grassland in between was light brown, looking parched and tired. And to the south, in the middle of the valley, the lurid surface of Lake Magadi appeared almost radioactive.

"Quite a place," said Max. "Pink lakes."

"Right," said Francis Dermenjian as he took a sip of coffee. "Pink lakes. Perfect for nourishing the pink flamingos. They love these natural alkaline sinks and all the red algae they produce. After all, it's what makes pink flamingos pink. Thank you for the coffee. It's quite good."

Max raised his cup as he tried to clear his brain. Too much Scotch, too little sleep. And in the background, Oscar Newman's loud snoring filtered through the otherwise still morning air.

"This is extraordinary," said Francis. "I must confess I cannot believe the Maasai agreed to this. They revere children above all else, even their cattle. And as you probably know by now, according to their beliefs, God granted the Maasai dominion over all the cattle on earth. I've been speaking with some of the Maasai elders lately. They're not all thrilled with the notion of this clinic. Not by any means."

Max set down a cutting board along with the remnants of a semi-stale loaf of bread and a nearly empty jar of peanut butter. Then he leveled his gaze at Francis. "Ever talk to the women around here?"

"Not very often," said Francis. "This is a fairly male-dominated society."

"Right. Well, I'm surrounded by them all day long. And while I'm still learning their language, I can tell you they're very worried about being able to feed all the children."

Francis was momentarily silenced. But whatever rejoinder he might have been contemplating was cut off by the sounds of an approaching vehicle.

"Sorry," said Max. "That's got to be Mr. Mboto. I need to go wake up Oscar."

Mr. Mboto arrived shortly, accompanied by a young nurse dressed all in white and a young soldier dressed in a beige uniform.

"Hello," said Max. "I'm Dr. Taylor."

"Good morning," said the minister as he brushed the swirling red dust off his dark-blue suit. "I trust that Dr. Newman is here?"

"Yes, sir," said Max, shaking hands. "I expect him to—"

But his voice was drowned out by a raucous hello as Oscar came bounding out of the spare tent, fully dressed and looking far less hung over than Max.

"Welcome, Mr. Mboto," he said, extending his huge hand in greeting. There were introductions all around. Yet Francis Dermenjian stood apart, momentarily unnoticed. Seeing him, Oscar turned and bolted in his general direction.

"And who do we have here?" he inquired as he shook hands with Francis.

"Francis Dermenjian, sir, and very pleased to meet you. I teach botany at the University of Nairobi."

"And I'm pleased to meet you as well, a professor, no less."

While the nurse and soldier poked around inside the examination tent and went over all the paperwork Max had left for them, minus a narrative statement, Oscar, Francis, and Mr. Mboto sat down at the picnic table. Oscar unfurled the aerial photos while Max found two jars of jam and his last two jars of peanut butter to hold down the corners.

"Amazing how these people move about," said Oscar. "But as I understand, the rains are soon to return and the center of the valley should green up. So I suggest we move this clinic westward, near the Ewaso Ngiro River here, as that area provides the most promising grazing. Or so I'm told. I only wish we could penetrate farther north. But unfortunately, there's an uprising out that way. Best to steer clear."

Max cleared his throat. "Excuse me," he said, "but what's this about an uprising?"

"Oh, nothing too serious," said Oscar. "Just a bunch of malcontents from Uganda trying to escape the local warlords. Happens all the time."

"Terrific," said Max.

"Hey now," said Oscar, "you joined the foundation because you wanted to see the real world, right? Well, here it is in all its beautiful, repulsive splendor, animals chasing down other animals, those too weak to survive, devouring them right down to the entrails. Why should humans be any different?"

Francis Dermenjian set his coffee mug down on the table. "Excuse me, Dr. Newman," he interjected, "but with all due respect, if you wish to compare wild animals with our own species, then you should bear in mind that *Homo sapiens* is

6

the only animal on earth that regularly engages in warfare, murdering its kind with no eye whatsoever toward feeding on its kill."

"Right you are," said Oscar, smiling at his new acquaintance. "Just as we're the only animal species on earth that is perpetually in heat. I believe the two go hand in hand."

"Fascinating theory," replied Francis, looking a bit dumbstruck. "But please, tell me. Is it true that you have over a thousand clinics such as this one spread all over the world?"

"Yes, we have 1,827 to be exact. For now, anyway. We have another three hundred or so on the drawing board."

Before Francis could respond the unmistakable staccato of an approaching helicopter halted their conversation. Oscar stood and squinted into the sun. He saw not only the helicopter but, worse, the large letters plastered along its side that indicated the media had found him once again.

"You can save your questions," he said to Francis. "Here come the professionals. I wonder what the hell they want now."

Chapter 2

The shrill whistle of the teakettle sliced through the quiet of the afternoon, stirring Elizabeth from her reverie. Comfortably seated on an old wicker chair out on the veranda, with her long legs tucked up beneath her, she had been watching her small flock of Scottish Blackface sheep work its way down the lush green slopes that ultimately led all the way to the rocky shore. Though a few stubborn clouds still clung to the skyway, casting great shadows on the verdant slopes and the deep emerald sea, the day was as bright and clear as days get in Scotland. And the Isle of Mull had never looked better.

To the west, the land fell gradually toward an inlet, then curved north to embrace it like a giant arm. It left a dramatic cleft that was only exaggerated in its grandeur by the seeming insignificance of the single-track road that ran along its top. Elizabeth stood up to tend to her seething teakettle, then stopped suddenly. A yellow car was steadily mounting the road to the southwest and had not turned off toward Tobermory. Was it a taxi? Could it be Oscar, on time for once? It wasn't long before it headed up the road that led to the cottage but then, without warning, turned down some hidden drive across the way.

Annoyed that she could have been so presumptuous, she rushed back to the kitchen and turned off the kettle. Oscar on schedule, really. But then a familiar voice, as scratchy as gorse, called out to her from the back door.

"Hello there, Ms. Elizabeth." Leaning against the doorjamb was a small, whiskered fellow in overalls with a pipe in his mouth and a brown tweed cap hovering above his curly, gray eyebrows.

"Good afternoon, Tommy," she replied. "Care for some tea?"

Tommy shook his head. "T'anks, but I've got chores to do. Any word from Oscar? He's due in, eh?"

"No, I'm afraid not."

"Aye, well, I see you got a message waitin'."

She turned around to see that he was right. The little red light on the old landline was blinking. How could she have missed it? She had been checking for messages from Oscar for a couple of days, awaiting confirmation, or not, that he was on schedule. It must have come in while the teakettle was whistling, while she followed the path of the deceptive yellow car.

Her heart pounded as she lifted the receiver and dialed her voice mail. Tommy looked on in anticipation. She despised these moments, knowing how often Oscar's life had been threatened, how he spent his time traveling through third-world nations where crime and poverty were often rampant. There was a target on his back, no doubt, perhaps a bounty. Finally, she heard his voice.

"Hello, my darling," he began, before detailing the reasons he'd been detained and was running behind schedule. Tommy looked on, watching the relieved expression on Elizabeth's face. Then she rolled her eyes and began shaking her head from side to side before suddenly erupting, perhaps in anger or just mere frustration with Oscar's unpredictable adventures.

"Incroyable!" she exclaimed, her jaw tightening. She slammed the phone down on its cradle and began to pace about the room, muttering to herself in her native French. Tommy seemed quite taken aback as she finally ceased her pacing and turned toward him.

"First he says everything's fine, 'Having a productive trip.' Then he says he will be delayed in Kenya for a couple of extra days, catching up on business. Then an unanticipated stop in Paris. And then," she began. But she could not continue.

Tommy moved toward her but she started pacing again.

"And then he has the nerve to ask me…"

"Aye," said Tommy, "to ask ye…"

"He wants to know if I'll…" But she caught herself just in time. The last thing she needed to do was tell Tommy that the message closed with a rather significant question composed of four short words: "Will you marry me?" If she told Tommy, then all of Mull, and most likely the entire world beyond, would know very quickly. "He wants to know if I'll forgive him for being late again."

"Ach, that sounds like Oscar. Always late, always apologizin' for it."

"So it seems," said Elizabeth.

Tommy excused himself, referring again to his chores. Elizabeth knew he was more likely off to check on the ale supply than tend to any chores. But it was just as well. She needed time, time to think clearly. Oscar had finally proposed to her, in a voice mail! It was infuriating. What on earth had possessed him? Why not pop the question upon his return? She picked up the kettle and brought it toward the teapot. Then she put it back on the stove. Teatime would have to wait. She grabbed a sweater and headed out the back door.

What was she going to do? She had known and worked with Oscar in his research laboratory for six years and had lived with him—when he was in town, at least—for the last two. And though he was overweight, swore and drank too much, and was occasionally coarse to the point of being absolutely crude, she knew she loved him. For when they were together, which seemed to be less and less the case, he made her feel the way no man had ever made her feel before. He made her laugh. He gave her strength and encouragement, doted on her, told her she was beautiful, intelligent, even funny.

She walked briskly, gradually climbing the hillside above the cottage until she stopped just short of an old stone building that at one time had been an integral part of the Scottish wool industry. But now just a few sheep scurried out of the building as she approached. At this familiar spot, she often imagined the shearers of long ago busily herding their large flocks of sheep and deftly removing fleece after fleece. She imagined the excitement that must have prevailed back in the days when the textile trade was in full swing. That would have been at least fifty years ago, before all the woolen mills closed. Too much foreign competition. She wondered if anyone had ever considered making cheese from the sheep's milk, as in southern France, where she was raised, instead of relying on the wool.

She stopped abruptly as the image of Provence struck like a bolt of lightning. For it occurred to her that if she did decide to marry Oscar, she would have to break the news to her mother somehow. Worse, her mother would insist, if she survived the news in the first place, that the wedding take place in Balgères, at Sainte-Marie, as Elizabeth had promised her father before he died. Slowly, the lightning in her head turned to thunder.

She made her way across the various pastures and through the several turnstiles that led back to the cottage. Once again she put the kettle on. Oscar might not tolerate a religious ceremony to begin with. Furthermore, being wed in a Catholic church might be impossible, considering his occupation. But Mother would insist on it, if for no other reason than to irritate Oscar, whom she despised with a passion.

The warmth and fragrance of the tea provided comfort and helped her focus. By evening she had convinced herself that the status quo was perfectly satisfactory and Oscar would have to find someone else if he needed to be married. Having thus reached what she felt at the time was a final decision, she went to bed. But sleep was elusive as the weight of the question, the timing, and the method of transmission in particular left her battling a plague of conflicting emotions.

She arose early and put on the kettle before strolling out to her flower garden. Though it was early October, a few stubborn autumn crocuses were still in bloom amid the heather. She went back inside, toasted a crumpet, and brewed her tea. Afterward she let her sheep out of the paddock, then returned to the veranda to watch them graze while she pondered exactly how she would deliver her response to Oscar's audacious inquiry. Once weary of this unpleasant exercise, she decided to turn on the news. Any kind of distraction would do.

She sat down on the sofa, reached for the remote control, and turned on CNN. Once again there was breaking news, something about Kenya. She froze. The camera focused on a young, rather attractive Asian woman dressed all in khaki.

"Good morning. This is Melanie Woo reporting to you from Lake Magadi in the Rift Valley of Kenya. I'm here with Dr. Oscar Newman, whom some have dubbed the 'King of Contraception,' not just for developing the safest and most effective contraceptive device ever but for all the work his foundation has done to make safe birth control an option for women all over the globe."

As the camera panned back, Oscar came into full view, bigger than life.

"Dr. Newman," she said, "I've been informed that you are about to be selected as this year's recipient of the Nobel Peace Prize. What's your reaction?"

Oscar looked at her in disbelief, then exploded with laughter.

"You can't be serious," he said, gradually composing himself. "Well, I suppose I should be quite honored, although I don't believe that conferring the Peace Prize on me would be in the best interests of world peace!"

Elizabeth dropped the remote. "Oscar? The Nobel Peace Prize? That's impossible!"

Chapter 3

"Here's to your good health, one and all," said Oscar, raising a glass. "And especially to Ms. Woo, whose courage and persistence I find quite inspiring. How you found me in the middle of this vast expanse is quite beyond me."

"Thank you, Dr. Newman," she replied. "I know my visit was the last thing you wanted, but what can I say? You are big news today. When we learned you were meeting with the minister of health this morning, we simply made a few inquiries and, well—"

"I understand perfectly," said Oscar. "And though I thoroughly contest your hypothesis about this Nobel nonsense, I appreciate that you would take the time to see the success we are having here among the Maasai. They understand their situation. They see the limitations."

"Are you certain of that?" said Mr. Mboto.

Oscar evinced a smile as he wiped some chicken grease off his chin. "Such are the indications, but who can ever be certain of anything?" he replied. "Especially in Africa."

Max stood nearby, tending the coals on the grill that was roasting the last of the chickens Mr. Mboto had brought along, live, for the noon-hour meal. Max had personally slaughtered, plucked, cleaned, seasoned, and grilled them, and looked on while the others helped themselves. And though he was quite hungry, he was content to keep a safe distance from the conversation while preserving his unobstructed view of the lovely Melanie Woo, who continued to probe Oscar about this Nobel business but to no avail.

"Ms. Woo," Oscar began once again.

"Please," she interrupted, "call me Melanie. After all, I'm not on assignment anymore. I got my interview."

"Very well, Melanie, but reporters are always on assignment, are they not? Do you mean to tell me that if I were to suddenly drop dead on the spot here, you wouldn't report it?" Oscar peered at her with raised eyebrows, his head generally inclined toward his plate.

"Well, I suppose I would, but as you see I am without a cameraman, so how could I report it?" she replied. This was true. Edward, her cameraman and pilot, had flown back to Nairobi the moment she'd agreed to stay for lunch.

"Well, you have plenty of footage from this morning and certainly a cell phone. You could easily record our conversations, including perhaps my last words as I agonized in the throes of death, and have a stunning story for this evening's news. A simple voice-over would do the trick. It would be most impressive, I should think."

Melanie dropped her fork and stared him down. "Dr. Newman," she began.

"Please, call me Oscar. And I am definitely *not* on assignment," he said, laughing before inhaling half a glass of wine.

"All right, Oscar," she continued, "but surely you understand that journalists like me have certain ethical codes we must abide by that prohibit the secret recording of conversations, if that's what you're driving at."

"Please, Melanie," said Oscar, barely controlling his laughter, "I don't mean to suggest that at all. But reporters have exceptionally long antennae that enable them to root out certain truths as well as certain exaggerations, such as this report that I am about to be awarded a Nobel Peace Prize."

He placed his head on his hands and stared at her with wide, intensely curious eyes.

"Do you still deny it then?" she asked.

Oscar roared with laughter. "You see," he said, looking to the others. "I told you she was still on assignment!"

Francis smiled halfheartedly through tight jaws while Mr. Mboto ignored the comment altogether. Max felt the impulse to rescue Melanie from another of Oscar's assaults but hesitated as he glanced over her body to see if he could spot any sign of a cell phone tucked up her sleeve. Or perhaps in a back pocket. Her sleeveless khaki blouse was rather snug at the waist, as were the shorts she wore below. He concluded that everything seemed to be very much in its proper place. Absolutely everything.

"Perhaps we should change the subject," Melanie suggested. "What do you intend to do while here in Maasai country?"

"Actually," Oscar began, "I intend to meet with elders from the nearby villages to discuss the nature of…"

But he failed to complete his sentence. For at that moment he saw three men approaching the tents. Two were clearly Maasai elders but the third man, dressed in Western clothes, was clutching his hand and seemed to be in great pain. Francis jumped up from the picnic bench.

13

"Joseph!" he cried out.

Joseph Ole Saikele, the chief elder, or *Alaigwanani*, of the Maasai of southern Kenya, responded warmly, referring to Francis with a strange Maasai name. The two spoke briefly in the Maasai language before Joseph introduced his companions. The one to his left, with two good hands, was named Senento. They had come to ask Max if he would circumcise Senento's son since the man who normally performed such duties was clutching a hand swollen to the size of a small melon. This man was a Ndorobo tribesman, who, in his current condition, could not even hold a knife, much less use one to delicately carve the foreskin off a boy's penis.

Max quickly examined the hand. Several bones were broken. When asked how this had happened, Joseph explained that they had been attempting to subdue an angry bull. The bull, however, not wishing to be subdued, had stepped on this poor fellow's hand.

"He'll need X-rays before these bones can be properly set," said Max. "It'll probably require surgery. He needs to get to a hospital."

Mr. Mboto volunteered. "Dr. Newman," he said, "I'm afraid we must leave now. Can you gather your affairs?"

Oscar froze. It was much too soon.

"Please," said Francis, "I would be more than happy to offer Dr. Newman a lift back to Nairobi whenever he is ready to leave."

"That's very kind of you," said Oscar. "I wouldn't be taking you out of your way?"

"Not at all. But if you have an extra day or so, I could show you around a bit."

"Excellent," Oscar replied. "I really should be getting back home, but I would so love to see more of this magnificent country. Thank you so much."

Though reeling in pain, the injured man protested as he was helped into Mr. Mboto's vehicle. Once they and the ever-vigilant inspection team were gone, Max turned to Joseph and Senento to learn more about this circumcision. By agreeing to do it, Max knew he would be venturing into a rather sacred Maasai tradition, a rite of passage that tested a boy's courage in a very painful and unforgiving manner. Yet circumcision is normally a fairly basic medical procedure and, given the conditions for establishing the clinic in the first place, Max knew it would be difficult to refuse. Besides, the opportunity to immerse himself in another culture had been a major factor in his decision to work for Oscar.

Joseph did all the talking. He was quite tall, like many Maasai, and wore a large orange blanket, distinguishing him as an elder. He held a black club in one hand and a fly brush made from the tail of a wildebeest in the other. Slung over one shoulder was a calabash, a drinking vessel made from a hollowed-out gourd. His head was shaved, and from his partially slit pendulous earlobes hung beads and fine metal ornaments. After listening to and understanding most of what Joseph had said, Max indicated it would be no problem. When did they want it done?

"Tomorrow at dawn," Joseph replied.

Max said he would be ready. Joseph thanked him and offered him the calabash filled with soured milk. Max drank from it, as did Joseph and Senento. Joseph then scattered a few herbs on the ground.

Max introduced the others, beginning with Melanie. Joseph bowed ever so slightly toward her, as did Senento. To everyone's surprise, she responded to them in the Maa language, wishing Senento and his family well on this important occasion. Max then introduced Oscar, the man who was responsible for this clinic and many others.

Senento nodded but said nothing. Joseph stepped forward and looked Oscar squarely in the eye. Oscar, quite out of character, simply stared back, apparently speechless. He was about to offer his hand when Joseph turned away rather abruptly and began speaking to Max once again. Max turned to Francis for some help, as Joseph was speaking quite rapidly.

"He says you are all invited to witness the circumcision," Francis responded. "Even you, Oscar. There will be festivities this evening, part of the preparation for the actual ceremony. Joseph says he will send some escorts later in the afternoon to lead us there."

"Wonderful," said Oscar enthusiastically. "Please tell them I would be delighted to offer a goat as a gift to Senento's family in honor of this occasion."

Max eyed Oscar somewhat suspiciously. Here was a man who seemed to know how to take advantage of every situation. For a goat had actually been penned up at the clinic for weeks, mere lion bait, a gift from one grateful patron of the clinic.

"So, Melanie," said Oscar, "would you like to accompany us? I've known many women who would love nothing better than to see a man's penis whittled down to size. How about it?"

Melanie stared at him in disbelief. Max cringed.

"Actually," said Melanie, taking it all in stride, "I was once a student of East African culture and the Maasai have long been of great interest to me. So thank you. I will radio Edward to pick me up tomorrow morning."

"Excellent!" exclaimed Oscar.

Max told Joseph and Senento they would all be ready when the escorts arrived. He thanked them for the opportunity to be a part of such an important event.

"Joseph doesn't seem to share that fellow's appreciation for the services your clinic provides," observed Melanie once the visitors were out of range.

"Oh well," said Oscar, "the men are the hardest to please, in general. But the chap who offered up the goat has twelve daughters. Paying the dowry for that lot might just break him. In any case, it does appear as though the women are appreciative."

He was referring to several Maasai women who had arrived while they were eating lunch. They were sitting in a circle near the main examination tent and were singing softly among themselves.

"I think I need to get back to work," said Max.

"If you don't mind," said Melanie, "I'm really tired. Is there some place I could lie down for a bit until our escorts arrive? I just got back from a quick trip to San Francisco for my sister's wedding, and I can guarantee tonight's festivities will keep us all up rather late. I'm afraid my body hasn't yet adjusted to the time change."

"No problem," said Max. "There's an empty tent with a cot right over here."

It seemed to him, as they headed toward the tent, that her body was very well adjusted in every way possible. He tried to resist looking at her too directly, knowing all too well how the sight of a beautiful woman can suddenly hijack all the synapses in a man's brain. He even found himself wondering if she, too, might be sporting a Newman Insert.

Chapter 4

Engrossed in their tea and conversation, none of them noticed the arrival of their colorful escorts—three moran standing tall at the edge of the circle of tents, their long, ochre-infused braids brushing their broad shoulders. Bright ornaments dangled from their sculpted ears and colorful beads and amulets hung from their slender necks. Each one wore an orange cloth about his waist like a short, tight skirt. Their legs were strikingly painted with more ochre, and within the ochre were vivid finger-painted patterns. Their feet were bare, though one wore beads around his ankles. And all were fully armed with spear, shield, and scabbard.

Oscar, Max, and Melanie marveled at their guides as they all wound their way carefully through the wait-a-bit thorn, slowly descending toward the bottom of the Rift Valley. The sun still rode high over the Nguruman Escarpment some thirty miles to the west. Occasionally, they would startle some Thomson's gazelles, or a solitary impala would bolt from some hiding place. They flushed birds of all kinds. Francis urged them not to worry about any large carnivores. These moran were the fiercest warriors in the world and they were there to protect them. No one seemed too concerned about his or her safety.

At one point they encountered a number of tall, rather phallic-looking mounds that quickly drew the morans' attention. They were termite mounds, and the moran proceeded to capture the large white insects between their fingers and toss them in their mouths. Francis explained to the others that this was like candy to the Maasai. As if for show, Francis popped one into his own mouth while Melanie, Oscar, and Max looked on in disbelief.

"You should try it," he said.

They all declined rather emphatically.

Eventually, they perceived what looked like giant mushrooms nestled among a grove of thorn trees. As they approached, it became evident that these were Maasai dwellings. Francis explained that this was the ceremonial *manyatta*. Each house, or more precisely, each hut, was built of branches that were stuck into the ground and then bent over to form a roof. Grass was woven through the branches and the roof was heavily plastered with cow dung mixed with mud.

These huts were arranged in a large circle with the center reserved for cattle. Surrounding the entire settlement was a large fence consisting of thorny brush arranged in such a fashion as to deter predators.

Once they were inside the brush enclosure, the density of flies increased dramatically with every step they took, even though the cattle were all currently grazing somewhere well outside the compound. Many of the women of the village were busily applying fresh coats of mud and manure to the roofs of the huts while others gathered around large cooking pots that simmered away over smoldering wood fires. The younger girls, all wearing their finest ceremonial beadwork, were tending to the horde of little children that scampered about. Many of the youngest boys were already clutching little stick spears.

The men had gathered in the center, engaged in heated discussion about the location for each aspect of the upcoming ceremony. As soon as Max, Oscar, Francis, and Melanie entered the ring of Maasai houses, their moran escorts shouted to the entire gathering, announcing the arrival of the new cutter and his entourage. The women all stopped their home repair work, the girls and children all ceased their chatter, and the men stood solemnly, neither smiling nor frowning. Everyone simply stared at the non-African newcomers. Max recognized Senento and finally Joseph, who walked over, slowly and with great dignity, to greet them.

Francis translated as Joseph thanked them for coming, saying all of the villagers were honored by their presence. He then called to the group of elders. The men moved aside to make way for someone who clearly held a rank of some distinction. In sharp contrast with the others, cloaked in the more traditional orange *shukas* and plaid blankets, this gentleman was wrapped in navy blue. What distinguished him even more was a dark cape made from the hide of some wild animal. Francis explained that this was Nilenga, the *laibon*, or spiritual leader. He and Senento walked forward, Senento remaining slightly behind as they approached.

Joseph spoke rapidly, nodding his head as he reinforced each point. Nilenga listened. His face remained stern and seemingly frozen as Joseph explained who each visitor was and why they had come. When he had finished speaking, Nilenga approached Max. Without changing his facial expression in the slightest, he grabbed Max's right hand, raised it, and then, bending forward, spat upon it.

"Don't be alarmed," whispered Francis. "He just bestowed a great blessing upon you."

Max smiled at Nilenga as best he could and thanked him. Nilenga greeted Francis in similar fashion. He then approached Oscar, completely ignoring Melanie Woo, who was next in line. Oscar smiled rather sheepishly, awaiting his own anointment as Nilenga looked him up and down as well as side to side. He started to raise his hand when Nilenga suddenly turned away and began speaking with Joseph and Senento. Senento nodded and called out in the direction of one of the houses. A rather short woman emerged and walked slowly toward them, her head slightly bowed. Senento introduced her as Meko, his second wife. It was their third son who was to be circumcised.

Max greeted her first and in his best Maa said how pleased he was to be of service to them. She and Senento both thanked him. After greeting the others, she took Melanie by the hand and led her back toward the house where other Maasai women, young and old, instantly surrounded her and began to examine her with great curiosity. Had they never seen an Asian woman before?

Joseph announced that it was time to instruct Max in the details of the circumcision ceremony. He asked Francis to join them as a translator, just to be certain that Max understood every aspect of the procedure. Max and Francis voiced their consent, and they departed with Joseph and Nilenga toward a larger house near the entrance to the manyatta.

Senento and Oscar stood alone in the center of the ring of houses. The other men had dispersed, and soon Senento uttered something incomprehensible before he, too, returned to one of the houses.

Oscar stood in silence, looking around to see if someone was about to join him, but his comrades and the villagers had completely abandoned him. So he gazed in absolute amazement at the scene before him. Here was a village made entirely of sticks, grass, mud, and dung, the most basic of natural ingredients. No electricity, no running water, no plumbing, and no need for them among a people who clearly depended only on the earth, the sun, the rain, and the grass these elements provided for their cattle that in turn provided not only sustenance but also roofing material. It was all so simple and efficient.

After a moment of contemplation, he heard a noise behind him and turned to see a young lad of three or four stalking him with a small stick. He squealed as Oscar faced him, crouching and speaking to him with strange new words. The little one backed off and then laughed as Oscar got down on all fours and began to crawl forward, growling softly. The boy resumed his stalking, giggling wildly as he feigned several attacks before launching his stick and catching Oscar squarely in the ribs. Oscar caught the little spear with his hands and clutched it to his side, rolling over and howling like a dying lion, which he resembled in many ways. He

19

seemed nearly as large, and with his thick mane of dark hair and his large beard, he could easily have been the king of beasts. His little assailant leaped on Oscar as if he were a large stuffed toy, laughing so hard he could barely breathe. It took but a moment before a dozen or so other little boys noticed the commotion and swarmed all over Oscar, alternately laughing and threatening with their own little sticks.

This was how Senento found Oscar moments later, sitting in the dirt playing catch and release with a small horde of young boys who wrestled with him and charged at him from all directions. Oscar looked up when he noticed Senento's slender legs standing in front of him. He was holding a long orange gourd and seemed to be offering it to Oscar. Oscar stood up slowly and dusted himself off while patting some of the boys on the head.

Oscar accepted the gourd, eyeing it suspiciously. Senento uttered a coarse command and the boys all dispersed immediately.

"Thank you, Senento," said Oscar, still catching his breath after all the laughing and roughhousing. He sniffed the gourd. The aroma was familiar but not immediately identifiable. He took a small sip and smiled. It was beer, or at least something approaching beer. Senento explained it was honey beer brewed especially for the circumcision ceremony. Oscar pretended he understood.

"Yes," he said, "it's very good. Thank you."

Meanwhile, Max, seated inside Joseph's musty and claustrophobic house, which reeked of stale smoke mixed with the fetid aroma of dried manure, listened intently as Francis translated Joseph's instructions into English. Nilenga sat by silently, nodding with his eyes half closed. Joseph began to explain the procedures for actually cutting the foreskin. Max interrupted as politely as he knew how. Reaching into his bag, he produced a fresh scalpel. He peeled back the aseptic wrapping, and its stainless-steel finish gleamed in spite of the dim lighting afforded by the small hole in the roof that served as a crude skylight and chimney.

"I have these," he said. "They are very sharp."

Nilenga protested. He quickly produced a small, hide-covered box from which he withdrew a crude-looking knife made from antelope horn and some old scrap metal. He gave it to Joseph.

"This is the circumcision knife," said Francis.

Max froze. "Uh, wait a minute," he said nervously. "This won't work. Tell them I will only use a scalpel."

Francis looked at Max with apprehension but conveyed his message to Joseph and Nilenga. They in turn looked upon Max with an air of great disappointment but nonetheless inspected the scalpel very closely. They turned it over and over and traded a few words before Nilenga ran his index finger down the curve of the blade. Before he even winced his finger began to bleed. He gave Max a rather fierce look before uttering some words that Max immediately recognized as disapproval.

"He says it will not do," said Francis. "It is too sharp. All of the boys must endure the same test. There can be no shortcuts along the road to manhood."

Max stared in disbelief. He turned to Francis, speaking softly while stifling more than a bit of outrage. "This thing they're calling a knife is completely dull," he said. "I wouldn't perform the most minor surgical procedure with anything this primitive, especially circumcision. We're talking about the highest density of nerve endings anywhere on the body and doing it without anesthesia to boot. Not only that, but with a knife—and that's being generous—that has sat around for who knows how long in that animal skin. There's a serious risk of infection. Tell them I refuse to do it unless I can use proper medical procedures."

"If you say so," said Francis, whereupon he conveyed to them the essence of Max's concerns. The two Maasai seemed quite taken aback as they turned toward each other and began speaking rapidly. Francis translated.

"They say there is really no problem. The boy is responsible for sharpening the knife. Whatever happens will be due to his own efforts, not yours. Unless, of course, you should slip."

Max was aghast, wondering how the Hippocratic oath pertained to this particular situation. Clearly, there was no dire medical emergency. In fact, like the incisions in their earlobes, it was more like cosmetic surgery. Perhaps "cultural surgery" was a more accurate term.

Then he remembered that he, too, had been circumcised once upon a time, probably without any anesthesia other than his own infantile consciousness. And who knew what scars that may have left. But gradually, the politics of the situation gained some ground and he began to understand with more clarity than ever before the commitment he had made not only to Oscar but more importantly to the Maasai. He was well aware that the single most important event in a Maasai male's life was the circumcision ceremony. If a boy could endure the circumcision without flinching, crying, or otherwise betraying his pain, he would be admitted

21

into the next stage of life, moran-hood, while keeping his family's honor intact. If, however, he should cry out, he would be ridiculed and his family disgraced. The months of preparation for the ceremony would end in disaster.

"When can I meet the boy?" Max inquired.

"Soon," said Francis. "He should return from his wanderings this evening."

When Joseph and Nilenga were satisfied that their surrogate cutter had been properly instructed and understood every facet of the Maasai-style circumcision procedure, Joseph rummaged through an old wooden box and produced a long leather cape. He handed it to Max. It smelled musty and reeked of wood smoke. He tried it on. It was ornamented with fine beadwork and was obviously meant to be worn on ceremonial occasions such as this. Max thanked them politely, indicating he would be very pleased to wear this during the ceremony. It wasn't exactly a surgical smock but it would do. He began to remove it but Nilenga objected. Apparently, the festivities had begun.

As they emerged from Joseph's home, it was evident that more visitors had arrived. Squinting into the late-afternoon sun that hung low in the sky before him, Max saw silhouettes of many new Maasai, most of whom were engaged in animated conversation with the local residents. He recognized Senento surrounded by guests who were offering him gifts of all kinds, including sheep and goats. There were more fires burning, with large skewers of meat roasting over them. He noticed that the goat that had been tethered near Senento's home, a gift from Oscar, was now missing. And so was Oscar.

From just outside the manyatta came a sudden cheering and hollering. Twenty or more young Maasai in charcoal capes came charging into the center of the circle of houses, laughing and chanting and pointing at someone whom Max could not distinguish. Yet above their heads he could see the top of a sapling dancing in the air. As the youths gradually parted, Max saw a boy whom he guessed to be about sixteen carrying the slender young tree. He carried it across the center of the manyatta as those gathered there for the ceremony cheered him on.

"It's an *alatim* tree," said Francis. "A type of olive. It is a symbol of fertility. The women will plant it next to his home."

"What's the boy's name?" Max inquired.

"Matthew," said Francis. "Matthew Ole Senento."

"Can I meet him now?"

Without speaking, Joseph grabbed Max by the arm and led him toward the center of the manyatta. He called to Senento and to Matthew. The crowd fell silent. Matthew approached, holding his head very high and wearing an expression that concealed all feeling and emotion. Senento greeted his son, telling him that the honor of his family depended entirely on him. Matthew nodded but said nothing.

Joseph introduced Max as Nilenga stood by with the knife. Again Matthew nodded without speaking. He wore an orange-plaid shuka. His head had been recently shaved and around his neck were several strings of beadwork and an intricate brass amulet that hung from a single strand of leather.

The boy said nothing and Max wondered how disappointed he must be to have this *mzungu* standing in for the traditional circumciser. Yet the boy's face belied nothing in the way of apprehension or fear. His narrow eyes, set above high cheekbones, seemed to stare past Max and the others to some distant dream or vision. He was good looking, and from the breadth of his shoulders seemed well enough advanced into early manhood to merit the operation.

Nilenga stepped forward and presented the knife. Matthew accepted it and finally uttered a few words, no doubt in respect for the powers that Nilenga was reputed to possess. Matthew then nodded, turned, and walked back to the hut where he had left the sapling tree. Immediately, the boys in the charcoal capes began to taunt him and jeer at him.

"They are from the same age class," said Francis. "They have already been circumcised and are basically telling him he doesn't stand a chance, especially with the white butcher."

Max winced, but before he could respond he heard Oscar's gruff voice approaching.

"Well, Dr. Taylor," said Oscar, still clutching his gourd, "lovely outfit. Looks like you're in for the procedure of a lifetime. Tell me, how many doctors do you know who will be able to say they took a knife to a man's penis while all his friends and relatives stood about cheering for him?"

"Very funny, Oscar," he replied. "You know as well as I do that if this kid screams, I'm the goat. Did you see that knife?"

"Don't worry," he said, "everything will be fine. I can feel it."

Chapter 5

Joseph led Max, Francis, Oscar, and Senento to a series of small, rather crude tables. From there they could see the entire assemblage of villagers and guests as they all seated themselves in a large circle. Food was brought out in large wooden bowls and set before them. There was roasted goat meat, some strange-looking fruits and vegetables, and what looked like polenta.

Max was licking the drippings from some goat meat off his fingers when someone moved in from behind to claim the seat next to him. It was Melanie. She had been escorted by Meko, who showed her to her place and then vanished.

"Good evening, Dr. Taylor," she said. "I hope you don't mind if I join you for dinner."

"Uh no, not at all," he said quite insincerely. For in truth he knew that the last thing he needed at this time was the distraction of a beautiful woman. "Looks like you did okay at the local jewelry store."

"The women are so kind," she said as she fingered the colorful new necklaces that hung down to the top of her loosely buttoned white blouse, highlighting just a soupçon of cleavage. "They kept insisting I take it all. I offered them money but they refused, saying that what you are doing for them has saved them from so much disappointment."

"Yeah, I know," he replied, struggling to focus on his dinner.

"Hey, cheer up. I'm sure you'll do fine. By the way," she added with a slight giggle, "your robe is magnificent."

"Thanks," he said, feeling his face burning red with embarrassment.

He asked about her work and she described the various stories she had been following, including the uprising in Uganda. Oscar, seated far to their left, waved on occasion and once Max thought he saw Oscar wink at him. So, he thought to himself, Oscar's behind all this.

When the meal had been consumed, they heard some chanting in the distance that grew steadily louder. In a few moments the real guests of honor arrived. At least a hundred moran, their long braids matted with ochre, came dancing and singing into the center of the manyatta. They formed a circle and, one by one, took turns singing and dancing in the center of the ring. Holding their spears and shields, they would jump straight up, high into the air. They were all slender and well muscled, each one clutching a spray of *leleshwa*, or camphor leaves, under one arm.

The sun was now fully set and a large, orange moon was rising. They danced until the moon was high in the sky and all the guests were well fed and fairly inebriated. Their songs told stories of their bravery, their great hunting skills, and their passion for various young women. Max listened closely but found himself struggling at times to understand. Melanie noticed his puzzled expression and began translating for him, blushing only slightly as she described particular nuances of certain songs concerning matters of sexual prowess.

But when the moon had reached its zenith, the moran departed as quickly as they had arrived. The crowd cheered them as they danced and sang their way out of the manyatta and back into the hills from whence they had come. When all was quiet, Matthew stood while Nilenga made a few pronouncements. Matthew then proceeded to distribute gifts to many of those present.

"What's he doing?" Oscar inquired of Francis.

"He is giving away all of his belongings," Francis replied. "A man has no need of those worldly things he acquired as a boy."

Matthew gave away his shukas, his small spear, and various trinkets and bits of jewelry. When he had nothing left but a small loincloth around his waist, he thanked his father and his mother for all they had done for him, picked up the circumcision knife, and then turned and walked out through the entrance to the manyatta. No one said a word as he disappeared into the brush to spend the night in solitude.

"Fantastic!" said Oscar.

People then rose, some staggering, and slowly made their way to various sleeping quarters. Nilenga found Max and led him to his house, where he would spend the night. There was a small cot covered with hides next to a pen where three young goats lay bleating at him. Unconcerned, he made up his bed and laid himself down upon it. Only after he was comfortable did he notice that there were at least four other people in the tiny room, nestled in small cots tucked into the darkness. No one spoke, although Nilenga did utter a few words before leaving, presumably saying good night. Or maybe he was saying, "You had better not fuck up tomorrow." Max couldn't begin to understand him.

Sleep eluded him most of the night. Men talked outside the hut until quite late and then the sounds of the cattle within the kraal and the wildlife in the distance kept awakening him. In between, his own thoughts churned as he kept trying to retrace the events in his life that had led him to this particular bizarre situation.

It was still dark when Nilenga tapped Max's foot with his long walking stick and indicated it was time to rise. Max began to put on his ceremonial cape when Nilenga stopped him, leading him to the other small room within his house. There he covered Max's face with a white chalky substance, which dribbled down through his red beard. He wanted to find a mirror but thought better of it. He donned the leather cape and emerged from Nilenga's hut to find people already preparing for the big event. There was a large hide in the center of the manyatta and the Maasai, at least the men, were gathering around it. He remembered that women were generally not allowed to watch. The sun had yet to appear but the eastern sky was becoming lighter by the minute. He saw Oscar and Francis emerge from one of the houses and even caught Oscar trying to conceal a trace of laughter as he beheld Max in all his splendor.

Walking slowly toward the leather hide where the circumcision would take place, Max felt as if he must be dreaming. How had all those years of medical school and training, his years in emergency rooms, his own failed practice, and his failed marriage led to all of this? What had ever possessed him to abandon his profession—his own life, in fact—to work for this madman who now stood there staring at him as if he were some sort of circus freak? All sorts of questions and doubts flooded his mind, but it was too late. He had committed. He noticed that beyond the center of the manyatta, tethered to a post, was a large bull, no doubt the one that had crushed the real circumciser's hand. Silently, he cursed the bovine son of a bitch.

When the first rays of sunlight struck the beast's horns, there came a cheering as Matthew entered the manyatta. He walked stiffly and erectly to the center and stood before the hide. He bowed and presented Max with the knife. It was gleaming and razor sharp. There wasn't a trace of rust. Matthew acknowledged no one else, seeming to gaze straight through and past all those present.

As Max accepted the knife he heard a slight rustling from the entourage. He looked up to see Melanie standing between Oscar and Francis. She was dressed in tight jeans and a snug little orange top that, apart from complementing her fine new jewelry, placed in splendid perspective her firm, well-rounded breasts. In the crisp morning air her nipples stood at attention. Max felt his own passion rising within him, which in turn caused him to clench his teeth in anger and embarrassment.

What the hell was she trying to do? His job was to concentrate on Matthew's penis but now, thanks to Melanie, his own was begging for some attention.

Melanie smiled at him and Max thought he caught her concealing her own laughter. He knew he looked absolutely ridiculous, even to the Maasai. He imagined how people would react to him walking into LA General to check in on one of his patients, cloaked in this dark leather cape with his red hair and beard drizzled with chalk. They'd lock him up. Yet here he was about to perform surgery that, under normal circumstances, would classify as a rudimentary procedure.

Max took one last look at the crowd and at Melanie. Matthew was sitting down on the hide with his legs spread apart. An older Maasai slipped behind him to help support his back. All was ready. Max glanced at Nilenga, who simply nodded.

Then Max took a small pitcher and splashed Matthew's face with the same mixture of chalk and milk as he wore on his face. "One cut," he said in his best Maa as he raised the knife. Then he cut into the foreskin, starting at the top. Matthew's eyes widened slightly but he remained steady. Slowly, Max worked the knife around, discovering that it was quite adequate for the task at hand. Blood quickly covered the hide and Max had to concentrate hard to ignore it and, above all, to not even think about looking up at Melanie. Within five minutes the last bit of skin had yielded to the knife and Matthew had withstood the test. He sighed heavily as Max removed the foreskin for him to see.

Senento spoke first. "Wake up," he said slowly. "You are now a man."

Matthew's mother then appeared along with a few other women who helped escort Matthew to the hut where the *alatim* tree had been planted. The men wrestled with the bull and drove into its neck an arrow, which they immediately withdrew. They quickly filled a gourd with blood, mixed it with milk, and took it to Matthew, who bowed his head in gratitude. People were lining up to bestow gifts upon him and all the village seemed to have been relieved of an immense burden. Senento thanked Max profusely. He was clearly overjoyed. Oscar and Francis offered their congratulations. Max simply felt stunned, wishing he would awaken from this strange dream world. Melanie shook his hand, saying how much she admired his willingness to help in what must be a rather unusual service for an American doctor. He thanked her, but before he could say anything further he felt a tugging at his arm. It was a Maasai woman who clearly wanted his assistance urgently.

She led him to another of the huts. As he stooped inside he saw a young girl of about twelve being held down by four other women. She was naked and the woman who had led Max there motioned to him to use the knife on her. In a horrifying instant Max understood what she wanted him to do.

"No way!" he said frantically. "Joseph never said anything about—"

But before he could finish the woman grabbed the knife from him in disgust and slashed away the young girl's clitoris and the outer lips of her vagina. The girl screamed horribly as blood gushed down her legs. The others laughed as they struggled to hold her still.

Max stood outside the dung house for a moment trying desperately to regain his composure. Finally, he threw off his cape and ran to Joseph's house to retrieve his medical supplies. He was well aware that the Maasai generally ignored the laws prohibiting female circumcision. Every woman who came to see him had been circumcised. Yet he could not believe that not only did the Maasai women condone such a cruel practice, invented by men to suppress the sexual appetites of their various wives or lovers, but worse, they inflicted it upon themselves.

When he returned to the hut where the girl lay writhing in pain, nearly in convulsions, the women were chatting as if this was simply a part of their daily routine. Max had already removed some bandages from his bag when he noticed that the women had applied some sort of poultice to the young girl's wounds. She saw him looking at her as she lay weeping helplessly on the ground. She shook her head slowly, signaling to him that this was none of his affair.

He stood outside again, breathing heavily. It was useless. These people were barbaric. They had no need of him nor was he particularly inclined to be of further service. When he looked up he saw Oscar approaching.

"Max," he said, "you were magnificent. But the party's just begun! Come, join us. You've done a wonderful thing for these people."

"To hell with these people," he said, still breathing heavily. "Go look in there if you want to see what these people are really about."

Oscar raised his curly eyebrows but did as Max suggested. He emerged in a moment, shaking his head. "Ah yes, female circumcision as well. It happens in some cultures. But listen. We are not here to dictate our values to them. That is their business. We are only here to lend them our technology in order to help keep their culture alive."

Max stared at Oscar as the weight of his words sank in. Oscar approached and put his arm on Max's shoulder, slowly leading him back toward the crowd.

"Look, Oscar," he said, "I did my part here. I'd like to go back to camp now."

"Not a bad idea," said Oscar. "This little junket has been quite extraordinary but I suppose I, too, should be moving on. Elizabeth will be quite vexed with me by now. Besides, Ms. Woo has a civil war to attend to. I imagine she'll be anxious to leave as well. And speaking of Melanie, I don't suppose she revealed any little trade secrets to you last night?"

Max stopped suddenly and turned to face Oscar. "I get it," he said. "You arranged for her to sit next to me, thinking she might get careless and drop some little tidbit about how she really scooped this Nobel story. Well, sorry, Oscar, but we never discussed it. Look, why don't you stop fighting this whole thing and just accept what's happened. Hell, you spent your whole life trying to convince the world that unlimited population growth is a one-way ticket to disaster and you showed people how to get it under control safely. So why not stand up and take a bow? God knows you've earned it."

Oscar stopped for a moment and looked at Max, noticing what an enormous amount of emotional strain he seemed to be under. Yet he delivered this plea with a passion that seemed rather detached from the circumstances of the moment, or of his recent past. "You really think I should go through with it?" he asked.

"Absolutely. Anyway, you don't have any choice now. The whole world knows."

Oscar laughed his usual mischievous laugh and slapped Max on the back. "What the hell," he said. "I suppose it could do the program quite a bit of good. We'll just need to beef up security, right?"

Suddenly, Max looked a little less enthusiastic. "Yeah," he said, "we'll just beef up security."

They found Francis and Melanie and said their good-byes to Joseph and Senento. When Oscar inquired about Nilenga, Joseph indicated he was occupied with some spiritual matters.

"Just hope he's not working up a curse for you, Oscar," said Francis.

"Very funny. Please give him my regards and wish the lad well."

Chapter 6

The journey back to camp was uneventful. Only one of the three moran who had originally escorted them to the ceremonial manyatta accompanied them. And he, not wanting to miss the festivities, turned back after a mile or so, indicating that they need only return the way they had come. Fortunately, Francis seemed to recognize every tree and shrub, having by virtue of his profession an abiding interest in every facet of the landscape. He led them straight to the camp, where Edward and his helicopter were waiting to carry Melanie off to her next assignment.

Melanie took a few moments to change into the khaki outfit she wore when she had first arrived. Max had offered her the use of his private shower to wash away the dust but she declined. She said Edward had arranged a stopover at one of the tourist lodges near the Mara River, on the way to Kisumu, where they could both freshen up. Max felt his jaws tighten.

"Good-bye," she said at last. "You know, Max, you really should find someone to help you out here. I don't like the thought of you being all alone in the middle of this wilderness."

"Don't worry," he said, "I'll be all right. But I am looking for an assistant, preferably one who speaks both English and Maa."

Melanie laughed. "I'll think about it," she said. "Meanwhile, you take care. I hope to see you again one of these days."

"Feel free to drop in for tea any time."

"Thanks. Perhaps I will. After all, you never know where the next story will break." She then turned to Oscar. "As for you," she said, "I'll look for you in Oslo. Thank you so much for asking me to stay. It was an experience I know I will never forget."

"Our pleasure, Melanie. And best of luck out on the front. You be careful, too."

"Don't worry," she said. "See you in Oslo?"

Oscar said nothing but simply winked at her. She smiled back, seemingly quite pleased with herself. She then said good-bye to Francis and gave each of them a generous hug before climbing into the helicopter. Oscar, Max, and Francis stood by as the chopper veered off into the sky and disappeared out over the dry savannah. An emptiness seemed to descend over the threesome as the sounds of the helicopter faded.

"Hell of a woman," said Oscar.

"Yeah," said Max, "hell of a woman, all right. Just what I didn't need. Look, I have to get this crud off me. Do you mind?"

"Go right ahead while we gather our belongings," said Francis. They were ready to depart by the time Max emerged from his crude shower.

"Well," Francis began, "I suggest we take off and see if we can make our way to Nairobi by tomorrow night."

"Very well, then," said Oscar, "we'll be off. Thank you so much, Dr. Taylor, for a most entertaining sojourn."

"My pleasure, really," said Max. "After all, I wouldn't be here if it weren't for you."

"And there'd be bugger all, no Newman Foundation whatsoever, if not for young doctors like you who care more for saving the world than leading the life of your average, much wealthier physician," Oscar replied. With that he gave Max an enormous hug.

"Thanks, Oscar," he said. He said good-bye to Francis and then watched them drive off in a cloud of dust. He could see the dust for quite some time, slowly rising above the tops of the trees as they circled to the east and then headed northward. As he watched the dust settle for several moments, an intense, almost suffocating loneliness settled over him, while visions of Melanie danced in his head.

Francis drove deftly and kept up a brisk pace despite the roughness of the road they followed and the decided list Oscar's great weight imparted to the overall balance of the Jeep. It soon became obvious to Oscar that Francis and his Jeep were as one, that years of traveling through country such as this had helped to meld man and machine into a single organism that bounded freely through the rugged countryside.

From time to time they came upon various large animals, including a variety of antelope, zebra, and a few gangly giraffes. They all ran away at first, somewhat startled by the Jeep, but did not appear to be terribly frightened and ambled off to safe distances before resuming their ruminations.

Francis made several stops to collect various plant specimens, explaining to Oscar the significance of each one. They explored a number of draws and ambled on foot up steep slopes where Francis would then spend time carefully combing through the local flora looking for certain rare specimens.

They had left Maasai country far behind and were now entering Kikuyu land, where traditional farming had taken over much of the landscape. They waved to the workers tending to their crops. Some but not all of them waved back. It was getting on toward late afternoon and high above them they noticed an occasional hot-air balloon. Francis explained that this had rapidly become one of the more popular, albeit expensive, ways for tourists to view the wonders of the Rift Valley.

Finally, they came upon a steep, well-incised draw that cut deep into the eastern escarpment. They had left farmland well behind again and were facing a very rough trail that led upward into a canyon.

"This will be our last stop for today," said Francis. "I have never shown this spot to anyone, mind you, and its very existence is a well kept secret. In many ways it is like an ancient archaeological treasure whose exact location must be closely guarded."

"There's absolutely no chance whatsoever that I could ever find my way back here," Oscar replied, "so don't worry. But what the hell are you talking about, if you don't mind my asking?"

"You'll see," said Francis.

With that he slipped the Jeep into first gear and began to climb. The narrow roadway became rougher as they proceeded. Francis had been peering often at the gauges for the last hour or two, evincing a rather concerned expression from time to time that was not at all lost on Oscar.

"Is there a problem?" Oscar inquired at last.

"No, not really," said Francis. "The oil pressure is not exactly ideal but the overall temperature is within tolerance."

"We could walk, you know," said Oscar.

"Yes, I suppose," said Francis, "but we still have about two miles to go before we reach our destination. It's quite a climb, about two thousand feet. I believe we can make it as long as I don't overdo it."

The question of overdoing it was precisely what worried Francis most. Oscar's enormous weight proved to be an unknown that defied factoring in. Before they had gone a half mile, the engine erupted in a large cloud of black smoke. Upon

32

inspection, Francis discovered that the oil pump had given out and sprayed oil all over. Fortunately, the engine had not caught fire.

"Well," said Francis after the smoke had cleared somewhat, "I do believe we're in one of those situations that we all try our utmost to avoid."

There was a certain nervousness in his voice. It was the tone that said, "We have really not done our utmost to avoid this situation, although we thought we had."

"Life is full of risks," Oscar said. "Since you spend a great deal of time navigating through this countryside in this rather decrepit Jeep of yours, I'm sure you have a contingency plan. Am I right?"

"Yes, of course," said Francis. "I've another oil pump right under this seat here…" His voice faded as he reached under the passenger seat and came up empty. "That's impossible! I know I had a spare. I specifically made a point of bringing along an extra. I put it right there under the seat!"

Francis paced about, trying to remain calm but obviously concerned. "All I can think is that one of the native boys took it. They are always looking for interesting trinkets from Western culture with which to impress their friends. All I know is it was there when I left Nairobi. I suppose we'll have to radio for help. I'm terribly sorry about this, Oscar, really I am."

"I've been in many worse predicaments than this," said Oscar. "I just hope that your radio hasn't suffered the same fate as your spare oil pump."

"Oh, no," said Francis, "it's right here in the glove compartment, which I keep locked at all times. The only problem is we'll have to hike up to higher ground. A radio signal would not get far from down in this draw. In fact, I suggest we gather up our gear and hike to our original destination. From there it's but a short hike up to the top of the plateau. We should be able to broadcast a decent signal from up there."

"I defer to your wisdom and experience in a situation such as this," Oscar replied.

And so they gathered the most critical of their gear, consisting mainly of water, sleeping bags, food for the night, a pistol, and, of course, the radio. They followed the rough track they had been pursuing in the Jeep, noticing that as they climbed it became more and more obscure until there was hardly any trail at all. Francis guided them onward, through thick brush that disguised the presence of an ephemeral stream somewhere within.

After twenty minutes or so, Francis headed for the high ground. They broke out of the riparian vegetation and entered more open but even steeper ground. All along Francis called out the names of this shrub and that shrub, describing each plant's peculiarities and special uses. Finally, he stopped and turned to see how Oscar was holding up.

"I'm okay," he said, panting and sweating profusely. "How much farther?"

"We're nearly to our original destination. Then it's about a five-hundred-foot climb to the rim."

As he spoke, he pointed up to the lip of the canyon, where the land suddenly leveled off, high above. To think that the earth's skin had just stretched to the breaking point, causing the Rift Valley behind them to simply fall away, leaving this steep escarpment upon which they were situated, required a mental stretch on Oscar's part. Getting to the top, however, would require an even greater physical stretch. He took a deep breath and headed onward and upward.

After another fifteen minutes or so, Francis stopped. He waited patiently for Oscar to catch up to him. They each took a large drink from their respective water bottles before Francis spoke.

"Oscar," he said, "I'd like you to take a look at this bush here."

He was pointing to a shrub about five feet high that was covered with reddish-brown berries. It had bright green leaves that were slightly leathery in texture but really had no features that might immediately lead the layperson to consider it special.

"Very nice," said Oscar. "Is this what you wanted to show me?"

"Yes," said Francis, nearly shivering with excitement. "I'd like you to meet *Coffea arabica*, a native coffee plant, one of less than several hundred upon which the world's entire coffee industry depends for the genetic diversity necessary to keep pace with evolution. The majority of these native plants are found to the north in the Ethiopian highlands. Kenya is one of the world's largest coffee producers. Yet all the coffee bushes you see in Kenya, including those first planted long ago by the English colonialists, are almost exact genetic replicas of each other. They are well adapted to this climate and are fairly hardy, but if a new blight should suddenly develop for which there is no defense system, then here perhaps lies the answer."

Oscar gazed in subdued astonishment as Francis began picking the berries. He examined each one carefully before stuffing it into a small sack. Oscar wanted to help but wasn't certain he was qualified.

"What will you do with them?" he asked.

"Send them to a seed bank," said Francis. "I have been collecting seeds from this plant for sixteen years now. Some will be allowed to develop into mature plants in hothouses. Some of those could be cross-fertilized with other native varieties to develop new types that have higher resistance to whatever coffee blight is at issue."

It suddenly dawned on Oscar, as he gazed at Francis, how devoted he was to preserving the gene pool of modern agriculture. After all, without it, civilization as we know it wouldn't stand a chance. What, for instance, would become of the modern world if the global workforce were suddenly deprived of coffee every morning? Would the world economy come to a grinding halt? Or, worse, was the barley that produced his much-esteemed Scotch whisky equally at risk?

"If this plant is so valuable," Oscar inquired, "why hasn't someone done something to protect it? After all, what's to prevent the landowner from turning all this into more rangeland?"

"Good question," Francis replied. "The truth is, it's too remote from the pastoralists like the Maasai. Besides, *I* own it. But we haven't really time to discuss such points. We must get to higher ground before dark."

From there on the slope was steep and sparsely vegetated. As a result, footing was poor and both Francis and Oscar had to resort at times to climbing on all fours. Francis continued to explain to Oscar what each shrub was called as they grabbed an occasional branch to help hoist themselves higher and higher. Oscar thanked Francis for the botany lesson but expressed greater interest in finding a more decent route, one with a much more humane angle of repose.

"Sorry, Oscar," he said, "but this is a rift valley, after all, and a young one at that. We're climbing up the eastern aspect of a normal fault plane. You should be thankful that it's not a sheer vertical cliff."

"It might as well be, as far as I'm concerned," said Oscar, obviously quite fatigued.

Within a half hour they had successfully mounted the slope. They hiked out to a promontory that divided the draw through which they had just ascended from its neighbor to the south and made camp. The brilliant ambers of the setting sun were just beginning to fade into twilight.

"There's hardly any daylight left," said Francis. "I suggest you start gathering some firewood, lots of it, while I try to reach someone on the radio."

"Right," said Oscar.

"Here," said Francis, handing him the pistol. "You'd better take this as well. I trust you know how to handle one of these."

"Certainly," said Oscar in an unconvincing tone.

As it was still the dry season, Oscar managed to find enough dead branches to keep them more than comfortably warm throughout the evening. But warmth was not the main concern. It was more important to be seen. Even if Francis did succeed in contacting someone, a fire by which to locate them in this vast wilderness was essential. Francis kept encouraging Oscar to find more wood while he continued to send messages out on various frequencies. Finally, Oscar dropped his last armload of dead branches and sat down.

"So," he said, "is there no one listening?"

"I believe I've gotten a message through but I'm having trouble picking up an answer," Francis replied. "I'm trying quite a number of frequencies. I'm sure we'll have better luck in the morning if we don't hear from anyone tonight. I wouldn't worry, however. Breakdowns such as we have experienced are not uncommon. It may be that no one wishes to reply until morning, when a new crew will be in. Such rescue operations are much easier in the daytime."

Oscar seemed satisfied with this explanation. They built a fire and prepared a simple supper of canned foods and some freeze-dried vegetables. When they had finished eating, they laid out their sleeping bags and made themselves comfortable. Behind them, a brilliant amber moon began to rise above the trees. Oscar reached for his knapsack.

"Care for a little moonshine, my friend?" he inquired.

"I beg your pardon?" Francis responded.

"Whisky," he replied, "eighteen years old. The Highlands' finest, in my estimation."

"Just a touch, perhaps," said Francis, "to help me sleep."

Oscar rustled through both their packs until he found two metal cups and filled them. "To our impending rescue," Oscar intoned.

"Yes," said Francis, "to our rescue."

"Do you believe we are safe here?"

"Yes, especially on this promontory. With the forest behind us, there is only a small chance of any wild animal attacking us. The large predators prefer to hunt on the open savannah."

"All the better then, I suppose," said Oscar contentedly, "to witness, from a front-row seat, the Great Rift Valley *au clair de lune*."

Oscar laughed then began to hum a few strains of Debussy as the fire flickered behind them and the moonlight illuminated the immense chasm before them. All the rough features of the land far below were discernible, as were the howls of the monkeys and nocturnal cries of other beasts of the forest behind them.

"This is a most remarkable and beautiful land," Oscar mused, settling in comfortably with his whisky and using his sleeping bag as a pillow. "But since our rescue does not appear to be terribly imminent, would you mind telling me how you came to live here? Do you have family? Are your parents still alive?"

Francis lay still for a moment, his head propped up upon his pack. He took a small sip of Scotch. "Oscar," he said, "I will tell you how I came to live here, if you like. But I warn you it is a strange story."

"All the better," said Oscar.

"Very well, then. Have you ever heard of Count Teleki von Szek?"

"No," he replied, "I'm afraid not."

"He was a Hungarian explorer, a geographer and sportsman and such, who set out to explore East Africa in 1887. He began his exploration in Pangani, along the coast in what is now Tanzania, and proceeded inland to the northwest, past Kilimanjaro, Lake Naivasha, and on up to Lake Rudolph, then back to Mombasa. It was an enormous expedition, financed by Teleki himself, and included hundreds of porters. Most of the secrets of East Africa had already been discovered, such as the source of the Nile and all that rubbish. The expedition seems to have been one of wanton killing of wildlife by white Europeans intent on proving themselves superior to the wildlife as well as the native Africans. In any case, there was a certain archaeologist along on this expedition who happened to be my great-great-grandfather. He returned to our ancestral home in Hungary with a small fortune in raw diamonds, which he left with my great-great-grandmother. He returned almost immediately to Africa on his own, presumably to recover the rest of the treasure he had apparently unearthed. Unfortunately, he was never seen again and to this day the origins of those diamonds are a mystery."

Francis paused to take another sip of whisky.

"And?" Oscar inquired, rather wide eyed, as he refilled his glass.

"Suffice to say that the suspicion that the rest of the diamonds lay somewhere within the Rift Valley was enough to entice his descendants to spend a good portion of their lives combing the entire valley, searching for the roots of the family fortune. Such expeditions were costly, however, and dangerous. Eventually, my grandfather, tiring of the hunt, set up shop in the diamond trade, establishing a flourishing business in Antwerp, Belgium, the diamond capital of the world. My father, however, found the diamond-trading business rather boring. The stories he had heard as a child about his great-grandfather, the archaeologist, stumbling upon a rich deposit of diamonds somewhere in the wilds of the Rift Valley posed too much of a temptation. We moved from Antwerp to Nairobi when my brother and I were quite young. Although he was heir to a considerable fortune, my father wasted much of it, financing extensive exploration efforts using modern seismological testing equipment and such, looking for the elusive diamonds. He refused to borrow money or seek investors, wanting to maintain exclusive control over the finds. He died twenty years ago in a plane crash near Mount Kenya. My mother then proceeded to drink herself to death within the next two years. It was a terrible time."

"Yes," said Oscar, "I imagine it was. But what then became of you and your brother?"

"Oh, we survived all right. My brother still runs the family diamond business in Antwerp, though he spends a fair amount of time in the Rift Valley, still hoping to come across the missing diamonds somehow. I, on the other hand, came to loathe the whole obsession with these diamonds. I saw how it had turned my father into a desperate man. As he grew older he became more bitter and despondent. The money dwindled. We moved from house to house, each a bit more modest than the previous one. Who knows how much he squandered.

"Often he would take my brother and me along on his excursions, retracing the route Count Teleki followed, more or less. We visited some terribly remote areas. I found the whole idea of digging through various types of terrain, searching for certain incredibly rare and very small minerals, exceedingly boring. What fascinated me were the people, the wildlife, and the plant life we encountered. To me, these were the Rift Valley's real gems. I began to learn the native languages and I found that my real passion in life was to learn more about this great valley

38

and its inhabitants. Once I was able to drive, I would venture out on my own to visit some of the Maasai settlements. The Maasai taught me many things, among them their tremendous knowledge of plants and their many uses. That's when I developed an obsession with botany, when I was about seventeen. The Maasai were especially friendly toward me and since then we have only grown closer. So I studied botany at the university, eventually receiving my PhD and, well, now here I am, a full-fledged professor. So there you have it."

"Fascinating," said Oscar, "absolutely fascinating. But surely there are others, cousins, perhaps?"

"All deceased, I'm afraid," said Francis. "There's an awful lot of family history in between, but the bottom line is that my brother and I are the sole remaining heirs to the family's diamond business, which, as I said, is run by my brother. I could care less about it, to tell the truth. I sold my share of the business to him not long after my parents died."

"And what have you done with the money, if you don't mind my asking?" said Oscar, filling his glass once again and chuckling to himself. "Invested it in all the plots of wild coffee plants here about?"

"Some of it, yes. Much is tied up in various small 'investments,' so to speak, in Maasailand, developing some springs here and there to improve their water supply, financing a number of small shops where the Maasai women can sell their jewelry to tourists. There's a fair amount in savings. But the majority is indeed invested in land. Have you ever heard of a Vavilovian center?"

"A what?"

"A Vavilovian center, named for the famous Russian geneticist Nikolai Vavilov. It is a geographic area where some of the world's agricultural crops were first discovered. There are about a dozen worldwide, mostly scattered about the equator. We are near one of the largest of these centers, where wheat, barley, sorghum, and coffee were discovered, among other commodities. I have purchased over a hundred parcels throughout the Rift Valley where these native species still flourish. It doesn't guarantee their survival, but it's the only way I know to assure they are protected from encroaching development. Cattle can, in theory, disturb them but most of these parcels, like the one below us, are rather inaccessible."

"Extraordinary," said Oscar as he rose and threw a few more pieces of wood on the fire. "You are quite a remarkable man, Francis. But how do you know your great-great-grandfather didn't simply return to wherever it was he found them, dug up the rest, and then headed for America or somewhere else to start life anew? Perhaps he feared the Hungarian government would get wind of his findings and confiscate them?"

"Believe me, Oscar, all those possibilities have been thought through and fully researched. The most likely conclusion is that he was killed somewhere along the way. Whether or not he discovered the diamonds on his own or came across them through some other means, perhaps illicitly, is completely unknown. The nearest diamond mines are in north central Tanzania, at Shinyanga. That's about six hundred miles from here, well off of Teleki's route. But it is not inconceivable that he could have encountered some tradesmen en route and robbed them. That, at least, is my theory. How all of this occurred without Teleki's knowledge is what puzzles me. In any event, it's all history and I do not concern myself with it. My brother, however, still believes that my reason for living here is to find the missing diamonds. He thinks this botany obsession is just a front, an excuse to roam through remote parts of the valley in pursuit of the family fortune. Try as I might to convince him that I am not the least bit interested in perpetuating this destructive family obsession and that the geology is simply not conducive to producing a diamond deposit, he persists in his suspicions of me."

"Sounds like sibling rivalry, if you ask me. Do you see one another often?"

"Too often for my liking, if you want to know the truth. My brother—Peter is his name—has 'diversified' his diamond business and become an extremely wealthy man. I do not respect the company he keeps or the type of business I believe he engages in."

Oscar raised a bushy eyebrow and eyed Francis somewhat curiously. He concluded from the bitterness in Francis's voice that he had probed far enough into the Dermenjian family's history. He filled his glass and offered the bottle to Francis, who declined.

"You are right, my friend," he said, "that is a strange story. You spurn the prospect of immense wealth to embrace a land and a culture that are as far removed from your Hungarian roots as I imagine any culture could possibly be. But I must say I can't blame you for falling in love with this valley."

Oscar had stood up and was walking slowly toward the edge of the promontory just beyond where they had made camp. The full moon had climbed far enough into the sky to flood the valley below, highlighting the various folds and ripples of the valley floor and its western escarpment. Oscar walked precariously close to the precipitous edge. Francis joined him. They stood there for several moments, watching and listening in silence.

"As amazing as your story is," said Oscar at last, "what I find even more amazing is that we are standing here gazing down at the proverbial cradle of humankind. To think that a few million years ago this place was crawling with early hominids, our ancestors, struggling to survive in what must have been frightful conditions. How do you think they did it, Francis? With so many ferocious creatures to contend with, and such a harsh landscape, how in the world did *Homo sapiens* ever manage to rise above the other creatures?"

"Well," said Francis, "looking about the world today, I suppose one could argue that humankind hasn't exactly risen above anything. We may well end up destroying the world before we're through, just another evolutionary blind alley, like the Neanderthals. But the remarkable evolution that took place here happened under much more favorable conditions, climatically, at least. Most of the fossil remains, such as those at Koobi Fora and Olduvai, were recovered from what used to be shallow lake beds. Evidently, there were quite a number of large, shallow lakes and more lush vegetation than exists today.

"But what ignited the incredible evolution of our species from our apelike ancestors to the cunning, creative beings we are today is a topic of much speculation. According to certain well-respected anthropologists such as Richard Leakey, our species grabbed the evolutionary upper hand, so to speak, by virtue of what's been called 'reciprocal altruism.'"

"I beg your pardon?" said Oscar.

"Reciprocal altruism. Meaning that the early hominids, perhaps even our prehominid ancestors, the australopithecines, developed an economy based on food sharing as opposed to solitary feeding. There is much evidence to support the notion that our ancestors lived in small, nomadic bands that roamed the countryside hunting and gathering food, but consumed it together at camps, many of which may have been along the shores of the lakes that occupied the Rift Valley in those days. The altruistic behavior of sharing food lends tremendous stability to a society. For instance, if one member of the band should fail to catch some game or find a supply of nuts, roots, or berries, others will provide. The favor is reciprocated when the same individual succeeds and others fail. Otherwise they might all eventually perish. For all the attention that the early stone tools receive as evidence of the emergence of a rational, thinking creature, I find it rather ironic

41

that the invention of a handbag with which to carry nuts, roots, and berries back to camp—probably made from leaves and twigs that are too ephemeral to be a part of the fossil record—is what no doubt propelled us on our remarkable evolutionary journey."

Oscar laughed quite loudly. "That's fantastic," he said. "You're saying that the first significant achievement of humankind was to invent a shopping bag to gather food from nature's warehouse of nutrition? Remarkable! No doubt it was invented by a woman!"

They both laughed at that as Francis nodded his head in general agreement. "Yes," he said, "it may well have been a woman. The fossil record seems to support the notion that men did most of the hunting while the women gathered more of the edible plants. It's still that way in most of today's hunting and gathering societies."

"So do you believe that the Maasai are the most direct descendants of these early hominids?"

"No, not at all. There is a fair amount of evidence to indicate that the Maasai moved to the Rift Valley several thousand years ago from up north, perhaps from Ethiopia. But it is their home now."

"So it is. You know," Oscar continued, "I can't seem to forget that boy, the one who was circumcised. His stoicism, his wandering off to spend the night alone in the bush, basically naked, giving away all of his belongings before entering manhood. I suppose that's an example of reciprocal altruism, giving away all of his possessions in anticipation of receiving others' possessions in return. I don't know, perhaps it seems crazy, but I feel a kinship with him. Here I am, approaching middle age and about to be married for the first and hopefully last time in my life, about to embark on what for me will be a completely new chapter in my life. Tell me, Francis, have you never married? You're not gay, are you?"

Francis laughed. "No, Oscar, I am not gay. I have had a few relationships with women but for some reason nothing has worked out. I suppose I should work harder at it, but then I am perfectly content being who I am, living the way I do."

"Bully for you, then," said Oscar. "But about that boy. I feel as though I, too, need such an experience, a chance to reflect upon the next stage of my life, to look back from where I have come and to prepare for my new commitment. Don't get me wrong now, I've already been circumcised."

He laughed and then became suddenly excited as he gazed along the Rift Valley below.

"Say, I'll bet you've been to Olduvai, haven't you?"

"Why yes I have," said Francis. "It's only about 150 miles to the south. You just follow the crevice of the rift down past Lake Natron and turn right at Ngorongoro Crater. Why do you ask?"

"Because that is where I would like to go before I marry, to see where the first traces of human life were found, to walk in the same earth that clung to the feet of our early ancestors, to connect, so to speak, with the real roots of humanity before I pass on my own genes. And perhaps, since I never had a father who could teach me, I could even glean some enlightenment regarding how to serve as a proper trustee of my own genetic endowment. Don't you think that would be a fitting pilgrimage?"

"Why yes, I suppose that for a man as concerned as you are about the survival of our species, a visit to such a place might be quite appropriate."

"Yes indeed, it certainly would, just to feel the magic of the place that gave birth to a species so all powerful and yet, pitifully, so shortsighted as ours. Alas, Francis, would you take me there? Not on this trip but sometime soon, when I return to this magnificent country? I would gladly pay all expenses."

"Damn the expenses, Oscar, it would be a great privilege. I'm planning a trip to Lake Natron this December. Perhaps you could join me then and we could just continue on to Olduvai. The road is a bit rough but certainly passable."

"That would be splendid—perfect, in fact. With luck, Elizabeth and I will be married in January. There will no doubt be numerous tedious preparations for the wedding, to which you are hereby most cordially invited. Elizabeth's mother, who detests me, by the way, will certainly insist that the wedding take place in Balgères, in southern France. She would be delighted if I were completely in absentia until the last detestable moment. Therefore, the timing would be perfect, assuming I can convince Elizabeth that my presence for the few weeks prior to the wedding is not needed."

"That may require some convincing. Am I to understand then that you and Elizabeth have yet to pick a precise date for your wedding? I believe most couples that are engaged to be married make all such arrangements many months ahead of time."

43

"Well," said Oscar, "we're not exactly engaged. You see, I just proposed to her two days ago."

"I'm sorry," said Francis, quite stunned. "But you were here, in Africa. Was she here, too?"

"No, she wasn't," he replied. "You see, I left her a voice mail, which contained a certain pointed question, if you know what I mean."

"You what?" shouted Francis, thoroughly in disbelief. "You proposed to her in a voice mail? Why, there's hardly a less romantic way to pose the question! Do you really think she will say yes?"

Oscar rubbed his forehead with his one free hand and then drained his glass. "By God," he said at last, "I don't know what the hell I'll do if she doesn't. I love her with all my heart and soul."

Francis stared at him. The two stood there for a moment or two in silence, watching the land far below as the full moon continued to rise above them.

"Well then," said Francis, raising his glass, "here's wishing you a warm and connubial greeting upon your return to Scotland."

"Aye," said Oscar softly, wiping one eye with his sleeve, "thank you so much. She just has to say yes."

Chapter 7

They awoke to the crackling of static from the radio. Francis rolled over in his sleeping bag and fiddled with the controls. It was the Kenyan National Police wishing to know their whereabouts. It was really quite simple. Just head west from Nairobi, then follow the eastern escarpment northward and look for their campfire about five miles south of Hell's Gate, on the southern flanks of Mount Longonot.

"You can't miss us. We are camped on a promontory just to the south of a deeply incised draw."

Oscar looked on with excitement.

"Excellent," said Francis, "thank you very much."

"How soon will they be here?" asked Oscar.

"It will likely be a few hours," Francis replied. "Hopefully no more than that. One never knows in such situations."

"Fantastic," said Oscar as he emerged from his sleeping bag. He took a deep breath. "Such wonderfully clean air. Feels as though it's crammed with vitamins, it's so pure."

"Well, you'd better breathe it in quickly," said Francis. "We need to rebuild the fire if they're going to find us."

Once they had a sizable blaze going, they sipped coffee and nibbled on some stale biscuits. The mist that had covered the valley floor earlier was dissipating, slowly unveiling the topography below. Francis explained that the valley floor dropped several hundred feet between Hell's Gate, just above Lake Naivasha to the north, and the area near Lake Magadi, where their journey had begun, about sixty miles to the south. Before them the valley floor was jagged and broken, looking as though it had been tossed up like the sea and then frozen in place. Farther south it became gradually wider and they could see farmland, with a few buildings scattered here and there, transected by a road that, as Francis explained, led across the Rift Valley to Narok. Beyond was a vast savannah that was still shrouded in mist, or was it smoke? Francis grabbed his binoculars.

"The Maasai are burning the grasslands," he explained, "to retard the invasion of thorn trees that, in that particular segment of the rift, constitute the climax vegetation."

"I beg your pardon," said Oscar. "What do you mean by 'climax vegetation'?"

"Sorry," he replied. "That's simply a term that describes the ultimate ecological steady state, after all of the various successional or seral stages of plant communities have been allowed to compete against one another without outside interference. After a fire, for example, whether it is set deliberately or not, the race begins again, so to speak. The grasses and herbs, whose seeds are either tolerant of fire or imported by the wind or animals, such as birds who leave them in their droppings, take hold first. Gradually, shrubs may begin to encroach, although herbivores may do them in when they are seedlings if the area is heavily grazed. Ultimately, however, the thorn trees will begin to take over, shading out the sun-loving grasses and herbs and finally dominating the landscape. As the trees have little value for cattle, the Maasai and other tribes will often burn the savannah to retard the succession. Am I being clear?"

"Yes, Francis, I understand completely. Otherwise the thorn trees would then become a climax species, just like us."

"I beg your pardon?" said Francis.

"The thorn trees would take over the valley floor just as *Homo sapiens* have taken over the world, controlling what grows in what places, where the sun may fall, and basically what may exist and what may not. Don't you agree?"

"I must admit I have never thought about our fate in those terms but, in an ecological sense, I suppose it is a valid concept. There are few places on earth that have not been affected to one extent or another by human activities. Yet the term has always been applied strictly to plant communities, usually an association of species that dictates what other plants may coexist in a subordinate yet stable relationship. But all of that can disappear in a moment since, as geologists are often prone to point out, life exists only by virtue of geologic consent. Look behind you, for example."

Oscar turned with a perplexed look and saw looming above them to the northeast a huge volcano that had been previously concealed by clouds.

"That is Longonot," said Francis, "now dormant but by no means extinct as volcanoes go. In order to get to this point, we climbed up through hundreds of years of ash laid down in successive layers from a few inches to several feet in thickness. The forest behind us exists only by virtue of the moisture that Longonot is able to steal from the clouds as they pass overhead."

The summit of Longonot was at least ten miles away. Yet it appeared so close that Oscar could not believe its immense presence had thus far escaped his notice.

"How tall is it?" he inquired.

"Over nine thousand feet, about four thousand feet higher than we are at present. Consider that Kilimanjaro is another ten thousand feet higher than Longonot and you may begin to appreciate the incredible geologic forces at work right beneath us."

"Believe me," said Oscar, "I can appreciate them."

They sat for some time in silence as shadows diminished and the heat began to rise. Francis and Oscar took turns with the binoculars, examining the landscape and its inhabitants, such as the various colorful birds that came to pick over their campsite. Soon they could see the air along the valley floor wavering. Lammergeyers, large African vultures, began soaring on thermals that rose from the base of the escarpment. Francis was measuring the flight of one such creature when he noticed another flying object in the distance.

"Look," he said, "there's a hot-air balloon. Should be a good day for sightseeing." He handed Oscar the binoculars.

"Yes," he said, "I see it. Whoever they are, they seem to be headed our way."

Francis retrieved the binoculars quickly. It was not immediately evident but Francis finally concluded that, yes, the balloon seemed to be heading straight toward them. "I wonder who that could be," he mused.

They took turns looking through the binoculars as the balloon continued its course in their direction. It was very colorful, with red and yellow diamonds patterned beneath a sky-blue dome. Gradually, they were able to distinguish two figures standing in the hanging basket, one clutching the propane control, the other peering back at them with his own binoculars. The latter put the binoculars aside and began waving.

"Good God," said Francis, looking stunned and suddenly pale. "It's Peter!"

"Peter?" queried Oscar. "You mean your brother, Peter?"

"Yes," said Francis, "the very one."

They stood speechless for several moments as the balloon approached slowly. Finally, it hovered over the clearing at the edge of the promontory. The roar of the propane jets died down as the gentleman at the controls lowered the flame.

"Hello there, dear brother!" yelled Peter. "Grab a rope, will you?"

Francis stepped forward and seized a long rope that Peter had tossed overboard. He tied it to a nearby shrubby tree and turned to face his brother, who was climbing out of the basket just as it settled to the ground.

"Hello, Peter," he said with an air of amazement. "What on earth are you doing here?"

"Coming to your rescue, as usual," he said with a laugh as he stepped forward and hugged Francis. "What have you done now? Finally run that Jeep into the ground?"

"More or less, I suppose. But before we get into how you happened upon us, I'd like you to meet a new acquaintance of mine, Dr. Oscar Newman."

Peter gave Francis a look of astonishment as he turned to greet Oscar. "My, my, Francis, you do keep interesting company. Certainly a refreshing change from the pastoralists with whom you normally associate. Peter Dermenjian, sir, pleased to meet you. May I congratulate you on your impending Nobel Prize?"

"Thank you, Peter," said Oscar. "I'm most pleased to meet you as well, particularly in these unusual circumstances. I trust you'll be offering us a lift?"

"Absolutely," he replied. "My companion, Dr. Meinz, and I intercepted your radio message this morning. As we happened to be in the vicinity, we volunteered to fetch you back to civilization."

"I see," said Francis, seeming rather subdued. "Very well, then. But are you certain that this balloon can accommodate all of us?"

"Quite comfortably," Peter replied, "but we're wasting fuel. Gather your things and let's be off."

It took only a moment or two for Francis and Oscar to extinguish the fire, collect their bags, and climb into the basket. Dr. Meinz, oddly attired in a faded blue suit, greeted them with a simple nod of his balding head. Peter untied the safety rope and climbed aboard. With a sudden roar of propane they were soon aloft. The balloon quickly climbed well clear of the promontory. There was no wind to speak of and Dr. Meinz repositioned a large fan attached to the rim of the basket so as to gently propel them in a more southerly direction.

Peter was right. The basket had ample room for the four of them, even Oscar, who lodged himself in a corner, clutching the sides. This was a new experience for him. He had long since conquered any fear of flying, yet the sensation of near weightlessness and the exposure to the elements made him almost giddy. Francis pointed out various natural features below, most notably Hell's Gate and Lake Naivasha in the distance, while Peter rummaged through a large ice chest. Within moments he produced a bottle of well-chilled champagne, glasses, and a plate of hors d'oeuvres. Once they had reached a suitable altitude, Dr. Meinz throttled back and the roar of the propane subsided.

"To your health, gentlemen," said Peter, passing the glasses around.

"Thank you," said Francis. "A bit early for champagne don't you think?"

"Nonsense," replied Peter, "not when in such distinguished company. Besides, according to what I've read, Dr. Newman rarely refuses a drink. Am I right?"

Oscar accepted his glass and smiled politely. "Certainly not genuine French champagne. Thank you."

Dr. Meinz, who still remained silent, accepted his as well. The foursome clinked their glasses together and sipped the delicate, bubbly liquid as they floated effortlessly, like a bubble themselves, over the great valley.

"Incredible, isn't it?" said Peter. "Meeting like this. I was going to phone you when we returned to Nairobi. However, fate has been so kind as to bring us together sooner than expected. And in such exquisite surroundings. But tell me, Dr. Newman, what brings you to Kenya? Surely you haven't been trying to interest my brother's Maasai friends in your birth-control business."

"Actually, he has been quite successful with the Maasai," said Francis on Oscar's behalf. "It's astounding."

"Really?" said Peter. "And who's next? The Turkana? The Afar? I dare you to approach anyone in the Danakil. They'd skin you alive."

"Perhaps," said Oscar, "and perhaps all their killing ways are keeping their numbers in check, so why bother?"

They were soaring over farmland now, with fields of well-organized row crops on the flat valley bottom and coffee plantations along the slopes on either side. Black people were working the fields and gathering the coffee beans.

"God bless the Kikuyu," said Peter. "These are people who understand how to carve a living from the land. Look how industrious they are, how productive. Quite a contrast to the Maasai, who squander thousands of acres on their filthy cattle and their scrawny sheep and goats. Look, to the south you can see them burning the savannah, polluting this magnificent air. When will the Kenyan government ever learn to control these fools?"

"That's enough, Peter!" said Francis, quite angered by his brother's remarks about the Maasai, which he knew were meant for him.

"It's quite all right," said Oscar. "Your brother has a valid point, at least with respect to stretching our resources to make do. No one really knows how many people the earth can sustain. Certainly, if people combine the forces of water, sunlight, and the soil correctly, we can produce more food for more people, perhaps for a longer time. But tell me, Peter, how long will it be before the soil's productivity has been mined? Before it is all eroded away? How long can we continue to augment the soil with nonrenewable petroleum-based fertilizers to make up the difference? What you're seeing below us here simply isn't sustainable. The Maasai, on the other hand, may have a better shot at survival in the long term, if they can control their numbers and if others would stop stealing their land. They seem to have achieved a balance between what nature provides and what they need as a people."

He winked at Francis.

"Let's forget the Kikuyu and the Maasai for a moment," said Francis. "I'd like to know what you're doing here, Peter, and since when have you taken up the sport of hot-air ballooning?"

"Well," said Peter, refilling their glasses with the last of the champagne, "it's quite simple. Dr. Meinz has always had a fascination with these contraptions. He used to give lessons in Germany. I told him there was no finer spot in the world than the Rift Valley for hot-air ballooning. Isn't that correct, Conrad?"

Dr. Meinz simply gave an affirmative nod.

"Then how is it," Francis continued, "that you were able to monitor our radio messages? That seems a rather odd coincidence."

"Yes, it is quite a coincidence, I suppose, but then safety is of paramount importance. We were simply trying various frequencies, listening for an up-to-date weather forecast, when we happened upon your transmission. Isn't that right, Conrad?"

Dr. Meinz nodded again, smiling. "Yes, that is correct," he said.

Francis looked at the two of them rather suspiciously. Oscar drained his glass, thanked Peter for the champagne and hors d'oeuvres, most of which he had consumed himself, and began to lift the lid of a large wicker basket. Peter quickly intervened.

"Please," he said, "allow me to take that."

He then placed the glass into an identical wicker basket next to the one Oscar had nearly opened. Francis immediately reached down and flung open the other basket. Inside was a large shortwave radio, a spotting scope, and various pieces of photographic equipment, including several long-range lenses.

"So, Peter," he said accusingly, "it looks like you've been eavesdropping on more than our transmissions. Let me guess, you're on your way toward Narok. No doubt you have an interest in what becomes of the Ugandan refugees."

"Have you lost your mind?" Peter said. "We're simply here to photograph the wildlife. Isn't that right, Conrad?"

Once again Dr. Meinz nodded affirmatively.

"Don't give me that nonsense," Francis said. "You never cared a damn about African wildlife. Only Father's obsession with the mythical diamonds ever interested you."

"Tut, now, let's leave our dear father out of this. And diamonds are my business. I never said it was I who was interested in the wildlife. Dr. Meinz happens to be a great photographer who has been studying up on the creatures of the Rift Valley. Why look, there go three ostriches. Do you see them?"

Dr. Meinz glanced down below, hardly with any keen interest. "Yes, I see them," he said. "Lovely creatures."

"But since you've inquired," Peter continued, "I do find the events in western Kenya rather interesting and rather upsetting—so many people being displaced so rapidly. It seems as though Uganda has simply ruptured at the seams and thousands of people are spilling over into Kenya. I suppose, Dr. Newman, that you would simply chalk this all up to excessive breeding, am I right?"

Oscar looked at Peter and paused before answering. "I understand a warlord or two is creating quite a bit of havoc," said Oscar. "But no, it really doesn't surprise me, given that the center of unrest is one of the most densely populated regions on earth."

"Perhaps," said Peter, "but what right do we have to pass judgment? Conflicts like these are as natural as can be. People have always fought one another and always will. It's our nature. Don't you agree, Francis?"

"Whatever you say."

"Now, don't be so sullen, brother. You're not worried about your poor Maasai friends being overrun, are you? After all, it's just a matter of time before civilization finally creeps in to fill that particular void in the Rift Valley's productivity."

"Enough!" said Francis. "I am sick and tired of your constant needling about the Maasai. The truth is, they are quite concerned. Just last week I passed through Mosiro. There are no intruders yet but you could hear gunfire far in the distance.

51

The Maasai pretend to be unconcerned but you can see the worry in their faces, especially the women."

"My, but you two do go at it," observed Oscar. "Has it always been like this?" Peter laughed. "It's all in good fun," he said, "isn't it, Francis?"

"Whatever you say, Peter."

Francis turned away. They were just passing over the Kedong Valley, heading for a small airfield about thirty miles west of Nairobi. Dr. Meinz gave the balloon a blast of propane and they rose again rather swiftly. The sun was still quite high. Oscar glanced at his watch and began to realize that within an hour or two he would likely be saying good-bye to Francis. There was a flight from Nairobi leaving for Paris at four.

The airfield soon came into view. Dr. Meinz guided the balloon gently to a landing just beyond a cluster of small planes. A Land Rover approached and from it emerged a young black man who quickly gathered up Francis's and Oscar's meager belongings. They thanked Peter and Dr. Meinz for coming to their aid and transporting them back to safety.

"Dr. Newman," said Peter as they were about to part ways, "there's one thing I must ask you."

"Go right ahead," Oscar replied.

"If birth control is, in your estimation, so vital to the survival of our species, why can't we simply rely on condoms? Do you really need to impose your IUD on all these women? It doesn't do anything to retard the spread of AIDS, does it?"

"Believe me, Peter," he replied, "I have nothing against condoms. They are vital to controlling the spread of AIDS among sexually active people. My only interest is in family planning. Are you married?"

"No," he responded. "Why do you ask?"

"Perhaps you own a swimming pool?"

"Yes, as a matter of fact I do."

"Then it's quite simple. After going to all the trouble and expense of building your very own swimming pool, you wouldn't want to have to don a wet suit every time you took a dip, would you?"

"I beg your pardon?"

"Never mind," said Oscar. "Thank you again for all your help."

Chapter 8

The heavy rain showed no sign of letting up. Elizabeth gathered her groceries, opened the car door, and made a run for it. But it was useless. By the time she reached the front door of their apartment, just blocks from the University of Glasgow, she was soaked. She entered dripping wet and set the soggy bags down on the table by the entry, mere seconds before they might have burst. She caught a glimpse of herself in the hallway mirror and paused to gaze at her own sorry reflection.

"What's the use?" she said aloud. "Why do I even bother? There's no one here to appreciate me even if I could manage to look decent."

As she was hanging her coat to dry, she noticed the telephone blinking at her. More messages.

"Good evening, this is Reginald MacArthur of the *Glasgow Daily Times*. I was hoping to chat with Dr. Newman. I'll try again later."

She pressed the delete button.

"Hello. Rodney McEwan here, *Belfast Telegraph*. I'd like a word with Oscar, could be an exclusive. Plenty of money in it. Ring you later."

And so on. She listened to them all, hoping one might just be Oscar himself. Finally, she heard his familiar voice.

"Hello, my dear. Oscar here, in Paris. I'm just wrapping things up and should be in late this evening. Don't bother coming to fetch me, I'll hire a taxi. I hope all's well. I've had a fantastic trip but I miss you terribly. Can't wait to be home. Love you."

End of message. Neither a hint of anxiety nor any mention at all of his proposal. Had it all been another tasteless joke?

She put away the groceries, put on the kettle, and sat down with the evening paper. Three teenagers murdered outside a pub in Manchester. Prime minister's wife suffers a heart attack. Unrest in Uganda. It was all bad news, once again.

Speaking of which, how would she break her own news to Oscar? Would it mean the end of their relationship? Would he accept her plea to leave things as they were? Is that what she really wanted? Or was it time to get serious about her life, to find a truly decent man with whom she could settle down, who would always be there for her and their children? Did such a man exist and could she ever find him if he did?

These were the same questions that had haunted her for days and, as she sat sipping her tea, continued to haunt. But one thing was certain. She would not, could not bring herself to marry Oscar.

Though she had little appetite, she reheated the stew that had once been the lamb she had been saving for Oscar's return. After a few bites she returned the rest of her modest serving back into the pot. She read until eleven, then flicked on the news. There were graphic close-ups of the murdered teenagers. A clip on the prime minister's wife. Then they shifted to a live scene at the Glasgow airport. Protesters were being held at bay by several police officers. Then Oscar came into view with a sea of reporters rushing at him, each one clutching a microphone.

"Dr. Newman," said the one who had managed to get his microphone in Oscar's face just slightly before the others. "Let me first congratulate you on being selected to receive the Nobel Peace Prize."

"Thank you," said Oscar as he smiled and waved at the ranting protesters, pretending they were his fan club.

"Obviously your efforts to lower birthrates are not universally appreciated. Were you surprised at being selected by the Nobel Committee?"

"Yes, I was quite astonished."

"Well then, what are your plans for the future, after receiving the Peace Prize?"

"My plans?" said Oscar, laughing as usual. "This may astound you all, but I plan to marry the woman I love and to focus my energy toward making babies of my own!"

And with that he was off, leaving the reporters with their mouths agape while the protesters continued to taunt. Elizabeth abruptly stood up and turned off the TV.

"You presumptuous bastard!" she screamed as she slammed her book to the floor. "Just try to find someone to have your babies. It sure as hell won't be me!"

With that outburst she ran to her bedroom, threw on her nightgown, and went to bed. But it was useless. She was far too angry to sleep. She returned to the sofa, folded her arms before her, and waited. Finally, she heard a car door slam, heard his footsteps and then the key as it turned the lock in the front door. She watched as the door slowly opened. There was Oscar with a ragged suitcase in one hand and a large bouquet of flowers in the other.

"Hello, darling," he said, standing dripping wet in the doorway as Elizabeth, still seated on the sofa, stared at him with fierce eyes.

"Hello, Oscar," she said rather frigidly.

"I brought you some flowers," he said.

"I can see that," she replied.

"Shall I put them in a vase for you?"

"No, that won't be necessary. Perhaps you should save your energy," she declared bitterly, "for making babies!"

"Ah," he said, "well then, I'll just set them here on the hall table."

Oscar set down his suitcase and removed his coat slowly, always with an eye on Elizabeth.

"So you watched the news," he said amid the deafening silence. "Just throwing them off stride, the pesky bastards. I hope you weren't offended."

Elizabeth glanced up at him. "Offended? Why should I be offended? You wander off to the ends of the earth for weeks and weeks, leave me that ridiculous voice mail, and then announce to the world before we've even spoken that not only are we engaged to be married but we're having babies as soon as you can 'focus' your energy. Well, I'll tell you where you can focus your energy, Oscar. Out that door."

"Elizabeth, please, calm down. I certainly meant no harm," he pleaded. "It's just that suddenly everything has become so clear to me." He approached her slowly, then paused to kneel before her as he took her hand in his. "I'm terribly sorry if I've been inconsiderate," he said, gazing into her eyes in a searching and yet adoring manner. "I suppose this Nobel business has shaken me a bit off of my foundations. But it means so little to me, next to you. Something happened to me on this trip. I realized more than ever before how much I love you, how much more important you are to me than anything else on earth, including my work and this damn Nobel Prize. Perhaps my methods seem crude but I am most sincere. Elizabeth, the only thing that really matters to me is you. Please say that you'll marry me."

She looked at him carefully, staring deep into his forlorn eyes, seeing the pain in his expression as he awaited her answer. She stood up and walked away, stopping only to stare out the window toward the lights of Glasgow in the distance. After what seemed an eternity to Oscar, she turned and spoke.

"Oscar," she said, "I'm afraid it won't work. I love you very much. You know that. But I can't marry you."

Oscar was still kneeling by the sofa. He closed his eyes and lowered his head, shaking it slowly.

"Please don't take it too hard," she continued. "The last thing I want is to come between you and your work. But it is hard enough being away from you as it is, and if it's children you want, you can't expect me to spend over half of my time as a single parent while you risk your life time and again traveling through some of the most dangerous places on earth. And you simply are not dependable. I've been waiting four weeks for you, double what I expected. You're always delayed and you always seem to find time to squeeze in some extra work, like this little jaunt to Paris. For all your talk, I'm really not the most important thing in your life. It's quite obvious. Don't you see?"

"Yes," said Oscar, finally standing, "I see perfectly well what you mean. And you are right, I would be a terrible husband and father if I were to keep traveling about the way I've done for these past ten years. But I must tell you about my trip to Paris."

"Please, Oscar," said Elizabeth, "I'm really not in the mood. However, I appreciate your taking my answer so well."

"Quite the contrary," he replied somewhat sternly. "I haven't taken it well at all. And if you think you'll be rid of me this easily, you've another think coming. I need to tell you about Paris. Come, sit down next to me."

She hesitated while Oscar made room for her on the sofa. She slowly moved in beside him. Holding her delicate hands between his, he began to relate the events that had just taken place.

"You remember Dr. Bayard, from the French Institute for Global Stabilization?"

"Yes," she replied, "vaguely."

"Dr. Bayard has been pestering me for years to allow his organization to become more involved in our operation. I suppose it was partly my enormous ego that refused to relinquish any control. But all that's changed."

"What do you mean?" she said.

"Well, I decided to pay him a visit in Paris on my way home. It went very well. The institute has agreed to take over the day-to-day operation of all of the clinics and to establish at least one hundred per year for the next ten years."

"What do you mean, 'take over'?"

"I mean they have agreed to all of my terms. I'll be a member of their board of directors, but as for the hands-on work, they will take care of it."

"Meaning?"

"Meaning that I will no longer be away traveling all over the world. An occasional trip to Paris, the usual speaking engagements, et cetera, but I plan to return to teaching and," he paused, stroking Elizabeth's long, light-brown hair, "to focus my energy on you."

Elizabeth stood up again and began pacing the floor, obviously quite stunned. "You mean you are giving it up? The Newman Foundation for a Sustainable Future has been turned over to the French? I don't believe it!"

"It's true, my dear," he said. "And speaking of turning things over to the French, I'm all yours now. Unless, of course, you are serious about shoving me out the door."

"Not just yet. Am I to understand," she continued somewhat angrily, "that you have singlehandedly relinquished control over the foundation? You might have at least consulted me, not to mention all the others."

"But my dear, I am consulting you. After all, I'm asking you to marry me. What more sincere form of consultation could there be? If you approve, then all's well."

"Oh, Oscar," she said, thrusting her arms to the ceiling in disbelief. "What on earth has come over you? Getting married is one thing, but selling out your entire foundation without even talking to those who will be most affected will infuriate the entire organization. What will happen to everyone?"

"No one will be fired. That was a prime consideration. As people move on, Bayard will replace them with people of his choosing. There will be very little disruption."

"And does that include me, your research assistant?"

"You may do as you wish. However, should you decide to marry me, I can assure you that you will have little time to devote to your career."

"And why is that?"

"Because," he said, suddenly rushing to her and hoisting her into the air with his massive arms, "I intend to consume you with love and devotion."

Oscar feigned an attack on her upper torso before burying his face in her neck as he slowly brought her down to earth. Elizabeth recoiled in laughter, then became more subdued as she stood again near the window.

"Oscar," she said, "when did you get this sudden desire to father my children?"

"Sudden desire?" he said, quite wide eyed. "Why, there's nothing the least bit sudden about it. I've always wanted to father your children. It just never seemed terribly practical. That's changed now. And so have I. I'm ready to take on different responsibilities, much more domestic ones."

"I see," she said. "What you mean is, you're getting old, and so am I. But to propose via voice mail certainly cheapens the occasion. Whatever came over you?"

"Elizabeth, I could not help myself. For some insane reason, all the pieces fell together this past week as soon as I reached Kenya. I was flying in a small plane over the Rift Valley, peering down at what is undeniably the cradle of humankind, when it hit me. For there below me countless generations of our ancestors had bred and multiplied, while the forces of evolution carved away at their genetic material and all that it transfixes, leaving the likes of you and me to rule the world. I realized quite forcibly that the only thing we can do that is of any significance whatsoever in this lifetime is to reproduce, to pass on our genetic material, our DNA."

Elizabeth stared at him, clearly stunned. "That's quite a statement from one who spends his entire life trying to evoke quite the opposite."

"Yes, but that's in number only. Everyone should have a shot at it, so to speak, at raising children. Anyway, when I reached Magadi, I had barely any battery left on my phone. I knew I'd be off the grid and it was my last chance for some time to reach you. And you know how I am. When I decide something must be done, then best it be done quickly."

"You really should stop to think sometimes, Oscar," she replied. "You are so impetuous."

"Yes, I am," he admitted. "But so be it. Enough of this diversion, let's cut to the chase. Is it yes, or the door?"

Elizabeth laughed, beginning to enjoy this tender torment. "Let me ask you this," she replied. "Would you be capable of dealing with my mother through all of this?"

"My dear, when it comes to marrying you, I am capable of dealing with anyone and anything, including your mother. Just so long as it's done and done fairly soon."

"And why the hurry?"

"Because we're going to either do it or not do it. I don't wish to spend months agonizing over a decision that seems relatively straightforward."

"Straightforward to you, perhaps. Have you thought about what our wedding would be like at Sainte-Marie? I made a promise to my father, you know. The press would have a field day with you being married in a Catholic church."

"Hell," he said, "I grew up Catholic. In fact, my mother once put me in a Catholic school. Take a look at these knuckles. I can still show you scars where the nuns smashed them with a ruler when I was a lad. They'd have to let me in."

"After a healthy confession," she teased. "But Oscar, have you really thought long and hard about the adjustments you'd need to make? Are you indeed ready to stay put, to tend to babies and their smelly nappies? Life would be quite different."

"Yes, believe me, I have thought about it long and hard. I am more than ready and willing. But it's not at all what I would consider a hardship. I wish you could have been with me when we visited the Maasai. Now there are people who know about hardship. One of our physicians, for example, Dr. Taylor, was called upon to circumcise a young lad of sixteen or so. It's a rite of passage into manhood, done at dawn, without anesthesia, in front of a large crowd. If the poor lad cries out or even winces, he fails the test and is completely ostracized. That rarely occurs, you see, because these lads have thought about this moment their entire lives. Before the ceremony, they give away all their belongings to friends and relatives. And so they enter manhood stark naked and penniless, not to mention foreskin-less, having withstood incredible pain simply by being mentally prepared for it. Now, if the Maasai can adjust to changes such as that, I can certainly adjust to living a warm, cozy life with you and our children."

"Ah," said Elizabeth, "and that's how you see yourself, giving everything up and, rather than being circumcised without anesthesia, having to face my mother at our wedding?"

Oscar laughed so hard the apartment nearly shook. "Very good," he said. "The point I was trying to make is that life is full of adjustments, some easy and some not. But settling down with you and removing the strain of constantly traveling about the world is about as pleasant an adjustment as I could imagine. That is, if you'll have me."

He stared apprehensively at his beloved. Elizabeth pursed her lips, her chin trembling slightly.

"Oh, Oscar," she said at last, moving closer to him. "I can't believe you did this for me. It's not right."

"Now, now," he said as he folded his arms around her, "I did it for us. For you and me and, with a little luck, for our children."

She looked at him with an expression that conveyed relief, puzzlement, and tenderness. "With luck," she said, breaking into a large smile, "and a little focus."

She raised her mouth to his and they kissed long and deeply. She loosened his necktie and he, in turn, helped her off with her robe as he escorted her to the bedroom. They made love rather tenderly, as they had always done, but with a certain sense of conviction that seemed to say with more power than any words could convey that yes, the wedding plan was on after all.

"You're beautiful, my dear," he whispered once their passion had crested and was slowly receding. "Would it be impertinent of me to presume that this warm reception constitutes a positive response to my recent inquiry?"

He looked at her intently. This time she smiled but did not laugh.

"Oscar," she said at last, "I would love to have your children."

"Then you will marry me?"

"Of course I will, you silly bull."

They embraced again and kissed each other gently.

"Thank you," said Oscar, beaming like a harvest moon on a cloudless night. "Ah, I just remembered," he continued, "I have something for you. Wait right here."

He left the bedroom but returned shortly with a small box, which he handed to Elizabeth.

"I was going to show this to you earlier but in the heat of battle, or whatever, it slipped my mind."

She opened it slowly and, in the dim light from her reading lamp, saw the sparkle and glistening of diamonds. Oscar told her to look at the underside. The name "Elizabeth" was engraved on it.

"It's a beautiful ring, Oscar."

She studied every stone carefully. There were seven in all, six small diamonds circling one large one. Oscar looked on, stroking her hair once more.

Soon they were asleep in each other's arms, resting peacefully, almost blissfully, until another reporter called much too early in the morning. Oscar told him as politely as he could to bugger off and then disconnected the phone.

After they spent another hour nestled in each other's arms, Oscar rose and made them both coffee, which they sipped tranquilly in bed. Elizabeth continued to examine her diamond ring, watching it shimmer in the sunlight that streamed in from the east-facing window.

"It's exquisite," she said. "I've never owned a diamond. In fact, I was beginning to think I never would."

"Elizabeth, my dear," Oscar replied, "I'm certain that if I were to suddenly disappear, for good, you would have gentlemen by the dozens lining up at your door with diamond engagement rings. But speaking of diamonds, I must tell you about this extraordinary fellow I met in Africa, Francis Dermenjian. He and his brother—a lout, in my opinion—are sole heirs to a fortune in diamonds ostensibly discovered somewhere in the Great Rift Valley. And while they are heirs to a fortune, they have never found where the original family diamonds came from!"

"Oscar, what on earth are you talking about?"

He proceeded to relate aspects of his most recent journey, highlighting the episodes concerning the Maasai as well as the sudden appearance of Melanie Woo, the reporter, and his astonishing rescue by Francis's brother, Peter. Having constructed a miniature Rift Valley by rearranging various folds in the sheets between them, he traced the route he and Francis had taken, pointing out Lake Magadi, the location of the circumcision, the rescue site, et cetera.

"In sum, my dear, it was a remarkable journey. But above all, it was an awakening. One that was long overdue. I saw very clearly that I have been derelict in fulfilling my primary function on this earth, which is to pass on my genes. In limited quantities, of course, and to who knows what end ultimately? But that is part of the human condition, is it not? Our faith that if we procreate, future generations will thank us."

"I wouldn't bet on it," Elizabeth replied, "but it's worth trying, I suppose. After all, human nature seems to insist on it."

"Incessantly, I'm afraid," he replied, stroking her soft cheek with his large, hairy hand and feeling for her nearest breast with the other. It was but a moment before they were locked together in another heated embrace, their bodies rapidly transforming the miniature Rift Valley Oscar had formed in the sheet beneath them into a complex series of very flat cotton escarpments.

Afterward Elizabeth arose, showered, and dressed, then fixed them some scones and leftover lamb stew. Oscar, who had lingered in bed, finally ventured to the table. He thanked Elizabeth for preparing such a nice meal and immediately resumed his discourse on the Rift Valley. Elizabeth sensed from his tone of voice and his rapid speech that he was leading up to something she probably did not want to hear. At last, however, he turned the conversation to their wedding plans.

"So, my dear," he resumed, "I was thinking that if we left for Balgères after the Nobel ceremonies, that would leave about three weeks before our wedding."

"But Oscar, we haven't even spoken to my mother about all of this. We can hardly make any definite plans just yet."

"Of course, my dear," he said, "but let's suppose that we were to be wed in early January. Do you think you would need my services during those few weeks before the wedding? Wouldn't it be better, quite honestly, if I were to be somewhere out of the way while you and your mother worked out all the details of the wedding plans?"

"Hold it right there," Elizabeth said sternly. "You just told me not more than a few hours ago that you were through traveling all about, that you were 'ready and willing' to stay put. Now here you go again. Just what are you talking about?"

"It will be but a short trip and it has nothing to do with my work. It has to do with me. I must go back to the Rift Valley, to walk upon the same earth that our earliest ancestors walked upon. I cannot tell you why. It's some sort of rite of passage, I suppose. But it is very important to me. Something began to happen to me down there, and I would like to finish with it before I wed. I shall be in the best of company, with Francis Dermenjian, a fellow of exceptional integrity and a walking geography text to boot."

Elizabeth stared back at him with suspicious eyes. "I'll agree to talk about it," she said firmly, "but that's all I'll agree to."

Chapter 9

The weeks passed slowly for Maxwell Taylor as he waited anxiously for help from Nairobi, which, as he'd come to expect, never arrived. It wasn't that he really wanted some help. It was just knowing that someone was about to invade his life again, someone with whom he would spend a great deal of time, someone who would be, in short, a complete stranger.

The number of Maasai women who visited him had declined significantly. There were, in fact, days when he saw no one. It was during one of these idle periods that he ventured off to check on a herdsman he'd stitched up the week before. The man had been gored by a warthog while trying to protect one of his calves.

When Max arrived at the manyatta, there was no one. All was abandoned. The slurry of cow dung and mud plastered on the roofs of the houses was all cracked and weathered to a light gray. Somewhat like the wildebeest, the migration of the Maasai was afoot. He realized it was time for him to be moving on as well.

Driving back in the Scout, he watched the dry landscape pass quickly by, waiting for a gazelle or some other large creature to leap in front of him, but none emerged. It seemed as though all the wild animals had left as well.

Max found his thoughts drifting off to other realms and eventually settling on vivid memories of Melanie Woo as she'd appeared to him the morning of the circumcision, her face and figure as clear in his mind's eye as they had been in the moment itself. He wondered where her migrations might have taken her and if she and Edward were still reporting on the conflict in Uganda. And he couldn't help but wonder what else they might be doing.

He turned in early that evening and fell into a delightful yet disturbing reverie. He and Melanie were dancing slowly around a fire. They were surrounded by moran, some of whom were holding spears while others held forceps with Newman Inserts in them. He was trying to motion them away and move closer to Melanie's gently swaying, barely clad torso when something awakened him. As he sat up he felt something wet on the mattress beside him. Then the loud beating on the roof of the tent told him it wasn't just rain, it was a deluge. The short rains, long overdue, had finally arrived. He moved the cot to avoid one leaky spot only to find another.

To his surprise he received a transmission shortly after 7:00 a.m. saying that a fellow American, a Chris Olson, would be along the following morning to help guide him to his next destination. He should be ready to leave at that time.

He listened as a young African woman, or so he presumed by her accent, read a message to him in rather crude English. He interrupted several times only to find that she had no information other than what was written on the computer screen in front of her. She was merely part of the foundation's answering service, following through on orders. Over and out.

"Incredible," he muttered to himself.

In his last communication, they had said he'd have at least a week's notice before the move. Fortunately, he had already begun packing. With so few women to treat, he had made good use of the spare time, sensing that the move was imminent. Still, wrestling with the large main examination tent on his own, in the pouring rain, did little to soothe the anger he bore toward the Newman Foundation for a Sustainable Future.

He spent all day carefully breaking everything down and packing it all away, wondering why this Chris Olson hadn't been sent a day earlier to help him. He understood why the following morning when a Land Rover arrived and a young woman in her mid-twenties hopped out from the passenger side.

"Fucking mud," she exclaimed as she alighted on the ground, only to have it swallow her up to her ankles.

"Hello," said Max. "You must be Chris Olson, a fellow American."

"Close. Try Christine," she said, "and you're Dr. Taylor, I presume."

"That's right. Max, to you."

Never had it crossed his mind that Chris Olson might be a Christine, and certainly not a pretty blond Christine with a certain Southern Californian spoiled-child air about her. She was wearing khaki shorts and a UCLA T-shirt under a hooded rain parka. The driver was a young Kenyan who wished them luck getting to their destination. As he drove off his tires spun and slithered in the sea of mud that had once been the terra firma of Maasai Clinic Number One.

"Well," said Max, watching the Land Rover disappear, "I'm glad you're here. There's no way I could find my way to wherever it is I'm going on my own. I trust you know where that is."

"Yeah, more or less. I should have been there a week ago."

She walked slowly through the mud to the Scout and threw her pack inside. Max stared at her, trying to avoid the temptation to check out her tan, slender legs as she leaned through the back of the Scout to make sure her pack was secure. The legs won out. They were fabulously well proportioned, shapely but not too muscular. His faced tightened up as he quickly looked away.

"I planned my whole schedule around getting back to Kalema before the rainy season set in," she said as she turned around. "But now we have to cross this godforsaken valley in the rain and mud. I hope you've got a winch and a good radio because we're probably going to need them."

"Yes," he replied, "I've got a winch and a good radio. You don't work for the Newman Foundation, do you?"

"No, I'm not working for the Newman Foundation, thank you. Apparently, somebody found out that I needed a lift to Kalema and you needed directions to David's, which is kind of on the way. Someone put two and two together, so here I am. You got plenty of gas?"

"Yeah, about fifty gallons. Mud tires, too. This rig will get us there okay."

"It better," she replied. Max watched as she jumped into the passenger seat and slammed the door shut. He checked to make sure everything was secure on top of the Scout before climbing aboard and starting the engine.

"So who is David?" he inquired as they worked their way through the mud toward the main track leading back toward Lake Magadi.

"He's a missionary. Apparently, he knows where you're supposed to go."

"Oh," said Max, "and how does he come to know that?"

"How would I know? I guess he knows Oscar Newman and all about your clinic."

"A missionary? Oscar doesn't make friends with too many missionaries, from what I hear."

"Don't worry, David's very reliable. He'll know where you're supposed to go."

"I see. So you know him."

"Yeah. He's been out in that part of the Rift Valley for years. He runs a school for the Maasai."

"Ah, that explains it. Oscar generally contacts the school districts wherever he tries to set up clinics. They know more about local politics than anyone."

Max was suddenly feeling much better, trusting that there was someone out there who knew where he was supposed to go and evidently knew the Maasai as well.

"So what's going on in Kalema?" he asked.

"I'm working on my PhD in anthropology through UCLA. I've been studying the Maasai women for nearly two years now, trying to figure out why the hell they put up with being so totally repressed by their men. I just spent a month in the States trying to get my financing sorted out."

"Ah," he said, once again at a loss for words.

"If you really want to help them control their birthrate," she added, "I'd start with the men."

"Really?" he said.

"Yeah," she continued, "especially the moran. Vasectomies all around for starters. Castration might be the answer."

"No kidding?" he replied. "Well, I very nearly did castrate one of them."

"You did?" she said, her eyes wide. "What happened?" For the very first time she seemed interested in something Max might have to say. And now she was actually looking at him, her pale-green eyes wide and waiting for answers. Though trying to keep his eyes on the road, he couldn't help stealing a glance at her soft, well-proportioned nose and small but delicate lips. All in all, a very pretty sight. He gripped the wheel tighter and pressed slightly harder against the accelerator. He told her about the circumcision ceremony, about Oscar's visit, and somehow managed to leave Melanie Woo out of the story altogether, though he did make mention of a reporter.

They reached Magadi by noon, picked up the latest weather report, and continued westward, hoping to beat the next storm front that was due in.

They crossed the causeway that divided Lake Magadi into two lobes of caustic hell, bodies of water that were saturated with soda that bubbled up from the bowels of the earth, creating an environment fit for only two things, soda miners and flamingos. To the south mounds of soda dredged out by the Magadi Soda Company loomed like small white starch volcanoes over the eerie lake bed, which was stained red with algae. In the distance they could see the silhouettes of a few lanky pink flamingos.

They were but a few miles past Magadi when it began to rain again. The Scout was already moving much more slowly than normal.

"It's a different kind of soil out here," said Christine. "It sticks like glue."

"No kidding," said Max. "I can see why you wanted to get across the Rift Valley before the rains."

"Beating the mud isn't the real reason I wanted to get back there," she said. "I needed to be there when the Maasai started to move down to the lowlands. I needed to watch how the decisions were made about where and when to go, to see what part, if any, the women play in the decisions about the move and how to go about it."

"Really?" said Max. "And just how would you determine all that?"

"It doesn't matter. They're probably gone by now."

They drove for another hour or so, the rain picking up now and then but for the most part refraining from any cloudbursts like those of the day and night before. The road was passable but only at a very slow speed that accommodated all of the deeper ruts and chuckholes along the way, all of which were filled with the glue-like mud. The tents and other equipment lashed to the roof sloshed from side to side as the Scout rolled and careened its way toward Kalema. But Max finally had to pull to a halt, for the road had suddenly disappeared altogether.

The rains of the past few days had coalesced into a serious gully washer that had blown away the rusty metal culvert that used to guide the water safely beneath the roadway. All the rock and dirt that had surrounded it were gone as well. Instead of a road there was a chasm ten feet wide and three feet deep. Through it ran a torrent of brown water.

They both stepped out and walked slowly to the edge of the stream channel. The banks were full.

"We might have to wait this out," said Max. "There's no way to get across with the water that high and running that fast."

"What if it keeps raining? It could get higher, you know."

"Yeah, I guess that's possible," he said. "Let's take a look downstream, see if there's a place to cross." He walked over to the Scout and pulled out a rifle.

"What's that for?"

"Protection, what else? Don't you ever carry a gun out here?"

"No, never. I've been out in the bush a lot and I've never had any trouble. I don't like guns."

"I don't like them, either. I just feel safer with one whenever I venture out into lion country."

67

"Suit yourself," she said, shaking her head. "Just don't aim it near me."

They walked about half a mile, finding that the stream channel only began to cut deeper into the earth. They turned back and headed upstream. Thick riparian shrubs obscured their view of the stream itself for the most part. Finally, they found an area of braided channels where the water was lower but the stream was over a hundred feet wide.

"Hard to tell where the main channel is," said Max.

They looked around. The water closest to them swept by in a gurgling channel about a half-foot deep. It carried dead leaves and small branches and a silt load that turned it a light brown. Max knelt down and dipped his hand in the stream.

"Amazing stuff," he muttered.

"What's amazing?" Christine responded.

Max looked suddenly embarrassed. "Uh, water," he said hesitantly. "It's like the blood of the earth. Draining away the dead leaves, all the tired old cells, which feed the healthy ones downstream."

Christine stared at him. "You really are a doctor, aren't you?"

"Yeah, I'm afraid so."

"Sounds like you think the earth is just a big liver or something."

"I guess you could say that, with a bad case of cirrhosis. Actually, it's more like a heart, a heart that beats every time the earth spins around."

Christine gave him a look that made Max wonder if she was questioning his sanity. "Okay, now you've lost me," she said.

Max stood up and looked at her quite seriously. "Well, the earth heats up in the daytime and cools off at night," he said. "The heat evaporates the water, making clouds, and the coolness condenses the water, making rain. It's like a big pump, and all life depends on it."

She looked at him with raised eyebrows. "I think you've been out here on your own for too long," she said.

Max considered the comment. "You may be right about that," he replied. "But we have a little predicament here. I think this spot is probably our best bet. I'll check it out."

He took off his shoes and waded out into the water, crossing each braid of the larger stream until he reached the other side. The water never reached above his knees.

"Let's give it a try," he shouted as he headed back toward Christine, who stood with arms folded, looking skeptical.

"I hope you know what you're doing."

"So do I. The bottom's a little soft in places but we should be able to make it."

Fortunately for both of them, he was right. The Scout crept deftly across the various stream channels, sinking a few times to a precarious depth but always managing to regain traction until they emerged from the potentially perilous waters and found drier ground. Within minutes the Scout nudged up the side slope of the roadway they had left hours earlier.

Chapter 10

They encountered no other major obstacles though progress was excruciatingly slow. The gathering clouds, threatening at times, finally gave way to full-blown sunshine as they approached the Ewaso Ngiro. They had seen a number of Maasai as they drove along and now they were seeing more and more.

"Stop," said Christine.

"What?" said Max. "Here?"

"Yes, right here."

So Max stopped and Christine jumped out of the Scout and ran into the brush along the roadside.

"Where the hell are you going?" he yelled. As she didn't respond, he assumed she was simply answering nature's call. But ten minutes went by and then fifteen. He was about to go look for her when she suddenly emerged from the brush with three Maasai women.

"I found them!" she said, beaming.

"Found who?"

"My friends, the Maasai I have been studying. This is Elisa, Kipu, and Molema. I looked in the rearview mirror just back there and saw them crossing the road. Their new manyatta is a mile or so to the north."

Max said hello as Christine removed her pack from the Scout. Her Maasai friends chatted incessantly and seemed genuinely pleased to see her again.

"So this is it?" said Max. "You're bailing out on me already? Where the hell am I supposed to go?"

"Oh, you'll find it. Just go another ten miles or so until the road forks. Stay left and go about one more mile till you see an old brown building. That's David's school. I'm sure he's expecting you. Please say hi for me, okay? And let him know I got back all right."

"Yeah, sure," said Max, "no problem." He cleared his throat. "Guess I'll probably run into you out there somewhere," he continued, pointing to the bush in general that surrounded them.

"I'm sure you will. Hey, thanks for the lift. It was an adventure."

She laughed and then walked off into the brush with her Maasai friends, never pausing to look back at Max, who sat for some time in the Scout, tapping his fingers on the steering wheel.

"Unbelievable" was all he could say.

Fortunately, Christine was right. The road was in better shape and the fork in the road was obvious. Now, as he headed in a southerly direction, the number of Maasai walking beside the road was increasing and Max was happy to see them. He waved as he drove by, seeing more and more cattle as well and, in general, more and more signs that began to suggest there was a human civilization within these wildlands after all.

David's schoolhouse was a modest single-story building that stood off on the east side of the road, about a hundred yards into the brush. Max followed a faint set of tracks leading up to it. He stopped in front and looked for any signs of recent habitation. All was still. Evidently, school was not in session.

As Max stepped down from the Scout, a man emerged from a door in the side of the building. He was a white man wearing a dark robe, a dark cap, and a dark beard. A bit portly, he was, unlike Oscar, of medium height.

"Hello," said Max, "you must be David."

"Yes," he said as they shook hands. "I am Father David Sebastian, at your service. I trust you are Dr. Taylor. I've been expecting you. Please come in."

Max thanked him and followed him inside. He seemed quite friendly, speaking with a deep, soothing voice and a heavy foreign accent. "Are you French?" said Max.

"Yes," he replied. "But come. Have a seat and I'll pour you a drink. You have had a long journey."

He led him back to his private quarters, which consisted of a single room with a large window that looked out onto the savannah. There was a sleeping loft above and below it a kitchen area with stove, sink, and a small refrigerator.

"You've got electricity?"

"There are solar panels on the roof. I use lanterns for lighting and usually wood for cooking. The solar panels were a gift from Oscar."

"Really?" said Max. "How did you get to know him?"

"I helped him with the Kenyan government when he first started talking about a mobile clinic to deal with the Maasai."

"Oh?" said Max, looking even more perplexed as he studied the robe David was wearing. "But, uh, aren't you Catholic?"

"Yes, more or less. Doesn't matter. In any event, that's how I met Oscar. But please, have a seat. What can I pour you?"

"Anything cold would be good, thanks."

David reached into his small refrigerator and handed Max a cold beer.

"Incredible. Thanks, I haven't had a beer in months."

They sat outside on a small veranda attached to the back of the schoolhouse. It was late afternoon. The land rolled away gently toward a small creek bed obscured by thick brush. Many colorful birds darted in and out of the bushes as Max told David about his journey across the Rift Valley with Christine, not forgetting to pass on her salutation. David nodded and said he was glad she had made it back safely.

"But tell me more about yourself, if you please," said David. "I imagine that you have found working among the Maasai to be interesting, if not challenging?"

He spoke like a Frenchman, turning what would otherwise be a statement into a question.

"Very interesting and very challenging. But the most challenging part is Oscar, or at least the foundation. I guess I expected to have a little more contact with them. Other than getting a load of supplies from them every couple of months, I don't hear a peep from them."

"That's Oscar for you. The foundation operates on very little overhead, often depending on favors from acquaintances like me to keep his clinics running smoothly."

"But he never mentioned you," said Max, hesitating, "and you're a Catholic."

"Yes, I believe we've been over that. Look, I saved enough hot water for you to take a shower if you like. Would you like to clean up while I prepare a little supper?"

"That would be great."

David pointed the way to his crude shower stall. The water was a mere trickle, but it was quite hot and Max was able to cleanse himself more thoroughly than he had in weeks. He combed his hair, even trimmed his scraggly beard before joining David back in the inner sanctum.

"I trust you eat meat?" said David.

"Absolutely," said Max, seeing that the table was set and a rather dusty bottle of wine had been opened.

The meal featured roast leg of warthog served with a dark gravy that mingled with fresh potatoes and excellent bread that David had baked himself. The wine was a well-aged Château Margaux.

"I can tell you're a priest," said Max. "I feel like I've died and gone to heaven. That is one of the best meals ever. Do you always cook like this?"

David laughed. "Only when I have a special guest. But I do enjoy cooking, and eating." He reinforced the last point with a gesture toward his midsection. Once Max had finished mopping his plate with another slice of bread, David poured them each a small glass of cognac.

"So tell me," he said, "how does it feel to spend all of this time out in the wild, alone with the Maasai?"

Max studied his glass. "It's pretty amazing," he said. "I can't believe that less than a year ago I was just one more doctor running around Los Angeles as fast as I could from patient to patient, from my office to different hospitals, spending hours fighting freeway traffic when I could have been saving lives. But I can't say I miss it. I like the Maasai. And they seem to like me okay."

"So I've heard."

Max looked surprised. "You have? How?"

"I heard that you circumcised a young boy and that his people were very grateful."

"News travels fast."

"Yes. Stories like that travel well. But you have some family somewhere, yes?"

"Had some family, for a while, anyway. My wife and I separated about a year ago. The divorce papers were signed just before I left to come here. But I suppose you heard that, too."

"I did, in fact. That is what concerned Oscar most about you, to be quite honest. He wasn't sure if you'd be able to handle the isolation, given what you've been through."

"Actually, I came here to try to get away from women for a while," said Max as David refilled his glass. "I need some time to get over this divorce. But it's not that easy. You see, I met these two women. Well, actually, Christine's one of them. The other one was a reporter, Melanie Woo. Just between you and me, they are two of the most attractive women I've met in a long time. Look, I know you're a priest, but heck, I was married for five years."

"I see," he said. "But when it comes to women, we all must learn to manage, somehow. Even me."

They both laughed.

"The amazing thing is," Max continued after another healthy swig of cognac, "that's what it's all about, isn't it? That's why I'm here, to try to do something to help prevent our all-powerful sex drive from dooming us and all other species to a completely unsustainable future. And you know how sexually active the Maasai are."

"Probably no more active than most societies, but then what would I know?"

Max laughed again. "Yeah, well, sometimes I lie awake at night and I can hear the Maasai cattle bellow and the wild cats cry and I know the Maasai are busy finding each other and clawing at each other and making love, and sometimes it seems like the entire Rift Valley is just teetering on the edge of a huge orgasm. Especially when the moon's out, when it's easier for them to find each other and everyone's acting a little crazy anyway."

David shook his head and smiled. "Listen," he said, "we've a big day ahead of us tomorrow. I'm taking you to your new location where you can set up again. I therefore suggest we get a good night's sleep. You look like you could use one."

Max smiled and then lowered his head. "No doubt about that," he said. "And from the way I've been talking, the sooner the better. Thanks for a great dinner."

David showed Max to a cot up in the loft, not far from his own bed. It took but a moment before David was fast asleep and snoring in a low, resonating patter. Max tossed and turned, fading into sleep but awakening time and again to David's sudden snorting.

Sometime toward early morning he awoke to the sounds of what he presumed to be a large truck going by. But then he realized that his bed was quivering far more than could be accounted for by a passing truck. The rumbling quickly subsided and he realized, as years of inbred Southern California panic receded, that he had just felt a moderate earthquake. David snored on, oblivious to the earth's contortions, and eventually, Max succumbed to his fatigue. He awoke to the smell of freshly brewed coffee and heard David shuffling about down below while he languished in his cot.

He was drifting off when again he heard a familiar rumbling, like another truck. He sat upright in his cot, listening attentively as another jolt of adrenaline raced through him. An aftershock? Then he realized it really was a truck. He heard the engine cut out and a car door slam. Then footsteps and the front door opening.

"David!" said a familiar voice. Creeping quietly to the railing at the edge of the loft, he peered down as Christine entered and ran to David. She gave him a huge hug, one that lingered far too long.

"Oh, I missed you so much," she said.

David stepped back and straightened his arms, holding her soft shoulders between his large furry hands. "I've missed you, too," he said somewhat nervously, glancing up to the loft only to see Max quickly retract his head from view.

"The refugees, did you know they're moving into Maasailand up north?"

"Yes, I know," he replied, "these are difficult times. We must talk."

But before they could talk any further, Max announced his presence with a loud yawn from up above. He descended the steep staircase while buttoning his shirt.

"Good morning, Christine. How in the world did you get here? And what's this about refugees moving in?"

"Road crew," she said. "I spotted them this morning as they were out looking for washouts. They let me borrow a truck for a while. And it's true. The refugees are why I came to see David."

Max walked toward the stove to pour himself a cup of coffee. David smiled, looking a trifle embarrassed.

"Hey, did you guys feel that earthquake last night?" said Max.

"No," said David. "Are you sure it was an earthquake?"

"It was. I felt it," said Christine.

David laughed to himself.

"What's so funny?" said Max.

"Perhaps it was merely the Rift Valley," he responded, "having another orgasm."

Chapter 11

Oscar, draped in a black woolen overcoat, walked slowly toward Tobermory Manor. The sprawling red-brick building, trimmed in white, featured a modest gold cupola in the shape of a thistle. It stood atop a gentle rise that afforded views all the way back to the harbor. Oscar mounted the steps leading to the ornate entry and made his way inside.

"Hello, Dr. Newman. Congratulations are in order, I believe."

"Thank you, Isabelle," he replied to the receptionist, a redheaded woman in her forties whom Oscar had known for well over a decade. "How's Mother?"

"Anxious to see you, I would imagine."

"Right," he said as he signed in. "I'll just go see her, then."

The nurses in attendance all smiled and said hello as he walked by. The door to room 108 was open, as if they were expecting him.

"Hello, Mother," he said as he entered. "Happy birthday."

Eleanor Newman sat in her special chair by the window, wrapped in a standard hospital gown, holding her head off to one side and staring at the wall. From the side of her mouth a bit of drool hung down, ready to join the pool of spittle already collected in the stainless-steel bowl anchored to the chair below. There wasn't a hint of recognition or any sign whatsoever that Eleanor Newman was "at home."

"I have some big news," said Oscar as he set a bouquet of flowers in a vase next to her bed. "I'm leaving for Oslo today. I'm to be given the Nobel Peace Prize."

Still no reaction, not that Oscar expected one. For ever since the stroke Oscar had operated on the assumption, however ill founded, that although his mother could no longer speak or evince any emotion whatsoever, she could still quite possibly understand all that was said to her perfectly well.

"And afterward," he continued, "I'm going to Africa, back to the Great Rift Valley. It's an amazing place. I suppose you may be wondering why but it's all because, when I return from Africa, I'm going to marry Elizabeth. It's a bit difficult to explain, I suppose, but Elizabeth and I would like to start a family, odd as that may seem."

More silence. He wiped her chin with a wad of tissue.

"And the idea frightens me, to be quite honest. I never knew my father, so I don't have much to go on. I mean, what does it take to be a good father? How do you go about it? Well, I thought, why not take a trip back to the Rift Valley, the place where it all started. I believe it will help me to prepare myself mentally, emotionally, and, I daresay, spiritually for this whole notion of procreation."

Much to his amazement, she blinked.

"Mornin', Oscar," came a voice behind him. He turned to see another familiar face, Tommy's wife, Ethel, who had been working at the manor for over ten years.

"Good morning, my dear," he cried. "Mother just blinked!"

"Did she now? It does happen, you know. Tommy said ye'd be comin' by. The old girl's doin' jes' fine."

"I suppose," said Oscar. "Well, I hate to leave but I must be on my way to Oslo. Give my best to Tommy. I'll be back in a month or so."

He leaned over and kissed his poor mother on the forehead.

"By God, she blinked," he muttered as he exited the room. And then he was off to gather Elizabeth and head to the airport. The flight was remarkably smooth and offered exceptional views of Norway's fjord-rich coastline. The bumpy ride was still ahead. Elizabeth gripped Oscar's hand tightly as they proceeded through the gangway and into the airport, where a crowd of reporters and a throng of protesters waited in ambush.

"Hello, Oslo," Oscar cried to the cameras.

"Oscar!" shouted Francis. "Over here, quickly."

"Francis!" Oscar yelled back, so pleased Francis had accepted his invitation to attend the ceremonies as a special guest of the Nobel Laureate. Security had provided a corridor of uniformed officers and Francis showed them the way with a wave of his arms. A waiting limousine whisked them quickly to the Grand Hotel on Karl Johans gate. Another crowd awaited them outside. Many carried rude signs expressing their disdain for the Nobel Committee's selection. Oscar noted that many of the signs bore the Birth First insignia. Fortunately, Oslo police had walled them off, which enabled Oscar, Elizabeth, and Francis to enter the hotel unscathed, though insults and threats were launched at them in several languages. Hotel staff quickly ushered Oscar and Elizabeth, along with Francis, to the Nobel Suite.

"Magnificent!" said Elizabeth.

There was a large sitting area with a balcony looking out toward the parliament building. On the left was a dining area. And to the right French doors led to a large bedroom with its own balcony. Upon the dining table was a bottle of champagne in a sterling-silver bucket filled with ice and a congratulatory note from the hotel manager.

"Elizabeth," said Oscar, who had ventured beyond the French doors, "come look at this bathroom. I do hope you weren't planning on sleeping tonight."

Freshly cut roses were neatly arranged in between his and her sinks. Farther on was a large sunken Jacuzzi next to their own private sauna.

"Oh my" was all she could manage as she sniffed the roses.

"I suppose the only proper thing to do would be to drink that blasted champagne," said Oscar.

"Why not?" said Francis. "When's your next engagement?"

"Dinner with the Nobel Committee chair and the mayor of Oslo at eight o'clock," said Elizabeth.

"Plenty of time," said Oscar as he popped the cork.

"To the Nobel Laureate," said Francis, raising a glass.

"To Oscar," said Elizabeth.

"To the both of you," said Oscar, "without whom I would never survive the next forty-eight hours."

Oscar and Elizabeth met the Nobel Committee chair, Professor Olefsun, a tall, white-haired Norwegian with a ruddy complexion who looked like he had spent his entire life on skis, and his wife, Marthe, in a private dining hall within a dimly lit restaurant that boasted acres of old wood paneling. They were joined by the mayor of Oslo, Gunnar Ranstad, and his wife, Ilse. After a delicious meal and good conversation, followed by too much brandy and more conversation, Oscar and Elizabeth returned to their room, where Oscar followed through on his earlier comments about depriving Elizabeth of sleep.

Yet they looked quite refreshed when they joined Francis for a breakfast of smoked fish, eggs, and dark Norwegian bread and coffee. Francis, contrary to his nature, spoke hardly a word.

"Is there anything the matter?" Oscar asked at last.

"Yes," Francis replied, "there is. Have you seen today's paper?"

"No I haven't as a matter of fact. No doubt the press has made some outrageous comments about me again."

"No, it doesn't concern you at all. Here, look at this."

Francis handed Oscar a copy of the London Times. Oscar evinced a touch of embarrassment at having been so presumptuous but then, as he read the headline, his eyes began to widen considerably. He picked up his napkin to wipe his chin as he handed the paper to Elizabeth. She bit her lip as she saw the headline. "TERRORISTS SEIZE SHIPMENT OF NUCLEAR WASTE!"

"Good Lord," said Elizabeth, "it says here the ship may have been carrying enough plutonium oxide to build an atomic bomb!"

"Yes," said Francis, "there were apparently several containers holding eighty to two hundred kilograms each in heavily shielded packaging. The attack ship, a Liberian registered tanker, had radioed for help and was seen listing to one side. All a ruse, of course. Once the transport ship came up broadside, the attackers killed the entire crew with nerve gas before transferring the plutonium oxide to a small submarine, like the ones they use for smuggling drugs. They all escaped and no one has any idea who they were, where they came from, or where they may be headed."

"No doubt an inside job," said Oscar. "I imagine that those who engage in such trafficking are offering a very high price for such a commodity."

"No doubt," Francis responded.

"Well," said Elizabeth, "let's not let such sobering news prevent us from enjoying this lovely day. Oscar, I would love to see a bit of Oslo, if it can be managed."

"Yes, dear," he replied. "Perhaps Francis would be so kind as to escort you. I need to spend time on my notes for tomorrow's lecture. And there's that blasted press conference at five."

"I would be delighted to accompany you," said Francis, brightening considerably. "I was contemplating a visit to Frogner Park, actually. It's full of sculptures by Gustav Vigeland, a bit out of the ordinary. The park's not too far away."

"Yes," said Elizabeth, "it's a beautiful day for a walk in the park. Oscar, are you certain you won't be able to join us for a little while, at least? It would do you good, help you forget about this nuclear waste business."

"No, my dear, I really must prepare myself. You two run along."

And so they did. Francis hailed a cab, and ten minutes later they arrived at a park on the outskirts of the city. Bare trees towered above the snow-covered ground on either side of a broad, formal avenue that led uphill in a series of rises toward quite a number of massive sculptures. A magnificent fountain stood at the bottom of the incline, spouting columns of water. Francis and Elizabeth slowly climbed the incline until they were surrounded by huge sculptures of humans in various contortions displaying all aspects of the human condition, from anger to joy, from youth to old age, each with a snowy cap about a half-foot thick.

"Remarkable," said Elizabeth. "I've never seen anything quite like it."

The centerpiece was a particularly striking sculpture that depicted over one hundred human beings writhing one atop the other in a massive phallus that rose sixty feet into the crisp December air.

"This is called *The Monolith*," said Francis. "Vigeland said it depicted his 'religion.'"

"Really?" she replied. "Pity Oscar isn't here. He would find it all quite fascinating."

That he would, but Oscar Newman, the imminent Nobel Laureate, was at that moment downing his third shot of aquavit. And Oddvar, his new found friend, was ordering another round.

"Vite!" he exclaimed to the young, tattooed bartender. *"Encore un aquavit!"*

All Oscar had meant to do was find an out-of-the-way place, perhaps a quiet bar or, better yet, a pub where he could quaff a pint while reviewing his notes, a place where no one would recognize him, and he could also perhaps come to terms with the morning news. Oddvar hadn't a clue who the burly man seated at the bar might be, nor did he care. What was important was showing him the photos of his dogs. They were both quite taken aback several rounds later when Elizabeth and Francis suddenly appeared behind them.

"Oscar!" Elizabeth shouted. "We've been looking everywhere for you."

He turned around on his stool, holding on to the bar for stability. His notes were strewn all about along with the morning paper.

"Elizabeth, my dear," he stammered, "how nice to see you and Francis. How was the park? Look, I'd like you to meet my new friend Oddvar here. He was just telling me about his dogs."

"I see," she replied. "Do you realize that in one hour you will be facing a sea of reporters?"

"One hour?" he repeated. "Why, I was just getting started."

They helped Oscar back to the room, availing themselves of the freight elevator to avoid general embarrassment. Elizabeth ordered a pot of coffee, then another, from room service. Finally, time running out, she straightened Oscar's tie.

"Please don't embarrass yourself too much. Or me, for that matter."

"Not to worry," said Oscar as he kissed her on the cheek. Francis escorted him down the hallway, to the elevator, and on to the conference room, where he handed him off to the Nobel Committee's security staff.

"Break a leg," said Francis. "Preferably theirs. I'll see you back in the room."

Elizabeth turned on the flat-screen TV and played with the controls until she saw Oscar standing next to a podium, struggling to hook a tiny microphone onto his necktie as the Nobel Committee chair was introducing him. A young woman quickly interceded and helped secure it. Surrounded by dozens of much larger, more intrusive microphones from TV and radio stations all around the world, Oscar smiled at her. Cameras flashed nonstop while in front of him a throng of reporters sat anxiously, ready to pounce. In the background a nearby cathedral's bell resonated throughout the room.

"Thank you, Mr. Chairman, for that kind introduction," said Oscar as the last ring faded to near silence. "And good evening, ladies and gentlemen. It's now five o'clock. Do you all know where your nuclear waste is?"

He held up the morning paper with its unsettling news. Elizabeth covered her eyes.

"Pity that thieves are now succeeding in purloining the deadliest substance our civilization has yet produced. Makes a mockery of Alfred Nobel's belief that his invention, dynamite, now well over a hundred years old, was so deadly that it would deter anyone from engaging in future warfare. Oh yes, it was only to be used for good, just like uranium. How naive. And how ironic, this Nobel *Peace* Prize, for which I am, rest assured, most grateful."

Oscar paused to fill a glass of water from a nearby pitcher. As he was pouring, however, his hand and wrist failed him and he spilled water all over the podium and all over his notes.

"This is disastrous!" cried Elizabeth.

"Well," said Oscar, recovering quickly, "there you have it. A perfect demonstration of what we mean by 'carrying capacity.' Here we have a glass, which, like our earth, is finite. And here we have a pitcher of water, which, like our ability to reproduce, is seemingly inexhaustible. At any rate, ladies and gentlemen, I apologize. Fire away."

And so they did, peppering him with questions regarding the future of his foundation, what his role would be in his new capacity, what he would do with the prize money. He responded directly to each question, generally keeping on point, for nearly half an hour.

"How about all the protesters, Dr. Newman?" shouted a young man near the back of the room.

"Yes," he replied, "how about them. Next question."

Then Melanie Woo stood up in the second row. "Dr. Newman," she began.

"Melanie," said Oscar, "how nice to see you again."

"Yes, Dr. Newman, it's nice to see you as well. Congratulations on your Nobel Prize. What I would like to know is, given how rampant pornography is on the Internet, what are your views on masturbation, particularly as a means to perhaps short-circuit the male sex drive?"

She remained standing, lovely as ever in a tight-fitting pants suit, all eyes fixed upon her.

"Fascinating question," said Oscar. Elizabeth stood up and began pacing about the room. "I would respond by saying that rather than short-circuit, it might well serve to further energize the beast but, in any event, there's no point in crying over spilt milt!"

Oscar began to howl with laughter, at which point the Nobel Committee chair declared that the press conference had run its course, thank you all for coming.

Chapter 12

The next forty-eight hours were an endless procession of ceremonies, each with the same general intent—honoring the Nobel Laureate. Aids and escorts arrived at Oscar's door to ensure that he appeared at the proper place at the proper time and hopefully in the proper condition. Didn't they trust him? There was dinner with the Nobel Committee, a reception with the king and queen of Norway the following morning, and finally the ceremony itself in the early afternoon.

The limousine dropped them at Oslo City Hall, where more fanfare and paparazzi awaited, happily well roped off. It was an immense red-brick building, with two rectangular wings flanking each side of a wide plaza, heavy with security. A brass band played a rousing Norwegian tune. The Nobel Committee chair greeted Oscar and Elizabeth and guided them toward the entrance. Cameras flashed all about. As previously instructed, Oscar turned before entering and waved to the crowd, to a fervent but mixed reaction—the Population Connection versus Birth First.

Once inside the entry, in a long, narrow foyer that adjoined the *grande salle*, he turned to Elizabeth.

"Got to go now," he said. The Nobel Committee, fully assembled, was waiting.

"Love you," said Elizabeth as she kissed him lightly on the lips.

"Is that all?" said Oscar.

"Here," she said, reaching into her purse and handing him a large red apple Oscar had removed from the daily fruit basket delivered to their room at the Grand Hotel. "I still don't understand, but…"

"Don't worry," he replied. "On second thought, perhaps I should start calling you Eve?"

She laughed and kissed him again before Francis took her arm and escorted her to their seats. They entered the grande salle, a space of very large proportions whose walls were covered with murals of Norwegian life in its many aspects. Blues and yellows, some bright and some muted, mixed with the colors of the sea and forests and the native rock, while figures from all walks of Norwegian life populated the grand scenery on high. Below the largest mural of all was a broad stage with windows that looked out at the tall ships in the harbor beyond. A grand piano stood to the left while seating for the Nobel Laureate and the Nobel

Committee members was off to the right. In the center was a large podium. Several hundred people were already seated, engaged in friendly conversation for the most part. Many recognized Elizabeth and conveyed their fondest regards as she and Francis proceeded down the aisle. Evidently, the vast majority of those present supported, or at least did not overtly oppose, the cause.

Soon after everyone was seated, apart from the royal family, trumpeting from on high announced the arrival of the Nobel Laureate. Everyone stood, turned, and watched Oscar walk at a slow ceremonial clip down the center aisle alongside the Nobel Committee chair, with the rest of the committee members in tow. When they reached the head of the room, they all turned and bowed toward the crowd. Applause erupted from every corner. Once everyone was seated, a string quartet launched into a beautiful Mozart concerto.

Then the royal trumpeters erupted again to announce the arrival of the king and queen. It was another long procession, as the king, queen, prince, and princess took their royal time assuming their royal places at the head of the assembly while the crowd stood and applauded. At long last the committee chair arose and walked to the podium.

He spoke for nearly forty-five minutes, explaining the history of the Nobel Peace Prize, the role of the committee, the selection process, and finally the basis for this year's choice. He spoke of Oscar's invention, the Newman Insert, which on its own could merit a Nobel Prize in Medicine as, he allowed, the Royal Swedish Academy of Sciences had strongly considered. But Oscar had not been satisfied with merely producing the world's safest and most effective contraceptive. "To the contrary," he said, "here is a man who is fully committed to his belief that the current rate of growth of our human population is unsustainable and will ultimately lead us—and indeed is leading us—inevitably toward our own destruction. Here is a man so committed to fostering world peace that he has devoted his own share of the fortunes arising from the sales of his invention to the free dissemination of the Newman Insert throughout the third world, where growth rates are among the highest. And not only do the doctors who dispense this remarkable contraceptive provide for family-planning services, they are often the only professional medical services available."

He continued by citing some statistics regarding declining birthrates in countries where Oscar had established his clinics. Coinciding with the declining birthrates was a decrease in what might be considered an index of human frustration, the number of outbreaks of violence involving different societies who shared a common resource base. And he cited the resurgence of wildlife in areas where efforts to aid family planning had apparently been successful. Finally, he asked Dr. Newman to join him at the podium.

"Dr. Newman," he said, "it is with great pleasure, gratitude, and admiration that the Nobel Committee bestows upon you this year's Nobel Peace Prize."

Oscar stepped forward as the chair handed him a large folding diploma and a small box that held his peace prize gold medal, which featured the profile of Alfred Nobel himself.

"Thank you very much, sir," he replied. "I am deeply honored."

The chair extended his hand in congratulations. Oscar ignored it rather unceremoniously, preferring instead to give him a huge bear hug. The assembly erupted with applause and laughter, culminating in a standing ovation. When all had settled down, a rather large dark-haired woman joined the string quartet and sang a beautiful aria from *La Traviata*.

At last the time had come. The committee chair walked to the podium once more and turned toward Oscar. "And now," he said, "I would like to ask Dr. Newman to deliver this year's Nobel lecture."

Elizabeth squirmed in her seat as Oscar stood and walked to the podium, looking quite good in his nicely tailored tuxedo. His hair was neatly combed and his beard freshly trimmed. As he approached the lectern, he flipped the apple from his right hand to his left and back again.

"Thank you, Professor Olefsun," he began in a commanding voice before turning toward the general assembly.

"Your majesties, your royal highnesses, excellencies, distinguished members of the Norwegian Nobel Committee, dear friends, and colleagues throughout the world. Mere words could never express the gratitude and humility I feel at this moment. The Nobel Peace Prize is indeed the finest honor anyone could ever receive. I accept it on behalf of all the hardworking members of my foundation, and all the officials and citizens around the world who have assisted in making rational family-planning assistance and care available to millions and millions of people living well below the poverty level, most of them scattered in countries whose people and resources, not surprisingly, have often been ravaged by war.

"I thought I would begin by telling you a bit about myself, about how I ended up in the particular line of work I have chosen. So let me begin with my childhood.

"I was born near Redruth, Cornwall, in the southwest corner of England. My father was a tin miner and my mother cleaned houses to help with expenses. When I was but a month old, my father was killed in a cave-in at the mine where he was working. I was an only child and my mother worked very hard to raise me properly. We were quite poor, but I managed as best I could to achieve a decent education and to withstand the taunting by other children who seemed to scorn me for being so poor and having no family other than my mother, a hardworking woman who could often be seen scrubbing sidewalks in front of the village stores.

"I remember distinctly how, when I was a lad of about ten, one of my rivals in school earned the admiration of our teacher by bringing her a nice ripe apple. He had polished it quite well, I noticed, but in those days no one would even think of eating an apple with the skin still on it. The soot from the coal-fired steam plants and the poisons sprayed on nearly all the fruit grown in the area dictated that one should remove the skin of any apple prior to eating it. So, on my way home from school that day, I stopped by a nearby orchard and picked the largest, ripest apple I could find. I took it home that night and I very, very carefully peeled it."

As he was speaking, Oscar pulled from his pocket a small knife and began to peel the apple he had carried with him to the podium.

"I peeled it so that it was still perfectly round, as if it had grown up as a perfect, skinless apple. And when I was through, I placed the apple in my coat pocket so I would be sure to have it the following day when I went to school."

And to illustrate this point, Oscar placed the now perfectly shaped, skinless apple in the pocket of his tuxedo jacket.

"I managed to do fairly well in school and supplemented my academic achievements with a bit of athletic prowess, most notably by heaving the shot put, discus, and javelin a fair distance. All of this was sufficient to earn me a scholarship to the University of Glasgow, where I discovered the biological sciences. Perhaps it was the myriad hormones rushing through my body—you know, the ones that propel us to procreate—that guided me toward the study of the human reproductive system. Or perhaps it was simply the incredible miracle of our own existence, with all its improbabilities, that led me to learn how all this could be possible. In any event, I became obsessed with the biology of human reproduction, through study much more so than practice, I must say, until one day I happened upon a lecture by a visiting American professor. He was speaking about limits, about the earth's carrying capacity and how it had already been exceeded. And that was some thirty years ago.

"Just look where we are now. The rate of extinction of species is now as high as it was during the great extinctions of the Pleistocene era, when vast sheets of ice covered much of the world. It is no wonder. We dam and redirect mighty rivers; we slash and burn vast tracts of atmosphere-enriching forest to make way for agriculture that runs entirely on nonrenewable, fossil fuel–based fertilizers. We displace entire mountains in our quest for fuel and precious metals, and we have so altered our atmosphere through our addiction to fossil fuels that we have wrought climatic changes that are raising the level of the sea, threatening our many coastal cities, spawning hurricanes of biblical proportions, and killing off northern forests and burning them to the ground while acidifying our oceans. But worst of all, ladies and gentlemen, we are running out of food."

He paused to take a drink of water while the words settled in. Elizabeth bit her lip, afraid Oscar might make another mess. But he replaced the glass without incident and smiled at the king and queen, seated right in front of the podium along with the prince and princess.

"Within the last twenty years," he continued, "the price of wheat and corn has tripled while rice is selling for over five times what it cost early in the century. Can anyone guess why? It was not because of bad weather or a poor harvest. In fact, during this period wheat, corn, and rice harvests were all quite high, with record production in one year. No. The sharp increase of these commodity prices is due to the disturbing fact that for most of the twenty-first century, humankind has been consuming more food than it is producing. So it's simply a matter of supply and demand. And with a world population expected to reach nine billion by midcentury, the experts tell us we will need to double current food production rates by 2030. Now there's a challenge."

He paused again for a sip of water.

"Many people are of course skeptical when they hear such talk. They point to the green revolution of the late twentieth century. A remarkable success—new varieties of wheat and rice that out produced their predecessors several fold. They produced so much grain that schools in India were closed early to provide more room to store the surplus. And it worked, provided these crops were fed copious amounts of fossil fuel–based fertilizers. Another dead-end strategy, all things considered."

"The promise of genetic engineering? A ray of hope, but one that will certainly lead us back toward monocultures, to genetically unequipped monocrops that despite their built-in, genetically engineered armor, have no clue as to what new parasite may come knocking at their door.

"My overall point is that the current rate of human population growth is now overwhelming our ability to share the earth's productivity in an equitable, peaceful manner, not only with respect to each other as human beings but with respect to the other magnificent creatures with whom we share this incredible, rare, and beautiful planet.

"Now some may argue, and they do, that competition is what evolution is all about, that our ability to compete more successfully than other species has led to our current state of domination over the earth's resources. We are indeed unique as a species, with our downturned nostrils, our bipedalism, and our perennial desire—indeed, our seemingly constant desire and ability to mate and reproduce, which, along with our terribly enlarged brains, render us entirely dominant among the creatures of this earth. We are what I call the 'climax species' of this planet, the species that dictates whether, where, and how other species may live.

"But how long can we coexist as long as our numbers increase at current rates, intensifying competition for finite resources while we produce weapons of mass destruction that are now finding their way into the hands of terrorists, despots, and the insane demagogues of various developing nations, those willing to fight for what they perceive as their rightful share of the world's resources?

"Many have argued, and of course they still do, that war is generally a conflict among cultures, that hatred bred from generations of ethnic disparity is more responsible for war than competition for finite resources. I respond by saying that ethnic and cultural differences represent merely the stress fractures of the bedrock of humanity which, when stretched thin, tear and break along these fault lines, like the contact planes between differing types of rock. At the bottom of every conflict is competition for resources, whether it is the local well or the fields where one's ancestors are buried.

"The world we have now created presents a scenario for disaster that prior generations could never have imagined. Again, how foolish Alfred Nobel would feel if he knew that destructive power was now measured not in tons but in megatons of TNT. And that destructive force, as we have seen recently, is no longer controlled by the global 'superpowers.' Can you imagine how suddenly dangerous an impoverished third-world nation, to whom the 'superpowers' have denied access to nuclear weapons, would become if suddenly they revealed their new found capacity for destruction? And we who live in urbanized areas have grown to know all too well the intense fear that inner-city gangs can generate as they steal and murder and proliferate their drug-based culture. Can you imagine global gangs wielding not assault rifles but atomic bombs? Impossible, you say, yet we see today that there are those twisted minds whose obsession for power will not be abated until they control the deadliest weapons known to humankind.

"Yes, my friends, I'm afraid the gun of nuclear annihilation is still loaded and pointed at our heads, as it was throughout the Cold War years. Now, however, the world has become a decidedly less orderly place. The balance of power has been altered, but the power has not been banished. Try as we do to discard the deadly seeds of the nuclear age, they still persist among us, some, no doubt, in the hands of madmen."

Oscar paused and took another sip of water. His audience remained still and silent, many almost rigid, as he resumed his oratory.

"Well then, what can we do to disarm and defuse this latest scenario for Armageddon? Certainly, we can do a better job of policing the nuclear decommissioning process, and perhaps one day we will actually come up with a viable solution for the long-term disposal of nuclear waste. Wouldn't that be amazing? But even if we could finally abolish the threat of nuclear destruction forever, there are plenty of other weapons at large that are capable of killing and maiming people en masse.

"The key lies elsewhere. We must attack the threat of war by building a sustainable future. Like it or not, we find ourselves at a crossroad in our evolutionary journey. To continue as we are will surely spell disaster. The balloon will simply burst. Yet we haven't the time to evolve in the Darwinian sense. The evolutionary race is over and we humans have won handily, for now, at least. In fact, the past few centuries seem to me like one long and wild victory party, as we have celebrated our victory over other creatures, celebrated our 'domination' of nature. But we have finally learned, I believe, that there can be no domination of nature, for we depend on nature for our very lives, like any other creature. No, we must take humanity in a bold new direction, wherein we recognize that we have reached the edge and to survive we must tiptoe very carefully to keep from falling off. There is no more land.

"So what does this new road toward sustainability look like? What must we do to find it, to build it, in fact, so that generations to come may easily follow? I for one have endeavored to promote the art of family planning, not just as a way of reducing competition among individuals but to help promote peace among families, to help the family survive as the principal building block of humanity. Some may call me naive, and indeed they do, yet I continue to believe that families that are at peace produce societies at peace and hopefully, in turn, nations at peace.

"I firmly believe that the true road to a sustainable future lies right before us. But we can no longer wait for government, inept as it has always been, to effect a solution to our current dilemma. We can no longer wait for the 'other country' to change its policies or for our neighbors to act first. We must each as individuals strive to reduce and, in effect, minimize our own impact upon the finite resources of this beautiful planet. That is the only way forward."

Oscar paused once more for a drink of water and then reached into his pocket. He withdrew the apple he had peeled earlier and inspected it. It was no longer a white, fresh-looking fruit but a brownish, fuzzy orb.

"I suppose you have been wondering about this apple. As you can see, it now has neither peel nor appeal."

He paused to laugh. There was a muffled chuckling from a few members of the assembly.

"This is what I mean, you see. I peeled a similar apple long ago, thinking it would please my teacher. But it turned all brown and began to rot on me, as this one is doing. I sincerely believed that I was doing a wonderful thing, improving on nature, so to speak. You cannot imagine the embarrassment I felt when I reached into my coat pocket and handed my teacher such a foul piece of fruit in front of all my classmates. My fellow students ridiculed me for months.

"But we are not speaking of apples here. We are speaking of the future of earth, our home. Think about it for a moment. Are we not, each one of us, collectively peeling the living skin from this beautiful, ripe, and bountiful planet? Does not each one of us take a little bite, a small paring from this planetary apple we call earth that fortunately still clings to the tree of our solar system by some ethereal stem connecting us to the sun? And isn't it by virtue of that lingering connection to the sun that the earth is sometimes able to heal itself, to allow the scars that we inflict upon it daily to mend? Or is the earth beginning to turn brown like the apple I hold here in my hand? Have we gouged too deep? Are there too many lacerations upon the delicate epithelium of the earth for it to heal and to continue to function? Can we ever restore the immense rain forests that renew our fresh oxygen supply? Can our atmosphere, for example, which is part of that protective skin, undo the damage done by ever-increasing concentrations of greenhouse gases? Can the oceans, which we have polluted and overfished for decades, ever recover so as to continue to feed our children and future generations? And have we destroyed so much of earth's beauty that the opportunities for spiritual renewal provided by unspoiled natural systems, such as free-flowing, unpolluted streams and virgin forests, are now so rare that humanity is condemned to life in four-walled rooms surrounded by squalor and desolation?

"Yes, my friends, the key to a sustainable future lies within each of us. We must each take responsibility for the imprint, the traces, the scars that we inflict on this planet that sustains us, to help keep the earth's skin alive. That means taking responsibility for one's own life at all times and, in particular, for one's own sex drive. It means taking responsibility for preventing unplanned pregnancies, currently estimated at one out of two in the United States, a so-called developed country. It has been said that we are but vehicles for our DNA, that our true purpose in life is to procreate, assuring the survival of our DNA and thus the species. This is the evolutionary life force that propels and motivates us in many aspects of our daily lives. And it is precisely that drive that threatens to send us and all the other inhabitants of this planet over the edge.

"I have had the good fortune to have developed a birth-control device that, unlike many other similar products, is safe to use and highly effective. Couples are free to engage their sex drive as often as they like and to plan sustainable families. By that I mean two children, of course, one to replace each parent. The development of such a device was my sole purpose in life for many years. For I believe that no matter how well we each minimize our impact on earth's limited resources, no matter how small a paring we each make in the earth's living crust, the most critical element of our survival strategy must be to maintain a global population that allows for the integration of each of our inevitable little scars in a sustainable manner. Dissemination of my birth-control device to where it is most needed, in rapidly growing, non-sustaining third-world countries, was merely a logical extension of my previous work.

"Alas, as I have made clear, it is now my intention to relinquish much of my responsibility with the foundation and, perhaps somewhat ironically, to settle down and hopefully become a family man myself, assuming my lovely fiancée here doesn't have a change of heart."

Oscar gestured with one hand toward Elizabeth, seated in the front row, who blushed immediately but still managed to smile.

"And so we look forward to settling down and raising a family, and we can only hope and pray that our children, if we are blessed with children, and yours, will look back upon us and on what we have bequeathed them, and be able to say thank you, thank you for leaving us an earth that is still intact, that is still vibrant and bountiful and not an ugly, skinless, lifeless, slowly rotting earth that, like this apple I hold in my hand, is dying. For we must remember that it is our children who will ultimately judge us and decide whether we have succeeded or whether we have failed to provide a future for them that is worth living.

"Thank you very much, ladies and gentlemen. I wish you all the very best."

Chapter 13

Following the photo sessions with the royal family, the Nobel Committee, and a host of affiliates, Oscar and Elizabeth were returned to the Nobel Suite in time to watch the parade held every year in honor of the Nobel Laureate. Bands, acrobats, and hordes of citizens of Oslo and beyond filed below them while Oscar and Elizabeth looked on from their balcony. Oscar waved and the crowds cheered him. Most of the protesters had dispersed and all was peaceful amid the yuletide scenery, colorful lights, and general merriment below.

When the parade was over, they were escorted down to the great dining hall in the Grand Hotel for the Nobel banquet. Oscar, seated beside Elizabeth at the head table, wasted no time diving into the delicious fare. He had spoken with far too many people of late and his appetite beckoned. It was all exquisite—pickled fish from the northern seas, *coquilles Saint Jacques,* followed by rack of lamb *á la norvegienne*, impeccably seasoned and accompanied by exquisite French wines. Then came the cheeses, the desserts, more wine, and more shaking of hands in between. But that was not the end of it. The following day featured the Nobel concert with popular musicians, celebrities by the dozens, and far too much fanfare. They returned to their room that evening much later than expected and collapsed on the bed, keenly aware that in just a few hours they would be departing for southern France.

Francis joined them in their suite for an early breakfast.

"I can't thank you enough," said Oscar as he poured some coffee for his new friend. "I don't know how I would have survived these last few days without your steady hand. And thanks for looking after Elizabeth. In fact, are you certain you can't spare a few more days? I could certainly benefit from your charming demeanor while dealing with Elizabeth's mother."

Francis laughed. "Terribly sorry," he replied. "As much as I have enjoyed these past few days, I must return to Nairobi to prepare for our ensuing journey and to take care of a few personal matters."

"Are you worried about my mother again, Oscar?" Elizabeth chimed in. "You're not getting cold feet all of a sudden?"

"My feet," Oscar replied, "are quite comfortable. It's my testicles that concern me most."

They had a good laugh as Oscar pulled his hotel bathrobe tighter around his sizable waist.

"Well, my friends," said Francis, "I must be on my way. It's an early flight, otherwise I'd ride with you to the airport."

"We shall meet again soon enough, when we begin our little trek to Olduvai," said Oscar as they embraced.

Elizabeth kissed Francis on both cheeks. "You will keep him out of trouble, won't you?" she said with pleading eyes.

"I will certainly do my very best," said Francis, "provided they let him in the country! And I trust that you will stand by this man, no matter what transpires between him and your mother."

Elizabeth laughed. "Don't worry, Francis. Nothing can come between us now. Mother will just have to accept Oscar for what he is and, more importantly, for what he is about to become—my husband."

Their flight to Marseille was fairly calm. Elizabeth covered Oscar with a blanket as he nestled into his first-class seat. Then she covered his eyes with a black mask to block out the light as well as help conceal his identity. No one recognized him and he was able to doze peacefully while Elizabeth sat next to him, unable to focus on anything but their impending reunion with *Maman*, the irascible Madame Le Clerc.

Elizabeth's younger brother, Edouard, met them in the baggage claim area. He was dressed in gray slacks and a tight-fitting lavender shirt with a beige sweater draped loosely about his shoulders. He and Elizabeth embraced and spoke a few words in French before Oscar reached them.

"Good to see you again," he said to Oscar with a thick French accent as they hugged briefly.

"Always a pleasure, Edouard," said Oscar, stepping back from a cloud of cologne. "Thanks for coming to fetch us."

"Tu ne croiras pas tout ce qui vous attend," said Edouard once they were headed away from the airport in Edouard's car.

"Please," said Elizabeth, "in English, for Oscar's sake."

"Okay," said Edouard, "you should know that Mother has convinced Father Brodard that Oscar should be excommunicated from the Catholic Church. In other words, no wedding, at least not at Sainte-Marie."

"Excellent," said Oscar, laughing.

"This is outrageous!" Elizabeth declared angrily. "I spoke to Mother but a few days ago and she assured me—much to my surprise, I admit—that she was doing everything possible to secure our wedding arrangements, despite her own feelings about it."

"Elizabeth," Edouard said as he drove deftly along a crowded thoroughfare, "did you really believe she would ever agree to this? She has been working on Father Brodard for the last two months, ever since you broke the news to her. Oscar would be required to endure a long and dreadful series of instructions involving considerable penance, including relinquishing all involvement with his foundation, before they would even consider readmittance to the Catholic Church, much less allow the two of you to be married at Sainte-Marie."

"But I have a letter signed by Father Brodard indicating that our wedding date and time are confirmed. I thought that would be the end of it."

"My dear sister, as long as Mother is alive and you are intent on marrying Oscar, you will never know the end of it."

They exited the major roadway they had been traveling and began to climb another, much narrower one that led up through olive groves and barren vineyards. The road finally reached a ridge top that afforded spectacular views of the Mediterranean far to the south. They had left the sprawl of Marseille far behind and looked down upon the ancient village of Balgères. Rising from the midst of antique houses were the tall spires of Sainte-Marie.

At last they arrived at a pair of massive stone pillars that supported two exquisite wrought-iron gates that swung slowly open as Edouard's vehicle approached. He drove them down a long drive until a large estate loomed before them. It was made of stone, much of it covered in ivy, with a mansarded roof made of slate that hung at precipitous angles. The driveway led to an enormous, ivy-covered entry with massive oak doors. Edouard pulled to a halt. As he did the front doors opened and a distinguished-looking fellow came out to greet them.

"Bonjour, Jacques," said Elizabeth with a huge smile, *"ça fait longtemps."*

"Oui, mademoiselle," he replied, *"c'est un grand plaisir de vous revoir, et vous aussi Monsieur Newman."*

Oscar smiled and said merci, resisting any further attempts to display his meager, ill-pronounced French. Better to save what little he could remember for his future mother-in-law.

They entered the main *salle*, where the fading daylight filtering through the high front windows did little to dispel the darkness. Richly colored Oriental rugs covered the ancient wooden floor while enormous tapestries hung all about the room, set between tall Corinthian columns. The furniture was old and built on a scale that complemented that of the room itself. A magnificent hearth loomed at the far end with large andirons in front, and nearby a sizable suit of armor guarded the entrance to the library. This room provided the only serious source of illumination to the otherwise somber chamber. And it was toward that shaft of light emanating from the library that Elizabeth and her brother led Oscar.

Seated in an overstuffed chair, with her glasses resting just above the tip of her nose, Madame Le Clerc sat reading by the light of a lamp situated just behind her. She looked up as they entered the room, her expression not changing in the slightest as she set her Bible down on the table beside her.

"Bonjour, Maman," said Elizabeth as she leaned over and kissed her mother on both cheeks.

"Bonjour, ma petite," she replied.

Edouard approached and, kneeling, took his mother's hand and kissed it.

It was Oscar's turn. He smiled at her but stood his ground. *"Bonjour, madame,"* he said with a slight nod of his head.

"Bonjour, Oscar," she replied, as the smile reserved for her only son quickly receded.

"So," said Edouard, seeking to lighten the atmosphere a bit, "anyone care for an aperitif?"

"Sans doute," replied Madame Le Clerc with a frigid glance toward Oscar.

Edouard poured a pastis for Oscar and himself while Elizabeth took a small glass of sherry. Madame Le Clerc abstained. After a bit of stunted conversation, Edouard invited Oscar to take a little tour of the house. He accepted without hesitation.

Left alone, Elizabeth sat quietly, holding her mother's hand, awaiting the inevitable lecture.

"Ma chère fille," it began, as her mother launched into a long discourse about how she was her only daughter, about how well she loved her, how well her father had loved her, and how happy he would be that she was keeping the promise she had made to him as he lay upon his deathbed, to be married in the church where she had been baptized. Elizabeth interjected a polite "merci, Maman," knowing

precisely where all this was leading but not knowing in the least how she would respond.

At last there came the unwelcome words. Madame Le Clerc looked at her daughter, squeezed her hand and sighed. "I respect your decision to marry Oscar," she said, "in spite of my feelings toward him. But it is not so simple. I'm afraid that Father Brodard has taken a very dim view of Oscar and his work and has determined that he is not fit to be married as a Catholic."

Elizabeth stared coldly at her mother and withdrew her hand. She felt the anger welling up within her, anger she had repressed for many years but now boiled within. Despite Edouard's forewarning, nothing would now dissuade her from venting her wrath. As she struggled to frame the precise words she would use to express her anger, however, the chimes of the doorbell resonated throughout the house.

"Ah, c'est Monsieur Brodard," said her mother, indicating further that she had invited him to dinner so that Elizabeth and Oscar could plead their case directly with him. Elizabeth looked at her with a blank stare, bit her lip, and said nothing as her mother rose to greet her guest.

He was not as tall as she had remembered him, and his hair was considerably thinner and much grayer. He was still rather lean and his smile had not changed, a smile that many years of priesthood had taught him to turn on and off as the occasion demanded.

"Elizabeth," he cried, *"comment vas-tu? Ça fait longtemps."*

"Oui, Monsieur Brodard, longtemps," she replied as politely as she could, trying to remember just how many years it had been as he kissed her once on each cheek. She concluded that it had not been long enough.

At last Edouard and Oscar descended the stairs that led to the second floor and the various bedrooms of the palatial estate. Oscar approached the darkly clad priest with all the grace and charm he could muster, which was considerable under the circumstances, and in his very best French said how delighted he was to meet him. Father Brodard smiled affably and congratulated Oscar for his Nobel Prize. Further conversation was curtailed, however, as Jacques reappeared to announce that dinner was served.

Madame Le Clerc took her place at the head of the magnificently set table, with Father Brodard to her right and Elizabeth to her left. Edouard occupied the opposite end with Oscar to his right, next to Elizabeth. A small, dark-skinned

97

woman wearing a light-blue smock served them each a generous helping of soup from a large silver tureen. Jacques stood by, on the alert for any transgression of protocol. Before anyone dared touch a spoon, however, Madame Le Clerc folded her hands before her and called upon Father Brodard to say a blessing. He issued his familiar smile and began a long discourse that was lost on Oscar but seemed to have something to do with kowtowing to the will of God.

The soup was delicious, a simple potage of local garden vegetables blended with herbs and cream that only the French seem capable of combining in precisely optimal proportions. Subsequent courses included quail and veal and, thanks to Edouard's subtle cues to Jacques, some of the most exquisite wines Oscar had ever tasted. Throughout the meal the conversation was quite innocent, if sparse, focusing on the weather in Scotland and bits of inquiry about Oscar's impending return to Kenya. Elizabeth translated for Oscar and he marveled at her as she spoke in her native tongue. Her manner and expression were quite different, yet he loved her all the more for it, especially the way the tip of her nose would twitch and bend as she spoke, quite unlike the bonny lass he'd met years ago who spoke English almost like a proper Londoner.

At last the inevitable moment came as the dishes were cleared away. Elizabeth reached below the table and gripped Oscar's hand while the coffee was served. She looked at her mother, whose stern expression and sideward glances toward Father Brodard signaled that the moment for serious conversation had arrived.

"Dr. Newman," he began, speaking suddenly in rather fluent English, "I have given much thought to your situation and have beseeched the Lord for help in what is, for me, a difficult matter. I have known this family for many, many years and have personally baptized both of the Le Clerc children. I was greatly saddened when Elizabeth moved to England, but I have kept her in my prayers all these years. Her mother assures me that she has been faithful to the Catholic Church and I realize that she loves you very much. But you must understand that the Vatican does not condone the practice of birth control. While I have received a copy of your certificate of baptism, I'm afraid that your devotion to spreading the use of your contraceptive device forces me to reconsider marrying the two of you as you have requested."

He paused to take a sip of coffee but then raised his eyes and stared directly, unflinchingly, at Oscar.

"In short," he continued, "I regret to say that I have recommended that you be excommunicated from the Catholic Church."

Silence pervaded the room as these words settled like poison. Elizabeth gripped Oscar's hand tighter as she felt her eyes beginning to well up with tears. She was beyond anger now.

"I see," said Oscar as he slowly swirled the coffee in his cup. "I must say this comes as quite a shock. But there has apparently been some misunderstanding. While Elizabeth and I agreed that we would be married in the church where she was baptized, Sainte-Marie, we agreed to be married by a priest of my choosing."

Elizabeth gripped Oscar's hand even more tightly as she tried not to let her facial expression belie the fact that she had absolutely no idea what he was talking about.

"Ah, but that is very complicated, I'm afraid," replied Father Brodard. "Only the archbishop of Marseille can agree to such an arrangement. And I doubt he would grant such a request."

"Au contraire," Oscar replied, reaching into his coat pocket and handing an envelope across the table to Father Brodard, whose shocked expression was nothing compared to that of Madame Le Clerc. Father Brodard opened the envelope and removed a letter written in English. He read it over a number of times.

Dear Dr. Newman,

I am in receipt of your request to allow Father David Sebastian to perform a wedding ceremony for you and Elizabeth Le Clerc, a longtime parishioner, at the church of Sainte-Marie in the village of Balgères. I have known David Sebastian since he was a student of theology and a deacon within my own archdiocese many years ago. I have a great love and respect for him and for the missionary work he has performed so admirably in Kenya.

He has written to me on your behalf and speaks very highly of you. While the matter of birth control is of great concern, Father Sebastian assures me that, despite your profession, you do not personally use birth-control devices. In that case, I shall be happy to speak with Father Brodard at Sainte-Marie and to help with arrangements for your wedding as soon as your plans are set.

I would also like to thank you for your generous contribution to the archdiocese's restoration fund. It is only through such kind donations that aging churches such as Sainte-Marie can continue to provide a beautiful and safe sanctuary for our parishioners.

It was signed by Monsieur Bernard Jossard, archbishop of Marseille. Enclosed with it was the letter from David, written in French, of course, which Father Brodard set down upon the table, having barely glanced at it. Elizabeth, whose spirits had brightened considerably, read it over and stifled her laughter as she read the part that argued that if the Catholic Church could admit soldiers of war, then surely it could retain someone whose only sin was helping families live within their means.

"Well," said Father Brodard, clearing his throat, "this does seem to take the matter out of my hands."

He glanced cautiously at Madame Le Clerc, who glared at him in return and then rose abruptly from the table and left the room without speaking. Elizabeth turned to Oscar and hugged him tightly while Edouard asked a terribly embarrassed Father Brodard if he would care for a spot of cognac.

Chapter 14

It was again closing time for Max and daylight was beginning to fade. It was December 21, the winter solstice. He examined his inventory of supplies as he did at the end of nearly every day. Concentrating on his clipboard, he failed to hear Christine as she entered the tent.

"Knock," she said quietly, almost timidly.

Max turned around, quite startled. He hadn't seen her in a few weeks, not since she had stopped by looking for some help fixing a broken bicycle chain. "Hello," he said, "what brings you here?"

"Oh, I was just in the neighborhood. How have you been?"

"Fine, thanks, and you?"

"Okay, more or less." She looked around the tent and noticed the small shrub Max had placed in one corner. It was decorated with little Christmas ornaments made from red and green seedpods and feathers and such, whatever seemed festive that Max had been able to scavenge from his surroundings.

"I like your Christmas tree," she said.

"Thanks," he responded, looking a little embarrassed. "It hardly qualifies as a Christmas tree but heck, somehow Christmas and Africa just don't seem to go together. Happy Kwanzaa. Anyway, what do you mean, you're doing fine, 'more or less'?"

She looked down at her feet, drawing a circle in the dirt floor with the toe of her sandal-clad right foot. Her long, slender legs were even tanner than before. "It's not easy living with the Maasai," she said, looking up at him. Her pretty green eyes weren't as piercing as usual. In fact, they looked rather sad, almost warm.

"Are they treating you okay?" he asked.

"Pretty much," she replied. "But I just can't stand the way some of the men treat their wives. They beat them and the women just take it in stride. And there's nothing I can do about it."

"Yeah, I know," he replied. "I've seen the bruises. They always make excuses when I ask how it happened. But heck, this is their society and we aren't going to change it. Not much different from what I used to see in LA. You want to sit down?"

He motioned toward the cot and the chair next to it. She sat down on the edge of the cot, the one usually reserved for the Maasai women who came to see him.

"So this is where you do it," she said. Max looked at her curiously as she stared at the ground. He noticed for the first time that she was wearing a touch of makeup. Her lips were glossy and moist. What was she up to? Did she come here for a Newman Insert? She was acting far too meek, quite out of character, somewhat like a child whose feelings had been hurt.

"Max," she said, looking up at him.

"Yes?"

"I need a favor."

"Well, sure," he said as he sat down in the chair beside her. "What is it?"

"It's not for me. It's for a friend. She needs your help."

Max rose as the pieces all fell into place. He paced back and forth, feeling the anger mount within as he anticipated her next words.

"She's eight weeks pregnant, Max, and her husband hasn't slept with her in over six months. Some of them can deal with this but not him. He'll beat the living shit out of her if he finds out. You've got to abort it, Max."

He turned around and watched her recoil once she saw his expression. She squirmed on the cot as he walked toward her.

"Christine," he said, his voice trembling, "you know goddamned well I can't do any abortions. I can't believe you even asked."

She sat back on the cot, looking almost frightened. "But you have to," she said defiantly.

"Like hell I do."

"Fine," she said, "turn your back on her now, and you can stitch up her head and set her bones after he's done with her."

He paced back and forth momentarily before facing her. "Maybe that's what it will come to, but she should have thought about that before she messed around. Christ, if she didn't want to get pregnant, she could have paid me a visit."

"Maybe she should have but it's too late now. I just don't get it. If you guys are so obsessed with birth control, I don't see why you can't do a simple abortion."

Max glared at her, struggling to maintain his composure. "It's not the same thing," he said as calmly as he could. "There's a big difference between preventing conception and aborting a fetus. Besides, Oscar guarantees there will be no abortions at any of his clinics. It's condition number one for every clinic he sets up.

If that rule's broken and the government finds out, or even worse, the press, you can kiss the whole foundation good-bye."

"Oh, come on," she said, "nobody would ever know."

"How can you be sure? She'd probably tell her friends. I'm sure at least some of them know she's pregnant. They'd want to know what happened."

Her stern eyes refused to yield any ground. "She could just tell them she miscarried. It happens all the time."

Max looked at her and then began to walk in circles, the veins on his temples bulging. He stopped in front of her with his face close to hers. "Look," he said, his facial muscles taut and his voice nearly quivering, "you're not hearing me real well. I can't do it and that's it."

She stared back at him until he turned and walked away, moving toward the center of the tent. "Fine," she said, "if that's the way you want it. But just think how you'd feel. How would you like it if your wife gave birth to somebody else's baby?"

Max stopped suddenly but then resumed walking in small circles, feeling the rage within slowly explode as the dam burst. Then he turned and walked toward her, his face red and contorted in an expression unlike any she had seen before. His eyes were bulging, on fire.

"Get the hell out of here!" he screamed at the top of his lungs, just inches from her face. "Just get out of here and don't ever come back!"

Yet she sat on the cot, frozen, staring at him as he walked away, trembling and clenching his fists. "Oh my God," she said, rising slowly. She walked toward him as he stood in the center of the tent, still shaking as tears welled up and slid down his cheeks. She moved behind him and put her arms around his waist.

"I'm so sorry," she said as she held him close. "I didn't know. How could I? You never talked about your divorce."

An interminable silence ensued as Christine held on to Max and he stood still, feeling her arms around him, her hands holding on to his, feeling for the first time in months the warmth of a woman's touch, a sincere touch that slowly melted away the pain, the anger, and the bitterness that had turned an otherwise compassionate heart to stone. He swallowed hard.

"It's okay," he managed at last, nearly whispering. "I'm sorry I yelled at you. It was my partner. I wish to hell I'd never met him. Julie, my ex-wife, she really liked him. I don't know. Maybe she liked his Maserati more. Anyway, she thought a successful guy like that could really help launch my career."

"When did you figure it out?" she asked.

Max turned around and faced her as she slowly let go of him. "When Amy was two years old. I was just giving her a routine exam when it hit me. There's no way she could have type B blood if she was my kid. I'm A positive and my ex-wife is type O. It had to be someone with type B blood, like my partner."

"Oh my God, that must have been devastating," she said, leading him back toward the cot. They sat down while she held on to one of his hands and Max wiped his teary eyes with the other. "So where are they now?"

"Back in LA, probably married by now. Here's a picture of her."

He reached toward his desk and turned the frame around. Christine studied it carefully.

"She's beautiful. Look at those dimples and those little blond curls."

"Just like her mother," he said, taking a deep breath. "I was the happiest guy in the world, completely in love with both of them. And then poof, just like that it was all gone."

Christine looked at him tenderly and he noticed tears in her eyes as well. "She was a fool, if you ask me," she said.

"Thanks," he said softly as his vocal cords wrestled with the enormous lump in his throat. He looked at her amid the emotions tearing through him and marveled at how moments ago he had been absolutely furious with her but now it was all he could do to fight off the impulse to plant a major kiss on her sweet little lips. He was moving closer to her when the honking of a car horn rudely interrupted their tender interlude.

They emerged together from inside the tent and watched as a white Land Rover pulled to an abrupt halt in front of them. It looked brand new, except for the mud splattered all over the front bumper and sides. The doors opened slowly and out stepped first Oscar from the passenger side and then Francis from the driver side. Then David came out the rear door.

Max pulled out a handkerchief and quickly wiped his face. Christine stood erect and ran her fingers through her hair.

"Hello there, Dr. Taylor," bellowed Oscar.

"Hello," said Max, "didn't expect to see you so soon. In fact, I heard you'd retired. But it's great to see you. What's up?"

"Just passing through," he replied. "Thought I'd drop in to see how you are getting on."

Max looked more than slightly bewildered. He glanced at Christine, who still stood by his side. "We're getting on just fine," he replied as he shook hands with Oscar and then Francis and finally David. "Good to see you all again."

"Likewise," said Francis.

"Nice to see you," said David, "and Christine. What a pleasant surprise. Oscar, have you met Christine Olson?"

"I'm afraid I haven't yet had the pleasure," he replied as he stepped forward to shake her hand.

"Hi," she said, looking slightly embarrassed as she shook hands with Oscar and Francis.

"What brings you to Africa?" said Oscar.

"Oh, I'm doing some anthropological work with the Maasai. I, uh, just stopped by to talk to Max about one of his patients. I've been a little worried about her."

"She's seems to be suffering from a distended abdomen," said Max. "Nothing that time won't cure."

"I see," said Oscar, who quickly understood what had just transpired between them. Or at least most of it.

"Actually," said David, "we came by to tell you it's time to move the clinic again. The latest reports from Maasai scouts indicate that more refugees have moved south. Joseph and I have just been to a meeting with government officials, and they are urging the Maasai to move south of the Kalema Road until this situation has been resolved."

Both Max and Christine looked at him in disbelief. The clinic was now located about five miles north of the Kalema Road, in a very pleasant area nestled below the Nguruman Escarpment, just a mile from the Ewaso Ngiro. There was fresh water nearby, plenty of trees for shelter, and the grass was greening up. Max had been there nearly two months and had come to feel comfortable, almost at home, despite still having no one to help in the clinic. He did not like the idea of leaving, especially for the reasons just stated.

"I don't get it," he said. "Why doesn't the government just send some troops and move these refugees out of here? This is Maasai country."

"It is not so simple," said David. "Kenyan troops have nearly sealed off the road from Nairobi to the Mara Reserve, which runs through Narok. But quite a few

Ugandan refugees have slipped through and have occupied Maasailand just north of here. The government has been attempting to negotiate with them, but they are weary of being persecuted and they are surprisingly well armed."

"No surprise to me," muttered Francis.

"I'm sorry," said David, "I couldn't quite hear you."

"It's nothing," replied Francis.

"Actually," added Oscar, "Francis was merely expressing my very thoughts as well. Surprising, you say? Not at all. For one reason or another, weapons always seem to find those who have been uprooted and are therefore rather desperate."

"Perhaps," David continued. "But the government doesn't expect these people to move farther south, nor do they expect more refugees to slip through and join them. The army simply wishes to establish another line of defense, the Kalema Road, in the event these refugees cannot be persuaded to move out peacefully. If the negotiations do not succeed, the army would like to be able to move in quickly and push them back north, without having to worry about the Maasai being caught in the middle. The government officials with whom we spoke are confident that the refugees will agree to being relocated very soon."

"Really?" said Max. "Where to?"

"I don't know where, frankly. Hopefully back to Uganda. Joseph is conferring with the elders as we speak. I believe he will succeed in convincing them that it would be in everyone's best interest to move south temporarily. In any case, it will be months before the dry season returns and the Maasai head north again to the occupied area. Besides, there is plenty of good grass to the south."

Max shook his head. "Fine," he said. "I guess it's none of my business, anyway. So what do I do? Start packing or wait till we hear what Joseph and his buddies decide?"

"Joseph said he would get word to me in the morning," David said. "I told him, at Oscar's suggestion, that I would be spending the night here. Oscar assured me there would be adequate accommodations. That way, assuming the decision is to head south, we can all help you with the move tomorrow."

"I certainly hope I haven't inconvenienced you," said Oscar, with a subtle glance toward Christine. "Francis and I have our own tents, so I thought we could all sit about the campfire, have a bite of supper and perhaps a bit of merriment, if possible, given these unfortunate circumstances. After all, it's only a few days until Christmas. How does that sound to you?"

"Well," said Max, "I guess that sounds all right, as long as you don't mind canned stew."

"Don't even think about it," returned Oscar. "Dinner is on me. Just get a nice campfire going and I will do the rest. Francis and I made a stop at the market in Nairobi, and we have a veritable feast on hand."

"In that case," said Christine, "I'll just get on back to my trailer. You guys have fun. Sounds like I'd better start packing, anyway."

"Nonsense," said Oscar, "there's no great rush. Please, do me the honor of joining us for supper. And I'm sure there are ample accommodations for you as well, are there not, Max?"

Max looked more than slightly uncomfortable, feeling David's eyes upon him. "Uh yeah," he said, "there's an extra examination tent with a spare cot and blankets. It's all yours, Christine, if you want it."

"Please join us," interjected David. "We'd love your company. And besides, I'm sure Oscar would be interested in hearing about your research."

Christine forced a smile. "I guess it is getting a little late to be bicycling back to my trailer."

"Splendid," said Oscar. "Then let's get that fire going."

Max set about building a fire while Christine and David gathered more wood and Francis and Oscar prepared the food they had brought. There were fillets of fresh tilapia, an assortment of potatoes, and various legumes that Max had never seen before. They grilled the fish and the vegetables; Francis provided some fresh herbs to enhance the flavor. Oscar rummaged through the back of Francis's vehicle, and from one of the coolers he produced two bottles of French wine as well as glasses for them all. And by the time darkness set in, they were all seated at the large table with candles aglow and a delicious meal before them.

"Bless you all," said Oscar, raising his glass, "and my heartfelt thanks for the excellent work you do, and especially to David for all he has done for the Maasai and for me personally as well."

"Hear, hear," added Francis.

"Thank you, Oscar," said David. "I am very happy to be of service to you and to your foundation. But I feel that at this time, in view of the circumstances, it would be appropriate to offer a simple prayer, if you do not object."

"Certainly not," Oscar replied.

David lowered his head and put his hands together, as did the others. "Oh Lord," he began, "please grant us the wisdom to see clearly in these difficult times and, in particular, to keep the Maasai safe from all harm."

They all remained silent with their heads bowed until Oscar raised his glass again.

"Thank you, David," he said, "that was a lovely sentiment. But tell me honestly, do you really believe that the 'Lord' might intervene in the affairs of the Maasai, or in anyone's affairs, for that matter?"

"That is a rather complex question," said David, with a somewhat perturbed glance toward Oscar. "Or perhaps I should say the answer is quite complex. I suggest we leave it for another time."

"Very well, then," said Oscar as he passed the fish platter to Max. "But speaking of divine intervention, I wish you could have seen the look on Elizabeth's mother's face when she realized there was no way she could keep you from marrying her daughter and me at Sainte-Marie. I almost felt sorry for her. I hated to invoke our little insurance policy, but then I really had no choice."

"I am most happy to be of service to you and Elizabeth," said David. "Besides, I have not been back to France in three years. The fact that you are paying my expenses makes it all the more painless. My only concern is leaving here when things are in such a state of disarray."

"Perhaps by the time I return from this little junket with Francis, all will be well," Oscar returned. "It sounds as though the military will soon be here to send these intruders back where they belong."

"Let us hope that they depart, for one reason or another, before the Maasai determine to take matters into their own hands," said David.

Chapter 15

Word from Joseph came early, just after sunrise. He arrived with a small entourage of Maasai elders who stood by as Joseph conferred with David, speaking with sharp intonations and decisive arm motions. Francis, who had been the first to arise and had kindled a small fire, remained at a distance.

It was a difficult situation. Ordinarily, the Maasai do not back down or shy away from adversity. Many of the elders, not trusting the Kenyan government to come to their defense, felt it was time to take action against the intruders. But the decision was to comply, to move south until the long rains began. By then the intruders would be gone and they could all move back north. The government guaranteed it. Joseph departed with his escorts as soon as the message was delivered, heading off into the bush amid heated discussion.

After the various tents were dismantled and stowed, along with all the equipment and medical supplies, either inside or on top of the two vehicles, Max, Francis, and Oscar headed off to help Christine with her trailer. She needed a tow, which would not be a problem. The Scout could handle it. The problem was Christine.

It all started when Oscar asked about her research methods as they were packing up the last of her affairs. After she explained her interview process, he asked if she'd ever considered teaming up with Max, since he was surrounded by Maasai women all day long. "You could help him in the clinic," said Oscar, "and it might prove to be a less intrusive method for gathering your data."

"I am not intrusive," she exclaimed. "I simply conduct my research out in the open. If you're suggesting I should eavesdrop and spy on these women like some undercover agent, then you have no idea how professional anthropologists operate."

"I admit," responded Oscar, "that I am not familiar with the procedures employed by anthropologists, but I do know from my own endeavors that observation is the key. You were explaining last night around the campfire how your research is focused on determining how much influence Maasai women have when important decisions affecting their society are made. I would bet that the vast majority of women who come to see Max decide all on their own if—and if so, when—they will conceive a child, without regard to what their husbands might think. Now that's real power, if you ask me!"

"Wait a minute," said Max. "I'm getting along just fine at this clinic all by myself. Besides, I'd need someone who knows a little bit about medicine."

"Christine, didn't you tell me that your father was a doctor, and that you used to work in his office during the summers?" David said.

Christine looked at them all as if they were a pack of hyenas that had her surrounded. "Yeah," she said coldly. "But all I did was take care of the paperwork. Maybe give a few shots now and then, or sterilize equipment."

"And that's precisely what Max needs," said Oscar.

Max began to object, but before he could summon the words, David interrupted.

"Actually," he said, "in view of the circumstances, it might not be a bad idea. I have never been comfortable with you working so independently, and with the refugees possibly moving farther south, I hate to think what might happen to you if you were to encounter them on your own."

Christine stood next to her trailer, which was now firmly hitched to Max's wagon, apparently in more ways than one. "Holy shit," she said to herself.

She looked at Max, who pursed his lips and gave a slight shrug of his shoulders, indicating there would be no further argument from him, even though the house within was completely divided on the issue.

"Ready?" said Max.

She glared back. "Ready as I'll ever be."

They drove slowly through the melee of the Maasai attempting to once again pick up their lives and move all their animals and goods toward some unknown destination to the south. Many of the men remained engaged in animated conversation while the women labored to gather their utensils, their store of firewood, and their children. The dissension created great delay, and by evening the majority of the Maasai were still well north of the Kalema Road. Even the cattle seemed to resist the move south, content with the good grass that surrounded them.

But by the end of the following day, the Maasai were busy establishing new settlements in an area east of David's schoolhouse, well south of the Kalema Road and just north of the salt marshes along the north shore of Lake Natron. And so it was not until noon on the day after that Oscar and Francis, having done what they could to help with the sudden southward migration, bid their good-byes to Max,

David, and Christine. Standing outside the schoolhouse, they listened politely to David's pleas for them to remain for Christmas, just a day away.

"Oscar," said David, "I know how well you enjoy a good party. After a simple Mass in the morning, there will be a great feast. Everything is in such disarray; we could all use a little cheering up. The Maasai will be dancing and singing and I still have some excellent wines on hand."

Oscar listened and smiled. "Thank you, my dear friend. It sounds delightful. But Francis and I are already behind schedule, and Lord knows I cannot afford to be late getting back to Elizabeth this time. Speaking of which, our flight to Marseille leaves at noon on the fifth. Max, are you sure you can get David to the airport on time?"

"No problem," he said. "I'll make sure he's there."

"Excellent," said Oscar, who proceeded to embrace David, Max, and a slightly reticent Christine. "Until then, have a very merry Christmas and good luck settling in."

Francis bid them good-bye and thanked them again before they headed off in the new Land Rover. As they drove slowly up the steep, muddy tracks that ascended the Nguruman Escarpment along the western edge of the Rift Valley, Oscar and Francis reflected on the plight of the Maasai. What could they do? The once-fierce Maasai with their spears and their shields were no match for well-armed, desperate refugees looking for a new homeland. Was the usurping of Maasailand inevitable? Or was it a merely transitory threat? And, most importantly, would the government troops ever come? There were no answers, and as they moved farther up the steep escarpment they each glanced anxiously back from time to time at the land far below that was gradually receding from view.

"That Joseph fellow certainly has his hands full," Oscar remarked. "How does he manage to maintain control? Seems as though he has to speak for thousands of Maasai over such a large territory."

"Yes, he does," replied Francis, "but he has been the leader of his age class since I first met him, back when he was a moran. He's not only what the Maasai call the *Alaigwanani*, or chief elder, he's also the government-appointed administrator for all Maasai between the walls of the Rift Valley south of Mosiro. He has gained the respect of all Maasai as well as government officials in Nairobi. He's struggled terribly to keep the culture from disintegrating. But he's never faced such a challenge as this."

111

Once atop the escarpment, they seemed to enter another land altogether, a more temperate and more diverse landscape that hinted strongly of the incredible wildlife that the plains to the west and south, the Maasai Mara and Serengeti, held in store. The Maasai they met along the way displayed a greater familiarity with westerners, approaching the shiny, new white Land Rover without hesitation, presenting trinkets and jewelry for sale and offering, for money of course, to be photographed with them. Francis joked with them as they drove slowly along the rutted dirt track that would lead them to the Mara Reserve. The Maasai soon backed away, realizing that anyone who spoke their language as well as Francis had no need of being photographed with them. Oscar sat still meantime, smiling and saying nothing as the Maasai chattered at him and nearly stuck their entire heads inside the vehicle, the better to show off their wares.

Eventually, the crude dirt road intercepted a much-improved roadway that led them by late afternoon to an old lodge deep in the heart of the Mara Reserve. It was well beyond the periphery of the park, where the Maasai were still permitted to graze their cattle. A young Kenyan lad led them to a room overlooking a marsh where game was plentiful in the waning daylight. Francis and Oscar stood for a while on a small balcony, swatting at mosquitoes as they watched reedbuck and gazelles sip from small pools amid the tall reeds.

They dined in a large hall built of heavy timbers. Waiters brought large plates of food while Christmas music poured into the room from speakers hidden behind large, potted palms. The strains of "White Christmas" seemed entirely out of place.

"To your good health," said Oscar, raising a glass. "Thank you so much for spending your Christmas holiday with me. I am so looking forward to tomorrow. What better way to spend Christmas than amid the wilds of Africa, where perhaps the only traces of true freedom still prevail and the order of nature still reigns supreme."

Francis raised his glass in return. "Well, I am most delighted to serve as your personal safari guide, but I hope you won't be disappointed. The order of nature may still be more or less intact, but I can assure you that Mother Nature does not reign supreme. The tourists, like us, see to that. I wish Elizabeth could be here."

"No more than I."

"I still find it quite remarkable that she allowed you to come on this journey at all. How did you manage it, with Christmas and your wedding so close at hand?"

Oscar wiped his mouth with his napkin. "It wasn't easy, I can assure you. We celebrated Christmas a tad early at her mother's home. I gave her the tickets for our honeymoon trip to Tahiti as a present, so she would be assured that I would not renege on my promise. That helped ease some discomfort. In the end, we agreed that my absence would help considerably in keeping her mother from hatching any further plots to derail our wedding plans."

Their conversation was interrupted by an older, distinguished-looking gentleman who approached their table with an air of excitement.

"Francis Dermenjian," he bellowed as he drew near, "what a pleasant surprise. So good to see you. Why, it's been ages."

Francis stood and reached out to shake hands. "Good to see you, Reggie," he said. "It has been quite a while. I'd like you to meet my traveling companion, Oscar Newman."

"Most delighted," he said, pulling up a chair and hailing a waiter as if he owned the place, which, as Francis explained to Oscar, was indeed the case.

"You're that Nobel chap, aren't you?" said Reggie, who, speaking with a thick British accent, seemed like a veritable relic from earlier colonial days. "Why, I was simply looking over the guest register when I saw your names. It's quite an honor. How long are you staying?"

"Just tonight," said Francis. "We're heading off in the morning on safari through the Mara, Serengeti, Ngorongoro, and beyond. We plan on about two weeks."

"Well, you're in luck, Dr. Newman. This is the finest guide we ever had here. Knows this country like the back of his hand, can read it like a book. You'll see plenty of wildlife, I guarantee it."

"So you used to work here?" Oscar inquired of Francis as a waiter opened a bottle of champagne and began filling fresh glasses.

"Yes, many years ago. I worked about five summers here. Reggie was a friend of my father's, helped me get hired, in fact."

"And there's always a job waiting for you," he said.

"I'm afraid I'm a bit too old for that now. My patience with tourists these days has worn much too thin, and besides, it's hard work. I've had to push so many vehicles out of the mud that I'm amazed my vertebrae are still intact."

Before leaving them, Reggie asked if they would mind posing for a photograph. A photo of Oscar would go well on the walls, which featured pictures of various celebrities, from Hemingway to the pope. Oscar obliged, unaccustomed as he was to such celebrity status.

They rose very early on Christmas morning, the air clear with just a trace of humidity. After a light breakfast, they headed toward the Land Rover. Safari vehicles of all types were lining up in front of the lodge, and in a distant clearing Oscar noticed several hot-air balloons being readied for some early-morning flights.

"Looks like we just beat the commuter rush," observed Oscar.

"That's exactly what I had in mind," replied Francis as he started the engine and looked about to assure himself that all was ready. Then he proceeded to drive toward a faint set of dirt tracks that led toward a large, grassy plain where the silhouettes of various hoofed creatures far in the distance stood out in the dim morning light.

As they approached, binoculars at the ready, Francis began describing the different varieties of antelope, distinguishing the stately impala, the sleek Thomson's and Grant's gazelles, and the handsome topi from one another, all of whom were grazing quite comfortably side by side. A few gangly, unmistakable wildebeest and a fair number of zebra milled about as well. Francis stopped the vehicle at a slight rise in the nearly invisible roadway that provided a better perspective for viewing the herd, which must have numbered well over two hundred animals. Oscar was about to speak when Francis made a quick movement with his hand, indicating that silence was in order. He pointed to the west, where the tall grass was wavering slightly. As Oscar watched, the grass suddenly parted and a large cheetah came bounding straight toward them. Oscar gasped, but before he could utter a word the cheetah bounded up onto the hood of the Land Rover, as if he planned to join them in the front seat. Instead the magnificent feline creature gave them a look of mild tolerance, then sat upright, alert and completely focused on the herd before them.

"As you can see," Francis whispered, "some of the wildlife have grown quite accustomed to tourists. He's just using us, trying to get a better fix on the herd, which to him means breakfast."

"Absolutely incredible," whispered a very awe-inspired Oscar in return. After a few moments the cheetah jumped quite suddenly and began following a circular course to the east. They watched as he disappeared and then momentarily reappeared, moving ever closer to the herd of animals. Francis pointed out one particular topi that stood as sentinel atop an old termite mound while the other animals grazed quietly. Suddenly, the topi began to wave his tail wildly before bolting from his perch. In an instant the entire herd was in motion, moving rapidly toward the west as the cheetah emerged from the tall grass at full speed. He closed the distance between himself and the herd very rapidly. One of the younger gazelles fell behind the pack, and in an instant the cheetah had him by the snout, pulling him down and out of sight. Francis and Oscar continued watching, but all they saw were the flailing legs of the young gazelle and the occasional shifting of the cheetah's hindquarters as he easily overpowered his quarry.

"Breathtaking," said Oscar, quite startled at seeing such a kill so soon after leaving the comfort of the lodge.

"The terrible beauty of nature," said Francis, as they watched another cheetah emerge from the grass to join in the feast. "Most people spend days waiting to see a kill such as that. We're quite fortunate."

"Best Christmas present ever," said Oscar, feeling his heart race.

"For us, perhaps," replied Francis, "but certainly not for that young gazelle."

Chapter 16

They watched for another ten minutes or so as hordes of vultures descended from the sky, ultimately forcing the cheetahs off the kill. Francis started the engine and they moved on. They spent the next few hours driving slowly across the plains, passing various herds of hoofed animals, seeing more cheetahs but no further kills. Occasionally, they would come across the bleached bones of wildebeest who had clearly failed to make the return migration to the Serengeti. Francis explained the cycle of the wildebeest migration, how the volcanic soils of the Serengeti would dry out in July or August, leading to the annual trek north to the Mara, where they would graze until the rains returned to the Serengeti in September.

By midday the ferocious heat forced them off the plains. Francis headed for a gallery forest along the Talek River, where Maasai manyattas were again evident and various camps held a profusion of tourists. Nonetheless, they saw numerous Cape buffalo, bushbuck, and finally, enormous elephants pulling down pods from some abnormally large acacias near the river. They stopped to watch them, emerging from the Land Rover but not venturing too far from it. The trees were rich with birdlife and Francis did not hesitate to identify them all, often merely by their calls before he'd even seen them.

"Reggie was quite right," said Oscar. "Did you know we would find elephants here?"

"I had a good hunch. They favor the seedpods from these particular trees, which I thought would be ripe this time of year. Just a lucky guess."

"Luck? Hardly. You're too modest, my friend," said Oscar as they gazed at these enormous creatures with their prehensile snouts that deftly pulled the pods from the trees. A large bull stood to one side, moving his large front leg from side to side amid the grass.

"That bull is eating grass," said Francis. "They have very sharp toenails that function like scythes, so there's no need to lower their heads to graze."

Oscar watched as the elephant lowered his trunk, swirled it one time, and raised a large sheaf of grass, which he stuffed into his mouth. "Extraordinary," said Oscar.

Francis drove deftly, barely watching where he was driving, giving Oscar the impression that the Land Rover was really just part of an amusement ride in one vast fantasy game park. They stopped for lunch at the edge of the plains beneath a grove of sausage trees, whose low-hanging fruit is so prized by the Maasai for making their calabashes. They ate some sandwiches and watched as a troop of baboons, curious yet wary, moved slowly from the trees out onto the grassy plains, searching for grubs. The colorful baboons turned and looked at the two humans from time to time before disappearing in the lush, tall grasses, only to reappear occasionally as they stood on their hind legs to look about for predators.

"There you have it," said Francis. "That's how we did it!"

"I beg your pardon?" inquired Oscar.

"This is precisely the situation that gave rise to our species. You saw how they moved out of the forest on all fours, yet stood on their hind legs to look for predators?"

"Yes," said Oscar.

"Our ancestors did likewise, only at that time the Rift Valley was just forming and the climate was becoming drier. Grasslands were expanding, and the ability to move from one patch of forest, where our simian ancestors were most at home, across the grasslands to the next patch was greatly enhanced by the ability to stand on two legs, just like those baboons, to keep an eye out for predators. Later on, bipedalism proved useful for spotting prey as we developed into a carnivorous species."

"Ah yes," said Oscar, suddenly rising to his feet to gain a better view of the departing baboons. "While no doubt nurturing a penchant for reciprocal altruism."

"Perhaps," offered Francis, who smiled at such a suggestion.

They spent the afternoon driving along the edge of the forest, where game was not as plentiful as on the plains but the chances were better for spotting both leopards and lions. Most importantly, from Francis's viewpoint, there were fewer chances of encountering other tourists and thus spoiling the sense of wilderness about them. But it was not until quite late in the afternoon that they finally saw a pride of lions lying about in tall grass beneath some trees about fifty yards off the rough dirt track. The lions barely raised their heads as the Land Rover came into view and slowed to a halt.

Oscar and Francis sat silently, watching carefully through their binoculars as these magnificent beasts lolled about. They appeared as docile as could be, their only movement consisting of an occasional lick of a massive paw or a sweep of a tail at flies. Yet one large male with a thick mane of dark-brown fur kept a faithful eye on both Francis and Oscar. The others completely ignored them.

"They don't appear too terribly frightening," whispered Oscar, who was nonetheless breathing more heavily than usual.

"These animals are quite used to humans," replied Francis. "It is highly unlikely they would charge. But one would be well advised to remain in one's vehicle and under no circumstances to approach them."

"No argument there," said Oscar as he lowered his binoculars and gazed at the mighty cats, particularly the male, with whom he felt he had made eye contact that sent shivers down his spine.

They watched the lions for nearly half an hour, waiting for them to move, growl, or do something other than lie about. The lions clearly had no interest in doing so and Francis moved on. By early evening they reached the Mara River. Here they encountered many more tourists, who were intent on seeing hippos wading in the river or the crocodiles sleeping along its shores.

They found a decent campsite relatively far removed from other humans and ate a light, early supper before venturing to a small overlook by the river. The water was chocolate brown and running high. Fifty yards upriver, several hippos were bathing in midstream, while two more were grazing in the reed grass along the shore. One of them emerged from the water and ambled up along the opposite riverbank, its tiny ears set high above its bloated body. With a quick shifting of its enormous bulk, it turned and let loose a huge spray of manure that covered a swath of trees along the shore for a distance of at least fifty feet. Oscar nearly doubled over in hysterics.

"It's really no laughing matter," said Francis. "The hippos play a very important role in river ecology, spreading enormous quantities of fertilizer, as you just saw, as they move about consuming hundreds and hundreds of pounds of vegetation every day."

"I've no doubt that every bit of every animal's excrement plays an important role for some creature somehow in the intricate web of life on this amazing continent," said Oscar, still reeling with laughter. "But watching that hippo reminded me of, well, certain people I've known. Mostly politicians!"

They slept peacefully and awoke before dawn. Once they had broken camp, Francis headed out to the east along another set of faint dirt tracks toward more open country. The eastern sky harbored a number of clouds that changed slowly from dark-gray silhouettes to fiery-red medallions that heralded the birth of a new day. As it peeked above the distant hills, the sun spread glorious light upon the rich grass of the Mara, and long shadows loomed wherever wild animals stood grazing. They passed herds of zebra and antelope, witnessed the occasional cheetah in pursuit of gazelles, and watched eagles and hawks circling and diving in search of lowlier creatures such as mice and voles, whose numbers, though unseen, were tremendously high. Or at least that was what Francis maintained as he continued to provide a running monologue concerning the ecology of the Mara plains, describing the life history of every species they encountered.

By midmorning they reached the border with Tanzania and entered Serengeti National Park. Yet what lay before them was not the Serengeti of Oscar's imaginings. There were no vast, grassy plains teeming with wildlife, just more woodlands. The plains were many miles to the south. But it was glorious country, heavily wooded in places but quite open in others, with more relief than they had seen throughout the Mara. Here they saw klipspringer standing high atop rocky hills like mountain goats, whose niche, according to Francis, they occupied in this equatorial zone. They watched stately giraffes prance amid the levelheaded acacias and saw the broken branches—and in some cases, trunks—of many other trees where elephants had blazed new trails. Occasionally, they would glimpse through the trees a band of these enormous pachyderms that would quickly disappear into deeper woodlands, wary of potential poachers.

By noon they had rejoined the main road through the park, where dust trails from the vehicles before them tempered their progress. They had entered a more sensitive area, known for its leopards, where off-road travel was prohibited. Yet they made good time, undeterred by sightings of large predators that normally beckon vehicles to a halt. By midafternoon they had arrived at Seronera Wildlife Lodge, a well-fortified structure built into a rocky outcrop. Here they were obliged to check in with Tanzanian immigration. Francis breathed a sigh of relief when their blacklist failed to cite Oscar among those who were not welcomed in this country.

They quenched their thirst at the bar before heading out again into the African terrain, where the acacia woodland was beginning to thin out as they approached the famous Serengeti plains. They had traveled but half a mile when Francis turned off the main road onto a faint track that ran alongside a small stream.

"With luck we may sight a leopard or two," he said.

The stream course was lined with trees, which Francis periodically stopped to examine. Finally, they saw dangling from one of the trees a large, spotted leg. Francis pulled to a halt. They watched as the leg was raised up into the foliage, out of sight. Then a large male leopard descended from the tree and leaped onto the ground. He gave a casual glance toward them and then walked slowly into the thick, tall grass. They followed him with their binoculars, watching the ripples of his sleek, muscular body undulate beneath his dappled coat, his long tail swinging lazily behind him. At last only the wavering of the grass belied his whereabouts. It was a brief encounter but another unforgettable sighting for Oscar, who sat shaking his head.

"Can't believe any human would even think of wearing the hide of such a creature," said Oscar. "We're simply not worthy. And to think they were hunted nearly to extinction because of their beautiful skins."

"They're not exactly out of the woods, if you'll excuse the pun," Francis responded. "Poachers are still taking quite a toll on them."

They returned to the main road and drove on for several more miles before Francis ventured off road again in search of a suitable campsite. They stopped at what appeared to be the edge of the woodlands, where only the vastness of the Serengeti savannah loomed before them.

"It means the 'empty place,'" said Francis as they were setting up their tent.

"The empty place?" said Oscar.

"Yes, that's what 'Serengeti' means in the Maa language. We'll see for ourselves tomorrow."

They made camp as the lowering sun set the sky afire once again, spraying hues of purple across the clouds while auburn tones rippled through the sea of waving grass. Not a single silhouette of any savannah inhabitant interrupted the view to the south as they sat before their campfire, eating the last of the fresh food they had brought from Nairobi, and watched the immense expanse of grass before them shift and sway in the fading daylight. A thin sliver of a new moon appeared in the western sky until it too dipped slowly below the horizon, leaving only the bright band of the Milky Way as celestial illumination.

They slept peacefully but were awakened early by the grunting of wildebeest. They looked out from their tent to find the formerly empty savannah pulsing with a new tide of wildlife. The wildebeest had moved north overnight and were spread by the thousands in a vast stain of black upon the grasslands to the south.

Throughout the day, as Francis drove slowly overland, the herds did not thin but instead became even denser. At times they were so immersed in wildebeest that Francis would come to a halt, waiting for the animals to move aside and let the Land Rover pass.

"I feel we're intruding right into the heart of their domicile," Oscar remarked.

"Indeed we are," said Francis, "but their domicile is constantly on the move. We simply happened into the midst of their current wanderings, and it seems we have them all to ourselves."

"Perhaps it's the other way around," returned Oscar, a bit uncomfortable with their proximity to several thousand tons of snorting and grunting, foul-smelling bovine creatures whose menacing horns more than once came close to putting a few dents and scratches in the Land Rover's virgin paint job. Yet the exhilaration of finding himself engulfed in such a massive horde of truly wild animals was completely new, and Oscar found himself laughing, quite nervously at times.

"Remarkable creatures!" shouted Oscar above the din. "They look like they're part horse, with those long, large heads, and part ox, with those droopy horns."

"Perhaps part goat as well, considering their bearded chins," Francis replied. "Someone once suggested they resemble an animal designed by a committee. What I find remarkable is how they share the grasslands with the other inhabitants of the savannah, like the zebra you see grazing among them. They both eat the same grasses, but zebra prefer the tougher stems while the wildebeest eat the more tender, moist blades of grass. And the Thomson's gazelles feed on only the most tender shoots. It's quite an efficient partitioning of resources. Speaking of which, there's a congregation of vultures over that way; let's see what they're feasting on."

Within ten minutes they came upon a fairly fresh zebra carcass, where a lone lioness was attempting to fend off not only the vultures but a pack of at least a dozen hyenas. Francis and Oscar watched for several minutes, from a distance so they would not interfere, as the hyenas ultimately chased off the lioness and gorged themselves while the vultures sat patiently, for the most part, awaiting their turn. The bloodied faces of the hyenas were a sight indeed, but it was more their shrill howls and yips that gave Oscar the willies.

"I still do not comprehend how humankind ever emerged from such a setting as this," he offered. "Without this vehicle, we'd be dead meat, quite literally."

"Well," said Francis, "back then we didn't have to worry so much about these creatures. Only saber-toothed tigers."

"Thank you," said Oscar. "I feel much better now."

By the time they had passed through the herds, it was late afternoon. They had traveled only fifteen miles or so, since navigating through the vast sea of wildebeest intermixed with zebra and assorted antelope had required very slow, careful driving by Francis. Once beyond them, Francis made considerably better time. They exited the tall grasslands and entered the short-grass range, where they saw mostly Grant's gazelles and the occasional jackal until they began climbing up to much higher ground.

"These are the Naabi Hills," said Francis. "We should have some nice views from up here."

They climbed slowly, winding through stunted trees rooted among outcroppings of well-rounded boulders. They saw lions once again and cheetahs resting in the shade of the trees. Once at the summit, they pulled to a stop under a grove of *Commiphora* trees. From there they could see quite clearly in all directions. The savannah they had traversed all day lay to the north, and in the lowering sun they could see the silhouettes of the large herds far in the distance. Rising above the savannah here and there were small hills, arranged like island archipelagoes amid the sea of grass. Far to the east were the crater highlands, and behind them, to the southeast, was Olduvai.

"You see those rocky outcroppings in the distance, peeking up through the grasslands?" Francis inquired, as he pointed them out to Oscar.

"Yes, they seem a bit out of place," he responded.

"They are the very tops of mountains that have been slowly buried by the eruptions from those volcanoes you see over there, to the east. They are called kopjes, meaning 'little heads,' and, like these Naabi Hills, they have their own remnant vegetation and wildlife, isolated as they are from each other. The lodge at Seronera is actually built into one of them. Did you notice the fig trees growing there, and the little hyrax peeking in and out of the rocks? They're like survivors on a ship that is slowly sinking as the ash from those volcanoes ever so slowly engulfs the landscape before us. But just as the ash has buried all but the very tops of the old mountains, it has created the vast grasslands that we see below. The ash is quite porous and does not hold water well. However, salts in the ash are leached away by the rain to form a dense hardpan three feet below the surface that inhibits trees from rooting there, thus assuring the survival of the grasslands. And the ash is rich in calcium, which has been literally transformed, via the grass, into the flesh and bones of these immense herds."

"As well as ours, I suppose," Oscar responded. "Dust to dust, and all that."

"Yes," said Francis, "and ours. This is indeed where it's believed our species emerged. For there you have, below us, Olduvai Gorge, where the waters from the heavens have slowly exposed the traces of our ancestors, long since buried under the trillions of tons of ash that created the plains we see today."

Oscar looked to the southeast, where the land fell away and faint traces of the layers upon layers of volcanic ash could be seen in the side slopes of the gorge he had come so far to see firsthand. He shivered in anticipation of the following day's encounter with his, and everyone's, past.

Chapter 17

They camped several miles away near the wooded edge of a marsh bordering Lake Ndutu. Game was quite abundant. Graceful eland nibbled on brush nearby while impala, steenbok, and an occasional giraffe wandered within sight of their camp. They heard the roar of lions during the night but managed to sleep fairly well despite the realization that they, too, were potential prey.

"Just be sure to keep the tent zipped up tight," said Francis.

"With pleasure," said Oscar as he extinguished the lantern and lay listening to the sounds of these ferocious creatures of the night through the painfully thin walls of the tent. Once asleep, he dreamed about Elizabeth and saw her running through herds of wildebeest trying desperately to reach him, but the wildebeest would not let her through to him. Nor could he get to her, as he found himself unable to run, as if his legs were rooted in the volcanic soil. The unsettling effects of the dream were soon lost, however, as he awoke and realized that this was the day he had long awaited.

"This marsh," said Francis, "is part of the headwaters that drain to Olduvai, which is actually now properly called Oldupai Gorge. I thought it would be a fitting place to begin today's journey."

"Olduvai or Oldupai, whatever. Ready or not, here we come!" Oscar responded, feeling quite invigorated as he finished packing his sleeping bag and other belongings.

They ate a light breakfast of dried fruit and grains before heading out, winding back around the various fingers of the marsh, retracing the route they had taken from the Naabi Hills. It ran along the stream that carved away the gorge where the Leakeys made the discoveries that first established East Africa as the undeniable birthplace of humankind.

"Many years ago this area was occupied by a soda lake," said Francis as he drove slowly, "but faulting and uplift caused the drainage pattern to shift, allowing this stream to carve this three-hundred-foot-deep gorge through various layers of volcanic ash, exposing our ancestral roots, as it were."

"I'm already a bit giddy at the prospect of seeing it all firsthand," Oscar replied.

"And you will. I took the liberty of hiring a guide to give us a private walking tour beginning at ten o'clock. It would be best to view the gorge before it gets too hot."

"I couldn't agree more."

They met their guide just outside the Olduvai Gorge Museum, which overlooked the full depth and breadth of the gorge. He was a young Tanzanian who had studied archaeology at UC Berkeley. He spoke English quite well and happily, after introductions, appeared to have never heard of the Nobel Peace Prize Laureate Professor Oscar Newman. As they descended a steep path, he pointed out the various beds of lava and ash that contained fossils and relics from different periods of human occupation going back nearly two million years. "So we are literally walking back through time as we descend," he said.

"So we are," said Oscar, who was paying careful attention to where their guide was pointing. "The beds are fairly discernible. Yet it's hard to imagine the vastly different worlds that occupied this very place. It makes you wonder how long it will be before more eruptions doom this area once again."

"We'll get a good look in a day or two at the active volcanoes that are currently threatening to send more ash this way," said Francis, "but those that buried these bones and these tools have long since eroded away. Do you see that spiky plant growing in abundance over there? It's what the Maasai call *oldupai*, hence the name of the gorge. It's really just a type of wild sisal."

"Yes, I see," said Oscar as he stared at the sparsely vegetated, crumbling walls of the gorge. Once they reached rock bottom, their guide led them to a small monument marking the discovery site of *Zinjanthropus* or, as later renamed according to the plaque on top, *Australopithecus boisei*.

"You are now standing on the basement rock," said the guide, "black lava that is 1.8 million years old. Back then, the area was occupied by a lake, as evidenced by the many fossilized fish bones found in some of the strata. And the abundance of primitive stone tools found here by Dr. Louis Leakey during his initial explorations back in 1931, along with a fossilized skull allegedly found nearby in 1913, led him to believe the area had been occupied by early man. So he and his team began digging through nearly two million years of history, conveniently exposed by the river, which over the last thirty thousand years has carved through the various layers of rock and volcanic ash to create Olduvai Gorge. They were looking for the creature, or creatures, that made those stone tools. It took them twenty-eight years of intermittent exploration to dig through the overlying strata before they finally came upon the remains of someone who might have made such tools.

"On July 17, 1959, while Louis was sick and back in camp, his wife, Mary Leakey, discovered a few teeth sticking up from the ground at this very location. She hurried back to camp and yelled to her husband, 'Louis, I found him!' Over the next few weeks they unearthed pieces of a skull, generally known as 'Zinj,' whose reconstruction can be seen in the museum collection."

"Fascinating," said Oscar. "Such perseverance."

"Yes, they were obviously quite dedicated," the guide continued, "but was it Zinj, or *Zinjanthropus*, later renamed *Australopithecus boisei* and now known as *Paranthropus boisei*, who made those tools? Very doubtful, as he was a vegetarian. He has an apelike skull with a sagittal crest and powerful jaws. The Leakeys dubbed him 'nutcracker man.' The following year, in 1960, the Leakey team discovered fossil remains not far away—still in the oldest bed here, Bed I—of *Homo habilis*, which means 'handyman.' His cranial capacity was much larger and they also found an abundance of stone tools, including hand axes. Both of these sets of fossil remains date to 1.8 million years, and the two species likely coexisted, for perhaps as long as five hundred thousand years. But *Homo habilis*, or handyman, is viewed as the first member of the genus *Homo* due to his larger cranial capacity and clear ability to make and use stone tools. They apparently lived communally near the shore of the lake that once occupied this area.

"The discoveries continued that year, and later in 1960, while excavating in the younger Bed II, the Leakey team found the 1.4-million-year-old skullcap of another early hominid with a cranial capacity of greater than one thousand cubic centimeters. Later discoveries proved this creature was fully bipedal and nearly as big as we are today. They called this species *Homo erectus*, upright man. He appeared about 1.6 million years ago, as *Homo habilis* was going extinct, and later spread throughout parts of Africa and Eurasia. And it was *Homo erectus* who first discovered how to make fire. There are many paleoanthropologists who believe we *Homo sapiens* are direct descendants of *Homo erectus*, who disappeared about 140,000 years ago, by far the longest-lived species in the genus *Homo*.

"Beds III and IV have yielded very little in terms of the fossil record, though many fine stone tools have been found. The geology of these beds is not good for preserving and fossilizing bones. There are not the right minerals present. But Bed

V has revealed fossilized remains of *Homo sapiens*, dating back four hundred thousand years."

"Extraordinary," Oscar remarked as he surveyed the breadth of the excavations.

"Yes," said the guide. "And there are several ongoing digs within the gorge. There are still many questions to be answered about our human origins."

"But there's no doubt," said Oscar, "that we all came from here, from this Great Rift Valley, this veritable cradle of humankind. And that means that we are all, to one degree or another, cousins. We are all family."

"If only we could admit it," said Francis.

They visited the Bed I stone circle, thought to be the earliest human-made shelter discovered to date. Then their guide led them to an assortment of ancient stone tools lying out upon the ground.

"These are hand axes," he said. "The more crudely shaped ones were made by *Homo habilis*. The others, which are more symmetrical, are the work of *Homo erectus*." He explained how the tools were made and what type of rock was used, and showed how *Homo erectus* would use them to butcher their kills or, more likely, their scavenged meat. Then they visited the site of an ongoing dig by students from the University of Wisconsin. Oscar pelted them with questions regarding their work, to which they were most happy to respond, showing him bits of fossilized bones that they were hoping would help them better understand the ecological setting that existed there long ago and the myriad ancient animal species that once lived within it.

After two hours of walking through the gorge, Oscar, Francis, and their guide found their way back to the steep trail leading uphill to the museum. They thanked their guide profusely and tipped him quite generously. Francis grabbed some sandwiches and drinks from the cooler in the back of the Land Rover, and they settled down for lunch under one of the thatched-roof shelters near the museum that afforded perfect views of the gorge.

Francis looked at Oscar, who, despite his keen interest in visiting Olduvai, seemed rather glum. He was just staring out into the gorge, his face expressionless.

"Are you all right?" Francis inquired.

"Yes," said Oscar, wiping his brow. "That was quite a walk back through a considerable span of time. It's all quite overwhelming. There's so much to absorb here. My mind isn't capable of fully grasping the meaning of it all. To think these people roamed about over a million and a half years ago. So much has evolved since then, and this is where it began. Those stone tools, whose idea were they and where did the spark of inspiration to create them originate? And did they only use them to carve away at the animals they killed? Or did they, as your brother would have it, use them on each other?"

"Those are all good questions, the type that keep archaeologists and paleoanthropologists hard at work, I suppose," said Francis. He hesitated before resuming the conversation, noting the worried, almost haggard look on Oscar's face. He hadn't even touched his sandwich.

"It's not meeting your expectations somehow, is it?" said Francis. "This visit to Olduvai Gorge."

"No, it's not that. This has been a marvelous morning of discovery. It's just that while all this is so stimulating intellectually, I still have such fears about procreating. That's what I'm struggling with, and I thought perhaps seeing where it all began would somehow wash those fears away. I was just being foolish to have such high hopes."

"I don't know," said Francis. "But what exactly are you afraid of? Elizabeth will certainly make a good mother. And I don't see why a compassionate man like you wouldn't make a good father."

Oscar breathed a sigh and finally took a bite of the sandwich followed by a healthy swig of water. "It's like this," he began. "My father was killed when I was but a month old, trying to renovate an old tin mine back in Cornwall. The walls collapsed around him. Besides having no fatherly role model, I had no younger or older siblings, so I was never around babies much. And now whenever someone hands me a newborn child, an infant to hold, I simply hand the child back as quickly as possible. It frightens me, frankly, to hold such a small, vulnerable person in my hands. And the prospect of having my own child to hold frightens me even more, to be perfectly honest. I wouldn't know where to begin."

"My goodness," said Francis. "There are plenty of books on parenting, books that should be able to help you to—how did you put it?—'serve as a proper trustee of your own genetic endowment'!"

Oscar took another bite of his sandwich and began chewing, as much on the words just spoken as on the bread and what lay in between.

"Yes, I suppose you're right," he said at last.

After lunch, they visited the museum, which held not only the famous Zinj skull but those of *Homo habilis* and *Homo erectus*. There were also displays of ancient animal fossils, both Olduwan and Acheulean-era stone tools and of course a large display devoted to the Leakeys. But Oscar remained glued to the reconstructed skull of Zinj, and next to it, also from Bed I, his neighbor in time and space, "handyman."

"Quite impressive, aren't they?" said Francis.

"They certainly are. But try as I may, I just can't seem to breathe any life into them."

"Perhaps give it a bit more time," said Francis. "Or better yet, have a look around at the other exhibits. I'm going to visit the restroom."

Oscar tore himself away from the mesmerizing fossilized faces of our ancient ancestors, who had somehow lived without fire for a million years. He glanced at the collections of stone tools and the fossilized horns of ancient antelope. Turning a corner, he entered an entirely new room that featured a large mural, a depiction of life as it might have been way back then, with upright hominids walking through a mudflat. Surely this is *Homo erectus*, he thought, until he read the descriptions and saw the re-created footprints of these very people laid horizontally in front of him. This was not *Homo erectus*; this was *Australopithecus afarensis*, the same species as Lucy, who was discovered as an almost intact skeleton in the Afar region of Ethiopia. And these footprints, recreated from castings of the actual footprints discovered in 1978 by Mary Leakey and her crew at Laetoli, thirty miles away, were 3.6 million years old! And they were walking upright!

Oscar began reading every interpretive sign describing how those who left these footprints had been walking through a mudflat when volcanic eruptions covered their footsteps with ash and no doubt buried them as well. The imprint of the arches and the array of the toes indicated these creatures were bipedal, walking upright. There were three sets of footprints, two that were close together, one set much larger than the other. Though the mural depicted a man and a woman walking side by side, Oscar saw it much differently. He stood next to the cast of the footprints and retraced their steps, only he held his arm out to one side, as if sheltering someone from the falling ash. This is how Francis found Oscar upon his return, and tears were streaming down his face.

"Good heavens, Oscar, what's wrong?" he cried.

"Nothing, my friend," he replied, "nothing at all."

"Then why are you crying?"

Oscar took a deep breath. "Do you remember when I said I wanted to walk in the dirt that clung to the feet of my ancestors? Well, this is as close as I'm going to get. But as I contemplated what was happening here, I saw not a man and a woman, but a man and a child. He was doing his best to shelter him, his son, from the rain of ash that was pouring down upon them. I tried to imagine how they must have felt when suddenly, it was my father trying to protect someone, possibly me, from the failing walls and rotted timbers of the old tin mine. Had I been there with him, he surely would have tried to protect me, just as this father was trying to protect his son 3.6 million years ago. And then it hit me. We are all still animals. The instinct is there, rooted in our genes for so many generations. It is nothing more than the will to live, and to keep on living and surviving from generation to generation. What I'm saying is I understand now. When and if the time comes, I believe I will be ready."

Chapter 18

They left Olduvai and headed for their next stop, Ngorongoro Crater. By late afternoon they had reached the upper slopes of the famed caldera and stopped to take in the view to the west, over the area they had just crossed. The air was very clear, thanks to a stiff breeze blowing from the north.

"Beautiful," said Oscar, contemplating the vast expanse of wildland before them, land that stretched all the way to Lake Victoria. "Like out of a dream."

"Yes," said Francis, "a dream that helped produce an animal as crafty as us."

"Amen," Oscar replied. "But what's that eerie noise? Sounds like it could be the ghosts of all the lost souls who once lived in this valley below, still searching for eternity in these hills."

"It's the whistling thorn," said Francis as he grabbed Oscar by the arm and led him toward one of the many scrawny-looking trees nearby, each one covered in gray, flaky bark infected here and there with large, puffy galls.

"The whistling is caused by ants. They burrow into the galls, creating these tiny holes that make a whistling sound when the wind blows. The ants secrete formic acid, which is an irritant to any browsing animal, thus helping to protect the tree. Classic example of symbiosis. Interesting hypothesis, however, these ghosts. If you're correct, they may simply be trying to find their way back to Eden. For that is where we are headed."

Oscar gave a puzzled look. "Ngorongoro?"

"Yes. Ngorongoro Crater, one of the true natural wonders of the world."

They stopped for the night at a lodge built into the side of the crater rim that circled all the world before them. The broad, round valley, twelve miles in diameter with a sizable lake near the center, was otherwise covered in grasses. The forested slopes flowing down from the crater rim were the lushest and greenest hues in Mother Nature's palette. Standing on a terrace nestled between stone ramparts, Oscar and Francis sipped Scotch whisky and toasted one another.

"What a remarkable day," said Oscar. "A journey through time, to see ourselves as we once were long, long ago. And now this. I can't thank you enough, Francis."

"No need, Oscar, I'm enjoying this journey as much as you. Ngorongoro means 'Gift of Life' in Maa," said Francis. "I still find it so difficult to fathom the

131

immensity of the explosion that occurred here some three million years ago to create a caldera as big as this. Can you imagine?"

Oscar thought of the 3.6-million-year-old humanlike footprints he had just seen, preserved for so long by volcanic ash.

"Yes, Francis," he said. "I think I can. It's what helped create the Serengeti, isn't it? And from what you tell me, it's a gift of life in more ways than one."

"How's that?"

"Didn't you say that the ash is rich in calcium, calcium that helped build the bones of the vast herds in the Serengeti? And ours too, no doubt?"

"Yes, there's some truth to that, depending on the particular volcano." Francis polished off his whisky. Oscar's was long gone.

They dined at a table next to a large window, eating like kings, drinking good wine, marveling at the view, and generally making the most of their stay. They slept in but it was just as well. Thick morning fog covered the entire valley.

"No sense venturing down there just yet," said Francis. So they treated themselves to a nice English breakfast while watching the fog slowly dissipate, like a heavenly veil yielding to the rising sun.

"Shall we get on with it?" said Oscar, wiping his chin. "I'm ready to see downtown Eden."

They descended a steep roadway, winding through a forest of giant candelabra trees while the last wisps of fog faded away. They caught glimpses of elephant and buffalo. At one point a female lion crossed the road in front of them, turning her head slowly to briefly inspect their vehicle before continuing nonchalantly on her way, clearly disinterested and not the least bit frightened. At the bottom of their descent they encountered a lovely pool of water, on the far side of which was a stand of trees whose bark was peeling off in large chunks, revealing the yellow trunks underneath.

"This is called Seneto Springs," said Francis, "and those are fever trees on the other side. Bit of a misnomer, really. They always grow near the water and the early settlers blamed them for the outbreaks of malaria before anyone knew anything about the *Anopheles* mosquito."

They continued on amid short-grass plains as the sun climbed higher over the far rim of the crater. They passed more wildebeest and gazelles and spotted the resident pride of lions that laid claim to that particular sector of Ngorongoro. Their bellies were full and so Francis moved on, seeing they were in no mood for

132

hunting. They passed by small pools where flocks of Egyptian geese and sacred ibis preened in the morning sun. Soon the shoreline of a soda lake came into view, and Francis drove slowly, not wanting to disturb the horde of flamingos that bathed in the freshwater springs along its western shore, washing encrusted soda from their elegant pink feathers. Beyond them, hundreds more stood in the shallow waters of the lake, dipping their strange inverted beaks into the soapy waters to feed.

"This, too, is called Lake Magadi," said Francis. "Magadi means 'soda' to the Maasai. The water is actually toxic for the flamingos to drink, but they have evolved an incredible beak that allows them to filter out tiny crustaceans that grow in abundance in the alkaline waters but not ingest the water itself. They drink from freshwater springs, like the one in the foreground where they are bathing themselves."

"Fascinating," said Oscar once again, as he marveled at them through his binoculars, "and so beautiful, the way they move as one large mass, like avian ballerinas. Must be at least a thousand of them."

"There are at least three million flamingos that live in the various lakes of the Rift Valley. Most of them breed far out in the middle of Lake Natron, our next destination."

"It's simply spectacular," said Oscar. "I don't know how much more beauty I can take. You were absolutely correct, Francis. If ever there was an Eden, this is it."

They ventured on, slowly skirting the edges of Mandusi Swamp, where they saw saddle-billed storks and black-headed herons stalking through the tall grass of the marsh. At one point they observed a bull elephant sunk well up to his chest wading through a pool within the marsh, trumpeting loudly as he moved along slowly among the reeds, as if signaling to some nearby hippos that they had better make room for him. They drove to the top of Round Table Hill, the remains of an old volcanic cone, and from there watched the inhabitants of the marsh below as they suffered through another day in paradise. There were lion cubs bouncing through the tall grass, their mothers in casual pursuit. There were numerous waterfowl nibbling and occasionally diving and more often preening in the now-midday sun as they lolled about on some old rock or stunted tree trunk. In the shallower areas zebra were grazing and on occasion sipping from small pools.

"Magnificent," said Oscar. "Wilderness in absolute harmony. An ecological horn o' plenty. It's a wonder they deign to let us in on the fun."

"Just another day on the crater floor, everyone doing his or her best to stay alive," said Francis. "And all these wild animals have all they need for survival right here, no need to migrate to anywhere else. Let's just hope it lasts forever."

They camped at a modest tented campsite located halfway up the side of the crater. It was a decided departure in terms of comfort from the previous night's accommodations, but the staff was friendly, the evening meal was passable, and the beds were quite comfortable. Most importantly, wildlife was plentiful. Elephants came into view, along with plenty of zebra and colorful birds.

Light rain fell that night, and when Oscar and Francis awoke the land around them seemed cleansed and renewed, ready for another day's bout between predator and prey. They rose early and were on their way before their companions in camp had even begun to stir. The roads were a bit muddy but certainly passable, and as they began to climb the steep wall of Ngorongoro Crater they stopped where a curve in the roadway afforded a vista of the land below. Parts of the crater floor were still covered with mist, like the previous day. They watched it slowly dissipate before their eyes as the cool, damp ground met the warming air of a new African morning.

"One might almost expect to see a band of angels flitting about on top of the mist," said Oscar.

"It is indeed a lovely sight," returned Francis, "quite a magical place, really. I never cease to be awed by it."

"Understandably so," said Oscar. "In any event, where to now?"

Francis slipped the Land Rover into gear. "Today we're heading for Lake Natron," he said. "It will be quite a contrast, I can guarantee that. Some think it quite an inhospitable area and indeed it is, I suppose. Very few people venture out that way. It's quite desolate and unbelievably hot. Natron is where I've been conducting research for the past several years, studying the ecology of the local hot springs. There are remarkably different types of algae that grow in different hot springs near the shore of the lake. I've been trying to determine what factors favor one type of algae over another and how those changes may affect the food web within these small, self-contained hot spring ecosystems."

"Sounds rather academic," Oscar observed.

"Yes, I suppose. But someday lowly algae may help solve the energy crisis. In any event, it's the reason for my trip here in the first place. So I suggest we get this piece of business out of the way. Then we'll decide about Manyara and Kilimanjaro. I doubt we'll have time for both."

"As you wish," said Oscar. "After all, I'm really just along for the ride."

They drove eastward along the southern rim of the crater, savoring the last glimpses of the interior of Ngorongoro until the road began to descend through thick forest. Bright-yellow *Crotalaria* bushes lined the roadside, and beyond them stood the silver trunks of stately pillar wood trees. At times there were views of the bamboo-covered flanks of Oldeani Volcano to the south and beyond it, far in the distance, Lake Manyara.

After exiting the forest, they crossed fertile farmlands where coffee plantations and wheat fields dominated the landscape. Francis explained that they had now entered the land of the Mbulu tribe, originally from the Horn of Africa. The farms were of some concern insofar as they blocked certain migration routes for wildlife.

Oscar shrugged his shoulders. "It's always something that gets done in," he said, "no matter where we go."

The road then descended in steep, winding curves. At the bottom they entered a bustling village with a lively marketplace and a thriving shopping bazaar where the local people, including numerous Maasai, were hawking their wares to throngs of tourists.

"This is Mto wa Mbu. It means 'Mosquito River,'" said Francis. "This is where we would turn off if we were headed for Lake Manyara. But let's check out the market scene, grab a bite of lunch and provisions for the next couple of days. This might be a good spot to pick up a nice souvenir for Elizabeth as well. But we'll be back in a couple of days on our way to Lake Manyara."

"Okay, I'm following you," said Oscar as he glanced southward to see if any part of the lake was visible through the sprawl of hastily constructed buildings.

They located some vendors selling curried bananas, rice, and maize, which they washed down with warm banana beer. Another vendor had fresh goat meat for sale. Francis loaded up on odd-looking fresh fruits and vegetables while Oscar cruised the art stalls. Nearly all of them were run by Maasai women who were quite anxious to strike a deal.

"See anything you like?" said Francis, who now held two shopping bags full of provisions.

"I think I'll hold off for now," said Oscar. "Maybe when we return."

Francis made some comments to the women, who laughed as he and Oscar turned and headed back to the Land Rover.

Once beyond the village Francis made a sharp left turn that eventually led to a very poorly marked track that headed into entirely new terrain, dry and desolate as Francis had promised, that skirted the eastern flanks of Ngorongoro.

"We're heading down the Avenue of the Volcanoes," said Francis, "the heart of Maasailand, if you ask me. That's Kitumbeine volcano before us, not quite ten thousand feet tall, and beyond it through the haze is Gelai. To the east are Losiminguri, Burko, and Monduli, as well as several others which aren't quite visible from here. And ahead of us to the left is Loolmalassin, which is well over ten thousand feet."

Oscar examined the landscape all about him, feeling rather small and quite vulnerable. He wasn't sure he liked the idea of traveling through an area full of active volcanoes, and freshly acquired images of ash-entombed, fossilized skulls did nothing to ease his sense of discomfort.

The land all about was green yet the road was quite dry, in spite of the previous evening's rains. There were ruts and gullies of eroded earth all about them, signs of overgrazing. They passed several herds of rather scrawny Maasai cattle, sighting on occasion a Maasai herdsman as well, who would wave to them and smile. As they headed down into the Engaruka Basin, the temperature continued to climb until Francis was forced at last to turn on the air conditioning.

"Beastly hot," said Oscar, who had been wiping his brow steadily for the last several miles.

"Just the beginning," said Francis. "Wait till we get to Natron."

Unfortunately, the road was deteriorating rapidly, just as the temperature was soaring. They were forced to stop on several occasions where streams draining the eastern slopes of Loolmalassin had taken out part of the roadway. They managed either to restore the roadway using shovels or to push the Land Rover up over the lip of a stubborn washout. It was hard work and Francis kept a close eye on Oscar, often telling him to relax and by all means not to overexert himself.

At one point they picked up a young Maasai hitchhiker who, after traveling half a mile with them, complained that it was too cold in their vehicle and decided he would rather walk. He told Francis that his family's manyatta was not far off and invited them to come and visit. Francis thanked him but said they had a schedule to keep. The Maasai fellow gave him a curious look and shook his head slowly as he walked off into the savannah, clutching his spear to his side.

As they continued on they found themselves completely surrounded by volcanoes. Kitumbeine rose high into the sky five miles to the east, with herds of wildebeest and gazelles grazing peacefully at its base. Loolmalassin towered above them to the west. The eroding flanks of Gelai lay straight ahead. And as they rounded a bend in the scant roadway, there appeared before them another immense, perfectly symmetrical volcano whose minutely furrowed slopes disclosed every tiny crease where sparse rains had worn away its veneer of recently deposited ash.

"That, my friend," said Francis, "is Ol Doinyo Lengai, the Maasai Mountain of God. It is the home of their god and creator, Engai."

"So we have now entered the Maasai holy land," said Oscar.

"We certainly have. Lengai is still an active volcano, and every so often it puts on a spectacular show, spewing black ash for miles that, after contact with the air, turns into pure-white calcium carbonate, or washing soda. It comes from the same subterranean source as the soda springs that feed Lake Natron."

Oscar stared up at the summit of Lengai to the left and then across at Gelai, which towered above to the right as they mounted a slight rise, a saddle between the two enormous volcanoes. Then Oscar looked ahead and saw the strange red-and-white surface of Lake Natron stretching out to merge with the blue sky far beyond. Its shores, composed of white soda flats, were still several miles away, but the pockmarked surface of the lake beyond, where soda springs broke through the crust in eerie red-and-white swirls, looked like some ghastly cauldron where the devil, or perhaps Engai, was concocting some lethal brew.

Francis pulled to a halt and opened the door on his side. The hot, dry air struck Oscar like a blast furnace. He, too, exited and joined Francis in front of the Land Rover, wiping the perspiration from his face. It was late afternoon and the sun was sitting high above but just west of Lengai's summit. The shadows cast by the many ridges and fissures, the many small rivers of virgin ash that ran down its flanks, covered in soft green vegetation, lent a stark relief, a dramatic sense of dimension and an invitation to wallow in the cool, dark folds of this majestic mountain, out of the path of the infernal African sun. Francis turned his attention, however, toward Lake Natron.

"Do you see those soda flats to the west of Gelai?" he inquired.

Oscar nodded.

"The springs I've been studying are right out there. We'll need to get to sleep very early and rise well before dawn so we can dash in and get the samples I need and be gone before the sun is too high. It can climb to 140 degrees Fahrenheit out on that lake in midday."

"A veritable hell on earth," said Oscar. "Yet it's quite beautiful in its own way. I simply can't believe that all those flamingos could raise their young out on that foul, outlandishly hot, caustic excuse for a lake."

"Yes, two and a half million lesser flamingos breed out there," said Francis. "That's 75 percent of the world's population. There's very little chance of being bothered by predators and the red algae provide plenty of nutrition for young and adults alike."

"While turning them all that lovely shade of pink," said Oscar, as he again wiped the perspiration from his brow. "So where do we find a bit of shade in this outrageous, volcano-clad land you've brought me to? I'm about to perish in this heat."

"Don't worry," Francis replied, "we're not far from our campsite, which I think you'll find much to your liking."

They drove for another few miles, though progress was slow due to the presence of many small fingers of ash that swept across the faint trace of the road they had been following. The ash was like fine sand and traction was quite poor. Nevertheless, they eventually came to a tree-lined stream that wound its way around Lengai toward Natron, feeding steamy marshes in the distance.

"Now this is more like it," said Oscar as he waded barefoot through the stream in the shade of overhanging acacias.

"Tell you what," said Francis, after examining the arc of the sun through the trees as he, too, plied the gravel-bottomed yet alkaline waters of the Ngare Sero. "Let's take a little walk upstream."

And so they did, after donning old tennis shoes to help preserve the skin on the bottoms of their feet. After half an hour of plodding through the winding course of the lower stream, the water never rising above their knees, they entered a spectacular gorge with ever-narrowing walls covered first with succulent euphorbia, then a seemingly tropical oasis of wild date palms and fig trees that hung above them. And then they heard the rush of cascading water and came upon a spectacular waterfall. They waded beneath an overarching natural bridge and immersed themselves in the cool, rushing water that, while soapy from its alkaline origins, refreshed and soothed in a most satisfying manner.

"Unbelievable," said Oscar, feeling jets of cool water circle about him while Francis floated peacefully, his eyes closed. "You were right, I never expected anything like this. It's absolute paradise compared to that inferno where we started. I never dreamed heaven and hell could coexist in such harmony."

Chapter 19

They returned to the Land Rover as the sun was fading away beyond the lower reaches of the Nguruman Escarpment that rose high above the western shores of Lake Natron. The campsite showed signs of previous inhabitants, but on this night, New Year's Eve, it was all theirs. The fading light upon the eerie surface of Lake Natron, still a few miles away, seemed almost supernatural as small, scattered clouds above the lake reflected the red shades of the setting sun as well as the crimson tones of the lake below. The broad hulk of Gelai to the east stood basking in the afterglow, its serrated slopes dropping steadily into the starkness of Natron's soda-encrusted shoreline.

Francis built a fire and proceeded to grill the goat meat they had procured at the market. There were more curried bananas and various greens for a salad. Oscar pulled from their only operative cooler a bottle of champagne he'd been saving to ring in the New Year as stars began to peek out from behind the thin veil of daylight.

"Francis, my good friend," said Oscar, raising his glass, "this has been the journey of a lifetime. I have traveled all over this world, through the jungles of Sumatra and the rain forests of Brazil, through the swollen lowlands of India to the Great Wall of China. But never, in all my travels, have I felt so close to the deep secrets of the earth and all its mysterious beauty as on this particular journey. It has been more rewarding than I ever could have imagined and once again I thank you. More than that, I would like to drink to your good health and to wish you a very happy New Year."

They clinked their glasses together as the fire crackled and the heat of the day gave way to the tepid stillness of evening.

"Thank you, Oscar," Francis replied. "And may I wish you a very happy New Year as well. What better way to start than by marrying the woman you love?"

"Hear, hear," chimed Oscar, "I'll certainly drink to that. I must say, I certainly do feel ready. I can't wait to see Elizabeth again. I'd almost as soon skip Manyara and Kilimanjaro and get back to her immediately. As far as I'm concerned, my mission has been accomplished. In fact, looking back on this past year, it seems as though so many of my life's dreams have been realized. And yet, after this journey through time, a year seems so insignificant. Look at this landscape. What does a year mean? The volcanoes sit and brood, casting their shadows about, maybe a puff of ash every now and then, but a year to them—to Engai as well, no doubt—must be like one small fleck of ash among the tons and tons that have been spewed forth over the ages."

Francis laughed. "Actually, this landscape can change drastically over the course of a year," he began. "Just one eruption will see to that. Not long ago the Maasai, who used to be quite numerous in this area, moved farther south because of rumblings within Lengai and a few small eruptions. But in a geologic sense you are of course correct. We are facing due north, looking straight up through the heart of the Rift Valley, which extends all the way to the Afar Triangle and the Red Sea. In several million years this entire area will be underwater, just like the Red Sea itself, which was created as what is now Yemen was sheared off the top of the Afar Triangle and moved north. Eventually, the sea will reclaim this valley as well, and the area to our east will become another island, like Madagascar."

"Quite remarkable, isn't it?" said Oscar. "It's as if the earth itself is alive, its skin crawling and contorting and convulsing while every plant and animal simply does its best to hang on for the ride."

"No animal so successfully as us. But I suggest that if we are to continue to be successful, you and I get some sleep. It will definitely be in our best interest to rise very early."

They slept comfortably, their tent a mere speck of blue nestled at the foot of the immense volcanic cone of Lengai. At 4:00 a.m., Francis shook Oscar and they quietly dismantled and folded their tent amid the sounds of owls and other night creatures. They drove slowly toward Gelai, careful not to crush any of the hundreds of nocturnal rodents that skittered about the barren track that soon faded to no track at all. Francis navigated carefully, following landmarks noted on a crude hand-drawn map.

"Why not use the GPS, for which you paid rather dearly, I'm sure?" Oscar inquired. "That map looks like something out of *Treasure Island*."

"I might if I knew the exact coordinates of the hot spring. Never had GPS before. But I've relied on this map for years to guide me."

"So I see," said Oscar.

The moon hovered above the western flanks of Lengai, and though just past half full, it cast enough light to enable them to see clearly the awesome outline of Gelai and the major ridges that ran down its flanks.

They traveled several miles before arriving at the base of Gelai where it plunged into Lake Natron. Francis drove carefully along the lakeshore, taking advantage of thick soda flats that created a good driving surface. The soda crackled under the weight of the Land Rover, and Oscar did not seem too concerned with the notion of driving on part of Lake Natron itself until Francis came to a large boulder near the shoreline. There he made a sharp left turn and headed right for the center of the lake.

"What the hell are you doing?" he shouted as Francis continued to drive out toward the center of Natron.

"Trust me," Francis replied, "I have driven out here many times. I've taken corings of the soda and consulted with our engineering department at the university. It's more than dense enough to support a tank, at least where we're headed, and it certainly beats walking. The idea is to get in and out quickly, before the sun is up. It's not quite half a mile to the springs, and then it will take me but half an hour to get the samples I need. Then we can head back toward Manyara."

Oscar looked unconvinced but said nothing further as Francis continued to study the map, the odometer, and the compass mounted on the dash. Then up ahead they saw, in the faint light afforded by the newly rising sun far behind Gelai, a small opening in the soda from which a plume of steam was rising. Oscar sighed as he realized they had apparently arrived at their destination. Francis pulled to a stop.

"I don't understand," said Francis. "I must have misread the odometer at the start. We should have another two-tenths of a mile to go. In fact, this doesn't look quite right."

He gave Oscar a puzzled look that turned to one of great alarm as the Land Rover suddenly heaved to the left, then abruptly to the right as it plunged through the soda into a steaming pool of hot water.

"Oh my God, no!" shouted Francis as the Land Rover sank slowly but soon came to rest on the bottom of the lake, with water halfway up its sides.

"This wasn't exactly part of your plan, was it?" said Oscar, who had remained perfectly still.

"No, it certainly wasn't," said Francis, who was literally shaking. "We must remain calm. I need to think."

They sat side by side, both of them breathing heavily. Francis glanced at his watch.

"We have about two hours before the sun will be unbearable. If we exit through the sunroof, we might be able to break through some of this crust and perhaps make some room to maneuver."

He tried the ignition and the engine caught.

"At least we still have power, but who knows for how long. Fortunately, this model is equipped with a snorkel, designed for driving while partially submerged, like when fording a river. Yet this water is so caustic it will eventually corrode the metal, and any electrical connection it contacts may soon be useless."

Francis opened the sunroof and then cut the engine. He climbed out and then realized as he peered back in at Oscar, who stared up at him forlornly, that Oscar was too large to fit through the opening.

"Tell you what, let me pop open the rear window. Oh, and be sure to grab the satellite phone."

Francis did his part while Oscar retrieved his satellite phone, their only link to the rest of the world, from the glove compartment. Then he began rearranging all their food and various pieces of clothing and equipment in the rear of the vehicle to clear a path. As he climbed toward the back, however, the shifting of his weight caused the rear end of the Land Rover to suddenly sink deeper. Hot water spilled over the tailgate into the vehicle, and the sudden tilting caused Oscar to tumble forward. As he thrust out his arms to cushion himself, the satellite phone slipped from his hand and fell into the pool of water that was slowly causing the rear of the vehicle to sink even farther.

"Quick," Francis shouted, "hand me the phone. If it's damaged, we're really in trouble."

Oscar fished about amid all the recently inundated supplies. Once he located it, he quickly passed it out to Francis.

"I'm terribly sorry," he said. "I can't believe I could be so clumsy."

Francis ignored him as he repeatedly pressed buttons on the phone, listening carefully for any sound other than the faint static he was picking up. Oscar struggled on his own but finally managed to squeeze through the rear window, though by the time he fully emerged from the recesses of the swamped Land Rover and set foot upon the hard soda, he was saturated with the hot, soapy waters of Lake Natron.

Francis was frantically punching at the phone, which he had come to realize was now perfectly useless. Oscar approached him cautiously.

"It's beyond hope, isn't it?"

Francis stared at him without uttering a word. The expression on his face fully conveyed the seriousness of their situation. How he missed the trusty old shortwave radio he carried with him at all times in his Jeep! He handed the defunct satellite phone to Oscar and leaned over to peer into the back of the Land Rover. Their cooler had fallen over and flipped open, and all their food was sitting in at least a foot of foul water.

"Like our food supply, I'm afraid," said Francis. "But at least we stowed the camping gear on the roof. I don't know how alkaline this water is. It doesn't feel too bad but it could easily damage all sorts of materials, including our skin."

Oscar felt his skin begin to tingle slightly beneath his soaking-wet clothes. It tingled but fortunately did not burn. Then he looked down at his feet and noticed that the old tennis shoes he was wearing were turning black and the soles were beginning to disintegrate.

"Hand me my rubber boots, if you will," he said. "The soda is beginning to eat away at these flimsy old tennies."

Francis handed him the boots, which Oscar quickly put on, while Francis tried to extract all he could from the flooded Land Rover. He threw their duffel bags up on the roof.

"Help me spread these things out on top," he said, "and don't let anything touch the soda crust or it will be ruined."

Oscar obliged by standing on the edge of the crust and leaning over to help Francis spread out their spare clothing on the roof. The eastern sky was aglow and they could see the light of day hitting the top of the Nguruman Escarpment far across the lake. After the clothes were set out to dry, Francis rejoined Oscar and began walking around the Land Rover, trying to understand what had gone wrong and trying even harder to figure out how to make it right. He walked out to where the steam was rising from the opening in the soda crust. Then at last he returned, walking briskly toward Oscar.

"The earthquake," he said, breathing rapidly, "last October. Its epicenter was near Lake Natron. It wasn't that large, but that's the only explanation I can conceive of as to why there's suddenly a hot spring here that wasn't here last summer."

Oscar looked puzzled.

"Who knows what the plumbing is like beneath this lake bed," Francis continued. "There are springs everywhere. Evidently, that earthquake created a new fissure or reopened an old one that had been plugged. I know I was on the right course. This isn't like the hot spring I've been monitoring. There's hardly any algae growing in it and the water doesn't appear to be as hot. It may even be slightly fresher. Can't tell without taking some samples. But we haven't the time. You can already see the shadow of Gelai projected onto the surface of the lake. It's getting smaller by the minute."

Oscar looked to the west and saw that indeed they were situated within the shrinking shadow of the great volcano to the east. "What do you suggest we do?"

"Let's get the shovel and see if we can break this crust behind the Land Rover. We might be able to back on out of this mess."

There were two shovels, a large one and a small one. They hacked at the stubborn crust, and while they were able to chip it away little by little, they were not able to break off any large pieces. It was taking too long and the shadow of Gelai now extended only halfway across the lake. Looking behind them they could see the fiery outline of its silhouette as the sun climbed higher.

"I have an idea," said Francis, who began stripping down to his underwear. "I'm going to see if there are any large chunks of lava down below. If so, we might be able to smash the soda crust away with them."

Before slipping into the hot water, Francis climbed back into the Land Rover and switched on the headlights. Then he climbed back out and slowly immersed himself in the mysterious water in front of the Land Rover, being careful to avoid contact with the highly alkaline crust.

"It's not too terribly hot," he said before submerging and swimming beneath the crust in search of any large object that might serve as a wrecking ball. The bottom was composed primarily of loose sediments, but he could feel that there was a solid substrate beneath. The water was murky and it stung his eyes. He returned to the opening next to the Land Rover to renew his breath and then dove again, this time feeling his way through the muck and grabbing hold of a piece of rock. Much to his amazement, it broke free. It was nearly a foot in diameter, heavy, but by summoning all his strength he was able to roll it along the bottom to the opening next to the Land Rover. He came up gasping for breath and then lifted the rock to the surface and placed it on the stable crust. Then he climbed onto the Land

Rover, dried himself, and put his shoes on again. Oscar helped him pick up the rock and carry it to the rear of the Land Rover.

"Let's toss it high in the air, so it lands about two feet behind the rear bumper," said Francis, "on the count of three."

Francis counted to three and they tossed the rock ten feet in the air. It came crashing down right on target and shattered into a thousand yellowish-brown fragments.

"So much for that theory," said Oscar, who then looked at Francis and was quite taken aback by the expression on his face. "Francis, what's wrong? You look as if you've seen a ghost."

Francis looked back at him, not changing his expression in the least. "Yes, I believe I have seen a ghost. That's kimberlite."

"I'm sorry," said Oscar, "I'm not following you."

"That rock, it's kimberlite," he repeated, as he bent down to study the pieces of shattered stone. He picked up a small, shiny fragment and turned it over in his hand. Oscar moved beside him. Francis showed him the bit of rock that had caught his eye and the penny dropped.

"This is no ordinary hot spring, Oscar. This is a kimberlite pipe. A diamond pipe."

Chapter 20

It was several moments before either of them spoke. Oscar remained crouched, turning the stone, the size of a pebble, over and over in his hand. It was cool to the touch, and though no direct sunlight yet fell upon his hand, there seemed to be light trapped within the stone, trying to escape. It was a brilliant, raw diamond with a decidedly amber hue. Oscar looked at Francis, who had stood up and was now staring silently to the south, toward the beautifully sculpted volcano, Ol Doinyo Lengai, basking in the golden light of early morning like a giant sentinel keeping watch over Lake Natron.

"Seems our luck has returned," said Oscar.

Francis turned toward him and scowled. It was quite striking. Oscar had never seen such an expression from his mild-mannered friend. Not only was it scornful, it was the look of fear.

"Luck? You call this luck?" he countered rather forcefully. "This is a curse if ever there was one. Do you realize what will happen if anyone finds out about this? We are sitting at the foot of the temple wherein Engai, the great god of the Maasai, resides. And out there, in the middle of this seemingly dreadful lake, is where two and a half million flamingos from all over East Africa come to breed and nest. Have you ever been to Kimberly? Ever seen a diamond mine? Imagine a huge, cavernous pit a mile wide or more, with immense ore trucks everywhere and blasting equipment blowing the rock to bits and pieces every time you turn around. There would be waste piles as far as the eye can see and people starting new towns that would feed off the ever-spreading destruction. Forget about the flamingos. Natron would be transformed into just one more industrialized wasteland where the only god is greed itself."

Oscar stared at Francis and scratched at his chin through his scraggly beard. "Hell of a way to start a new year," he said at last. "You are quite right. I suggest we forget about this diamond discovery and set about trying to survive. That's the important thing."

"Yes," said Francis, still obviously quite shaken. "Let's gather what we will need. There's a lava tube up on Gelai where we can take shelter. We had better start heading there now so we can contemplate our next move. There's nothing more we can do here."

Before leaving, however, Francis retrieved a silver space blanket from his emergency kit and, with Oscar's help, spread it out beside their trapped vehicle.

"I doubt anyone would notice the Land Rover," said Francis. "It's as white as this crust."

They then gathered up their sleeping bags and stuffed them, along with some spare clothes and what little uncontaminated food was left, into a large green duffel bag. Oscar retrieved a five-gallon jug of water from the back while Francis removed a pistol from the glove compartment. He then reached for a long wooden box that was tied to the roof rack. Nestled within auburn folds of velvet was a large shotgun that looked brand new.

"It was my father's," said Francis, as he picked up the weapon and placed two large shells in the twin barrels. Oscar stood by silently, somewhat alarmed that his peaceful friend seemed so at ease with such a deadly instrument.

They followed the tracks the Land Rover had made in the hard soda, trying in vain to stay ahead of the shrinking shadow of Gelai. When they were halfway to shore, the sun crested the northern ridgeline of Gelai and the intense light reflecting off the pure-white soda nearly blinded them. The temperature immediately began to soar.

"Only eight o'clock and it feels like midday," said Oscar.

"We'll be all right," said Francis, "if we just keep moving."

Though possibly true, these were not the words Oscar wished to hear. The jug of water he was carrying weighed over forty pounds alone and, with all the other equipment strapped to his back, the going was rather slow. The crusty soda formed strange polygons such that every few yards or so the edges would meet and rise and crack open. Walking across them caused the soda to crunch loudly underfoot. And even at that early hour it was like walking on a hot griddle. Oscar was already drenched in sweat. It was quite some time before either of them spoke.

"It must have been the earthquake," Francis said at last, still trying to convince himself. "There's no other possible explanation. That diamond pipe must be connected near its bottom to whatever volcanic source feeds Lengai. The hot spring it tapped into obviously dissolved away the soda crust, leaving the thin layer we unfortunately ventured onto. But it's completely out of place."

"Why do you say that?" said Oscar.

"Because all the diamond pipes in Africa were formed at least a hundred million years ago. Some, like the pipes at the Cullinan Diamond Mine in South

Africa, are nearly two billion years old. Most of them have eroded away, as this one should have. Yet, unless I'm mistaken, it floated about for eons, while the Rift Valley was forming, like a cork on a sea of molten crust. And that rock I retrieved, it was definitely kimberlite, only exposed, oxidized kimberlite. You saw how yellowish it was in color? Well, that means that we've stumbled upon the very top of the pipe, where the kimberlite has at times been exposed to oxygen. Below, it will be a denser blue-black stone with fewer diamonds. You see, kimberlite pipes originate deep in the mantle of the earth, from molten magma at least a hundred miles deep. The kimberlite finds a fissure in the crust, usually due to weakening by volcanic activity, and it rises like a soufflé through a pinhole in the earth. It then collapses as gas escapes and settles back into the hole. The entire deposit may only be a few hundred yards in diameter. That's one reason they are so hard to find."

"I see," said Oscar, as they finally reached the shoreline and stood staring up into the harsh sunlight at the severely inclined slopes of Gelai. They set down their loads. There were no trees in sight, only rough scree slopes that rose steeply up the side of the volcano.

"Let's leave everything here," said Francis. "I can't remember the exact location of the lava tube but it's up there somewhere. In view of our predicament, I suggest we split up. Time is of the essence. If you should find the entrance, approach it very cautiously. It may be occupied. If you encounter any large predator, remember that they are not at all used to humans. We're not inside a park anymore. Whatever you do, don't run away. That only incites them to attack. You're better off staring them down, making a lot of noise."

Francis could read the unsettling effects of these words on Oscar by the look on his face.

"Here, take this," he said, handing Oscar the pistol, "if it will make you feel better."

"Thank you," said Oscar, who accepted the pistol with some hesitation and then rolled it over in his hands. The metal felt cool, like the diamond in his pocket.

They each quenched their thirst before heading uphill. The slopes were rocky rather than ash covered, with small bushes growing low to the ground, offering no shade. The sun that had crested the ridgeline made looking directly upslope nearly impossible. They moved from side to side, slowly working their way uphill, sometimes on all fours. Francis shouted directions to Oscar, telling him to look farther south, to look for game trails that might lead to a lava tube. He said not to worry about staying within sight of each other. Oscar complied reluctantly, venturing into draws that cut him off completely from Francis, leaving him isolated within a very hot, very desolate, and very frightening wilderness.

There were many game trails amid the stunted shrubs. Oscar followed them until they disappeared or became too obscured by undergrowth. He found a particularly well-used trail and was following it, part of him hoping it would lead to shelter and part of him fearing it would lead only to the jaws of death, when he heard a cry from Francis. He had found something. Oscar scurried to find his friend, all the while keeping his pistol at the ready.

Dense growth almost entirely obscured the lava tube. Close inspection showed the faint trace of an overgrown game trail leading to it. Fortunately, Francis had noticed, from a distance, an aberration in the pattern of vegetation where the condensation of moisture at the mouth of the cave had evidently induced more exuberant growth than in the surroundings. And some of the species growing there were out of place, sprouted from seeds that had clearly been imported from another neighborhood by whatever creatures had sought shelter within.

Francis cut away at the shrubs guarding the entrance and, crawling on hands and knees, entered the cool, dark depths of Gelai's internal passageways, where once upon a time lava had hemorrhaged from within the bowels of the now-silent volcano.

"There appears to be a vacancy," shouted Francis, as he shined his flashlight all around. The walls of the lava tube, which was just high enough for him to stand, looked to be made of frozen butterscotch. The lava stood out in sharp peaks and hung in long, droopy curls along the sides of the cave. The floor was littered with bits of bone and piles of dried grass that had once been the nests of some former inhabitants. Oscar pulled himself through the opening Francis had cleared and attempted to stand.

"Not exactly the Ritz but I suppose it will do," he quipped.

"It will have to," Francis replied, "but hopefully not for long."

They transported all the supplies they had brought from the Land Rover and began to arrange their new living quarters. Francis cut away at the rest of the overhanging vegetation outside the entrance to the cave while Oscar gathered grasses and soft leaves to place under their sleeping bags. They erected a grill and a fire pit just outside the entrance. From there they could just make out the wavering image of the Land Rover, a captive of Natron's crusty surface. Only a

150

faint trace of the silver space blanket remained, eaten away by the caustic soda crust beneath it.

As the temperature climbed every sortie outside the cave became carefully measured. They were a few hundred yards up the northwest slope of Gelai and the only shade to be found was within the cave itself. Once they had done all the arranging possible, they laid themselves down upon their sleeping bags.

"As I see it," said Francis, "we have two choices. We can stay and try to extricate the Land Rover, or we can try to hike to one of the Maasai villages nearby."

"Technically, that's two options and hence only one choice," Oscar replied, "but how far away is the nearest village?"

"I stand corrected," said Francis. "Make that one choice. I'd say it's at least ten, perhaps fifteen miles. We would have to hike at night, but that wouldn't be too difficult since the moon is over half full."

"And if we stay put and try to recover the Land Rover, how would we go about it?"

"Good question. The fundamental problem is that the crust behind the Land Rover gets thicker and thicker as the lake gets shallower. We might have better luck smashing through the crust in front, closer to the source of the hot spring, but that only leads us into deeper water. Even if we could break through, where would we go? Besides, it may not be long before the engine wiring is shot."

"Well," said Oscar, "life would certainly be simpler if we could somehow manage to free your vehicle from its current state of bondage. Even if we made it to a Maasai village, then what? We would still have to find transportation. And I absolutely must get to the airport by the fifth. That's only a few days away. I say let's give it another go. If we fail to liberate the Land Rover, then we will have more moonlight tomorrow or the next day by which to seek out your Maasai comrades."

Francis peered over at his friend. "What do you mean, tomorrow or the next day? If we can't find a way to free the Land Rover this evening, then we must head out tomorrow. Unless, of course, you are really thinking about how to liberate the diamonds instead."

Oscar glanced over at Francis. "Actually," he replied, "I suppose that does raise another option. We could simply remain here, smashing rocks to bits, searching for more diamonds, until someone comes and finds us. Unfortunately, that would not accommodate my schedule."

"Then it's not an option," said Francis, "and it wouldn't accommodate my schedule, either. I say we sleep on it. There's nothing we can do during the daytime. So let's try to get some rest and see what we can accomplish after the sun goes down."

Oscar agreed but neither of them was able to sleep. They both lay there, staring at the dimly lit rock wall of the lava tube, studying the strange, contorted patterns where flowing, molten rock had suddenly turned to solid stone. Occasionally, one of them would speak, tossing out an idea for how to free the Land Rover. They talked about an explosive device, but neither could figure out how to make one. They thought about trying to siphon some gas and set the soda crust on fire. Neither of them was certain what effect that would have, other than to deplete their fuel supply, which they would need to get back to Nairobi. They talked about trying to cut through the crust, but neither could devise a way to construct a saw that would be long enough or sturdy enough to penetrate what was no doubt two or three feet of crust. But they did agree that if they could somehow smash away the crust behind the Land Rover, and let it settle below, they might be able to construct a ramp on which to back out of their predicament. Neither of them commented on the potential for recovering a fortune in diamonds in the process.

They ate lightly and drank sparingly from the jug of water. When the sun had set, they ventured carefully down the steep slope to the lake, dodging the thorny shrubs beneath another brilliant African sky. Rays of amber arched over the horizon and the flecks of clouds overhead turned crimson as the light faded. As it did the temperature of the air slowly moderated. Francis glanced at the small thermometer attached to his vest. It was down to one hundred degrees.

By the time they reached the Land Rover, they had their strategy well in hand. Oscar, being the stronger of the two and a fair swimmer as well, would scour the lake bed in front of the Land Rover for good-sized rocks to stockpile over the recalcitrant crust. Meanwhile, Francis would use a shovel to dig a U-shaped groove behind the Land Rover. In such a manner they hoped to sufficiently weaken the crust such that the rocks they gathered from the bottom would break through and offer a way to back out of their predicament.

Francis climbed inside the Land Rover, slid the key into the ignition and, crossing his fingers, twisted the key to the left. The engine began to turn over, signaling that the electrical connections were still intact. In a few seconds the engine caught and he switched on the lights, the better for Oscar to see. He climbed back out, letting the engine idle, grabbed the large shovel, and started digging at the hard, stubborn crust.

Oscar donned some shorts for the occasion and climbed carefully up onto the hood of the Land Rover before gently lowering himself into the water. It was hot but certainly not unbearable. He hesitated before finally submerging his entire head and body and was surprised to find that the water was remarkably clear, and rather than stinging it felt soothing, almost like eyewash. It seemed as though the farther he roamed from the Land Rover, the fresher the water became. But there was only three feet of water separating the bottom of the lake from the bottom of the wretched crust above, which he knew he must avoid touching. A foot or so of soft mud covered the bottom, and as Oscar glided along, feeling through the muck for a handhold in the kimberlite below, he realized that the density of the highly mineralized water was buoying him toward the surface. He found himself bouncing off the bottom of the crust and quickly turned back and swam toward the Land Rover, closing his eyes to avoid being blinded by the headlights. He took an enormous breath as he broke the surface, his oxygen spent, feeling the flesh on his back beginning to burn.

He submerged himself once more and managed to break off a few bits of rock from beneath the muck. He shoved them into his pockets until they provided just enough weight to keep him neutrally buoyant.

After surfacing for another breath of air, Oscar plunged back below the crust. He felt along the bottom again, not venturing more than ten feet from where he'd begun, feeling for crevices or handholds of any kind. He found the rock to be quite rough and highly fractured, and deep inside some of the fissures there was undissolved soda that burned the ends of his fingers. Still, he inserted them as deeply as he could and pulled with all his considerable might.

The sediments he disturbed in the process swirled before his eyes and obscured his vision. But vision was of only secondary importance, since he could not see the rock below that he was trying to liberate in the first place. On the first few tries he succeeded in breaking off only small pieces, like those in his pockets. He could tell the rock was quite brittle, perhaps too brittle. He returned to the Land Rover and broke the surface gasping for breath again.

"Any luck?" said Francis, who was leaning over beside the vehicle.

"Not yet," Oscar replied. "Tell you what, hand me the smaller of the two shovels. I need better leverage."

Francis obliged and Oscar dove once again. He lodged the shovel deep into one of the crevices and pried it back and forth. Finally, he felt something give. He reached both hands deep within the fractures on either side and was surprised at how easily the mass of rock tore loose. After resurfacing for another breath, he was able to lift it free of the surrounding rock and roll it along the bottom toward the opening in the crust. It was at least twice as large and twice as heavy as the rock Francis had retrieved much earlier that same day. Oscar took a deep breath and then submerged himself only to surface a moment later with the huge piece of kimberlite. He heaved it onto the crust beside the Land Rover.

"Freeing the rocks is not a problem," he told Francis after he'd caught his breath, "it's moving them that's a challenge. There has to be an easier way."

"How about using the winch?" said Francis. "We'll just need to make a basket of some sort to hold the rocks and then let the winch tow them back to the Land Rover. The cable's at least a hundred feet long."

"I've got an idea," said Oscar. "Let's use one of the duffel bags."

"Perfect," said Francis. He then turned and began to unload a large canvas bag sitting on top of the Land Rover, removing the spare water, leftover biscuits, and extra clothing they had brought along for the evening's activities. Once it was emptied, he handed it to Oscar.

"I suggest we begin stockpiling rocks up here for our assault on the crust once you've managed to cut a sufficiently deep groove around the back," said Oscar. "How long do you think that will take?"

"Hard to say, really," Francis replied. "It's been about half an hour and I'd say I've managed to remove barely an inch of crust at most."

"Then I'd better keep busy. Who knows how much force it will require to ultimately break through?"

Oscar surveyed the situation from below. This task required an orderly approach. He decided to first swim straight toward the center of the hot spring, where the crust had thinned and then given way to open water, perhaps a hundred feet from the Land Rover. Then he would move from right to left.

He took a huge breath of air and pushed off. In the considerable light provided by the headlights, he could see the mud-laden bottom quite clearly. The white crust above reflected the light very well and he was able to discern the many particles of suspended sediment swirling before him as he plied through the hot water. But he could not see the opening in the crust near the source of the hot spring and had to rely on thermal sensors. Holding the handle of the duffel bag in his teeth, he steered by extending his arms to either side, in order to detect the waves of heat emanating from the pinhole in the earthly crust below that may have once upon a time delivered this incredible rocky soufflé of diamond-bearing kimberlite.

Though the heat was becoming close to intolerable, he could see that not far ahead of him the white crust above disappeared. He swam as rapidly as he could, realizing that he was well past the point of turning back. His lungs were on fire and it felt as if the rest of his body were as well, but he finally reached the opening and surfaced like a breaching whale.

The water was considerably deeper and in an instant he realized that his only option was to tread water. He was exhausted from his long underwater swim and had hoped to rest a bit before returning to the Land Rover. But the water was so hot and the steam rising from it so thick and laced with hydrogen sulfide gas that even catching his breath was difficult. Looking back toward the Land Rover, he could see the ripening moon sitting high above Gelai. He stared at it for a while, somewhat mesmerized, and then suddenly wished he could dive deeper, to the source of the springs, and peer down through the orifice toward the center of the earth to where this body of diamond ore had originated. He wanted to at least feel the opening in the earthen crust that led to the depths of the fiery engine responsible for molding and moving entire continents and creating majestic mountains like Gelai and Lengai, whose beautiful, moonlit symmetry dominated the view to the south.

Oscar took as deep a breath as was possible and began swimming back toward the lights of the Land Rover, realizing that he would have to abandon the notion of surfacing close to the source of all this hot water. Francis looked quite relieved when he saw Oscar surface.

"I thought you'd drowned!" he said. "I've been standing here for several minutes waiting for you."

"Swam out to the opening," Oscar replied, panting heavily. "Thought I might be able to work from both ends, with two sources of fresh air. But the air's not fresh out there by any means and it's too hot and too far."

"Are you out of your mind? How many rocks do you think we're going to need?"

"Who knows? I felt it made sense to scope out the possibilities, the limits of what we can achieve here. Having done that, I'll get to work. How's the digging progressing?"

"Very slowly, I'm afraid," said Francis.

Oscar rubbed his bearded chin. "I'll keep after the rocks. How's the petrol?"

"Slightly over three-quarters full. It should be plenty to keep the engine idling for several hours, so long as the wiring doesn't give out."

"Good. Then let's have at it."

Oscar started by gathering as many rocks as he could loosen close to the Land Rover and then worked his way outward. Within an hour he'd recovered a dozen or so fairly good-sized pieces and moved them close to the Land Rover using the winch and duffel-bag system they had devised. When he ran out of room with his stockpile, he began lifting them up to the surface, one by one, using the duffel bag as the handles made lifting much easier. After all the rocks were on top, he pulled himself out of the water, dried himself, and slipped on his shoes.

Francis had made considerable progress. He had scored the crust by a depth of a few inches in a U-shaped pattern that was as wide as the Land Rover and a good fifteen feet long. Oscar stuffed one of the rocks back into the duffel bag and carried it to the rear.

"It's been a while since I tossed the hammer, but I think I still remember how," he said.

Francis looked slightly confused but quickly understood as Oscar picked up the duffel bag with both hands, spread his legs wide, and began to spin. He turned slowly at first but then gradually gained speed as his huge upper body moved in an elliptical motion. He lifted the bag high into the air on the side closest to the target zone and lowered it on the other. After several spins he released the bag with a loud grunting sound, and they both watched it fly high into the night air. They could see quite well by virtue of the moonlight and the taillights of the Land Rover. The bag spun around as it ascended and then seemed to stop spinning as it reached its zenith. Then it slowly picked up momentum and came crashing down with a thud right in the center of the U.

The soda crust won. There wasn't the slightest crack. Oscar rushed to the bag and unzipped it. Then he dumped out the rubble within, which was fairly well pulverized. He reloaded and repeated the exercise with the same results. He dumped the next mound of rubble alongside the other. He repeated these movements until all the rocks were reduced to rubble and formed a decent-sized mound in the center of the U.

"Well," he said, "looks like we'll need more rocks. And you'll need to keep on digging."

Francis looked slightly discouraged but managed a faint smile. "I guess we've no other choice. But you're going to give yourself a hernia heaving these rocks up in the air like that. Sheer mass will make do. If you set the rocks on top, I can maneuver them into place."

"Nonsense. This is simply a matter of gravity. We need to take advantage any way we can."

"Yes, but it will do us no good if you should wrench your back or strain a muscle. We need to be prepared to hike our way to the nearest village, in case this strategy should ultimately fail us."

"Fail us? How can it fail? This crust has to give way at some point. I'll wager we break through by sunup."

"I only hope that's true."

Unfortunately, it wasn't. By the time the rays of the new day's sun crested Gelai, they had amassed a very large pile of rubble behind the Land Rover. But the crust had not yielded. Oscar stared in disbelief at the mound of crushed kimberlite spread out before him. Francis shook his head, almost despairing. The gouge in the crust was nearly six inches deep, but clearly a deeper incision was required.

Oscar was thoroughly exhausted. He had moved heavy rocks all night long and his fingers were bleeding from handling all the rough, heavy rocks. The whites of his eyes were completely bloodshot and his eyelids were red and swollen. The skin on his back was badly burned but his spirit was strong. He just knew it was only a matter of time until the crust gave in. But the shadow of Gelai was moving quickly toward them, and the air in the distance was already wavering in the heat of the morning.

"I believe it's time to push all this rubble back into the water," said Francis rather despondently. Oscar could not believe his ears.

"Are you insane?" he inquired. "We worked all night to build up this mound. With another couple of hours work, we'd likely break through. Tonight we can finish the job."

"Tonight we must head off for the nearest village," said Francis firmly. "We gave it our best shot here but it didn't work. Who knows how many more pounds of rubble it would take to break through. We haven't much food left and we need to conserve our strength. But first we must remove all evidence of our discovery."

Oscar stared at his companion in disbelief. "Remove all evidence of our discovery?" he repeated. "Why, it's simply a pile of rocks we dredged up from the bottom of the lake. Only a well-trained eye like yours would notice anything peculiar about these rocks. Aside from being rather brittle and rather yellowish, they just look like a pile of everyday stones to me."

"Perhaps to you," said Francis as he picked up one of the shovels and began to push the pieces of rock fragments back into the water. "But if my brother should find us, it would be disastrous."

"Disastrous?" shouted Oscar. "Disastrous? Why, for one thing we'd be saved. But why would anyone, particularly your brother, be looking for us? We're not due back in Nairobi for a few days. And I'm certain we'll break through tomorrow night."

"Don't be absurd!" shouted Francis in return, becoming more agitated by the moment as he continued to push the rubble back into the lake while Oscar attempted to restrain him. "If you won't help, then get out of my way," he continued, glaring at Oscar. "The sun will be on top of us in a few minutes."

Oscar stepped back and watched in horror as Francis continued to shovel the mass of broken stone into the water behind the Land Rover. The shadow of Gelai crept steadily closer as Francis began to work ever more frantically and Oscar simply paced back and forth, shaking his head.

"This is absolutely insane!" he shouted. "You're undoing our only hope for escape! It took us all night to…"

But before he could finish his discourse, a remarkable thing occurred. The sun's intense rays overtook them. Francis stopped his shoveling. He stood up and stepped back slowly until he was next to Oscar, covering his eyes. Sharp points of light reflected like laser beams from the pile of stones—or, to be more precise, from the unconcealed edges of a certain carbon-based mineral found within the pile of stones that is the hardest, and one of the rarest, substances on earth.

Chapter 21

By the time the brutal heat of the midmorning sun chased them back to the cool darkness of their lava tube, they were both badly sunburned and seriously dehydrated. What was left of the pile of rubble remained behind the Land Rover, testimony to Oscar's prevailing argument that the best way to hide the evidence of their discovery without jeopardizing their chances for escape was to simply remove the material that might attract the eye of any unexpected guests in the first place. It also required much less labor.

Oscar had managed to fill a sock half full of kimberlite-encrusted diamonds. Most of them were quite small, less than half a carat. Others were sizable and Oscar, lying on his stomach upon his sleeping bag, examined each one very carefully. Francis, meanwhile, lay on his back, staring at the roof of the cave, furious but silent.

"I realize you are quite vexed with me," said Oscar after several moments of uncomfortable silence. "But you have no idea what this discovery will mean to the foundation. With these diamonds I can establish hundreds more clinics and perhaps pay our staff something closer to what they deserve. What do you suppose these are worth?"

"I don't know," replied Francis rather coldly. "Quite a bit, no doubt. But that doesn't really matter. There's no point in even discussing their worth since you cannot possibly redeem them. I suggest you concentrate more on how to stay alive today rather than speculate about your worth tomorrow. We're almost out of food and water, and it's a miracle we don't both have sunstroke by now."

Oscar turned onto his side, wincing as he rolled over on a patch of sunburned skin. "Francis," he said, "you're taking this a bit too far. What do you mean, we can't possibly redeem them?"

Francis remained rigid, his arms firmly folded upon his chest. "You don't understand," he said. "My brother is a sight holder in London on the diamond exchange. The minute these diamonds appeared on the market, he'd know. Then he'd come looking. They would be easily traced back to you and, ultimately, to me."

Oscar stared, not comprehending.

"Look," Francis continued, "diamonds are sold in lots. Once a month or so the sight holders, about three hundred select and terribly wealthy individuals in all, meet in London. Eighty percent of all the diamonds sold in the world pass through their hands. And they can tell where practically every diamond came from by its color and clarity. It wouldn't take long before they realized there has been a new discovery, and my brother would certainly recognize these as the long-sought-after Dermenjian diamonds."

"I see," said Oscar, scratching his beard. "But how can you be sure these are, in fact, the famous Dermenjian diamonds?"

"It was obvious to me when I saw that first diamond yesterday morning."

"But you hardly looked at it. Perhaps you should examine these to make certain."

Francis sat on his sleeping bag and looked at Oscar with tired, drooping eyes. He rubbed his wiry fingers through his thinning hair and then ran his hand slowly down over his face. "Okay," he said at last, "I'll have another look."

He reached into his knapsack and pulled out a small hand lens that he used for keying out plants. Oscar handed him a few of the larger diamonds. Francis took them and examined them close to the entrance to the cave, where there was better light. He scrutinized them for quite some time, turning each one over and over, studying every facet. Then he walked back to where Oscar lay waiting.

"They are nearly flawless. There's a telltale reddish, slightly amber coloring, not an imperfection by any means. They are quite distinctive, identical, in fact, as I'd expected, to the so-called sunset diamonds my ancestor brought back to Hungary all those years ago."

Francis sat back down on his sleeping bag, looking lost and bewildered.

"I still cannot believe we stumbled upon them," he continued wearily. "Why should it fall on me to chance upon the very thing that I have come to abhor more than anything else in this world, right in the midst of that which I love best?"

Oscar's eyes opened wide. "Well," he said, clearing his throat, "that's one question I suppose we will never be able to answer. Suffice to say that you have stumbled upon them and, ironically, we have invested our chances of escape on further stockpiling of the body of kimberlite that plays host to them."

Francis lay down and stared at the roof of the cave. "So we have. But we could still simply strike out for the nearest village. The moon is almost full. We should have plenty of light."

"True," said Oscar, "but there will be even more light tomorrow. As long as the Land Rover is fully functional, I say we stick with our original plan. Another few hundred pounds is all we'll need, I'm sure of it."

Francis turned on his side, looking skeptical. "But are you sure you are up to it? You're certain to wrench your back if you work as hard as you did last night. We can't risk injury. And besides, you must promise me that you are not promoting this strategy simply to reap the diamonds hidden in these stones."

Oscar stared at his traveling companion. "Well," he said at last, "the diamonds are really just bits of rock, aren't they? Unusual rock but nothing more, I suppose. Don't see why everyone makes such a fuss over them."

"Ah, but they do," said Francis, suddenly animated.

"Yes, of course they do," Oscar replied. "Can't get married without one, it seems."

"That's simply an artifact of marketing," said Francis, sitting up, "one of the greatest marketing strategies ever. Convince every man, and better yet every woman, that the only way to express true love is to give her a diamond, the most enduring substance on earth. Why, it's the fast track to sexual commitment. Just show her a diamond and she'll be your sex slave forever."

"Francis," said Oscar, "you sound awfully bitter."

"Bitter? Bitter?" he responded, swinging his legs before him as he turned toward Oscar and began speaking louder than before. "Why, you have no idea. I'm well beyond bitter. Don't you see what our civilization's become? We don't respect honest, hard work any longer, or sound character. We worship whatever will bring the most wealth as quickly as possible. Entire economies are inextricably tied to the price of various rare substances which are inherently worthless, like those perfect carbon crystals you hold in your hand."

Oscar looked at the tumble of gems before responding. "Yes, but it's always been that way. And besides, it's not necessarily evil. Think of all the good we could do. Think of all the parcels of land you could purchase and protect, the stability it would bring to the foundation. And we haven't harmed anything here."

Francis eyed Oscar with a look of disdain that made Oscar recoil slightly as he lay upon his sleeping bag. "You don't understand," he said sharply. "I've already told you how devastating a diamond mine right here, in the middle of Lake Natron, would be to the millions of flamingos that have nested here every year for Lord knows how long. It's been called the greatest avian spectacle in the entire world!

You've seen them prancing about like avian ballerinas. I believe that's how you described them. But a diamond mine would surely destroy their prime nesting habitat out here in the middle of this seemingly godforsaken lake. But it isn't godforsaken, either, is it? All this sits at the foot of Mount Lengai, the Maasai Mountain of God, where their god Engai apparently resides. It would be such a desecration to dig all this up just to extract more of those rare gems you're holding. And, as I said, the moment these diamonds hit the market, you might as well just kiss this place good-bye."

Oscar squeezed his fist, feeling the hard edges of the diamonds press into his skin. He looked up at his friend, who was staring out toward the harsh sunlight beyond the entrance to the cave.

"All right," said Oscar solemnly. "It's as you wish."

Francis turned around abruptly. "Meaning?"

"Meaning that these diamonds will remain a secret between you and me. I shall not divulge a thing about our discovery so long as we both shall live."

Francis stared, clearly stunned by Oscar's pronouncement. "Are you certain you can do that?"

"Yes. I can and I will. I promise you, as a friend. And friends—friends like you, Francis—are much more precious than diamonds. Far more rare."

Francis sat back down and stared at Oscar with piercing eyes that seemed to be searching for another clue, for some sign of betrayal. "Thank you," he said at last, softly. "Now let's get some rest."

Francis lay back down and was asleep within minutes. Oscar lay still, watching his friend breathe slowly, listening to the rhythm of the air moving in and out of his long and slender nostrils in time with the slow raising and lowering of his chest. All was quiet outside, as the heat of midday sent every creature packing into some sort of burrow or refuge, much like them.

Once again Oscar found sleep difficult. His mind was racing, partially from exhaustion. He was also accustomed to sleeping on his back, which was impossible due to the soda burns. Finally, exhaustion won out and he fell asleep on his stomach, still clutching the sock full of diamonds.

After several hours they were both awake and felt somewhat refreshed, though Oscar had slept intermittently at best, awakening every time he tried to roll over. Francis rubbed some lotion on Oscar's back and afterward they prepared a very meager supper. They still had one sack of flour, and Francis made more biscuits that Oscar cooked, with the aid of some aluminum foil, over a small fire while Francis ventured off to see what other edibles he could procure. By the time the biscuits were done, Francis had returned with handfuls of berries and more wild onions.

As they were eating, Oscar wondered aloud what would have caused Francis's great-great-grandfather to venture out onto the hostile surface of Lake Natron.

"Who knows? Perhaps he was looking for fresh water," Francis replied. "There certainly isn't much about. Perhaps he didn't realize that all of Natron is just one immense cauldron of soda. He might have ventured out across the crust to the nearest spring, hoping to slake his thirst or to find water for the entire party."

"Yes, what was that fellow's name?"

"Who? Teleki von Szek?"

"Yes. Perhaps he was one of Teleki's scouts."

"It seems plausible, as good an explanation as any so far. Teleki's route was slightly farther to the east but within a day's hike from here, as far as we know. In any case, it doesn't much matter, does it? But speaking of fresh water, we are running low and we are nearly out of food. If we don't break through tonight, we have no choice but to leave. I can't believe I even consented to wait another day."

"Well," said Oscar, "I still maintain that as long as your vehicle is running, it offers the best chance for a timely escape. As for food and water, there is plenty of game and surely there's a stream that drains this mountain somewhere. I'll bet a naturalist like you could live off the land for weeks if you absolutely had to. These onions are actually quite tasty."

Francis glared at Oscar once again with a look of exasperation. "Oscar, don't even think about it. I may have developed fairly good survival skills but we are leaving here tomorrow night. You seriously jeopardized our chances of escape by staying so long out in the sun. We can't take any chances. We may need all the skill and experience I have, plus a fair amount of luck as well, just to reach a Maasai village safely."

They spent the night building the pile of kimberlite rubble behind the Land Rover even higher. But the crust still did not yield, so they removed the telltale traces of their discovery in the first rays of the morning light, as they had done before, and filled one more sock half full with diamonds. By the time they arrived back at their sleeping bags, they were far more exhausted and far more disappointed than they had been the previous day. Before they could express any sentiments about their physical and mental condition, however, they made another frightening discovery.

"Lion tracks," said Francis as he examined the large paw prints upon their now-tattered sleeping bags. "We're fortunate that our food cache, such as it is, wasn't destroyed."

Oscar glanced over at the rocks they had piled up on top of their last cooler, not that it was cool inside. The rocks hadn't been disturbed. But his sleeping bag was badly torn up.

"Good thing we're out of meat," he said. "Do you think he'll be back?"

"Let's hope not. In any case, it wouldn't hurt to keep the shotgun and pistol handy. Chances are he wouldn't return until it's dark again. Lions hunt at night, you know. They're essentially nocturnal."

"So are we, it seems," Oscar replied.

"And we'll be gone by tonight. The moon will be full and we'll be hiking back to that Maasai village our hitchhiking friend invited us to. I believe it is the closest settlement."

"Can we make it in one night?"

"Yes, if we travel light."

"Shouldn't be a problem. We've not much left."

Francis glanced at the sock full of diamonds that Oscar still clutched in his hand. "And you'll have even less once you've returned those diamonds to their original owner, Lake Natron. Along with the others."

Oscar looked somewhat despondently at the sock of priceless gemstones that hung forlornly at his side. "As you wish," he sighed. "But please, let me sleep on it. It was an awful lot of work."

"Fine," said Francis, "but before we bed down we had better set up an alarm system. In case that lion returns."

Together they began collecting metal cups and bits of silverware. Francis tied them all together with some twine and strung them out near the entrance to the cave.

"I'll keep the shotgun beside me," said Francis as Oscar placed the newly gem-filled sock next to its twin under his pillow and laid himself down upon his tattered sleeping bag.

"How comforting," said Oscar as he tried to forget that mere hours ago a huge carnivore may have slept in that very spot.

The lion did not return, but late in the afternoon an enormous clap of thunder rousted them from their slumber. Francis jumped to his feet. He moved toward the entrance to the lava tube and carefully dismantled his crude alarm system. What he saw was quite disconcerting.

The sky was nearly black. Large clouds were rumbling along at a brisk pace, threatening rain. Streaks of lightning darted at the ground at regular intervals, followed by successive peals of raucous thunder.

"It's come up from the Indian Ocean," said Francis. "Not too common this time of year but not unheard of."

By the time Oscar joined Francis near the entrance of the cave, it had begun to rain. At least, it began as rain but soon it became a downpour, a drenching that beat upon every leaf, every blade of grass, and every exposed grain of sand for miles around. And it continued steadily for the next few hours. Francis prepared more onion soup over his camp stove, set just within the confines of their cave, while Oscar put their only spare pot outside to collect the precious raindrops that were the size of pearls.

"Interesting syncopation," Oscar observed before posing the question that had been pestering him for some time. "So, are we off for the village or not?"

Francis stirred the soup and did not respond.

"Francis," Oscar pressed, "are we off to the village tonight? As far as I'm concerned, it's entirely up to you. You'll hear no argument if you think we can withstand this weather."

Francis continued to stare into the steamy pot before him. "It would be unwise to travel under these conditions," he said at last. "The clouds show no sign of abating. There'll be no moon tonight, I'm afraid."

"Then what will we do?"

Francis looked up. "Nothing," he said. "We'll conserve our strength for tomorrow. Exert ourselves as little as possible, rest up."

"But I am rested. Why not throw another load on the rock pile? I mean, as long as we're still here."

Francis gave him a cold look. "I thought you were putting matters in my hands."

Oscar hesitated, as if searching the air for a response. "Well, yes, as far as getting to the nearest village. But as long as we're still here, let's not give up. As long as the Land Rover continues to function, we have all the light we need. And I may be worn down a bit, but I am more than ready for another go. In fact, I doubt I could just sit here in this cave doing nothing. It would drive me insane."

Francis countered rather feebly and soon capitulated, realizing that their situation was quickly turning from dangerous to desperate. Oscar was right. They could not afford to waste time. They put away their dishes and ventured out into the rain, which had lost some of its force. The lightning had moved on as well. There was still enough daylight by which to see their way down the hill, but by the time they reached the Land Rover, it had darkened considerably.

Francis hit the ignition. There was silence. He tried it a second time. Again nothing. He looked over at Oscar, his jaw set tight. He tried one more time and there was a faint click. He tried again and the starter engaged, and on the next try the engine caught. Francis let out an enormous sigh and gave Oscar the thumbs-up sign as the latter climbed onto the hood before submerging himself once again into the steamy waters of Lake Natron. Francis turned on the headlights.

"The water is higher," said Oscar. "And slightly fresher."

"It's all the runoff," Francis replied. "We must hurry. The lake could rise significantly and very quickly."

"Right," said Oscar, who submerged himself only to reappear moments later with the first stone of the evening.

Francis resumed his digging. The U-shaped gouge in the crust behind the Land Rover was now a foot and a half deep, and the rainwater that filled the trough helped soften the crust so that he made more rapid progress than before. But then he noticed that the water was actually covering the bottom of his boots and turning them black.

"Oscar," he cried, hearing his friend emerge from the shallows. "Be careful where you walk. The water has risen and the crust is turning into a highly caustic slush."

Oscar looked about. He held in his hands a duffel bag full of kimberlite. He was about to set it down on the crust but thought better of it and set it on top of the hood instead. He walked around to the back and examined the progress Francis had made.

"Excellent. I'll bet you that within…"

But before he could finish his thought, a large wave of water came tumbling over his feet as the immense slab of crust piled high with kimberlite finally, and rather silently, fell out of sight. It moved in one mass, slowly downward, the pile of rubble settling like a sinking volcano. Only the tip of it remained in view, a small island in a strange sea of witch's brew.

Oscar and Francis stood side by side, not believing their eyes.

"Yes!" they cried in unison.

"I can't believe it," gasped Oscar. "It finally gave in."

"It was the water," said Francis. "The lake is rising, and it was surely the weight of the water that made it give way. We had better set to work immediately building a ramp out of the crushed stones. Who knows how long the lake will continue to rise. It could flood the engine."

They both plunged into the water and quickly reshaped the pile of sharp-edged stones into something resembling an inclined plane.

"This will have to do," said Francis. The water had risen another two inches. He climbed into the driver seat.

"Do something with that duffel bag on the hood," he said before reaching down and examining various levers and gearshifts. Oscar retrieved it and threw it on top, next to the spare tent. The engine had been idling for several hours but responded well when Francis depressed the accelerator, which was now partially underwater. Then he depressed the clutch pedal, engaged four-wheel drive, and slid the Land Rover into reverse. He slowly let out the clutch.

To both his and Oscar's astonishment, the Land Rover began to move for the first time in days. Francis gripped the wheel with all his might as he slowly guided the Land Rover backward up the makeshift ramp. The water was much higher now, completely covering the alkali crust.

"It needs to be compacted," Francis shouted over the roar of the engine. "The wheels are spinning."

Much to Oscar's alarm Francis put the vehicle in neutral and slowly moved back down the ramp. He applied the brakes, then put it in reverse and climbed higher until the wheels began spinning again. But he had advanced considerably.

"Just one more go should do it," he shouted before shifting back into neutral. He carefully guided the Land Rover back down the incline, pressing down on the brake pedal before depressing the clutch. He reached for the gearshift, but before he could shift into reverse, the Land Rover lunged forward into much deeper water. And then all went dark.

Chapter 22

Francis's repeated attempts to restart the engine merely demonstrated that whatever electrical connections had preexisted were now defunct. He slammed his fist against the dashboard before climbing out through the sunroof. Once he had regained the slushy crust, he walked to the front of their hopelessly stranded vehicle now semi-submerged in Natron's corrosive waters. He jumped in and popped open the hood. The water now covered two-thirds of the engine.

"Wonderful, nearly all of the wiring is underwater now. The rising waters surely helped the crust break away, but now it's too deep and the engine is literally flooded."

Oscar remained silent, having fully comprehended the significance of these words. "One hand giveth," he said calmly, "while the other taketh away."

"That's nonsense," exclaimed Francis. "I didn't expect the brakes to fail like that, but the water is so caustic it must have eaten away at the brake lines. Let's try pushing it up the ramp. Maybe the engine will start if it gets to dry out a bit."

Oscar looked the situation over, slowly rubbing his beard with one hand. "That's quite an angle," he said.

Together they pushed with all their might. But it wouldn't budge. Aside from the sheer weight of the vehicle itself, it was now half filled with water.

Weary and despondent, they returned to the shelter of the lava tube and collapsed onto their respective sleeping bags. Had the lion appeared, he would have encountered no resistance whatsoever.

They both slept soundly, oblivious to the conditions outside, until Francis awoke to a sound that he did not immediately recognize. It was a soft wail, a low moaning noise. As he slowly awakened, it seemed as if the strange sound was coming from a source somewhere within the cave. Then he realized the sound was coming from Oscar. At first Francis assumed he was merely having a bad dream until he noticed that his friend was drenched in sweat. He leaned over and felt his forehead.

"Francis," said Oscar, shivering as he awakened to the touch, "I'm freezing. Is there another blanket?"

Francis glanced at his friend and without speaking threw his tattered sleeping bag over him. "You're burning up."

"Yes," said Oscar, his teeth chattering, "I know."

Francis looked suddenly more anxious. "You're the doctor," he said. "What do you think it is?"

"Nothing serious," he replied rather faintly, "just a bug of some kind."

"It's no wonder, the way you've been overexerting yourself and sleeping and eating so poorly. On the other hand, you have been taking all the necessary precautions, haven't you? I mean, about traveling in the equatorial zone?"

Oscar did not immediately respond. "Of course I have," he said at last. "I'm certain to be fine after a bit more rest."

Francis stared at his companion, who lay still but breathed rapidly, panting like a dog. "Well, whatever it is," he said, "you'll need to stay well hydrated. The storm was kind in that regard but the water we were able to collect is almost gone. I'm going to look for more. I'll leave the pistol for you in case that lion comes back. Just fire a couple of shots in the air and you'll be sure to scare him off."

With Oscar thus left in charge of holding down the fort, Francis headed off to survey the landscape along the northern slopes of Gelai. He headed for the deepest draw he could see, noting the renewed greenery of the sparse vegetation since the rains had fallen. Two slopes converged in a small valley about half a mile from the lava tube. There was a telltale corridor of thicker and darker riparian brush that ran a slightly sinuous course more or less down its center. Francis studied the brush carefully as he moved down the slope. He found a small opening amid the thick vegetation, an old game trail, and crawled along on his belly to the center of the brush, to the valley's thalweg, where he found a slight trickle of a stream. When he stuck his finger in to feel the flow, it barely wet his fingernail. From his pocket he produced a small, square piece of metal that he shoved into the middle of the tiny stream, forming a miniature dam. There was a little notch cut out of the center to which he attached a piece of plastic that directed the flow into some rubber tubing that led to a large, collapsible container placed several feet downstream. While waiting for the container to fill, he cut a number of slender green shoots from shrubs that grew alongside the miniature stream and fashioned them into snares, as the Maasai had taught him. He carefully concealed each one along separate small game trails. Meanwhile, the water was slowly accumulating behind the tiny dam, and within an hour the plastic container was nearly two-thirds full, with several inches of sediment on the bottom. Francis carried the container back to the cave as the sun was setting, closely surveying the land before him and behind him, looking for any oddly moving shrubs or wavering blades of tall grass.

Oscar was asleep, his chills having subsided. But Francis felt his forehead again. His fever was still running high.

"Fantastic," he said to himself, "this is just what we needed."

Once more the thought of hiking out to the nearest Maasai village would have to wait. Oscar was in no shape to go walking, even if it did mean missing his own wedding. The only positive aspect of their current predicament, if indeed there was one, was that their failure to appear at the Nairobi airport the following day would at least render them officially missing. Surely someone would come looking for them soon.

But still they must survive. The food they had left might feed them for a couple of days at most. And aside from the onions and a few wild berries, he had seen little in the way of edible plant life growing upon the dry, scorched slopes of Gelai. Hopefully, the snares would provide a meal or two.

He prepared a very thin soup that he ate sparingly, saving the better half for Oscar, who continued to sleep despite repeated efforts by Francis to awaken him and make him eat and, more importantly, take fluids. He finally gave up and scribbled out a note that he placed under the pistol next to Oscar. Then he grabbed the shotgun and headed back down to the Land Rover.

The inside was now completely flooded and all hope of driving away from this nightmare was gone. But that was not why Francis had come back. He had come to scatter all the rubble they had shaped into the ramp, to remove all traces of their discovery.

He labored all night, to a point where he felt no one would notice any disturbance of the lake bottom. Fortunately, the moon was now quite full and its rays helped illuminate the opening in the crust. He scattered the kimberlite rubble Oscar had labored so hard to gather in a large circle, feeling with his hands to be sure it was all buried beneath the fine sediments that covered the lake bottom. When he had finished and the glimmer of a new dawn began to turn the sky a soft pink once again, he headed back toward the lava tube.

Exhausted from another night's hard work, he still managed to find enough strength to hike back to the draw where he had set the snares. They were all as he had left them, with not even a trace of fresh tracks along the narrow, dusty pathways. He cut away some of the brush and lashed it to his back. It would not only serve as firewood but also be useful for creating a sign, a message that he would lay out on Natron's crust to advertise their whereabouts.

As he approached the entrance to the lava tube, carrying the huge bundle of brush upon his back, he shouted for Oscar. He did not want to take him by surprise. Hearing no response, he continued on until suddenly two shots rang out. Francis could almost feel the bullets passing next to his head as he dove for cover.

Opening his eyes and peering up from his crouched position, he saw Oscar standing at the cave entrance looking completely bewildered as he held the pistol in his hand and stared down at Francis. He was shaking and squinting, with his free hand shading his eyes, as if he was trying to make out exactly who or what had approached the cave entrance.

"Oscar," shouted Francis, "it's me. There's no need to be alarmed."

Oscar stood still, wavering slightly, as he continued to peer out into the new daylight that illuminated the land about him and, in particular, at Francis whose bundle of shrubbery stood out somewhat like a lion's mane.

"Father," said Oscar, "is that you?"

Francis lowered his head. "No, Oscar," he replied, "it's me, Francis. You're a bit delirious. I suggest you rest some more and by all means put down that pistol. You nearly killed me."

Oscar's expression continued to be that of a man whose mind had left him temporarily, displaced by an intense fever that had done anything but subside. Without speaking, however, he turned back toward the inside of the cave and lay back down on his sleeping bag. Francis approached him cautiously, waiting until he had set the pistol aside before moving in next to him. He was breathing hard again, seeming to stare off to a distant place far removed from their current whereabouts. Francis placed one hand upon Oscar's stomach and began to probe. He could feel his liver and lower ribs, despite his still-enormous but rapidly shrinking girth. Then he found the spleen, swollen and hard. Again he shook his head and felt tears coming to his eyes as his earlier suspicions were now confirmed.

He stared at Oscar's fever-ridden body, visualizing the billions of parasites that were busily multiplying within him, causing his red blood cells to swell until they burst, which in turn gave rise to the fever. These were the same parasites that had killed Alexander the Great, decimated vast armies throughout history, and effectively guided the course of civilization since time immemorial. But the fever would subside in a day or two as the first generation of parasites broke free from the cells that nourished them, only to begin reproducing once again.

"Oscar," said Francis in a firm voice, shaking him as he spoke but hearing no response. He tried once more and Oscar groaned as he rolled over and slowly opened his eyes. "Oscar," Francis repeated, "it's me, Francis. You're suffering from malaria. You stopped taking your pills, didn't you?"

Oscar looked straight ahead at the ceiling of the cave, still breathing hard and not answering.

"Oscar," Francis shouted, "you're very ill. I have only one dose of an antimalarial drug. It should help quell the fever—for a while, at least."

Oscar stared at Francis but still did not respond. Francis reached for his knapsack and rummaged through it until he found the one dose of chloroquine he kept in his first aid kit. Inserting one arm behind Oscar's massive neck, he managed with some difficulty to lift his head and shoulders. Then he forced the medicine into his mouth and made him swallow a large sip of water. Oscar gagged at first, as the water was quite alkaline and the capsule rather large. But it went down and, as Francis was laying Oscar's enormous head back down onto the pillow, he made another startling discovery. The diamonds were gone.

"Oscar!" shouted Francis as he grabbed him by the shirt with both hands and shook him violently. "Where are the diamonds?"

Oscar opened his eyes slowly, sweat continuing to pour off his forehead. He muttered something incomprehensible and Francis shook him again.

"Where are the diamonds?" he shouted once more.

Oscar's reply was rather faint but Francis thought he heard him utter that they were safe.

"Safe where?" he demanded.

"Safe," Oscar mumbled as he turned away, "moonbeams safe."

"Moonbeams?" repeated Francis in disbelief. "Moonbeams? Where are they? Where are the moonbeams, Oscar?"

But Oscar only shook his head slowly from side to side. "Moonbeams safe," he repeated.

Francis stood up and moved toward the entrance to their cave. "This is just too fantastic. Now I've a raving lunatic on my hands."

He chose not to bother any longer with Oscar but to wait until the medicine took effect. Hopefully, the fever would subside and Oscar would return to his senses. But where could the diamonds be? He looked all around their sleeping area and found nothing. He took the flashlight and searched all around the cave, venturing a hundred feet or more into its depths, which continued on for some unknown distance. There were large rocks, huge chunks of lava that had peeled away from the sides of the lava tube and littered the floor of the cave. The diamonds could easily be hidden in any one of hundreds of crevices between them. His only hope was for Oscar to come back to his senses, to remember where he had hidden them.

It was now midmorning and he had not eaten or slept in many hours. Francis lit a fire outside the cave and prepared a bit of hot cereal that he consumed with a few sips of water. He left the fire to smolder and then settled down on his sleeping bag.

He slept quite peacefully for several hours, dreaming about the woman he had nearly married many years before. They were together again, joyful and in love, when the sound of gunfire shattered his reverie. Francis leaped up from his sleeping bag and saw Oscar holding the pistol once again, pointing it toward the opening of the cave.

"The lion," he said, "he came back."

Francis jumped up without a word and ran to the entrance of the cave. He saw the tail of a large feline creature wavering above the shrubs as it ventured away from them. Then he looked back at Oscar and saw a familiar and welcomed look in his eye.

"Oscar," he said, "you're feeling better, I presume?"

Oscar looked away before responding. "Yes," he said, "I believe I'm a bit recovered."

"Good. But tell me. What happened? You stopped taking your malaria pills, didn't you?"

"I had just run out," he replied, sitting back down on his sleeping bag and wiping his brow. "I was about to renew the prescription when I thought, no, I want this to be a special trip. I didn't want to deal with the nausea. After all, I've been taking those pills for years. I thought I had plenty of resistance."

"This is a special trip, all right. But nausea is the least of your worries. Have you had such attacks before?"

"Yes," he replied rather faintly, "several years ago in India. Should have been cured by now."

"Well, either you've picked up a new strain or it's been hiding in your liver all these years. All this exertion has clearly weakened your system."

"I suppose so," he said. "But what have you done with the diamonds? You've tossed them back into the lake, no doubt."

Francis looked at him with a stunned expression. "Please tell me you're joking."

Oscar looked slightly perplexed. "Joking?" he said. "Why would I joke about those bloody diamonds? I do believe they are a curse after all."

Francis rubbed his weary eyes and shook his head slowly from side to side. "I haven't done anything with them, Oscar, but we must find them. What about the moonbeams? You were quite delirious but you kept indicating they were safe somewhere. Can't you remember?"

"Moonbeams? You mean the diamonds?"

"Yes, that's what you called them."

Oscar began to laugh but soon he was coughing. Francis handed him some water. "My, but that water is wretched," he continued as he wiped his mouth. "Moonbeams, eh? I haven't any idea whatsoever. But then I can't remember much of anything since our failed attempts to dislodge the Land Rover."

"Well, we can't leave here until we find them. Do you feel up to traveling?"

"I believe so," said Oscar, who then attempted to stand. He wobbled slightly before Francis grabbed his arm to steady him. Then Oscar turned abruptly and grabbed Francis by the shoulders.

"Wait!" he exclaimed. "What day is it?"

"It's Friday the fifth."

"No! It can't be," he shouted. "I'm due back in France this evening. The wedding is only two days off! We must leave now."

"Yes, but first we must find the diamonds."

"Don't be ridiculous. No one will find them."

"I won't take that chance," Francis replied. "Think. What did you do with them?"

"I told you I don't know," he snapped.

"Then let's start searching. I'll use the flashlight and you can use the lantern. Or perhaps you hid them outside the cave."

"Perhaps the lion took them."

"Don't be silly. But then I suppose it's possible that someone, perhaps a Maasai, came by and took them from you while you were asleep."

"Highly unlikely."

"Yes, but not impossible. Perhaps they heard the gunfire. All the more reason to find them. You look outside while I continue searching within."

And without further discussion, Francis reached for the flashlight and began probing once again. Oscar sat for a few moments, struggling to remember what he may have done with his two socks full of diamonds. His head was still swimming, yet the frightening realization that he was almost certain to miss his wedding day, the most important event in his entire life, gradually took hold. Elizabeth would be terrified.

The search proved fruitless. After a few hours they decided to rest. Oscar was famished, having not eaten anything substantial in well over twenty-four hours. Francis ventured off to check the snares and to see if he could replenish their water supply. Daylight was nearly spent but he could just see clearly enough to make his way back to the draw where he had procured their last water and set the snares. At first he could not believe his eyes, for there was a small springhare trapped in one of the snares, still struggling to free himself. Francis pulled out a knife and slit its throat, then gutted and skinned it. Before returning to Oscar he checked the tiny stream only to find it was completely dry.

Though unaccustomed to eating meat, let alone killing it and preparing it, Francis agreed with Oscar that it was tasty after all. Nonetheless, in view of Oscar's weakened condition, he let him devour nearly all of it. They washed it down with almost the last of the bitter water and then began debating their next move as they stared into a roaring, crackling fire while a bright, full moon beckoned.

It was now Oscar who demanded that they set out for the nearest village and Francis who resisted, convinced that their failure to appear at the airport at the appointed hour would most certainly result in a search party being sent out to find them.

Oscar countered that he could not wait any longer. The only chance of being on time for his own wedding depended on getting to a village as soon as possible. Surely the villagers could arrange some sort of transportation to Nairobi.

"Yes, most likely they would just tell you to walk to Nairobi. That's what they would do," Francis replied. "But assuming we would be stuck at the village, no one would find us. It's not part of the itinerary. Besides, we don't even know exactly where it is. And if you were to have a recurrence of that fever, you could very well die. No, the more I ponder it, the more obvious it is to me that we should stay put and await our impending rescue."

"And my wedding?"

"You'll just have to postpone it. But at least you'll be alive to experience it."

"And how can you be sure? We're nearly out of food and water. Just because you got lucky with that rabbit, who's to say we'll find other nourishment in this barren landscape?"

"They'll find us within a couple of days. I'm positive. All we need to do is to set all that brush out on the lake so that anyone flying over will see it. I submitted our itinerary to the proper authorities, and if the government doesn't send out a search party, then the university certainly will. And they know the exact location of the hot springs."

"And if they don't come? At least the Maasai would feed us. We could starve here."

"We won't starve, I promise. Besides, we're not leaving until we find those diamonds."

Oscar stood and walked a few steps away from the fire before turning abruptly to face Francis. "You don't trust me, do you?"

"Why, of course I trust you," said Francis.

"Are you sure you're not just worried that I really do know where the diamonds are and that I might come back and retrieve them without you? Is that it?"

"No, not at all. I trust you implicitly. You gave me your word."

Oscar stared at Francis for some time, still breathing more heavily than usual. "All right," he said at last. "We'll wait it out."

Chapter 23

No help arrived that day or the following day. All remained still, just an occasional gust of wind or the distant howling of some nocturnal creature breaking the impenetrable silence outside the cave. They had set all the brush out on Lake Natron's slushy crust, spelling out "SOS" in large letters not far from the entombed Land Rover. But thus far to no avail.

Francis continued to search for food and water, venturing farther and farther from the cave. On one sortie he came across a small herd of Thomson's gazelles and managed to pick off the slowest of the group with his shotgun. But a pack of hyenas appeared as he was skinning the poor creature and efforts to scare them away did no good.

He found other small drainages and tried digging for water but managed to create only small mud holes. By now his lips were cracked and swollen, for he had spared nearly all the water for Oscar. He squeezed what little moisture he could from clumps of mud and managed to moisten his lips and his swollen tongue.

On the third day Oscar's fever returned, as expected. The parasites had no doubt suffered a setback due to the effects of the medicine Francis had administered, but it was not enough to entirely halt their debilitating progress. By midday he was again shaking with severe chills and bordering on delirium, sometimes calling to Elizabeth to come keep him warm.

Francis threw both of the tattered sleeping bags on top of him before heading back to the draw. He walked with a determined stride, bent on alleviating their hunger. But the snares were still empty. He stood up to have a look around, certain that this comparatively lush fold in Gelai's northern flanks must harbor some sort of sustenance. Yet all was still, with no trace of wind. Then suddenly, as he turned to go, a springhare came bounding out of the brush. There was no time to ready the shotgun. Instead he dropped everything he was carrying and began chasing it, running as fast as he could while keeping an eye on the animal's long, floppy ears, as the Maasai had taught him. The instant the ears lay straight back, Francis dove to his right and, having guessed correctly, he scooped up the small furry animal as it attempted to make a sharp turn out of harm's way.

After skinning and cleaning it, he returned to the cave and set his quarry on a spit over a small fire. Oscar arose to the smells of the impending meal, wiping his brow and staggering slowly, looking bewildered once more but awake and, most importantly, alive.

"I got lucky," said Francis.

Oscar did not respond. He simply sat down next to Francis, who handed him a juicy thigh to gnaw on. Francis picked up a small bit of loin, but before it even touched his lips he heard a faint sound in the distance. He stood suddenly and looked to the north. At first he thought he was just imagining it, but then his eyes helped to convince him that what he thought he heard was indeed quite real. For there, some distance off yet steadily approaching, was a helicopter. And there could be no doubt that it was headed straight for them.

Francis immediately abandoned the roasted springhare and went bounding down the hill, leaving Oscar alone with the freshly cooked meat. He wasted no time in devouring it while staring at the strange machine that was undeniably headed their way. He watched as the helicopter approached and finally came to rest near the forsaken Land Rover, its whirling blades scattering the brush he and Francis had so carefully placed to mark their whereabouts.

Having run all the way, Francis stood near the Land Rover, panting and trying to recover his breath. Daylight was slowly fading but he could see clearly enough to recognize the yellow diamond symbol on the side of the helicopter.

"Peter!" he shouted as his brother stepped out of the helicopter and walked toward him with a deliberate stride. He was dressed in his usual handsome attire with fine leather gloves to protect his delicate hands from the desert heat. Dr. Meinz followed close behind, still wearing his faded blue suit and tie.

"Francis," returned Peter sharply, "what the hell kind of fix have you gotten yourself into now? I've been looking all over for you along with plenty of others."

"Thank God you've arrived!" Francis replied, breaking into tears of joy and relief. "We've been stranded for days. Oscar's come down with malaria and needs medical attention badly. The fever's coming on strong. He's up there on Gelai. We've taken refuge in an old lava tube."

Francis pointed in the general vicinity of their accommodations before the two shared a quick embrace. Francis attempted to explain all that had transpired but Peter interrupted. It was clear that his patience had worn thin.

"Enough," he said sharply. "I have been searching for you for two days now, two days out of my itinerary that I can ill afford."

He then turned toward Dr. Meinz. "Conrad," he shouted, "see what you can salvage from the Land Rover while Francis and I fetch Dr. Newman. With luck I'll make my flight back to London."

"There's really nothing worth bothering about," Francis rejoined.

"No doubt," said Peter, "but we might as well salvage what we can as long as we've come this far."

Francis offered no further objection. Dr. Meinz complied immediately and began by reaching for the various items stored on top of the Land Rover as Peter and Francis began walking toward the shore. Francis looked back just in time to see Dr. Meinz retrieve the crudely folded tent and then a rather sorry-looking, well-worn duffel bag that had somehow made its way to the Land Rover's rooftop.

"Wait," he shouted, "don't worry about that."

Dr. Meinz stopped and looked back at them. "As you wish," he replied with a trace of a smile. "It's quite heavy. Feels like it's full of rocks."

Francis forced a bit of a laugh but his brother reined up short.

"Rocks?" he inquired with a wry look toward Francis. "Are you sure? But why would my brother the botanist be collecting rocks?"

Francis attempted in vain to conceal the enormous shock of adrenaline that pulsed through his body as he suddenly realized that, despite all his efforts to remove every trace of kimberlite from the area, he had overlooked the duffel bag that Oscar had apparently stowed on top of the Land Rover the night it had rained so hard and the stubborn crust had finally given way. He could not believe his eyes.

"Uh, ballast," he stammered. "We needed more weight to get out of the mud several miles back. So we threw some rocks on top. It appears we forgot all about them once we got free."

Peter looked askance, clearly unconvinced. "Really? Well, let's have a look. I'm always interested in rocks. One never knows what might lie hidden within them."

"Don't be silly," rejoined Francis rather anxiously. "We must get to Oscar immediately. He's delirious with fever."

But it was too late. Peter was already walking back toward the Land Rover and Dr. Meinz was proceeding to lower the duffel bag. He handed it to Peter, who gave his brother a curious look before setting it down on the soda crust and opening the metal zipper.

As he peered inside the duffel bag, his expression remained rather dubious. But when he reached inside and pulled out a large chunk of yellowish-brown rock that the setting sun illuminated in reddish hues, his body began to tremble. He held it up in the fading light and turned it in every direction. His breathing was heavier than usual and he glanced quickly at his brother, his jaw set tight.

"Francis," he said firmly, "where did you find this kimberlite?"

His brother looked rather dumbfounded. "Kimberlite?" he replied. "What on earth are you talking about?"

Peter turned and gave Francis a fierce look that clearly indicated he would tolerate no shenanigans. "Don't you try to fool with me. Where did you find this rock? I must know."

"Why, it was—it was—several miles back, I'm not at all sure where. We encountered some rough going and simply needed to improve our traction, that's all. It was just lying beside the road. It couldn't possibly be kimberlite."

"Just lying beside the road, eh? I'll tell you what's lying—it's you. Don't think you can fool me for a minute. To think I believed all this rubbish about your passion for plants and all that nonsense. Now tell me once and for all: Where did you find this piece of kimberlite?"

Francis froze, trying to cope with this unbelievable twist of events. "I tell you I don't know. I suppose we could backtrack and look for the area of washouts, but that's of no importance now. We must get Oscar to hospital quickly."

"To hell with Oscar," replied Peter, his eyes fixed firmly upon his brother. "Conrad, see what else you can find in this wretched vehicle."

Dr. Meinz complied again and set about searching the roof rack for more bags of rocks. Coming up empty, he then began to rummage through the interior while Peter kept his gaze fixed on Francis like a hunter locked onto his prey.

"Nothing inside," said Dr. Meinz as he searched the rear of the Land Rover.

"I told you," said Francis.

"Hold on," said Dr. Meinz unexpectedly. "Here's something in the glove compartment."

He walked toward Peter as he removed the cloth that surrounded the pistol Francis had deliberately hidden from a delirious Oscar Newman.

"Well, well," said Peter, "now here's a relic. It looks like one of Father's. But how did you end up with it? I thought he had bequeathed them all to me, you being such a pacifist."

Francis became suddenly alarmed as he watched his brother examine the pistol as if admiring the dull luster of the gray metal. "He gave it to me," said Francis. "It was half of a matching pair. You have the other one, but it's no doubt rather inconspicuous amid your entire collection of firearms."

Peter sneered, clearly losing patience. "Don't toy with me," he rejoined angrily. "Just tell me where you found the kimberlite, damn it!"

Francis stiffened. "Is that a threat?" he countered, noting that his brother was gripping the pistol harder and had one finger upon the trigger.

"A threat?" he replied. "Why no, of course not. Why should I threaten my own brother, my former partner, who has absolutely no reason to withhold any information that might lead to the discovery of our mutual birthright?"

Francis looked at his brother in disgust. "Birthright, is it? And why is that? Just because an ancient relative of ours managed to find a few remarkable gemstones many, many years ago? None of that gives you or me any rights to them whatsoever. All I can tell you is that if I did know something, you're the last person on earth I would ever confide in."

Peter recoiled at these last words and turned away for a moment. His face was reddening and the veins on his neck were beginning to thicken. He took a deep breath before facing his brother once again.

"Francis," he began, waving the pistol before him to make his points, "I said don't toy with me. I believe you know exactly where these stones came from, and if you don't tell me right this instant—"

"Don't you dare point that at me," Francis countered before his brother could finish. And as he spoke these words, he reached for the barrel of the gun.

Oscar, meanwhile, looked on, gazing as best he could through his binoculars. Though his fever was again running high, the arrival of Peter and the notion of being rescued and perhaps being soon reunited with Elizabeth helped to clear, at least momentarily, his foggy mind. Yet he could not quite believe what he saw as Francis folded suddenly and then fell slowly. His slumped body had nearly reached the hard crust of Natron when the sound of a gunshot reached his ears and the sudden realization that Francis had been shot seared his entire being. He watched in horror as Peter and his companion tried to revive Francis but ended by carrying his limp body to the helicopter.

Oscar remained staring, unbelieving, taking stock of his own bewildered senses before his body overcame his weakened mental state and emitted a resounding *"No!"* that may very well have carried clear to the other side of the Rift Valley.

Peter evidently took note of the source of his cry, as he left Dr. Meinz to tend to Francis and headed off at a rapid pace in search of Oscar, who remained frozen, uncertain as to whether he should flee or surrender.

"Dr. Newman!" shouted Peter as he reached the shoreline and began ascending the northwestern slopes of Gelai. "There's been a terrible accident. My brother has been shot. Please, you're a doctor, you must help him."

Oscar did not move. Horrified, he watched Peter come in and out of view as he quickly mounted the steep slopes. Yet the challenge to his Hippocratic oath added another dimension to his turmoil.

"There's nothing I can do," he shouted in reply. "I have no instruments or medical supplies. Surely Dr. Meinz is capable…"

But there was no response, only the sound of Peter running up the brushy slopes. Oscar could hear his heavy breathing and the pounding of his footsteps on the broken terrain as he approached. Yet the sound paled relative to the wild pounding of his own heart.

Time was running short as the footsteps came closer. To flee would be so ironic, he thought, after waiting so long to be rescued. But he found himself backing slowly into the lava tube, with fear his only motivation and his loathing for Peter Dermenjian growing steadily by the minute.

"Dr. Newman," Peter called once more as he searched for the entrance to the lava tube. "Please, we need your help. And you need ours."

Oscar remained still, crouching within the darkness of the cave, feeling his head swirling in shock and disbelief and gripped with terror. Perhaps he was dreaming all this. Perhaps Francis would return momentarily and he would awaken from a terrible nightmare. But then he heard Peter's voice again, much closer than before.

"Dr. Newman, please, you mustn't be frightened. My brother and I had a terrible misunderstanding. No harm will come to you, I promise. Just tell me where you found the diamonds."

Oscar gripped the lantern that, though unlit, was the only item he had thought to take with him as he began his retreat farther into the recesses of the lava tube. His breathing was more rapid than before and he was sweating profusely. In the darkness, he tripped over some pieces of broken lava but kept feeling his way slowly backward while his eyes were trained on the entrance to the cave. At last he saw Peter silhouetted against the pink sky outside.

"Dr. Newman," he shouted once more, the sounds echoing loudly. "I know you are in there. Certainly, you must realize you have no choice but to come with me. If I leave you here, you will most certainly die a horrible death. This is your only means of escape."

The word "escape" resonated over and over as Oscar hovered behind some fallen rocks.

"Dr. Newman, I am losing patience. I realize you are very ill. You must come with me now if you wish to survive. Just tell me where you found the kimberlite and I'll see to it that you get the best of medical attention."

Oscar remained hidden behind a jumble of rocks, shaking with fever and fear and torn apart inside by his desire to save Francis. In a relatively short time he had come to regard Francis as perhaps his best friend, not that he had many to choose from. And he no doubt lay dying, or was perhaps already dead, at the hands of his brother, who was now approaching, still clutching the pistol that had fired the deadly shot. Finally, Oscar stood up, his fear overcome by his love for Francis and by his sense of sworn duty to render whatever aid he could in such circumstances. He knew there was likely very little he could do, especially considering his own weakened condition. But he had to try. And so he stood up and was about to announce his intentions when he saw another dark figure silhouetted at the entrance to the cave.

"Peter," said Dr. Meinz, "your brother is dead."

Chapter 24

An involuntary shriek escaped from Oscar. Peter cursed as Dr. Meinz approached.

"Newman!" shouted Peter. "Tell us where you found those diamonds or you're a dead man, just like my brother."

"Never!" Oscar replied frantically. "You murderer! How could you kill your own flesh and blood?"

He recoiled still farther into the depths of the cave.

"It was an accident," Peter replied, advancing slowly. "He shouldn't have reached for the gun. But my brother was a weakling. And as you know, only the strong survive. So tell me where you found the diamonds and you'll be among them. Otherwise I will be forced to leave you here to die as well."

Oscar felt his way carefully along the rocky floor of the cave, which was beginning to twist and slowly eclipse the trace of daylight from the opening. Still, he could see the silhouettes of Peter and Dr. Meinz moving cautiously forward, feeling their way as well. And then they were gone. He slowed his retreat, listening carefully for their footsteps. But all he could hear were their voices. They had apparently stopped advancing upon encountering the total darkness of the cave. There was some further discussion, rather heated at times, which Oscar could not comprehend, followed by silence. Oscar waited patiently for quite some time until he heard the sounds of the helicopter engine. It was quite audible at first but then subsided as the helicopter departed, leaving him alone to die. Or so he believed.

He crept closer to the entrance and was quite startled to see a fire outside the cave and Dr. Meinz huddled before it, holding his head in his hands. Beside him was the shotgun. Oscar retreated once again, surmising that Peter would return in the morning better prepared for a proper search of the cave. Perhaps he could reason with Dr. Meinz or overtake him. But to what end? It was becoming harder to reason and Oscar felt the fever gradually overwhelm him. He began to withdraw farther into the darkness, into the belly of the volcano.

He felt his way for a hundred yards or so, stumbling over the broken rocks and banging his shins time and again. At last he felt he was far enough from the entrance that he could dare to light the lantern. He found some matches in one of his pockets and soon it was aglow. The brightness made his eyes hurt at first but then they grew accustomed to the light that illuminated the haunting shapes of molten, twisted rock all around him. After half an hour of mindlessly trudging toward the center of the volcano, Oscar felt his fever begin to twist his perception, and the walls began to crawl with images of ghoulish faces. They seemed to breathe and writhe and taunt at him, but he kept up his pace, wondering with what shred of consciousness remained if he wasn't already dead and was simply marching into hell all on his own. He finally stopped to rest, setting the lantern down on a large, flat chunk of lava. He sat down, leaning back against the wall of lava, and drifted off to another world.

He had no idea how long he had been in such a position, barely conscious, when he heard another voice. It called to him, rather eerily, from somewhere beyond the cave.

"Oscar," it said, "I knew ye'd come back. I've kept them safe jes' like I promised."

Oscar raised a weary head and looked about. The cave walls were flickering in the lantern light and the butterscotch lava curls were undulating and pulsating with each flicker. He was certain it was a dream. Then the voice called to him again.

"Oscar, please, you must help me. I've been trapped here for years."

Oscar was well beyond frightened, having crossed over to what felt like another dimension, one that admitted neither human reason nor emotion. He simply looked about, seeing nothing but the ghostly faces and swirling images his fever concocted. He picked up the lantern to get a better look. What he saw was indeed quite frightening. For not twenty yards beyond lay the end. The lava tube came to an abrupt halt, and if he had had any notions of finding another exit from the internal workings of Gelai, they were all extinguished when he saw that there was nowhere else to go. He stood still, trembling, realizing that escape was impossible. He stared at the wall before him, trying to remember what had brought him to this place, watching the swirling images and haunting faces within the frozen lava.

He saw his mother searching for him, and Elizabeth as well. Their faces came and went in the flickering light, but then he heard the voice again and thought he saw someone trapped beneath a large pile of rocks that marked the end of the cave. He moved closer.

"Help me!" cried the voice once more.

Oscar began to move the rocks aside until he came upon a face that looked somewhat familiar.

"Father," he said, "I remember now. Just lie still and I'll save you."

He began to dig and claw at the rocks that seemed to hold his father pinned to the floor of the cave. His face was haggard and looked rather ancient, but that did not matter. He had to set him free. He dug frantically, pulling rocks aside and flinging them some distance away. His father was bleeding profusely but nothing mattered except to extricate him from the fallen rocks. But the more he dug, the more his father remained trapped and the more exhausted Oscar became until he finally collapsed.

He came to several hours later and found himself alone and shivering in the dark. The lantern had gone out and he was lying facedown in a depression of some kind. He sat up and struck a match that illuminated his surroundings momentarily before being extinguished. He lit another but it, too, soon was out. He felt around him, trying to piece together the events that had brought him there, deep within the silent volcano, when he felt what he thought at first were two feet. He gasped as the recollection of his attempts to save his own father came rushing back. Then his senses cleared momentarily, and he realized that what he held in his hands were the two socks full of diamonds.

His breathing slowed as he rolled onto his back and stared at the roof of what now appeared to be his prison cell, still clutching the socks filled with diamonds. There was really no point in trying to light the lantern, for there was nowhere to go, other than back to the entrance to surrender himself along with the diamonds. He had no idea how far he had wandered but there was clearly no point in remaining. Eventually, he came to accept that surrendering to Peter was his only choice. And Peter would no doubt take the diamonds and then kill him just like he'd killed Francis. But none of that seemed to matter since he would soon be dead no matter what.

He lit one more match to see if he could get the lantern, which was apparently out of fuel, to function once more. As he struck the match it flared up and then died down as the others had done. Oscar assumed the matches were wet but he tried striking another. It, too, began to burn but the flame wavered before going out. Though still struggling with the fever, his dull mind reasoned that if the matches were wet, they wouldn't light in the first place. Something was causing them to go out. He placed his palms out, facing up, and felt them turning cold and clammy. He lit another match and noticed, before it extinguished, that the cave seemed to be a bit misty. That made no sense, and he attributed the mist to the fever and began reminding himself that he could not trust his own senses. Nonetheless, he struck one more match and placed it inside the lantern. As expected, the lantern did not light, yet the match continued to burn for a moment, which was enough time for Oscar to see that the chamber at the end of the lava tube was indeed filling up with mist.

Oscar began immediately to search his pockets for any scraps of paper. He reached into his wallet and removed a few pound notes that he stuffed inside the lantern. Then he lit them, stood up, and lifted the now somewhat more functional lantern as high as he could. The light revealed a slow swirling of the mist but in a downward direction that clearly suggested that the source came from above, from a hole in the roof! Oscar grabbed the two socks and tied them together and flung them about his neck. Then he tried scaling the walls of the lava tube, probing for the opening, but the light gradually faded and he was forced to stop.

He found his handkerchief, placed it inside the lantern, and after setting it on fire, resumed his search for an exit. He could feel the mist descending, and by the time the light faded once again, he had located a narrow crevice in the rock above that clearly served as a conduit to the outside. He could feel the cool mist flowing past his fingers as he stood on rocks he had piled one atop the other to serve as a platform for his explorations. The crevice was wide in one direction but narrow in the other. He would never fit through. Yet he pulled at the rock and was astonished and nearly crushed when a large chunk broke loose. He reached again, now in darkness, and felt a ledge where he was able to find a grip. By pressing his feet against the side of the lava tube, he was able to walk his lower body up the sides and hoist himself up into a small compartment within what amounted to a vent for the river of lava that had passed through thousands of years before.

He lit another match and saw that the passageway above was congested with rocks of various sizes. He probed and pried and managed to loosen them one by one. Then, by pressing his body and legs against the opposite sides of the narrow chimney of rock, he was able to climb higher. But there were still more rocks above obstructing his passage. He turned his face away each time a rock broke free. And while he was fortunate that none hit him on the head, he could not move his legs out of harm's way. If he did, he would certainly fall, risking more serious injury. In addition to the considerable pain of the rocks falling on his thighs and shins, the muscles in his legs started burning from the constant exertion required to maintain his position, pressed between the sides of the rocky passageway. But despite the excruciating pain and the fever that still wracked his body, his hopes of escaping grew stronger as he inched his way upward.

There was no way he could know just how far he needed to climb or whether he would encounter an absolute impasse, either a passage too narrow or rocks he could not dislodge. But after what seemed like an eternity, he felt the cool mist flowing past him more forcefully and, as he reached upward for another handhold in the rock, all he grasped was air. It was still pitch black as he pulled himself up out of the rocky crevice onto the invisible slopes of Gelai and into a dark, dense cloud of vapor. The surface was quite steep, and before he could gain decent footing, he fell and began rolling downhill, adding bruises to his upper body to match those on his legs, until he came to rest against some thorny shrubs. He felt warm blood trickling down his face but in his fevered stupor thought nothing of it. He stood up and, shivering in the cold, misty air, simply allowed his body to travel downhill, stumbling like a blind man as he felt his way amid the brush.

Though he tripped and fell several times more, and his vision was clouded, he discerned that he was traveling within a narrow draw along the western face of Gelai. He had been following a rather straight line back toward Natron, but as the lighting slowly improved, he sought the deeper recesses of the draw. Though the shrubbery became thicker with each step, he was driven by an overwhelming thirst and a desire to remain hidden.

When he arrived at what he surmised must be the center of the draw, however, there was no water to be found. Still, he followed it downslope to where it finally converged with the crusty surface of Natron. No water had surfaced, and as he stood panting and watching the fog slowly recede, he muttered a few curses under his breath. The outline of Lengai at the southern end of the lake was barely visible. He was thinking about the Maasai god, Engai, that supposedly inhabited the great volcano, but as he began to trudge in its direction, his right foot suddenly broke through the thin crust. The mud below was quite thick and sticky, and while he tried to extricate his right foot, the other one broke through.

Whatever fresh water flowed down the slope now traveled beneath the surface and only served to weaken the ordinarily sturdy crust. Oscar struggled mightily once again to free himself from the tenacious mud, which was alkaline enough that, by the time he freed himself, had begun burning the skin on his legs. His clothes were in tatters but the socks filled with diamonds still hung about his neck as he trudged along Natron's shores, resuming his journey to the south. Looking up at the sun-drenched slopes of Lengai, he prayed to its eponymous god to help him reach a Maasai village before being found by Peter, who by then must have resumed his search.

As he stumbled along, paralleling the shoreline, Oscar felt like his legs were but stumps that the rest of his body somehow managed to place one in front of the other. He knew it was only thirst and hunger, and a strong will to survive, that kept them churning slowly forward as the temperature climbed and the outline of Lengai became larger and larger. How he wished he had paid better attention when Francis had explained the usefulness of the various plants about him, especially which ones were edible. He tried nibbling on various stalks but ended by gagging and nearly retching from their natural alkalinity.

Eventually he veered away from the shore, guessing it to be midmorning by the aspect of the intense sun. He had set a course toward the eastern slopes of Lengai when, mounting a slight rise, he saw a vaguely familiar sight. There were several large termite mounds. He remembered how Francis had said they were like candy and, however repulsed, his empty stomach forced him to investigate. There were several of the large white insects crawling along the surface of the first mound he inspected. He grabbed one between his fingers and stuffed it into his mouth. No sooner had he done so when he felt an intense stinging on his tongue.

"Why, you little bastard," he muttered as he spat out the impertinent insect. Realizing, however, that his weakened body required some kind of sustenance, he picked up another. This time he squeezed it between his fingers to make sure it wouldn't bite. He put it in his mouth and made a face as he swallowed it. It definitely wasn't candy but the taste was not objectionable. He picked up another and squeezed it, popped it in his mouth, and repeated with another and another. Before long he had consumed all the termites crawling on the outside of the mound. Then he laughed and began to search for a stick. He found one that seemed suitable and began screeching and scratching like a chimpanzee in some Jane Goodall film as he probed one of the entrances to the termite mound. He withdrew the stick, which was covered with termites. But the termites were very active and there were more of them than he could pinch before they began crawling up his arm and biting back. He brushed them off and abandoned that particular mound. Moving to another, he inserted the stick inside a large, promising entry tunnel, but when he pulled it out it was empty. He moved his face closer to examine the opening and recoiled with a loud shriek as a deadly black mamba snake emerged, flicking its forked tongue at him.

He threw the stick aside and continued his journey to find a safe refuge where there would be real food and water. The ash-swept countryside was brutally hot and desolate, and he could feel his already-weakened system growing even weaker by the moment. Yet there were still miles to go before he could rest, before he might find some friendly Maasai to help him. As he mounted the next rise, he saw at last a welcomed sight. It was nothing more than a tree, a large tree that at the very least offered some shade and a suitable place to rest.

He sat down beneath it and tried to estimate how much farther he needed to travel and how much strength remained in his bruised and battered, alkaline-burned and fever-plagued body. His mouth was as dry as the sand around him, and the empty pit in his stomach felt like it was beginning to digest his own entrails.

Somehow, the meager flow of energy to his brain reminded him that he was carrying on his person an enormous wealth of gems. How would he explain them in the unlikely event that he actually encountered someone? The answer was obvious. He couldn't. He must bury them. He dug a pit about two feet deep and placed the two socks side by side before covering them up. He scattered bits of brush on top to obscure the freshly dug hole, not that he was too worried anyone would be suspicious. He even wondered if any human had ever sat beneath this tree before, or ever would again. Why would they? For this was no doubt the most isolated and desolate place on earth.

After nearly falling asleep, he forced himself back to his feet, knowing that he must find a better refuge before the heat of day peaked. He continued to trudge toward Lengai, mounting and descending progressive swales of windblown ash. Then he remembered the cool waters near the place he had camped with Francis at the base of Lengai. With renewed courage he picked up his pace, believing that such a place could not be too much farther. Perhaps over the next rise he would see a landmark of some kind, a place he would remember.

He was almost beginning to feel optimistic, that there was perhaps a shred of hope left, that maybe he would see Elizabeth once again. But his hopes were dashed as he mounted one last rise and saw before him, square in his path, what he had dreaded most all along. For there, in all his African glory, stood the veritable king of beasts. The huge lion gave a soft growl at first as Oscar stopped in his tracks, hoping against hope that he was again hallucinating from the fever. But then he heard the lion roar more loudly and he tried to remember what Francis had told him. Whatever you do, he had said, don't run. Remain calm, make loud noises.

"Go away!" he screamed. Yet the lion, with a thick, majestic mane, simply stood staring at him with his enormous head lowered.

"Please!" he cried. "Leave me alone! Just go away!"

Yet the lion began to pace, his fierce eyes maintaining contact all the while with Oscar's.

"Help!" screamed Oscar, who was feeling rather faint and began praying he would simply awaken. "Elizabeth!" he screamed. "Make me wake up! This can't be happening! Francis! Anyone! Help me! Please, make me wake up!"

But he did not awaken. For it was too late. The lion began to pace more briskly until he finally turned and began to charge. His immense and powerful frame quickly closed the distance between them. Oscar, frozen in place, watched in disbelief as the grotesque face of the beast, with large jaws and huge, gleaming teeth, bore down on him. Then all that remained, amid fleeting thoughts of Elizabeth and his mother, was the foul stench of the predator's breath as his world went completely dark and completely quiet.

Chapter 25

To say that a pall had settled over the stately home of Madame Le Clerc would be like saying some volcanic ash had once settled over the Serengeti Plain. Intense remorse permeated every room and the anxiety in the air was electric.

Tommy and Ethel sat quietly, wringing their hands and daubing their eyes with wet handkerchiefs, stirring only to assist Mrs. Newman, whom they had brought along as a surprise for Oscar. She sat in her wheelchair beside a large fire that attempted in vain to brighten the somber main salon. She remained nearly passive, saliva dribbling into her metal bowl, though on occasion she would break out in slight convulsions.

"She knows," said Ethel.

"Aye," said Tommy.

Edouard paced anxiously up and down before the hearth, smoking a cigarette, while off in the library David Sebastian continued to hold council as best he could with Madame Le Clerc and Father Brodard. Jacques stood vigil upstairs, just outside of Elizabeth's bedroom.

Nothing inside the room had changed over the years. But no matter what consolation her dolls and other mementos had provided during her youth, they were completely worthless now. Jacques waited and listened carefully for any stirrings. There were none. All that he heard was a soft yet relentless wail, a cry stemming from the extreme depths of someone's being. And that would be Elizabeth of course, who, after days of no word, had been sent reeling by reports that not only was Oscar missing and presumed dead, but he had apparently killed Francis.

The newspaper lay next to the bed. She had read it a dozen times and still could not believe it. Yet the headline was clear.

Missing Nobel Laureate Wanted for Murder of Nairobi Professor

Nairobi. Dr. Oscar Newman, who last month was awarded the Nobel Peace Prize and has been missing for over a week in the wilds of northern Tanzania, is the chief suspect in the murder of Dr. Francis Dermenjian, professor of botany at the University of Nairobi.

The body of Dr. Dermenjian was discovered last Tuesday by his brother, Peter Dermenjian, head of the international diamond cartel Dermenjian Diamonds, Ltd. According to his diary, Francis Dermenjian had been traveling with Dr. Newman when they became stranded along the shores of Lake Natron.

After taking shelter in a cave situated on the slopes of the nine-thousand-foot-tall volcano Gelai, Dr. Newman apparently came down with malaria. The diary records that he became delirious and attempted to shoot Dermenjian. Authorities strongly suspect that he ultimately succeeded since Dermenjian was shot at very close range. And the only fingerprints found on the gun, according to Nairobi police, were Dr. Newman's.

Authorities say there is little chance Dr. Newman could survive on his own this long in the hostile terrain east of Lake Natron. Search parties, however, continue to comb the area.

Though the news was now old, it was no less devastating. From the moment the Kenya National Police had phoned three days earlier, Elizabeth's anxious moments awaiting Oscar's return had turned into a horrendous, never-ending nightmare. Edouard had tried desperately to comfort her. And David—who had flown to Marseille without Oscar, praying he had somehow taken a different flight—had spent hours at Elizabeth's side. He had even managed to fill her with hope, for a while, at least, by assuring her that rescue operations would locate Oscar very soon. But now he remained apart from her, consulting with her mother instead while sharing in the remorse and admitting to no one but himself that Oscar was lost for good.

"How much longer must we wait?" bemoaned Madame Le Clerc. "Surely he is dead by now. We must get on with our lives. Perhaps we should begin to arrange a service for him."

Father Brodard nodded at the suggestion.

"That would be premature," replied David. "He hasn't been missing that long."

Despite his own pessimism, David had urged everyone to remain strong, to have patience, to pray for Oscar's safe return. Yet his own show of strength, such as it was, was but a thin veneer covering the intense pain inflicted on him not only by the likely death of Oscar but by the certain death of Francis. There were few men in Kenya whom David had admired as well and now, suddenly, he was gone.

"May I suggest," offered Father Brodard, "that we at least begin making arrangements for a service? While we beseech God's mercy on him, we must admit that it is very unlikely Oscar is still alive."

David pondered a moment. He had spent an entire week with Elizabeth's family and Oscar's clan, intent on performing a wedding ceremony. But now, in the wake of disaster, he seemed to be head cheerleader, a role he did not relish. His own mother, who was eighty-three and long since widowed, had been awaiting the arrival of her youngest son for several days. And he was already overdue in Kenya, where classes should have resumed.

"As you wish," he said. "But I must go now. I will leave a number in Marseille where you can reach me if there is further news."

"Very well," said Madame Le Clerc.

Without ceremony, they all rose. David simply nodded as he went off to gather his things. Madame Le Clerc and Father Brodard remained in the library, still standing but sharing a hint of a smile, if not overtly with their lips, then with a subtle darting of the eyes toward one another.

No one suspected that at that very moment two visitors were approaching, unannounced and uninvited. They had traveled far and had slept very little in the past several days, having been fully occupied searching for the groom at large by helicopter, by car, and on foot. They had begun with the cave, believing it impossible for Oscar to have found a way out. Yet he was gone. They had followed his trail from the apex of the vent in the lava tube to the shores of Natron. Once his track ventured away from the shore, however, all trace of Oscar was lost in the shifting swales of windblown ash.

Peter had organized a search party of his own to complement that of the Tanzanian Police Force and the Kenya National Police. They had scoured the countryside, investigating every recess of Gelai's mighty fortress as well as all the land between Gelai and Mto wa Mbu. But all they had found were piercing thorns amid dry scrub, occasional thickets of impenetrable forest, and endless dunes of blowing ash. They had visited every Maasai settlement in the area and interviewed every villager and herdsman they'd encountered, probing for information about Oscar. But the only Maasai who had apparently laid eyes on him was the young hitchhiker. He remembered Oscar as the biggest *mzungu* he'd ever seen. But news of such an old sighting was useless. Only his comment about seeing big rocks and dirty shovels inside the Land Rover, obtained after endless questioning by Peter's operatives, offered any hope. But after several days it had become evident to Peter that either Oscar was dead, and his remains eaten and obliterated by some wild creature, or he had somehow managed to escape. And if he had escaped, there was no doubt where he would have headed or, perhaps, left some word of his plans.

The Ferrari gripped the pavement as Peter depressed the accelerator. He leaned into the turn as the engine propelled the car forward at an ever-faster pace. They climbed higher into the ancient hills of Provence while Dr. Meinz did his best to navigate. More than once they had missed a turn. As they finally neared the village of Balgères, however, the roadway turned from pavement to cobbles. They adapted their speed to the new terrain, and though a few of the locals were forced to quicken their pace while crossing narrow streets, the sleek, black machine snaked its way safely through town. It hugged the tiny sidewalks that ran beside ancient timber and stone buildings that leaned inward and threatened to constrict the roadway altogether. When they emerged from the village, they continued to climb until the large, stone pillars and wrought-iron gate came into view.

"This is it," said Dr. Meinz.

Peter pulled to a halt next to the gatepost and pushed a red button below a black metal speaker. After a few seconds of silence, he pushed the button again.

The sound of the gate bell resonated throughout the house like a jolt of adrenaline. Every downcast face suddenly lifted, drawing breath, eyes wide. For days they had waited for any sign, any signal, any communication. Whenever the telephone would ring, every stomach muscle would tighten and slack jaw stiffen with anticipation. But not until now had an unexpected visitor arrived. It did not bode well. Such were the habits of those who bore sad news.

The speaker hissed.

"Bonjour," said Jacques.

Peter announced himself, apologizing for his tardiness. Jacques politely explained that tardiness was not an issue since they had not been alerted to his visit in the first place. Peter fumed but quickly apologized. Evidently, he and his secretary had miscommunicated. Everything had been so difficult lately. Jacques assured him he was most welcomed and the gates swung open, as if by magic.

As soon as she heard the gate bell, what little color was left in Elizabeth's cheeks drained quickly from them. She rose from her bed at the rather rude recall from the timeless remorse that had enveloped her for days. Her heart was beating so loudly she barely heard the soft tapping at her door.

"Who is it?" she inquired, trying to remain calm.

"It's me, David. You have a visitor. Peter Dermenjian."

The news of Peter's unexpected arrival hit Elizabeth like one more shock wave in a series that seemed to be of tsunami-like proportions. She was completely unprepared. All sorts of speculations were possible. Why had he come? Had he found Oscar? Or was he simply bent on revenge for his brother's wrongful and untimely death?

"I can't face him," she pleaded.

"You must," he replied. "Please, may I come in? We must talk."

Elizabeth opened the door slowly and David entered, still wearing his priestly garb. She stood next to the door, her arms at her sides. Her expression was listless, nearly extinguished. David looked at her for a moment but he had run out of soothing words. He opened his arms and held them out to her. She fell toward him and placed her head upon his shoulder.

"It will be all right," he whispered, "sooner or later. It's hard to tell. But have faith. *Ça ira mieux.* Only now you must deal with your guest."

"He is not my guest. I did not invite him."

"Yes, but you must pay your respects. I am certain he has come to pay his."

Elizabeth took a step back and looked at David with a grim face, grim but pretty in spite of the puffiness and the dark circles about her eyes.

"Give me a few moments, please. I can't see him looking like this."

David smiled at her before stepping back through the door and proceeding toward the stairs. He paused, however, before descending, eyeing the foyer where Jacques stood resolute, preparing to greet Monsieur Dermenjian. He heard a faint squeal of rubber as the Ferrari pulled to a stop. Car doors opened and then closed with dull thuds. There was silence followed by a rapping on the hard oaken door, to which Jacques responded very calmly but with an air of precision, as if his sole purpose in life were to open doors for people.

Peter entered, followed by Dr. Meinz. Jacques offered to take their coats. Peter wore a dark leather jacket, dark pants, and dark shoes. Only his gray silk shirt provided any contrast to the rest of his attire. He slowly removed his driving gloves as he surveyed the interior of Madame Le Clerc's spacious and ornately decorated home.

The next to approach and bid him welcome was Edouard. He shook Peter's hand and that of Dr. Meinz, who stood to Peter's left, his dark suit less disheveled than usual. Edouard kindly extended his regrets regarding the loss of Peter's brother. Peter lowered his eyes very slightly and thanked him.

Edouard guided them toward the main salon, where Tommy and Ethel had been keeping vigil over a distraught Mrs. Newman. Peter cast a curious look their way as he followed Edouard to the library, where Madame Le Clerc sat quietly in her chair, wrapped in her shawl with her glasses perched on the end of her nose. Father Brodard stood beside her.

"Madame Le Clerc," said Peter, not waiting for introductions, "I am Peter Dermenjian. Francis Dermenjian was my brother."

As he spoke he bowed gracefully in her direction. Then he approached and extended his right hand. She extended hers as he bent down slowly to kiss it, stopping far short of the deed in deference to her age. It was a delicate move, one that appeared well practiced. His hands were soft and supple, the nails impeccably manicured. He was very handsome and his attire bespoke position and fine taste. Short notice notwithstanding, whatever expectations Madame Le Clerc might have generated regarding Peter Dermenjian were soon surpassed.

"I apologize for the gross negligence on my part of not assuring that you had been advised of my impending visit," he said.

Madame Le Clerc studied him for a moment before replying. "It is nothing," she said. "We are most pleased that you have come. Obviously we have been very concerned about Oscar and welcome any news you may bring. But first we must extend our deepest condolences regarding the tragic death of your brother."

Peter bowed his head. "It is most regrettable. No doubt a terribly unfortunate accident. But no one can save him now. Oscar, however, is another matter. I have been searching for him for several days and have found no trace whatsoever. He simply must be found, dead or alive. I trust you have received no news of him?"

"Not a word," came a voice from behind him. Peter turned and saw Elizabeth silhouetted in the entry to the library, backlit by the fire in the hearth in the main salon. "I am Elizabeth Le Clerc. If you have no news of Oscar, please tell me what you found. What did you tell the police? I must know everything there is to know."

Peter stood motionless, surprised but entranced as Elizabeth entered the room, wearing a long dress cinched tightly above the waist. She had brushed her hair and folded it into a long French braid. As she came into view, her cheeks bore new found color and her lips were no longer dry but glossy and full of luster. And her eyes, however darkened by days of sleepless sadness, now searched like lasers for some inkling of the truth.

"Elizabeth, really," interjected Madame Le Clerc with a huff.

"Please, Mother," Elizabeth responded sternly. "Leave us."

The look on her mother's face conveyed clearly the depth of her humiliation, yet she rose slowly, grabbed Edouard by the arm, and walked from the room without uttering a word, followed by Father Brodard and Dr. Meinz, who carefully closed the door behind him.

Left alone, the two stood silently in the somber atmosphere of the library, where many volumes of leather-bound books lined the walls. Only the light from Madame Le Clerc's reading lamp provided any relief from the oppressive darkness that seemed to have enveloped the entire house. But there was enough light for Elizabeth to see clearly the expression on Peter's face as it turned from a look of surprise to one that was soberer and slightly downcast.

"Elizabeth," he began, "I will tell you all that I know, as you desire. But first I must convey my deepest regrets regarding Oscar. I wish I had some better news but I do believe he is dead."

Elizabeth bit her lower lip but remained rigid, fighting back the tears that began to rise once again. It was one thing to read such words, but to hear them spoken, spoken with such conviction by one who was perhaps in the best position to render such an opinion, was a terrible blow. Her chest heaved as she struggled to maintain her composure.

"Thank you," she said, or at least attempted to say. The words, bottled up in emotion, barely escaped her lips. "It is a terrible tragedy," she continued, recovering slightly. "And I, too, would like to offer my sincerest regrets regarding Francis."

She lowered her head, unable to resist the tears that now insisted on rising from her swollen eyelids. Peter took a step toward her but she quickly stiffened and faced him. He stopped short.

"Thank you," he replied with a slight bow. He folded his hands in front of him. Elizabeth could not help but notice the gold ring he wore on his right hand. It held the largest diamond she had ever seen. And his eyes were also sad, with dark circles as evidence of the hours he had spent in pursuit of the elusive Oscar Newman.

"Elizabeth," he continued, "I want you to know that above all I bear no grudge toward Oscar. If he did indeed kill my brother, as all the evidence would suggest, it was either an accident or an act of a delirious man. Did he have a history of malaria?"

"Hardly," she replied. "Once, several years ago, he had a brief spell in India. Lord knows he'd been exposed constantly in his travels. But never an outbreak like this."

"According to my brother's diary, he'd stopped taking his malaria tablets. Why would he do such a thing?"

"I don't know. He always complained of the nausea but took them nonetheless whenever he traveled to the tropics. Perhaps he ran out or grabbed the wrong pills. He always did his own packing. But please, the Kenya National Police have told me nothing. All they do is ask me questions. I am tired of questions. I would like some answers. Where did you find Francis?"

Peter pursed his lips and looked away, sighing heavily. "I found Francis beside their campfire," he began as he turned back toward her. "I could see the smoke from the air when I set the helicopter down on the hard soda crust of Lake Natron, not far from the swamped Land Rover. My guess is that Oscar was frightened by the helicopter and began shooting. Francis tried to stop him but was shot accidentally. Oscar must have then fled into the bush. Dr. Meinz and I searched for him briefly and shouted for him as loudly as we could, but he did not respond. We then carried Francis back to the helicopter. We circled Gelai looking for Oscar, but it was getting dark and I needed to get Francis to a doctor. We took him to the best hospital in Nairobi. But it was too late. I returned the next day to resume the search for Oscar along with Kenyan troops and the Tanzanian Police Force. We combed every inch of the mountain and searched all the wilderness for miles around. We interviewed every Maasai in the area. But we have found no trace whatsoever of Oscar. One can only presume he was consumed by predators and his bones scattered or buried in the shifting sands."

Elizabeth took all this in without flinching, standing still, her hands clasped over her heart. Tears that she didn't seem to notice rolled down her cheeks, and through clouded vision she saw that tears were beginning to form in Peter's eyes as well. She felt her resistance slowly crumble, and though she had only just met him, she soon found herself sobbing on Peter's shoulder and clinging to him as if he represented what little remained of Francis and, in some strange way, of Oscar as well.

"You must grieve," he said, holding her close. "We all must grieve. But you are tired. You must also get some rest. I have a villa not far from here. I am on my way to London and may not return for several days, but you are most welcome to make use of it."

Elizabeth stepped back and dried her eyes with her sleeve. "That is most kind of you. But I must stay. Oscar's mother is here. She is an invalid and must be cared for."

"Then bring her as well. My staff would be completely at your disposal."

She hesitated. Peter handed her a card.

"The address is right here. I will advise my staff."

"That won't be necessary," she said.

"Very well. But in case you should have a change of heart, I will advise them anyway."

Elizabeth smiled hesitantly. "Thank you for coming," she said. "And thank you for helping in the search for Oscar."

"Please, it is the least I could do. And it shall continue. My people are still working with the local officials. They are posting signs everywhere advertising a reward of one million Kenyan shillings, worth ten thousand euros, for whoever finds him, dead or alive."

"Ten thousand euros?"

"Yes. It will be more than sufficient to coerce the Maasai into joining the search. He will be found, Elizabeth, I assure you."

"Let us hope so," she said, biting her lip and still clinging to a belief that he would be found alive. "Perhaps we should join the others. We have kept them waiting long enough."

Peter smiled demurely. "As you wish. But permit me to say that it has been a pleasure to meet you at last, in spite of the circumstances."

He reached for her hand but she withdrew it as she headed for the door separating the library from the main salon, where the others remained gathered.

"I would like to offer a toast," said David, once Jacques had served the aperitif, "to Oscar and Francis. May they find peace, wherever they are. And may the terrible wounds inflicted on us all by their sudden parting be healed, through the grace of God."

Everyone bowed and said amen. Then they all continued sighing and found conversation difficult to sustain. When the glasses were drained Peter announced that he must be off. Madame Le Clerc objected, begging him to remain for supper, to remain for the night. He declined, citing important business obligations. As he was bidding her good night, however, he squeezed a small bottle of pills into her hands.

"This is from Dr. Meinz," he whispered. "It will help her sleep."

Madame Le Clerc thanked him and tucked the bottle into the folds of her dress. Peter then turned toward Elizabeth.

"Thank you for your kind hospitality. I am sorry I cannot bring you better news."

"I understand," she replied. "Yet I cannot thank you enough for coming so far to share the news you have."

"Sad as it is," he replied as he took hold of her hand and bowed. "For the moment, at least. I trust that we will meet again."

His departure was soon followed by that of David. Unlike Peter Dermenjian, he left with little fanfare but offered encouragement and hope. He challenged them to remain strong. He embraced Madame Le Clerc and Father Brodard, and the two men, presumably cut from the same cloth, however unevenly, exchanged a few private words. Lastly, he embraced Elizabeth.

"Keep some distance," he whispered. "I do not trust him."

If she was at all perplexed by this last remark, she did not let it show. She returned to the main salon and stood before the hearth. Tommy had not stopped talking about Peter Dermenjian since he had left. What a gentleman, a genuine billionaire. He wanted to know if he and Ethel had been invited to the villa. Elizabeth understood their desire to get away. Her mother had not said one word to them since their arrival. Nor had she inquired after Mrs. Newman. Clearly, they were beginning to feel quite unwelcomed.

"We're all staying right here," Elizabeth told them, "at least until there's further word."

But days rolled by and there was no further word. Only a call from David to say that he was returning to Africa, and that the search continued.

Chapter 26

The search for Oscar did indeed continue, but without the services of the one person who undoubtedly wished more than anyone else in Kenya that he could be a part of it. Unfortunately, Dr. Maxwell Taylor was far too busy at Maasai Clinic Number One to offer any assistance whatsoever.

It had been nearly four weeks since Oscar and Francis had passed through, urging them all to move south. At least a dozen new manyattas had been built within a half hour's walk of David's schoolhouse. Many others were in progress across the Ewaso Ngiro. Everything was more compact than usual, squeezed into the southernmost stretches of Maasai cattle country south of the Kalema Road and north of the extensive marshes bordering Lake Natron. Yet it appeared to Max that the Maasai had managed to readjust, more or less. Tensions had been held in check for the most part. But then came the devastating news.

Max found himself at a complete loss. Though he'd spent little time with either Francis or Oscar, he could not believe that Oscar could have done such a thing. He and Francis seemed the best of friends. And the thought of Oscar deliriously at large in the remote wilds of the Rift Valley to the south made him want to jump in the Scout immediately and help find him.

But while Max was bewildered and thoroughly despondent, the Maasai were angry, especially the elders. A group of them arrived at the clinic early one morning, with Joseph leading the charge, demanding an explanation as to why this Oscar Newman, the man who had brought them this clinic, would have murdered Francis.

Max could understand their anger. Francis Dermenjian had been a great friend of the Maasai. More than that, he had been their benefactor, a man who had invested substantially in various Maasai enterprises. He had even taught them a few things about the native plant life. But now he was dead, shot at point-blank range by Oscar, according to reliable sources.

Max did his best to calm them down, telling them again and again that the investigation was not over, that many people were still searching for Oscar, that the truth would be discovered. His words seemed to pacify them somewhat, but as they were leaving, he realized there was no way he could possibly join in the search now. If he left, they'd tear his clinic apart.

But he was forced to leave after all. Joseph demanded he drive him to Francis's funeral and Max had no choice but to oblige. It was the least he could do.

The funeral was a very stately affair, with much pomp supplied by the university. A long cavalcade of black limousines carried various faculty members and several of Kenya's political elite, including Joseph. When they arrived at the cemetery, a very plain wooden casket lay poised above a large, rectangular hole in the ground. Francis had apparently wanted to be buried next to his parents, leaving the one remaining family plot for his brother, who, looking somberly elegant in his exquisitely tailored suit, offered some very kind words about the dearly departed.

It seemed to Max, however, that Peter hurried through his eulogy, in which he described their childhood together and his brother's fascination with the wilds of the Rift Valley. Various others offered their separate testimonials, but once it was over Francis was still dead, Oscar was still missing, and Joseph was still angry. In fact, he had hardly uttered a word to Max the entire trip. But fortunately, and no doubt because he was doing Joseph a favor, Max found the clinic still intact upon their return.

In addition to his deteriorating relations with Joseph and the Maasai, Max was still adjusting to working with his new assistant. Christine's resentment at having been talked into working with him and "spying" on her research subjects was quite evident. She also did not appreciate using as a cover the administration of birth-control services to the very people she was trying to study quite objectively.

All things considered, however, Max felt that everyone was adjusting fairly well to the move and to the tense circumstances surrounding it. But that assessment did not account for some of the moran, who had remained out of sight and clearly disagreed with the majority opinion of the elders. They had ventured north, ignoring the general decree to not interfere with, nor in any event provoke, the refugees. They had taunted them and, in return, had been fired upon.

Whatever modicum of peace that had prevailed at the clinic was shattered early one morning as a troop of moran came rushing into the circle of tents, shouting and holding their spears high. In the center were three moran carrying a fallen comrade.

Max took one look and showed them the way into the main examination tent. Christine was listening to recordings of Maasai women conversing and didn't hear them coming. She recoiled in horror as they laid the blood-smeared body on the cot.

Max examined the wound. The young moran had been shot just below the ribs. He asked the others if anyone had notified his family. None of them replied. In fact, the tent became quite hushed until the entry flap flew open and Joseph walked in. He gave a fierce, angry look at the rest of the moran, who all quickly filed out. Then he looked at Max. He said this was Ntanda, his oldest son. He added that he was also his most foolish son.

Max said he would do all he could. What he didn't say was that if the bullet had pierced the liver, chances were very slim. He looked at Christine.

"We'll need to scrub up. Put on some hot water."

She looked at him as if he were absolutely insane. "Don't be ridiculous," she said. "I'm not qualified for anything like this."

"Don't worry," he replied as he put on a surgical smock and handed one to Christine. "I'll talk you through it. But I need your help or he's going to die."

She continued to stare at him in disbelief. Then she took a look at the patient. Though barely conscious, he was breathing hard, almost convulsing at times. Christine looked at Max with an air of resignation and began putting on the smock.

They labored for over an hour. The bullet was very deep, resting up against the back of his lower ribs. But it had missed the liver. Max explained to Christine everything he saw, and she gradually found herself drawn into the operation, mesmerized by the complexities of the human body and impressed with how well Max seemed to know his way around inside it.

"I think he'll be all right," he said as he handed her a bloody sponge that she added to the basket of bloody sponges amassed during the course of the morning. Then he grabbed a pair of forceps and slowly began to dislodge the bullet. It was a long shell and the young patient's body writhed again as he started to pull.

"Another shot of morphine," he said. Christine gave a push on the syringe. In a few seconds the body was still once more. Max continued to pull very carefully, keeping the sharp edges of the bullet from doing any more serious damage. Fifteen minutes later he was examining the shell he had removed.

"AK-47," he said. "Now where do you suppose they came by one of those?"

Christine shook her head again. Things were getting really crazy.

Max cauterized the wound before dressing it properly and strapping his patient down to the cot. He would be out for a few more hours. Christine stood by, repulsed by the smell of burning flesh but marveling at the fact that their patient was still alive.

"Now, wasn't that fun?" said Max as they were washing up.

"I didn't come here to be a nurse," she replied sharply.

He simply shook his head. "And I thought I'd be through patching up gunshot wounds once I got out of LA."

Max found Joseph waiting outside. He told him that the chances his son would live were good. Joseph nodded without smiling and thanked him. Then he turned and walked away.

Max spent the night in the main examination tent, keeping watch over his patient. Christine returned to her trailer, which was parked a hundred yards or so away. Neither of them slept very well. Max was bothered by the moaning and occasional fitful shouts from Joseph's son, who lay semiconscious, slowly awakening to his pain.

In the morning, Max took stock of his supplies once again. He was already rather low on most ordinary items, but the operation on Joseph's son had totally depleted his supply of morphine. He hoped he wouldn't need any more, but this latest incident suggested more trouble might be in store. He had been trying to get through on his shortwave radio to a frequency he had been given by the Newman Foundation but without success. So he borrowed Christine's fancy satellite phone and tried once again to reach Nairobi. All he encountered after repeated attempts was a voice mail box that was full. It all seemed to fit. He'd never even heard back from them after reporting his new location.

He looked at his patient, whose consciousness was approaching fast.

"How is he?" whispered Christine as she entered the tent.

"He's coming around. All I have left is Percodan. I hope it's strong enough." He administered a shot in his buttocks and the writhing body began to relax immediately. "I'm thinking about taking him into Nairobi. I can't seem to get through to anybody to bring me any supplies."

No sooner had he spoken than his antiquated shortwave radio began to crackle. Max grabbed the headphones and began adjusting a dial to lock onto the right frequency. But it was not the Newman Foundation at all. It was David, saying he would be arriving in Nairobi Wednesday morning. Max took down the flight information and said he'd be there. David asked how things were going, to which Max simply responded, *"Comme si, comme ça."* Better to save the details until they were face to face.

"That settles that," he said after signing off. "David gets in day after tomorrow. I guess I am going to Nairobi."

Christine's startled eyes locked onto his. "I'm coming with you," she said.

Max looked at her with arched eyebrows and shook his head from side to side. "Just can't wait to see him, can you?"

"No, it's not that at all. It's my advisor, she's arriving, too."

His eyebrows reached for even greater heights. "Wait a minute," he said, "I thought she decided to wait until things settle down out here."

Christine pursed her lips, not looking too pleased herself. "There's nothing I can do. I got a message from her a couple of days ago. But it's been so crazy around here I was afraid to even mention it."

"So when does she arrive?"

"Thursday. I was going to ask you if I could borrow the Scout. But if you're already going, then we could all just ride together."

Max thought it over a moment. "Yeah, fine," he said. "Besides, I could use some help with Junior here."

It would mean three days away from the clinic, but that was certainly better than having to make two trips. Besides, when was the last time he'd had a real break? Certainly not the trip to the funeral. And that had been his only excursion out of the bush in over six months. But with Christine and her academic advisor?

That evening he stopped by her trailer to see if all was ready. He wanted to get an early start. She swung open the aluminum door just as he was about to knock.

"Hi," she said, smiling for a change, "come on in."

He ducked through the small doorway and entered the inner sanctum of the trailer. Papers were strewn about a table at one end, next to her laptop.

"Hungry?" she inquired.

Max hadn't really thought much about food all day. "Well, sure, I could use a bite."

She motioned him to a seat and cleared a space for him at the table. Then she went to the tiny kitchen area and returned with two steaming bowls of what looked like Chinese food. Max sniffed it before tasting. There were some odd bits he didn't recognize.

"Interesting," he said after a couple of mouthfuls. "What is it?"

"Mostly rice," she replied, "and some kind of marinated root that Molema gave me."

"I see," he said. "Got anything to wash it down with?"

She rose and, much to his surprise, reached into a small cupboard and produced a bottle of wine.

"Very nice," he said as she produced two glasses and handed him a corkscrew. "What's the big occasion?"

She looked at him with her sad green eyes. "Nothing. I have to get rid of the alcohol before Gertie gets here. We might as well drink it up right now. I was saving it for David."

"But he'll be here in a couple of days."

"So will she."

"Gertie?"

"Yeah, Dr. Gertrude Brecht, professor of anthropology. She has strict policies about that stuff. So now I have to get everything cleaned up and organized. Do you mind if we don't tell her about me working in the clinic?"

Max just had to laugh. "Don't worry," he said. "But why did she change her mind? Things should be back to normal in a month or two. Hopefully sooner."

"That's just it. She's spent plenty of time with the Maasai when things were normal. But here's a chance to see firsthand how they behave as a society under severe pressure."

Max nodded and then looked around the small trailer. "Whatever," he said. "But where's she going to sleep?"

One look in Christine's direction revealed not only the answer but why he was being wined and dined.

"Come on," she said with a soft smile and pleading eyes. "You've got plenty of room. It would only be for a few weeks."

"A few weeks?" he said. "Well then, why don't you just let her stay here and you sleep in one of the tents? I don't know that I want to be neighbors with some teetotaling grande dame of anthropology."

Christine started to laugh but stopped quickly and just looked down at her food. "It's bad enough I'm working with you," she said. "I wouldn't want her to get the idea I might be, well, sleeping with you, too."

Max shook his head and laughed. "That's right," he said. "We wouldn't want anyone thinking that."

They finished the meal and most of the wine before Max excused himself. It was time to change bandages again. He walked slowly back to the cluster of tents, listening to wild noises in the night while admiring the myriad stars and the overall immensity of the dark African sky. But when he arrived back at the clinic, Ntanda was gone.

Max wasn't that surprised. He had been slowly returning to his senses, and though he was in great pain, Max knew he was anxious to leave. He had demanded Max cut away the strapping that bound him to the cot. Max did so but only after giving him another injection that would keep a normal person down for several more hours. What he had ignored, however, was that Ntanda was Maasai, a moran and leader of his own age class. Ntanda apparently had other plans.

Chapter 27

The Kalema Road was in much better shape than the last time Max and Christine had crossed it several months ago, traveling in the opposite, inbound direction. Things had dried out considerably, leaving ruts that were fairly deep and quite hard in places, but Max was able to avoid most of them as he carefully guided the Scout forward. Christine kept her eyes focused on the area to the north, looking for any potential hijackers that might be lurking by the roadway.

"According to Maasai scouts," said Max, "the refugees are still miles north of here."

"They better be," said Christine.

"And if they aren't," Max scoffed, "what are you going to do about it?"

Christine just crossed her arms a little tighter and didn't respond. The only signs of trouble were the few Kenyan soldiers guarding the causeway across Lake Magadi. Clearly, the soda miners had paid their dues. They asked for identification and pelted them with questions, eyeing Christine very closely all the while. Discovering no transgressions and apparently judging that neither Max nor Christine was likely to have any affiliation with the refugees, they let them pass. Max wondered what they would have done if he'd had his patient with him. When they reached the east side of the lake, they found the paved highway that delivered them with unaccustomed speed, in spite of the many potholes perforating the well-aged asphalt, north to Nairobi.

By four in the afternoon, they were sipping drinks by the pool at the Hilton. This wasn't part of the original plan, but since the door to the Newman Foundation's office was locked and no one seemed to know when anyone could be expected, Max vented his wrath on his credit card. Christine had objected at first but relented once Max offered to cover all expenses beyond what her stipend would support.

"Just try to relax," he said as the waiter departed. "Think of it as just another anthropology lab."

There were a few Europeans, two Africans, and several Americans gathered around the pool. The jacaranda and bougainvillea were in bloom. Christine sipped her gin and tonic as a welcomed breeze stirred the blossoms.

"Okay," she said, nestling into her deck chair. "I'll do my best. You could stand to lighten up, too. Ever since we went to the Newman Foundation, you've been unbearable."

"So why do you think we're here? They're driving me crazy! Six months working for them and the only person I've ever really talked to is Oscar, and now he's off who knows where, probably dead, and the office is closed. I thought he ran a first-class operation. That's why I signed up."

"Maybe you should call that new guy. What's his name?"

Max polished off his Scotch and soda. "Bayard. That's a good idea." He hailed the waiter again and asked for another round of drinks. Then he reached for his cell phone, struggling to recall when he'd last tried to use it. He dialed the Newman Foundation's main office in London, brightening slightly as the call actually went through. But a recorded message referred him to a new number.

"Got a pen?"

Christine rummaged through her bag, found a writing utensil, and handed it to him. Max wrote the number down on the bar tab and dialed again, this time to Paris.

"Oh great, another recording," he said. "Only it's all in French."

"Here," said Christine, "give it to me."

Max handed her his phone with a look of astonishment that grew more intense as she began pushing buttons and ended up conversing in excellent French with someone on the other end. Her expression became rather serious and after a few moments he heard her saying, *"D'accord, merci."* Then she hung up.

"Well?" said Max. "What did you find out?"

"It's not good," she sighed. "This whole transaction between Oscar and Bayard hasn't been completed. The guy I talked to says everything was moving along okay, but when Oscar disappeared it all came to a halt, including the cash flow. So much of the Newman Foundation's assets are directly under Oscar's control that with him missing and presumed dead, it's like his whole estate is tied up in probate. It could be a while before things clear up."

Max stared at her, realizing that the fate of Maasai Clinic Number One was entirely in his hands, at least for the time being. "Thanks," he said, "I guess. Where did you learn to speak French like that?"

"I spent some time at the Sorbonne long ago. But what I want to know is, what are you going to do about your medical supplies?"

"I don't know," he said. "I guess I'll just have to stop by the hospital and hopefully pick some up tomorrow."

"Good," she said with a rare smile in his direction.

Max watched as she donned some sunglasses and lay back down in her chair. Her youthful skin, drenched with oil in all the places her newly purchased lime-colored bikini failed to cover, which was nearly everywhere, glistened in the equatorial sun. He took a deep breath and headed for the pool.

The water felt like cool, liquid silk. He swam a length underwater, then surfaced and swam another few laps. He felt surprisingly fit, having lost at least ten pounds since coming to Africa. Memories of his college swimming days came back to him as he churned the water. But he quickly returned to the present as he surfaced at the far end of the pool and found Christine standing before him, looking down with that expression he knew all too well. It simply meant something wasn't quite right.

"I'm hungry."

He ran his fingers through his auburn hair, wringing out the water that had felt so cool and soothing. "Okay," he said. "Meet you in the lobby in half an hour."

Forty-five minutes later she arrived, wearing a short yellow skirt and a white cotton blouse. She had also put on some lipstick and makeup, and Max even caught a delicate whiff of perfume as he stared at her in disbelief. Her blond hair was pinned up high on her head, revealing the sleek and elegant lines of her neck.

"My goodness," he said. "You look very nice. Where'd you get that skirt?"

"Oh, this?" she said. "When I bought the bathing suit."

"At the Hilton gift shop? Charged to the room?"

"Oh come on, it was on sale."

"Right," he said with a slightly scolding look, not that he was at all displeased. This was almost like going on a date, and she was very attractive.

"The concierge said there's a good Ethiopian restaurant not too far from here."

"Lead on, MacDuff," she said. "I love Ethiopian."

They found the restaurant easily and their meal was exceptional, as advertised. And although Christine talked mostly about all that was going wrong with her research project and worried about what Dr. Brecht would say, Max was happy to be with her, sharing a bottle of wine and the best food they had eaten in months. He paid the tab and they walked back out into the Nairobi evening. The sun had set but fortunately the streets were well lit.

"I think I feel safer out on the savannah," said Christine as some of the locals eyed her a bit lasciviously. She grabbed on to Max's arm, catching him by surprise. But they arrived back at the Hilton without incident.

"Thanks for a lovely dinner," said Christine once they were back in the lobby.

"Nice to have your company," said Max. "Look, I'm going to go have a drink in the bar. Sounds like there's some live music. Want to join me for a nightcap?"

Christine thought for a moment. "Okay, but just one. David gets in pretty early tomorrow."

"Right," said Max. "David the priest."

The bar was about half full and a jazz trio consisting of piano, bass, and drums were playing off in one corner. A waiter showed them to a table just above the dance floor, where a few couples were drifting along in and out of each other's arms to an old Cole Porter tune. Max ordered a couple of Negronis. They arrived moments later in large martini glasses, pale red with large twists of lemon.

"Cheers," said Max.

"Cheers," said Christine as their glasses clinked. She took one sip and opened her eyes wide as the alcohol began to burn. "Wow! These are strong," she said.

"I know," said Max, smiling as he clinked glasses with her once more.

They chatted about the situation back at the clinic, about the refugee crisis. Max did his best to allay her fears, mostly by concealing his. When the waiter came by again, he ordered another round before Christine could object.

"Hey," she pouted, "I said just one drink."

"Oh come on, relax. We're on vacation. Tomorrow it's back to the salt mine."

"Right," she said, "with Dr. Brecht."

The band then launched into another, livelier tune, joined by a fellow on clarinet, who played marvelously. More folks ventured onto the dance floor. Christine took another sip of Negroni and looked at Max.

"You wanna dance?" she asked.

Clearly caught off guard, Max stammered that he used to dance some, but it had been a long time.

"So what if you're a little rusty," she said. "After all, we're on vacation."

She stood up and took him by the hand. What could he say? That his ex-wife liked to dance? That she'd forced him to take dance classes? That dancing would only bring back more of the memories he was trying to leave behind?

213

They were playing "Fever," a simple fox-trot. Easy enough. Christine smiled as he held her about the waist while holding her right hand in his left, gliding her backward, then forward, a step to the side. And again. After a few more goes, they embellished a bit. He spun her about, leading as he had been taught by that gay dance instructor his ex-wife had found somewhere.

"You're very good at this," said Christine.

"Ah"—he shrugged—"just a little something I learned at day care."

When they returned to their table, they found fresh drinks waiting for them, complements of an elderly gent seated across the room with not one but two prostitutes clinging to him. He nodded at them and winked, raising his glass in their direction. Max nodded back, mouthing the words "thank you" while Christine sat down momentarily. She took another long swig of Negroni, looking confused by the presence of a third cocktail as she had yet to finish the second one. She looked up at Max accusingly but he just shrugged his shoulders, pointing to their benefactor across the way. He waved back at her and blew her a kiss. Then the band lit into another tune, much faster than the last.

"Okay," said Christine, taking one more gulp, "let's see what you're made of."

She was holding on to both his hands now and pulling him toward the dance floor. But not only was the music faster, it had more of a Latin beat. And another drummer had stepped in, playing congas. Then a beautiful, dark-haired young singer stepped to the microphone and began singing a Brazilian number. The whole place was hopping, and Christine was putting all her moves on display, the ones mastered after years of teaching jazz dance to help get through college. Max stood back and marveled, attempting to keep with the rhythm while Christine stole the show. Everyone was watching her as she focused all her energy on Max, coming at him quite seductively, placing her body so close to his until he spun her away. The short yellow skirt rode even higher as she twirled, showing off more of her perfect dancer's legs. She was clearly energized by the music, the alcohol, and the need to just let loose for once.

When the band finally took a break, Max paid the bill. He collected Christine, exhausted and quite intoxicated, and led her to the elevator. She leaned on his shoulder for support as they ascended. Their rooms were on the same floor, adjacent but not connected. Max stopped at his and fumbled for his key card while Christine continued to lean on him.

"You wanna come in?" he asked nervously.

Christine laughed. "What, you wanna play doctor or something?"

Max hesitated. "Yeah, maybe something like that," he said as they tumbled through the door together. He led her in and sat her down on one of the beds. "I'll be right back," he said.

She looked at him and put her lips together as if to blow him a kiss but began laughing instead. He ventured to the bathroom and took a good look at himself in the mirror. He splashed some cold water on his face and shook his head. Then he riffled through his shaving kit until he found a condom. He wondered how long it had been in there.

But when he returned to the bedroom, Christine was lying on her side, out cold. He shook her once, then twice, but it was useless. Uncertain what to do, he simply stood beside her, admiring the soft and delicate lines of her face, the lips still pouting even in sleep. He found a spare blanket and placed it over her after slipping off her shoes. Then he gently kissed her on the forehead.

"Sweet dreams, my dear," he whispered. "I'm sure there'll be hell to pay in the morning."

Chapter 28

The trip from Marseille had been pleasantly uneventful. The flight was fairly smooth, it was nearly on time, and the food had been well packaged. But as they approached Nairobi, the pilot began to swing the plane back north in a wide arc. As it tilted, splitting the clear airway between sets of high, billowing clouds, David found himself staring down below at the Rift Valley, catching his first glimpse of it in many days. What he saw upset him far more than he was prepared to accept.

It reminded him of the Serengeti, but he knew full well that those were not wildebeest. They were people. Poor, desperate, displaced people who had somehow found their way for many, many miles, avoiding all serious confrontations, determined to negotiate all ranks of resistance, until they could find an unoccupied area where they might settle, at least for a while, like gravel in a turbulent stream tumbling out of the mountains.

And like stones in a streambed, these people were hard in character and hard in spirit. But whether they had succeeded in avoiding the Kenyan troops, or whether they had essentially been herded past the more populated areas of western Kenya toward a more open, unfarmed area, was a matter of much debate. Regardless, it was quite clear that the refugees could not return to Uganda, and it was quite clear they would not be tolerated in Busia or Kakamega or Kisumu or Kericho and certainly not in the Mara Reserve.

And so they settled out in Maasailand to the east of the Mara, in very dry, hot, and inhospitable country. It was open and there was good reason for it. Unfortunately for Joseph and all the Maasai under his jurisdiction, it just happened to be their land, where they lived, where their ancestors had lived, even though they had probably stolen it to begin with.

But somehow the refugees had managed to move in. They had established one huge makeshift village out of dingy old tarps and surplus Army camouflage. There were a few Red Cross tents amid the general chaos, but it was primarily people, poor ragged people huddling under scraps of tarp and each other, desperately seeking some shade. As the plane descended, heading north and leaving all clouds high above, David could see the huge stain of humanity stretching south from Mosiro, nearly to the shores of Lake Magadi.

Max and Christine were waiting for him at the baggage claim but he barely said hello to them. He was too enraged. He shook hands with Max and hugged

216

Christine almost mechanically, saying how good it was to see them but that he must get to a phone immediately. He must speak with the authorities. He railed at the *sacré* Kenya army and their inability, or perhaps unwillingness, to protect the Maasai homeland, which also happened to be his homeland, for the moment, at least.

"I wonder who he's calling," said Max, watching David grip the public pay phone as if he wanted to strangle the person on the other end of the conversation.

Christine did not respond. She merely leaned against the nearest wall while staring at Max with venom in her eyes.

"Still not talking, eh?"

"Damn right," she said. "Don't you ever get me drunk like that again. You could have raped me for all I know."

"Hey, you got yourself drunk," he said, rubbing his eyes as he tried in vain to fend off his own world-class hangover. "And I told you nothing happened. But you're a hell of a dancer."

"Right," she said, "so you decided to dance me all the way to your room."

Just then David hung up the phone and turned toward them. She brushed her hair back with one hand, trying to regain composure despite her anger and the worst headache of her life.

"We have an appointment with Captain Olengi of the Kenya National Police in one hour. He's apparently the man in charge of dealing with this refugee crisis. I will show you the way."

They gathered David's baggage and were soon headed for downtown Nairobi once more. David shared the front with Max while Christine slumped in the rear, holding her stomach and concentrating on not losing her breakfast.

"So tell me," said David, "how are the Maasai dealing with all of this? They must be absolutely livid. Have you spoken with Joseph recently?"

Max tried to swallow but his mouth was still too dry. "Well, yeah," he said, "I saw him not too long ago."

"And?"

"He really didn't say too much."

"What? Surely he must have told you something. What was it?"

Max gritted his teeth. "Okay," he said, preparing to open up. "He thanked me for saving his son's life. The refugees shot him."

David stared at Max as if he'd just uttered pure nonsense. "What? Tell me you are not serious."

Max glanced over at him. "I'm serious," he said, "it's true. Only he's going to be all right. Christine helped me. I couldn't have done it without her. Right?"

There was nothing but silence. Max looked for Christine in the rearview mirror, but she was too far down in the seat, either asleep or pretending to be.

"That is outrageous," said David. He was now fuming even more than before. "I swear the Kenyan government has allowed this to happen. It gives them one more excuse to carve away at what little land is left for the Maasai."

The Kenya National Police headquarters was located in one of the old colonial structures, and as they walked through the halls it reeked of bureaucracy and musty papers. They found Captain Olengi in his office. A young soldier led them in and asked them to have a seat. Captain Olengi did not even look up. He was occupied with paperwork. After a few moments of uncomfortable silence, he put down the report he had been reading and stared at them with an air of impunity.

"State your business," he said rather coldly. His face was perfectly round and his skin very dark. Max guessed him to be in his mid to late forties.

"My name is David Sebastian. I run a school for the Maasai, south of Kalema. I want to know why the Kenyan government has allowed these refugees to occupy lands belonging to the Maasai. They must be moved immediately."

Captain Olengi stared at David without expression for a moment and then broke into laughter. He stood up, as if to show off more of his neatly pressed khaki uniform with all its medals and other adornments.

"And by what authority do you come here demanding such things? You, a schoolteacher and a missionary no less. What authority do you carry? None!" he shouted. "Get out, you are wasting my time."

David stood up, his black robe billowing, and faced Captain Olengi, not backing down an inch. "I come here as a servant of God and as a friend of the Maasai." He was shaking, he was so angry.

"A servant of God?" said Captain Olengi, who was still laughing as he began pacing behind the desk. "Indeed. And your friends?"

Max stood up and introduced himself. He said he was working for Oscar Newman. Captain Olengi stopped pacing and took a step toward him.

"Oscar Newman," he repeated. "Well, well. You cannot imagine how much trouble that man has caused me. In the middle of this crisis, I am forced to send an

218

entire unit to the Tanzanian border region to search for him. Why? Because I am told he is an important man, because I am told I must. So be it. I will take orders from my superiors even if I do not like them, but I will not take orders from the likes of you."

The last remark was directed back to David, who still stood erect with an expression that indicated he was not about to budge. Christine remained seated, her arms folded over her stomach and her head bowed, wanting no part of this discussion.

"And this one," said Captain Olengi, "who is she?"

Christine looked up. "Me?" she said weakly. "I'm not anybody."

Max covered for her. "She's an anthropology student studying the Maasai. At least, she was until these refugees moved in."

Captain Olengi stared at them both for a moment, clearly unimpressed. "I suggest you both go back to America. This is no time to be visiting Maasai country. No one can guarantee your safety."

David was about to speak when Max cut in.

"Do you think the refugees will move farther south?"

Captain Olengi shrugged his shoulders. "They have been ordered to remain north of the Kalema Road, but who knows what they will do," he replied. "For now we have a stable situation."

None of them had noticed the large aerial photo on the wall right behind them. They were all too busy glaring at Captain Olengi, who stepped around from behind his desk to show them the location of the refugee camp, situated right in the middle of the Rift Valley northwest of Lake Magadi.

"Do you mean that you are going to just let them stay there?" said David, nearly shouting. "For how long?"

"We are not only allowing them to stay there but we are feeding them as well. For how long, I cannot say. We are busily negotiating with Ugandan officials but right now it is not safe for them to return. For many, it will never be safe."

"But again you are stealing land from the Maasai!" objected David quite forcefully. Max noticed that his fists were clenched tight in a rather unpriestly fashion. Captain Olengi wheeled and walked toward him, then stopped not six inches from David's face.

"We are not stealing anything from the Maasai!" he returned crisply. "They have agreed to this arrangement. The Maasai will be compensated."

Jaws dropped all around. Even Christine was alarmed enough to finally stand up and walk toward Captain Olengi with a worried look, as if he were speaking total nonsense. The notion of the Maasai as landlords of these ruthless refugees was more than they could comprehend.

"And just who agreed to this?" asked David, dumbfounded but still rather puffed up.

"Joseph Ole Saikele," he replied.

David turned toward Max.

"He never mentioned anything to me," said Max. "No one from the Kenyan government has even been out to visit, as far as I know."

"I spoke with Joseph at Francis Dermenjian's funeral," said Captain Olengi. "He signed some papers."

The anger in David's eyes turned slowly from a decided scowl to a softer, wide-eyed stare of pure disbelief. "Er, please excuse me," he said after a moment's silence, during which he managed to gather his composure a bit. "Perhaps I have behaved rather badly. My apologies. I shall speak with Joseph. But how long can this arrangement last? The Maasai need that land for their cattle."

"Of course they do. We have a few more months. Then we will see."

"But what if they move south in the meantime?" said Max. "These people are armed."

Captain Olengi raised one eyebrow. "Do you have proof of that?"

"Are you serious?" said Max. "Joseph's son was nearly killed. I pulled a bullet two inches long out of him. Missed his heart by inches."

Captain Olengi paced back and forth, deep in thought. This news clearly disturbed him. "I will station more troops along the Kalema Road," he said at last, "and if I ever catch the bastard who is supplying them with weapons, I will rip his heart out."

"What do you mean, *more* troops?" said Max. "There's not a Kenyan soldier west of Lake Magadi."

Captain Olengi flashed angry eyes his way, as if to say he would tolerate no further impudence. "They are carefully concealed," he replied sharply, "keeping an eye on the refugees."

Max didn't respond but his one raised eyebrow conveyed plenty of doubt. Concealed where? It was pretty open country. He looked at David, who seemed newly perturbed. The refugees were certainly a problem, but the idea of Kenyan troops that close to Maasai settlements was just as troubling.

Before leaving, Max inquired about the search for Oscar. Captain Olengi said it might soon be abandoned as they had still found no trace of him. Besides, he needed his troops back to help patrol the Kalema Road.

They left Captain Olengi's office in various states of disarray. David had even more questions than before but only Joseph could answer them. Max was troubled over the fact that there was far more going on all around him than he'd ever imagined possible, and he was angry with Joseph for keeping him so much in the dark. And Christine, in a state of pure misery, was still dwelling on Olengi's words about their safety, or lack thereof.

David led them to a small restaurant a few blocks away. He knew the owner, a small, dark, and wiry man who greeted them warmly and led them to a private table in the rear where they could talk things over. The man never even asked them for their orders. The food simply appeared.

David said a quick grace before diving into a heaping plateful. There was fruit and rice and bits of marinated meat. It was all quite spicy but the cool, dark beer took the edge off. In between bites David fired question after question at Max and Christine, wanting to know what was being said about Oscar, who this Dr. Brecht woman was, when she was due in, how long she would stay, and what they thought about the need for Kenyan soldiers to protect them. He asked all about Joseph's son, Ntanda, why he was shot, and what the Maasai were planning to do for revenge. Max tried his best to supply answers. Unlike David, he picked through the food, trying to isolate the little morsels that were so full of fire. His stomach needed a rest. Christine stayed with the fruit and a few bites of rice.

David told them about his time in France and his efforts to comfort Oscar's poor fiancée, Elizabeth Le Clerc, and all her entourage. He asked if they'd had any contact with Peter Dermenjian. Max said he'd met him at the funeral, but that all they had done was to shake hands while Max passed on his condolences. David seemed troubled.

"What's wrong?" said Max.

"I don't know," he replied. "It's just that somehow I feel he is connected to all of this, to Oscar's troubles."

Max drank the last of his beer and looked David square in the eye. "Look," he said, "I don't have a clue what's going on. All I know is there's a medical clinic

I'm responsible for, and the Newman Foundation has closed shop and left me high and dry. I need to get some supplies. I believe there's a hospital nearby."

"Yes," said David, "it's not too far."

David called for the check and Max paid for it. They found the Scout and without too much difficulty they found the hospital. The hospital had nearly everything Max felt he needed but at retail prices, extreme retail prices. Fortunately, they accepted his credit card, and within an hour the Scout was fully packed, with scant room left on the luggage rack. Max tied it all down under a tarp.

It was late afternoon. Dr. Brecht was arriving early the following morning on a red-eye flight from Frankfurt. They piled back into the Scout and began discussing lodging possibilities for the night. David insisted he knew people who would gladly put them up for free but Max objected, saying the extra bed in his room at the Hilton was available at no charge. Besides, it was too late to cancel the reservation.

Later on, as he lay in the cool, fresh sheets that still smelled of laundry detergent and a hint of bleach, Max began to reconsider having invited David to share his room. He tried stuffing small wads of tissue in his ears, but nothing would block out David's snoring. All Max wanted was to get some sleep. The last thing he needed was to lie awake one more night playing back in his mind all that had gone wrong in his life. And there was definitely a chance that things could get much worse in a hurry. After all, there were no guarantees. As if there ever were.

Chapter 29

They arrived at the airport in plenty of time only to find Dr. Gertrude Brecht waiting impatiently beside her luggage. The plane had been early. She was a large woman in her early fifties with dark but graying hair piled in a bun. Rectangular reading glasses sat on the end of her slightly bulbous nose as she poured over a set of notes. She wore dark, baggy shorts and a dark, baggy blouse. Other than her enormous bosom, nothing but her serious demeanor seemed to distinguish her.

"Hello, Dr. Brecht," said Christine with a touch of nervousness in her voice.

Dr. Brecht looked up at her and, without speaking, quickly examined her and both of her companions before standing. "How do you do, Miss Olson?" she inquired in a thick German accent. It came across more as a statement, a greeting that was mandatory in such a situation.

Christine said she was fine and introduced David and Max, who each said they were pleased to meet her, et cetera, though neither of them sounded very convincing. It didn't matter, for it became quite clear that this woman was all business.

Max offered to carry her large suitcase. It weighed a ton due to the fact that it contained more books than clothes. David grabbed her other bags, and as they worked their way back to the Scout, she began her cross-examination. She had prepared a series of questions for Christine and wasted no time as she inquired all about her research. Occasionally, she would direct a question to David or Max, who rode up front once they set off in the Scout. They would answer her and occasionally throw in a bit of unsolicited information before Dr. Brecht would cut them off and return to her line of questioning. She exhibited no interest whatsoever in the troubled market for soda from Lake Magadi or the fate of Oscar Newman.

When they reached Magadi the troops stationed there asked to see identification. She handed Max her passport, and he could not help but notice that it was covered with visas. It looked like she had been to every country in the world. Fortunately, the guards let them pass but not until warning them to be on the lookout for Ugandan refugees who might try to hijack the vehicle. Max thanked them, and later down the road he asked about her travels, but she said there wasn't time to discuss it and besides it was really none of his business. David sat quietly, staring out the window, trying to remember how long Christine had said Dr. Brecht would be visiting but not daring to restate the question.

The roadway was still in fairly good condition and they made reasonably good time. Once more they saw no sign of the refugees, but then again they saw little sign of any life whatsoever. Normally David would have expected to see at least a herd or two of gazelles grazing at their leisure or the occasional giraffe, but on this journey all was still. All he saw were songbirds and some bearded vultures circling high above. It did not bode well.

A few miles from the clinic they encountered two Maasai women walking along the roadside. Upon seeing David and Max in the Scout, they began waving, motioning them to a halt. They approached David on the passenger side and spoke rapidly, too rapidly for Max to understand, but they were clearly pointing in the direction of the clinic. David translated.

"They're saying we must hurry, that yesterday a white man stumbled into the clinic. They say he is crazy with fever and that he needs help badly, unless he's already dead."

"It has to be Oscar," said Max as he threw the Scout into gear and stomped on the accelerator.

They drove the rest of the way at breakneck speed. Dr. Brecht bounced around in the back of the Scout and repeatedly asked Max to slow down, but he would hear none of it.

When they arrived at the clinic, quite a few ochre-stained moran seemed to be standing guard. Upon seeing Max, they parted to make room as he made his way quickly, with David just behind, toward the main examination tent. Max threw open the flap and, upon entering, saw a skinny, naked man dancing what looked like a hula and singing something about his beautiful island.

"Welcome," said Max as he walked slowly toward the deranged fellow, who was still turning in slow circles in the center of the tent. "My name's Max."

The naked man did not respond or acknowledge Max in any way. He continued to dance ever so slowly, occasionally raising his arms up high and lowering them again.

"His name's Jack McGraw," said Christine from behind. "He's a prospector. The refugees took all he had, and obviously, he got a little too much sun. The moran found him. All he had on him was this."

Christine handed Max a small duffel bag. He accepted it with something less than enthusiasm, conveying his disappointment not only at not having found Oscar but in having acquired, much to the contrary, another charge who would likely prove to be quite a challenge.

This was indeed the case. Max needed the help of both David and Christine to subdue the newcomer while he inserted a needle in his buttocks. Once he was fully sedated, Max set him up in the tent he'd reserved for Dr. Brecht, with an IV drip to replace the fluids he'd lost and a sheet to cover his wiry and seriously dehydrated body.

With his newest patient comfortably settled, sedated, and apparently out of danger, Max rummaged through the duffel bag. The identification tag held the man's business card. He was indeed Jack McGraw, exploration geologist for Orion Minerals, Ltd., headquartered in Houston, Texas. According to the passport he found in a side pocket, his full name was John David McGraw, and he was from Tulsa, Oklahoma. He was fifty-seven years old. Inside he found some badly soiled clothes, an old shaving kit, and a bag full of rock fragments. Each fragment was in its own smaller plastic bag and was labeled with letters and numbers that had nothing to do with the periodic table or any convention Max could think of. The rocks were streaked with green and encrusted with pyrite crystals. What the hell was he prospecting for? And where? And how did he end up here?

When Max emerged from the tent, he found Christine and Dr. Brecht standing by, looking somewhat impatient. Where was he going to put her now that the spare tent was occupied?

"They ate his mule," said Christine.

Max looked more confused than usual.

"The refugees," she continued, "they ate his mule."

"Oh," he said, catching on. "No wonder he's delirious. He must have traveled miles on his own without food or water."

"That's not all," added Dr. Brecht. "According to the moran, the refugees not only killed his mule but are killing the Maasai cattle as well. The Maasai are extremely angry. They will not stand for this."

The two women looked at Max as if it were all his fault. Then David approached. He had gone off searching for news of Joseph.

"Did you find him?" asked Max.

"No," said David, "he's gone off to talk with the refugees. They're poaching Maasai cattle."

"Wait a minute," said Max. "How can the refugees be killing Maasai cattle when they're all north of the road and the cattle are all south of it?"

"They are desperate," said Dr. Brecht. "And the cattle are, too. It is too crowded for them here, squeezed between the Kalema Road and the marshes to the south. They'd rather be up north where there is better grass. So if a herdsman doesn't pay very close attention, one may stray across the road and, well..."

David and Max looked at each other. She had not been in camp for more than an hour, but already she knew more about what was going on than either of them. Clearly, Dr. Brecht had wasted no time sizing up the situation. While Max had been dealing with Crazy Jack McGraw and David had gone off searching for Joseph, Dr. Brecht had endeavored to do what she did best, get the facts. She had been interviewing all the moran who had helped bring Crazy Jack McGraw to the clinic.

David joined Max in the big tent, away from the women. "I'm worried about Joseph," he said. "Who knows what kind of reception he can expect."

"Yeah," said Max, "and I'm worried about his son."

"As well you should be."

"Why do you say that?"

"Because he's not doing well. According to one of the moran I spoke to, he's been very much in pain, barely able to walk."

"I'm not surprised. He needs medication. Anyone know where he is?"

"Yes. The moran have made camp up on the escarpment to the west, where they can watch the movements of the refugees. I could send word to him but I doubt it would do much good. You might have to visit him on your own."

"If that's what it takes. I'd like to see him."

"I'll talk to you tomorrow," David said. "But now I must get ready for school once again. There is much catching up to do."

David turned and exited the tent, stroking his beard. Max followed him outside and was greeted rather coldly by Christine.

"So," she said, "what about Dr. Brecht's accommodations?"

Max took a deep breath. There was still one more tent but it was packed away. The last thing he felt like doing was setting it up. But what choice did he have?

"Dr. Brecht," he said, "you can put your things in there."

He was pointing toward his own tent. Christine opened her eyes wide and was ready to speak, but he cut her off.

"I wasn't exactly expecting Mr. McGraw. I had to put him in the tent I had set aside for you. I'll set up another tent for you tomorrow. Meanwhile, you're welcome to mine. I'll stay in the big tent tonight."

"That's awfully kind of you," said Dr. Brecht.

"Damn straight," he muttered under his breath as he brushed past Christine to grab a few things he needed for the night.

He went back to the big tent and poured himself a stiff drink. He lay down on the cot, his head propped up by a few pillows. He could hear Christine and Dr. Brecht talking outside, and he wished he had some kind of lock for the door. Surely they would find something that was not quite right that only he could remedy.

He came to just after midnight. Dr. Brecht was screaming in German. Apparently, there had been an intruder. Max jumped up and ran outside. He could not believe his eyes. David was backing away from Dr. Brecht, who, emerging from what was now her tent, held a large knife in her hand.

"I'm terribly sorry," he was saying as he nervously moved away from the tent. "I was simply looking for Max," he said as she continued to leer at him as if he were some sort of priestly pervert.

"What is it?" said Max, noting the look of alarm on David's face and the quivering manner in which he was speaking. He looked frightened, nearly trembling.

"Come with me," David said as he began leading Max away from the immediate vicinity of the clinic, leaving Dr. Brecht to rant as Christine came running from her trailer to see what was the matter.

"What's going on?" said Max. "Is it Joseph? Is he all right?"

"It's nothing to do with Joseph," said David as they walked off into the darkness.

Suddenly, two fierce-looking moran stepped out from behind a large bush.

"These moran," said David, looking pained but at the same time rather excited. "These moran, they've come for the reward."

"The reward?" said Max.

"Yes, the reward. They've got Oscar."

Chapter 30

Enveloped in darkness, David and Max covered their faces with their arms to fend off the invisible branches that repeatedly whipped their entire bodies. They stumbled down the streambed as fast as they could, trying to keep up with their Tanzanian guides, trying in vain to somehow avoid tripping or stubbing their toes on the large stones that lined the narrow channel. Max had brought a flashlight, but every time he clicked it on his stealthy guides turned on him and attempted to rip it out of his hands. It soon became clear how they had managed to avoid the search parties. Why they had done so was still not clear but presumably it had something to do with the reward.

Peter Dermenjian had offered one million Kenyan shillings to whoever could lead them to Oscar. So why were they demanding two million? And why would they ever think a poor missionary would have anything approaching such a large sum of money available in ready cash? What would these nomads do with so much money, anyway? There were many questions to be answered. The most pressing had been where to come up with at least a down payment, which the men had indicated would be necessary before they would even lead them to Oscar. Fortunately, they had accepted David's gold chalice, given to him by his uncle as a gift when he was ordained. Surely he would get it back once Oscar settled up with them, assuming Oscar was alive, and assuming he and Max weren't being lured out of sight simply to be murdered for the gold chalice.

They continued to follow the winding depression that ran south, well beyond the rickety schoolhouse and onward into darkness. The water, which had begun as a mere trace of mud between the hard rocks, had increased to a discrete laminar flow fed by groundwater that bled off the past winter's rain into this small capillary and was slowly cutting a deeper incision into the volcanic ash as it drained to the marshes just north of Natron.

It seemed to take forever as they penetrated the narrow tunnel the stream had carved through dense riparian brush. But gradually the hard stems gave way to softer blades of tall grass as the narrow stream channel broadened and the large stones disappeared and the earth became softer. They felt their way through towering marsh grass as the rotten-egg stench of anoxic decay filtered up through

228

the thick mud that grabbed at their feet. To their right they could still feel the occasional hard stems that told them they were skirting the edge of the huge marsh.

When they finally stopped, panting heavily and gasping for air, it was still pitch black, for no moon graced the heavens on this particular night. One of their guides made a soft sound, like a cooing dove. Seconds later there was an echo. They immediately plied their way through the towering sheaves of grass toward its source.

Oscar was lying at the base of a small tree near the edge of the marsh. Two more moran stood guard. Max knelt down beside him and put his head to his chest, listening carefully for a sign of life. He was unconscious but still breathing, still clinging to life, if only by a thread. Max clicked on his flashlight and focused its narrow beam on Oscar's face. This time the moran did not object. No doubt they realized that, for them to receive the reward, it was important for Max to ascertain whether this immense but pitiful man was still alive.

Oscar's eyelids were very red and quite swollen, his lips cracked and caked with dried blood. Despite many days of exposure to the intense African sun, his face looked rather wan, almost gray. He was still gripped with fever. Max peeled back Oscar's shirt and saw the festering wounds across his enormous chest where the lion's claws had dug into his flesh. He pressed lightly on one of the areas where the skin had been ripped apart. Yellow pus flowed from the wound. Max grabbed a stethoscope from the small bag of medical supplies he had brought with him. He rubbed it with his hands and pressed it to Oscar's chest, avoiding as best he could the areas of inflamed skin. His heartbeat was stronger than he'd expected, but the beat was quite irregular, another sign, along with a terribly swollen tongue, of his extreme state of dehydration.

Max looked up at David. "He's in pretty bad shape," he said.

"I can't believe he's even alive," said David as he bent down and took hold of Oscar's hand, which felt like an enormous limp rag. But then, much to his amazement, he felt the hand squeeze his own ever so lightly.

"He might be coming to," said David.

Max turned the light upon Oscar's face once more. Oscar gently turned his head away and tried to speak.

"David," he whispered in a hoarse, barely audible voice. Max gave a twist to his flashlight. The sharp beam dissipated into a soft light that permeated the whole of the small enclave where Oscar lay in pain. His head turned slowly back toward them and his weary eyes began to open. They were mere slits between swollen eyelids.

"Oscar," David said, "it is so wonderful to see you again. Do not worry, you're going to be all right."

A faint smile appeared on Oscar's cracked, swollen, and peeling lips. He shook his head ever so slightly from side to side.

"Yes, you are," said David. "Max is here to make certain. But these moran, your saviors, they say that you have promised them a great sum of money. Is this true?"

Oscar closed his eyes and labored to draw in a deep breath. Then he gently nodded as he exhaled and his massive chest subsided.

"They say we must pay them two million Kenyan shillings, twice the reward that Peter Dermenjian has offered."

Suddenly, Oscar's eyes opened much wider. He tried to speak but no sound emerged. David lowered an ear to Oscar's lips, the better to comprehend.

"Pay them," he whispered.

The words, though barely audible, hung in the air for a moment as David tried to imagine all that had transpired, tried desperately to understand why Oscar would be willing to bestow such a large sum of money on these poor nomads who had dragged him almost twenty-five miles at least, when rescue had been so close at hand. Again there were many questions and very few answers.

"As you wish," he replied.

He released Oscar's hand and stood up to face the fierce young warriors while Max resumed his investigation of Oscar's vital signs. Of the four Tanzanian Maasai, David approached the one whom he presumed to be the leader of the pack, the one who had nearly scared him to death when he'd come tapping at his window hours before. He noticed for the first time that a fresh pair of lion ears hung from the top of his spear.

David thanked them once again for their efforts to save Oscar's life. Then he promised, upon his word as a servant of God, that they would have their reward. He explained, however, that it would take a bit of time. He would have to travel to Nairobi, where there are banks. In the meantime, they could hold on to the gold chalice, which he assured them was extremely valuable.

The fellow with the lion ears laughed in a mocking tone. He told David that they would indeed have their reward, that they had traveled very far under great duress carrying this enormous pig of a man. They had endured many a hardship, carefully avoiding the people who had been hunting for him. And as for this vessel, he said, holding up the chalice, it was not worthy of holding his piss. He said that if they did not receive their money before the next new moon, they would come back for Oscar. And if they did not find him, they would find the man in the helicopter who wanted him dead or alive, and tell him all they knew.

David stared for a moment in silence and slowly shook his head. He could bear it no longer. He asked them all to please sit down, to please explain why the man in the helicopter wanted Oscar so badly. At first his hosts refused, stating they must be gone, they could not afford to be caught.

"Caught?" asked David. "Caught by whom?"

They spoke quickly for a moment among themselves. The one with the lion ears, who called himself Olabon, said he believed the game police were after them for killing the lion.

"Oh, I see," said David, seeming quite impressed. "But please tell me, how did you manage to kill this lion?"

Olabon did not answer. David rubbed his eyes and then reached into a pocket and pulled out a pack of cigarettes. He lit one for himself and offered them around. They were made from a fine, black Turkish blend, the kind Joseph fancied. At first Olabon refused, but as the smoke wafted about him and his comrades appeared eager to partake, he relented. David offered the packet one more time. They each grabbed one and David helped them with a light. Then he motioned again for them to please sit, to tell them about the lion kill. They mumbled briefly to one another before assembling themselves into a small circle amid the shrubs bordering the marsh. Without consulting Max, David reached into the medicine kit and produced a bottle of brandy. Then he asked Olabon for the chalice and filled it half full.

"To your bravery," he said, raising the chalice. He took a small sip and passed it to Olabon, who looked back with a fierce, mistrustful look. Then he grabbed the chalice and took a larger sip before passing it to his friend on his right.

"So," continued David, "please tell us how you killed the lion."

Olabon still looked wary.

"Do not worry. After all you have done for Oscar, we would never betray you."

Olabon looked around again, eyeing everyone cautiously. Then he took the chalice and helped himself once more. With careful expression and immense pride, he began to tell his story.

He had been out hunting early one morning, stalking small game. It was a very still morning, with just a slight breeze from the south. The fog was very thick and the hunting was poor. After several hours with nothing to show for his efforts, he heard a man crying for help. It was obviously some *mzungu* who had no business being out in Maasai country. But they were very foolish, these mzungu. He ran quickly until he heard the roar of the lion. He knew immediately, from the sounds the beast made, that it was threatening to charge.

He crawled upon his belly, careful to remain downwind, until he mounted a slight rise and saw Oscar. His back was toward him, and he was deep within a U-shaped blind alley the wind had carved in the tiny grains of volcanic glass. Peering through a small bush, Olabon could see the fire in the lion's eyes, focused on its prey. He waited to see if the beast would merely go away on its own, knowing it would not. It was too lean. When the lion began to charge, he resisted the urge to rise. Instead he hesitated, not wanting to launch his spear until the beast was in closer range, not wanting the lion to suddenly change its mind about whom it was intending to kill. So he waited until the lion had committed itself, waited until the powerful hind legs had dug deep into the ash, planted firmly for the kill. As the massive muscles uncoiled and the beast launched itself into midair, its huge front claws fully extended in front of its powerful frame and its great jaws wide open, Olabon rose as if in slow motion. He gripped his spear firmly, feeling its perfect balance in his hand as he became the spear, and with all of his might he unleashed it. He was no more than ten meters from the lion when the spear made contact just as the lion made contact with Oscar.

Man and beast collapsed together. Olabon quickly ran to inspect them, pulling his knife from its sheath just in case. But there was no movement. Oscar lay motionless, covered with blood, the beast's massive head and magnificent ruff resting on his chest. It was difficult to tell whether the blood was Oscar's or the lion's. No doubt it belonged to both of them. He stared for a moment, yet the lion still did not move. He had pierced it through the chest, right through the heart.

Oscar was unconscious, maybe dead. He listened for his breath and discovered he had simply fainted, like any mzungu would when attacked by a lion. He tried to push the lion off of Oscar but the beast was much too heavy. So he went searching for his comrades. Together they moved the lion aside and carried Oscar back to their camp hidden deep within the thick forest on the east side of Gelai. Then they went back to butcher the lion. They ate its heart for supper.

The following morning search parties arrived. Olabon feared they were after him for killing the lion. But from Oscar's reaction to the sight of the blue helicopter with the yellow diamond on the side, it was clear that whoever was in the helicopter was searching for Oscar and it was clear that Oscar did not wish to be found. So they hid him in another secret recess within Gelai, applying their traditional medicine to treat Oscar's wounds, waiting for the helicopter to leave.

They decided he must be a criminal who was badly wanted by the authorities. He promised them lots of money to keep him hidden. But hiding him was difficult. Sometimes he would begin screaming in his sleep and they would have to muzzle him. Then one day they found a sign with a picture of Oscar. It said that whoever found him dead or alive would receive a million Kenyan shillings!

"I see," said David as the chalice was passed around one more time and the subject of money resurfaced. Somehow Oscar, when not delirious, had led them to understand that the man offering the reward was very evil. He had drawn a map in the dirt, showing them approximately where the schoolhouse lay in relation to Gelai. He had written "DAVID" next to the schoolhouse and had circled his name. Then he had crossed out the "one million KSH" on the reward sign and written in "two million." With this last statement Olabon rose and drained the last of the brandy.

"I have told you about the lion," he said, "so where is the money?"

David shook his head. "Help us deliver him to my schoolhouse," he replied, "and we will make arrangements for the payment."

"We want the money now," said Olabon.

"I told you," said David, "you can keep the chalice until we can get you the money. Besides, the instructions were to deliver Oscar to my schoolhouse. You are not there yet."

Olabon again conferred with his tribesmen. "We will carry him no farther. This is close enough."

David explained that Oscar was too heavy for the two of them to carry alone. His patience was wearing thin. "You want the money, you carry him," he said.

Olabon gave him a disgusted look. He then picked up the chalice and studied it for a moment. With a laugh and a wry look toward his comrades, he reached one hand inside his *shuka*, grabbed his penis, and held it directly over the chalice. Before he could summon his urine, however, David leaped to his feet and knocked him to the ground. The chalice went flying. The three other moran stood up and grabbed their spears. Max stood up as well, wishing he had thought to bring a weapon of his own.

"Don't you dare commit such blasphemy!" shouted David, unable to control his rage. He stared at Olabon for a moment before his priestly compassion returned and he offered his hand to help him to his feet. Olabon brushed it aside and rose on his own. David shook his head. "What a fool I am," he muttered in English. "I don't know what I was thinking, trying to give you this holy vessel, whose worth you cannot begin to comprehend. Then filling you with brandy."

Olabon approached him. Standing some six inches from David's face, he hurled all manner of insults. David flinched momentarily before returning fire, speaking rapidly and with great emotion. Olabon tried to interrupt but David kept on lecturing and staring down the young Maasai, whose swagger seemed to be losing ground. Max, unable to comprehend, watched as Olabon's expression changed slowly. At first he was indignant, then somewhat confused but still angry. He tried again to interrupt, but David would not relent, shaking the chalice to make his points and motioning on occasion toward Oscar, who still lay semiconscious on the pallet. The other Maasai looked at each other and seemed rather uncomfortable.

Finally, David concluded and asked for their decision. Olabon looked at his comrades. They looked at each other again and exchanged but a few words. With an angry look at David and one for Max, Olabon picked up his spear and walked over toward Oscar. He snapped a command at the other three, and they each took their accustomed place and lifted the pallet holding Oscar. Then, without further discussion, they began retracing the route back to the schoolhouse.

"What the hell did you say to them?" said Max as he and David followed behind.

"Nothing too outrageous. Mostly I appealed to their pride as Maasai, as moran, as people whose honor was only as good as their word."

"Is that all?" said Max, disbelieving.

"No, that's not all. I told them that if they did not live up to their word, there would be no money whatsoever, and that in view of their disrespect for the chalice, I was withdrawing that offer as well."

"But they could have just taken it and left. What could you and I have done to stop them?"

"Nothing, I suppose, but after I explained that the chalice represents the vessel Jesus Christ used to convert water into wine, symbolizing his blood, and that it is extremely sacred, I believe they were spooked. I also said that as a priest I knew all about their own spiritual matters, that I knew their elders and their witch doctors, and that if they did not wish for bad things to befall them, they would follow through on their word."

Max couldn't help but laugh. "So, in essence, you threatened to put a curse on them."

"Eh, something like that, I suppose."

"Brilliant."

They arrived at the schoolhouse as the first glimmers of sunlight illuminated the clouds atop the Nguruman Escarpment to the west in soft shades of pink and gray. They made Oscar as comfortable as possible on one of the cots and then turned to deal with their visitors. David offered them some bread and milk, which they gladly accepted. He promised to meet them on the next new moon at the spot by the marsh where they had found Oscar. Olabon took one last look at Oscar, who was now sleeping comfortably, and muttered a few words before heading out the door along with his friends.

"What did he say?" said Max.

"He said the old fart better not die now, not after all this."

"Is that all?"

"No. He repeated that if they don't get the money as agreed, they'll be back for Oscar."

Chapter 31

While Max carefully cleaned all of Oscar's wounds, which were extensive, and hooked him up to an IV, David cleaned the chalice. He even gave it a bit of polish before placing it back into the red velvet sack that bore David's initials. He drew the gold drawstring tight and placed it on the table. Oscar remained sleeping on the cot, his breathing still quite labored.

"I've got to get him to a hospital," said Max. "He needs a major transfusion. But I don't know what to do about that Crazy Jack character. I hate to leave him. And who knows what he's up to by now."

"I only hope that Joseph hasn't encountered any hardships," said David.

"That's all we need. But right now I need plenty of antiseptic. I'm going back to the clinic to get some supplies and to check on things. I'll be back in a while. Can you keep an eye on him?"

"I'll try," said David. "But the children will be here soon so don't be too long."

"I won't."

Max hurried back to the clinic, apprehensive and extremely tired but intent on getting back to Oscar as quickly as possible with proper medication. He passed a number of schoolchildren on his way and exchanged greetings with them. One of the boys said, "Hello, how do you do?" to show off his command of English before falling all about laughing along with his friends at such silly-sounding words.

As he came within view of the canvas tents that seemed to sag more than usual in the still morning air, he heard Dr. Brecht utter, "There he is!" He wished he could hide but it was too late. Christine was already walking toward him.

"And just where the hell have you been?" she asked. "We've been trying to keep this maniac under control. He refuses to get dressed, and every time we get near him he just wants to do the hula with us."

Max walked past her without speaking, rubbing his scalp. What should he tell them?

"Don't you just walk past me like that without even saying good morning. We've been worried sick about you. Where have you been?" She was trailing after him, trying to make eye contact, but he kept staring straight ahead as he walked on.

"I was helping David. His generator broke and he needed it for school today. I was pretty tired so I just spent the night there."

Christine looked at his mud-covered boots and the tears in his shirt. "Bullshit," she said. "What the hell were you two doing?"

Max ignored her and walked over to the tent where he'd left Jack McGraw. It was empty. "Great," said Max. "One more lunatic on the loose."

"He's in the big tent," she said, "totally bonkers."

And so he was, leaning stark naked against the filing cabinet as Max entered and singing "The Yellow Rose of Texas." Next to him was the bottle of Scotch lying on its side.

"I see you went and helped yourself," said Max. He walked up to the poor wretch and pulled him into the light. He was still singing but the words were unintelligible. Max grabbed his jaw and twisted his face toward the light. Then he let him go, satisfied by the rapid constriction of his pupils that Crazy Jack was returning to some semblance of sanity.

"Ain't you got nothin' else to drink around here?" said Crazy Jack.

"Sorry, pal, but I'm putting you back on the IV."

It was a struggle, but with Christine's begrudging help the mission was accomplished. Max then gave Crazy Jack enough sedative to keep him subdued until he returned.

"And where are you going now?" she demanded as Max packed his medical bag.

"Look," he said, "I need to tend to someone."

"Who?" she snapped. "It's not Joseph, is it?"

"No," said Max, "it's not Joseph."

"Then it's his son, isn't it? I'll bet he just refuses to come back to the clinic."

Max looked at her and just rubbed his eyes. "It's something like that," he said. "Just keep an eye on Crazy Jack for me, okay?"

"When will you be back?"

"As soon as possible."

Finally back at the schoolhouse, Max backed the Scout up to the door of David's living quarters. Oscar was still lying unconscious on the cot. Max stepped outside and peeked into the side window of the schoolroom, catching David's eye. He gave his students a math problem to solve and told them all to remain seated. He then headed outside to help Max place Oscar into the back of the Scout. Max had folded up the rear seats so there was room for Oscar to lie down in what was now a makeshift ambulance, with a jury-rigged IV to boot.

"Do you think he'll be all right?" asked David. "Perhaps I should go with you."

"He's sleeping soundly and should be fine. You have enough to do here, and once I get him to the hospital, he'll be in good hands."

"I'm not so sure about that. He'll have to deal with the police and…"

"Yes, I know," said Max. "But we haven't any choice."

David nodded and then wished him well, advising him to do everything possible to keep Oscar's identity concealed. But he knew all too well that as soon as Oscar appeared in public, he would be swarmed with media as well as the police. These were unsettling thoughts but he knew there was no choice. It was simply a matter of life and death. And surely justice would prevail.

Max drove carefully, going much slower than usual in view of Oscar's delicate condition. Oscar muttered a few words every now and then, but he was still a long way from resuming full consciousness.

As he approached the bridge over the Ewaso Ngiro, Max noticed a few soldiers beside the road. He couldn't believe that Captain Olengi had kept his promise. Max slowed down and waved, hoping they would not impede his progress. But one of the soldiers stepped into the middle of the roadway, holding his rifle at the ready. Max reluctantly pulled to a halt.

"*Jambo,*" he said, flashing his best toothy smile.

"Jambo," returned the soldier blocking his way. "I am sorry," he said in English, "but the road is closed. It is too dangerous."

Max could not believe what he was hearing. "What do you mean, the road is closed?" he inquired as calmly as he could. Fatigue was draining what little patience he held in reserve. "I have to get this man to a hospital."

"I am sorry," said the soldier, "but we have our orders. Besides, there is a doctor who lives back the way you have come. It should not be too hard to find him."

Max was confused for an instant; then he shook his head. "Look," he said, "I am that doctor. And this man needs to get to a hospital."

"I am sorry," said the soldier, "I cannot let you pass. You must choose another way."

Max muttered a few expletives beneath his breath before throwing his hands in the air. "What other way? If I don't get this man to a hospital pretty soon, he'll probably die on me."

The soldier stood his ground. "It is too dangerous," he said. "The refugees have refused to remain north of the road as they have been instructed. They are armed and have been poaching Maasai cattle to the south. Your vehicle could very well be hijacked. They would not think twice about killing you or your companion."

Max again lowered his head and rubbed his eyes. He was too tired to argue.

Class was still in session when Max arrived back at David's schoolhouse. He sat in the Scout for a few minutes, looking at Oscar and then staring at his dashboard. He hated to disrupt any lessons but it was already too late. David came bounding out of the front doorway, surrounded by a few dozen children delighted to suddenly have the afternoon free.

"What's happened?" said David once the children had fled.

"The road to Nairobi," he said, "it's been closed."

"Closed?" David roared back. "Why, that's impossible! What about the troops that Captain Olengi was sending?"

"They're there, all right. I think closing the road was their idea. It sure makes life easier, for them, at least."

"But how are we supposed to get supplies in and out? And what about Oscar?"

"I don't know about supplies," said Max, "but we need to get Oscar better situated."

They managed with some difficulty to rearrange Oscar back on the cot in the middle of David's living area. Max restored the IV, though he found it even more difficult to locate a suitable vein.

"His blood pressure's getting pretty low. No telling how much he's lost."

"What's his blood type?"

"It's A negative. Not very common. But I need to find a donor."

"I would gladly give mine. I'm A positive."

"Me too, and that won't work. It's got to be Rh negative, just like his. I need to go check with Christine and Dr. Brecht."

Max hopped back in the Scout and drove cross-country to the clinic. He found Christine and Dr. Brecht seated at a table, pouring over sets of statistics Christine had compiled concerning the Maasai women.

"How's the patient?" said Christine.

"He's doing all right but I need some Rh negative blood."

"Well, don't look at me," she replied. "I'm O positive."

"And don't look at me," said Dr. Brecht. Max waited for her to divulge her blood type, but she was not forthcoming.

"How's our other patient?" he asked.

"Sleeping like a baby."

Max peered into the tent. Crazy Jack was snoring peacefully. "I hate to wake him but I don't have any choice." Then he thought it over a moment. "Well, maybe I don't have to wake him."

Max stepped inside the tent and carefully took hold of Jack's hand. He pulled a needle from a small blood-testing kit and deftly pricked his finger. The patient winced but did not awaken. Max dripped some blood onto the little card that came with the kit before placing a small Band-Aid over the tiny pinhole in Crazy Jack's finger. Then he looked at the card and smiled. He had found some matching blood!

"Eureka," he whispered. Christine was waiting for him outside. He motioned her back into the tent. "Look," he began, "I really need your help."

"With what?"

"I need a quart of Jack McGraw's blood. All you need to do is divert his attention. I'll pretend I'm just taking a sample or two."

"And just who's going to receive this blood? I won't do it unless you tell me."

Max rubbed his weary eyes. This had to be kept a secret. "It's for Oscar Newman. He's alive, barely."

"Oscar Newman?" she nearly shouted. "Where is he?"

"In David's schoolhouse. Please, he's lost quite a bit."

"But...," she began before Max cut her off.

"Look," he begged, "we don't have much time. I'll fill you in later. And don't breathe a word about Oscar."

"Okay," she said. "I get the picture."

They took their positions alongside Crazy Jack McGraw.

"Hello there," said Christine, smiling as she took hold of his hand. "I just need to check your pulse."

Jack McGraw, entirely focused on the lovely young woman who had awakened him and was delicately gripping his wrist, barely noticed as Max inserted a needle in his arm and proceeded to fill two small plastic bags with Jack's recently rehydrated and sedated blood while Christine kept him occupied with questions and conversation. It wasn't top-quality blood, but it was the best, and only, matching blood in town. Max rushed back to the schoolhouse.

"If you want to know the truth," said Max to David as they both watched Crazy Jack's blood trickle into Oscar's system, "I've never treated a case of malaria before. I've given him the best medication I have, but beyond that and some fresh blood, such as it is, I don't know what else I can do."

"And what more could they do in a hospital?" asked David, who was slicing up some fruit and cheese.

"Well, for one thing, I'm sure they'd have better blood. Whole blood transfusions can be risky, but what choice do we have? And no doubt they have some better drugs."

"Perhaps," David replied as he set out a few plates and a fresh bottle of water. "I wonder what Oscar would choose."

"Who knows," said Max. If Oscar had any opinion on the matter, he was not about to voice it. He was lying on his cot, sleeping as the blood Max had drained from Crazy Jack slowly inflated his sagging arteries. Once the transfusion was complete, Max removed the needles and rubber tubing and placed a Band-Aid over the puncture in the crook of Oscar's right elbow.

They picked away at the cheese, the fruit, and some old stale bread. They sipped at the water but neither of them spoke for some time. David was the first to break the heavy silence.

"We're nearly penned in, you know, with the road closed."

Max looked up from his plate. "So?"

"So?" said David. "Haven't you considered the fact that we are quite vulnerable here? The refugees are well armed, out of food, and clearly unconcerned with whatever the Kenyan government has given them in the way of mandates. Perhaps you should take Christine and Dr. Brecht with you, along with Oscar, of course."

"With me?" said Max. "You mean if they ever reopen the road?"

"Yes, I think Captain Olengi was right. It is time for you to leave. It is too dangerous here now."

Max sat pensively, laboring over a morsel of bread. He couldn't quite believe what he was hearing. "Leave?" he said. "You want us to leave? What about the clinic?"

"I don't want you to leave, but I am concerned about your safety. Besides, when's the last time you administered to one of the Maasai women? That's what you came here for. I believe you've fulfilled your mission."

"Well, business has been pretty slow in that department, but what about Crazy Jack? What about Joseph's son? And who knows what may have happened to Joseph himself and all his buddies during their visit with the now-well-armed refugees? Besides, what about you? What about your safety?"

"God will look after me. And I have a duty, a responsibility to the Maasai," he replied. "But you, you don't have a dog in this fight. You are free to go."

Max stared intently at David. "No dog in this fight, huh? Is that what you think? Well, let me tell you something. I used to have a dog, a damn fine dog, purebred golden retriever. But where is he now? With my ex-wife, along with just about everything else I ever owned."

"Your point?" David replied demurely.

Max rose from the table abruptly. "My point is that I don't have any other goddamn place in this world to go. I don't have a goddamn dog anymore anywhere, so I might as well stick it out here, where there's a damn good chance I might do somebody some good."

He was pacing now, flushed with anger.

"Might I request you to please mind your language?" said David. "I am still a priest and you are in my house."

"Still a priest?" said Max with renewed vigor. "Still a priest? While you're off doing who knows what with a young American anthropology student? And helping the Maasai with birth control? And beating up young Maasai warriors?"

David stared at Max and then lowered his eyes. "I am not perfect," he replied. "I have my demons like everyone else. I try to do my best. Just like you. So stay if you like. I was only thinking of your best interests."

Max stopped his pacing. "Look," he said, "I guess I'm just a little tired after last night's ordeal with Oscar and Crazy Jack, and the road closed and all. I'm sorry. I should just keep my mouth shut."

"We're all very tired," said David. "Why don't you take a little rest? Oscar seems comfortable enough."

"Sounds good, but I need to change his bandages again. His blood isn't clotting like it should. Hopefully, that transfusion will help."

"Very well," said David as he cleared their dishes away. "But I'm going off to find Joseph. I must know what's going on around here. He must be back by now."

Chapter 32

It was a good half-hour walk to Joseph's new quarters, halfway to the Ewaso Ngiro. The country here was open, with only a few young acacias growing amid the thick green grasses that thrived on the alluvial soil.

A young lad tending to a small herd of goats just outside the manyatta told David that Joseph had indeed returned. But he recommended to David that he not seek him out. He said he was very, very angry. David raised his bushy eyebrows in apprehension and thanked the lad for the advice. But then he told him that, no matter what, he must see Joseph.

"You will find him down by the big tree, with the elders," said the lad, pointing to the west. "They are all very angry."

"Can you take me there?"

The lad agreed, leading him back in the direction he had come, the goats ambling along behind them. Within five minutes David heard Joseph speaking, nearly shouting. He could see a large, solitary thorn tree off to the south. He thanked the lad and told him he would find his way. The boy shook his head and repeated that Joseph was very angry, but David would not be deterred.

Making his way through the tall grass, he finally spotted Joseph standing beneath the large tree with the usual consort of elders seated on the ground before him. He was speaking rapidly and shaking what looked like a large white stick. As he moved closer, David realized it was not a stick. It was a large bone, a thigh bone. Joseph waved it in the air as he spoke. Then he pointed it to the north before slamming it into the palm of his left hand and staring angrily, in silence, at the elders seated before him. David surmised that his encounter with the Ugandan refugees had not gone well. But at least they were all alive.

"Jambo," said David.

Joseph had not seen him approaching. He motioned him to come forward, offering a terse greeting, more like a series of grunts. A few of the elders nodded, not so much in greeting but more to acknowledge David's presence.

"What happened?" David asked in Maa. "Did the refugees agree to leave your cattle alone?"

Joseph began pacing, slapping the bone against the palm of his hand several times before speaking. Never in all his years in Joseph's district had David seen him so angry. Joseph cursed the refugees as he explained what had transpired.

They were ten: Joseph, four of the elders, and five moran. They had approached the most southerly hovel of tents and demanded to speak with whoever was in charge. They were told to wait, to retreat from the decrepit city of lean-tos and tarps and all the filth. They obliged, in part because they were asked to and in part because of the stench of human excrement.

They waited for nearly half an hour. Finally, Joseph sent one of the moran to find out what the delay was, to tell them they must talk, that the Maasai would not tolerate the killing of their cattle. The moran returned, saying someone would join them shortly. Again they waited. At last they saw four of the Ugandans exit the largest of the tents. Three of them carried rifles. The fourth, a squatty man dressed in army fatigues, was carrying something else, something rather long wrapped up in cloth.

The moran gripped their spears, ready to launch them if any of the Ugandans so much as lowered the tips of their rifles. But they kept them shouldered, barrels pointed toward the sky. When the distance between them had narrowed to but a few yards, the Ugandans stopped. The squatty one without the weapon stepped forward. He spoke a very crude Swahili. He said their leader was not able to receive them. He said they would need to make an appointment.

This was such an affront that Joseph spat and cursed. He told them they must talk now, that they would not tolerate any further killing of Maasai cattle. He told them they must turn in their rifles, that his agreement to lease the land back to the Kenyan government for the sake of the refugees stated there would be no weapons. And certainly no killing of Maasai cattle!

The Ugandans looked at him and laughed, pausing only to reiterate that, to see their leader, he must make an appointment. Joseph, quite indignant, tried to brush them aside, but they blocked his way with their rifles. Then their spokesman told Joseph he was very sorry but asked him to please accept a gift from their leader. Joseph asked for the name of this leader but received no answer except that he would reveal his name when he was ready. Until then, the spokesman said, he had sent along this token of appreciation, which he handed to Joseph. Removing the cloth, Joseph saw that it was merely a bone, a sun-bleached thigh bone from a Maasai cow.

"And what am I to do with this?" Joseph asked. The Ugandans then all broke into laughter.

Their spokesman said, "Our leader says that, as far as he is concerned, you can shove it up your ass!"

Again the Ugandans fell about laughing. The moran gripped their spears tighter and began to raise them, but Joseph, with a wave of his hand, commanded them to stand down.

"We are all very hungry," the Ugandan spokesman had said. "All the Red Cross brings us is rice and soybeans. We are fighting men and we must have meat. And we will take what nature provides."

David listened to this story and felt his insides tighten and the anger rise once again within him. His temples were throbbing. But as angered as he was by the refugees' outrageous behavior toward the Maasai, their hosts, he had not forgotten that the alleged agreement to allow them to occupy Maasailand in the first place made no sense at all. He wanted to ask Joseph what, if anything, he had agreed to. But this was neither the time nor the place, among all the elders. He listened to Joseph and the elders discuss strategy, reviewing options ranging from a midnight raid to simply removing their cattle. The latter option, noted Senento, would likely only spur the refugees to move farther south, to occupy more unauthorized Maasailand. The others agreed. After much heated debate they settled on summoning all of the moran within the district and putting them on around-the-clock surveillance of the Kalema Road to prevent further poaching of their cattle.

When the elders had dispersed, David asked Joseph if they could speak in private for a moment. Joseph, always cordial if not exuberant, invited David back to his house and showed him to a small stool made from olive wood and leather. His wife brewed some strong tea that they sipped while making small talk, as was customary, commenting on how difficult the refugees were being but how good the grass was in this particular area near the Ewaso Ngiro. Finally, David told Joseph about his meeting with Captain Olengi, about their conversation and Captain Olengi's assertion that the Maasai, and Joseph in particular, had agreed to let the Ugandans occupy their lands. He asked how this could be true.

Joseph sipped his tea, swirling his small metal cup as he stared into it, as if looking for clues to the future. Though the light was poor, it was sufficient for David to see clearly the strain in Joseph's expression, which was never anything more than somber to begin with. But now the deep lines in his face seemed to cut deeper; his furrowed brow seemed more bundled up than usual. It was a long face, with high cheekbones and really no cheeks at all, only hollow spaces that joined his hard-set jaw. His slit earlobes hung halfway down his neck.

"It is true," he said, as if confessing to some awful wrongdoing.

"But why?" David asked. "Why would you surrender your land even temporarily, land you have fought hard to keep others from taking away?"

Joseph said nothing but merely reached behind him and opened a small wooden box. From it he removed an envelope and handed it to David. He opened it carefully and removed a three-page document written on the letterhead of McDonald, Schlepp, and Greevey, attorneys-at-law.

David studied the document for several minutes. He stood up in order to hold the paper closer to the light, closer to the hole in the roof of Joseph's house, so that he might better comprehend and perhaps come to believe what was written down, sworn to, and signed not just by Joseph and several other Maasai leaders but by the president himself.

According to the document, the Maasai agreed to lease their land from the Kalema Road north to Mosiro for a period not to exceed six months to the government of Kenya, to accommodate an international crisis that, under the leadership of the United Nations, would be swiftly resolved. In return, the government would extinguish all prior pending claims to Maasailand, including mineral, grazing, and water rights on lands described in exhibit A; would secure, on behalf of all Maasai, guarantees against all external claims of ownership of said lands, including mineral, grazing, and water rights as described in exhibit A; would develop and operate no fewer than twenty new water sources on sites to be determined; would implement grazing improvements on all leased lands as well as on no less than ten thousand hectares, sites to be determined; and would substantially upgrade current educational institutions on Maasai lands.

Exhibit A was attached. It was a map that encompassed all Maasai lands in Kenya from the southern border north to Mosiro and from the edge of the Nguruman Escarpment to the eastern edge of the Rift Valley. David read it over not twice but three times, carefully examining the signatures, looking for any hint of fraud. Joseph assured him it was binding. Maasai attorneys had been working on an agreement like this for several years. Only the crisis provoked by the Ugandans had provided the leverage needed for the Kenyan government to actually sign it.

David sat back down. He was aware that the Maasai had a cadre of attorneys available to them to help settle land ownership disputes. And like tribes everywhere, who were frequently shoved into the most remote and desolate corners of the world, the borders of their lands were often contested. But this agreement granted the Maasai far more control than David had ever thought possible. Grazing rights and water rights he could understand, but mineral rights? And there was no doubt that the promise of upgrading "the currently inadequate educational institutions" was a clear slap in the face.

"Why?" he pleaded. "Why would the Kenyan government agree to such things? They have fought the Maasai on all these points for many years."

Joseph shrugged his shoulders and told David they had had no choice. If they had not agreed, there would have been such bloodshed, such turmoil that all the world would have taken notice.

"What do you mean?" David asked.

Joseph told him how he had explained to the government that without this agreement, the Maasai would have fought the refugees to the death. There would have been so much bloodshed, so much suffering, that all of Kenya would have been shamed. And, most importantly, such a conflict would certainly have sent all the tourists packing.

David left Joseph with words of thanks and encouragement, congratulating him on having negotiated what was certain to be an historic agreement if, as Joseph claimed, it was indeed binding. Even more surprising was that Joseph appeared entirely unconcerned with the road closure. What did the Maasai need with roads? After all, they were only for the tourists.

With his hands thrust deep into the pockets of his dark robe, David walked alone through the ordinarily dusty but now suddenly verdant savannah, looking down, lost in his thoughts and completely unconcerned with the possibility of being pursued by man or beast. The fact that he'd been isolated from all of Joseph's and the other Maasai leaders' negotiations with the government left him with a peculiar feeling, not quite a sense of betrayal but certainly one of intense futility. There was no question that it hurt, especially the bit about the quality of education. All these years he'd taught Western concepts and values to the Maasai, to prepare them for the inevitable clash with the outer world, while trying to provide lessons that pertained more directly to their own agrarian, semi-nomadic ways. And all this on absurdly minimal funding from both the Kenyan government and the Jesuit Missionary Foundation. If anything was missing, it certainly hadn't been communicated to him.

Chapter 33

David would have much preferred an evening to himself, the better to digest the news regarding his apparent subpar performance as well as Joseph's stunning contract with the government of Kenya. But that was not to be. With Oscar's sudden reappearance, his humble and very small quarters behind the schoolhouse were now at capacity, an apparent secret annex of Maasai Clinic Number One. Somehow he managed to scrape together a meager supper for all of his guests.

Christine had suddenly turned into Florence Nightingale, tending to Oscar's every need, wiping his still-sweaty brow, spoon-feeding him his first solid food in days. Dr. Brecht had revealed another side of her staid personality by sitting back quietly with paper and pen, drawing sketches of the infamous Oscar Newman in his first stages of convalescence. And a much more subdued Jack McGraw sat close by Oscar the whole while, marveling at the man who now carried his own blood within him and who seemed all the more fit because of it. Oscar indeed seemed more alert than he'd been earlier, perhaps because of the fresh blood, or perhaps because of the two cups of coffee he had consumed. Regardless, he seemed willing, if not entirely able, to tell his story. Max asked what he remembered about the past few weeks.

"Not very much," said Oscar rather faintly in a very raspy voice.

But little by little, upon gentle probing by Max and David, who asked only for yes or no answers to their questions, Oscar began revealing bits and pieces of his recent misadventures. Much of it was still a mystery to him. He remembered the Serengeti and Ngorongoro, even camping near Natron, but the rest was largely a blur.

"Do you know what happened to Francis?" said David at last.

"Yes," said Oscar after some hesitation. Max glanced at the monitor and saw that Oscar's pulse was quickening.

"His brother, Peter…," Oscar began, but he was too overcome with either emotion or pain, or both, to continue. His chest began to heave again and his breathing was labored.

"It's okay," Max assured him, "just rest easy. We want you to stay comfortable. We'll talk more later."

David glared at Max for attempting to halt what was amounting to a revelation, perhaps a confession, or quite possibly an accusation—in any event, an answer to a question they had all held foremost in their minds for some time now.

"What about his brother?" said David, ignoring Max and his pleas entirely, anxious for some kind of answer before Oscar relapsed into his feverish delirium once again.

Oscar continued breathing heavily, his eyes shut tight. Then he started shaking all over.

"It's okay," said Max, "you don't need to answer. We'll have time for that later. You just need to rest. And stop breathing so hard. You might rip your stitches out."

But it was too late. Oscar continued to take deep breaths and Max could see tears welling up, a sign that he was better hydrated than before, but this state of agitation was not good. Finally, Oscar put his lips together and tried once more to speak.

"His brother," he began, gasping for air and trembling terribly, "his brother shot him in cold blood."

"Peter Dermenjian shot him?" said Max, suddenly quite interested in whatever Oscar might have to say. "But why? Why would he shoot his own brother?"

Oscar turned his eyes away. "That I cannot tell you," he whispered.

"Well," said Max as he removed some pillows and lowered Oscar's head, "it's pretty clear why Peter Dermenjian posted a reward for you. But you've done enough talking for today. You need more rest. And I'm afraid you're going to need a good lawyer as well."

The words might as well have been sharp needles jabbed straight into Oscar's brain.

"No!" he pleaded. "No lawyers! Just fetch Elizabeth, I must see Elizabeth."

Max stared back at Oscar, wishing he'd just kept his mouth shut. "All right," he said. "We'll see if we can get through to her in the morning somehow. And we can talk about your condition then. But sooner or later you're going to have to face up to your situation. I hate to say it, but you're wanted for murder."

It wasn't the best of notes on which to bring the evening to a close. But visiting hours were over and everyone needed rest. Over the next few days Oscar continued to convalesce, making steady progress with no signs of rejecting the blood Crazy Jack had donated, albeit unwittingly. Jack McGraw was now his roommate, sleeping in the cot next to Oscar so Max could keep an eye on both of them. Oscar began to recall and to relate more of what had transpired back at Lake Natron, speaking of the swamped Land Rover. But he made no mention of any diamond discovery.

Max slept on David's couch, not far from his two patients. Early one morning he had a dream that the refugees were chasing him, firing their automatic weapons. When he awoke, shaking and covered in sweat, he saw that it was nearly light out and that the dreamy sound of the machine guns was in reality the sound of an approaching helicopter. He sprang to the doorway in time to see it beginning to descend. It was blue with a large yellow diamond painted on the side.

"Quick," said David, who'd been awakened by the sounds as well, "help me with Oscar."

Max didn't immediately understand what he meant until he watched David grab the rug beneath his dining table and pull it, table and all, far to one side of the room. David then reached down and grabbed the latch to a small door that led down to his priest hole, a dark, hidden compartment barely high enough for a man to stand, originally built as a hiding place for missionaries who may be under siege. He lit a candle in the darkness below and then mounted the steep stairs. Without speaking, they rousted Jack McGraw and nearly threw him off his cot where, until that very moment, he had been sleeping soundly despite all the noise.

"What in hell are you two…," he began, but David made it very clear that silence was essential.

They grabbed the cot Jack had been lying on and rushed back down to set it up in the priest hole. Then they returned and quickly ushered Oscar, who, perhaps accustomed to being squirreled away quickly by his Tanzanian rescuers, complied with David's urging to stow himself down in the safety of his secret hideaway. He stumbled as Max helped him down the steep steps, but luckily David was able to catch him and help him lie back down upon the cot.

"Just keep still and be very quiet," said David in a harsh whisper. "We'll let you out as soon as they are gone."

"As soon as who's gone?" Oscar whispered back. He was barely awake.

"I don't know, but it could be Peter Dermenjian."

David climbed back up the steps and shut the small hatch. Then, with help from Max, they slid the rug and table back over to the middle of the room.

"Jack," said David, pointing to the cot that Oscar had occupied, "lie down quickly."

"What am I, somebody's dog?" he muttered as he nonetheless lay back down on Oscar's cot. Max grabbed a role of adhesive tape and wrapped some of Oscar's dirty bandages over his chest. Then he threw a couple of pillows on top of him and covered him with a blanket.

"Remember," he said, "you're very sick. In fact, you're not even conscious. Don't say a word no matter what."

Jack looked at him as if he were the one who was very sick.

"Look," Max whispered, "this will earn you some serious whisky."

By then the helicopter had landed and a tall black man dressed in military green and a Kenya Army beret approached the schoolhouse, followed by an armed soldier and, much to Max's and David's alarm, Olabon.

"That son of a bitch couldn't wait," said Max.

"Don't be so sure," said David, noting that Olabon did not seem at all happy about this affair. In fact, the soldier was prodding him along with his rifle.

"Jambo," said David as he stepped outside his schoolhouse.

"Jambo," said the tall black man in a gruff tone of voice. Despite his military attire, he bore no identification. "We are searching for Oscar Newman. He is wanted for the murder of Francis Dermenjian. This Maasai tells us he helped bring a man here who fits his description."

"Why yes," said David. "Yes, this is the fellow who brought us our latest guest. Nice to see you again. Come look, he's doing much better. But if it's Oscar Newman you're seeking, I'm afraid you'll be quite disappointed."

David led them both into his small quarters, where Jack McGraw lay upon the cot, his head turned to one side, facing away from them. The IV stand was still next to the cot. The soldier remained outside. Max knelt down next to Jack and felt his pulse.

"We think he's going to make it," he said, "thanks to this fellow."

He was gesturing toward Olabon, who wore an expression that conveyed both fear and confusion. The black man with the Kenya Army beret approached the cot.

"Let me see his face," he demanded.

"Certainly," said Max as he grabbed the back of Jack's head and turned it toward him. Jack let his tongue fall out of his mouth but kept his eyes shut, clearly overdoing it. The black man in the beret pulled a picture from his shirt pocket. He examined it carefully, then knelt down next to Jack and held the photograph next to his face. There was indeed a slight resemblance, mostly the broad face and beard, but this was not Oscar Newman.

"Olabon!" he shouted. Words were exchanged in Swahili. David, standing behind the black man in the beret, kept his eyes locked onto Olabon's.

"Is this the man you rescued?"

Olabon, Maasai to the core, showed but little interest in this questioning as he slowly stepped toward him and peered down at Jack McGraw. As Olabon raised his head, David caught his attention. He was holding a piece of paper upon which he had quickly scribbled, legibly enough, "3,000,000."

Olabon rubbed his chin. The black man in the beret, who was even taller than Olabon, glared at him, awaiting his response.

Olabon looked at David, then at Max, then at the black man who'd brought him to this spot once again.

"Yes," he said, "yes, of course this is the man I rescued." He spoke in Swahili with a sharpness, a disdain that said, "You have wasted enough of my time—now take me home."

"Damn you," shouted the tall black man.

Before David could reprimand him for his use of foul language, he bolted through the door and headed back toward the helicopter. A half-dozen moran had gathered nearby and were busy examining the large metal craft.

"Get back," the man shouted as he approached. The soldier, with Olabon in tow, followed behind. The Maasai laughed, amused by this large fellow's impatience.

"What are you staring at?" he yelled as all eyes focused upon him. "Get your sorry asses out of the way before you get your heads cut off."

The pilot, who had remained in the craft, had already fired up the engines. As soon as the blades began to spin, the young warriors quickly stepped back out of the way and crouched in unison. Something in their movements struck the black man as funny. With a wave of his hand he signaled to the pilot to cut the power. He walked toward them, laughing to himself, and asked how they were faring.

"Well enough," said one of the moran, a tall fellow who was a bit hunched over as he kept a close eye on the blades of the helicopter.

"What is your name?" asked the black man.

"Ntanda," he said.

"Do you speak for your comrades?"

The young Maasai stepped forward, one hand clutching his spear, the other clutching his side. "Yes," he replied, "I speak for my people."

"What's the matter with you?" he inquired. "Are you injured?"

His friends began to laugh, knowing he would deny it.

"It is nothing," he replied.

"Let me see," said the stranger as he reached out to pull Ntanda's arm away from his side. There was pus dripping from a small puncture wound. "What happened?"

Ntanda remained silent.

"He was shot," said one of the other moran, "by the Ugandans."

"Ah," said the black fellow, "I see. Well, you should go and see the doctor over there. He can treat your wound. But first please tell me, how do you plan to defend yourselves when the Ugandans come to take your cattle, come to take your food, come to take your women? With your spears? And your shields, will they stop bullets as well?"

He began to laugh again as if it was the funniest thing he could imagine, the Maasai attempting to hold off, with their primitive spears and shields, hundreds of well-armed, malnourished, and consequently desperate refugees intent on survival at all costs.

Ntanda walked toward him, unamused by this chiding. "And what would you suggest?" he asked.

The black man turned and made a motion with one hand toward the soldier who was standing with Olabon next to the helicopter. He apparently understood, as he removed a long wooden box from a compartment on the side of the helicopter and carried it over to him. The black man removed a large knife from his belt and pried the box open. Inside were a dozen new rifles, dull green but with a luster that indicated they had never been fired.

The black man picked one up and handed it to Ntanda. Then he passed the rest around to the others and showed them how to aim, how to pull the trigger.

"AK-47," he said, "most reliable weapon around." He pulled a round of shells from inside the wooden box and inserted the clip. "Metal-piercing bullets, top of the line."

Ntanda said he did not believe that any bullets could pass through metal. "Let us see you shoot one through your flying machine," he said, pointing to the helicopter. The black man laughed once more.

"Don't be stupid," he scoffed. "Why would I want to shoot my own helicopter?" He scouted the land for something equally substantial, something metallic.

"What is that?" he inquired, pointing toward a rusted old tank set a short way up the hill beyond the schoolhouse.

"Just an old water tank," said one of the moran.

"If I can shoot a hole in that tank, will you buy some of these rifles? You will surely need them."

Ntanda looked at the ground before replying. "We can only offer you cattle," he said.

The black man laughed once again. "No, you can indeed offer much more than cattle. My boss is fond of these," he said, producing a small handful of gemstones from his coat pocket.

"We have no stones such as those," said Ntanda.

"Perhaps you do," the black man replied, "but you just haven't found them. All we ask is permission to look for them."

Ntanda laughed. This was crazy. All they wanted in return for guns the Maasai needed to defend themselves was the chance to look for stones they would never find?

"This is too easy," said Ntanda. "Let us see you pierce the metal with your bullet."

The black man smiled a very broad smile, slowly nodded, and raised the rifle. He paused for a split second to aim and then pulled the trigger.

Perhaps it had once been an old water tank, but now it was clearly full of petrol—or at least it was until the bullet pierced the container and detonated the contents in one huge blast that sent flames shooting high into the sky, igniting the trees and shrubs nearby. David and Max came barreling out of the schoolhouse in a state of great alarm. David ran behind the schoolhouse and began cranking on the generator.

"Grab the hose!" he shouted to Max, who searched alongside the schoolhouse until he found a long garden hose and began to unfurl it, moving as quickly as he could toward the fire.

The explosion was heard throughout Maasailand. Joseph had been stirring his morning tea when the blast occurred and was so alarmed he dropped his cup in his lap. He stepped outside and saw everyone running. Then he turned and looked to the west, where he saw the huge column of billowing smoke. By the time he arrived, there were already hundreds of Maasai attempting to beat down the flames that, in spite of the rains the night before, were spreading rapidly.

The black man was shouting orders to the soldier, telling him to help put out the fire. But he was too frightened, clearly bent on fleeing as he tried to force Olabon back into the helicopter. Joseph saw his son standing nearby, still holding a rifle in his hands.

"Ntanda!" his father shouted.

He turned around, defiant as always.

"What have you done?" he screamed.

"He did it," said Ntanda, pointing to the black man, who was still trying to coerce the soldier into helping to stop the fire. Joseph stared at the man with instinctive, abject hatred.

"Who are you?" Joseph demanded in Swahili, "and why do you come and start fires in Maasailand?"

"I am sorry," he said, "I was just showing these boys how to fire a weapon. They said it was an old water tank."

"Get out of here with your weapons," Joseph shouted, "before we throw *you* into that fire!"

"Whatever you say," he replied. "But I'll tell you what, you can keep the rifles. You're going to need them."

He simply turned his back and walked toward the helicopter. Joseph shouted at him to come take his weapons, but the man kept on walking. As he climbed into the large glass bubble, Joseph motioned to Ntanda and the other moran to throw the rifles in with him.

They quickly picked up the rifles, threw them into the wooden box, and carried it as fast as they could toward the helicopter. The pilot had started the engines, and as the blades began to twirl, they had to stoop as they ran. They reached the glass bubble just as the black man closed the door. He waved and smiled at them through the roar of the engines. The blades picked up considerable speed, and the rush of air sent the many ochred braids of the young moran flying in all directions. As the helicopter began to lift off, they crouched down low and heaved the box up onto the two parallel landing skids. One end rested precariously up against one of the struts that descended from the body of the aircraft. As the machine took off, the other end of the rifle box slammed up against the other strut. The moran all covered their faces as a dense cloud of dust and tiny stones swirled about them at great speed. Joseph watched the blue machine rise and hover before the blades tilted forward and it moved out, right in the direction of the fire. It passed no more than fifty feet directly above. The huge blast of air delivered by its powerful blades caught the flames and nourished them in a wild rush that radiated from the ring of fire, sending flames shooting up into the faces of some of the Maasai as they used their shields and spare hides to quell the fire. Far worse, however, was the inevitable flight of the box of AK-47 assault rifles, complete with several ammunition cartridges, right down into the middle of the flames.

Ntanda and his friends watched in awe as the box slipped off the skids and spilled its contents, each weapon and the ammunition clips tumbling slowly through the air toward the burning grasses and forbs below.

"Entapal!" shouted Ntanda. Clear out!

It was difficult for him to be heard, but as the helicopter veered off to the north and the noise and wind dissipated, Ntanda began running frantically along the edge of the fire, yelling at everyone to duck and cover. Few of them complied, but when the first ammunition clip exploded they quickly understood. The remaining cartridges exploded like strings of firecrackers. Miraculously, no one was injured.

Once the fire was more or less extinguished and disaster had been averted, Joseph looked at the charred rifles strewn among the ashes, then turned toward Ntanda.

"Dig a pit and throw them in. These weapons do not belong in Maasailand."

"As you wish, Father," his son replied. "Besides, they are useless. All the ammunition has been destroyed."

While Ntanda and his friends buried the rifles, David and Max made sure the schoolhouse had been sufficiently wetted down and would not succumb to the flames that had crept to within ten feet of the old wooden structure.

"That was close," said Max. "But it's safe now and I need to check on Oscar."

David merely nodded, then cast his gaze sadly toward all the smoldering ashes that had once been more or less his front yard.

Max slid the rug, table and all, to one side and lifted the hatch. The first step of the small ladder was just visible, but then it descended into darkness. It smelled stale and musty.

"Oscar?" Max whispered, not wishing to alarm him in case he was sleeping. There was no reply.

"Oscar?" he repeated as he crouched and felt his way toward the cot until Oscar's voice erupted, stronger than the night before.

"Yes?" he replied at long last.

"Oscar, are you okay?" said Max, grabbing him by the arm. His eyes were beginning to adjust. The small patch of light from the modest opening above was just enough for Max to see that Oscar was alert, that he was lying comfortably, staring straight up at the ceiling.

"I can't say," he replied. "What in God's name happened out there?"

"It was Dermenjian's agents," said Max, "looking for you. But we threw them off the trail. Unfortunately, they set the whole place on fire and we've been fighting the flames ever since. Are you sure you're all right?"

"Well," he said, "I believe I'm still alive, if nothing else."

"That will have to do for now. Give me your hand and I'll help you up," said Max, sliding his hand down Oscar's forearm.

"Try the other hand," said Oscar.

"The other hand?" Max replied. "But what's wrong with this one?"

"Nothing's wrong with it. It's merely occupied."

Max looked at the hand that at first glance appeared quite unencumbered. But as he stared at it a moment longer, peering through the darkness, he noticed that the hand was shaped like a cup, as if it was holding something.

"What are you talking about?" said Max. "What have you got in your hand?"

"Semen," said Oscar.

"What?" cried Max.

"Hush," said Oscar. "I said I have semen in my hand."

Max couldn't believe his ears. Had Oscar gone delirious again? He placed one hand on his forehead. For the first time since they'd recovered him, it felt cool. The fever was really gone.

"Whose semen have you got, Oscar?"

There came a large sigh. "Mine, you idiot."

258

Max took a deep breath, feeling another rush of anger and frustration overwhelm his tired body.

"I can't believe it," he said. "I just can't believe it. We've been out there saving your goddamn life—again, mind you. Not just David and me but all the Maasai for miles around have been trying to keep the schoolhouse from burning down, with you in it, while you're down here merrily whacking off. Besides, you shouldn't overexert like that."

Oscar turned his head toward Max. "I did not overexert," he said rather calmly. "It's been quite a while since I've been with a woman."

This was unbelievable.

"Yeah, tell me about it," said Max, newly infuriated.

"I trust you have a good microscope on hand?" Oscar inquired, catching Max quite off guard.

"A microscope?"

"Yes, a microscope. I have been suffering from high fever for far too long. And you know very well what that can do to a fellow."

But of course. It made perfect sense, for once.

Chapter 34

The air was soft and delicate and the jalousies, mounted on the French doors along the thick, south-facing wall, were turned downward, admitting but a tiny fraction of the midmorning light. Wisps of steam scented with jasmine filled the room. The only sounds breaking the silence were the periodic groans emitted by Peter Dermenjian as he suffered through the long, slow, and very deep kneading of his back, shoulder, and thigh muscles by a tall, blond masseuse. She was a good six feet in height, with a straw-colored braid tightly wound into a knot on top of her head.

But in an instant the tranquility was gone. From somewhere nearby came the whining of a cell phone. Every muscle in Peter's face tightened as he rolled over. The tall masseuse handed him the wafer-thin phone, and he immediately dismissed her with a wave of his hand.

"Banyon," he said, "did you get him?"

There was a long silence. As he listened his demeanor changed from one of deep interest to one of deep concern to one of intense anger.

"Are you telling me it wasn't him?" he shouted.

He listened until he could no longer bear it, interrupting only to emphasize his extreme displeasure. To mistake Oscar for another stranded wayfarer was one travesty costing him plenty, but setting fire to Maasailand was another.

"What about the weapons?"

Again he listened closely but his expression turned even more dour. Dr. Meinz entered the room just as Peter was hanging up in disgust.

"Damn it!" he shouted.

"Then it was not Newman after all," said Dr. Meinz.

Peter rose abruptly from the table, wrapping a white robe all about himself. "No, it was not Newman," he fumed. "It was some American prospector who apparently bore some resemblance."

Dr. Meinz looked rather perplexed. "But the Maasai swore he had brought the man all the way from Gelai. How can it be that two white men both become stranded in such a remote area at the same time? What are the odds?"

"Yes," said Peter, "what are the odds. Unless there were three of them."

"The third being the prospector."

"Of course, a prospector, a geologist. But surely we would have seen him. Perhaps he was camped elsewhere, closer to the kimberlite. We must speak with him. Get Banyon on the line again."

Dr. Meinz nodded before turning to leave, sweat dripping from his brow. As he reached the door to the steam room, he turned back.

"And what happened to the Maasai boy?" he said.

"According to Banyon," Peter replied with a trace of a smile, "he received his just reward."

"Pity," said Dr. Meinz as he studied the condensation on one sleeve of his faded blue jacket. "He might have told us more."

Dr. Meinz exited just as Natalia, a slim, young Russian woman with short black hair, entered. Without speaking, she grasped Peter's hand and led him to a plush leather chair. She placed his fingers into precast molds that were fixed to the sides of the chair and filled with oils. Then she walked behind him and placed her hands alongside his temples.

"It has been a hard time, yes?" she inquired. Her soft, throaty voice was soothing and she began to massage his scalp very gently, beginning with the temples and working slowly back toward the base of his skull.

"Yes," he replied in a subdued whisper, "far too difficult a time."

"Then you will let me know how I may help with the tension."

"Without fail," he replied as he attempted to relax once again. She pressed her fingertips firmly against his forehead and pulled the skin upward, forcing his eyes to open wide and exposing his tear ducts to the soft, steamy air.

"I am sorry to interrupt but I cannot reach him," Dr. Meinz reported as he reentered the room. Peter remained momentarily silent while Natalia's hands massaged the facial muscles just beneath his cheekbones.

"Then where the hell is he?" he asked in a measured tone.

"No doubt somewhere well removed from a place where you might reach him," Dr. Meinz replied.

"No doubt," he shouted, quickly losing whatever self-control he had found earlier. "I don't care where he is. Just get hold of him and tell him to go back for the prospector. We need to find out all he knows about these bloody diamonds."

"Very well, sir."

"And what about Elizabeth?" Peter continued as he settled back into the chair again, straining to compose himself. "Are you certain she is comfortable?"

"Absolutely," Dr. Meinz replied. "I can assure you she is very comfortable. She is on the lower terrace, by the pool, if you wish to see her."

Peter closed his eyes as Natalia grasped his right hand and began to massage his cuticles. "Yes," he said, "I believe I will join her for lunch."

The lower terrace was immense, offering a panoramic view of the Mediterranean. It was situated at the base of the villa, all of which was nestled into the seaward side of the dark red volcanic rock that forms the Massif de l'Estérel to the southwest of Cannes. Lying just below a ridgeline, it afforded splendid views while turning its back on the cold mistral winds. From a distance, the crisp whiteness and columned walkways of the estate stood in stark contrast to the red rock and the dull *garrigue* that covered these hills wherever the bedrock permitted. It was indeed quite a fortress.

And upon the lower terrace, beside the soft-blue water of a long, sleek pool that reflected the perfect Mediterranean sky, Elizabeth Le Clerc sat alone in a wrought-iron chair before a round, glass-topped table, sipping a cup of tea. Behind her rows of lavender rimmed the walkway beside the pool. Just a few feet from the table was a long stone wall that bordered the entire terrace, beyond which the land simply fell away. She sat quietly and rather calmly, gazing out at the vista toward the deep-blue Mediterranean, and beyond the Mediterranean, toward Africa.

She was dressed in black, her clothes loose and flowing in the breeze rising up the face of the cliff. It was like a soft, familiar caress, reminiscent of childhood. Her dark glasses obscured the light and seemed to shield her from the rest of the world as well. She took another sip from her cup.

"More tea, mademoiselle?"

It was a voice that seemed to come from nowhere in particular, familiar but somehow foreign. She looked up and saw a face staring down at her. It belonged to a young, dark-haired man, another member of Peter's staff.

"Yes," she replied, "that would be very nice."

"Monsieur Dermenjian wishes to know if he might join you," he added as he filled her cup from a sterling-silver decanter.

Elizabeth stared blankly. "Of course," she replied. "I would welcome his company." Somewhere in her muddled thoughts it seemed there was something else she had to say, but whatever it was soon vanished from her mind and she returned to sipping her tea and staring off into the distance.

"Excellent," replied the young server, who then quickly disappeared.

She remained staring out toward the vast Mediterranean, motionless, quite listless, thinking she should perhaps check on Eleanor, Oscar's poor mother, who Peter had insisted would be most welcome. She was in a room somewhere upstairs. But thankfully, Dr. Meinz was looking after her and she could visit later, when she had a bit more energy.

"It is nice to see you out among the elements on this beautiful day."

She turned her head slowly. Peter Dermenjian was approaching her small table. He smiled as he sat down before her, wearing but a white robe and slippers. His dark hair was moist and combed straight back. There was just a slight tinge of gray above the ears.

"I trust you are finding everything to your satisfaction?" he inquired.

She hesitated before responding, apparently content to simply stare at this gracious and very handsome man who had afforded her every courtesy and every comfort since Oscar's disappearance. Despite the tinges of gray, he seemed rather youthful, with all his features quite alive and attentive, particularly his riveting blue eyes set beneath a very inquisitive brow.

"Yes," she said at last, "everything here is quite satisfactory. I cannot thank you enough."

"There is no need to thank me. It is indeed my pleasure to have you as my guest. I was hoping you wouldn't mind if I joined you for lunch here on the terrace. André has prepared a wonderful bouillabaisse. Would that appeal to you?"

Was it already lunchtime? Elizabeth could not remember what she had eaten earlier, but there seemed no reason to refuse.

"Yes, that would be lovely," she replied.

Peter waved his hand, and within seconds the young staff member who had kept her teacup full all morning appeared. Peter submitted to him precise orders for André. As the young man departed, Peter turned to face Elizabeth once again. She stared at him in silence, as if in a trance.

"You have remarkable hands," she said.

If this comment caught him off guard, he did not let it show. He had been gesturing with his hands while ordering lunch and assumed it was the sparkle of the large reddish-yellow diamond set in the gold ring on his right hand that had caught her eye.

"You mean the ring?" he replied. "It was a gift from my father."

"I wasn't talking about the ring," she said. "I meant that you have remarkable hands."

"Why, thank you," said Peter, maintaining his aplomb. "I do my best to take care of them. They're important tools of the trade."

She appeared slightly confused. "I don't understand."

"It's quite simple," he continued. "I buy and sell diamonds for a living. Occasionally, other precious gems as well. I can tell you more about the quality of a particular gemstone just from the feel of it than most others in the profession can with all their hand lenses and microscopes. The cut, the carat, the purity—all these attributes can be sensed by these delicate instruments."

He was holding his hands out before her, turning them over for her to inspect, as if in awe of them himself.

"Do you mean you can detect flaws in the cut of a diamond simply by feeling it?" she asked.

"Oh yes, much more readily than by tedious visual examination."

"That's amazing."

"Yes," he replied, "but not as amazing as André's bouillabaisse."

For as he was speaking, one of André's minions was serving the *soupe de poissons*. Another followed behind with a platter of fish and then another with the rouille and other side dishes to round out the meal.

"This is all quite delicious," she said.

"André is the envy of all my friends. I cannot tell you how much I've been offered for his services."

"I can well imagine," she replied, feeling a bit out of her element, but with all the strangeness that had befallen her lately, she did not dwell on it. The wine, a nicely chilled rosé, was cold and crisp, and it almost seemed as though her arms and hands were simply bent on feeding her even though she still wasn't sure if she had an appetite for such rich food. It didn't seem to matter.

"I will be leaving for London tomorrow," said Peter.

"Really?" said Elizabeth.

"No need to worry," he reassured her. "I will be back in a few days, and you will be well looked after in my absence."

"But we must be getting back to Scotland."

"Nonsense," he replied. "Why return to that dismal old country when it's so beautiful right here? Besides, I want you to remain, at least until we've received some definitive word about Oscar."

Upon hearing Oscar's name Elizabeth lowered her head. "That's very kind of you," she said softly. "But it just seems as though we should be getting back. I feel we've already overstayed our welcome, and we may never receive definitive word about Oscar."

"That may be," he conceded, "but my people are doing everything in their power to locate him. Besides, you've only been here a few days. I want you to simply feel at home."

"Home was never like this," she confessed. "But why must you go to London?"

"London?" he replied, wiping his chin with his napkin. "Why, De Beers is in London. The Diamond Trading Company. Nearly eighty percent of all the raw diamonds sold anywhere in the world are sold there, bought by fortunate people such as me. We're known as sight holders. We put in our orders some weeks in advance, and about ten times a year the De Beers company offers us each a small box of diamonds. Price fixed, take it or leave it."

"That doesn't sound very fair," she observed.

"Fair?" he responded. "If you mean that one ought to be able to haggle over the prices and which diamonds are acceptable and which ones aren't, then I suppose you're right. But it's really the only game in town. And it's been going on like this for decades, so, in the end, I suppose it must be fair or people like me wouldn't put up with it."

"And what sort of diamonds are you looking for this time?"

Peter froze. He lowered his fork. "I am looking for diamonds like this one," he said as he set down his spoon and extended his right hand toward her. She gazed at the large diamond embedded in the gold ring.

"Look at it carefully," he said. "Have you ever seen anything quite like it?"

The tone of his voice, suddenly much more intense, and the expression in his eyes, almost flecked with anger, told her she should look very carefully.

"It's beautiful," she said, "such an unusual color. It's so yellow and red, like the setting sun. I don't believe I've ever seen a diamond like that before."

"Yes, in fact, that's what we call them, the sunset diamonds. There are only a few of them besides this one, and they are all in my vault. But I have heard that recently there's been a discovery, in Africa, of diamonds that are very similar in nature."

"Really?" She looked into his eyes and nearly jumped back into her chair; his expression looked like that of a madman. "Are you all right?" she asked.

"Yes," he replied, calming himself a bit. "I'm quite all right. It's just that I've been searching all my life for the source of this very diamond. It was found by my great-great-grandfather."

"Yes," she replied, "I know. Oscar told me all about it."

"All about what?" he responded, tossing his napkin to the ground.

"All about the Dermenjian family diamonds, about your obsession with finding the source."

It was more than he could bear. He stood up and began to pace.

"It's nothing, really," she pleaded. "Francis told him all about it. I don't know why. It's such a fascinating story."

"Indeed it is," he replied, taking his seat once again and composing himself. He raised one hand to hail the young server. "Would you care for coffee?"

Chapter 35

Charterhouse Street had all the appearances of a not-so-normal workday, one that occurred every fifth Monday when three hundred or so diamond dealers and manufacturers came to town to see what De Beers had to offer. Peter carried no briefcase and no overcoat despite the crisp air that held the last wisps of the morning's slowly dissipating fog. He nodded politely to a few familiar faces as he made his way to the Diamond Trading Company. Once through the front door, with its diamond-shaped panels, he quickly headed up two flights of stairs, avoiding the elevator. There was a briskness and purpose in his step as he made his way through surprisingly uncongested corridors to one of a number of small rooms. There was a coded entry, and he pressed several small buttons to the left of the door before it clicked and opened automatically. He closed the door and approached a small sliding-glass window. A young woman, blond and quite attractive, smiled and slid open the two-by-two-foot pane of glass within the wall that separated them.

"Good day to you, Mr. Dermenjian," she said as she took a seat on the side opposite from Peter. "I think you'll like what we have for you today."

She reached down and took hold of a small wooden box and then placed it on the surface between them and pushed it through the window. Peter took hold of it with trembling hands. He could not help himself. No matter how many times he'd approached this window with no fanfare whatsoever, merely to conduct a business transaction, his heart would race and near panic would ensue as he waited impatiently to find out whether the long-missing Dermenjian diamonds had been rediscovered. But this time was different. He himself held one of the new generation of Dermenjian sunset diamonds, albeit a very small one, one that had been embedded in a piece of kimberlite he'd found on top of his brother's Land Rover. So they had been rediscovered by his brother and his obese friend, both of whom appeared to be quite dead. He wondered if Banyon had found that prospector. But most of all he wondered what was in the box.

He turned and placed it on a countertop in front of a tall, north-facing window, the proper lighting for viewing diamonds. For it was under such conditions that raw, rough diamonds were graded and sorted by color, by shape, and by weight into over three thousand varieties, a very long and tedious process. As always, Peter had submitted his order for certain sizes and shapes of diamonds and, in particular, certain colors. Yet it was more like a request than an order since De Beers, while always doing its best to accommodate the desires of its sight holders, also had to be careful not to dole out too many exceptional diamonds at once, since to do so would risk flooding the market and lowering prices.

Peter took a seat before the window and opened the box. It was filled with many small white pieces of paper, each one labeled as "blue speculative spotted" or some other description whose meaning was abundantly clear to the sight holders and to few others. Peter did not bother to even open the folded pieces of paper, each one containing diamonds of corresponding character. He sorted them out until he came across one labeled "yellow unspotted." His hands began trembling again as he tried to carefully unfold the white paper, which seemed to hold a more generous than usual collection of stones. He closed his eyes as he opened the last two folds and felt the small pile of gems with his fingers. There were two of very good size and several "flats," or broken pieces, like small slivers of glass. One of the larger stones was a macle, two diamonds back to back, joined like Siamese twins. He didn't recall ordering any macles. Then he opened his eyes and cast his gaze over the rough stones. They were rather undistinguished except for the exceptional yellow hues that varied from one stone to another. Peter smiled. Although there were plenty of yellow stones, there were none with the distinctive amber hue that was the signature of the Dermenjian sunset diamonds. And since De Beers controlled eighty percent of the world diamond trade, odds were that his brother's discovery was still a secret.

He left all the gemstones there in the room and went down the hall to see who else might be about. He would come back later to finish looking them over, to perform the mundane work of determining whether he agreed with the way De Beers had graded and thus priced each individual gem, which he nearly always did. Only once had he protested the grading of a particular diamond and, after much haggling, De Beers had declared itself correct and the price still firm, take it or leave it. To press further would have only risked being excluded from the club.

There were a few of his acquaintances smoking cigars in the lounge. He nodded as he passed by, seeing no reason to enter and waste time with that pathetic lot. He exited the Diamond Trading Company and turned left down Charterhouse Street. He had in mind a certain eating establishment specializing in Indian cuisine. As he walked he felt that he was being followed. At one point he stopped and turned and saw a small, wiry man wearing a turban dart into a storefront. As he crossed over to Fleet Street, he saw what he thought might be the same dark figure, half a block behind him, pause at a kiosk to read some advertisements. Not unusual, given the large number of Pakistanis in London.

Some thought it rather careless that Peter, a man who relied heavily on all his various staff members, none more so than his personal physician, Dr. Meinz, would travel unaccompanied on these occasions. Yet Peter insisted on it and would not tolerate the suggestions that he employ a bodyguard for the sight holder meetings, when he would often travel with very large sums of money.

He lost sight of the dark, turbaned man until he reached the Nataraja. He entered through several beaded curtains to a darkened room with a number of small tables and booths, one of which he requested. The waiter handed him a menu and he ordered a glass of mineral water. He was still perusing the menu when a distinct, quite unpleasant aroma of garlic and human perspiration distracted him. He looked up as the dark, turbaned man slid into the booth across from him.

"Good day, Mr. Dermenjian," said the man in the turban. As he spoke he produced a large pistol, which he aimed at Peter's heart. His voice was rather rough and his accent was thick, perhaps Indian or Pakistani. He was smiling through a face full of whiskers, revealing a mouthful of heavily stained and very crooked teeth.

"Hello, Achmed, or whatever the hell you're calling yourself this week," said Peter. "What have you got for me? And put that silly thing away. I'm not interested in handguns."

The man looked around carefully, making certain that their conversation would not be overheard and that the gun would go unnoticed. "Oh, but this is no ordinary handgun," he said, rolling it over in what little light there was so Peter might appreciate its beauty. "It is a Luger from 1942, never been fired. I have a dozen or more, very reasonable, too. But, if you like, I have some other very exceptional devices that might interest you more." He giggled a bit as he placed the pistol below the table, well out of the way.

"Like what?"

"How would you like a few tanks, or a Humvee? Very good condition, 2011 model. Complete with antiaircraft guns and missile launchers."

"Too large for my tastes. All I need are serious guns, rifles."

"I know," said the man, again giggling to himself.

"What's so damn funny, you crazy Arab, or whatever the hell you are?"

269

There had been times when Achmed appeared to him as a gypsy or as a drunken sailor. No one seemed to know from where he originated or what allegiance he owed to any particular country, if any. It was rumored he grew up in Brooklyn.

"I heard about the mess you made in Kenya," he said, stifling more laughter. "It doesn't sound like your little scheme is working."

Peter took a sip of mineral water, trying to remain calm. Achmed asked the waiter for a pint of beer. "It will work, believe me. But I will need more rifles. And a little help."

"I can give you the same as last time," he continued, covering what little of his face was not obscured by his dark beard and filthy turban as he struggled to keep from bursting into hysterics. The smell of garlic and sweat was nearly overpowering.

"That would be fine," said Peter, ignoring his taunting. "But make it double. The refugees took more than I'd anticipated. I'll make the usual arrangements."

"Are you certain you wouldn't be interested in something a bit more exciting than AK-47s?"

"I told you I'm not interested in any tanks or Humvees."

"I'm not talking about tanks or Humvees. I'm talking serious weaponry."

"How serious?"

"How serious can you get?"

Peter gave him a curious look. The man was a maniac to be sure. He was nearly in tears, apparently finding this exchange terribly amusing. "What the hell are you talking about? How serious?"

"Well, shall we say *atomically* serious?"

Peter looked at him with disbelief. "Are you saying you've got some of that plutonium that was smuggled off that ship?"

"Perhaps," he replied, smiling as he took a sip of beer. "Are you a little more impressed with me now?"

Peter looked at him and shook his head. "No. And I'm not interested."

Chapter 36

The days following his rescue were rather difficult ones, made all the more so by the extreme depression that overwhelmed Oscar as the realization took hold that his manhood was no doubt extinguished forever. Max tried to tell him it might be only temporary, that such depressed motility was sometimes just a short-lived side effect of extreme malarial fever. Oscar agreed, but only in the context that his seeds, which he, too, saw under the microscope and all of which exhibited no motility whatsoever, were indeed very short lived. He saw them lying still and lifeless by the millions, their little tails dormant, not a squiggle in the bunch.

To make matters worse, there was the delicate matter of Elizabeth's whereabouts. Using Christine's satellite phone, David called the apartment in Glasgow. No answer and the voice mail was full. He tried the cottage on Mull but again no answer, mailbox full again. No wonder, he thought, with so many questions regarding Oscar's whereabouts.

"Can't you just call her cell phone?" said Christine.

"Right," said David. "Oscar, what's her number?"

Oscar lay still, looking somewhat perplexed. "I can't quite remember," he replied. "She's simply number one on my contact list."

"Wonderful," said Christine. "And I suppose your cell phone was eaten by the lion."

David finally managed to contact the University of Glasgow, where Elizabeth was still presumably employed, but no one there knew where Elizabeth might be, either. Oscar concluded she must still be at her mother's but that was certainly one phone number he had never committed to memory.

David, however, had written Madame Le Clerc's unlisted number down in his address book. Why hadn't he asked for Christine's cell phone number? All this information-age technology. He had never even owned such a device as it would be quite useless this far away from the most remote cell tower, unlike the satellite phone he now held in his hand.

David dialed the number. Much to his astonishment, Jacques answered on the second ring. They began speaking in French as Jacques provided an update regarding Elizabeth. David's entire expression froze as Jacques explained that she had accepted an invitation from Peter Dermenjian to spend a few days at his nearby villa while his associates continue the search for Oscar Newman. So far, no news.

David was mortified. Nevertheless he replied in kind that there was no news on his end either. He asked Jacques to pass along his regards to Elizabeth, and that he would phone again if there should be any news. Jacques provided the number for Peter's villa which David alleged he was writing down. Hanging up, he realized he needed to keep this dreadful news to himself, for now at least. It would be far too devastating for Oscar. And he certainly was not about to call Peter's villa, bearing the news that Oscar was indeed alive!

"Jacques has just informed me that Elizabeth is no longer staying with her mother," said David. "He believes she has returned to Scotland."

That disclosure, another pure fabrication by Father David, evinced more head scratching until Max suggested phoning the police in Marseille or asking the British embassy to intervene. Oscar recoiled in horror at such suggestions. He reiterated that he wanted no contact with any authorities whatsoever, at least not until he was safely reunited with Elizabeth. Nor would he permit David or Max to leave a message with anyone regarding his own state of affairs. For Oscar realized all too well that aside from being at least temporarily impotent, he was now a fugitive who was wanted by the authorities, as well as the actual perpetrator, for a crime he did not commit.

Far too many bleak thoughts stirred inside him as the fog that had enveloped his consciousness for weeks, ever since the fever first struck, slowly lifted, and he began to reassemble the shattered fragments of his life. For security reasons, he spent most of his time sequestered in David's priest hole, lying upon the cot, staring into the darkness. Max and David knew Peter Dermenjian's people would return. It was only a matter of time. But where else to hide him?

It was rank and musty down in this earthen pit that had been rather crudely excavated below David's living quarters. It smelled of damp earth and small rodents. But Oscar did not mind. The quiet darkness of the priest hole suited him. It was the closest thing he could imagine to death. For with all his fortunes turned against him, he came very close to feeling there was nothing left to live for. Every thought that he was able to formulate in any clear manner—such as how Elizabeth, if he did succeed somehow in getting back to her at all, would react to him now that he was merely a drone—brought him only more pain. Would she still marry him? Or would it matter? For it was also quite possible that he could end up spending the rest of his wretched life in some horrible prison or perhaps be mercifully executed for the alleged murder of Francis Dermenjian.

Aside from such dreadful anguish, the pain in his lion-clawed chest and alkali-burned legs and back had subsided only to the point of being barely tolerable without medication to numb it. Max offered to renew his prescription but Oscar refused, complaining that the medicine numbed his brain as well. What was more, his lips and tongue and the insides of his cheeks were still covered with blisters from all the exposure and dehydration. Max applied a special salve every morning to the open fissures in his lower lip, which resembled the creases in a loaf of bread that had been baked under the merciless African sun.

But beyond the sadness and the discomfort, what disturbed him most of all was the slowly dawning recognition that the new path he had chosen, his new track toward becoming a husband and a father, a "proper trustee of his own genetic endowment," beginning with this idiotic pilgrimage to the cradle of civilization, had merely succeeded in derailing his entire life. He had already forsaken his foremost accomplishment, one to which he had dedicated nearly all his energy and resources, the Newman Foundation. It was now presumably in the hands of another presumably capable man, in another country. But reports from Max indicated that the Newman Foundation was falling on its knees without Oscar Newman, its founder, the man who had garnered not only fame but a Nobel Prize as well for all his selfless efforts. Yet this thought, the idea of returning to help revive the Newman Foundation, to help achieve its many lofty goals, had no appeal whatsoever. As a drone, what did it matter? He was no longer a part of the human equation.

He had lain for quite some time in the priest hole, rolling all these ugly thoughts around in the dim recesses of his mind, when the trapdoor opened unexpectedly. He could hear the sound of footsteps on the treads of the steep, narrow stairs, but he could not identify them. It wasn't David or Max and certainly not Christine. He briefly wondered if it might not be Peter Dermenjian or one of his agents coming to either interrogate him or put him out of his misery. That would be all right. Might as well get it over with.

"Hey, Oscar," came a familiar voice. "You awake?"

The lanky frame of Jack McGraw was silhouetted against the dim light that fell through the trapdoor. Oscar did not respond.

273

"Ain't ya got no light down here?" said Jack as he tried to feel his way toward Oscar's cot. "Must be a candle or somethin' somewhere."

Oscar heaved a great sigh. "I thought you would have gone back to your prospecting by now," he said, his voice less rough than in previous days but still sounding like there was a handful of gravel in his vocal cords. And his swollen tongue and swollen lips made speaking that much more of an effort. His words were all a bit slurred.

"Ouch!" said Jack as he bumped his head on a low, rough-hewn beam after closing the trapdoor. He paused and struck a match. Oscar covered his eyes.

"There," said Jack as he made his way toward a small table. "I knew there had to be a candle or somethin'." Jack also found a small stool that he brought close to Oscar's side, along with the candle. "So how're ya feelin'?" he asked. "Need any more blood?"

Oscar almost laughed in spite of his state of depression. "I think I'll be all right for a while," he replied, "as long as the fever stays away. Thank you again for the donation."

"Don't mention it," said Jack as he peered around at the dilapidated cupboards and shelves that lined the small space. "We all got to help each other out when we can."

The words, though innocently spoken, resonated deeply.

"Yes," said Oscar, "reciprocal altruism, that's what it's all about."

"What in blazes are you talking about? You still crazy?"

Oscar heaved another large sigh. "Oh, it's nothing," he said. "Just something Francis used to talk about, helping one another."

"Too bad about that fella. But I still don't get why his brother killed him."

Oscar stiffened as the vision of Francis slumping to the ground beside the stranded Land Rover returned, a vision that had come to haunt him in the past few days as his memory slowly recovered.

"Perhaps it was an accident," said Oscar.

"Well," said Jack, "you seen it. You said he wasn't but two feet away. That don't sound like no accident. And then he blames it on you, for God's sake. That don't sound like no accident. What d'ya suppose the old padré's got in all these cupboards?"

Oscar thought about replying, but Jack was already up peeking through drawers full of papers and prospecting behind old pieces of canvas that covered many of the shelves.

"Hey, look at this," said Jack, producing an old photo album that contained pictures of David in his youth. There were also some photos of his ordainment, showing him kissing the ring of some bishop who was wearing a brilliant red robe trimmed with gold and wearing a large double-pointed bishop's hat that was also red and gold. He showed the photos to Oscar, who smiled politely but then suggested that these were personal items and wouldn't it be better to respect David's privacy.

Jack returned the photo album but continued to snoop, peeking behind the canvas drapes and looking through various cupboards filled with canned goods. He found some tins of foie gras and caviar, jars of who-knows-what-type of delicacies or condiments, for all the labels were in French. Jack showed each item to Oscar, who kept imploring him to stop his snooping. Besides, he was stirring up a considerable amount of dust and Oscar was beginning to cough. Finally, Jack said he'd seen enough.

But he couldn't help himself. There was one more set of shelves, covered with a dingy, oil-stained cloth. He pulled it back and, much to his delight, discovered four cases of wine stacked two by two. He pulled out one of the bottles.

"Hey, Oscar," he said, "look at this."

He brushed the thick layer of dust off the bottle and moved it toward the candle.

"Says here Château M-a-r-g-a-u-x, 1981. Ya think David would miss just one bottle?" Jack inquired without even looking to see Oscar's expression. He was already ripping off the lead foil and studying how to remove the cork. "Be right back," he said.

Before Oscar could raise any objections, Jack was up the stairs and had raised the trapdoor. He returned in a few minutes with a corkscrew and two glasses from David's tiny kitchen.

"You really shouldn't," said Oscar as he watched Jack deftly remove the cork and pour two glasses. He handed one to Oscar.

"Here's to your health," said Jack, grinning ear to ear. "You could use some."

"And you could use some manners," Oscar replied. "You've no right to go rummaging through David's belongings and certainly no right to be opening a very expensive bottle of wine that I'm certain David has been holding on to for some important occasion."

By now Oscar had raised himself up on one elbow and found himself taking a sniff of the delicately fragrant wine that had been imprisoned for so long in that little bottle. It seemed heaven sent. Jack had already consumed his first glass and was pouring another. Oscar concluded that there was no point in trying to keep Jack from imbibing. It was very clear that, without Oscar's help, Jack would drain the entire bottle on his own.

He took a sip. It was a small sip, but the response of his still-swollen tongue, or more precisely the taste buds upon it, as the delicate liquid—the refined essence of some of the world's most precious grapes—rolled over and penetrated these delicate sensory organs, producing an overall effect that was nearly orgasmic in nature. Oscar closed his eyes as the fruit and texture and fragrance attacked his inner senses. For all his misery, it was indeed a sublime moment. He took another sip.

When they had finished the Margaux, Jack opened a Haut-Brion, '86. It went down quite smoothly, but with a touch more tannin than the Margaux. They toasted numerous times to everyone's health, even Dr. Brecht's.

"She's just an old bat, an old German bat," said Jack as he attempted to imitate a bat flying about the room.

"And what about that Christine?" slurred Oscar, his swollen tongue even less functional than before. "She's certainly no bat. More like an angel, speaking of winged creatures."

They both found that remark quite hilarious.

"Ssshhhh," said Oscar, "we don't want to disturb David's classroom."

Jack covered his mouth with one hand but continued to flutter with the other like a bird with one wing. He tried in vain to control his laughter as he strutted about, holding one lanky arm out to his side and waving it up and down.

"Shush, you crazy bastard," whispered Oscar. "And sit down before you crack your skull on one of these beams. Besides, I want to know what the hell you're doing here."

Jack just laughed some more. "I'm gettin' drunk jes' like you," he said, clinging to the stool.

"That's not what I mean," said Oscar rather slowly as he attempted to straighten his jaw. "What I want to know is, if you really are a prospector, what are you looking for and who put you up to it?"

Jack turned suddenly, and his expression changed from the look of a complete drunken fool to one of a man who was guarding a huge secret. He looked around, as if anyone else might be listening, before pouring them each another glass.

"Oscar," he said, looking around again. "Oscar, I found me another gold mine."

He took a drink and then began to laugh once again. Oscar looked at him rather incredulously.

"What do you mean, 'another gold mine'? You've found others?"

"Oh sure, almost a dozen. I'm damn good. But the secret is you got to work alone. Lessee, there was that one in Borneo, that was my first, long time ago. Then way up there in Amazon country, in Brazil. But this one's a beauty. Once I get back to Houston and turn in my samples, I'll be settin' pretty. I'll get a big bonus and then I can pay off *Esmerelda*."

He finished off his glass and poured another. Oscar stared in amazement.

"Who's Esmerelda?" he inquired.

"*Esmerelda*'s my boat. How d'ya think I got all the way over here?"

"By boat? But we're practically in the middle of a desert!"

"Oh, she's parked over in Mombasa. Came the rest of the way by train and then by bus. I bought a mule from this Maasai fellow, only them refugees done shot and ate her. Nearly took all my rock samples, too, but I kept 'em hid till they was gone."

"I can't believe they didn't kill you, too."

"Couldn't catch me. I'm good at hidin' out. Besides, what would they want with me? They ain't cannibals, far as I can tell."

Oscar finished his glass and watched as Jack reached for another bottle. This time he didn't even bother to dust off the label. He just popped the cork and refilled Oscar's glass.

"So where is this bloody gold mine of yours?" said Oscar as he sniffed the bouquet of this next exquisite example of the French vintner's art.

"Oh, it's up in the Loita hills," said Jack, pointing at random to where he thought the Loita hills might be, "where the ol' rift stretched and left a huge crack in the almighty earth's crust, and that let the cauldron down below just bubble up and leave a thick slice of gold-inlaid quartz. But I ain't tellin' nobody exactly where, even you. Not till I get back to Houston, anyways."

The wine was affecting Oscar more than his normal constitution would have permitted. He began to laugh as well, for the first time in several weeks—since New Year's Eve, in fact, when he and Francis had shared a fine bottle of champagne while sitting around the campfire at the foot of Lengai.

"What's so damn funny?" Jack wanted to know.

"Nothing," said Oscar, pausing to wipe the tears of laughter from his eyes. "I was just wondering, have you ever searched for diamonds out this way?"

Jack looked puzzled, more so than usual. "Diamonds?" said Jack. "What, gold ain't good enough for ya?"

Oscar, feeling the full effects of all the wine he'd consumed, broke out into near hysterics. "Gold is golden," he mused, "but diamonds are a girl's best friend!"

For some strange reason Oscar thought that most hilarious. Jack, however, appeared slightly offended, sensing that Oscar was not the least bit impressed with his gold find.

"Ain't no diamonds around here. If there was, that Dermenjian fella, the one that killed his brother, woulda found 'em by now. He's been lookin' all his life."

"I know," said Oscar, still laughing so hard it was more difficult than usual to breathe. "Believe me," he said, "I know."

Jack gave Oscar a suspicious look. "Ain't no diamonds around here," he repeated.

"Oh yes, there are," said Oscar, still laughing but more in the style of a wide-eyed lunatic as he looked up toward the ceiling. Then he turned toward Jack and looked him in the eye while the candlelight flickered. "And I'm the only one alive who knows where they are."

Jack stared back, stunned, possibly spooked. "Goddamn, yer a fuckin' crazy man," he said. "You're still sufferin' from that fever. There ain't no diamonds in this valley. It ain't old enough. You probably just found some old quartz crystals. You may be a pretty good doctor but you ain't no geologist. That's a fact."

Oscar didn't reply. He just rested comfortably, leaning back once again against the stack of pillows behind him, gazing off into nowhere, wearing a silly grin. He sniffed at his wine before finishing it off. Jack looked at him and then downed his glass before pouring them both another.

"All right," said Jack, his prospector's curiosity getting the better of him. "If you ain't denyin' it, then tell me just where in this godforsaken valley you found these fuckin' diamonds."

"I can't tell you," Oscar replied as he held his glass beneath his nose to savor the delicate bouquet.

"Oscar," said Jack, after studying him for a while and noticing how suddenly pleased Oscar seemed with himself. "Maybe you did and maybe you didn't find them diamonds that asshole Dermenjian's been lookin' for. But I can tell you I've got somethin' better. Somethin' a whole lot better."

Oscar rolled onto his side and looked at Jack. He was having some difficulty focusing. "All right," said Oscar, "tell me. What have you got that's a whole lot better than a diamond mine?"

Jack looked around again and moved closer. "I've got my island," he whispered. Then he broke out into total hysteria and stood up, swaying his skinny hips back and forth again as he turned around and around, pretending he was some South Pacific wahine in a grass skirt, just as he had done when Max had first encountered him.

Oscar lay there staring at Crazy Jack as he did his little hula steps, watching and waiting for the oversized trousers Max had loaned him to fall down. His scrawny upper body, covered with a fair patch of gray, was as sinewy as a cheetah's. But what in blazes was he talking about now? What island? It occurred to him that maybe they were both crazy after all.

As this thought turned slowly inside his inebriated brain, Oscar failed to hear the trapdoor open. Nor did either of them hear the footsteps as Max descended into their midst, followed closely by David.

"What's going on here?" David shouted as he took in the scene before him. "And who gave you permission to drink my wine?"

He was staring at Crazy Jack, ignoring the fact that Oscar held half a glass of Chambertin in his hand and didn't seemed at all ashamed of it.

"Please," said Oscar, "Jack was just about to tell me about his island. Pray continue."

Max and David looked at each other in disbelief. Oscar was lying on his side, covering one eye to help him focus his blurry vision. Crazy Jack was back to performing his hula dance, his eyes closed. He ended by nearly tripping over David, who caught him at the last minute.

279

"Great," said Max. "This is really terrific. What the hell are we going to do with you two?"

There was a moment's silence broken only by Oscar.

"I'll tell you one thing you can do," he said, laughing but seemingly in some kind of discomfort as he attempted to stand. "You can help me outside. I could piss an ocean right now."

Max looked over at David, as if for guidance.

"I am very ashamed of both of you," said David as he moved to lend Oscar a hand. "We are facing a considerable crisis and you're not helping us at all."

All the while he was looking at Jack, the undoubted instigator of this little stunt, who was now clinging to the stool for much-needed stability.

"Don't blame it on me," Jack stammered. "I only found a gold mine. Oscar, he says he found a diamond mine. So it's his party, not mine."

Chapter 37

Until this time the motive for the murder of Francis Dermenjian had not been at all clear. Oscar had spoken of the intense jealousy between the two brothers as if that would suffice. That their relationship was very strained was not news to David, but it hardly seemed a sufficient reason for Peter to murder his own brother. Oscar had suggested that there may have been a struggle over the gun, that the murder was really just a tragic accident. But why the gun in the first place? And why would Peter then blame Oscar unless he wanted to be sure that Oscar would be apprehended? Yes, if Francis and Oscar had discovered the long-missing Dermenjian diamonds, David surmised, and if they had refused to divulge the source, then the murder, or at least the threat of violence, began to make more sense. But while the legend of the Dermenjian diamonds was quite familiar to David, to Max it just sounded like a bit of folklore.

"Do you really believe all that nonsense?" said Max as they stood outside the examination tent back at the clinic. Oscar was waiting inside, preparing to endure the drawing of another blood sample along with more probing of his vital signs. Despite the risk of Peter Dermenjian's return, Max had insisted on transferring him and Crazy Jack back to the clinic, where he had access to more proper medical supplies. David, still fuming over the pillaging of his precious wines, did not object.

"It's quite possible," David replied. "Francis told me the story once about his great-great-grandfather's discovery. Let's go inside. It's time we learned the truth."

They both approached Oscar as he lay upon the bed, covering his eyes to keep any light whatsoever from entering his inner world, one that had grown only darker with the after effects of the prior evening's indulgences.

"Oscar," David began, "we were wondering if we might speak to you again about what happened to Francis."

Oscar's body began trembling ever so slightly as these words were spoken. "Certainly," he replied, "but I've told you all I can."

"Yes," said David, "I believe you. But what parts have you left out, parts that you may feel for one reason or another that you can't tell us? For instance, is there any truth to what Crazy Jack said about finding a diamond mine?"

Oscar lay perfectly still, staring up at the canvas ceiling of the tent, watching it flutter as a gentle breeze began to stir outside. He remained silent.

"Oscar," David repeated, "is there any truth to it?"

Finally, Oscar turned his head to look at them. David was wearing his black priest's robe. Max wore his white lab coat.

"Yes," Oscar responded at long last. "It's true."

The manner in which he spoke these words, with a begrudging acknowledgment of a fact he wished he could undo, left no doubt in their minds that Oscar's situation was far more perilous than either of them had suspected.

"Thank you," said David. "That helps to explain quite a bit. The reward, the visit from that fellow with the rifles."

"Where did you find the diamonds?" said Max.

"I'd rather not tell you. Francis insisted it be kept a secret. I promised him I would not tell anyone so long as we both shall live. I believe those were the words I used." Oscar looked away as he finished his sentence.

"I don't suppose it really matters," David suggested.

"Oh, but it does," Oscar rejoined, turning back to look David straight in the eye. "It mattered very much to Francis."

"You mean the location?" said Max.

"Yes," Oscar returned. "It's a very bad place for a diamond mine. In fact, it's a very bad place for almost anything."

"But how did you manage to find these diamonds?" David inquired.

Oscar heaved a great sigh. "I can't tell you that, either."

David looked at Max and, with a subtle nod of his head, motioned him outside the tent where they could caucus. After they had exited, Oscar lay calmly upon the simple bed, somewhat detached yet worried that he was betraying his dearly departed comrade. His recollection of events surrounding their days marooned on the shores of Natron was still somewhat hazy. But he remembered clearly the shattering of stones, about which he had said nothing, and the extreme anguish with which Francis had greeted their discovery. He envisioned the flamingos, by the hundreds of thousands, tending their nests on Natron's soda-rich surface while the great Maasai god Engai stood guard over them from way atop the perfectly symmetrical volcano Ol Doinyo Lengai. Yes, it was a terrible place for a diamond mine.

David and Max reentered.

"We're going to see about moving you to a safer location," said David. "And we're going to keep Crazy Jack with you."

"That's right," said Max. "He's your lifeline in case the fever comes back or your blood refuses to clot."

"No," Oscar returned. "Jack should be free to do as he pleases. Besides, he needs to return to America. And when are you going to get in touch with Elizabeth and inform her that I am indeed alive, at least for the moment?"

This was a question that both David and Max had been expecting and one that neither of them cared to answer, at least not truthfully.

"We don't know where she is," David lied. "We've phoned all over Scotland and she's clearly not returned. We assume she's still at her mother's, but I haven't been able to locate the phone number. I'll keep searching, but your situation would certainly be more favorable, more credible, if you were willing to discuss this business about the diamonds with the authorities. That would be necessary to back up your claim that Peter's the murderer, not you."

"I can't do that," Oscar replied. "I promised Francis. Besides, I want nothing to do with any authorities, at least not until I have Elizabeth by my side."

"Didn't you say that you promised not to reveal the diamonds to anyone 'so long as you both shall live'?" said Max. "Well, unfortunately, Francis is dead. So that lets you off the hook, right?"

Oscar closed his weary eyes and shook his head slowly from side to side. "No one must know," he stated with conviction. "And you must both promise not to tell anyone."

"As you wish," said David, "for now, at least. But I must go see Joseph. I think I know where we can hide you."

"And where would that be?" Oscar inquired.

David winked at him and then departed without responding, leaving no clue. Max shrugged his shoulders and began his examination. He drew a blood sample and then checked all of Oscar's vital signs. They were much improved. His heartbeat was stronger and more regular and his lungs were clearer than before.

Oscar said nothing as Max examined him, poking him with needles, probing various orifices, and finishing by cleaning his flesh wounds once again. Thanks to Crazy Jack, his blood was now clotting properly and the healing process was coming along. The claw marks on his chest were still quite inflamed but the infection was clearing up.

"You're making good progress," said Max. "Maybe in a week or so we can get you off those antibiotics."

"That would be good," Oscar replied. "Then you can get me the hell out of this country and back where I belong."

"That might prove to be a little difficult," Max replied as he drew one last blood sample.

"We must try. If you can't bring Elizabeth to me, then I want to be back in Great Britain before anyone knows I wasn't eaten by that dreadful lion after all."

Max paused as he made some notes on Oscar's chart. "I don't know how we could pull that off, but we've got a couple of weeks to think about it. You're going to need at least that long before you're up to traveling that far abroad. Unless, of course, you've changed your mind and will let me take you to a hospital in Nairobi, where you'd receive more decent medical care."

"No," Oscar replied. "I believe you're doing just fine. And my situation is far too delicate to be taking such chances—with the authorities in Nairobi, that is. I'm certain that a man of Peter Dermenjian's means could muster a fair amount of influence."

"I guess you could be right about that," said Max as he removed a small wad of cotton that covered a tiny puncture wound in Oscar's right arm. He replaced it with a small bandage. Oscar just looked away, still enormously bothered by his stupidity, by his failure to control his ego once again by blabbing about the diamonds.

But his secret was out and there was nothing he could do to get it back. If only he'd kept his foolish mouth shut and said nothing to Crazy Jack, who would no doubt tell everyone about the diamonds. In fact, the news must surely have whetted his prospector's appetite. Perhaps there was a good reason for keeping him around after all. But then how long would it be before Peter Dermenjian realized that his long-sought-after diamonds lay directly beneath the spot where he had killed Francis, within the caustic confines of Lake Natron? It brought him but little comfort to think that if Peter did choose to search there and find the kimberlite, then perhaps he would be satisfied and leave him alone, despite the fact that he was an eyewitness to the murder. Such speculation served as nothing but slow torture as he lay upon the cot, staring up at the canvas roof, again watching it flutter very slightly in the soft breeze that stirred outside the tent, while Max stood nearby, hunched over a powerful microscope as he examined Oscar's blood.

He was looking for signs of malarial parasites and happily finding none, at least none that appeared to be alive. Soon the sound of Oscar's snoring filled the tent and Max found himself smiling, content that his patient seemed to be recovering and that, despite his predicament, there seemed to be some room for optimism.

But then he heard other noises, outside the tent. They began as a soft din but grew louder. David was returning and he obviously was not alone. Max exited the tent, hoping he could keep the voices down so as not to disturb Oscar, who needed all the rest he could get. But as soon as he saw Joseph and the other elders, and saw the anger on their faces, he realized it would be difficult, if not impossible, to keep them from bothering Oscar.

"Please, keep your voices down," he pleaded with them in the Maasai tongue as he stood before the entry to the tent. If he had hoped that standing there would in any way dissuade Joseph from confronting Oscar, he was quite mistaken. Joseph brushed by him without a second thought and walked into the tent, followed by Senento and several others.

None of them had been told, prior to David's visit, that this man named Oscar, the mzungu who had allegedly murdered Joseph's good friend Francis, was not only alive but being hidden in Maasailand right under their very noses. Joseph was clearly infuriated, his bloodshot eyes turning even redder as he shouted at David that this man must leave immediately. He made it very clear that in no way would he allow this murderer to remain on lands within his jurisdiction and that he would certainly not intentionally shelter him from the authorities who sought him for committing a most outrageous crime.

David paused before replying, then restated once again and rather emphatically that Oscar had not murdered Francis, that he was quite innocent of the crime and it would be proven beyond a shadow of a doubt.

"All he needs is a chance to recover from his illness and injuries," David pleaded, "and then he will be ready to stand trial."

"That would be fine," Joseph replied, "so long as he recovers somewhere else—anywhere but Maasai country."

Oscar, rudely awakened by this sudden intrusion, simply lay upon the cot, his hands folded behind his head. It was somewhat amusing to him until one of the elders, standing next to Senento, produced a piece of paper with Oscar's picture on it, a rather poor one at that. It stated in Swahili that this man was wanted for murder and that there was a reward of one million Kenyan shillings for whoever found him, preferably alive. Joseph grabbed the wanted poster and held it next to Oscar's face. Oscar smiled meekly.

"Not a very flattering photo, is it?" he spouted.

Joseph curled his lip in disgust as he tossed the paper to the ground.

"What's going on?" Oscar inquired with a look toward David. "Are they going to turn me in?"

"Not if I can help it," said David. "I told Joseph that you were here, that you had been brought to us by their Maasai cousins to the south, in Tanzania, and that we were trying to nurse you back to health, as is our duty as Christians. I simply asked if he would allow us to move you up to one of their camps, up in the hills to the west. Dermenjian would never find it, just as the authorities who searched for you all over Gelai never found you."

"I was just beginning to get comfortable in your priest hole, actually," he replied.

"Yes," said David, "far too comfortable."

Joseph interrupted, having conferred briefly with the rest of the elders. "Then who killed Francis Dermenjian if it wasn't this man?"

David looked at Oscar. "It was his brother," David replied in a very solemn tone of voice. If this news stunned him, Joseph did not let it show. But the elders all looked at him in disbelief.

"Why would a brother kill a brother?" Joseph asked as he cast a scornful look toward Oscar.

"These two brothers were very different," said David. "It happens sometimes."

Joseph snorted, clearly unpersuaded. "He must be gone by morning," he stated, pointing at Oscar, "or I will see that he is personally escorted out of Maasai country."

David let these words resonate a bit, wishing he could speak of the diamonds, wondering if Joseph knew anything at all about Peter Dermenjian. Max, who had stood aside, listening and watching as David and Joseph conversed, decided to step in.

"Do you realize your son would be dead by now if it hadn't been for this man?" he said rather boldly, formulating the question as precisely as he knew how given his limited fluency in Maa.

Joseph turned, looking to see who might have uttered such nonsense. He saw Max standing near his microscope. "That is not true," said Joseph. "You saved my son's life."

"I played a part," said Max. But there his grasp of the language ended. He turned toward David. "Tell them I work for this man. That he pays my salary. That he developed this clinic, not me. And that it was the mere presence of the clinic that saved his son's life. Any decent doctor could have done what I was able to do."

David promptly translated and then amplified this line of reasoning. "Therefore," he continued in Joseph's direction, "you might think about repaying that favor by giving this poor man permission to remain in Maasailand for another week or two. By then he should be well enough to travel far away, back to his homeland, where he very much wishes to be. Surely you would not turn a sick man away."

"I would not refuse to help a sick man," Joseph replied, "but I will not protect a murderer, a man who killed a good friend."

"But he is innocent and must be presumed innocent, at least until proven guilty in a court of law."

Joseph raised an eyebrow at the impudence David was displaying. He paced about in the center of the tent, his tall and dignified presence swathed in his plaid blanket as always. Then he turned to confer with his colleagues, who were gathered to one side of the entry. David backed up against the tent flap, as if to block the exit. He felt a tug at his sleeve and, looking to his right, saw Christine peering in through a small opening in the flap of canvas that covered the entrance to the tent.

"What the hell is going on?" she whispered. Behind her David could distinguish Dr. Brecht, who was craning an ear so as not to miss a bit of the dialogue. David made a face that clearly communicated the need for them to remain silent and not show their faces.

"Then present the evidence," said Joseph, suddenly turning around. "Are there any other witnesses?"

David looked shocked. Was he serious? While Joseph was clearly the leading Maasai authority in the area, he had no right to be holding trial. Yet he persisted, repeating his request for David to present the evidence, to provide witnesses.

"If you think you're going to try this man right here and now, you're quite mistaken. Kenyan law provides for—"

But this time it was Joseph who cut David off, saying that his questions had nothing to do with Kenyan law—only the law of the Maasai, which prohibited giving shelter to a fugitive, a man accused of wrongdoing. David was well aware that Maasai "law"—"custom" would be a better word—was silent on the matter of presumed innocence.

"And what does Maasai law say about helping to heal those afflicted by illness and injury?" David inquired while pointing at Oscar. "Here is a man who is not only recovering from a serious case of malaria but an attack by a lion!"

This was clearly news, and rather big news judging from the buzzing that ensued among the elders. Joseph asked to see the wounds.

Max had been following the line of conversation and approached Oscar first. He threw back the sheet that had covered him and pointed at the bandages.

"Tell them I just changed his bandages and I don't wish to do so again. Tell him I can vouch that there are serious wounds here, serious claw marks."

David did so, but Joseph replied on behalf of all the Maasai elders that they would like to see the wounds anyway. Max stared at Joseph without speaking. Then he turned and explained to Oscar what was going on, why he needed to replace his bandages—again—which he proceeded to do. By the time he finished, the elderly Maasai all seemed to agree that a lion's front claws could very well have made those ointment-laden, stitched-up slash marks that ran from his right shoulder nearly to his navel.

"Did this occur before or after he killed Francis?" Joseph inquired.

"This is getting us nowhere," Max muttered to David.

"Oscar Newman has killed no one," said David. "His mission in life is to help people. That is why he sets up these clinics, to help people."

"He helps them by denying them children," Joseph replied.

"No," said Max, feeling emboldened enough to address Joseph once again in his own tongue. "That is your choice. All he does is offer you that choice in a safe manner. Besides, the Maasai—you, in fact—agreed to this clinic, without which your son would certainly be dead."

Joseph raised his hand and swatted at an invisible fly with his wildebeest-tail fly brush. He looked at Max and then at David and then at Oscar before conferring once again with the elders.

288

A brief moment later he turned back toward them and said he would like to question Oscar. "Who will translate?" he asked. David, though quite flustered, offered to provide such a service, but Joseph said no, it was clear David was biased in his opinion and might not translate truthfully. Such words burned in David's ears and he turned red with anger. Before he could speak, however, the tent flap opened and in walked Dr. Brecht.

"I will translate for Dr. Newman," she pronounced.

Again the Maasai elders began talking rapidly among themselves. By now they were well acquainted with this brash woman who insisted on engaging them in conversation whenever she could. Apparently, they weren't the least bit surprised that she had been eavesdropping, since she seemed to make a living out of sticking her nose in other people's business.

Joseph watched her move among the small crowd, greeting each of his associates in her own special way. They were clearly amused by her, as was Joseph, for she spoke to each of them in a very personable manner, in the Maa language but with a stiff German accent. They all seemed quite comfortable with her serving as Oscar's translator. She took a seat next to Oscar as Christine slipped inside, unnoticed by everyone but Max.

Oscar, for his part in all this, looked more than slightly confused as he listened to them conversing in a foreign language. Yet he seemed rather detached, nearly resigned to the inevitability of being questioned by the Maasai. But what was Dr. Brecht doing? She advised him not to be cute, to just give straight answers.

"What in God's name is happening?" he inquired of David and Max as they approached.

"You're about to be tried for the murder of Francis Dermenjian," David replied. "Best to keep your wits about you."

"Tried?" said Oscar, looking suddenly more alarmed. "But who's to be the judge? And what if I'm found guilty? This is madness!"

"No," said David, "this is Maasai country. I believe the worst that could happen is that you would be expelled."

Oscar looked at David, then at Max, and then at David again. "Let's hope you are right. But who shall defend me?"

David turned toward Joseph. "If you insist on putting this man on trial, then I shall defend him."

Joseph looked confused. "No," he replied. "That will not be necessary. He will defend himself."

Chapter 38

Joseph assumed the role of chief prosecutor, pacing about in the middle of the tent. All eyes were upon him as he flicked his fly brush about before turning toward Oscar.

"Tell us your story," he said, "all of it."

Dr. Brecht dutifully translated Joseph's command. Oscar appeared quite stunned. He again looked at David and then at Max, his eyes seeking some counsel but receiving none, only pained grimaces. There being no objections, and no further counsel, Oscar looked all around the room, carefully studying each face. His jury consisted of a dozen *il-payiani*, Maasai elders, who were all glaring at him, their faces long and deeply furrowed, their heads nearly bald, and their earlobes hugely distended and heavily adorned with beads and trinkets. Though understandably apprehensive, with no idea what bounds there might be on their license to decide his fate, Oscar realized that all the elders were doing was seeking to protect their people from yet another menace in their neighborhood.

Now unperturbed, he proceeded to tell his story, to provide his own defense, speaking through Dr. Brecht, who was seated right where Max had been seated hours earlier while probing his physical well-being. Only now a different type of examination was underway, one in which Joseph was probing his moral well-being.

Oscar described the events that had led up to the tragic shooting, beginning with the journey through the Mara and the Serengeti. He described the visit to Olduvai, and the three-and-a-half-million-year-old hominid footprints side by side, like father and son. He described the journey through Ngorongoro and the ensuing descent into the basin of Lake Natron and onto the soda lake itself, where Francis was conducting his research and where the Land Rover had fallen through the soda crust. He spoke freely while staring at the ceiling of the tent, as if all the scenes he was relating were projected thereupon and he was seeing them all again from a fresh, detached perspective.

As he described the troubles with the stranded Land Rover and their failed attempts to revive it, omitting any mention of diamonds, he became more animated. Francis had said there were lions about and given him a pistol for his own protection. But then his recollection became quite dim, at least until the helicopter had arrived. He remembered that well and how Francis had been so excited and how he had run down the hill to greet his brother, only to be met by a bullet from a gun. He began to describe how he'd seen Peter and Francis facing each other only a few feet apart and how he'd seen Francis suddenly slump to the ground. Only then had he heard the shot.

At this point Oscar stopped. He continued to stare at the ceiling of the tent, but tears were rolling down his cheeks. David moved to comfort him but Oscar brushed him aside.

"And then they came after me," he continued, his voice choking, "no doubt to kill me. But the lion nearly beat them to it. Thank God for Olabon."

Joseph stopped his pacing. "Who is Olabon?" he asked.

"A Maasai like you. He killed the lion before it could kill me. Then he and his friends brought me here."

The elders began speaking rapidly to one another once again. Joseph shouted at them to be silent.

"Did anyone else see the murder?" Joseph inquired, turning back toward Oscar.

"Yes," said Oscar, "Peter Dermenjian's personal physician, a Dr. Meinz."

Again the buzzing ensued among the elders once Dr. Brecht finished translating.

"Who drove the helicopter?" Joseph continued.

In truth Oscar had never determined that. In fact, the question hadn't even occurred to him. Perhaps there was another eyewitness who, despite being another Dermenjian employee, might not be as loyal as Dr. Meinz. Joseph repeated the question.

"How would I know?" Oscar rejoined, still intrigued by the idea.

Joseph turned and addressed the elders. They offered a few words in return. And then, quite abruptly, Joseph announced a recess, stating that he and his jury needed to discuss some matters in private. David demanded to know when they would return.

"When we have decided," replied Senento, casting one last, confused look at Oscar, the man who had given him a goat on the occasion of his son's circumcision.

David stood outside the tent, watching Joseph and his merry men stride off toward the nearest council tree, knowing all too well that the upcoming deliberations might last days. Or they could be back within the hour. There was no way of knowing.

He stepped back inside the tent to face Oscar.

"What the hell just happened?" Oscar asked.

David shrugged his shoulders and then scratched at his beard. "I would not worry," he consoled Oscar. "They just needed some information. The only piece lacking is the motive. Why would a brother kill a brother, especially after spending days trying to track him down? Otherwise your story seems entirely plausible."

"Not only is it plausible, it is true," Oscar rejoined. "And what about my motive? That's not been established either but no one seems to care."

"They don't need a motive," said David. "They see the reward money."

It was not the best of notes on which to end the discussion. But they all fell silent, privately digesting all they had just witnessed and wondering not only what the outcome might be but what to do until Joseph and his jury returned with their verdict. Crazy Jack finally broke the silence.

"So what do we do now?" he asked as he stumbled into the middle of the exam room turned courtroom. "Just wait for them bastards to reach a verdict? Hell, we got to get this poor son of a bitch to a hidin' place somewhere." Apparently, he'd been eavesdropping, too. But unlike Christine and Dr. Brecht, he had been much more discreet.

"There's no time for that. Besides, I have faith in Joseph," said David.

"By the way," Max added, "I hope you're not in too big a hurry to get back to Texas."

Jack eyed him suspiciously. "Now, what the hell is that supposed to mean?"

"It means I'll take you back to Nairobi as soon as Oscar's well enough to travel and we can figure out a way to get him out of this country without him being apprehended by the Kenyan National Police. It could be a couple of weeks."

"That don't matter," Jack replied, eagerly casting an eye toward Christine. "I ain't gettin' too homesick just yet."

"Good," David replied. "Meanwhile, we'd like you to keep Oscar company."

"It'd be my pleasure," Jack replied as he smiled at Oscar. "We got lots to talk about."

Oscar returned a smile, albeit a faint one.

The verdict came back early the following morning. Joseph arrived at the tent with a small entourage that included another potent Maasai figure—Nilenga, the *laibon*. Both Max and Oscar were still asleep when the two entered the tent with nothing but a few grunts to signal their arrival. Max jumped up from his cot and greeted them, running a hand over his hair in a vain attempt to look less disheveled. Oscar opened his eyes and shuddered in both horror and surprise. The last time he'd seen Nilenga was after the circumcision ceremony. He remembered the words Francis had spoken—"Just hope he's not working up a curse for you, Oscar." Apparently, it was too late.

Nilenga approached Oscar without speaking and peered deep into his eyes, locking onto them as if plumbing the depths of his soul. He then placed a hand on Oscar's forehead and ran it down over his face and then over Oscar's chest, pausing just above his heart. The pressure of Nilenga's hands on his chest wounds was enough to make him wince, but Oscar said nothing, trusting that this was just another type of Maasai ritual. Nilenga uttered something in Joseph's direction that Max could not comprehend. But then Joseph shouted to those who remained outside the tent. Instantly, the tent flap was open and four fierce-looking moran entered. They seized Oscar and began to drag him to his feet. Max jumped to Oscar's defense.

"What do you think you're doing?" he shouted as he stood before the moran, blocking their way. "This man is my patient."

Joseph turned and addressed Max sharply, with an air of indignation. "He is my prisoner," he stated quite firmly.

"Prisoner?" Max shouted. "What do you mean, prisoner? He's innocent."

Joseph ignored him as the moran brushed Max aside and ushered Oscar outside the tent and set him down on a pallet similar to the one the Tanzanians had constructed. Only this time Oscar's legs were being tied and secured to the branches that provided the main structural support. As if he had anywhere to run to.

Max pleaded with Joseph, butchering the Maasai words he was searching for, but it didn't matter. "Where do you think you're taking him?" he shouted. "He needs medical attention."

"Then you may come with him," Joseph replied.

Before Max could reply, he heard David shouting in anger as he came bustling through the sparse woodland that separated his schoolhouse from the clinic. Apparently, Joseph had sent word to him.

"This is outrageous!" he shouted, adding a few other expletives, all in French. Joseph braced himself for the onslaught in a manner that suggested he was accustomed to such confrontations. David dispensed with decorum and was in Joseph's face before Oscar shouted from his prone position on the pallet and asked David, once again, what in the hell was going on. It seemed there was always someone asking him that question lately.

"You're being taken prisoner," David replied.

"Prisoner?" said Oscar. "For how long?"

David redirected the question to Joseph, who had backed off a few paces.

"That depends," Joseph replied.

"Depends on what?" David persisted.

"It depends on what we decide to do with him."

Even more infuriated, David turned on Joseph once again, demanding to know what right he had to hold Oscar Newman, a citizen of the United Kingdom, in captivity. He threatened to radio the British embassy but Joseph only laughed. He then took David by the arm and led him away, where they could speak in private.

Oscar looked up at Max, who had witnessed all this and was just as confused. Jack McGraw peeked out from inside his tent and asked if the coast was clear. When he saw the four moran standing beside Oscar, clutching spears and shields, he ducked back inside. Christine had heard the shouting and came running. Dr. Brecht appeared moments later.

"They're taking Oscar prisoner," said Max as he finished stuffing a duffel bag with all he figured he would need for the next couple of days, including medical supplies.

"Prisoner?" she said. "They can't do that, can they? And just where do you think you're going?"

"Somebody's got to take care of him," said Max.

"I'm goin', too," came a voice from behind as Jack McGraw again emerged from his tent carrying a small knapsack.

Christine looked more perplexed than usual. "Oh, no you don't," she said. "You're not leaving us here alone with fifty thousand starving refugees."

"Suit yourself," said Max. David and Joseph returned moments later, speaking amicably, though the sweat on David's brow bore evidence of the strain he was under.

"It will take a few hours to reach our destination," he said.

"We're going with you," said Christine.

David knew from the look in her eyes that there was no sense arguing. "As you wish," he replied.

"Where are they taking me?" said Oscar.

"To a Maasai settlement up in the hills, up there," David responded, pointing westward toward the towering Nguruman Escarpment, whose uppermost reaches were obscured by morning fog.

Oscar said nothing in response but merely stared at David, as if beseeching him some further explanation. David simply shrugged his shoulders. Matters were clearly well out of his hands.

Chapter 39

After well more than an hour, the open ground they had been crossing single file, like a safari with its prey already in hand, ended rather abruptly. With the steep face of the Nguruman Escarpment towering above them, it seemed they must be near their destination. But the faint trail soon turned sharply and began to rise as they entered a tall, dense thicket of shrub willow that enveloped the entire party. Several minutes later the willow began to fade, overshadowed by thick, dark forest that clung to the walls of a very narrow canyon. It was more like a huge crack in the escarpment, slicing into it at an oblique angle, barely perceptible from the heated plains beyond. But within its confines, the air felt almost cool and smelled strongly of decay.

Joseph barked out an order, and the four moran who had been carrying Oscar set him down. Four others immediately stepped forward to take their place, lifting Oscar in unison, their faces all rather stern and showing no trace of strain or even mild annoyance at having been chosen to carry this enormous fellow up the nearly sheer face of the escarpment. They were simply following orders from Joseph.

At first the trail ran along switchbacks that hugged the sides of the narrow canyon. A stream carried but a trickle of water through its middle, slowly carving away the uplifted portion of the massive fault block that formed the Nguruman Escarpment. Large ferns dominated the understory. As they all trudged onward, the trail gradually steepened, eventually becoming so steep that at times only the ropes that tied him to the pallet kept Oscar from sliding off.

From his quasi-horizontal vantage point, his head resting upon a mere pile of leaves wrapped in a tangle of young vines placed at one end of the pallet, Oscar could do nothing but stare at the tops of the trees, offering no resistance. All control of his life was now well beyond him. He was no longer a welcomed guest as he had once been, however suspect, when traveling with Francis. The tables had somehow shifted, and he was now a prisoner of the Maasai and presumably their enemy.

His legs were lashed to the bamboo staves of the pallet that rested upon the strong shoulders of his young captors. The position seemed almost familiar to him, though his recollection of having been borne aloft in a similar manner by Olabon and his comrades was still rather faint. Foremost in his mind, as always, was Elizabeth. With his eyes closed to obscure any further light of day, he could see her quite clearly as she sat by the fire in their cottage on Mull. And he watched her glide across the floor of their apartment, picking up his scattered books and papers. But most of all he remembered her tender embrace. If only he could let her know that he was still—for the moment, at least—a part of this mortal coil.

Max did his best to keep up, panting as he trudged along after the four moran who, despite their heavy burden, still evinced no sign of fatigue. In fact, they weren't even sweating. Christine and Dr. Brecht followed behind, breathing heavily. David made as though he was lying back with them in case they might be in need of a priest for some reason, plodding along in his black teaching attire and flat-soled shoes that were not up to this particular jaunt. Crazy Jack shadowed him for the most part. But every so often he would stop to examine a rock along the trail or, where the trail ran hard against the rocky face of the crevice-like canyon, he would stop to poke at it with his ever-present rock hammer.

They were a few miles along when Max finally learned the reason for the abrupt change in David's outlook on Oscar's "imprisonment." Joseph had told David that the elders were unable to reach a decision. But since the matter of Oscar's guilt regarding the murder of Francis Dermenjian was still pending, they all did agree that Oscar should be detained until they were able to reach consensus. The idea of stashing Oscar in the moran camp, originally suggested to Joseph by David, went over well. It would give the young warriors a chance to learn how to guard and how to treat a prisoner. And although he hadn't mentioned this to the other elders, it would also allow Joseph to agree to David's original request to shelter Oscar, albeit under very different conditions than initially envisioned, as they were soon to find out.

They were nearly two-thirds of the way to the top of the escarpment when they reached a patch of ground where the trail leveled off and just one last layer of treetops obscured the blue sky above. The sheer canyon walls, though largely hidden by the trees, stood farther back and were more sparsely vegetated. It was abundantly evident, to Crazy Jack at least, that they were standing on top of a chunk of ground that had broken loose from the terra non-firma up above and was now wedged between the lower walls of the narrow canyon. Joseph came to a halt, turned around, and, without saying a word, made it clear by the power of his expression that everyone was to be still and to remain silent.

Within minutes a small band of Maasai warriors emerged from the forest to greet them. Some were dressed in the typical moran garb, with orange shukas and

298

finger-painted legs, while others had short braids with no ochre at all and carried plugs of wood in their hollowed earlobes. These were some of the young initiates, the *il-keliani*, all dressed in charcoal-colored robes. With one exception, all the moran greeted Joseph with enthusiasm and with the proper deference to his rank. The lone exception was Ntanda, Joseph's son, who stepped forward, still slightly hunched over from his bullet wound. With a certain arrogance that might be associated with his position as leader of his own age class, Ntanda gave a terse greeting and then demanded to know why his father had approached the morans' camp with all these mzungus, in particular Oscar, whose guardians had set him back down on the ground.

Joseph responded in a manner that seemed even more abrupt than usual, pointing on occasion to Oscar with his fly brush and then to Max and the others. Ntanda responded in a similar tone, with grunts and gestures that suggested he was none too pleased with this visit and, no doubt, with the notion of guarding Oscar.

Max moved up next to David, who was standing alongside Oscar and listening carefully to the muted conversation between Joseph and his son. David could see from Max's expression that he was not comprehending.

"Ntanda is telling Joseph that this is highly inappropriate," he whispered, "that he and his senior moran are far too busy instructing the new initiates in the ways of a true Maasai warrior to babysit this old fart, that of course being you, Oscar."

"Silence!" Joseph shouted as he turned around and glared at David, Max, and Oscar. David lowered his head ever so slightly and said he was sorry.

Joseph and Ntanda then discussed matters further, their voices alternating between soft, near whispers to loud volleys punctuated by quick gestures with their hands. In the end it was Ntanda who turned and addressed those in the procession. First he looked hard at Christine and Dr. Brecht and spoke to them rather crisply. Dr. Brecht responded in his native tongue.

"What's going on?" said Christine.

"He asked if we were circumcised," said Dr. Brecht. "I told him no. I trust that is correct?"

"Of course it is, but it's none of his business."

"This is a feasting camp—where the young warriors will gorge themselves on meat to make them strong. But they are not allowed to eat meat in front of circumcised women."

"Of course," said Christine, looking slightly embarrassed. "I knew that."

Ntanda then shouted directions to the four moran who had been Oscar's porters of late. They nodded and then began to untie him. Ntanda motioned to Oscar to get up, stating for all to hear that if this man who had murdered Francis Dermenjian—a great friend of the Maasai—was to be his prisoner, then he would not be coddled but would be treated like a prisoner should be treated. He ridiculed those who had carried him, chiding them, along with his father, for having pretended this despicable man was an emperor instead of a murderer, bearing him aloft on this stupid litter. He then directed the moran to bind Oscar's hands behind him.

"Enough!" said David as he stepped forward and placed himself next to Oscar, ready to defend him.

Ntanda looked as though he was about to erupt when Joseph stepped forward and took David aside. A brief moment later David turned toward Ntanda and spoke to him in Maa, almost politely, saying, "You may bind him but please, not too tightly, for he has been very ill."

Max looked at David and then at Oscar. Once again he felt as though he'd been inserted into some type of strange play, one in which everyone knew their lines except him. Oscar gave a subtle nod of his head, signaling that he would be all right. For he understood, perhaps better than anyone, that as long as his jury was still deliberating, he would be considered guilty as charged and would be treated as such. His worst fear was that the elders would think that the problem was settled, that he was now a good subject on whom the young moran could practice their own brand of incarceration indefinitely.

Ntanda snapped a command to two of his comrades. Having finished lashing Oscar's wrists behind him, they gently prodded him in the ribs with the blunt end of their spears, signaling it was time to be underway once again.

Fortunately, the camp was nearby and in ten minutes' time they had gained its center. Here the forest was a bit more open and the noonday sun filtered through outstretched branches. There were three large cattle tethered to three large trees, and a small pen housed a few sheep and several goats. Oscar stumbled into the center of the clearing, prodded by his new escorts. All the moran gathered there stopped to stare at Oscar and his companions. The air was a bit hazy, for there were fires smoldering all around the periphery. And around each fire were large slabs of meat skewered onto crude wooden stakes. At each fire pit, half a dozen or more of the relatively drab young initiates sat in a semicircle, abiding their hunger, while the older moran, dressed in their full regalia, turned the meat from time to time, taunting the younger initiates.

Oscar's mouth began to water as the delicious scent of beef ribs, beef shanks, beef brisket, and beef steaks of every kind permeated the air. It was like some strange Maasai food circus for dedicated carnivores. But as much as the thought of biting into a nice, tender piece of sirloin appealed to him, at the moment he was much more interested in something to drink. The walking had been harder than he'd expected. Even though the ground was fairly level, it was the first time in weeks that he had actually traveled any significant distance under his own power. And his mouth once again felt as dry as desert sand.

He was surprised to see that among this mix of younger and older moran, there were a number of young girls, at most thirteen years of age, also tending to the fires as well as helping to cure fresh hides that hung from ropes strung between the trees. There were no Maasai dwellings, at least none that resembled the dung-and-mud-roofed huts that had become so familiar to him. There were instead only crude lean-tos made of sticks and leaves and tucked away in the woods. It reminded Oscar of his days as a youth when he and his comrades would go off fishing. They would build similar shelters and pretend they were Picts living off the land. They would roast the trout they caught over wood fires while they settled into their own crude huts and pretended the surrounding forest was filled with wild creatures. Only *this* forest was indeed filled with wild creatures and *this* was certainly no childhood fantasy.

David approached him, offering a drink of water. But Ntanda intervened once again, stating that he would decide when the prisoner would drink and when he would eat. So instead of the delightful sensation of cool water on his parched tongue, Oscar felt his two attendants poking him in his back, right where his soda burns were just beginning to scab over. They shouted something to him that he did not comprehend but that he assumed meant "keep walking," which he did. Several yards beyond, however, he stopped. A sudden chill overcame him as he watched three of the moran ahead of him move aside some brush piled up against the side of the canyon wall. He realized they were leading him toward a cave, or at least some type of large hole in the side of the escarpment, whose entrance had been obscured by the brush that now stood to one side.

The notion of entering was more than repulsive. He had already spent far too long in such a place, and memories of his days trapped with Francis in the lava tube on the flanks of Gelai filled him with dread. He began to tremble.

"David," he gasped, "please don't let them put me in there."

"I'm sorry," David replied, "I wish I could. But do not worry. You will be much safer here. I will do everything I can to ensure that you are treated well."

Oscar looked at him with mistrustful eyes, as if to remind David that he had only just arrived at his new "hideaway" and already his hands were lashed behind him and his "protectors" were threatening to run him through with their spears if he did not cooperate. Max stepped forward, but before he could utter any words of encouragement or offer any assistance, Ntanda intervened.

"No one may speak to the prisoner without my permission," he stated coldly in perfect English. "Keep moving."

Both David and Max backed away. A despondent Oscar paused to look at them, staring with a blank expression that somehow conveyed a sense of betrayal before he trudged onward.

Upon arriving at the entrance, Oscar ducked to avoid hitting his head and stumbled into the narrow opening. Though it was fairly dark, he was relieved to see that it was not another lava tube and no more than thirty feet deep. It was merely another fissure in the wall of the fault-laden escarpment that had been enlarged by repeated chipping away at it, no doubt over many generations of moran who apparently used this camp quite regularly. Ntanda motioned to direct those who had taken charge of the empty pallet to place it on the floor of the cave. This would be Oscar's bed.

His captors untied the leather straps that had bound Oscar's hands behind him and allowed him to lie down. He was utterly exhausted and still craving that cool drink of water David had offered him. Ntanda, standing by the entry, looked in the direction of one of the young girls and gave her an order. Moments later she arrived holding a fresh gourd and offered it to Oscar. He accepted it and thanked her before taking a drink. But the liquid had barely passed his lips when he suddenly spit it out quite forcefully.

"It's blood, for Christ's sake!" he bellowed. "I need water."

Max brushed past one of the moran and barged inside. He knelt next to Oscar, handing him his water bottle. Ntanda looked on with a disgusted air but did not intervene. Oscar drank until the bottle was nearly empty, though he was still close to retching from the initial shock of drinking warm cow's blood. Ntanda then barked out another order to one of his colleagues. The latter entered Oscar's new home and then bent down to remove a leather hide just a few feet from where Oscar was lying that he hadn't even noticed. Oscar heard the clang of metal and in the dim light was just able to make out the shapes of numerous spears piled together.

Ntanda then stepped forward, reached into the stack of spears, and produced a large metal file that he handed to Oscar. He looked at him for a moment before speaking.

"After you have rested, you will file them all until they are razor sharp," he said, again in perfect English.

Oscar looked up at Ntanda, then to Max and David, who stood just inside the cave. Once again Max had had enough of the Maasai mistreating his patient.

"He is too sick," he stated in the proper Maa dialect. "He needs rest."

Ntanda smiled, perhaps amused that this American would dare attempt to address him in his native tongue. Again he replied in English. "When he is tired of resting, he can work to pay us back for keeping him alive."

"He is already paying you back," Max replied, reverting to English. "He has agreed to replace all the cattle the refugees have stolen."

Ntanda's eyes flew into a rage. "And how many is that?" he shouted. "Have you counted them all? And when will he replace them? After all the Maasai have died from starvation? The Kenyan government has ignored the slaughter of our cattle. They are happy that we are able to provide food for all of these foul-smelling people. And even worse, they are now stealing our water."

He began cursing all the Ugandans, and then he cursed the Kenyan government for allowing them to invade and usurp their land, Maasailand. Max looked at David, who appeared quite stunned by this news. Hadn't Captain Olengi sent soldiers to guard the Kalema Road, to prevent the refugees from poaching more Maasai cattle? Max had seen them, or at least two of them, for they had prevented him from taking Oscar to Nairobi.

"It cannot be true," said David.

Ntanda turned and faced David, a man he had known for many years, a strange, foreign man who had even taught him in school. Too well, perhaps. "Come," said Ntanda, "I will show you."

303

With a few terse commands Ntanda made certain that Oscar's guards were at their posts. Joseph bid his farewell after one last look at Oscar, no doubt relieved to have found secure housing for this alleged criminal.

Ntanda led the others through the forest to a promontory not far from the camp that jutted out over the escarpment. Christine shrieked as they emerged from the forest cover to a spot where the earth suddenly fell away. Ntanda gave her a look of disdain before walking clear to the brink of a well-defined ledge. The others followed.

The view was spectacular. Before them lay the entire Rift Valley, from Mosiro to the north to dreaded Lake Natron to the south, its strange pink-and-white surface wavering beneath the enormous bulk of Lengai. Far to the southeast, the symmetrical peak of Kilimanjaro stood out in the haze, beyond Gelai, whose faint outline hugged Natron's eastern shore.

But what was most striking was what they saw in the foreground of this tableau. For there, less than a mile from the promontory on which they were perched, were the masses of refugees huddled under whatever meager tatter of tarps they could piece together, their numbers stretching for miles to the north and south.

"No one can ever replace all the cattle these invaders have stolen from us," said Ntanda, "but even if one did, who will give us back our land? And our water? Look. Do you see the drilling machine over there?"

Max pulled out a pair of binoculars. He scanned the scene before them, noting the occasional Red Cross tents with their unmistakable flags flying above. A few Red Cross vehicles moved through the throng, albeit rather slowly. For each one was engulfed in a crowd of desperate refugees, all of them begging for food. The volunteers were no doubt doing their best to dispense whatever insufficient rations, whatever table scraps could be garnered from one of the most impoverished nations on earth. But toward the southernmost reaches of this stream of people, whose numbers dwindled as they approached Magadi, Max noticed a tall red derrick and could see puffs of black smoke emanating from the diesel engine beside it.

"But your father has an agreement—" David began. Ntanda cut him short, his eyes full of anger.

304

"My father is a fool," he cried. "These people will never leave unless we force them out. Or unless we kill them all and let the vultures and hyenas carry them away bit by bit."

David and his party spent the night at the *olpul* camp, sequestered in small huts well away from the central meat-processing fray. They were well fed and well treated, though access to Oscar was strictly limited. From what Max could surmise, he was being fed regularly, though much of his intake was cow's milk mixed with blood, the staple for injured warriors. Upon one occasion Max was sure he saw the young girl who tended to him bring Oscar a substantial piece of meat. This was confirmed when Max and the others were allowed to say good-bye to him.

Oscar was lying on his side, resting. Crazy Jack sat nearby, inspecting one of the spears Oscar had recently sharpened. There were dozens left to be properly honed, to be made ready for battle.

"Oscar," said David, kneeling down beside him, "we are leaving now. I'm sure you will be safe here. I'll be back in a few days to check on you."

"So will I," said Max, who had crouched beside him and was checking his forehead to make sure the fever had not returned.

"I'm sure you'll be fine," said Christine, who stood just outside the cave.

Oscar looked at them askance, then glanced over at Jack. "And what about you?" he inquired.

"Me?" he replied. "Heck, I ain't got nowhere to go just yet. Might as well stay here and keep you company. Them rascals don't seem to mind. And the meat's damn tasty."

"So be it," Oscar replied, turning back toward David. "But don't be too long. And please try to bring me some word of Elizabeth."

David nodded and said he would do his best. As they left, one of Oscar's guards stepped inside and shoved a dull spear at him. Oscar picked it up with a disdainful look at his captor. Begrudgingly, he picked up the file and began running it over the blade. He looked up to see his friends retreating. For some reason the image of Peter Dermenjian crossed his mind, as it did all too frequently. He gripped the file harder and ran it crisply along the edge of the blade.

Their descent was far more pleasant than their journey in, owing not only to the reversed pitch of the terrain but also to where they were headed. For Max and Christine, it was back to their quarters just south of the Kalema Road. While the move there had been chaotic, and the ordeal with Oscar had certainly not been a part of their plans, it was nice to be closer to David's school and to Joseph's manyatta. And with the refugees so close and so numerous, a fact driven home by the enduring image of the impoverished masses they'd seen from Ntanda's overlook, sticking close to one another seemed a good idea.

For Max, returning to the clinic meant trying to pick up the tattered thread of his career as a physician. The birth-control business had come to a complete standstill, but there were certain to be plenty of other situations developing that would require his attention. All too soon, perhaps, judging from Ntanda's mood and what he perceived as preparations for battle. Why else would Oscar be sharpening all those spears?

Christine was especially anxious to return to her newly relocated home. Despite all the troubles, the relocation and the many adjustments it required, and even the ordeal with Oscar, she felt a strong sense that her project, her entire reason for being in Africa, was on good terms. In just a few more months she would have all the data she would need. She had even managed to find some distance to place between herself and Dr. Brecht, who was always trying to stick her big nose into her preliminary findings. It was all still in very rough form, but with her interviews, her value mapping, and her "off the record" observations, she felt confident she would be able to defend her work before any doctoral dissertation committee. No one would be able to disagree that her data clearly supported her original hypothesis that the Maasai women possess far more power in deciding everyday issues in Maasai life than anyone before had ever thought possible.

As they ambled down the path, Dr. Brecht droned on nonstop. She poured over every detail of the many fascinating behaviors she had observed among the young Maasai men as well as the girls, stopping short, however, of revealing who was having sexual encounters with whom between rounds of meat eating. David and Max were impressed once again with her powers of observation. But how strange it seemed to them both that this Teutonic terror of an anthropologist never ceased to recount her many astute observations to whoever cared to listen. Presumably, it was all for the benefit of her student, Christine, who would nod in agreement and occasionally offer her own observations, which invariably brought on another round of comments regarding what Christine had seen and all that she had failed to see. Max stole a sidelong glance at her and caught her gritting her teeth. But Dr.

Brecht went on, proffering a comment about the subtle differences in the way one of the moran had been circumcised. "Why would that be?" she wondered aloud.

Before any of them could respond, Christine began screaming obscenities and running toward her trailer. They were about fifty yards away, but through the scattered thorn trees Max could see that the door was torn from its hinges, the windows all broken. Papers lay scattered all about.

David and Max exchanged bewildered glances before they, too, began running toward what had once been Christine's private dormitory and study hall. But all was now in shambles. Whatever order she had imposed on her files, all the academically correct data gleaned from hundreds of interviews, was gone. Dr. Brecht flew at the wreckage of the trailer, assailing the absent perpetrators in her native tongue, while Christine belted out another long string of obscenities. Max looked at David, his eyes suddenly wide.

"The clinic!"

The words barely escaped his lips before he was off at a sprint. David raced after him.

It could have been worse, but not by much. The tents were still standing, but the files and supply cabinets were turned over, their contents strewn all over the earthen floor. And the shortwave radio was smashed to bits.

"Damn it!" cried Max as he picked up an empty folder. "They took Oscar's files."

"My God!" said David as he crouched down to help amass what scant records remained. But then he stopped quite suddenly. "The schoolhouse!" he cried, and took off in its direction in as fast a gait as he could manage in his clumsy shoes.

Max realized that there was nothing to be done in any short time frame to restore order to the clinic. He ran after David and caught up to him halfway to his schoolhouse, which stood just a quarter mile from the clinic. Neither of them spoke as they ran, but as they neared the clearing that surrounded the schoolhouse, where the children would play at lunchtime, David slowed down. Through the thorn trees and acacia scrub they could see smoke and could even hear raucous laughter emanating from his humble home.

"My God, they're in there," said Max, realizing that whoever had overrun the clinic and Christine's trailer wasn't quite through ransacking the general neighborhood. And he noticed his Scout parked just beyond the schoolhouse.

"Jesus, they even stole the Scout. Maybe we should wait on this. They're probably pretty well armed."

"Joseph will be livid," David replied. "He told me his moran were patrolling the entire area. I thought it would be safe to leave."

Chapter 40

Just a few miles to the north, a Red Cross ambulance worked its way through a seemingly endless throng, leaving a long and winding cloud of red dust that was slow to dissipate. Scores of refugees, choking in its wake but unable to flee, implored the vehicle to stop and administer aid, or maybe even some food. They clawed at the red-and-white box on wheels as it rapidly plied its way through their particular cramped neighborhood, which itself was lost within the vast expanse of landless humanity that had ventured so far from home for reasons few of them really quite understood.

Occasionally, the driver would shout at them to get out of his way. He had nothing, he yelled out. He was just going back for more supplies. But once beyond the hungry hordes, he abandoned the box on wheels and was promptly escorted to Nairobi in a new but dusty Mercedes that just happened to be passing by. He caught the first flight to Marseille the following morning.

When the immigration officer asked for his identification, he handed over his Red Cross badge along with his passport. He stated that his business was to consult with a medical specialist, a Dr. Meinz, regarding the condition of a particular refugee he was treating in Kenya. The officer expressed his dismay at what was transpiring there and let the man pass.

Two hours later he had reached the gatehouse to Peter Dermenjian's villa. He lowered the window of his SUV to speak, but before he could utter a sound, the gate opened. He quickly found a parking space beneath an ancient olive tree, and when he reached the front door it swung open before him as well. In a few lengthy strides he stood before an elevator, entered the pass code, and climbed into the small enclosure that quickly made the ascent to an upper floor devoted entirely to Dermenjian Diamonds, Ltd.

It was Peter Dermenjian's lair extraordinaire, a well-fortified, well-furnished, and well-equipped inner sanctum that floated above the rest of the villa, occupying a central position that afforded panoramic views of the Mediterranean beyond and the terrace below, as well as strategic views via hidden cameras of the comings and goings of those few brave souls who dared to render a visit unannounced. Dark shelves of intricately carved walnut lined the entire back wall, and upon those shelves were numerous video monitors displaying views from the driveway, the pool, and the kitchen, as well as his retail stores in Paris, London, Tokyo, and New York and his production facility in Antwerp. In the center of the room stood a large walnut desk, with more ornate carvings that portrayed various aspects of the grape harvest. Peter Dermenjian sat behind it in a sizable leather chair, tapping his fingers together in anticipation as the door of the elevator slowly opened.

"Banyon," said Peter, "what news?"

"Good to see you, Mr. Dermenjian," said the tall black man, clean shaven now and no longer dressed in his Red Cross garb. Peter rose and extended his hand in greeting. Banyon shook it firmly.

"I have some information that I believe will please you very much."

"I have no doubt," replied Peter, forcing a smile but clearly apprehensive. "Apparently, it's so important that I have to pay to fly you here to tell me in person."

The man known simply as Banyon—whose passport, at least the one he was using at the moment, said his first names were Jean Paul—smiled and walked past him to settle down in an overstuffed chair near the window. He carried a large briefcase, which he set down upon a small table made of red Italian marble. Dr. Meinz stood by near the elevator.

"So, what have you got?" Peter asked rather impatiently.

"Well," said Banyon, smiling, "I'll tell you this for sure."

"Yes," said Peter, "pray tell me. After all, that's why we're all here and why you're being paid—quite handsomely, too."

"I can tell you that for sure"—Banyon paused, carefully fingering the combination lock on the briefcase—"that for sure Oscar Newman is alive."

Peter evinced no change in expression as these words wormed their way into the various dark recesses of his tortured mind, recesses entirely consumed with the notion that only one man possibly alive actually knew where *they* were, where the infamous Dermenjian family sunset diamonds originated, those that were brother and sister to the various multicarat gems stored in the vault that lay within this very room. And suddenly this man, Oscar Newman, witness to his brother's killing, a man who was not only his sworn enemy but his potential savior, was now what— alive? It seemed so preposterous after all the reports of lion attacks and Maasai rescues of what had to have been the wrong man. But what he had just heard at last made his heart leap to his throat.

"How do you know?" Peter demanded.

310

"It's very simple," said Banyon. "I have his recent medical records here. Look at this. Nearly daily records of a Caucasian man who weighs 260 pounds. Can there be any doubt who that is? Suffering badly from malaria, yet just last week he was found fit to be relocated."

Peter carefully examined the files, mere handwritten data sheets with no name and, more importantly, no dates. "How do you know this is from last week?" he asked. "How do you know it's not the imposter?"

"Oh, that's simple. His records are right here. Prospector from Texas, born in Oklahoma, out of his mind. According to the charts, at least."

Banyon handed Peter another set of manila folders, all labeled Jack McGraw, who was only weighing in at 160 pounds. Alcoholic, heatstroke, dehydration. Suffered from delusions, thought he was on an island somewhere.

"All right, but you still haven't told me how you know these records are from last week," said Peter, holding aloft the first set of folders.

"Observations," replied Banyon. "All these files were created after the Maasai moved south to their current location. The clinic moved with them. We found everything from before the move all boxed up."

Peter stood up and began to pace the length of the long, narrow office space. He walked to the far end, where there were more neatly arranged bookshelves, then stopped and turned on one heel.

"Fine," he said calmly, staring directly and rather piercingly into Banyon's eyes. "Then where is he?"

The words hung in the air for what felt to Peter an eternity. Banyon's former bravado seemed to have been sapped from within. He cleared his throat.

"Not far," he said softly. "Not far."

Peter cocked his head slightly, his patience as thin as the air above Kilimanjaro.

"I mean," said Banyon, "we are certain he is still in Maasailand. No one has left the area, not in any vehicle, at least. And he's in no shape to walk anywhere soon."

"Really?" Peter countered. "Then how did he get there all the way from the godforsaken shores of Lake Natron? That's the last place he was seen alive."

"I don't know, but we were tricked," said Banyon. "He was hidden in the priest's cellar. We found more bandages down there full of blood. Why would there be bandages in his cellar if they hadn't been hiding someone? And who would they hide if not him? Everybody knows he's wanted for murdering your brother."

These words seemed to cut sharply and Peter backed away.

"Sorry," said Banyon. "But the reasoning is sound."

Peter nodded. "Yes," he said, "the reasoning is sound, but you still haven't answered my question. Where the hell is he?"

Banyon reached into his coat pocket and retrieved a pack of Gauloises. He offered one to Peter, who declined. Banyon lit a match and raised it to the short, fat stick of black Turkish tobacco. Blue smoke rose before them, threatening to engulf Peter. Dr. Meinz alertly switched on the ceiling fan.

"I believe they've hidden him up on the escarpment somewhere. It can be pretty wild up there, hard to track and hard to get to. The only other place would be down in the swamps where there's plenty of cover. But you don't go sending someone with malaria down to the swamps to recuperate."

Peter considered all this for a moment before responding. "What about the Maasai? How do you know he's not in one of their manyattas?"

"Very unlikely. There are wanted signs everywhere. The one called Joseph might be inclined to shelter him, but not in full view of a whole village that believes Oscar killed your brother, their friend."

"If I may remind you, he *did* kill my brother," Peter cut in. "So all I can say is find him, whatever it takes. And find him soon."

"That is my intention," Banyon replied, "but I will need more money."

Peter flinched slightly and then turned to renew his pacing. "Surely you've not spent what I've already allotted for this particular task?"

"And then some. Here's my estimate"—and he handed Peter a slip of paper.

Peter winced again. "Outrageous," he shouted.

Banyon remained silent, holding his ground.

"All right," said Peter at last, after sufficient pacing. "But remember that my accountants will be scrutinizing each and every expense of yours."

Banyon began to laugh. "Of course they will, of course. Then it's agreed."

Peter did not respond, but with a gesture of the hand motioned him toward the exit. "You keep me informed," was all Peter had to say as Banyon stepped into the elevator, still smiling to himself. He'd never even asked about the guns.

Dr. Meinz cleared his throat, as if begging permission to speak. "Well," he said rather nervously, "that's certainly encouraging news. I don't wish to change the

312

subject, but Ms. Le Clerc's brother has been calling here day and night wishing to know when she will be, uh, 'released,' as he put it. I don't suppose that you would be willing to speak with him?"

Peter, who'd been staring blankly toward the Mediterranean, turned sharply and looked at Dr. Meinz, incredulous and newly enraged. "How can you speak of such a thing at this particular moment?" he stated. "This news is unbearable. He is alive, but no one knows where. We must find him. And as for her, don't you realize that she is the first person he will seek out? No, I cannot let her out of my sight. Not now, especially not now."

Before Dr. Meinz could reply the elevator door slid open and Natalia appeared, her hair a newly tinted purple.

"It's time for your fitting, my dear," she said.

"My what?" said Peter. "What on earth are you talking about?"

"You haven't forgotten what day it is, have you? I need to have you try on your costume. And you won't want to hear this, but the escort service called to say your 'intended' came down with appendicitis last night. I'm afraid pickings are rather slim at this late date."

"Is it Saturday already?" Peter replied. "It can't be!"

"Yes, it can," said Natalia. "Put this on."

She handed him what looked like some type of deformed iron lung that was hinged along one side. She also had with her a baggy pair of knickers, long stockings, pointy shoes, and a strange-looking square hat with a piece torn away.

"What in the world—" he began.

"Come now," she scolded, "you're going as Don Quixote, don't you remember?"

"Don Quixote? And why not the Count of Monte Cristo?"

"Again? You've been the count for three years running. It's time for a change. Besides, we discussed all this."

Peter was beside himself, going on about the cheek of Elizabeth's brother to dare portray him as her imprisoner when all he was trying to do was to help console her in her time of loss—while also spending, let no one forget, an enormous sum trying to find the man who was causing them both so much grief. Meanwhile, Natalia helped him out of his trousers and helped him on with the stockings, knickers, blowsy shirt, phony chest armor, and the absurd hat.

"Nearly perfect," said Natalia. "We'll just need to shorten the sleeves a bit."

"And what about an escort? I suppose you think I should just take you?"

"Please," she replied in her husky voice as she began removing various pieces of the Don Quixote ensemble, "you're putting far too much strain on my feeble heart."

"Here's an idea," said Dr. Meinz, a bit sheepishly. "What about Ms. Le Clerc? Lord knows she could use a change of scenery."

Peter stepped back into his trousers and laughed. "Elizabeth?" he cried. "Such an idea! Excellent, in fact."

Apparently, the concept of spending the evening with Elizabeth—in fact, the entire night if history were to hold true—intrigued him to the point of absolute rapture. A certain radiance not seen for weeks, at least not since his brother's unfortunate death, overcame him.

"But who would she be, then, if I'm the great, errant knight from La Mancha?" he asked, clearly intrigued.

Natalia stared at him disbelief. "Why, Dulcinea, who else? And you're a knight-errant."

"Whatever. But Dulcinea? At least you have the first part right—dull! But we'd need supervision, Dr. Meinz, of course. Conrad, what have you for a costume for tonight?"

"I know," said Natalia. "I believe I could transform this plump little pudding into a rather simple Sancho Panza without too much trouble at all."

Peter looked at them all, his face aglow. "Excellent," he declared. "We leave in one hour."

Chapter 41

Dr. Meinz plodded steadfastly toward the large guest room where Elizabeth had been residing for the past few weeks. He tapped gently at the door. Hearing no reply, he carefully turned the ancient door handle and entered the bedroom.

Her light-brown hair lay in streaks across the white pillowcase, her face turned away.

"Ms. Le Clerc," said Dr. Meinz softly, "I've brought you a bite to eat. And some tea."

Elizabeth barely moved at first. Though slow to respond, she soon rolled over and lifted her weary head, blinking as she tried to focus her newly opened eyes upon him.

"Dr. Meinz?" she whispered, searching for her voice. Newspapers were strewn about the room, but the one that still lay upon the bed bore the headline "SEARCH FOR NOBEL PEACE LAUREATE ABANDONED."

"I've brought you some food," he said. "It's well past noon."

Elizabeth stared at him with a blank expression. "I'm not hungry," she replied, turning back away from him.

"But you must eat," he insisted, "and besides, we're going for a little boat ride today. Peter thought it might help restore your spirits."

Elizabeth lay in silence. "Nothing can restore my spirits," she replied somewhat faintly, "unless Oscar returns."

"That he may," said Dr. Meinz, though not too convincingly. "But until he does, or doesn't, we must keep up our strength. You must eat, and then we will all take a little ride on Peter's yacht. I know you will enjoy it."

With that, he poured Elizabeth a cup of tea and handed it to her, nearly spilling it as Elizabeth leaned forward in her loosely fitting flannel gown.

"This is different," she declared, sniffing at the steaming mug. "But nice."

"I thought you might like a change. Perhaps it will perk you up a bit."

Elizabeth smiled, and it took him by surprise. "Thank you," she said. "You are too kind to me."

"Nonsense," he replied, "I'm just looking after you. It's no burden. But please, if you can, be ready to leave within the hour."

Elizabeth sipped her tea. "Where are we going?"

315

"Just for a little cruise along the French Riviera."

She contemplated this a moment, glancing at the tear-stained newspaper. "All right," she said. "I'll be ready."

And so she was. Dr. Meinz drove Natalia in a separate car with the costumes. Peter, in his Ferrari, raced in the lead around the tight curves and steep declines that his private road had carved within the rich red volcanic rock of the Massif de l'Estérel. Peter braced for the last hairpin turn before joining the coast highway. He glanced to his right only to see Elizabeth laughing as she held her arms high, trying to gather in the cooling breeze as it passed over the windshield. No, apparently, he wasn't driving too fast.

Upon reaching the waterfront in Cannes, achieved by snaking his way through narrow back streets, Peter quickly found his accustomed valet. The latter helped Elizabeth out of the low-slung car seat and handed her off to Peter. He turned toward her and was shocked to see that her piercing blue eyes were nearly level with his and seemed to look clear through him. Much to his surprise, she let go of his hand and placed her arm through his.

They proceeded along the quay, well within view of the crowds gathered in the long arc of picturesque cafés and restaurants that embraced the harbor, as at every port along the Riviera. The patrons, engaged in idle chatter, were all sipping their drinks, adjusting their *lunettes de soleil*, and doing their best to ignore the attractive, well-groomed couple that was slowly making their way, arm in arm, toward a formidable assemblage of top-of-the-line yachts, the kind that often grace Riviera harbors.

Peter led her out along one of the piers toward an immensely sleek and modern-looking vessel, whose hull was a dark blue and whose upper cabins were white with plenty of windows. The mellow tones of well-oiled teak and mahogany, along with a number of guests dressed in chic Riviera attire, showed through them.

"Your name is Jacqueline," he whispered. "If anyone speaks to you, just smile. No one will expect you to be terribly conversant."

The remark nearly stopped her in her tracks, but somehow the appropriate response to such an insult, delivered so obliquely, failed her. She watched Peter continue on into the main cabin to greet his guests and, summoning courage, she ventured forth. Somewhere along the way, however, she decided that the insult didn't matter one bit and that she would take his directive quite literally. She simply bade her mouth grin and felt herself breaking into as large a smile as she had ever smiled. It was suddenly so easy, like she was born to smile.

Once inside, she was quickly introduced to the various suntanned and jewelry-laden guests. Natalia handed her a glass of champagne. She took a small sip and smiled at all the guests, grateful to be under a gag rule because all the words that came to mind seemed quite silly. It made her want to break into laughter, but she somehow managed to maintain her quickly receding composure.

Natalia appeared as Elizabeth was smiling down a gray-haired gentleman in an olivine suit whose name she hadn't quite caught. She grabbed Elizabeth by the hand and led her to one of the outside decks. The lovely port of Cannes was fading into the distance, far beyond the yacht's considerable wake as it sliced the blue Mediterranean into ribbons of arcing white foam. Elizabeth took a deep breath and felt the salt air fill her lungs. The scent of the sea pleased her, like the caress of an old friend. A bright Mediterranean sun surrounded her with warmth as they stood within the lee of the aft cabin. The bubbling champagne tickled her lips every time she took a sip and made her laugh.

"I can't believe I'm on a yacht!" Elizabeth shouted over the roar of the engines. "Where are we going?"

"Didn't he tell you?" Natalia replied incredulously.

"Who? Peter? He never tells me anything." But she continued to smile.

"Why, you're going to have the night of your life," said Natalia. "But we need to get you dressed. This could take a while."

They retreated to the interior of the spacious cruiser, to a large room where there were racks of strange-looking clothes and mirrors everywhere. Several black wigs were resting upon mannequin heads.

"We'll begin with your hair," said Natalia.

"Wait one minute!" Elizabeth protested. "I've never worn a wig in my life and I'm not beginning now."

"But you must," Natalia insisted as she attempted to attach Elizabeth to a tall stool in the middle of the salon. "It's part of your costume."

"My costume? What are you talking about?"

"Why, you're going to the *Fête de Venice* masquerade ball in Monte Carlo, at the world-famous casino. Peter will be Don Quixote. And you will be—"

"Dulcinea," replied Elizabeth before Natalia could finish.

"Yes," said Natalia, "that's very good. So now you must get ready."

Elizabeth looked momentarily confused yet quite intrigued. "But then why the dark wigs? Dulcinea was a blond."

"Nonsense," Natalia shot back. "She was Spanish."

"Yes," Elizabeth replied, "but she was blond. It is one of my favorite books."

Natalia appeared quite confused. What was she talking about? A blond? "All right," she said. "I don't have any blond wigs. But if you insist on being blond, that's fine with me. We'll just need to try a different approach."

Somewhere in this exchange, the notion that Elizabeth was destined to escort one of the wealthiest and most elusively eligible bachelors in all of Europe to perhaps the grandest exposé of extravagance along the Riviera was lost on her. She was far more concerned that her rendition of Dulcinea conform to her notions of this femme fatale who seared the heart of one of literature's most endearing idiots. Her insistence that she was but of peasant stock and that simplicity must reign was accommodated in part by the costume master, who saw to it that her waist was drawn as tight as could be and that, with a bit of help from a bustier, she displayed an adequate degree of cleavage. Peter would insist on it.

When the two of them emerged from the salon and entered the main cabin, they were greeted by a long series of oohs and ahhs and *magnifiques!* Peter Dermenjian had been chatting up the gentleman in olivine, who happened to own several diamond outlets in Italy. Upon seeing Elizabeth, however, he ceased speaking and stared in amazement. Her hair, now quite blond, hung in long ringlets that framed her lovely face, which was now more beautiful than he'd ever seen it before and more beautiful than he'd ever imagined it could be. Her exquisitely full lips were anointed with bright-red lipstick; her eyes were highlighted by intense blue and coral eye shadow that ran clear to her darkened and elongated eyebrows. The simple peasant blouse, billowing as it embraced her shoulders yet plunging quite nicely where it should, fit snugly about her and was tucked into a beautiful blue-and-red scarf tied tightly about her waist. Several gold necklaces attempted in vain to obscure her now-pronounced bosom, which Natalia had labored quite successfully to place *en evidence*.

"Il y a du monde sur le balcon," chuckled the gentleman with whom Peter had been speaking and whose eyes were clearly focused on her newly pronounced bust line, her "crowded balcony."

The latter remained speechless while Elizabeth, a.k.a. Jacqueline, spun slow circles before the wide-eyed crowd. Her simple dark skirt flew up as she stomped the hardwood floor with her high-heeled silver boots, flamenco style. Peter and the guests all marveled at the sight. But what amazed Peter more than any of her adornments was the fact that not only was she smiling, she was laughing! This was certainly a side of her he'd never seen or even dreamed existed. He cast a glance at Dr. Meinz, who turned away, looking a bit embarrassed.

"Come," said Natalia, grabbing his hand, "it is your turn."

Peter was still gawking at his, er, escort as Natalia led both him and Dr. Meinz away. The guests realized that they, too, had better ready their costumes and began to recede from the room, leaving Elizabeth alone with the rest of the hors d'oeuvres and several unfinished bottles of champagne, just as the sun was beginning to set over the Mediterranean.

When Peter and his guests returned in all their *bal masqué* finery, which ranged from a pathetic giant swan to an aging court jester, a crew member announced that dinner was served. Two enormous oak doors leading to the very interior of the vessel opened as if by magic, revealing an elegant table adorned with enough dishes and silver to signal to all aboard that a serious feast was at hand. Peter took a seat at the head of the table, motioning to Elizabeth to take the one to his left. The others found their various name tags. The ostrich would sit at the other end of the table, with the court jester to his right. Then came the swan, the mime, the Queen of Hearts, et cetera. Sancho Panza filled in the spot next to Elizabeth.

It was all quite delicious, though Elizabeth found that her appetite had vanished. Some of the wines were quite heady and rich, but she managed to consume each glass that was poured for her. The conversation was animated, taking off in a number of linguistic directions, French and Italian mostly, but with some smatterings of Spanish. She said nothing as instructed, and no one posed a question or made any comment in her direction, which she found rather odd. On another occasion it might have seemed quite rude, but she understood her orders and merely sat still, secretly amused by every facet of the behavior of this strange entourage. They all just sat there in their absurd-looking costumes, awkwardly stabbing at bits of food, swirling it in sauce, sipping their wine, and making endless comments about how delicious every dish was. By the time they had finished their pears poached in burgundy, they were rapidly approaching their destination. At last everyone ventured out onto the deck, and all were quite pleased to discover that night had fallen and that Monte Carlo was ablaze with lights as they approached the pier.

319

Colorful fireworks cascaded down from above. The yacht glided smoothly into a berth all its own, parting the sparkling carpet of reflections that the million points of exploding light above painted on the surface of the water. As the gangplank was lowered, a parade of beautiful horse-drawn carriages pulled up along the quay. The foremost was larger than the others, entirely black with ornate gold trim along every seam. Elizabeth expected to see Cinderella herself descend from it as the tuxedo-clad footman opened the door. Only when Peter nudged her forward did she realize that this particular carriage was meant for her.

"For me?" she inquired, her eyes wide and almost teary.

The handsome young footman took her gently by the hand and guided her up each step that led to the inner sanctum of the carriage. Plush pink cushions, a dozen fresh red roses, and a chilled bottle of champagne awaited. Peter moved in beside her while Dr. Meinz heeded subtle signals and clambered up beside the driver. They moved slowly along the quay, the clip-clop of the horse's hooves beating out a pleasant rhythm as they passed beneath the soft glow of gaslights. To their right the armada of luxury yachts bobbed in the protected confines of the harbor. Their cabin lights reflected in the dark, slowly swirling waters caught Elizabeth's gaze, and she remained fixated on their mesmerizing patterns until Peter interrupted.

"There's the Place du Casino," he said, pointing to his left, just as a rocket exploded above a pleasant square filled with greenery, several large fountains, and in the center a large, oval pool. And beyond the flowers and fountains stood the famous casino, with its two ornate towers standing like sentinels over the sumptuous entry.

Elizabeth turned to look. To see clearly out of the carriage window required her to lean halfway across Peter. He placed an arm upon her shoulder, touching her pale skin where the billowing blouse ended.

"It's marvelous," she cried.

"Yes, indeed it is," said Peter. He removed his gaze from her bare shoulder and looked back toward their rapidly approaching destination. Dozens of costumed revelers were slowly heading toward the casino, in front of which was a welcoming committee of high-hatted beefeaters that reinforced the impression that they were approaching Buckingham Palace rather than a mere gambling hall.

Elizabeth finished one last glass of champagne as the carriage pulled to a halt. The young driver helped her down, and without thinking she grabbed on to Peter's hand. "It's perfect," she said with a bit of a wild laugh. "And if you don't mind my saying so, Señor Quixote, you look ridiculously fabulous."

Now she was leaning on Peter, still laughing as he led her toward the wonderfully illuminated and thoroughly magnificent casino. Dr. Sancho Panza, with his large satchel, scurried to keep up.

As they passed through the center-most of the three enormous sets of doors that fit snugly between the byzantine-looking towers, Elizabeth raced ahead to touch one of the many pale-green marble pillars that stretched up to an enormous Victorian-era glass ceiling.

"This is the atrium," said Peter.

"It's beautiful," she replied as she continued to stare at the tons of glass and intricately stretched and shaped wrought iron above. She stood at the center of a large black-and-white star that was part of the marble floor and began twirling. Peter grabbed her hand and led her quickly into the adjacent salon.

If he had a notion that this might quell her enthusiasm for the surroundings, he was mistaken. For the Salle Europe proved even more exciting to her. The walls were covered in olive-green panels and pale-yellow columns framing beautiful nineteenth-century paintings. It seemed as though the entirety of this enormous room had been lifted directly from the Louvre. In the center stood several large gaming tables, each one surrounded by avid gamblers. And each gambler was masquerading as his or her own statement for the season, or perhaps for the ages. It was hard to tell. She recognized some from the yacht. But once again Peter intervened.

"Here," he said to Dr. Meinz, who was having some difficulty keeping his peasant's trousers aloft. He handed him a small bundle of bills. "See that she has a good time. When she's lost all that, you can show her around. I'll be in the Salle Médecin but I do not wish to be disturbed, not until I've fleeced that Greek bastard who laid into me last month. Be sure to keep an eye on her at all times. I don't know what was in that tea, but she's more lit up than all of Monte Carlo."

"Uh, very well, sir," he replied a bit more nervously than usual. "Nothing to be worried about."

"Elizabeth," Peter began, before catching himself. "Excuse me. I mean Dulcinea."

"Dulcinella," she quickly corrected with a bit of a giggle.

"Whatever," he replied. "I regret to inform you that I must be off in pursuit of new conquests to better defend my honor, and yours."

Elizabeth knelt before him, taking him quite by surprise. "May you win the day, in spades," she quipped.

"Yes," replied Peter. "Thank you. I've given Dr. Meinz—er, Sancho—enough money to keep you entertained. Assuming all this gambling is new to you, he will try to explain the rules. I wish you good fortune."

"Thank you. But don't be gone too long," she replied as she stood, leaned forward, and planted a kiss on his cheek.

Though temporarily stunned, he was clearly anxious to be headed to where stakes were more to his liking. He leaned over toward Dr. Meinz, who was still grasping the wad of bills in one hand and the rope that hung all too loosely around his middle in the other.

"You keep a close eye on her. She never leaves your sight."

Dr. Meinz simply nodded as the famous would-be knight-errant turned and, wiping the lipstick from his cheek, strutted off in his absurd iron lung toward some inner sanctum of the casino where only the wealthiest folk in Europe—or anywhere, for that matter—could tread. Thus were Don Quixote's servant and imaginary consort abandoned, left to mingle with the rest of the masquerading mob. And the mob appeared equally divided between attacking the gaming tables and attacking the hors d'oeuvres and trays of champagne flutes and shots of whisky supplied in seemingly endless quantity by dozens of black-and-white-clad servers—all wearing masks, of course. An orchestra, heretofore unnoticed, began to play. Elizabeth turned and saw that directly behind her a dozen or so musicians were launching into a vibrant jazz number that added still more energy to the incredible ambience. It made the evening seem even more dreamlike, and it reminded her that Dulcinea was but a figment of Don Quixote's imagination, a dream within Cervantes' dream, in fact. It seemed so right, like her life of late—a dream within perhaps several dreams, one of which was a very bad dream that she did not wish to revisit at this particular time. No, this was a good dream—and it beckoned.

She recognized the court jester standing by one of the roulette tables and decided she would approach him. His wife, she presumed, a plump woman in her midfifties dressed uncomfortably as a 1920s flapper, clung to him as if she'd already had far too much to drink. He nodded cordially toward Elizabeth and asked how she was faring, though his attention seemed fixated on the colorful wheel at the far end of the table that was about to perform its magic. Consistent with her oath of silence, Elizabeth simply smiled at the gentleman and watched him place his bet. She heard the cry of *"les jeux sont faits"* and watched closely as the little silver ball bounced and danced all about the glimmering roulette wheel as it spun quickly around and around. Despite the masks, the sudden burst in the collective anxiety of those surrounding the table was nearly palpable as they, too, all watched the little silver ball as it became more and more discernible, randomly careening and glancing off the raised surfaces that defined each one-thirty-sixth of the surface of the wheel, everyone impatient to know if the little silver ball would ultimately find temporary quarters in his or her minute piece of the action.

There was a collective groan as the ball finally came to a halt.

"Vingt-deux," signaled the marshal, an attractive gentleman in his forties who wore a cowboy hat, a red bandana, and a gold star and who presided over this particular table. Everyone stared at the empty space, number twenty-two, while the marshal raked in certain chips and left others and began distributing some to one of the gamblers, a fellow dressed like Teddy Roosevelt, complete with riding britches, handlebar mustache, and of course the classic monocle.

"Would you care to place a bet?" came a voice that Elizabeth finally recognized as Dr. Meinz, who was now standing beside her holding a tray of multicolored chips.

"I, uh, I don't know…," she began.

"It's very simple," offered the court jester. "You simply place a few chips on one of the squares and then you say good-bye to them."

"Why not?" said Elizabeth. She looked at the table and saw that number thirty-six was open. That was her age, so why not bet on it?

Dr. Meinz suggested she begin with five red chips. She carefully stacked them on the preselected square as the marshal again announced *"les jeux sont faits"* and spun the wheel once more. The little ball danced in circles, and now Elizabeth felt herself being drawn closer to the table, leaning over along with the others to see more clearly whether fate would smile on her particular patch of green felt.

"Trente-quatre," cried the marshal and again there was a collective sigh, yet the marshal somehow spared Elizabeth's chips.

"Did I win?" she asked.

"No," said the jester, "but you didn't lose, either. I'd leave it right there."

323

And so she did, but not before placing another five chips on top of the previous five. The marshal spun the wheel again, and again they all watched as the ball jumped and to her amazement stopped at…

"Trente-six!"

Amid the cries of *félicitations*, she watched as the marshal pushed a pile of chips toward her. It was a wonderful moment, but in an instant the wheel spun one more time and the ten chips, plus the next five she had added, were gone. No matter—she was highly engaged now and completely energized. Someone handed her a glass of champagne and toasted her. It was the lion tamer with all the rings, who had not ceased looking her over and over since she arrived. She smiled at him and winked, then placed another bet. This time she decided she would try to cover more spaces, the better to capture the flag.

"Dix-huit," yelled the marshal, and another pile of chips was pushed in her direction.

She squealed with delight as she carefully arranged her variously colored chips into neat piles. Her entire world was now completely focused on the wheel and the little silver ball, almost ignoring the strange assortment of oddly festooned characters, all hooting and shouting and getting quite drunk on the champagne and whisky. Dr. Meinz, ever attentive, just kept feeding her more chips whenever she ran low. Her winnings came and went. How many thousands of euros she was ahead or behind mattered little, just as long as the little silver ball kept spinning and dancing.

"Trente-six, encore," shouted the marshal, incredulous. Now she was on a tear. Emboldened, she stacked her chips as high as she could without toppling them.

"Vingt-trois," he yelled, and just as quickly her fortune began to recede.

"Douze!" he yelled, and again the rake carried off several piles that had once been hers.

"Perhaps we should stop now," Dr. Meinz offered.

She turned and gave him a furious look, one of defiance and near-complete inebriation. He had stopped counting the champagne glasses long ago. Foolishly, she took the whole pile and placed it on the corner, next to thirty-six.

"What the hell," she said amid gasps all around. The marshal gave her a look as if to say, "Are you certain about this bet?" but proceeded to spin the wheel.

"Dix-neuf," he yelled, and again the rake came forward and took away not only all her winnings but all the chips she had ever possessed during the course of

the evening. Everyone groaned in unison, including some of the fresh faces who had recently joined the table, perhaps to get a look at this tall, blond woman in the sexy peasant dress who was by far the main attraction at this particular table.

"That was quite risky," said Dr. Meinz, "but now we are done here and I'm to show you around. Come."

He motioned to her like a master calling his dog. She refused to budge. She looked around the table. All of them were looking at her, all these fabulously wealthy men who must be so completely bored to be honoring her with so much attention and with so much sympathy. What did they really look like, she wondered, behind those masks and all that makeup? Suddenly, a new course of action came to mind, a rather outrageous one, but after all, what was there for her to do? She had no one in the world any longer who cared for her. Not even Peter, wherever he was.

Just as the marshal placed his hand on the wheel to begin the next spin, she jumped onto the table and planted herself on the corner, next to thirty-six, standing on her tiptoes as best she could, which was clearly a challenge to her, as she began to waver.

The marshal directed her to get down but she refused. He motioned to someone and shook his head. He gave her one last chance but she would not move. So he spun the wheel.

Dr. Meinz was yelling at her while the others, especially the lion tamer, began to hoot and holler. The orchestra quickly changed tunes and lit into a flamenco number. Elizabeth, seeming to adore all the attention, began to stomp her stiletto-heeled silver boots while the little ball still spun around and around. The stomping of her boots made the little ball dance even more than usual while she yipped and spun and stomped wildly. Her skirt was flying high, an even larger crowd had gathered, and somewhere beyond men in uniform, not just casino security but several gendarmes, made their way into the room. Dr. Meinz panicked and went to find Peter.

When they returned at a run, the security forces and the gendarmes were still attempting to penetrate the hordes while three gentlemen—the lion tamer, Teddy Roosevelt, and, curiously, the pope—were each arguing vehemently that they had won the bet and that Elizabeth was now in their possession. The orchestra played on and Elizabeth continued to bear down rapidly with her boot heels, turning in slow circles while tearing the green felt to shreds, scattering all the various chips, and yet still laughing hysterically.

"Je suis á vous!" she exclaimed in the direction of the three men, who were now near to blows.

"Elizabeth!" shouted Peter with all his might.

She turned and waved at him but still refused to come down. The constables yelled as well until one of them produced a very harsh whistle and blew it so loudly that everyone had to cover his or her ears. The orchestra stopped immediately and everyone fell silent. Elizabeth stopped spinning, though she was very near to collapsing from dizziness and overall intoxication. Suddenly, from the entrance to the room, by the atrium, came a familiar voice.

"Elizabeth," it shouted, "get down this instant."

The entire entourage turned as one and watched as a slender young fellow wearing ballerina slippers, pink-and-white-striped leggings, a puffy purple shirt, and heart-shaped pink sunglasses approached the table.

"Edouard!" exclaimed Elizabeth as she quickly descended from the table and ran over to hug her brother.

"My God," said Peter, "it's the sugarplum fairy. Where the hell did he come from?"

And he watched in abject horror as Elizabeth slipped her arm through his and quickly departed without even a good-bye to the stunned crowd or to Peter, who, suddenly surrounded by the casino security and gendarmes, was clearly being held accountable for the damages. After all, it was his guest—some penniless hired escort, as usual—who had inflicted them, and besides, everyone knew who had the deepest pockets in town. He protested mightily, as did the lion tamer, Teddy Roosevelt, and the pope, but to no avail. Like a mirage, she was suddenly gone.

Chapter 42

"Such a pity," David groaned as he picked up an empty bottle of Pomerol, a rare survivor of the exceptional 1982 vintage. It was just one among his modest assemblage of France's finest wines, all of which were now strewn about his humble household, each one completely drained.

"This must have been the knockout punch," said Max.

He was peering inside a dusty green bottle, hoping a drop or two of the precious liquid—merely thirty-year-old Armagnac—might have survived. It was a tremendous loss for David but a sacrifice, considering their plight, that he would have to endure *quand même*. As they surveyed the lamentable state of affairs, Joseph reentered, waving his fly brush with his usual flair, and announced that the prisoners were ready to be escorted back to their camp.

The refugees, all six of them, were tied together like a human chain and surrounded by a dozen taunting moran who still held their spears at the ready. They represented a mere fraction of the strike force Joseph had assembled in order to reclaim David's schoolhouse, needlessly, as it were. For the early-morning raid, in which the spear-clenching moran stealthily invaded the temporary sanctuary of the gun-wielding invaders, proved unnecessary. Each of the refugees had passed out, victims of excess consumption, and each was rudely awakened by the sharp, cold touch of a Maasai spear pointed at his throat. Now they all stood hunched over in their greasy, tattered clothes, hung over and humiliated while the moran continued to assault them with trash talk of a most vulgar kind that David hoped they could not comprehend. The situation was already tense enough.

Max expressed his dismay at Joseph's apparent decision to let them go. Why not turn them in? Despite David's observation that there didn't appear to be any authority in the vicinity to whom they could "turn them in," Max could not believe Joseph would allow these malicious intruders to simply return to their decrepit homes, however provisional, without some element of punishment.

"This really sucks," said Max as he surveyed the damage to David's quarters. "But frankly, I'm a lot more concerned with what happened to Oscar's medical records. At least you can replace this stuff, if you had the money."

"I'll bet I know who has them," said David, who clearly didn't have "the money."

"Dermenjian?"

"Who else?"

Joseph himself led the parade northward, forbidding anyone besides a few of the elders and his moran security force to accompany them. This was a matter for the Maasai to deal with in their own way, pure and simple. Max helped David restore some semblance of order, picking up empty tins that once held foie gras, caviar, and escargots. All the French delicacies from his sizable warehouse, heretofore hidden away, had been rudely consumed by the invading party. Or if not entirely consumed, badly contaminated. Even his favorite andouille sausage, admittedly a very strong rustic sort, was going to waste. Perhaps it was a bit too pungent, even for starving refugees.

With the morning getting on and David's premises at least in some semblance of working order, Max turned his attention to the Scout, now stationed behind the schoolhouse. Whoever had hot-wired it had done so very crudely. But the key still worked. The engine cranked over and over but would not start. Max checked under the hood. David, still occupied indoors, grimaced as he heard Max shouting more obscenities.

"The bastards stole my distributor cap," he shouted as David approached. "Now why did they have to go and do that?"

"Can't you fix it?"

"Fix it?" said Max. "How do you fix what you don't have? There's no distributor cap."

"Dermenjian," said David. "He knows Oscar is here somewhere, so he cut off any means of escape."

"Well," said Max quite dejectedly, "looks like we're stuck here all right."

By noon he had restored the clinic as best he could, refiling what little paperwork remained in the now-upright metal cabinets. The medical supplies, at least those that were salvageable, had been returned to their respective drawers and cabinets. The smashed-up shortwave radio and all the rest of the unsalvageable rubble had been gathered up in plastic sacks and stowed behind one of the tents. But throughout the process of resurrecting the clinic, he could hear the distant sobbing, swearing, and intermittent screaming from Christine. All her years of research ruined. Even though the computer remained, its hard drive had been eviscerated and all her data files were gone. Even her thumb drives were missing. But worst of all, considering their collective plight, the invaders had destroyed the solar charger for her satellite phone, whose battery was already nearly drained. It was beyond comprehension. Dr. Brecht muttered away in German as she picked up and sorted through the debris the marauders had left behind, trying to make sense of it all.

But nothing made sense anymore. Dr. Maxwell Taylor, who had come to Africa to try to do some good, and perhaps revive a completely broken heart, no longer had a mission here, or at least not the one that had brought him. Somewhere inside, he knew there was a far greater likelihood that his next medical procedure would involve removing a bullet rather than installing another contraceptive device. And Christine knew that her thesis, born from all these years of hard work and sacrifice living among the Maasai, had just ended in complete failure. Even David, well aware that the Kenyan government had agreed to upgrade the educational opportunities available to the Maasai, felt as though his services were no longer required despite all his determined efforts for all these many years. But none of that mattered. They were all trapped now and could only await either their rescue or their ruin. And although neither Max nor David said anything to Christine or Dr. Brecht, they both knew that Dermenjian's people were bound to return.

David prepared a meal for everyone that evening. Though he'd lost his entire wine supply and all his French delicacies, he managed to fashion a delicious stew using various herbs and vegetables from his own little garden. They all needed to discuss their future, and what better place than *á table*.

"We must notify the authorities immediately," Dr. Brecht demanded.

Max wiped his chin. "I agree," he said. "I haven't seen any traces of those soldiers lately, and there's been too much cattle poaching by the refugees. Do you think anybody's paying attention to all this? The moran are spread out all along the Kalema Road to guard the cattle, the only real food around. It's just a matter of time before the refugees come and completely help themselves. The moran have their spears, but Christ, the refugees have all these rifles!"

"A sobering thought," David replied, "but not very constructive."

"Your point?" said Christine, glaring at Max.

"My point is I agree with Dr. Brecht. We need to let the Kenya National Police know what's up."

"Yes," David continued, "you are quite right. But more importantly, there are very few minutes of battery time left on the satellite phone and no way to charge it. The radio has been destroyed. This is our last chance. I suggest we first try to reach Elizabeth at her mother's again. We owe it to Oscar."

David still hadn't mentioned to anyone what Jacques had told him the last time they spoke—that Elizabeth was staying at Peter's villa! It terrified him to think she might still be there.

"I thought she was headed to Scotland," said Dr. Brecht. "No sense taking a chance with so little battery left."

"What about calling the American embassy?" Max suggested. "They'd make something happen, assuming it hasn't been bombed lately."

After considerable debate they reached a consensus. They would call the American embassy in the morning. If that failed, they would try to reach Captain Olengi.

That strategy might have been the optimum, but they would never know. After a restless night, they gathered back at David's schoolhouse. Max dialed up the American embassy only to encounter a phone-tree system that approached jungle proportions. There were endless routings, and he finally hung up as the phone began beeping, indicating the battery was very low.

David then tried Captain Olengi. All he was able to reach this time, however, was a voicemail box that was full.

"Look," said David, "if we get through to Elizabeth, we can pass along the news that Oscar is alive but we are all in grave danger. She can contact the authorities and tell them our plight and our location. It may be long distance, but it's all the same to the battery. And that's two birds with one stone."

"Could be our only hope at this point," said Max. "Do you have the number?"

"Actually, no," said David. "The invaders stole my address book, where I had written it down. But I think I remember the number."

When the Banc de Marseille answered, David barely had time to apologize before the phone went dead.

"Great," said Christine, sitting back in her chair. "Now we're really fucked."

Dr. Brecht looked appalled to hear her student speaking once again in such a manner, but what did Christine care? Her future was washed up anyway. She got up from her chair and started cleaning the dishes.

"Somebody's just going to have to go find somebody who's in charge around here, besides Joseph, and get us the hell out of here," she shouted.

"Somebody?" Max replied.

"Yes," she said, turning those intense green eyes on him once more. "You. You're the only one of us who can handle a gun."

David rose from his chair as if to rebut such a preposterous remark but fell short of words. Unfortunately, what Christine had just suggested made sense. There was no longer any means of communication unless they entrusted the Maasai to inform the authorities, wherever they might be. But the soldiers, as Max had already noted, seemed to have disappeared.

"Surely if one hiked along the Kalema Road," David began, "one would eventually encounter the Kenyan soldiers. If they knew your plight, they would send a convoy to help get you all out of here."

"What do you mean, 'your' plight?" said Max. "Your supplies can't get through either with the road closed."

"Joseph takes good care of me. I always have plenty of meat and milk. I make my own cheese that preserves the milk, and my garden supplies all the greens I need. I will be fine until this is all over."

"And just when will that be?" piped in Christine.

"Just a couple of more months, at the latest. That is what the agreement with the government stipulates. The refugees will be gone by the middle of June."

"Perhaps," muttered Dr. Brecht.

David turned toward her. She was seated by the window, gazing outside to see if there might be any activity worth observing besides the road dust blowing all about. Her wide-brimmed leather hat obscured just enough sunlight that her ordinarily strong features seemed somehow subdued. Perhaps she was right. Who knew? They were merely words on a piece of paper.

"How soon can you get started?" said Christine, staring at Max again in a manner that left no doubt that she considered him the only man for the job.

"Wait just a minute," he replied. "I'm not heading down that road all by myself."

"That is right," said Dr. Brecht. "I will go with you. I have heard you try to speak Maa and Swahili. You will need a good translator to speak with the soldiers and with the moran who must accompany us."

331

Once more David was at a loss for words. As much as he wanted to spare Max from this mission accompanied by this woman, he had to admit that she was absolutely right. Perhaps Max was a decent doctor, but he was certainly no linguist.

"I will speak with Joseph straightaway," he said, rising abruptly from his chair. "You will need an escort."

Without another word he headed out the door. Max remained speechless, too baffled by the sentence bestowed on him by his colleagues.

"What about you?" he inquired in Christine's direction.

"Me?" she responded. "What use would I be? You're good with a gun and Dr. Brecht speaks thirteen Maasai dialects plus Swahili. Besides, I should stay and help David keep an eye on things."

"Right." Max picked himself up and headed back to the clinic without further comment.

David returned at noon only to report that Joseph was still off on his mission of returning the marauding refugees back to their camp. Max and Dr. Brecht would simply have to go it alone. There was no telling when Joseph would return. Besides, there were moran patrolling the Kalema Road, all armed and on alert for poachers, according to reliable sources.

When Max returned to the schoolhouse with Dr. Brecht in tow, he found Christine in waiting. Once again she was full of surprises, busily cleaning up the one item the refugees had neglected to steal or destroy—her bicycle.

"Dr. Brecht," she said, "try it. You'll make much better time with this."

She proudly presented her with a bicycle any college kid would be proud to own, with knobby tires and a sturdy titanium frame. Dr. Brecht, a woman who normally showed very little excitement, appeared overjoyed.

"Magnificent!" she declared as she mounted the two-wheeled steed and began pedaling in circles. An incredulous Max looked on as David emerged from his classroom.

"Great," said Max. "Since she'll be traveling at the speed of light, speaks thirteen Maa dialects, and wants outta here like crazy, I guess my services won't be needed after all."

"Wait!" David shouted before running off toward the opposite side of the schoolhouse. A moment later he returned, proudly wheeling before him another two-wheeled vehicle, one that looked like a relic from a 1950s garage sale. It had fat tires—smooth and, in fact, quite bald—and old-fashioned straw baskets attached to the rear of a rusted but sturdy-looking frame that Max quickly figured weighed ten times what Christine's modern bicycle weighed.

"No way," he said flatly.

"Come now. It is a good, sturdy bike," David countered. "I used to ride it quite a bit. You may have to go clear to Lake Magadi before you find any soldiers. That's nearly thirty miles. This will save time, which is very important. Don't forget we have a rendezvous with Olabon and his friends the next new moon. That's just three days. So you must be back. I don't want to have to face him, empty handed as it were, alone."

Max rubbed his chin. "Fine," he said. "Three days. Shouldn't be a problem, as long as the roads aren't too full of ruts. Or refugees. Right, Dr. Brecht?"

She did not reply. She just kept making circles in the dirt before them, getting used to the pedals, the gears, and the rather high seat. But soon she came to a halt. "I am ready," she said quite confidently.

Max stared at the decrepit two-wheeled vehicle offered up for his alleged convenience. It had no gears, just one big sprocket and one little one. And those ridiculous baskets. The oversized fenders and the handlebars, devoid of rubber grips, were all rusted. David borrowed the pump attached to Christine's bike and inflated the tires until they were quite hard. All the spokes appeared to be intact. David found some pliers and an oilcan and set about adjusting the seat, which was covered with the remnants of an old towel, and oiling the chain. Then Max hopped on board.

To his amazement it felt solid, very solid. He retraced the circles Dr. Brecht had transcribed in the dirt. After three revolutions he came to an abrupt halt. He stuffed his clothes and a sleeping bag into the baskets that hugged the rear wheel and then lashed his rifle to the handlebars and circled the track a couple more times.

"Let's go," he said.

Dr. Brecht needed no prodding. She had tied her hair in a tight bun and stuffed it under her wide-brimmed leather hat, which she had securely fastened to her large head by means of two narrow leather straps tied beneath her chin. Her slightly bulbous nose featured a thick white stripe of sunscreen. The much more modern canvas bags that straddled her rear wheel held all her gear except for the sleeping bag and small tent, which rested behind the seat.

"Be careful," said Christine, standing next to David on the lower step of the schoolhouse.

"Yes," said David, "be very careful. And be sure to contact someone who has the means to convey our situation to Nairobi."

"Who knows," said Max, "we may end up in Nairobi."

Without further discussion, they were on their way. They passed through the large patch of burned ground that Banyon had set ablaze when he fired on the old fuel tank. New light-green grasses pushed up through the charred earth and covered the hillside to their left. On their right, low-lying shrubs that had escaped the inferno rambled off toward clusters of thorn trees in the distance. They coasted down a gentle slope that curved right before spilling them out onto the Kalema Road, which ran straight for the most part, slightly elevated above the surrounding terrain.

It occurred rather quickly to both cyclists that early afternoon was certainly not the best time to begin this trek. The heat was brutal. But suddenly, after months spent in the bush, where time seemed suspended, there was a genuine sense of urgency. Dr. Brecht seemed so intent on reaching the nearest official who might be of assistance that, once acclimated to the vibrations from her bike frame, she set a blistering pace. Of course she had a modern bicycle with a modern frame and shock absorbers, not to mention gears. Max had the bicycle equivalent of a dromedary camel. Having reached level ground, Dr. Brecht shifted her gears and began to pull away. Max strained to stay with her while keeping an eye out for anyone who might be lurking in the brush.

Once they reached the bridge over the Ewaso Ngiro, Dr. Brecht pulled to a halt. Despite the rains over the recent weeks, the riverbed bore a mere trickle of a flow. All serious waters had been diverted for more vital ends than replenishing the irreversible foulness of Lake Natron to the south. The rains had managed, however, to find their way to the roots of the young grasses. The savannah was greening up. Even the thorn trees were taking on a fresh hue, slightly yellower but a sign that young leaves were beginning to replace an older generation. Max pulled to a stop and grabbed for his water bottle.

"I see no one," said Dr. Brecht as she completed a U-turn and sidled up next to Max.

"Me neither," he said before taking one last swig of water. "But we're still a few miles shy of the main camp area. That's probably where Joseph is right now."

"Crazy fool," she replied. "He's just going to get himself killed."

"Maybe," said Max, "but he seemed pretty confident about just waltzing into the refugee camp and returning his captives."

"Confident?" she replied. "Have you ever seen a Maasai who didn't appear confident? They're all as arrogant as arrogant can be."

It surprised Max to hear Dr. Brecht speak so rudely about her much-esteemed Maasai friends. But then he noticed a small herd of giraffes racing across the savannah to the north. Dr. Brecht noticed them, too.

"There could be trouble," she stated as she lifted her field glasses and watched clouds of dust kicking up behind the long-legged beasts. Their heads bobbed gracefully atop their long, powerful necks.

"Maybe they just need to stretch their legs a bit," said Max.

"Nonsense," replied the German woman. "You have been in Africa long enough to recognize when wild animals are in distress. There is trouble."

Before Max could respond, Dr. Brecht resumed her pedaling at an even brisker pace. He stood up on his pedals and gave his single speed all the punishment it could take, or at least all that he could deliver. Try as he would, he couldn't catch her.

The fact that the moran reputed to be stationed at regular intervals were nowhere in sight raised Max's apprehension level considerably. Where were they? He saw a number of Maasai tending their cattle but no moran. After ten minutes, however, he caught up with Dr. Brecht.

"Listen," she said.

Max cocked an ear. At first he heard nothing unusual. But he began to discern a low wailing off in the distance. He said nothing, then looked at Dr. Brecht and nodded. They both jumped on their bicycles and continued on at an even faster pace. It wasn't long before the source of the wailing became apparent. At least fifty moran were gathered in the middle of the road, all of them seemingly quite agitated over some turn of events. Both Max and Dr. Brecht pulled to a halt, within sight but at a safe distance from the young warriors.

"Poachers," said Dr. Brecht.

"Poachers?" said Max. "That means there'll be more prisoners to return, assuming you're right."

"Perhaps not. Joseph might return them, but what would his son Ntanda do if the poachers were caught not merely ransacking some white man's domicile, but killing and attempting to steal Maasai cattle?"

"I think we'd better take a closer look," said Max.

As they approached the entourage of ochre-lathered young warriors, all of whom seemed more well muscled and generally fit than Max remembered, he noticed that within the crowd were a number of the new initiates still clad in their charcoal capes. Apparently, the olpul was over. One of the moran spotted Max and stared him down to a halt. He began spouting orders that Max could not comprehend.

"He says to turn around and go back to wherever we came from," said Dr. Brecht.

"Right," he said. "This could get real interesting."

He ignored the orders and continued to push through the throng toward the center of the congregation of angry moran, who were all busy shouting and jumping and thrusting spears high in the air. At its center were three of the Ugandan refugees, on their knees, hands bound behind their backs, enduring the wrath of Ntanda and his core of senior moran officers. But once Max came within view, Ntanda turned his wrath in a new direction. The precise meaning of whatever he was shouting at him wasn't clear, but Max assumed it all meant to get the hell out, to leave them to their business. Before he could begin to cobble together the most fundamental response, Dr. Brecht intervened. She took no deferential tone whatsoever, preferring to speak to Ntanda at his own decibel level and in his own cadence and, of course, in his own particular native dialect.

"What's going on?" Max inquired.

"They're debating whether to just kill them here and now, which Ntanda clearly prefers, or take them back to the camp," she responded. "Killing them here and now would be the simplest, most expedient method of vengeance, but others are concerned not only with the potential retaliation but also with the need to make their point to all the refugees, to make examples of these desperadoes."

Simple enough. But before Max could even begin to contemplate an appropriate course of action, another commotion developed. Authoritative shouts coming from the outskirts of the moran circle became even louder as Joseph, Senento, and the other elders sliced through toward the middle, toward the next provisional batch of prisoners. Joseph reared up in front of Ntanda, his oldest and,

336

as he had once said, his most foolish son. That was right before Max had removed a rather large bullet from his torso.

Again the father and the son discussed the situation and debated the proper course to take. Joseph had just spent considerable time with their Ugandan guests, emphasizing the rules by which they must abide in order to remain in Maasailand, in his land. Yet here was a clear breach of contract. Joseph had already seen the butchered carcasses. The Ugandans kneeling before him still had the fresh blood of the two slain cattle all over their arms and ragged T-shirts. It was even in their hair.

Joseph barked out a command. Ignoring Ntanda completely, each of the three moran guards prodded his respective detainee. They all stood up and followed Joseph as he turned and began retracing his steps back to the refugee camp, from whence he'd come, leading yet another set of wayward Ugandans back to their safety zone. Ntanda followed behind the prisoners, protesting mightily but to no avail.

Max and Dr. Brecht stared at one another. There was far too much noise and commotion for them to speak, noise which had no doubt drawn Joseph and his entourage to intercept this militant crew in the first place, a crew bent on serious revenge for the wanton slaughter of their most prized possession, their cattle. They followed at a safe distance, not wanting to be engulfed by the dust kicked up by the moran, who were all in fine form. They hopped and chanted quite loudly, their wild, plaited ochre hair dancing in the air as they headed toward the headquarters of Jocko, the chief of the refugees, with whom Joseph had recently parted company. They were not exactly on the best of terms.

Ever since the thigh-bone incident, Joseph and the elders had been determined to stop the killing of their cattle by these marauding thugs. The moran guards had successfully deterred nearly all the poachers. Only a few cattle had been lost in the last several weeks since Joseph had first paid the unwelcomed visit to the man he now knew as Jocko, a man whose physical appearance belied his violent, unscrupulous nature. The audacity of the act, the impudence of him to insist on an "appointment" when the refugees were squatters in the first place—albeit with the blessings of the Kenyan government and the begrudging acquiescence of Joseph himself—still lodged deep in Joseph's rather pronounced craw. His eyes burned with anger as they came upon the largest tent in the pathetic maze of jury-rigged shelters, lean-tos, and hovels situated on land that had once been home, and should again be soon, to the Maasai and their herds.

Most of the ragged refugees fled at the sight of Joseph and the moran, who were pushing and prodding their captives along as they hopped and chanted, spears always at the ready. They were well within sight of the main tent when the flap flew open and out stepped a pudgy little man dressed in fatigues, with a military cap and a slim band of black hair clinging to his cheeks and chin. He had a broad nose and piercing eyes, which seemed nearly as full of anger as Joseph's.

He began to shout and a stream of taller, similarly clad associates bearing automatic rifles filed out of the tent and flanked Jocko. He told them to hold their fire and walked up to Joseph.

"Why have you come back?" he demanded to know, speaking in broken Swahili.

"I am returning more of your flock," said Joseph in kind, as he pointed angrily with his fly brush to the fresh batch of prisoners surrounded by moran, each of whom held a spear mere inches from a captive's neck. "They have wandered out of bounds and killed two more of our cattle. My son and his friends would like to kill them but I will not allow it. There will be no killing, not of men or of cattle. Furthermore, you will surrender all your weapons to the Kenya National Police. They are forbidden here."

Jocko smiled. He looked at his various sergeants at arms, each with a freshly oiled, fully loaded AK-47, and began laughing. The guns were identical to the ones Ntanda had confiscated from the three poachers.

"You will leave now," he shouted. "And these guns will remain. You have your weapons, we must have ours. Hand over the prisoners, they are good men. They are just very hungry like all the rest of us. Then leave."

Joseph cast a glance at his troops. Ntanda was in more of a rage than usual, standing in front of the three helpless Ugandans, who were on their knees trembling slightly, their hands still tied behind them.

"Tell him we will kill the next refugee to cross the Kalema Road," he told his father in their Maa dialect. "And if they are not gone by the agreed-upon time, we will kill them all."

Before Joseph could respond, either to Jocko or Ntanda, Jocko took a bold step forward in Ntanda's direction. He was apparently more of a linguist than Ntanda had assumed, having clearly understood what he had just conveyed to his father.

"Get out!" he shouted at Ntanda in Maa. "We have a right to be here. You are trespassing and must leave immediately."

338

Trespassing? Spoken in Maa, in his own tongue, by a filthy rebel invader whose troops were not only occupying Maasailand and killing their cattle but now telling *him* he was trespassing? Beyond the boiling point, his Maasai pride deeply offended, Ntanda reached down to his waist. His hand emerged with a long knife that in one fluid motion sliced through the air, slitting the throat of the captive poacher who was kneeling directly behind him. He slumped to the ground in a gruesome, bloody heap. Ntanda turned to face Jocko as he approached in an absolute rage. One of his soldiers raised his rifle, taking aim at Ntanda. Joseph shouted, but there was such a sudden uproar no one could hear. Then Senento stepped forward to intercept Jocko. But what he intercepted instead was a bullet fired at Ntanda—but not soon enough—by one of Jocko's soldiers. The killing of Ntanda, Joseph's son, would have been serious enough. But shooting an elder, as even an African as far removed from Maasai culture as Jocko would know, was a far greater offense. At least Ntanda was a moran, a warrior. Jocko motioned to his men to hold their fire. Joseph, glaring at his son, signaled the moran to put down their spears.

As soon as Senento went down, Max rushed in. The bullet had gone through his left side and left a gaping hole. He was bleeding profusely and writhing in agony. Max had no supplies with him but ripped off his shirt and began applying pressure. He looked up at the crowd around him. One figure stood out from all the others. It was not Joseph or Ntanda. It was a young lad dressed in a charcoal cape, gripping a spear and weeping tears of rage. It was Matthew, the youngest of Senento's sons, the one he'd circumcised months before.

"We need to get him back to the clinic," said Max as Dr. Brecht knelt beside him.

"But how? Surely not with our bicycles."

At that moment they heard the sound of a vehicle approaching, honking its horn to help get through the large crowd that had gathered. Much to the surprise of Max and Dr. Brecht, it was a military Jeep. The driver appeared to be a mere soldier, but in the front passenger seat was an officer of some rank, judging from the medals on his uniform. He jumped down as the Jeep came to an abrupt and dusty halt in front of Jocko's tent. Not surprisingly, Jocko's henchmen had stowed their weapons out of sight.

"What's happened here?" the officer demanded to know, looking first at the slain poacher whose life was rapidly spilling out onto the bare earth. He was beyond saving. Then he walked over to where Senento lay in another pool of blood.

"You have to take us back to my clinic," Max shouted. "It's just a few miles down the road."

He was a young lieutenant from the Kenya National Police, part of the small contingent of troops assigned to keep order as best as possible within the refugee camp. And apparently he had studied some English.

"You are the American doctor," he said. "Very well. Put him in the back. Jocko, I will deal with you later." He then turned to face Joseph, whose expression conveyed a sense of outrage and sorrow all at once. After all, Senento was his best friend. "And I will deal with you as well."

They drove back to the clinic as rapidly as the bumpy Kalema Road would allow. Max continued to maintain pressure in an attempt to keep most of Senento's blood inside him until he could remove the bullet and sew him up, if he lasted that long. Senento had long since lost consciousness.

"Which way?" asked the driver.

Max directed him not to the clinic but first to David's schoolhouse. Once they were close he shouted out for Christine. David emerged in his bathrobe, looking at once very concerned but also somewhat embarrassed.

"Quick," said Max, "Senento's been shot. I need Christine's help in the clinic."

Clearly quite alarmed, David nodded and ducked back into his house. Christine emerged moments later, her blouse barely buttoned and her hair all a mess. Max said nothing as she hopped into the rear seat beside Senento, looking almost as much in shock over this sad turn of events as Senento, whose gums were rapidly fading to white. Dr. Brecht simply stared at Christine as she sat beside her and finished buttoning her blouse.

Once Senento was strapped to the operating table, the lieutenant said he needed to get back to Jocko and company, as well as the soldier he'd left standing guard. He asked Dr. Brecht if she wanted a ride back to Nairobi. As she had explained to the young captain, that was the reason for their sortie in the first place. But much to Max's surprise, she hesitated.

"No," she said at last. "I am not leaving, not yet."

"Very well," the lieutenant replied. "But it may be some time before we can return for you. There are very few of us here, and as you can see we are very busy trying to maintain order with the refugees. And what about you, Dr. Taylor? You told me you were intent on leaving as well."

"Right," said Max. "But as you can see, I'm a little preoccupied at the moment. But I'll tell you what…"

He took a moment to scribble out a note and handed it to the lieutenant.

"What's this—a prescription?"

"Of sorts. I need a distributor cap for a 1980 International Harvester Scout, six-cylinder engine. Here's 10,000 shillings—should cover it."

He handed him the money and returned to his scrubbing up.

"And a satellite phone charger," said Christine as she put on a large surgical smock and tucked her tattered hair into a plastic cap.

"Right," said the lieutenant, looking bewildered. "We'll see what we can do."

Chapter 43

Madame Le Clerc climbed the winding stairs on her own, slowly ascending to the *première étage* to check on her only daughter, who as a child had cherished the morning hours. But today she had slept past noon. Madame Le Clerc tapped upon the bedroom door, waited a moment, then entered unannounced.

"Elizabeth!" she cried.

Her daughter was shaking terribly, lost in a dream about Oscar, who was being stalked by a lion. She was trying in vain to warn him but could not find her voice.

"Wake up, my dear, wake up. It's simply a bad dream, *un cauchemar.*"

Elizabeth opened her eyes. "Maman!" she murmured, startled yet relieved to know that she had simply been dreaming, not that it mattered much.

"Yes, my dear. It is time for you to get up. You have been lying here sleeping off and on for more than twenty-four hours. Edouard will be here shortly, and we will be taking our *déjeuner* in the garden. Please join us."

Had it really been that long? It was all so much a dream. And part of the dream, a very bad part, had her dancing atop a roulette table somewhere far away. It was all much too embarrassing to imagine. But despite the fact that her head was still throbbing with every pulse, as if her heart were some giant bass drum, there was no question she felt more awake than she had since she'd arrived in the early dawn hours over a day ago.

"Very well," she replied, "I will get dressed."

Elizabeth lay still for a moment after her mother left the room. She rose very slowly from her bed and walked very carefully toward the window. She had to lean on her dresser midway but arrived, still slightly dizzy, and steadied herself on the windowsill. Looking down on the veranda, she could see that the vines atop the ancient arbor were just budding out. She remembered the sunny mornings when she and her father would take their breakfast there. It would just be the two of them, her father sipping his morning tea while she sipped her hot chocolate. They would quietly eat crumpets and croissants, listening to the buzzing of *les cigales* warming up for their daily chorus, while the rest of the household slept on.

Elizabeth managed to shower, apply some much-needed makeup, and slip into a loose-fitting dress that seemed to comport with her mood, simple and uncomplicated. At least, that's how she wished things to be. She left her room and slowly descended the long, winding stairs, carefully clutching the railing, and found her brother waiting for her in the main salon.

"Elizabeth!" he cried as he rushed up to greet her with alternating kisses on her cheeks. "How are you? You were in such a state the other night, but at least I rescued you from that Dermenjian fellow. By the way, Maman says he keeps calling. Says he's worried about you."

"Thank you for taking me away from that horrid scene at the casino," she said as they embraced. "I am so embarrassed. But I think Mr. Dermenjian means well. We both lost loved ones, you know. I should call to thank him for—"

"For holding you like a hostage!" Edouard interrupted.

"No, for taking me in. I just couldn't bear sitting by while Mother and Father Brodard insisted on making funeral arrangements. I still believe Oscar may be alive. And I believe that if anyone is to find him, it will be Peter Dermenjian."

"And then?"

Before she could reply Jacques appeared and announced that it was time to place themselves *á table*.

Madame Le Clerc was already on the veranda, arranging some freshly picked flowers from her garden. The three of them sat down at the rustic stone table covered with a lovely Provençal tablecloth, fine silver, and Faience dinnerware. Jacques carefully ladled out a serving of soup for each of them.

"Dr. Deveaux telephoned this morning," said Madame Le Clerc. "Your blood-test results arrived. It seems you've been consuming enormous quantities of barbiturates."

"Blood tests?" she inquired.

"Yes," she said. "We were quite worried about you. Dr. Deveaux examined you yesterday morning."

Silence followed as Elizabeth began to realize why she had been so lethargic and why, since Edouard had returned her to the home where she'd been raised, she had had such fantastically vivid dreams. It also explained why she now felt so suddenly anxious. Her hands were shaking quite visibly as she attempted to lift her spoon to her mouth.

"It must have been in the tea. Dr. Meinz, Peter Dermenjian's personal physician, insisted I drink it. I'm sure he meant no harm. It's not unusual to give a sedative to someone who's just lost a loved one."

"A cup of tea," her mother replied, "indeed. Then what is with all this blond hair, and what about this story of you dancing about wildly at the Monte Carlo casino where Edouard found you wearing that outrageous outfit that made you look like some Marseille whore?"

Edouard was quite stunned to hear his ordinarily pious mother utter such a word. He waited for his sister to reply, but to his surprise she remained quite calm, simply focused on getting her trembling hand to deliver a spoonful of potage to her lovely lips.

"It was a costume ball, like Mardi Gras," she responded. "Peter was Don Quixote and I was Dulcinea."

"Dulcinea? And that is why you were dancing so lasciviously on top of the roulette table?"

"Edouard, you didn't have to tell her about that!" Elizabeth said.

"Oh, but I didn't," he responded. "She saw your photo in the paper. Luckily, the caption simply referred to you as an unidentified guest of one of the patrons."

Elizabeth gasped as her mother handed her a clipping from *La Provence*, which featured a photograph of a woman with long, bared legs showing a bit of cleavage while whirling atop a roulette table in the unmistakable opulence of Monte Carlo's casino.

"I'm sorry," she said. "I don't know what ever possessed me. It must have been the barbiturates mixed with the champagne."

"And who knows what else," added Edouard as Jacques began removing the soup bowls to make way for the *gigot d'agneau*, a beautiful leg of spring lamb seasoned with rosemary, sage, and other *herbes de Provence.* "You're just lucky his secretary revealed your whereabouts when I called Peter Dermenjian to inform you that your mother had had a heart attack."

"You told them what?" said Madame Le Clerc, stunned once more.

"I needed to get his attention, albeit with a lie. And more importantly, I needed to find you and get you away from that man, and apparently his druggist as well," Edouard replied, glaring at his sister across the table.

"Well, that is all quite disturbing but it is behind us now. We are very happy you have returned to us," her mother continued. "But now you must realize you have many other matters to attend to. *Mon enfant*, what you have suffered and will no doubt continue to suffer for some time is a great loss. Losing a loved one, even someone others can't begin to comprehend, is tragic. I know, having lost your

344

father well before his time. But you must realize that you have your own life and you must return to it. You must deal with this calamity. The university has called repeatedly. They want you to come reclaim Oscar's affairs. Apparently, they've hired someone to take over his classes. His office and his laboratory must be cleaned out soon, or they will simply discard everything. There are no doubt papers to sign, and you are Oscar's beneficiary according to his will."

It was perhaps too bluntly put, but what her mother spoke was the truth. She had had a life, somewhere, once upon a time. The cottage, the apartment, and, of course, the laboratory.

"Yes," said Elizabeth, "I must go. But I will need a few days to make plans, to get ready. Edouard, would you come with me? I don't know if I can face all this on my own."

She looked at her brother pleadingly. He wiped his chin and dropped his napkin in his lap.

"Well," he replied, "I suppose I could ask Jean-Pierre to handle my affairs for a few days. In fact, I could use a bit of a getaway as well. Just as long as that Dermenjian chap isn't following us."

It was only two days later that they were able to solidify their plans and board a flight to Glasgow. Edouard hadn't been to Scotland in several years, not since Oscar and Elizabeth had invited him to spend a week with them at the cottage on Mull. Elizabeth had made an appointment at the university, an appointment she dreaded keeping. So all was set. She and Edouard would attend to the business at hand concerning Oscar, and then they would spend a few days at the cottage on Mull. The idea of spending time at the cottage appealed to her, and it would be good to visit with Tommy and Ethel. But the images that appeared in her mind of the quaint people of Mull brought with them a shocking realization.

"Eleanor!" she shouted, rousting Edouard, who was slumped over in the adjacent seat. Other passengers looked at her with alarm.

"What is it?" Edouard inquired.

"Oscar's mother, Eleanor; she's still at Peter Dermenjian's villa!"

"Oh my," said Edouard, "I had completely forgotten. What are you going to do?"

She could not answer, for she did not know. One thing at a time, she thought. Somehow she would get through all this.

Once they had landed she searched through her purse and found Peter Dermenjian's card. She still hadn't contacted him to thank him for his kindness and hospitality, largely due to her indignation at having been secretly sedated by Dr. Meinz. And what had he slipped in her tea the night of her outrageous behavior at the casino? Her hands were shaking so badly it took a couple of goes with Edouard's cell phone before she reached one of his staff. She started leaving a message of thanks to be delivered, but within an instant Peter was on the line.

"Elizabeth," he said, "I have been terribly worried about you."

"I am fine," she replied. "I need to attend to some affairs in Scotland. My brother, Edouard, alerted me to the urgency involved, and I'm afraid I needed to leave immediately. I am so sorry for any trouble I caused."

"Oh, that," he replied. "It is nothing."

"I cannot thank you enough for your kindness and your generosity. And I realize that I have placed you in a precarious position regarding the care of Mrs. Newman, Oscar's mother. As soon as I have finished my business here in Glasgow, I will come retrieve her."

"No hurry," Peter replied. "She has been well looked after and will continue to be."

"Thank you. And Oscar?" she whispered. "Any news?"

"We have not given up. I will phone you the minute I find him."

"Oh," she said, "I seem to have lost my cell phone. I no doubt left it at your villa, before we left for Monte Carlo. But you can contact me at this number."

Peter said he understood and that the number had been duly recorded. What he failed to mention was that she was right, she had left her cell phone at his villa, and it was being monitored 24/7.

Edouard had gathered their bags and procured a rental car, which he insisted on driving just for the fun of driving on the completely wrong side of the road. The route to the apartment featured several challenging roundabouts, which of course ran counter to the prevailing currents in France. But they made their way without incident, other than several unsavory hand gestures aimed in Edouard's general direction.

The feel of the apartment was more or less the same. It was just knowing that Oscar was not about to suddenly enter, as he used to after completing a long session in his lab or possibly a longer session down at the Black Bull, the local pub, that made it all feel so incomplete.

The following morning Edouard drove his sister to her appointment with Dr. McNeil at the School of Medicine. As they approached the university, they crossed over the River Kelvin and eventually came upon the modern glass facade of the Wolfson Medical Building, which stood in stark contrast to the historic stone buildings of the original institution, founded in 1451.

As they walked toward the entrance after parking, Elizabeth quickly noted that each white pillar that helped support the curving glass enclosure above was wrapped with a yellow ribbon. There were placards commemorating Oscar, hoping for his safe return. But by now many of them were showing signs of age, some torn and some covered with graffiti. She walked past them as they finally escaped the relentless Scottish drizzle and entered the building. She had no idea where she had placed her identity badge, but fortunately, the security guard recognized her. He expressed his condolences regarding Oscar and offered to escort her to Dr. McNeil's office. Elizabeth thanked him and said she knew the way.

"Edouard," she said, "please wait here. I won't be long."

Dr. McNeil, chairman of the Department of Obstetrics and Gynecology, rose from his seat behind a large oak desk as Elizabeth entered.

"Ms. Le Clerc," he said in a soft Scottish tone that conveyed a hearty welcome as well as a strong sense of remorse. "I am so happy to see you. About as happy as I am sad that Oscar is not with you."

He was a rather tall man with a shaggy head of white hair. Great bushy white eyebrows arched over his steel-blue eyes while more tufts of white protruded from his ears. His cheeks were as rosy as any Scot's could be, and in his white lab coat he appeared to be completely antiseptic. He stepped from behind his desk and clasped both of her hands in his.

"I am so sorry," he said. "We are all so sorry about Oscar. We have not given up all hope, but alas, we have a medical school to run and I'm afraid we must make some decisions. So thank you for coming."

Elizabeth smiled and lowered her eyes. "Thank you," she said. "Where shall we begin?"

He asked her to sit down as he explained the situation in more detail. First of all, there was the matter of Oscar's academic load. Though he taught only one class, it was quite popular. Fortunately, a visiting fellow from Germany agreed to take over, albeit provisionally. And attendance was, well, nearly back to normal. As for his office, his textbooks and paper files had been neatly boxed up and were

347

being stored in the basement. All his computer files had been archived. The limiting factor was cryogenic freezer space. The department was fortunate to have attracted a top name in embryology, a Dr. Andrews, whose research was entirely dependent on the preservation of human tissues at such extremely low temperatures, just like Oscar's research. And his laboratory, as Dr. McNeil pointed out, was vacant.

"For the moment," Elizabeth added.

"Yes, for the moment. But nevertheless, we need the space. And that is where we need your help. You were, or perhaps I should say you still are, Oscar's research assistant, and you know better than anyone what to do with all his frozen tissue samples. Cryogenic freezer space is especially limited, but we can't begin to determine which of the hundreds of samples are of little or no value. We can archive those that may be essential to his ongoing research projects, and to defend his past research, if necessary."

So that was why they had been so urgently in need of her—to sort through the hundreds, if not thousands, of tissue samples, bits of rat and rabbit and pig ovaries and jars of semen that had been sitting deep frozen for years and were no doubt of absolutely no value whatsoever to anyone. Yes, she and Oscar had been derelict in cleaning out samples that had long since revealed whatever traces of growth abnormalities occurred, or not, when these poor substitutes for human subjects were exposed to various perturbations of estrogen and progesterone and an endless variety of closely related substances. So many compounds had been tested on these unfortunate animals, all of which ultimately led, after years of trial and error, to the development of the enormously successful Newman Insert. But because it was so successful, Oscar had insisted on maintaining his lab samples in the not terribly unlikely event that there was a lawsuit against him and his IUD. Best to preserve the evidence he would argue whenever the department suggested he make a bit more room available.

"I would be happy to go through the samples and discard those that are no longer essential to Oscar's research. It would take me a day or two. Is that all you need from me?"

She was displaying tremendous strength, all things considered.

"There is one more thing," Dr. McNeil replied, "and that is, if you haven't forgotten, that you are still employed by this university. I understand the reasons for your absence of late, and I can understand if you desire more time before returning to resume work here. Obviously, we would need to find something for you that is a good fit."

"Oh, yes," she replied. "I suppose I just assumed that as Oscar's research assistant and with him missing…"

"Nonsense. As it so happens, Dr. Andrews is in need of a lab assistant. I think you would find the work quite interesting. Come, let me introduce you."

Reluctantly, Elizabeth followed Dr. McNeil as he ambled down the hallway until, turning a corner, he bumped into a diminutive woman with stringy dark hair streaked with gray who was moving far too fast.

"Dr. Andrews," he began.

"Excuse me, Dr. McNeil, but I need to see you in private," the woman said. "I can't keep running back and forth between these makeshift facilities that have completely inadequate ventilation and no room for my files and computers with antiquated software…"

"Yes, Dr. Andrews, but if I may, I'd like you to meet Elizabeth Le Clerc, Oscar Newman's research assistant. I told you she might be available to work with you."

Dr. Andrews, who was not only rather short but decidedly hunched over, had some difficulty looking up at Elizabeth, who seemed to tower above. She tilted her head slightly as she raised it and looked at Elizabeth without a trace of a smile or any inkling of inner warmth.

"When can you start?" she said. "I am terribly behind. Dr. McNeil says you are very capable in the laboratory."

"Well, I—" she began, but Dr. McNeil interrupted.

"Ms. Le Clerc has agreed to help us put Dr. Newman's laboratory in order, so I'm afraid it will be a few days at the earliest."

"Yes," said Elizabeth, "and if I may, I would like to begin going through the lab samples as soon as possible. But my brother is waiting for me. I will return after lunch."

And so she did. While Edouard strolled about the streets of Glasgow, admiring the shops and the old stone buildings and walkways made glossy by the ever-present drizzle, Elizabeth put on an extra heavy sweater beneath her lab coat and began the tedious work of matching the various batches of ultra-frozen tissue samples with the various spreadsheets she had printed out. These contained records, at least one for every rat, rabbit, and pig ovary; each corresponding batch of whatever semen had been used to try to inseminate each creature; and every brain or brain stem that might have shown some abnormality after prolonged exposure to whatever hormone Oscar happened to be testing at the time. There were also numerous entire uterine tracts. The samples were all coded by experiment, and Elizabeth was able to gradually arrange them in chronological order. That way she could look for a reasonable dividing line, a date before which all corresponding samples could be pitched.

By late afternoon of the second day, she had examined nearly every sample, found its code, checked it on the list, and either replaced it back in the dark-blue, liquid nitrogen–cooled cryogenic freezer or put it on the appropriate shelf to be discarded. The room itself was refrigerated, though not to −170 degrees Celsius like the cells and tissues she had returned to their cryogenic state of suspended animation. It was quite cold and she took frequent breaks from sorting the sealed containers, returning to the warmth of the adjacent office where she could look through electronic files. On what she presumed would be her last foray of the day, she worked through what she knew to be some of Oscar's earliest analyses. They were primarily parts of experiments devoted to finding a better spermicide, an avenue of research he had long since abandoned. So clearly, these were destined for disposal. They even predated Elizabeth's association with Oscar. She picked up one of the containers and was about to place it in the discard area when she noticed something rather peculiar. It was about the same size and shape as some of the smaller vessels made of ceramic or heavy glass, but this one was made of stainless steel. What was more, she could discern, through the considerable frost that clung to its sides, an engraving. She picked it up with her enormous mitts and held it up to the light. She grabbed a cloth and wiped it clean. It read:

"Congratulations, Oscar! You've now arrived!"

It was signed by Dr. Mortimer Stanley, Oscar's longtime advisor during his years at the University of London. It must have been a gift in honor of Oscar's receiving his doctorate of medicine. She turned it over and found a handwritten label on the bottom. It resembled Oscar's writing and appeared to be an identification number—"NO 666160." That was not a part of any code she recognized. She ran a search on the computer but found nothing. Oh well, she thought, at the very least it ought to go with the rest of the assorted trophies and tributes Oscar had received, not the least of which was his Nobel Prize, which was off gathering dust on the mantel back at their cottage on Mull.

She met Edouard at a pub on Byres Road. While she was understandably exhausted from her day and a half of sorting all those icy samples, Edouard was flying high, delighted with all he had seen and bought. He was also into his third pint of ale when Elizabeth arrived. He ordered her a glass of sherry off the wood. Though she was barely able to keep her eyes open, they remained there for a modest supper of fish and chips before retiring to the apartment. Elizabeth then went straight to bed.

She awoke, however, in the middle of the night, her mouth dry and in need of water. She pried herself out of bed and went into the small bathroom and turned on the faucet. As she grabbed for her glass, she noticed the stainless-steel container with its engraving. She wondered what manner of pig semen or whatever might be contained within. She put her hand on it. It was not yet thawed and ready to be cleaned out. She turned it over. Suddenly, she went white as a ghost. For the label on the bottom now read differently. Instead of what she had assumed to be an identification number, it now read 091999 ON. Could it be that it was really a date, September 19, 1999? And instead of signifying some sample number, did the reversed "NO" stand for "Oscar Newman"? Her thoughts were flying in every direction, but at the core was the question—could this really contain…Oscar?

She spent the night mostly pacing, trying to calm herself and perhaps even get some sleep, but she kept returning to stare at the metal container. She looked at the calendar. It was the twelfth day of her cycle. But could she even begin to think of such a thing?

In the morning she returned to the university and reviewed all the computer files once again. There was absolutely no record of this particular sample. The container was now room temperature and presumably whatever was inside, if anything, had recently thawed out. Did she dare look? She eyed it with great anxiety before placing her hands on it and attempting to unscrew the top. There was quite a bit of resistance, which at one point gave her some relief. Because if she couldn't open it, then there was really no point even contemplating…but then it suddenly gave way, and with a couple of twists the top came free. Inside was exactly what she had feared she would find—someone's, or some thing's, elixir of life. She quickly screwed the top back on, breathing heavily. There were microscopes next door, but even if by some miracle these little fellows had survived for so long in the deep freeze, there was the matter of bringing them up to body temperature. She closed her eyes as an idea swept through her mind, and before she could begin to stop herself, she had found a box of zip lock plastic bags in one of the drawers. The next thing she knew, she was transferring the contents of the stainless-steel container into one of the plastic bags. She then wrapped it all in another. Turning beet red, she rolled it all up and went searching for the women's room. For she had indeed thought of a place where the strange container's contents could reach body temperature. It might be a bit uncomfortable, but once she was able to confirm with a microscope that whatever or whoever's they were, they were indeed dead, then the suspense would be over and she could get back to her life. And with that last thought, she felt tears welling up again and in the confines of her private stall, alone in the women's room, she had a good cry.

The following morning, she finished up all the paperwork associated with the culling out of Oscar's frozen tissue samples, then managed to regain her composure enough to stop by to see Dr. McNeil. She wanted to let him know that she would need some time, perhaps a week, to decide whether she would come back to work with Dr. Andrews.

"Yes," he said, "I understand. Just give me a call. And by the way, did that French fellow ever catch up with you, the priest?"

Completely stunned, and already fighting emotions she could barely keep in check, she felt her entire body stiffen. "David?" she inquired.

"I believe that was his name. He seemed terribly anxious to get in touch. I believe he was in Africa somewhere."

"In Kenya. What did he say?"

"Nothing really, just wanted to know where you were, and unfortunately, we hadn't the slightest idea."

When she relayed this news to Edouard over lunch, he did not appear surprised in the least. Why, of course, David had called Mother's home as well. Hadn't she spoken with him? After all, he had given him the number for Peter Dermenjian's villa. Edouard had assumed all along that they had been in touch.

"Not at all," she responded. "Not at all."

They were due to catch the ferry to Mull at 4:30. It was a few hours' drive, but Elizabeth insisted they make a stop at the university just one more time. Edouard waited for her in the car while she attended to whatever affairs were remaining. She seemed so terribly agitated by it all. But when she returned to the car, she seemed even more so.

"Are they treating you all right?" he inquired.

"Yes," she said. "But before we head to the ferry, I need to stop by a pharmacy."

"As you wish. But I'd advise you to be more careful about what you put in your body these days."

Did she ever!

They made the ferry with a few minutes to spare. The clouds had finally given up their domination of the sky and allowed the late-afternoon sun to reign at least temporarily over the sea. Even the green, distant shore of Mull was washed in light. Edouard reached for his bag and unzipped it, withdrawing a fresh, unopened bottle of Oban single malt Scotch he had purchased at the distillery. He opened the bottle and poured himself a glass as they sat in the car, rocking to and fro with the rhythm of the sea and the ferry. He offered one to his sister. She politely declined.

It was dark by the time they reached the cottage, but their arrival did not go unnoticed. Ethel arrived within minutes, wrapped in a large woolen shawl. Tommy soon followed and was quite pleased to see Elizabeth and her brother, as well as the bottle of Oban. They asked for any news of Oscar, of which there was none, and inquired after the health of Eleanor Newman. How soon would she back at the manor over in Tobermory?

"She will be back soon," Elizabeth replied. "I am going back for her in a few days."

The cottage was musty and needed airing out. Ethel brought over some stew and they enjoyed a humble supper together before a roaring fire. Tommy showed Edouard the way to the cellar and returned with a few bottles of ale. They sat together telling stories, discussing the local news, mainly whose sheep were lambing now, the recent weather, and Tommy and Ethel's visit to southern France. They toasted Oscar a number of times and wished mightily for his safe return.

Once they had bid each other good night, Elizabeth put on her nightgown and, before turning in, took her temperature. She examined herself as well, the nature of her secretions and the firmness of her cervix. It was not yet time, if there was to be a time.

The following morning, she and Edouard cleaned the cottage and rummaged through many of Oscar's things. It was hard to concentrate, and she really didn't know what she was trying to accomplish, rearranging his belongings this way and that. By lunchtime the place appeared fresh and clean and the musty smell was gone. She had gone through the meager food supplies, finding evidence of small rodents here and there, but no real damage.

They drove over to Tobermory for lunch. The colorful buildings along the quay were lovely to behold, glistening in the sun after the morning's rain showers. They ate at a small teahouse overlooking the harbor and afterward stopped by the market to pick up some milk and other basic supplies. Edouard bought some fish to cook for their supper. On the way back to the cottage, they stopped by the nursing home. Elizabeth wanted to assure them that Mrs. Newman would be returning soon. Mrs. Hamilton, the director, offered her condolences regarding Oscar and expressed great relief to know that Mrs. Newman was being well taken care of.

That afternoon she took a walk upon the moors, following the same route she had taken so many months before when she was torn up over whether or not she should marry Oscar. Now she faced a much more difficult decision. What did the plastic bag rolled up inside her, which caused a bit of discomfort as she hiked up the hillside, really contain? Was she hiding a new version of the "Newman Insert," she wondered with a trace of amusement, or was this really some pig semen or perhaps that of some anonymous donor? It was all such a gamble, one her escapades at the Monte Carlo casino, throwing Peter Dermenjian's money around, had not prepared her for. But if it was a pig, or some other animal, surely it would not take. And if it belonged to some human other than Oscar, she could always give it up for adoption. But that was craziness. Surely the odds were that regardless of whatever or whoever's it was, nothing would ever happen. And then there was the haunting question of why Oscar would fill his little memento from his beloved mentor and academic advisor with someone else's seed? It was perfectly within his nature to play this little joke upon himself. You have arrived! Indeed! But while all these possibilities swirled in her mind, there was no mistaking the fact that she had seen them moving, not as actively as would be expected in a fresh sample, but there had indeed been signs of life when she had made the last stop at the university and peered through the microscope. Could she possibly go through with it?

Edouard did a superb job with the fish, and he even found a few potatoes out in the garden. But Elizabeth said little during supper, only that yes, she had had a nice walk, it was a lovely day, et cetera—but she seemed terribly distracted.

"Sister dear," he said at last, "I think you still need more rest. After I clean up these dishes, I'm going to finish my book and I may just finish that bottle of Scotch as well."

She looked at her brother and nodded. "Thank you for supper," she said. "I believe I should go lie down. That walk was perhaps more exertion than I was ready for."

In her room she again took her temperature and examined herself. It was time. The walk had helped make up her mind and she could tell that she would ovulate soon, perhaps that night. She had bought a small kit at the pharmacy for administering a douche, somewhat like a dull syringe. It was simple enough, a long, blunt tube with a plunger of sorts. She stared at it for some time, turning it over in her hands, before taking a deep breath. Then she moved to the bathroom and removed the plastic bags. She carefully transferred the contents to the strange-looking implement. Her thoughts, however, were far away, with Oscar.

"Please be you," she said to herself as she inserted the instrument deep inside. Looking out the bedroom window, she saw a full moon beginning to rise. She crossed herself and, in a manner of speaking, took the plunge.

Chapter 44

The clear, metallic tones of the weathered brass bell that sat on top of David's schoolhouse, a bell not rung in years, resonated throughout the recently settled portion of Maasailand that Joseph presumably still governed.

As David descended the crude ladder he had used to gain access to the rusting metal roof and thence to the belfry, his thoughts turned reluctantly toward Father Crawford, his predecessor. He would never have allowed his church bell to fall into such a sad state of disrepair. But finally, after years of neglect, David had cleaned out the twigs and dried grass and congealed guano that had held the big brass clapper in check for so long. And then he rang the bell, hailing his congregation. Normally it didn't matter. The few Maasai who cared when his Sunday service started didn't need any bells. Bells were for cattle.

But today was different. This was a special Mass, one for his longtime friend Senento. For the bullet intended for Joseph's son Ntanda had ripped clear through him, and by the time Max, with the help of Christine, had patched him up, too much blood had leaked out of his body to sustain his life. He had never even regained consciousness. David had delivered last rites, knowing that Senento was one of his flock. He had even told David he wished to be buried in the small cemetery behind the schoolhouse. There he would be in the company of a few dozen other converts who preferred spending eternity under the banner of the Catholic church to the more traditional Maasai ritual of being left out in the wild to be recycled by the carnivores of the savannah.

Adding to David's overall state of exhaustion was the fact that he and Max had kept their promise to rendezvous with Olabon the night before, waiting all night in utter darkness along the edges of the marsh bordering Natron's northern shore, where they had first found Oscar. But neither Olabon nor his comrades had appeared. It worried them both, for Olabon was due an enormous sum of money, which they of course did not have.

Inside his schoolhouse, the desks were gone and every chair David could find was carefully placed in neat rows. He had made the transformation from school to church many times but never to this degree. What was lacking was an altar, a serious altar. Someone to help in this effort would also have been nice, but that was out of the question. Christine and Dr. Brecht were busy trying to revive whatever records they could find from her disheveled trailer, and Max, though thoroughly exhausted not only by the long hours of surgery that had ended in vain but by the pointless trek to Natron's northern edge, was busy putting the final touches on Senento's eternal resting place. Grave diggers in Maasailand, he had discovered, had but a crude understanding of what a well-dug grave looked like.

Summoning all his strength, David pushed his massive wooden desk to the middle of the floor. Then he placed his old, rough-hewn coffee table on top. He threw on a few Maasai blankets, carefully placed some big brass candleholders, and then the chalice as the crowning touch. *Et voilà*, his own little chapel. And just in time. He could already hear the chanting of the moran as they approached.

Joseph was the first to enter, leading a procession of elders. They were followed by the women, many of whom surrounded Senento's widows. Some of them were weeping; others were more stoic. And then came the moran, clutching spears and shields as they continued to sing in lugubrious tones. Ntanda, displaying even more swagger than usual, was the first to enter. He and his comrades in arms filed in and lined up around the sides of the room, providing a fierce backdrop, as if standing sentry to the seated congregation.

With all seats taken and the chanting of the moran silenced, David stepped up to the makeshift altar to begin the Mass. Somehow the presence of Senento lying still in the coffin before him took the edge off. No one was really looking at David. All eyes, except Joseph's, seemed to be fixed on the crude wooden box that Max and David had quickly nailed together from some old boards hidden in David's priest hole and that now contained Senento's mortal remains. David knew they weren't marveling at the workmanship, or lack thereof. They all appeared somewhat spooked, no doubt due to the firm belief that a dead Maasai's spirit can linger for several weeks in his homeland. And only after such a prolonged period would the Maasai celebrate the deceased's life, once assured he or she may no longer be eavesdropping. Yet this ceremony, this Mass, was a nice tribute, wrapped up in Catholic tradition but with a Maasai twist. Senento would be proud and quite impressed if he happened to be looking on.

David welcomed everyone and thanked them for coming to say good-bye to one of their dearest tribesmen. Senento had been a successful man, amassing a herd of over one hundred cattle. He and his sons had tended them well. His wives had borne him many fine children of whom he could be very proud. And his counsel among the elders was frequently sought out by young and old alike. He was a caring man with a mild disposition. Trustworthy and honorable, he always spoke the truth.

This eulogy, spoken in near perfect Maa with only the slightest French accent, had no visible effect on those gathered to bid farewell to the poor dead man lying before them. The men remained rigid and expressionless while many of the women, with heads bowed, simply continued their low-key incantations as if David did not even exist.

David then launched into the rituals rife with all of God's mysteries. He poured the wine into his golden chalice and drank of it. He blessed the horribly outdated holy hosts he had placed in a silver bowl and served up communion. A healthy portion of the congregation took part, blessing themselves as David placed wretchedly stale, dry communion wafers on their outstretched tongues. Inwardly he prayed that no one would gag on them. All the moran wisely abstained.

David then placed the chalice and the silver bowl back on the instant altar before turning to face the congregation.

"My dear friends," said David after all were seated once again, "I wish our friend Senento well as he embarks on this new journey. May God receive him with all his grace."

David lowered his eyes and stood silent for a moment before lifting his head to survey his congregation.

"If any of you would like to say a few words, now is the time."

A pronounced grumbling ensued as those gathered to honor their fallen comrade contemplated what, if anything, they might say. Predictably, Joseph was the first to stand and slowly make his way to the head of Senento's coffin. He swatted at invisible flies with his fly brush and hoisted one shoulder to better secure the orange, red, and black plaid blanket that constituted his Sunday best. He looked down at the coffin, then slowly raised his head to confront the congregation. His gaze swept across the entire assemblage before stopping to focus solely on his oldest son, Ntanda, standing tall and looking ever the fiercely proud moran, head of his age class. Joseph took in a deep breath before setting his deeply incised face in the locked and loaded position.

"There will be no more killing," he stated in his deep, raspy voice. "Not of cattle, not of men."

The words were spoken slowly, with the conviction of a man who had just needlessly lost his best friend.

"Let me repeat. There will be no more poaching of our cattle," he continued, his voice growing louder as his fierce eyes moved from Ntanda to make contact with each and every moran standing beside the rear wall. Then he shifted his gaze, looking down at his dead friend. He stood silent for quite some time, his long face hanging low. He looked tired, very tired. And very sad.

"I am sorry, my friend," he said at last. "I am sorry you had to give up your life to save my son. And I am sorry we failed to prevent the intruders from invading our land in the first place. You know as well as I that they could not have been stopped. Even the Kenya army, had they been better prepared, would not have stopped them. We did what we needed to do to secure a better future for our people once the refugees are gone. And they will be gone, soon."

He raised his weary head and looked again at the congregation, at his people. Then he looked once more at his son and the rest of the moran.

"There will be no more forays north of the road to Kalema."

His eyes slowly swept across the back of the room as he took pains to visually confront every single moran one more time. They all looked back, not one daring to lower or divert his gaze either in submission or in fear.

"Sometimes," he continued, "sometimes we must remember that not only are we Maasai, we are Africans. And sometimes we must do what is right for Africa, and by so doing, we can do better for ourselves. But for now we must wait, patiently and vigilantly, but we must wait, here in this land of good grass and ample water. They will soon be gone, every one of them, I swear it.

"Senento," he said, looking down one last time at the corporeal remains of his old friend, "I will miss you and I will miss your good counsel in these difficult times. I promise you we will prevail. We will survive as a united people, the Maasai. May you rest in peace."

Joseph turned and, without looking up, quietly made his way back to his seat. David stepped forward and looked around his schoolroom.

"Very well spoken," he said, clearing his throat. "Now who is next?"

All he heard in reply were more low rumblings as the mourners grappled with the words just spoken and with their own thoughts and feelings toward this well-liked yet, save to Joseph and a few of Senento's wives, little-known man. Like Joseph, he had kept most things to himself.

Much to David's dismay, and certainly to Joseph's, Ntanda handed his spear to his moran neighbor and strolled somewhat leisurely up to the instant altar, bearing the look of an upstart challenger. He stopped at the head of the coffin and scanned the assembly, his expression conveying a deep and sincere sense of grief as well as one of disdain.

"Senento," he began, looking down at the coffin, "you were like an uncle to me. Like a second father. The bullet that took your life was meant for me. I wish you had not attempted to intervene."

He continued to stare down at the corpse for a moment or two, tears rolling down his cheeks. It was a state of emotion quite unbecoming to a moran.

"I want everyone to know that I, too, am sorry. I am very, very sorry," he continued, raising his head and looking all around the room. "But I was only doing what I have been taught by my father and by my elders, including you, Senento. They are killing our cattle. And they are killing us by stealing our precious resources. They must be driven from this land, our land, before they have completely fouled it, before their defecation and their wretchedness have completely rendered our soil incapable of producing the green grasses that ultimately sustain us all."

Pausing to allow these words to penetrate, he wiped his eyes in a defiant gesture.

"Despite what my father may say," he continued, "they have no right to it. The government has once again turned against us by supporting this occupation of our land. Yes, my father condones it. But what choice does he have? Believe me when I say I respect my father, but I fear that he has simply lost the will to fight. And I am sorry to say he has exchanged it for empty promises, pieces of paper with fancy words on them, but that is all they are, more worthless words on worthless pieces of paper. Do you really believe in all these empty promises? No more encroachment of big farming into our land. More water, better schools. How many times will we trust our fate to these mzungu lawyers whose only aim is to line their own pockets at our expense? I do not trust them and will never trust a government that has consistently turned its back on us. The only choice before us is to rout this wretched plague of human locusts from our land before they ruin it entirely and before they come to claim it as their own. I only hope we are not too late. Senento, I pledge to you that your death will be avenged in true Maasai tradition, and that every one of these invaders will be driven away very soon and forever."

The words hung in the air for quite some time as many of those gathered craned their necks in an effort to see how Joseph would react to such a brazen challenge from his son. Joseph merely kept his gaze focused on the coffin before him, his expression frozen with remorse. Many were busy with their fans. For despite the recentness of his death and a hefty layering of camphor leaves, the intense heat was quickly perpetuating Senento's inevitable decay. He needed to be buried, the sooner the better.

Seated nearest to the coffin were Senento's pallbearers, six of his seven sons. The seventh was the young Matthew, who still wore the charcoal cape and wooden plugs in his earlobes that marked him as an initiate. He looked pleadingly at his brothers, obviously hoping one or more of them would stand up and defend Ntanda or say something about their father. Perhaps it was their proximity to the slowly decaying body, but none of them said a word. David then hastily drew the ceremony to a close, thanking everyone for coming and inviting them to attend the ensuing burial. The crowd dispersed slowly and rather solemnly.

The wives and children and some of the closer relatives, about thirty in all, gathered around the grave site as David continued with the last bit of ritual. He shook the holy water over the now-closed coffin and watched as Senento's sons and a few of his widows lowered the box into the hole Max had dug. Matthew was the first to pick up a shovel and begin the process of entombing the father he so loved and respected. He stabbed at the pile of dry dirt, angry tears streaming down his youthful face, and threw several shovelfuls into the breach before relinquishing the tool to one of his brothers.

Max, Christine, and Dr. Brecht looked on from the schoolhouse porch, having kept their distance from the funeral at David's request. There was already a decided resentment among the Maasai toward their Ugandan invaders. David did not want to risk adding to the resentment by the presence of the other, albeit more familiar intruders. That of course included Max, the alleged great doctor of medicine who had failed to save Senento's life.

"Did you catch what Ntanda was saying?" said Max. He had been listening to the ceremony through the thin wall separating David's living quarters from the school turned mortuary. Christine and Dr. Brecht had returned from their futile efforts to piece together the scattered remnants of Christine's doctoral thesis halfway through the requiem.

"This situation is far too explosive," said Dr. Brecht, her brow more furrowed than usual. "Ntanda is correct in at least one sense. Sitting by and doing nothing while others occupy the land you and your ancestors have fought for over hundreds of years is as contrary to the Maasai spirit as anything you could possibly imagine. If the governments of Kenya and Uganda can't agree where to move these people, and if the United Nations can't either, this could end in nothing but bloodshed."

"They still have a couple of months to work things out," said Max.

"Yeah," piped Christine, "a few more months during which we are stuck here trying to pull bullets out of people instead of doing what we came here to do. I can't believe we didn't get out when we had a chance."

"Unless you've forgotten, we had a medical emergency on our hands," Max reminded her.

"Exactly my point. I'm sorry we couldn't save Senento but I didn't come here to play nurse. I had a thesis nearly completed and now it's all gone. What am I going to do? Three years' work down the fucking toilet."

"I would not feel so discouraged if I were you," said Dr. Brecht, a comment that brought an immediate rise out of Christine. She turned to look at this Gertrude Brecht, her thesis advisor, who had just told her not more than an hour earlier that her research project was beyond salvaging.

"Excuse me," she said, "but I've lost all my data. Data that represented thousands of hours of work just to collect, let alone interpret. And you just told me it was hopeless. So now I suddenly have something to look forward to besides serving up suture and sponge to Dr. Taylor here?"

The peacekeeper in Max wanted to intervene but sheer exhaustion, and maybe a little common sense, made him hold back.

"You may not realize it, but you are in a very enviable position as an aspiring anthropologist," said Dr. Brecht. "The events unfolding here are unprecedented. And you are right in the middle of them. To be able to bear witness to and describe the stresses and adaptations made to them by the people you have come to know so well and who are of great interest to anthropologists all over the world is a tremendous opportunity. If properly researched, documented, and exploited, this could earn you far more acclaim than purporting to prove that Maasai women wield more social power than previously acknowledged."

For once Christine was speechless. She just bit her lower lip and stared at Dr. Brecht. In a strange way, Max felt this was all somewhat amusing.

"Right," said Christine. "Just hunker down like some embedded reporter and jot down who shot whose cattle and who got killed in return. Where's the science in that?"

Dr. Brecht shook her head and nearly laughed. "This is life, my dear, how it really is. Science is nice when the world of randomness accommodates it. But the key is accurately reporting and documenting what you observe in whatever manner works. This isn't a time for surveys and questionnaires and interviews. It is a time for keen observation and clear and sober reporting. We may feel isolated and out of touch, but I can guarantee that the world is watching this."

Max yawned. "Good luck with all that," he said. "I'm going to catch a nap before the next body arrives. And if one doesn't arrive, I'm going up there to check on Oscar."

He pointed in the general direction of the Nguruman Escarpment to the west as he headed off across the dusty parking area, which was of course completely devoid of any functioning vehicle. It felt like he hadn't slept in days, which wasn't far from the truth.

Chapter 45

Unbeknownst to Max, someone was watching from high up on the Nguruman Escarpment. Having first heard the bell ringing, then the chanting of the moran, Crazy Jack McGraw had been looking on for some time. The air was so still that the sound wafted up to the lookout Ntanda had first shown him days before. Barely able to distinguish the schoolhouse through the wavering air, he nonetheless discerned that an event of some significance was unfolding down below. It was no doubt what had drawn nearly all the moran away from the olpul feasting, leaving but a skeleton crew to guard the ever-dangerous Oscar Newman, who remained for the most part sequestered in his mini-cave. He was granted the privilege of a morning and afternoon stroll around the grounds, under armed guard, but that was the extent of his daily exercise. The swords and spears were all fully sharpened, and there was little to do but rest and heal and perhaps learn how to better communicate with his captors.

To that end Oscar had attempted whenever possible to engage in conversation the young girl who regularly brought him his food. Her name was Sarna. She could not have been more than thirteen, but Oscar was willing to bet she had been to see Max. She was very pretty and seemed to be a favorite with many of the moran. He pointed at the gourd, which he feared would be full of that disgustingly foul-tasting mélange of cow's blood and soured milk.

"Ol-pikuri," she said.

Oscar attempted to repeat the sounds she had just uttered, but his rendition only caused Sarna to begin to giggle.

"What's so funny?" Oscar replied, smiling at her. Then she handed him the gourd.

"Ol-pikuri," she repeated. *"A-itook."*

With the last pronouncement she raised her hand as if she were bringing the gourd to her lips.

"A-itook," said Oscar. "Drink!"

He was so elated that he understood yet one more word in the Maa language that he lifted the gourd and drank it dry. He paused a moment afterward and contorted his face in such a way that Sarna fell about laughing. Oscar suddenly realized how long it had been since he had seen or heard anyone laugh. He laughed back at her and the wretched taste was quickly forgotten. He pointed to his face and then at hers.

"Laughing," he said slowly and very clearly. Sarna smiled in comprehension.

"En-kuenia," she replied, trying her best to stifle her giggles, but Oscar had resumed his facial antics, conveying—only partially in jest—just how rancid his last drink had tasted.

Sarna was still laughing when Crazy Jack suddenly burst into view. He was running as fast as he could across the open space beneath the overhanging canopy of branches that both shaded and concealed from aerial views this moran camp that had long been the site of the olpul.

"Oscar," he was yelling, "I seen where they all went! There's some kind of funeral goin' on. There's probably a hundred moran or more, and all the villagers come outta the schoolhouse with a coffin. They drug it over to that little cemetery plot and now they're about to bury somebody."

Oscar sat up and handed the gourd back to Sarna. His expression turned dour. Was this it? The beginning of the inevitable clash between the Maasai and the Ugandan invaders?

"What do you suppose happened?" he replied. "No wonder all the moran have departed, except for old Ollie Tuna over there."

Oscar was referring to one of the less gifted moran, who had been left behind to stand guard. His name was Olitunu. All he lived for was playing *bao*, the local version of the ancient game of mancala. He liked to play with Oscar, even though Oscar, a decidedly quick learner, usually won.

"Maybe we should ask him," said Crazy Jack.

"We could try."

After several futile attempts to engage Olitunu in any type of remotely comprehensible dialogue, Sarna piped in. Olitunu was too busy stripping pieces of cured hide and wrapping them around the handle of his newly sharpened spear to be bothered.

"Senento dead," she uttered in plain English.

"Senento?" said Oscar. The name had a familiar ring. Somewhere within the misty domains of his faded memory there appeared before him a brimming gourd filled with the ceremonial honey beer. The thought of a brimming gourd full of beer made his mouth water and his pulse quicken. "Wasn't he the poor fellow who had to have his son circumcised by Max? Why, I gave him a goat in honor of the occasion. I wonder what happened to him."

Sarna lowered her head. "Ugandans shoot him," she softly whispered, as if it were taboo for a young girl of her age to speak of such things.

"Damn," said Crazy Jack, shaking his head. "That ain't no good at all. Them moran ain't gonna let that go without some kinda retribution."

"Retribution?" Oscar said. "Now where did you learn a word like that?"

Crazy Jack took no time in answering. "Pops. Pops always use to say that so and so would get his retribution sooner or later. My guess is it's gonna be sooner."

They both sat by silently, letting the news of this calamity soak in. Jack was beginning to squirm.

"Oscar, you ought to come see what's goin' on down there. Come on out to the overlook. It's 'bout time for your afternoon walk anyway. Ready to head out a little beyond yer usual lap around the campfire?"

Oscar raised a bushy eyebrow. "I don't know. In any event I doubt Ollie would approve."

"Yo, Ollie," Jack shouted as he stood up. "Time for Oscar to get his fat legs movin'. How about we walk him out to the lookout?"

Jack grabbed Oscar's hand and raised him to his feet. Olitunu, who had been sitting on a nearby log, abruptly let his leatherwork fall to the ground as he, too, rose to his feet.

"A-a," he said, meaning no, as he approached them with his spear raised on high.

Jack objected, standing as tall as he could and looking defiant as he stepped in front of Oscar. It was a bold move, one that he never would have dared if Ntanda had been in camp. He said no more but began to imitate a man walking in place. The penny dropped as Olitunu glanced skyward to see the time of day. He motioned to Oscar to follow.

Oscar walked slowly but faster than he had in previous days, as the steady diet of meat, milk, and cow's blood had begun to help him regain some of his considerable former strength. They walked around the main fire pit, under the canopy of trees that surrounded the central part of the camp. It was the normal circuit. When they arrived at the far end of the campsite, however, Jack grabbed Oscar by the hand once again and started to lead him toward the overlook. Olitunu raised his spear and blocked their way.

"Jeez, can't he jus' go look at what's goin' on down there? He ain't done nothin' and he sure as hell ain't in no condition to go runnin' off."

His appeal to Olitunu gained him nothing. They stared each other down for a while before Olitunu spoke.

"Bao," he said, looking straight at Oscar.

"Bao," said Oscar, more than willing to be bribed into another game. After all, he had finished sharpening all the spears. There really wasn't much else to do.

They all walked carefully out toward the bluff, Oscar pausing every few steps to take a deep breath or two. He winced as his burly chest expanded, stretching the lion-clawed scar tissue that was still not fully healed. But this was his greatest self-propelled excursion in quite some time, and he was determined to stay the course. It wasn't more than a hundred yards to the overlook, but the crude path was interlaced with large, gnarly tree roots and many rocky sections that required delicate footwork. His prospector friend and seemingly constant companion helped to steady him every few steps. When they finally arrived at the spot where the path gave way to a barren, rocky outcrop, Olitunu stopped and turned to face his prisoner and his prisoner's accomplice. He motioned to them to crouch down and remain concealed from view as they approached the overlook.

Oscar and Crazy Jack both bent down on hands and knees and crawled out across the solid basalt that led to the precipice. As they neared the edge, Oscar felt not only the burning of his chest but the wild racing of his pulse. Perhaps it was because he was suspended nearly two thousand feet above the valley floor! But far more disturbing than these giddy heights was the spectacle of thousands of Ugandan refugees sprawled out across the Rift Valley floor below. It was hideous, as if some huge dike had failed and let loose a torrent of humanity that had spilled into the middle of Maasailand. It was nothing but a sea of blue and white tents and black people that began far to the north and swept southward almost as far as the Kalema Road. The remaining ribbon of green grassland south of the Kalema Road, now settled by the Maasai and their cattle, pushed up against the extensive marshes that extended all the way to Natron's salty shores. The Maasai were penned in.

This grim tableau was like a large dose of smelling salts, arousing Oscar from weeks of sensory deprivation. The state of depression and self-pity into which he had fallen suddenly disappeared, and in its stead there arose a rekindled affirmation of the cause to which he had devoted nearly his entire life. Here was a perfect example of far too many people competing for far too few resources. In fact, it was

367

quite evident that this enormous encampment of displaced foreigners was entirely at the mercy of the United Nations, the Red Cross, and other brothers and sisters of mercy.

He lifted his gaze from the squalid scene below to take in a more general sense of the landscape. The Great Rift Valley of East Africa stretched far north and south, exposing nearly a 180-degree panorama. To the north he could distinguish the gently sloping outline of Mount Longonot and beyond it Mount Kenya silhouetted against the blue, smoky haze emanating from Nairobi. Slowly, it dawned on him that it was over there, on the other side of the Rift Valley, where he and Francis had been stranded after the Jeep had broken down, and Peter had rescued them. That was the last time he had sat so precariously near the edge, albeit on the other side. It must have been months before. He recalled the majestic ride in the hot-air balloon. In fact, Peter had mentioned something about this uprising. Francis had even accused him of spying on it. Yes, Oscar began to recall this and many other details of his strange journey through the Rift Valley over the past several months. But the Great Rift Valley had never looked like this.

"Unbelievable," he half whispered to himself. It seemed as if the powers of procreation had suddenly gone wild. The irony was overwhelming. For had he not come to this place, this cradle of civilization, on some silly pilgrimage, searching for guidance and inspiration regarding what it meant to procreate after all his years of bachelorhood? How had he put it, something like learning how to serve as a proper trustee of his own genetic endowment? It certainly seemed that all those spread out below had utterly failed in that quest. And apparently, so had he. His genetic endowment was toast.

Oscar tried to dispel such thoughts by drinking in more of the spectacular view. As his eyes swept the horizon from north to south, they came to rest on the majestic outline of Kilimanjaro dominating the view to the southeast. But as he continued to gaze southward, he was struck by the site of Lake Natron and Gelai just beyond. His body froze as he recalled much too vividly all the nightmarish incidents that had occurred both outside and within that mass of volcanic rock, not the least of which was being mauled by a lion. And the diamonds—yes, the diamonds—they were all still there. But they had cost Francis his life and might, in fact, cost Oscar his own life. Time would tell.

"See all them folk over by the schoolhouse?" said Jack.

Oscar shifted his point of view southward and located the small congregation just beyond the tiny square of tin roof that had to be David's quarters.

"Yes, I see. They must have buried poor Senento in David's little cemetery."

"Poor bastard."

Their brief conversation was interrupted by a jab in Oscar's heel from the blunt end of Olitunu's spear. Recess was over. Oscar took one last look at the hordes of refugees, then turned to head back to his dungeon.

They had not even reached the central encampment area before they heard voices, one voice rising above the others in a familiar, angry tone. Ntanda had returned from the funeral, along with the other moran and initiates, only to find their one prisoner missing. Ntanda turned and looked upon this pathetic trio as they approached the clearing; he reserved his most severe scowl for Olitunu. He walked up to him shaking his spear and began shouting and no doubt cursing. Obviously, the walk to the lookout was not a part of Oscar's sanctioned routine. Olitunu apologized, or at least did his best to look as contrite as a moran possibly can. Ntanda then approached Oscar and began yelling and probably cursing at him as well. Oscar stood his ground.

Ntanda stared back at him with a look of utter disdain and handed him his spear. He told him in words Oscar could not understand but in gestures to get back in his cell and to sharpen his spear again. Oscar grabbed the spear and stared back at Ntanda. He gripped the spear by its shaft and turned his body ninety degrees, eyeing a large wild olive tree twenty yards off, at the edge of the clearing. With a sudden twisting of his great bulk and a heaving of his torso, Oscar launched the spear in a direct line such that its tip buried itself two inches deep and chest high smack in the middle of the trunk. Oscar looked back at Ntanda, who stood speechless for once, and walked off toward his digs. He needed a rest.

That left Ntanda, who had stepped out in front of all his ochre-slathered comrades to berate Oscar, standing alone in the center of the clearing, temporarily unarmed. One of the young initiates walked over to the tree to remove the spear. But he needed the help of two of the moran before he could pry it loose.

Ntanda flew into another rage. He snapped some orders, and several of his closest allies followed him off to a remote area beyond the clearing. When they returned several moments later, they were carrying a heavily charred wooden box that appeared to be quite heavy. Making their way toward the hand-dug cave that had become Oscar Newman's primary address of late, they stopped short of the entrance and set the box down. Ntanda called out to both Oscar and Crazy Jack. Oscar looked up from his pallet bed and reluctantly sat up. His side and his lion-scarred, semi-healed chest were screaming at him for heaving the spear so violently. It was one thing to throw the javelin at the University of Glasgow, where he had had a fair bit of success in the sport, and quite another to think he had the strength to do it again after all these years and in his compromised condition with a real spear! Nonetheless, he finally stood up and walked outside to see what Ntanda was going to demand of him now. Jack McGraw appeared from behind a cluster of bushes and walked over to stand next to Oscar. They both peered down at the box with curiosity. Ntanda motioned to one of his lieutenants to open it. One of the moran stepped up and stuck his spear in between two of the boards to pry off the lid.

Oscar closed his eyes, disbelieving. Crazy Jack let out a whistle. For inside the box were the AK-47s, the ones that had been tossed into the fire set by the crazy man in the blue helicopter who had come looking for Oscar a while back. They were severely tarnished and singed and, judging by the look on Ntanda's face, no longer operable. Not that any bullets had survived the fire.

"Fix them," said Ntanda in plain English as he looked alternately from Oscar to Crazy Jack.

Chapter 46

Elizabeth sat alone on an ancient stone bench deep within the protected enclave of her mother's garden, watching the morning sunlight dance upon the many facets of the diamond engagement ring Oscar had given to her months before. A thousand tiny shafts of light reflected in kaleidoscopic fashion off the many well-polished surfaces of the ancient gemstones. It was nearly hypnotic.

Wrapped in a dark-green woolen cape, she sat amid the roses and admired the swirling sparkles and the magical ways in which this hardest of natural substances sliced the incoming beams of Provençal sunlight into myriad rainbow colors. Though she was momentarily mesmerized, the pain of losing Oscar lingered within. It was an all-too-familiar feeling, one that was starting to seem like a very depressed relative who at first came to visit but who has decided to stay. Not too unlike herself.

It had been well over a month since her return to Balgères. And with each passing day her mother pestered her ever more with all manner of questions about what she intended to do with the rest of her life now that Oscar was certainly dead. There were far too many questions to be answered, the most troubling being whether Oscar was indeed dead as her mother, and perhaps the rest of the world, presumed. Deep in reverie, she never even heard her brother approaching.

"Elizabeth," said Edouard as he took a seat beside her. "Dr. McNeil called again. You really must talk to him."

She turned to look at him briefly before glancing down at the well-worn stones beneath her feet. "I've already told him," she said. "I need to take care of Oscar's mother before I can return to Glasgow."

"Yes, but he needs to know when. Dr. Andrews is apparently going apoplectic without an assistant. She may well have hired one already, for all we know."

"That would be fine with me," she replied.

"What are you saying?"

"I am saying I've felt more warmth off a snowman than from that woman."

"But Elizabeth, what will you do if you can't go back to your old position?"

"I don't know. The only thing I do know is that I must get Eleanor situated somewhere. She can't stay with Peter Dermenjian forever."

"Well then, why don't you just run over to his villa and get her?"

371

"He's away again. And I can't just steal her away without speaking with him. Surely there is a considerable sum of money due for all the care. I am not going to let him incur those expenses. I just need to speak with him. I don't think it will be too much longer."

"And then where will you take her?"

"I don't know."

Elizabeth stood up and began walking along the little stone path that meandered through the walled-in garden. Edouard followed her, hoping he hadn't pressed too hard.

"When will he be back?"

"I don't know."

Edouard paused. This conversation would require a bit more tact if he was to extract any information. The bottom line, of course, was being able to tell their mother what her daughter was going to do and when she was going to get about doing it.

"Do you have any idea where he went?" he inquired, picking up the pace again.

"Yes," she responded. "He's in Kenya looking for Oscar and helping with the relief efforts for the Ugandan refugees." She stopped to examine the buds on a rosebush, trying to gauge how soon the buds might burst into bloom.

"Really? Then you have recently spoken with him?"

She kept staring at the rosebuds. But her mind's eye replayed the news story she had seen the night before. There had indeed been a story from Kenya, reported by none other than Melanie Woo, the CNN reporter who had pounced on an unsuspecting Oscar some six months previously, telling him and the entire world that he'd been selected to receive the Nobel Peace Prize. But last night she had been interviewing Peter Dermenjian, a substantial contributor to the relief effort. Standing next to his private helicopter, with its distinctive sunset diamond emblazoned on a powder-blue background, Peter Dermenjian had responded to her questions, stating he had come to see for himself the plight of the refugees, to see how the significant sums of money he had contributed were helping to improve the tense situation. He wanted to see if there were any other ways to help with the cause, to help Kenya, the country he'd grown up in, recover from this sudden and tragic influx of so many horribly persecuted Ugandans.

"Just one more question," she said. "It is well known you have also helped considerably in the search for Dr. Oscar Newman, the Nobel Peace Prize winner who has been missing for weeks. Have you, too, like the Kenyan authorities, given up the search?"

Peter cleared his throat. "No," he stated, deadly serious, "I have not given up the search. I believe there is still hope he will be found alive."

And with that last comment he had turned to face the camera, as if the words were meant for Elizabeth herself. But it was Peter's expression, displaying such a strong sense of conviction, that had given her renewed hope. Lost in these reflections, she nearly forgot that her brother was still standing by, awaiting a response.

"No, I have not spoken with him, not directly. I saw him interviewed on the news last night. By that Melanie Woo."

She proceeded to relay the story to him. Edouard listened very carefully.

"That all sounds very noble of him," he replied at last. "But I still don't trust him. So you really have no idea when he'll return?"

"Perhaps another week? When I inquired at his residence, all his secretary would tell me was that he was out of the country and would return when he had completed his business. And he doesn't answer his cell phone. He's no doubt well out of range."

"That's not very helpful. But assuming he does return, and soon, what will you do with Oscar's mother? You know damn well she can't come here. Mother wants nothing to do with her."

As if she didn't know. The idea of bringing Eleanor Newman back to this house, or anywhere near her mother, wasn't even an option in her mind. The logical location would be Eleanor's accustomed nursing home in Tobermory, where Mrs. Hamilton was waiting for her. But that would mean that Elizabeth, too, would need to return to Scotland. For wherever Eleanor was, she would need to be close by. It was the very least she could do to remain near Eleanor, who had no other family besides Oscar, for as long as she insisted on clinging to her unfortunate life. But that line of reasoning always led her back to the notion of returning to the medical school. Apart from her instant disdain for Dr. Andrews, she doubted she could face working in Oscar's old laboratory, especially after her last discovery.

"You can tell Mother she has nothing to worry about."

Edouard reached out and grabbed Elizabeth's hand, forcing her to turn and face him. "Perhaps *you* should tell her. She says you've been acting quite strangely of late and that you refuse to speak with her."

Elizabeth retrieved her hand and turned away. What was there to say? She couldn't very well tell him or her mother that she was a week late with her period and that she was absolutely terrified what that might signify. She was perhaps a bit elated as well but nonetheless certainly terrified. She wondered just how long it would be before Peter returned from Africa.

That unfortunately depended on what Peter might learn, and how fast, on this particular quest for the exact whereabouts of Oscar Newman. For now that Peter knew he was alive, his patience with Banyon had worn thin. It was time for a private conversation with Jocko. All his other affairs would have to wait.

Riding along in the Kenya National Police Jeep, Peter mused over the interview that his publicist had helped to arrange the previous day with that very attractive reporter, Melanie Woo, right outside the confines of the refugee camp. Though pleased for the most part with the interview, he regretted his response to the last question regarding Oscar Newman. It would have been more in his own interest to go along with the current thinking that Oscar Newman was long dead, his bones scattered somewhere near the godforsaken shores of Lake Natron. But she had surprised him with the question. It certainly hadn't been discussed beforehand with his publicist. Regardless, only he and his closest associates had tangible evidence that Dr. Newman was indeed still alive, evidence for which the media would pay mightily. It brought a smile to his face. At least he hadn't divulged that he was determined to actually find Oscar Newman this time, now that he knew he was alive, before he would even consider returning to the continent.

The Jeep swayed steadily from side to side as it meandered through the hordes, swerving as needed to avoid either people or large ruts in the crude roadway. Captain Olengi was at the wheel, having insisted on accompanying Peter Dermenjian on this most unsanctioned visit. This meeting had to come off absolutely without incident and therefore very discreetly. There was no way he would trust such an assignment to one of his subordinate officers.

A few of Jocko's guards responded with raised weapons as the Jeep approached. But they quickly put them out of view when the Kenya National

Police vehicle arrived carrying what looked like an actual military official. Peter Dermenjian descended from the passenger side while Banyon and Dr. Meinz exited on their own from the rear. Captain Olengi, sizing up the situation, jumped out and told the guards that they were here to see Jocko. He also added that he was not going to put up with any of Jocko's shenanigans. The guards nodded and went back to the large tent from which they had just emerged. Minutes ticked by.

Just as Captain Olengi was preparing to burst in, Jocko came around the corner. He was all smiles.

"Captain Olengi," he cooed, "how good of you to leave the comfort of your office and come pay me a visit out here in the wilds of the Rift Valley. Isn't it beautiful? If only there weren't all these damned tents and all these starving people."

"Yes. This is a most unfortunate situation. You could have chosen a much more hospitable place to relocate your people."

"Perhaps," replied the jolly, round warlord. "But this is where we are, isn't it? So let us not be rude. Please introduce me to your friends."

Well done, thought Peter. It would not be wise to acknowledge that he and Jocko had an association that went well back in time. They weren't exactly friends, but they had collaborated often enough on various black-market transactions.

"This is Peter Dermenjian. He has contributed substantially to the relief fund. He wishes to know what you are thinking about the relocation options you have been tendered."

"Yes," interjected Peter, smiling a rather forced smile. "I might be able to help, shall we say, open some doors. These are my associates, Mr. Banyon and Dr. Meinz."

"You are most welcome," said Jocko. "Please come in."

As they all began to walk around to the entrance on the other side of the tent, Jocko quickly turned back to address Captain Olengi.

"Please make yourself comfortable. I doubt this will take very long."

He was motioning toward a small table and a few chairs by a fire pit that Captain Olengi quickly surmised was where they cooked the meat poached from the Maasai.

"I am sorry, but I must insist on accompanying Mr. Dermenjian."

"That won't be necessary," said Peter. "I need to have a private conversation. Surely you understand."

375

Every muscle in Captain Olengi's face objected, but he recognized the look returned to him by Peter. It was a look that said, "If I have managed to persuade your superiors to let me come this far, then don't think I wouldn't hesitate to have you demoted for interfering in my interview with this impudent rebel demagogue." He fumed in silence as Peter and company rounded the corner and entered the tent along with its primary occupant, Jocko.

Inside the tent, whose ceiling was quite high, there was ample room along the walls for a table, a large bed, and a desk. Upon the desk was a computer, its screen lit up and displaying a long list of messages. Next to it was a box containing Christine Olson's files, hard drive, and the Scout's missing distributor cap.

They sat down on plush cushions that circled a large, round table. The floor consisted of a Persian rug that stretched to all sides of the tent, keeping the dust and dirt at bay. It was quite comfortable inside, especially compared to the absolutely miserable conditions outside. There were scented candles burning, helping to fend off the offensive odors that permeated the entire sprawling encampment.

"So how may I help you?" Jocko inquired as he placed an array of dried meats and dried fruits before them and offered them each some bottled spring water.

"You have helped enormously already," Peter replied. "The raid of Oscar Newman's clinic provided some very useful information. I'm sorry your people were apprehended."

Jocko laughed. "Silly young fools. Couldn't resist the temptation of all that fine wine in the priest's cellar. No matter. They were all returned. If only they had thought to bring me a bottle!"

"That could be arranged," Peter replied. "I trust you have ample weapons to defend yourselves in the event the Maasai should have a change of heart and decide to attack?"

"Yes, we are well armed as far as the Maasai are concerned, thank you. Not well fed but well armed. But the Maasai cattle, as scrawny as they are, help to round out the diet a bit. Do you like the meat? I cured it myself."

Banyon nodded his head. Peter and Dr. Meinz had thus far abstained.

"Where do you think he is?" said Peter, obviously not wishing to waste time on small talk.

"Who? Oscar Newman? I don't know, and frankly, I don't give a damn. I was just doing you a favor by stealing the files from the clinic and from that student. By the way, what should we do with all that? It's of no use to us."

He was referring to the box with Christine's files.

"I have an idea," said Dr. Meinz rather meekly.

"Really, Conrad?" said Peter. "I'm all ears."

"No doubt that poor young anthropology student is quite distraught over losing all her data. I'd be willing to bet she knows where Oscar Newman is. Perhaps she could be, shall we say, persuaded to divulge his whereabouts in exchange for her missing files."

"Excellent idea, Conrad," said Peter. "What else? Jocko, I understand the Maasai killed one of your party? What was that about?"

"I assure you it had nothing to do with this Oscar Newman," he replied as he chewed away at a piece of jerky. "One of our less experienced young men was caught poaching Maasai cattle. Joseph's hotheaded son slit his throat. I'd keep an eye on that one. He clearly doesn't believe in this truce. In fact, he should be dead. We've already shot him once but that young doctor apparently saved him."

"Really?" said Peter, as if this were news. "I trust your people are keeping an eye on him."

Jocko began to laugh. "Of course. We are monitoring every movement along the Kalema Road. Occasionally, we see him giving orders to his moran lieutenants. They are so quaint, with their colorful shields and their spears. We could remove them and take their cattle in a matter of hours. And we may. But for now we wait for word when we can begin to return to our homeland."

Peter stared, then began shaking his head. "But your homeland is completely overrun by all the warring tribes that ran you and your people out. You must consider other locations."

Jocko began laughing once more. "Yes, of course. Like this one? My people are mainly fishermen, not cattlemen. We will return to our home on Lake Kyoga once those who now battle for it have been sufficiently weakened. For that effort we will need much better weapons. So if your mission here is to help us to leave, then bring us better news of the struggle up north and above all bring us better weapons to fight with. We will need rockets and mortars plus many more automatic rifles when the time comes."

"Right," said Peter, clenching his jaw. "Listen to me carefully. You will find Oscar Newman for me. That, and only that, will earn you all you will need."

On that note Peter stood up, thanked him for the visit, and departed, but only after first collecting the box with Christine's files and hard drive. Captain Olengi greeted them as they exited the tent, still enraged at the cheek of this Dermenjian to exclude him from the conversation.

"What is in the box?" he inquired. It looked like computer files, possibly some very sensitive information that might be of great interest to his superiors.

"You will take us to see the priest," said Peter. "The one with the school for the Maasai."

Captain Olengi was preparing to open the passenger door for him but stopped abruptly upon hearing these words. "I cannot do that. I am not authorized to cross the Kalema Road. I am only authorized to take you to see Jocko. We are done then, and I am taking you back to the airport."

Peter stared back at him with the intensity of a four-star general. "Listen to me," he began rather sternly. "I have come all this way to help these people. I have donated more money than you could even imagine to help reach some peaceful accord. That may take a lot more doing. But I have here the entire set of files that belong to the young American anthropologist. Some of Jocko's young bucks went on a bit of a rampage and ransacked her trailer. He asked me to take these back to her with apologies. As I am here on a humanitarian mission, surely you would not stand in the way of correcting at least one wrong."

The young American anthropologist? Why, he remembered her, along with the redheaded doctor and that impudent priest who had dared to challenge him. They were supposedly somewhere across the Kalema Road, on the other side of the Ewaso Ngiro. While his instincts said stick to the plan, a side trip to see how this band was faring had some appeal. And it would give him a chance to inquire about reports that the refugees had shot one of the Maasai elders.

"As you wish," he said. "I will take you there."

Banyon helped guide them. He was not at all afraid to admit that he had already visited Father Sebastian in a prior search for Oscar Newman. But he really didn't care to go into the details of what had occurred during that particular visit.

Chapter 47

The Jeep pulled to a halt in the clearing beside the schoolhouse. David, Max, and Christine peeked out from behind drawn curtains and watched in amazement as Captain Olengi emerged from the driver side. But the elation of finally making contact with a bona fide authority was quickly dashed as the man they knew as Banyon stepped out from the passenger side. Then a third, well-dressed man with dark hair exited the rear. David and Max both recognized him immediately.

"My God," said David, "it's Peter Dermenjian!"

"And Banyon," said Max.

Finally, Dr. Meinz appeared.

"You two wait here," said David before opening his front door to greet these unannounced but not entirely unexpected visitors. Max hesitated but could not resist.

"Right," he said before turning toward Christine. "You stay here with Dr. Brecht. This could get ugly."

Christine just watched as Max headed outside, running after David.

Captain Olengi took a good look around, assessing the situation. No imminent threat and a vehicle that appeared to be in working order. They could leave if they had to. He took a few steps and extended his hand as David approached. David clasped it with both of his, perhaps trying to compensate for his behavior during their previous encounter.

"Greetings. We are very, very pleased to see you," he said, reserving his intense blue-eyed gaze solely for Captain Olengi.

"I apologize for the intrusion, but Peter Dermenjian has something for the American girl. Is she here?"

Before David or Max could reply, Peter took a step forward and held out his hand toward David.

"It's nice to see you again, Father," he said.

"Mr. Dermenjian, welcome."

Peter smiled and reached over to shake Max's outstretched hand. It was getting very awkward.

"Max Taylor. Good to see you."

"It's a pleasure to meet one of Dr. Newman's dedicated physicians."

"Actually, we met once. At the, uh, funeral. I'm really sorry about Francis."

Peter shivered at the mention of his dead brother's name. "Why yes, I remember, you were with Joseph. Thank you. Such a terrible tragedy. But we must all move on. I suppose it's futile to ask if you've had any word about the other half of that tragedy, Oscar Newman?"

David looked at Max with an odd expression. Then he turned back toward Peter Dermenjian and Captain Olengi. Banyon and Dr. Meinz had remained by the Jeep.

"I am very sorry to say that we just buried him."

The expressions on Peter's and Captain Olengi's faces could not have been more divergent. Though each was clearly stunned to hear such news, neither could afford to truly express himself. Certainly, Peter could not begin to reveal the horror these words conveyed. The diamonds were lost, again! Nor could Captain Olengi breathe the sigh of relief he felt over finally being able to check "find Oscar Newman" off his to-do list.

Max looked over at David as if to say, "Okay, I can run with this."

"David is unfortunately correct. He had been mauled by a lion after contracting malaria and was brought here a few weeks ago by some of the moran across the border. We have been without powers of communication or transportation, so we weren't able to alert anyone. I did all I could to save him. He was making good progress, but then suddenly one morning he was gone. It's a miracle he'd been able to survive that long, considering all he'd been through."

Max looked from Peter to Captain Olengi and then back again, wondering if they bought it.

"Why didn't you take him to a hospital?" snapped Peter.

"I tried. My Scout was working then, but the Kalema Road was closed. Captain Olengi's troops wouldn't let us through."

Peter turned toward Captain Olengi. "Is this true?" He was newly agitated.

"It may well be. I am sorry that whoever you encountered was so foolish as to not see this was an extreme emergency."

"Whatever," huffed Peter. "So where is he buried?"

"Come," said David, "I'll show you."

They headed off around the front of the school and walked on toward the cemetery. They passed David's garden. Surrounded by a roughly hewn wooden fence were neat rows of lettuce and other greens and various trellises covered with fruiting vines. Beyond, in a clearing bordered by a weathered picket fence, was an assortment of graves, each one marked by a weathered wooden cross. Toward the back there loomed a fairly fresh mound of dirt with an unweathered wooden cross at the head of it.

"How can we be certain this is the grave of Oscar Newman?" Captain Olengi insisted. "What about the Maasai elder? One of my men delivered him here. Where is he?"

David looked over at Max, standing on the opposite side of Oscar's alleged grave site next to a very distraught Peter Dermenjian. David half expected to hear his molars crack, the way he was clenching his jaw.

"I'm afraid I was unable to save him as well," said Max.

"That is true," said David. "He was treated to a more traditional Maasai *burial*."

He emphasized the word "burial," but Captain Olengi understood. It was the Maasai way.

"What about that prospector?" snapped Peter.

"Oh, him," said Max. "He was just suffering from sunstroke. Once I was able to rehydrate him, he was fine. He's probably off looking for the gold mine he kept babbling about."

"Very well, then," said Captain Olengi, looking a tad confused. He didn't know a thing about any prospector. "I will make a report. No doubt there will be some follow-up, as this news will be of great interest to a great many people."

"Wait a minute," said Peter. "You mean you're just going to accept that—that this is where Oscar Newman is buried?"

Captain Olengi glared back at him with anger in his eyes. But he replied quite calmly. "Don't tell me you're going to doubt the word of a Roman Catholic priest?"

The remark took everyone by surprise. But Captain Olengi had had enough of Peter Dermenjian's abuse.

"Dr. Taylor," he continued, for he had apparently left Peter Dermenjian quite speechless, "I believe your skills would be best applied among the refugees. Since you seem to have succeeded in killing off nearly all of your patients in these quarters, I suggest you try applying yourself to helping the sick and starving refugees. They need your help far more than the Maasai."

Max stared back, wondering where that disturbing comment was really targeted. It was somewhere between insult and direct order. He presumed it was likely somewhere closer to the latter.

"Tell you what," he replied, "you get me a new distributor cap for my rig over there and a new satellite phone charger so we can let people know where we are, and I might consider it."

Captain Olengi stared back at him in anger. Such cheek from this American doctor! "Now I'll tell you what," he replied quite sternly. "You will do more than consider it if you choose to remain in my country. Where is your passport?"

"What?" Max could not believe this. "What do you want with my passport?"

"I presume you're here on a working visa. Otherwise you should have left by now."

Max fumbled through his pockets. Ever since the clinic had been ransacked, he'd taken to keeping all his vital documents, such as his passport, on him at all times. He handed it to Captain Olengi.

"Let's get out of here," Peter cut in. "I've seen quite enough."

He turned heel and began walking back to the Jeep at a rapid pace. Captain Olengi ignored him while he examined the passport. Then he looked over at David.

"Is this really Oscar Newman's grave?" he asked, maintaining his aura of supreme command.

David tried his very best not to blush. "Of course it is," he calmly lied.

The sound of the Jeep's horn cut through the air.

"Dr. Taylor," said the good captain, "in view of the current crisis we're dealing with, and given that your former employer is now apparently dead, you're going to help tend to the refugees until this crisis is over. It shouldn't be but a matter of weeks. I'll send along further directions. Meanwhile, I'm going to hold on to this."

He then simply turned and walked back to the Jeep, oblivious to all the protests Max hurled at him. Peter Dermenjian was already seated in the front of the Jeep, with Banyon and Dr. Meinz situated in the rear and the engine running. Without further comment Captain Olengi hopped into the driver seat, gave a mistrustful look toward Max and David, and sped away in a cloud of dust. And with him went not only Christine's files and hard drive but the missing distributor cap.

While David and a very shaken Maxwell Taylor did their best to field Christine's and Dr. Brecht's questions, Peter Dermenjian raced back to France to find

Elizabeth. He wanted to let her know, in person, what he had found out before she saw it plastered on some headline. Most of all, he wanted to see the expression on her face. For he still suspected her of knowing more than she would let on. While Father David Sebastian had sounded rather convincing, there were still other possibilities, however slim.

He phoned her at her mother's from Nairobi saying he would be home the following evening, and would she please join him for dinner at his villa high up in the Massif de l'Estérel? She said she would be delighted. After all, Peter had also relayed that he had some news of Oscar, news he wished to discuss with her in private.

And so she arrived at the appointed hour, wearing a dark-blue dress. It was fairly modest but quite stylish. Her hair was rolled into a bun, as if she were merely off to some business meeting. And that's what she had originally intended, just a transaction regarding poor Eleanor Newman, a settlement, and they would be gone. But then came the other agenda item. Oscar!

"Good evening," said Peter as he opened the door for her.

"Hello," she replied rather faintly, as they exchanged awkward *bisous* on alternate cheeks.

He led her into a large living room with a sweeping view of the Mediterranean. Out of nowhere appeared one of Peter's staff members with a tray of aperitifs and some hors d'oeuvres. Elizabeth accepted a Perrier with a slice of lemon. Peter poured himself a glass of gin.

"So you have been to Scotland since I last saw you," he began. "I trust you were able to clear up some of Oscar's affairs?"

"Well, yes," she replied, trembling slightly as she stared at the bubbles rising in her glass. "But I have some decisions to make. And they all seem to depend on finding some resolution regarding Oscar, whether he might still possibly return. So please, I can't wait any longer. What is it you wish to tell me?"

It was too soon. He had hoped to get at least partway through dinner before divulging the terrible news. But what else could he say?

"Elizabeth," he began, "I have been to Kenya."

"Yes, I know. I saw you on the news."

"Really?" he replied, quite flattered. "While I was there I stopped to see Father David. I visited him at his schoolhouse."

Elizabeth drew a breath. It was the moment of truth. She opened her eyes wide. "And?"

"He showed me a grave, which he swears is Oscar's."

Never in his life had he seen so beautiful a flower wilt so quickly and so completely. Elizabeth continued looking at him, her eyes rapidly welling up with tears. Then she buried her head in her hands and began sobbing, softly repeating the word "no" over and over again.

Peter moved across to comfort her. He put one arm around her and pulled her close. She did not resist. "There, there," he whispered. "Surely you knew it would come to this. He was a wonderful man. And you are a wonderful woman with so much life left to live, so much life left to give."

Little did he know. Her pregnancy test had been positive! Peter's butler signaled that dinner was ready but Peter waved him off. He began stroking her neck and then her cheek. She lifted her head and looked at him in a strange, rather detached manner. He stared back at her, admiring her lovely eyes swollen with tears, her soft cheeks awash with the traces of those tears, and her luscious, trembling lips. Much to his amazement, she leaned forward, and in the next instant he felt the sweet, tender warmth of those lips on his.

Chapter 48

Captain Olengi filed a report the following day concerning the location of Oscar Newman's alleged grave site. And as he'd hoped, the reports of Oscar Newman's death handed down by none other than his doctor and his priest convinced Olengi's superior officers there was no need for further investigation. They would notify the British embassy. He was directed to work up a press release and a communication strategy. And so he did. The press release was very straightforward, indicating that he, Captain Olengi, was the press contact as well as the officer in charge. As for the communication strategy, it too was quite simple. Notify the press, all the usual suspects, and they would notify everyone else. Within seconds of his hitting the "send" button, his phone began to ring. Naturally, it was that pesky Melanie Woo.

"Good morning, Captain Olengi," she said. "What a startling bit of news. We can have a CNN helicopter at your headquarters in five minutes. CNN and all its viewers would like an exclusive look at the grave site."

He paused, staring at the phone. "I'm afraid I would have to clear that with…"

"Yes, I know. Word is they are all anxious for a look themselves."

His jaws tightened. "Fucking CNN," he muttered under his breath. Well, at least it meant just one trip with just one reporter who just happened to be a very attractive woman. It could be worse.

"I'll be on the rooftop in fifteen," he replied then hung up.

He met her on the helipad and stood at attention as she approached, giving her a moment to marvel at his finest dress uniform adorned with every medal ever bestowed upon him by the Kenya National Police. At least he'd done some preparation for facing the media, a CNN exclusive! Melanie flattered him with a smile.

"Thank you," she said. "Let's get going." Edward, Melanie's dedicated pilot and ace photographer, already had the helicopter's engines engaged and the rotors spinning. Captain Olengi settled into the front passenger seat, buckled himself in, and wrapped his personal headset around his ears to drown out the noise. No sooner had he done so than he felt his stomach tighten as the giant machine lifted off and tilted forward. Suddenly, they were beyond the rooftop and staring straight down at the busy streets of Nairobi from a rather dizzying height.

Far across the Rift Valley, awaiting the certain arrival of the media in one form or another, David and Max did their best to once again fend off the relentless interrogation by Christine and Dr. Brecht. It was Christine in particular who was thoroughly incensed that an official from the Kenyan government had actually visited them and then departed without bothering to inquire as to what help they might need or what crimes might have been committed against them. All anyone seemed to care about was keeping the whereabouts of Oscar Newman secret.

"What about the guys who stole my files and wrecked your clinic?" she demanded to know once again. "Joseph didn't get squat out of them, and here comes the sheriff at long last and you show him some bogus grave site and…"

"Yes, yes," said David. They were seated at his table once again, sharing some homemade bread and a round of well-aged cheese. Fortunately, both Crazy Jack and the invaders had failed to find the remote compartment he had personally dug out years ago beneath his priest hole, where he aged his cheeses.

"Yes, I admit I acted a bit impulsively. But I didn't know what else to tell them. I just wanted Peter Dermenjian to go away and to stay away."

It may not have been much of an excuse, but it served to silence the room a moment. As they had hashed this out in several ways already, David's summary statement remained the crux of it all. And true enough, Peter Dermenjian and his entourage had been dispatched for the moment. But in the distance, drifting in over the casual bleating of a passing herd of goats, they heard the beating of the blades, soft at first but growing perceptibly louder every second.

"Here they come," said Max, propped up in the window seat. "I think it's time for me to pay Oscar another visit."

"Oh, no you don't," David objected. "You're staying right here to corroborate my story. Besides, it would look mighty suspicious if the doctor who had declared him dead were to suddenly disappear."

"Look, you started this game of deception," said Max.

"And you play it very well. Oscar's life is at stake here. Let us not falter," David replied.

The helicopter descended amid the usual flurry of dust and flying stones, but soon the blades slowed to the point where the parties within could descend. Stepping down onto the parking lot in front of David's schoolhouse was none other than Melanie Woo, looking even more lovely and fit then Max had remembered. Whatever notions he'd had about avoiding this particular interview quickly vanished, momentarily at least, for the next person to exit was Captain Olengi, dressed to the nines. David brushed past Max, who stood frozen near the door.

"Captain Olengi, Ms. Woo," he bellowed as he hurried out to greet them. "Welcome!"

Max looked on, admiring the way David turned on his priestly charm as necessary to take the edge off any potentially awkward situation. He shook their hands and bowed to them, as if honored by their presence, before turning to lead them back toward his quarters, precisely in Max's direction. Captain Olengi looked immaculately official with his neatly pressed uniform so generously decorated with sparkling gold and silver medals. But as impressive as Captain Olengi appeared, it was nothing compared to the gamma-ray radiance Melanie emitted. She walked toward him with such energy, wearing tight-fitting jeans and a snug little tan jacket. Her dark, shoulder-length hair bounced as she walked, and her splendid lips shone a glossy red. She appeared tanner than he'd remembered, no doubt since she'd been in Africa for months now, following the plight of the far-flung Ugandans. And she was about to pick up another significant thread, albeit a complete fabrication, regarding the plight of Oscar Newman. Max brushed back his hair, which had grown rather shaggy since their last encounter, and looked to make sure all his buttons were properly buttoned and his zippers were properly zipped.

"Hello again," he said as Melanie stepped forward to shake his hand. He remembered that firm handshake.

"Hello," she said, flashing her perfect smile, ivory teeth glistening in the sun. "It's very nice to see you."

Max did his best to stifle the rush of adrenaline and various other hormones. "It's nice to see you, too. I suppose you're here about Oscar," he responded.

"Yes, I'm afraid that's what drew me here. It is so sad. I have to admit I was still holding out some hope that he might be alive."

"I know, so was I," said Max with an awkward smile.

Edward caught up with them. He was carrying a large duffel bag filled with camera equipment. "Excuse me, Melanie, but where should I set up?"

He spoke with a heavy New Zealand accent. Melanie looked over at David and smiled. There was no need to state the obvious.

"Come this way," said David as he once again retraced the steps back toward the cemetery with Melanie and Edward in tow. Poor Senento, he thought, such disrespect. But there was no turning back now. Max watched them move on, wondering whether or not he was expected to join them graveside. He stood frozen in indecision as Captain Olengi approached.

"Dr. Taylor," he began, "I trust you have been making preparations to take up your new post."

Max looked away, scratching his head. "Well," he said, "this is all a bit sudden. I mean, I've got this clinic."

"Correction," Captain Olengi interrupted, "you *had* this clinic. Your Maasai women are all fully equipped now, and your employer is dead. It is time for you to move on."

Max looked up. Somewhere in what Captain Olengi had just spoken was at least one lean kernel of truth. It had been weeks since any of the women had come to see him. He had speculated that they were all just a little too crowded down here, several hundred Maasai squeezed between the Kalema Road and the marshes north of Lake Natron. He'd thought that perhaps they were all too afraid to come see him for personal security reasons. But deep down he knew Captain Olengi was right. The Maasai women, to the extent they were willing, were most likely all fully equipped with Newman Inserts. So what was he supposed to do? Just pick up and walk straight into the craziness and mayhem within the borders of the refugee camp? He could be shot and left for dead by any one of Jocko's goons. But then Captain Olengi surprised him. He reached into a small satchel he'd been carrying and produced nothing other than the Scout's missing distributor cap. Max could not believe his eyes.

"Perhaps this will provide you a bit more incentive," he said. "The relief effort needs not only volunteers, especially doctors, but also as many vehicles as we can find to disseminate food and water. You will also need this."

He reached into his vest pocket and handed Max a green laminated badge that bore the emblem of Kenya as well as Captain Olengi's signature. Then he handed him a map.

"Just present this badge to anyone who may question you. This map shows you the way to the encampment. Report to the hospital. It's the one with the blue United Nations flag flying above it. The medical staff is very limited. You will ask for Dr. Bichette."

Stunned and bewildered, Max felt like he'd just been handed his draft papers and military orders all in one. The inclination to argue with Captain Olengi that he had no authority whatsoever to condemn him to possibly months of servitude within the dreaded refugee camp receded as it dawned on him that the Kenyan equivalent of martial law must certainly be in play, given the refugee crisis and all the frayed nerves it engendered. Looking on the bright side, he was certainly elated to finally get back the missing piece to his trusty Scout.

"Okay. Thanks for the distributor cap," he said after a long pause. "Where did you find it?"

"That is immaterial," he replied, having of course found it in the box with all of Christine's files. No sense returning them as that would only encourage her to remain in the midst of a hostile situation. "I have told Dr. Bichette to expect you within the week. She looks forward to working with you."

"She does, does she? And what do I do with my clinic? I've got two tents filled with medical supplies and—"

"Yes," he replied calmly. "Bring them. Especially the tents."

Again Max stood looking extremely perplexed as one more scene in his African adventure began to tilt seriously in a direction he had never even contemplated. Before he could respond, not that he knew what to say, Christine came wheeling around the corner with Dr. Brecht behind her.

"Okay," she said. "This time you're not getting away until you hear me out. Listen, Captain Olengi, I have been robbed of my files, my computer's hard drive, my phone charger, and everything I have worked for in nearly three years here in Maasai country, and I'm not going to…"

Captain Olengi burst into laughter before she could state her meaningless ultimatums. Then he composed himself and looked at her with a very stern expression. "I told you it was not safe to remain here. You are fortunate to be alive. Be thankful for that. Now, assuming you are ready to leave, I'm certain there's room in Ms. Woo's helicopter."

He folded his arms and tilted his head back slightly, awaiting a response. Max recognized the burning green in Christine's eyes as she prepared to unload again. But fortunately, Dr. Brecht interceded.

"Hello, Captain Olengi," she said as she extended her hand in greeting. "Gertrude Brecht. I apologize for the rudeness displayed by my student. She has worked very hard studying the Maasai women. It is true that her files have been stolen. But I do not believe she wishes to leave. Nor do I."

Captain Olengi raised his eyebrows. "Very well, as you wish," he replied. "I will see what I can find out about your missing files. Meanwhile, you will accompany Dr. Taylor to the refugee camp. We are still very much in need of volunteers. And that is the only condition under which I will allow you to remain in Kenya."

"Wait a minute," said Max, who had been calculating just how much space he would have in his Scout, assuming he could even get it running. "I don't have that much room."

"You can make two trips if necessary. So long as you all report to Dr. Bichette within the week. Now, I must join Ms. Woo. Please excuse me."

And off he strode toward the cemetery, leaving no room for debate.

"Not so fast," shouted a thoroughly distraught Christine. "That's not exactly part of my research plan." But he ignored her and kept right on walking.

"Well," said Dr. Brecht, "have you ever visited a refugee camp? I should think there's no better classroom for an aspiring anthropologist to study our species. And this will give us an opportunity to document both sides of the Maasai-Ugandan interface. I will begin packing."

Max and Christine both looked at her like she was insane but remembered that, to Dr. Brecht, the entire world was nothing but an immense human library filled with all kinds of people to be carefully studied and catalogued. They then looked at one another while they each tried to digest this latest Hobson's choice that Captain Olengi had thrust on them. Join in the relief effort or leave, assuming Max could somehow retrieve his passport. He felt the need to confer with Oscar more than ever. But David was now calling his name.

"Max," said David as he now rounded the corner of the schoolhouse, "Melanie would like to interview you. Surely you understand…"

"Of course," he said. "I'll be right there."

He hesitated some before walking inside David's quarters behind the schoolhouse. He stopped to check himself out in the mirror. No major spots on the shirt as he tucked it in, just small circles of moisture in the armpits. Not bad, considering his nerves were shot. Facing Captain Olengi had been hard enough, but he dreaded having to face Melanie Woo and the entire world of CNN only to tell a most colossal lie, one that might even lead to the revoking of his license to practice medicine once the truth was known. He looked around for a comb but had to settle for running his fingers through his own rapidly thinning mess of red hair, just to make it settle down a bit.

He walked slowly, turning over and over in his mind the answers to the questions he knew were coming in his direction. Thankfully Melanie was still interviewing Captain Olengi alongside Senento's grave, a simple mound of brown dirt outlined by an oblong ring of stones. Max noticed there were more beads hung on the cross that stood at the head of the grave than the last time he'd visited, signs that Senento's family members and perhaps a friend or two had paid a visit. He hoped they wouldn't be popping by soon.

Standing erect with his head held high, Captain Olengi responded to Melanie's questions with affirmative nods. The last words Max heard him speak were something like, "Yes, the Kenyan government deeply regrets the situation. But at least we now have closure regarding Dr. Newman and can concentrate more on the relief effort and the relocation process."

Melanie thanked him and signaled Edward to cut the lights and all the action. Captain Olengi made a slight bow in her direction before abandoning the spotlight. He looked up at Max and smiled, as if to say "okay, next victim."

"Hello, Max," said Melanie as she took a sip from a bottle of Evian. "Care for some water?"

There was a small cooler nearby filled with ice. Ice! And there were still several more bottles of Evian left.

"Sure," he said, accepting one that was already on its way to him before he even spoke.

"So, Captain Olengi tells me you've offered to help with the relief effort now that Oscar Newman is unfortunately dead."

She looked down at the grave as she spoke. Offered to help?

"Well, you see, Captain Olengi can be very persuasive."

Once the lights were on and he was standing next to her, he began to somehow relax. They continued to talk quietly while Edward made some final adjustments to the sound, the lighting, and the camera. Melanie was as beautiful as ever, with an ability to keep smiling and charming him that no doubt stemmed from years of training and experience.

"Ready," said Edward.

Melanie smiled at Max one last time. "Ready?"

He returned a fraction of a smile, one that said "go ahead, shoot me."

"Good evening," she began. "This is Melanie Woo reporting to you from southernmost Kenya, in Maasai country. I am standing beside a grave that we are told belongs to Dr. Oscar Newman, inventor of the famous Newman Insert birth-control device. Dr. Newman was awarded the Nobel Peace Prize last December for his worldwide effort to promote and facilitate family planning. With me is Dr. Maxwell Taylor, a doctor who joined the Newman Foundation last year and has been, shall we say, tending to the Maasai women ever since.

"Dr. Taylor," she continued, waxing serious as she sidled up even closer, poking a microphone toward him. "Evidently, Oscar Newman was brought here by some Maasai from across the border. Please tell us what kind of condition he was in when you found him."

This wasn't too bad. It reminded him of ambulance-chasing reporters from the local news stations hounding him outside LA General, looking for fodder for the evening news after he'd treated some high-profile criminal for gunshot wounds.

"He was in pretty bad shape, racked with malaria and fever, seriously dehydrated, and suffering from infections in the chest area, where he'd been clawed by a lion. There were also some pretty bad soda burns on his back and legs from all the time he spent trying to cross Lake Natron. I did everything I could think of to save him."

"Yes," she replied, "I'm certain you did. Have you established a cause of death?"

"Well," he said, "it's hard to say. He had so many issues. It's a miracle he survived as long as he did."

"I see. And now, with the loss of your former employer, I understand that you'll be lending a hand with the refugees up north."

Trapped once more. "Yes, I'll do what I can. It's a very tense situation right now."

"Indeed it is. Thank you, Dr. Taylor, and good luck. Back to you, Wolf."

And like that the lights were cut and it was all over. Max was pleased that he had never actually been forced to state that Oscar was dead. After all, he *had* done all he could. If they only knew.

Melanie had just one last question, off the record.

"You were close to Oscar," she began. "Do you have any idea where we might find Elizabeth Le Clerc, his fiancée? I would love to interview her but she seems to have disappeared."

Thoroughly caught off guard, Max quickly reviewed what little he knew about Elizabeth, which was next to nothing.

"I really don't know where she is," he replied. "We haven't had any way to communicate with the world outside ever since the Ugandans sacked the place. But even though we've never met, if you see her, please give her my regards, and my regrets concerning Oscar."

"I will," Melanie replied, "when I find her. But I wouldn't be too surprised if she turned up here. I imagine there's a good chance she'll be down to have Oscar's body exhumed and returned to his homeland. What do you think?"

The prospect of Elizabeth's coming to dig up Oscar had never crossed his mind. He felt the blush, the redhead's curse, infusing his cheeks with crimson. He hoped Melanie wouldn't read too much into it.

"It's a distinct possibility," he responded. "But Oscar was on a journey of discovery, a journey to the cradle of humankind. So maybe that's where he'd like to remain, given his purpose in life."

"That purpose being *empty* cradles," Melanie replied with a smile and a slight cock of her head.

"Maybe," said Max, having no clue how to escape such potentially disastrous dialogue with this most appealing woman.

Edward saved him. Having finished repacking all his camera and sound equipment, he came to inform Melanie that Captain Olengi was very anxious to leave. David had begged them to stay for a meal, however meager, but to no avail. Captain Olengi insisted there were other important matters to attend to back in Nairobi. Left unstated was his desire to avoid, if at all possible, any encounter with Joseph. He would certainly have seen and heard the helicopter and would be on his way to see what was brewing. And he would certainly demand to know how the relocation efforts were proceeding. That was news Captain Olengi did not wish to divulge. For there had been much discussion but thus far little to no relocation of any refugees whatsoever. Fortunately, there were still three months left on the contract.

As Captain Olengi had anticipated, Joseph came charging up to the schoolhouse moments after liftoff, enraged once again. Even he recognized the helicopter as belonging to a TV news station. He demanded to know what was going on. Why had the TV news people come again to Maasailand without consulting him?

393

"It was nothing," David replied as he invited Joseph inside his house. "Someone apparently started a rumor that Oscar Newman is dead. Imagine that!"

Joseph looked even more bewildered but no less angry.

"And it's high time I paid him a visit," Max muttered to himself, eager to avoid any further discussion regarding who was dead or alive and who was buried where.

Chapter 49

It felt good to be off on foot, crossing the savannah that ran on toward the darkened slopes of the Nguruman Escarpment. Billowing white clouds hovered high above. Though it was the middle of the long rains, Max hoped he would have at least a day before the next deluge. For now, this was the Africa of his dreams. A herd of Thomson's gazelles pranced about and he passed a small troop of baboons off to raid their favorite termite mounds. A solitary giraffe loped along through the sparsely treed grassland. Yes, it was definitely good to be off on his own, away from Christine and her Teutonic mentor, walking through the savannah, feeling the long grasses brush past his thighs, breathing in the strong scent of wild herbs as he crushed them with his feet. He tried to ignore the fact that it might be some time before he could make this trip again. For who knew when he might again be able to break away to pay Oscar a visit? At least he had the Scout back. The question would likely be how to wrangle it away from this Dr. Bichette.

By the time he reached the obscure, well-shaded trail that switch-backed up the face of the escarpment, he was drenched with sweat. Nonetheless he climbed rapidly, anxious to be certain that all this deception was worth it. After all, in his own medical opinion, Oscar was still very much at risk, especially if the fever returned, which was always a possibility.

Once he neared the top of the escarpment where the trail leveled off, he stopped for a rest and drink of water. Melanie had left him a couple of Evians, and he took one from his pack and drained it in a matter of seconds. Then he headed in toward the now largely defunct olpul camp, hoping for the best.

He encountered no resistance—in fact, no one at all—until he came upon Oscar and Olitunu engaged in a heated game of *bao* outside of Oscar's digs. Neither of them heard him approach.

"So who's winning?" he said.

"Max," cried Oscar, who had been lying on his side on a braided straw mat. "How good of you to come at last."

Max chose to ignore the "at last" part. He was very lucky to be there at all. "How are you feeling, Oscar?"

"Less terrible than yesterday," he said, "and hopefully more so than tomorrow. But the party here seems to be over. All the moran are gone, except for my friend here. So what's going on down there? Jack tells me there was a news helicopter popping in on you. It wasn't that Melanie Woo, was it? I suppose she's out looking for me."

Max rubbed his hairy chin. "Well," he said, "not anymore."

Oscar was predictably perplexed by this last remark. He remained quiet while Olitunu urged him to plant his damn seeds and get on with the game.

"Tetono peno," said Oscar. Olitunu sighed, losing patience.

"Il-kiturrini, doc-tor," said Max for Olitunu's benefit. Then he turned back toward Oscar, clearly impressed that Oscar had just told, in Maa, his guard and *bao* opponent to sit tight. And not only that, Olitunu picked himself up and moped off to continue his rounds as the sole security guard of the olpul camp.

"I see you're learning a bit of the language," said Max.

"It can't hurt. And besides, it's something to do. So just what do you mean, she's not looking for me anymore?"

Max shook his head. He needed to know. "David told the government and the media that you're dead and buried."

Oscar looked back with a blank stare. "What did you say?"

"He was just trying to do you a favor to throw Peter Dermenjian, who's still looking for you, off course. Captain Olengi was there. He's the Kenya National Police official who's in charge of this whole refugee mess. And up until then, you as well."

Oscar chewed on this for a moment. "So they've called off the search?"

"All except Dermenjian. I don't know if he totally bought it or not. He's definitely in league with the refugees somehow, so I'm sure they're watching for you. They wrecked the clinic. We think Dermenjian knows you're alive because they took your medical records. Or I guess I should say you *were* alive until recently, according to CNN."

"Tell me more."

"Well, Peter Dermenjian himself dropped in asking about you. David admitted that, yes, you'd been brought to the schoolhouse by some Maasai from down south. You were delirious with malarial fever, torn up by a lion, and burned all over by Lake Natron's caustic waters. He told them I'd tried to save you but that you'd just recently died. Then, sad to say, he told them you were buried behind the schoolhouse in what is actually Senento's grave. He was killed by the refugees."

"Yes, so I've been told. Terribly sad."

"It certainly is. But nonetheless, the official word is that you are buried there, not Senento."

"I see," said Oscar as he rolled onto his back, ready for the impending exam. "I am officially a dead man. Well, isn't that just perfect. I come all the way to Africa to try to learn a little something about becoming a part of our evolutionary journey and I end up a dead man. Or so it seems, both to the world and, quite frankly, to myself. But tell me, who's going to inform Elizabeth that I am still alive here in Kenya?"

Max put on some latex gloves and began the process of removing Oscar's filthy bandages. "Well, first we need to find her, which brings me to my next topic."

"And that is?"

"I apparently have a new job. Captain Olengi is forcing me to go help with the relief effort. He says all the Maasai women have been serviced and that my boss is dead. So I either go work in the refugee camp or leave Kenya for good."

"Fairly sound reasoning, I'd say."

"Whatever," he replied, intent on studying every inch of Oscar's chest wounds. "What's this? You've got a little tear down here below the ribs. If it gets any worse, I may have to re-stitch you. You're supposed to be resting."

"A bit difficult to rest when you're forced to sharpen spears all day. Fortunately, they're all well honed and ready for battle. Only now they want their rifles fixed."

"Rifles? Where did they get rifles?"

"Beats me. Crazy Jack says he can fix them. Don't know what good it would do. There are no bullets to put in them, thank goodness. And they haven't a clue how to use them. But please continue. If you're off helping the refugees, who will look after me?"

"I'll be back to check on you. I suppose I'll get a day off now and then. I brought along more bandages and more antibiotics. They should keep you for a while. Any signs of fever?"

"None so far," he replied.

"Good. You seem to be healing all right, for the most part. But you need to take it easy. I'm going to check your heart before I replace the bandages. I'll try not to press too hard on your tender spots. But before I do, where the heck is Crazy

Jack?" Max rubbed the smooth surface of his stethoscope to warm it up before applying it to Oscar's chest.

"Who knows where he is? He's always off snooping about, no doubt poking his pick hammer into some unsuspecting rock."

But that was hardly the case. For Jack McGraw was stationed once again at the overlook, binoculars raised, studying the lay of the land. It reminded him of some game he used to play as a kid. Only this playing field was far too lopsided, not at all like the cowboys and Indians of his youth. After waiting far too long to see if the helicopter would return, he picked himself up off the ledge and headed back to see Oscar. He was delighted to find Max tending to him.

"Howdy," he cried as he got closer. "Think this old screwball's going to make it?"

But Max could not hear him. He was too busy listening to Oscar's heartbeat through his stethoscope. It was strong but still a bit irregular. Nothing to worry about, assuming he kept drinking his fluids.

"Well, well," said Max as Jack sat down on the dirt beside them, "look what the cheetah dragged in. You look like you've been prospecting pretty hard."

"Prospectin'?" Jack answered. "Ain't no prospects up here. Just a bunch of jumbled-up pieces of rock caught in the uplift. Nothin' too interestin'. I just been lookin' after Oscar. And tryin' to fix those damn guns."

"Terrific," said Max. "I'm sure you're earning your keep. What do they feed you?"

Oscar made an unpleasant face. "Seems as though the butcher has left town," he said. "Haven't had a decent steak in days. But there is no shortage of milk. And cornmeal mixed with God knows what kind of greens and spices. I've convinced Sarna to hold back on the blood rations."

As if she'd been hiding in some recess and just heard her name pronounced, the young girl appeared bearing a gourd of something or other. It was mealtime.

Max introduced himself and sniffed at the gourd. "Nothing wrong with that concoction," he said, smiling at the young girl, who stood quite rigid before them, "so long as you can keep it down."

Oscar looked on, clearly finding no humor in that remark as he accepted the gourd that Sarna handed to him.

"Here you go," said Jack, reaching into a back pocket and producing a small brown packet that he then handed over to Oscar.

"What's that?" Max inquired.

"Nothin' much," said Jack, "just a little cocoa powder to help coax it down. It ain't so bad that way."

"Now where the hell did you get that?" asked Max.

"Oh, you know, I guess I have been out prospectin' some. So Doc, you figure he's going to make it?"

Max rubbed his chin. "Looks that way. But frankly, I'm still examining him. So if you don't mind…"

"Okay," said Jack. "Guess I'll go work on them rifles. The action ought to be better now that they've been stewin' in all that fat."

And so he departed, leaving Max and his patient alone once again.

"You still haven't told me how you're going to get word to Elizabeth that I am still alive," said Oscar once Jack was out of earshot. He had already drained the contents of the gourd. Sarna retreated until the next feeding.

"Right," said Max as he began to replace the bandages. "Well, here's a thought. How about if you tell her?"

If it hadn't been for the pressure Max was applying on his bandages, Oscar might have sat straight up.

"What nonsense is this?" he inquired.

"Look," said Max, "don't you think this hoax has gone far enough? We're back in touch with the rest of the world. It's okay to come forward and say, hey, look, I'm alive, instead of having the whole world thinking you're dead."

"But I will be dead, or worse, if Dermenjian catches up to me. He knows I'm the only man alive who knows where to find his bloody diamonds."

Max stopped his gauze cutting for a moment. "So what?" he said. "You don't have to tell him."

"I'm sorry," Oscar replied, "but he murdered his brother for failing to tell him. Just what do you think he wouldn't do to me to obtain the information? I promised Francis I would never divulge the location. And I intend to keep that promise."

"Fine," said Max as he began picking up the scraps of gauze and adhesive tape that the bandaging process had spun off. "But about getting word to Elizabeth. Like I said, Captain Olengi's forcing me to go join the relief program. I assume he's within his rights."

"No doubt. But even if he isn't, what could you do about it?"

"Good point," said Max. "So I've been thinking that the United Nations is there, and they must have good communication with Nairobi and who knows where else. I should be able to find a way to get through to the rest of the world."

"Excellent," Oscar responded. "I'm sure you'll have no trouble getting a secure line. Just try her at her mother's in Balgères. David has the number."

"Well," he replied, "he *had* the number. It was in his address book that was stolen by the refugees. First they ransacked Christine's trailer and stole all her data on the Maasai women. Then they wrecked my clinic and stole all your files. And next they invaded David's quarters and helped themselves to pretty much everything, including the address book."

Oscar covered his eyes. "I'm afraid I can't recall it, either," he said. "You'd understand if you'd ever met her. But whatever the case may be, as a former employee of mine, you have not only my permission to help out the refugees but my blessings as well. However, brace yourself. I know you've seen your fair share of humans abusing other humans, but I guarantee this experience will assault your senses and all your concepts regarding the limits of human brutality. So just remember, reciprocal altruism. It's what got us all this far."

Max gave him a quizzical look and then began to replace the bandages on the still-puffed-up and slightly scarlet wounds on Oscar's chest. "I don't have a choice other than leaving Kenya altogether. And I'm not about to do that with you in this condition."

Oscar smiled. "Thank you," he said. "Thank you for saving my life. And I hope that, one day, I will truly mean that."

Chapter 50

The moran still guarded the roadway every few hundred yards. Each of them clutched his spear while standing vigilant, slightly hunched over. The pouring rain dripped off ochre-plastered braids in various hues of reddish brown, streaking their orange capes. They all recognized the Scout by now and the passengers within. Each one raised his head slightly as the Scout rolled by as if to say, "I don't know why, but I'll let you pass." Max nodded and smiled at each of them in turn, but his overall focus was mainly to the north, keeping a lookout for any Ugandan carjackers.

Clouds of smoke hovered over the landscape beyond the scrub brush that bordered the road. The camp was out there, within a mile or so, but the only signs of life were a few darkly caped women out gathering firewood.

"Will you watch where you're going?" Christine shouted as Max ventured too close to the edge of the raised roadway.

"Sorry," he replied, "but did you see those women? Definitely not Maasai."

He glanced over at Dr. Brecht, awaiting her pronouncement of just who these women were and from where exactly they hailed. But, quite out of character, she said nothing. He looked in the rearview mirror. Christine was seriously squeezed between the left rear door and a large sack of bedding material. No response from her, either. Just more pensive brooding.

The muddy road was thus far not a problem nor were there any signs of a washout. They crossed over the land bridge at Lake Magadi, the mounds of soda ash looking almost gray in the cloudy light. A security guard flagged them down, looking rather surprised. After all, the Kalema Road was supposed to be closed. Max flashed his green card.

"We're evacuating," he said as the guard approached. "Captain Olengi's orders."

The guard examined the neatly laminated document and peered inside at Dr. Brecht and Christine. Without a word he waved them on. Slowly, they headed north on a gentle climb toward the Ngong Hills, toward Nairobi, skirting the eastern shores of the northern portion of Lake Magadi. The road was paved and only mildly afflicted with potholes. Once beyond the lake and gaining some altitude, Max caught a few glimpses of the camp from a rather oblique but very troubling angle. He stopped for a moment at a point where the view opened up. It was just an endless sea of blue and white tarps beneath a dusty cloud of wood smoke. But once again, not a word from either anthropologist.

A few miles farther on, Max noticed a crude fence made of barbed wire. It curved away to the west. A dirt track appeared, marked with signs that generally encouraged anyone who might possibly consider entering to just go away, in several languages.

"We're getting close," he stated. He checked the rearview mirror. Christine looked even more depressed. The dusty cloud was much closer now, and as he turned off the main roadway, it was clear they were now headed straight for it.

"Here we go," said Max as he began following the rough dirt track that showed plenty of signs of recent use. There were ruts, of course, but also fresh tire tracks left by one or two large trucks. The barbed wire continued to line both sides of the roadway, which slowly descended through acacia scrubland dotted with termite mounds. Suddenly, it dawned on Max that this wasn't too far from where he'd first set up shop. What a crazy turn of events. The area had been so tranquil just months ago. Now it looked like a gateway to some foreign land that had simply dropped from the heavens, on its way to hell.

They came to a heavily guarded gatehouse from which two young soldiers quickly emerged, dressed in army fatigues and clutching semiautomatic rifles. They quickly moved to make absolutely certain the Scout would come to a halt. As if anyone would come crashing through the flimsy gate in the first place. Who would invade a refugee camp?

Max stopped, rolled down his window, and presented the green card with Captain Olengi's signature along with the passports belonging to Christine and Dr. Brecht. The noise from the camp was nearly deafening. The two guards conferred briefly, checked their names off on a clipboard, and returned the documents. One of the guards walked over to the gate, lifted it, and waved them through.

Max drove slowly down a very muddy track that was bordered on both sides by huge, dull-green army tents. They appeared to be warehouses to temporarily store the enormous quantities of bulk food required to keep this instant city of at least fifty thousand alive. For a while, at least. It was clearly the drop-off point for all that arrived from the world outside this compound. And from here emanated the web like network of roads and delivery routes he had seen from high up on the promontory.

And so they drove on, searching for the United Nations tent with the blue flag on top. The muddy avenue was now bordered with much smaller tents, each one carefully labeled in English and Swahili. This appeared to be the main administration area for the camp. Max took special note of the one marked "Communications." A mix of soldiers and civilians wandered from tent to tent, carrying boxes and folders and various pieces of office equipment.

The rain had stopped and Max drove with his window down. The din from beyond the tents grew louder. At last he spotted the blue United Nations flag flying high above the last of the tents. It was quite large, set somewhat apart from the others. It featured a large Red Cross symbol on each side. Behind it were three smaller tents also adorned with the Red Cross insignia. Once Max pulled to a halt, they all stepped out and studied their new situation.

Most striking were the long lines of refugees leading up to the hospital tent. Max assumed they were waiting to be admitted or otherwise processed. Trucks bearing more refugees were unloading to the north, supplying more streams of very haggard and distraught people to the already burgeoning lines. One was composed entirely of young children. This was clearly where the simply undernourished would be separated from the truly famine-stricken children who were far more at risk.

Off to the side was another entrance. Over the canvas doorway, proudly displayed in the faded blue, white, and red trifecta of France, were the words "Médecins Sans Frontières."

"This must be the place," said Max.

Once they were inside, it took a moment for their eyes to adjust. Nurses in blue and white scrubs raced about. He flagged one down.

"Uh, excuse me, but I need to see Dr. Bichette."

The young nurse looked startled. She quickly pointed behind them to a small paneled enclosure.

"Ashe naleng," said Max. Much thanks.

He knocked upon the flimsy bamboo door that separated Dr. Bichette and her modern office equipment from the rest of the hordes.

She opened the door herself. Max thought whoever directed the medical crew that cared for this entire set of atrocities ought to have at least one handler, one person to buffer her from needless interruptions. But she appeared to operate all on her own.

"Yes, may I help you?" she inquired.

Max guessed her to be in her early sixties, a thin woman wrapped in a white lab coat with gray hair tied in a bun and glasses ready to slide off the tip of her nose at any moment. But she was attractive in a refined sense typical of so many French women.

"Hello," said Max, "I'm Max Taylor. Well, Dr. Max Taylor, actually, and this is Dr. Brecht, a professor of anthropology, and Christine Olson, a graduate student in anthropology who has been working with the Maasai in this area for the past couple of years. Captain Olengi sent us."

In an instant the "why are you bothering me?" look she had failed to hide when she first opened the door disappeared. She almost broke into a smile.

"Welcome," she said, "please come in."

She led them into her office, a fairly large room situated between the exterior canvas and the tall, dull-gray partitions fitted with the narrow bamboo door that had clearly been recycled from prior campaigns. Though it was spacious, the vast majority of it was occupied by servers and plotters and computer screens that would be the envy of many emergency-response centers. In the middle was a small desk with a serious flat-screen monitor and keyboard off to one side.

"Wow!" said Max as he beheld the wealth of virtual potential situated in one of the most remote places on earth. "Where in the world did you get all this?"

Dr. Bichette smirked a bit. "We have excellent computer capability and hardware and the latest software applications, thanks to various charity organizations. And we have an excellent technician. What we don't have are enough volunteers experienced in dealing with people in a crisis situation such as this. So I am very happy to see you. Please, sit down."

There were a few old plastic chairs along one wall. Max rearranged them while Dr. Bichette sat down at her desk and began rereading the information Captain Olengi had e-mailed her regarding these three for-the-most-part-reluctant volunteers.

"Dr. Brecht," she began, "I see that you speak many dialects of Swahili and Maa. You and your student will be most useful helping to interview the men and women to find out what you can about the fate of their family members. And you will help us determine to which country they should best be deployed. You will work out of tent number thirteen. Here, let me show you."

404

She put her fingers on the keyboard and within a few seconds a fairly detailed map appeared on the screen. She pointed out a location on a map that made no sense at all to Christine but Dr. Brecht nodded, indicating she understood precisely where they were to go. It was over near the recently refurbished airstrip. Then she showed them how she could easily toggle between maps showing detailed relief and major hydrologic features and recent aerial photos downloaded from passing satellites.

"That's amazing," said Max. "You have all that information at your fingertips."

"Very impressive," said Dr. Brecht. "How many in the camp?"

"Just over fifty thousand."

"And how many more on their way?"

Dr. Bichette clicked a few more times and the view on the computer screen panned upward. She moved her mouse to the latest aerial view of the area north of the camp, which showed a steady stream of refugees headed their way.

"I don't know. But as you can see, the unrest continues." She turned toward Max. "You will stay here," she said. "The tents to the rear are a hospital of sorts. There are three departments. Infections, general malnutrition and, shall we say, battle wounds. That is where we need help the most. I was told you would bring tents. You did bring tents, didn't you?"

There was no doubt that housing was a major issue here.

"Yes," said Max, "I have three pretty good-sized tents in fair condition."

"And you have some medical supplies?"

"Pretty modest and pretty basic."

"It will all be useful, I'm sure. And what kind of medicine do you typically practice, Dr. Taylor?"

"I'm a general practitioner. I worked ER for years in LA, er, Los Angeles."

"So you can handle trauma cases?"

"I've just about seen it all."

"Have you, now?" she replied, raising a skeptical eyebrow. "Then let us get settled in. Dr. Brecht, Ms. Olson, I will get you an escort. You can share one of the tents you brought. We need the others for a microbiology lab and a post-surgery recovery room. Dr. Taylor, you will be bunking with Ivan. He's in charge of water and waste management."

"But I thought there would be separate quarters for medical staff."

"There is but it's not adequate. Don't worry. You won't see much of Ivan—he's far too busy. Besides, you'll only be sharing quarters while you're sleeping. And I'm afraid there won't be too much of that."

"Terrific," said Max under his breath.

Dr. Bichette picked up a phone and told whoever was on the other end of the line to bring a Jeep around. Then she stood up and extended her hand toward Dr. Brecht.

"Dr. Brecht, Ms. Olson, thank you for volunteering your services. We are sorely in need of people with your skills. When you arrive at tent thirteen, ask for Inga van Hoven. She's in charge there. Let me know if you encounter any serious difficulties."

"Thank you," said Dr. Brecht, looking almost cheerful at the prospect of working with a woman who sounded like she might be Dutch, or perhaps even German. Christine then shook Dr. Bichette's hand and smiled faintly but seemed too in shock to know quite what to say. How were they supposed to get in touch when she was sending them clear across to the other side of this enormous camp? Dr. Bichette escorted them outside, back into the blinding daylight. The sun had broken through and the ground was steaming.

Max unlashed one of the bulky tents from the top of the Scout while Christine and Dr. Brecht removed their bags. A young black man arrived moments later in an old green Jeep with a Red Cross insignia on the side.

"You girls ready?" said Max.

Christine peered at him with that familiar burning glare from beneath her LA Dodgers baseball cap. "Ready as ever," she deadpanned. Dr. Brecht had already grabbed her bag and was walking toward the Jeep.

The young driver smiled at them. He was missing several teeth up front. Christine looked at the squalor surrounding them, the lines of sick, injured, and malnourished Africans awaiting treatment in the hospital tent off to her right, and across the roadway the vast, sprawling field of soaking-wet bodies huddling beneath the most meager of shelters, bits of shredded blue UN tarps, old tattered remnants of green army tents, and such. What the hell was this guy smiling about?

Once seated in the Jeep, with Dr. Brecht again up front, they headed off at a very slow pace. They passed by the long line of thin, weak children, where a few mothers still hovered alongside their young. They passed by the next line of hunched-over refugees, some of whom looked over at them as they passed by.

Their eyes were all sunken and hollow. Some had distended bellies. Then they passed by a shorter line, mostly composed of men, perhaps a mere hundred or so, who were heavily bandaged. Several were assisted by canes and crutches fashioned from acacia branches. Just beyond, at the far end of the tent, were two ambulances in the process of unloading some recent arrivals. Christine's eyes were riveted to the two medics who withdrew one of the victims from the back of the closest ambulance. She turned away quickly as a stretcher bearing a blood-drenched body was transferred to a gurney of sorts near a rear entrance to the place.

The view on the other side was not any more inviting. The road curved to the left and soon there were refugees on both sides of them, so many of them women with small children in their laps. They sat on dirty straw mats for the most part, with bits of tarp draped over them. They had all just been rained upon and they were all soaking wet. But the clouds had parted and the sun was now high. It was past midday. The steam rose from everywhere, mixing with the wood smoke from the many smoldering campfires. It rose from the ground, and it rose from the tarps that had failed so miserably to keep the rain off them. The steam even rose from the tops of the children's heads as they sobbed and their mothers did their futile best to console them. The overall effect was surreal and Christine felt herself beginning to swoon.

They passed by a number of water pumps where men and women in long lines waited their turn to fill their respective jerrycans, all of which appeared to have served them for far too long judging from how dented and discolored they were. In one of the lines two men were fighting, no doubt jostling for a better spot in the queue.

A short distance from the water supplies were food dispensers, small convoy trucks doling out sacks of rice, corn, beans, and flour. More lines of refugees formed, and beyond them the landscape was entirely covered with various shapes and styles of shacks and tarps and crude structures built from sticks and straw. In between them were people, the women wrapped in colorful scarves and shawls, and what few men there were wearing mostly ragged Western clothes, with the occasional long robe. Some were sitting, some standing, some of them talking, but they all looked terribly forlorn and terribly frightened.

They passed a long line of latrines that ran north to south. There were at least fifty separate small buildings made of straw and bamboo, and their presence was evident long before they came into view. Waste management in this sector had clearly fallen behind.

As the Jeep plied the muddy ground, it attracted many an underfed Ugandan looking for another morsel of food. Christine looked into the eyes of these poor lost souls, mothers holding up their malnourished young, pleading for help with their sunken eyes. Many still wore fine beaded necklaces and earrings, quite in contrast with their decidedly impoverished situation.

Once they finally reached tent number thirteen, Dr. Brecht thanked the driver as he helped them with theirs bags. She had been conversing with him nonstop while Christine had been taking in the scenery and revisiting her decision to study anthropology, particularly in this setting. Whatever. It was much too late to turn back now. Dr. Brecht and Captain Olengi had seen to that.

Inga van Hoven was a tall woman with short, straight brown hair. She had a prominent forehead and a strong jawline. She led them to her small office and offered them seats on a rustic-looking bench, speaking English with a heavy Dutch accent.

"Ik spreek Nederlands," said Dr. Brecht, clearly trying to impress. Inga responded to her briefly in her native tongue before switching back to English.

"Dr. Brecht, I can assure you that all your language skills will be quite useful here. We have many refugees who have been separated from the rest of their families. Interviewing them can be straightforward in many cases. But some are very difficult to communicate with. Once we know all we can about the families here, we sort them according to their willingness to be rejoined with other family members who might provide a safe haven, either in their own countries or elsewhere. For those still searching for missing family members, we try nonetheless to find potential homes for them. Besides the United Nations, we work with many charitable organizations, many of them Christian, who are in the business of finding opportunities for the displaced people of the world, such as the people you see here."

"Yes, I understand," said Dr. Brecht, looking over toward Christine to make sure she was following. "And how many are now working with you?"

"Just twenty-five," said Inga, "including you. Ms. Olson, you will assist Dr. Brecht by taking good notes and by checking ID tags. These are very important. Without proper tagging all our work is for naught."

408

Great, thought Christine, like checking on branded livestock. Just what she needed.

"I suggest you set up your tent nearby. I will show you where. Come."

While Dr. Brecht and Christine were busy getting situated, Max took the opportunity to quickly explore what he considered "base camp" before heading back to rejoin Dr. Bichette and company. He had already thrown his meager personal effects into the tent allegedly inhabited by someone named Ivan. He wondered if Ivan had any clue he now had a roommate. Judging from the disarray within his new lodgings, Ivan was an abject slob. Just the guy to put in charge of waste management.

He returned to Dr. Bichette's office at the appointed hour to begin his orientation. It was late afternoon on what already felt like an extremely long day. He tapped on her door. To his surprise the door opened almost immediately and Dr. Bichette appeared. She handed him a white lab coat and a surgical mask.

"You'll want to wear that at all times once inside the wards."

Max nodded and proceeded to don both coat and mask as she led him through a maze of partitions that walled off small cubicles filled with nurses frantically entering medical records on many a spreadsheet. They were situated on either side of the main access corridor that ran down the center of the long canvas building. A double set of doors set into a heavy wall of resin-filled canvas lay ahead. Max adjusted his mask, wondering what manner of germs he was about to encounter.

The scene on the other side was not as bad as he had feared. Dr. Bichette explained that the children were all being fitted with MUAC tapes to measure their mid-upper arm circumference. The tapes were colored coded from green to orange to red. The red zone was mighty skinny, but at least a quarter of the children were registering in that zone and were being escorted into a small ward for further examination and some highly concentrated nutrition. All children were being vaccinated as they passed through. It occurred to Max that he could probably use a dose of whatever the nurses were doling out.

Farther on was another serious partition with another set of double doors. Inside were twenty or more examination tables, each one occupied. About half the examinees were lying down, submitting to the palpations of several attending medical staff, while the others sat upright. Most of them had stethoscopes pressed against their chests.

"In here we screen sick refugees for bacterial and viral infections, usually malaria or upper respiratory complications," said Dr. Bichette.

Max understood immediately what was going on. Thanks to Oscar he was quite familiar with the symptoms of malaria, such as the swelling of the spleen, and he had treated many a Maasai for respiratory problems. He blamed most of it on all the wood smoke they inhaled in their cramped, marginally ventilated quarters.

"This is all pretty routine," said Max. "But what happens back there?"

He was pointing to the opening to his right that stated "No Admittance." Yet certain of the examinees were being wheeled through the door for further medical processing.

"We'll get to that soon enough."

Dr. Bichette introduced Max to some of the other doctors. Shaking hands was not an option, but Max said that he looked forward to working with them, et cetera. He was amazed to discover how international a group it was. And many were quite young as doctors go, not unlike himself.

"Now I want to show you where you'll likely be spending most of your time. Come," said Dr. Bichette.

They passed through the third set of double doors. It was a very simple but important way to control to some extent the spread of different types of infections. And infections were definitely an issue on the other side of these doors.

Once again there were gurneys laden with bodies, only these were all quite bloody. Definitely the trauma ward. Nothing he couldn't handle.

"This is the work of one of the cruelest of all the warlords," said Dr. Bichette, "a madman who wants to overthrow the government of Uganda. Yet his method is to abduct young boys to serve in his armies and young girls to serve as his and his officers' sex slaves. Those who either try to escape or might say bad things about him and his forces are treated very cruelly. We recently picked these poor souls up along the refugee trail."

Max looked all around. There were easily thirty beds, and by each one there were IV drips and serious piles of bloody bandages. Many of the patients were screaming and writhing in pain while nurses and physicians attended to them. Others lay in morphine-induced stupors.

The first bed they approached held a young man who was missing a hand. Other parts of his body had been slashed by a machete, but he'd been stitched up. It was a wonder he had survived so much blood loss.

410

In the next bed was a young girl missing a nose. Her face was bandaged, yet it was clear that a certain bulge below her eyes was missing and blood was seeping through. Max took a deep breath. This was truly barbaric. He looked over at Dr. Bichette. She said nothing and moved on.

They came to a third bed where a young man lay on his side, turned away from them. This one didn't look too bad, Max thought. He guessed him to be in his mid-teens. His legs were intact and his back showed no signs of brutality. Yet he was trembling uncontrollably and sobbing loudly. Dr. Bichette grabbed him by the shoulder. As she rolled him over onto his back, Max shrieked, quite out of character for a well-seasoned ER physician. But what he saw before him went beyond any prior concept he'd held regarding the bounds of human cruelty. For this poor young man, whose eyes were still frozen with horror, had no lips. They had been cut away. All that was left was a gaping hole in his face revealing teeth and gums surrounded by a rough-hewn oval of scabbed-over flesh oozing pus. Max turned away, concentrating on keeping his stomach contents in place.

"Welcome to Africa," said Dr. Bichette, "the real Africa."

Chapter 51

Weeks passed slowly by, and while Max, Christine, and Dr. Brecht struggled to meet the challenges of their newly imposed "volunteerism," Elizabeth passed the days feeling her body transforming as her wedding day approached.

She tied her long, newly blond hair into a bun atop her head and tried the dress on one more time. It was a lovely wedding gown, strapless and a pale cream color, close enough to white. The top was rather snug, perhaps too snug, as more cleavage than she was comfortable showing billowed up above the satin and the stays that attempted to hold it all in place. Beneath Elizabeth's swelling waistline, layers of silk-embroidered satin embedded with pearls cascaded down to the floor. A long train of delicate lace embedded with more pearls trailed behind.

She gazed at her reflection in the full-length mirror fitted into one door of her ancient armoire, reluctantly admitting she would have to ask Natalia to let it out one more time. And there were still another two weeks to go!

Before turning away to disrobe, she caught a last glimpse of herself in a slightly different, somewhat darker light. A flood of shame gripped her senses, and once again the guilt overwhelmed her. She sat down upon her bed, placed her head in her hands, and went back over it all once again.

Certainly, anyone who knew the truth would argue that her marrying Peter Dermenjian was not only the height of deceit but a despicable act of cowardice. Why couldn't she just admit what she had done? Surely everyone would understand, eventually. Perhaps her mother might even find a way to forgive her, someday. After all, she *had* been going to marry Oscar and they *had* planned to at least attempt to start a family. And if Oscar just happened to be dead and she just happened to have found what she believed to be some trace of him, some of his well-aged semen, long since frozen yet evidently still viable, surely people would understand. This way he would live on, assuming it really was Oscar and not some graduate student eager to earn a quid or two for making a deposit that would help "fuel" one of Oscar's many experiments.

But no, she had chosen a different path. It had all happened so suddenly, as if she hadn't really chosen anything. Despite all her efforts to prepare herself for the seemingly inevitable tragic news, once delivered it seemed to take on a life of its own. Beginning with Peter. She didn't really mean to seduce him. True, she needed comforting after hearing the awful truth. And true, Peter was more than willing. In fact, it was he who in the end did more of the seducing. She had merely acquiesced, and it had been quite the release both for her and for him. But why? Deep down she knew why, but it was a truth she could never divulge. She had done it for Oscar, the man she truly loved, and for the furtherance of his and her "genetic endowments."

But it wasn't a shameful act! It was merely the act of a mother protecting her young, the most ancient of parental instincts. After all, why had Oscar, who never knew his own father, gone off to Africa again, to the "cradle of humankind," on this senseless and tragic journey, if not to discover how to do the most human of things, raising a child?

The moment Peter had revealed his unfortunate news, she had understood in an instant that she just could not let history repeat itself. Not with her child—not with her and Oscar's child. He or she would have a father. A very good father, a man who had suffered a loss almost comparable to hers. He had lost his only brother. And by all accounts Oscar had killed him.

Despite those awful discoveries—the body near the cave, Oscar's fingerprints all over the gun—Peter had looked after her as well as Oscar's seriously infirm mother. And more than that, he had financed at no small expense the ongoing search for Oscar. Unfortunately, to say the least, the search had ended badly. But at least she knew, thanks to Peter. And at least she had made her own discovery, and her efforts thus far to plant her own small patch of humanity had been successful. All that was needed was love and nourishment. Peter could certainly supply the latter, and perhaps even the former. Time would tell.

She heard the steps approaching and then a knock upon her bedroom door. Nothing could have elevated her more from her reverie than hearing her mother's voice requesting permission to enter.

"Come in," she said, standing to properly greet her with kisses astride her mother's rouge-rich and heavily powdered cheeks.

"My darling daughter," she began, "you look absolutely ravishing. Quick, turn around for me."

Elizabeth made her best effort to smile, which was easiest when her thoughts turned to the developing fetus within her. She prayed her mother wouldn't mention the extraordinarily tight fit of the dress or the pronounced bulges in her abdomen and bosom as she performed a slow 360. The right time would come to clue her mother in, but for now she and Peter had agreed their little secret would remain a secret. And certainly the secret within the secret would remain a secret as long as she lived.

"I cannot tell you how delighted I am." Her mother beamed. "Father Brodard is downstairs. We have been going over the ceremony. Madame Lafitte will take care of all the flowers. I've ordered a hundred cases of champagne. And Peter's secretary phoned to say they have ordered limousine service for all the wedding guests. It will be magnificent."

Her mother stood before her, as joyful as Elizabeth had ever seen her, completely enthralled with the prospect of her only daughter marrying one of the wealthiest men in all of France. And so handsome! Plus his villa, at least the one he kept in southern France, was not that far away. They would visit often, unlike Oscar, who would have kept her child far, far away in that awful northern country.

"My, but your father would be so proud of you," she continued. "Peter is marvelous. He and your father could have talked for hours. Global markets, commerce, and such. And those diamonds! Where are they? I'm sure they're simply exquisite with that gown."

She was referring to the diamond tiara and matching necklace Peter had presented to Elizabeth at their engagement dinner. Everyone had been quite stunned, especially Elizabeth. Her mother had nearly fainted.

Elizabeth opened a dresser drawer and removed the aforementioned pieces of jewelry. They were indeed dazzling. She placed the tiny tiara on her head. It was subtle, for a diamond-encrusted ornament.

"It's like a halo," her mother cooed, "for my pretty angel. Now the necklace."

Halo? Angel? How far from the truth! Nonetheless, she clasped the necklace behind her long, lovely neck and posed in the center of her room, slowly turning another 360.

"Magnifique! Magnifique!" cried Madame Le Clerc. "You will be the most beautiful bride in all of France. And that reminds me. Reporters have been calling. The word is finally out that Peter Dermenjian, one of the most eligible bachelors in all of Europe, is about to be married. And I'm afraid they're making quite a story out of who it is he's marrying. Not my daughter, oh no, but the would-be bride of the late Nobel Laureate Oscar Newman. I keep telling them to go away but they are very persistent. Some are offering a handsome sum of money for a private

interview with you. And that Ms. Wong, or whoever she is. She wants to do an exclusive televised interview for one of the big networks."

"Not Melanie Woo?" Elizabeth shrieked.

"Why yes, I believe that's right."

"No," Elizabeth cried. She was the one! She had broken the Nobel story! "Just tell her I am still in mourning and I don't wish to be disturbed."

"Still in mourning?" her mother asked incredulously. "Still in mourning yet planning to be married to another man altogether? My darling, I think you had better get your facts straight."

"Good idea," she replied quite sternly. "And if you don't mind, I would prefer to do that all on my own."

Her mother looked shocked once again. "Very well," she replied, "but Father Brodard is waiting. He needs your concurrence on the readings he's selected."

"He selected?"

"Well, actually, I suggested them and—"

"I'm sure they're just fine, then," Elizabeth replied. "Tell Father Brodard I'll look them over but not to worry. I really need to lie down for a bit. I'll see you at dinner, okay?"

"Very well," her mother replied. "Edouard will be joining us. He's very anxious to speak with you."

Terrific. Once her mother was gone, she undressed and carefully hung the gown up in her closet. She lay down upon her bed and began to gently rub her stomach, gauging the swelling compared to yesterday. Was it her imagination or was she even bigger?

She slept for nearly two hours, dreaming restless dreams mostly about Oscar. She had been so tired lately. But these were nice dreams, not at all like the nightmares she had experienced when Oscar was missing and merely presumed dead. They were back at the cottage on Mull, with Oscar smiling like his old living self while she stood before the fire rubbing her belly, which in her dreams was well into the third trimester.

She awoke, slowly at first, to a light tapping on her door, followed by a soft yodeling of sorts. She recognized the familiar call that could only be her brother employing the signal they had both used as children to hail one another. She rose and wrapped herself in her bathrobe. She opened her bedroom door and saw her dear brother before her, holding forth a bottle of champagne in one hand and two champagne flutes in the other. In his mouth was a long-stemmed rose.

She had to laugh. "Come in," she said. "Please, come in."

"Thank you," he replied as she removed the rose from his mouth and gave him a kiss on each cheek. "Father Brodard is still here. Mother invited him to dinner. So I thought that perhaps we could *prendre l'apéritif à nous deux.*"

"Bonne idée," she replied, closing the door behind him. They moved over to a small table by the window. The late-afternoon sun streamed in, turning shades of pink and violet as evening approached. Edouard popped the cork and poured them each a glass. The champagne bubbled up and nearly overflowed before finally settling down so they could drink.

"Santé," said Edouard.

"Yes," his sister replied, *"santé."*

He lifted the flute to his lips and tilted it toward the ceiling, while she barely sniffed at hers.

"Such horrible traffic," he said as he set his glass down. "Marseille was like a million cars driving through invisible concrete. I kept waiting for it all to set up and there we'd be. Frozen in time."

"Sounds awful," she replied. "But thank you for coming all this way. It's so nice to see you."

"Yes, it's nice to see you, too," he replied. "You know, we really didn't get to talk at the engagement party. Although it wasn't much of an engagement, was it? Just a few short weeks. But still, it was quite a party."

"Really just a dinner," she countered.

"A diamond-studded dinner. Were they for real?" He gave her a menacing look.

"Most certainly they are for real. Peter would never even dream of using fake diamonds. What on earth are you suggesting?"

"Oh, nothing. It's just that, you know, I don't trust him in the least. And it scares me. After all, you're my only sister. I need to look out for you."

"I can look out for myself, thank you."

"Can you, now? Then how is it you're able to transition so quickly from the grief-stricken would-be widow to the love-struck would-be wife of one of France's most notorious billionaires? He may be single but he's certainly not celibate. Not in the least."

Elizabeth cleared her throat. "Look," she said, "if this is why you came here, to tell me how much you despise Peter, then you can leave right now. And take your champagne with you!" She was so angry she stood up and began pacing.

"I notice you've barely touched yours. You love champagne. What's wrong?"

"Perhaps it's the conversation!"

"Really? Or perhaps it's something else. You look nice in that bathrobe. But is there an extra pillow in there as well? Or some other *object*? I noticed you seemed awfully voluptuous the other night. I've known you for a very long time, Elizabeth, and you've never in your life been renowned for your bosom. But I can see from here it's even grown since last week. The bastard's knocked you up, hasn't he? That's why all the rush."

Elizabeth turned back toward him, her eyes filled with anger and tears. She began to tremble, struggling to find some form of expression to counter, to neutralize those stinging words. Knocked her up? She longed to tell him the truth but that was not an option. Instead she just stood her ground.

"Please forgive me," she pleaded as tears flowed down her cheeks.

"My God," said Edouard, stepping forward to embrace his only sister with a big huge hug. "I'm so sorry," he said. "I…I just had to know. That was terribly rude of me…"

They stood there for some time while Elizabeth sobbed.

"It's all right," said Edouard quite softly. "Everything will be all right."

"Please don't tell Mother," she replied. "I've never seen her so happy."

"I know," he replied. "And you're finally going to grant our father his last wish."

"For me to be married at Sainte-Marie?"

"No, you silly. His last real wish—to have his genes carried on. Lord knows I'm of no use in that regard!"

He laughed a bit halfheartedly at his own little joke, and Elizabeth laughed along with him. She stepped back and gazed at him, at his lanky frame and delicate features, and his sheepish grin.

"Thank you," she said. "I probably would have told you anyway. We never were much for hiding secrets from one another. But it feels good to finally be able to admit that, yes, I am pregnant."

She turned away, not wanting her perceptive brother to potentially read any guilt whatsoever in the expression she bore while admitting to such a state of affairs, as it were. To her surprise, he began to laugh.

"I can't believe it!" he exclaimed. "My sister's not only going to marry Peter Dermenjian, one of France's most notorious playboys, but going to bear him a child! Extraordinary. Why, the entire female population of France—all Europe, for that matter—will be in mourning. I just can't believe it myself. How on earth did he take the news? You know quite well that other women before you have made such claims and he's always vehemently denied any responsibility whatsoever."

Edouard refilled his glass and waited in anticipation for his sister's reply. She stood up and walked toward the window and stared outside.

They were dining at the villa. Elizabeth had just paid a visit to her once-upon-a-time future mother-in-law, who was still faring as well as ever in the room Peter had refurbished for her overlooking the Mediterranean. It contained all the amenities necessary for taking care of a poor woman in Eleanor Newman's sad condition. Elizabeth had insisted on paying for all her care but Peter wouldn't hear of it. He asked her to stay to dine with him and of course she had obliged. After all, they needed to talk. They were halfway through their *blanquette de veau* when Peter inquired whether Elizabeth found the wine perhaps a bit too astringent.

"No," she replied. "I just don't care for any wine today."

"Really?" he asked. "Not feeling well?"

She wiped her lips and put down her napkin. "Peter," she said, "do you remember the night you told me about Oscar?"

"Why, of course I remember. How could I ever forget a night like that? Everything was magnificent. Why do you ask?"

"Because I'm pregnant," she replied.

She remembered the look, the expression that had gone from stunned to incredulous.

"Surely you're joking," he countered. "How can that be? Don't tell me the world's most famous IUD has failed you? Why, Oscar would be furious!"

"As you may recall," she replied, "I was expecting to be married to Oscar back in January. I removed the IUD Christmas Day."

"No!" Peter exclaimed. "You can't be serious!"

Elizabeth recalled how terrified she had been that he might claim to have had a vasectomy. That would have ruined everything. Fortunately, he had proceeded to interrogate her regarding any other affairs she might have had recently.

"What about that trip to Scotland? Surely you have some, shall we say, close acquaintances up north?"

"I beg your pardon!" she said. "In case you have forgotten I have been in mourning over the loss of my fiancé. Besides, my brother, Edouard, was with me the entire time. He will vouch for me that no other man dared to get close to me, let alone…"

"I see," Peter replied. "You are convinced that our particular moment of weakness, of our—shall we say—succumbing to the powers of the flesh in our hour of grief, has led to this?"

"Absolutely," she lied, although in a way it was the truth, however twisted. "I saw a doctor yesterday and he confirmed what I've been suspecting for some time."

"My God," he said. "Then tell me, what do you propose to do about this?"

"Au contraire," she said. "What do you propose?"

"Propose?"

"Yes," she replied, "why not? We would make a fine couple. And I would not begrudge you your, shall we say, dalliances."

That invoked a seriously raised brow on the part of Peter. "Do you know the sex?"

Such a question!

"No, but I imagine it is a boy. There are very few female Le Clercs, and you had but one brother and no sisters, so…"

Suddenly, Peter's expression changed, slowly at first, but then he broke into a genuine smile. "A son? You think you're bearing my son?"

With that he was at her side, holding her hand. It certainly hadn't been lost on Elizabeth that Peter Dermenjian was in his mid-forties. And while abiding the bonds of matrimony seemed completely anathema to his character, fathering a son, or a daughter, an heir to his enormous fortune, might have tremendous appeal to him. Especially if the more traditional elements of the bonds of marriage, such as fidelity, could be somehow suspended indefinitely. And as for her fidelity, well, there were other priorities, such as loyalty to her child, who would at least have a father in name if not in blood.

"I'm afraid I would have to insist on a rather rigid prenuptial agreement," he stated.

"Of course," she replied. After all, such an instrument must be de rigueur for a man of his means, and ways, to insulate his immense wealth from any marauding femme fatale.

"Astounding!" Edouard exclaimed after listening to Elizabeth describe Peter's reactions to her news, minus the bit about a prenuptial agreement. "And evidently, when all was said and done, he surrendered."

"Evidently," she replied, smiling demurely as she patted her tummy.

"So here you are, pregnant. Which means I get to play *oncle* Edouard before too long. That's a role I am certain to cherish." He smiled at her and then glanced at his watch. "Oh my. It is getting on toward evening. I will leave you to dress for dinner. But rest assured. Your little secret is safe with me."

With that he gave her another kiss on her cheek and took his leave of her.

Chapter 52

The young man looked to be about twenty. He'd been hit hard in the shins by some blunt object, hard enough to break the tibia in two places. Max set about administering morphine while preparing to set the bones, just as another gurney arrived delivering another victim to the on-deck circle.

It never stopped. It was all part of a steady stream of badly maimed people, victims of horrendous hate crimes, going on for six weeks now. But it was early June and supposedly they would all be gone by mid-July. Right. He hadn't seen Christine for a few weeks and wondered how she and Dr. Brecht were getting along, and whether they and the others were making any progress finding homes for all these poor souls.

She showed up the following day, having caught a ride over in an empty supply truck, claiming she needed some medicine for a rash she had developed. Max gave her a salve to try. He had never seen her so distraught. He made her some tea and sat her down in his tent.

"It's so horrible," she said, shaking her head from side to side as tears rolled down her cheeks. "The mothers are all beside themselves. So many sons are missing, young ones, abducted to serve in some maniac's army. And their daughters are missing in huge numbers. I hate to think what's happening to them."

"Sounds like a harsh lesson in deep anthropology," said Max.

"Way too deep," she replied, looking down at the dirt floor.

"How's Dr. Brecht handling it?" he asked, refilling her teacup.

"She's eating it up, interviewing family after family, taking tons and tons of notes, and ordering me around like I'm ten graduate students rolled into one."

"Any progress with the relocation?"

"Pretty slow. A lot of countries are still figuring out their allocation, how many refugees they'd accept, even if we could figure out what families, or parts thereof, we can send off to begin with."

It was all way beyond them, the immense suffering caused by such immense cruelty, the root of which just might be the immense overcrowding in a nation with one of the highest birthrates in the world. At least this was what Max was pondering when they heard a horn honking outside.

"It's my ride," said Christine. Once outside the tent, she gave Max a big hug. "Thanks for the medicine and the tea. You should come visit our neck of the woods sometime," she said, green eyes almost pleading.

"Love to," he replied. "I'll see if I can wrangle a hall pass out of Dr. Bichette."

The driver opened the passenger door and Christine climbed in. Max leaned over to give her a kiss on the cheek, but he came up short as the face of the driver came into view. It was a face he recognized but he didn't dare say a word. Maybe Christine wouldn't even notice. It was Banyon.

"Say hello to Dr. Brecht," he said, seeing a look in Banyon's eyes that said, "I know you, too."

Thoroughly shaken, he wandered back inside the tent and poked his head into Dr. Bichette's office. She was busy reviewing spreadsheets, marking them up with a red pen.

"Uh, excuse me," said Max. "That driver, do you know him? The one who just gave Christine a ride back to tent thirteen."

Glasses perched again on the tip of her nose, she peered up at him as if such a question was so preposterous as to not even merit a response. "Dr. Taylor," she replied, "in case you hadn't noticed, I am busy trying to attend to the medical needs of all these patients that fate happened to deliver to this field hospital. I do not make a point of getting to know every truck driver and every messenger who happens to volunteer for this sad mission. Why do you ask?"

"Oh, it's nothing," Max replied. "He looked familiar, that's all."

"Well, next time you see him, why don't you simply introduce yourself. Meanwhile, I need to reconcile these medical records." She gave him that look he'd come to recognize, the one that said "time's up."

"I don't suppose—" he began.

"That you could check your e-mail again?" she replied. "Come back in a few hours after you've completed all your rounds. Besides, the satellites are not conveniently aligned at the moment."

That's great, he thought. All the best of modern-day technology, provided the satellites are willing. But he'd already come to half expect to be shut out again, due to Dr. Bichette's long work hours, if nothing else. He had been at it for some time now, logging on to the Internet when she permitted, which was only a couple of times per week. The field hospital's server was somehow directly linked to

Nairobi, and when the whims of space technology allowed, it linked up to the virtual world far beyond the remoteness of the refugee camp.

He had performed numerous searches for Elizabeth Le Clerc that had produced a number of leads but no contact as of yet. He'd e-mailed the School of Medicine at the University of Glasgow and had actually received a reply. It stated that Ms. Le Clerc was no longer employed there and that they were not at liberty to divulge contact information for former, or even current, employees unless such information was already available on the school's website, which it was not. He had managed to obtain the e-mail addresses of quite a few Elizabeth Le Clercs, but thus far the few who had bothered to reply swore they had never met and had no knowledge of Dr. Oscar Newman, the missing Nobel Laureate.

Max thanked Dr. Bichette and continued on his way back to the third tent, where a fresh truckload of maimed refugees awaited, the product of the weekly reconnaissance along the refugee trail. It was the same story all over again.

When the last patient was suitably stitched up and heavily medicated, Max cleaned up and headed back to see Dr. Bichette. Not only did he want to check his e-mail, he wanted to ask her about taking a day off. Like he'd told her from the start, he had some obligations to the Maasai, and it was high time he checked up on some patients he'd been caring for back across the Kalema Road.

When he arrived at her office, she was gone. So he took a seat in front of her computer screen, preparing to help himself to a bit of cyberspace. Hoping the satellites would be kind, he tapped on the keyboard to awaken the dormant screen. It zapped to life, and in an instant images from around the world appeared before him. It was dialed in to CNN's home page. No doubt Dr. Bichette had been looking to pick up news from the world outside. There were the usual stories about instability in the Middle East, various stories about the state of the world economy, football scores, and the like. He was about to log on to his e-mail account when he noticed a very disturbing headline in the entertainment section: "French Playboy to Wed Nobel Laureate's Ex-Fiancée."

He immediately clicked on the link, which brought up not simply a story but a video interview by none other than Melanie Woo, featuring Peter Dermenjian as well as the object of his recent cybersearches, Elizabeth Le Clerc. Max sat back and felt a shiver run through him.

"My God," he said to himself. "Look what we've done!"

He fumbled to find the volume control so he could listen more closely. They were all seated in what Max guessed must be someone's living room, no doubt Peter's, all very plush and modern with windows in the background overlooking the Mediterranean. Melanie looked as lovely as ever but Max found he could not stop staring at Elizabeth. He had never even seen a picture of her. Yet there she was seated beside Peter, who was holding her hand.

Peter did most of the talking, responding to Melanie's questions about the irony of their meeting and apparently falling in love while both were obviously in mourning over their respective tragic losses. Suddenly, Max understood Oscar's devotion to Elizabeth. She was absolutely beautiful. All the more reason to panic. Finally, Melanie turned toward Elizabeth.

"Ms. Le Clerc, I'm sure you're tired of all these questions about Oscar Newman, but I am very curious. Have you given any thought to recovering Dr. Newman's body and returning him to his homeland?"

That was unfair. Max could tell Elizabeth was extremely uncomfortable.

"Yes, I have," she replied. "Oscar loved the Great Rift Valley of East Africa. I believe he is at peace now and I therefore have no plans to have him moved."

"Well then," she continued, "do you plan on making a visit to his grave any time soon?"

At this Peter cut in. "Yes, after the wedding we plan to take a trip to Kenya, one that will surely include a visit to the small cemetery deep in the heart of the Rift Valley where he is apparently buried."

Max thought he saw an element of surprise in Elizabeth's expression as Peter delivered this bit of news. Perhaps it was news to her as well.

Melanie thanked them both and closed the interview by saying the couple were to be married this coming Saturday at an undisclosed location.

"Oh shit!" said Max, glancing over at the calendar hung by the door. Only three days away!

"I beg your pardon?" said Dr. Bichette as she reentered her office. She did not appear the least bit surprised to find Max sitting before her computer spouting expletives. "What is wrong?"

Max, caught off guard and quite stunned by what he had just learned, turned away from the computer. "What isn't wrong?" he replied. "The whole world's gone to hell. Listen, Dr. Bichette, I really appreciate you letting me use your computer and all. But I was wondering. Do you think I could have a couple of days off? I've been at it nearly six solid weeks, and my nerves are kind of shot. And I really should pay a visit to Joseph and see how the Maasai south of the Kalema Road are doing. I made a commitment to them and there are a few former patients I'd like to check up on. I'd need the Scout, though."

Dr. Bichette rifled through some papers in her in-box and then turned to face him. "That would be fine with me," she replied. Max breathed a heavy sigh of relief. "But I'm afraid you've been reassigned."

Max thought he must have heard wrong. "What did you say? How can I be reassigned?"

"Jocko says he needs a doctor. He specifically asked for you."

"Jocko? The warlord whose goons ransacked my clinic? You must be joking."

"I'm afraid not. These are orders from Nairobi."

"What's Nairobi got to do with this? Please tell me it's not Captain Olengi again."

Dr. Bichette simply stared back at him. "You have tomorrow to arrange for transferring your patients here to the rest of the staff, to brief them on your patients' conditions and treatments."

"What about the Scout?"

"Yes, you can take it with you. Jocko will no doubt want you to be fetching supplies for him."

This was unbelievable.

"And what about some time off?"

"That will be up to Jocko to decide. Good luck."

She reached out to shake his hand, signaling that the orders had been issued and the conversation was over. Then she grabbed a stack of papers and walked out, leaving Max to contemplate his next move. He felt like his head was about to explode.

He reported to work the next morning as usual and began the process of educating his medical colleagues regarding the needs and troubles of his nearly two dozen current patients. His fellow doctors all rolled their eyes at the notion of tending to Jocko, a notorious hypochondriac who insisted that his encounters with the medical profession be confined to house calls. Max was only slightly relieved to learn that he wasn't the first to get pegged for "Jocko duty."

His comrades in scrubs were all quite dedicated and likeable folk. Thierry, a Belgian doctor from Liege, agreed to take on the worst of his lot, a few of whom weren't likely to make it. Genevieve, from Paris, took on several more, and between a couple of Dutch and Norwegian doctors, he managed to pass his entire medical workload off to these highly skilled physicians, all of whom seemed to have a much better grasp of what they were doing there in the first place. He made the rounds to all his patients. He wanted to pay his respects and make sure those who really needed it had the best pain medication around.

After lunch he packed up his gear and retrieved the Scout from the motor pool. It looked surprisingly good for having been drafted into service to haul supplies around the sprawling camp. Dr. Bichette had drawn a map for him, so he had little trouble finding Jocko's "compound," as it were. It occupied all the southernmost area of the camp, east of the Ewaso Ngiro. But finding Jocko's private quarters within his compound was another matter altogether. A young soldier wielding a semiautomatic rifle, one of Jocko's goons, helped him. Once he understood that Max was the doctor Jocko was expecting, he climbed onto the hood of the Scout and simply began pointing, showing Max the way through this highly militarized zone of the refugee camp, where the tents were substantial and the standard of living seemed much higher than parts farther north.

And certainly Jocko's quarters were of an even higher standard than his immediate neighbors'. His personal tent was easily twice as large as any of those in this rather upscale neighborhood, and the plush Persian carpet, large double bed, and sizable sofa and matching chairs were testament to this individual's superior rank. He lived in comfort and, as Max immediately surmised upon entering and spotting the laptop on his long wooden desk, was very much in touch with the world within and outside of the camp.

"Dr. Taylor," said the pudgy warlord, king of the campground, "thank you for coming. My troops and I are badly in need of medical attention."

He was seated on his sofa, drinking a Coke while puffing on a large cigar. According to the other doctors, he was a relatively harmless and, some might say, ineffective dictator who had done his best to look after the needs of those he had claimed to rule back along the shores of Lake Kyoga. That is, until the neighboring warlords kicked his ass and began slaughtering many of his devotees. And, as Max could certainly attest, the slaughter was not over.

"What seems to be the problem?" Max inquired, anxious to simply get down to business. He hoped that it would entail medical business, but the sighting of

426

Banyon and this abrupt change of duty suggested other agendas were at play. Jocko pointed down at his feet.

"My gout has been acting up lately," he stated as he began to unlace his ankle-high black leather boots.

"Which foot?" said Max.

"Both of them, but the right one is the worst."

Max stared at the man's feet as he removed his long black socks as well. They were slightly swollen and smelled terrible, but from a gout perspective, they seemed fairly close to normal.

"I suppose I could give you some balm to rub on them. Your joints are somewhat swollen. Perhaps a bit of arthritis. May I ask how old you are?"

"Forty-two," he replied.

"Maybe you should try a different pair of boots. These look too small."

Jocko snorted, obviously offended by the suggestion that he did not dress himself in a manner befitting a man of his stature, a military commander. But at last he smiled and replied that he would consider doing so next time he was in downtown Nairobi.

"What else can I help you with?" said Max.

"Well," he replied, "you could check my men over; they may need medical attention. And there's a girl next door. I would like you to confirm that she is, shall we say, clean."

That was it. Max felt the anger welling up and it was all he could manage to keep his composure. He took a deep breath.

"Let's cut the horseshit," he said. "What do you want with me? I was just about to take a couple of days off. Tell you what, I'll even bring you back a nice new pair of shoes."

Jocko laughed. "That's very kind of you," he replied. "But let me tell you what you can bring me."

And he leaned forward to look Max directly in the eye. His cigar breath was disgusting but the expression he wore was far more bothersome.

"You can bring me Oscar Newman, dead or alive."

Max moved up off the ground where he'd been stationed during the perfunctory foot exam. He thought it best to stay on message. "Oscar Newman is dead, buried in the small cemetery behind Father Sebastian's schoolhouse. It's across the Kalema Road on the other side of the Ewaso Ngiro. In case you didn't know."

Jocko laughed again. "Is he now?"

"What the hell do you care, anyway? What's he got to do with all this?"

Jocko continued to laugh as he relit his cigar. "Let's just say that this land we are now occupying, much against our wishes, would be back in the hands of the Maasai much sooner if I was able to deliver Oscar Newman over to the authorities. There is a sizable reward out for him."

"Not anymore," Max responded. "Like I said, he's dead. The search is over and there's no more reward money on the table."

Max actually assumed that was true. Not that it mattered. The reward money that Peter had offered up in the first place would never be enough to arm this mob, at least not going up against the demons that now ruled Jocko's homeland. But if Peter Dermenjian could lay his hands on Oscar, and force him to divulge the source of the long-lost Dermenjian diamonds, he'd no doubt do his best to fortify all the armies in the world if that's what it took.

"Let us just say that, for lack of better terms, the reward money is indeed still on the table. And believe me, the search is still on. There are rumors among the Maasai that Oscar Newman is indeed still alive. And I intend to find him, even if I have to dig him up myself!"

Jocko spoke these last words with such conviction and with such menace that Max felt his skin begin to crawl. How he longed for the good old days back at LA General, patching up victims of gang wars.

"Jocko," said Max, "let's just say I understand."

"Of course you understand." Jocko replied. "You say he is dead. Where is the proof? Where is the death certificate? It has not been filed."

That was true. Not exactly an oversight. Max just didn't want to commit perjury if he didn't have to.

"Look," said Max, "I'm out here alone in the bush trying to manage this clinic for the Maasai. I packed contraceptives, not death certificates."

Jocko laughed once more before his look turned dead serious once again.

"All right," said Max, "you want real proof Oscar's dead, I can get that for you. Photographs, DNA samples. But if you're thinking you and your boys can just waltz over across the Kalema Road and exhume him, you're in for a rude awakening. There are moran stationed all along the road. They're not about to let

428

any of your soldiers—if that's what you call them—just saunter into town and start digging up bodies. You don't need that kind of confrontation with the Maasai right now. Things are tense enough. But if you really need proof, I can save you all that bother. And if there are any lingering doubts about my word as the doctor who treated Oscar during his ordeal, I definitely want to put those to rest."

"What kind of proof?"

It was just the question Max had been dreading as he tried to swagger his way out of this predicament.

"Photographs in the coffin if you want."

"Yes, a recent photograph of Oscar Newman dead in his coffin, in his freshly exhumed state, that might suffice."

Freshly exhumed? Now that would be difficult. But he sensed Jocko was close to approving his travel papers, so to speak, and once Oscar found out about the marriage, he'd surely drop this ridiculous hiding act and come forward to meet his fate. After seeing her online, Max was sure Oscar would agree to step forward, reaffirm his existence and his innocence regarding the murder of Francis Dermenjian, and deal with Peter Dermenjian *mano e mano*. This had gone far enough. As to how Max would explain his "mistake" regarding premature reports of Oscar's death, that would require more thinking later on. Right now he just needed to put a little space, actually a lot of space, between Jocko and himself.

"I can do that. I have a digital camera. I'll make sure the date and time are set when the photo is taken. I can be back in a few days."

He couldn't tell if Jocko was buying it. Besides, Jocko was looking for proof Oscar was alive, not dead. Maybe the certainty was worth something, though, from a negotiations standpoint.

"So what you are saying is you will exhume the body, take photographs, and return them to me within a matter of days."

This was unfortunately the deal on the table. How to pull it off, credibly if at all, was another matter altogether. He just needed to get clear, get to Oscar, and let him, the man at the epicenter of this shit storm, decide the next move.

"That about sums it up," said Max.

"Very well. But just to be safe, I will send my own witness. He will meet you at the schoolhouse at dawn in two days."

"Two days?" said Max. "At dawn. Right."

"But before you go, please, the girl." He motioned toward the tent just in front of his.

"Sure thing," said Max. Anything to get clear.

Chapter 53

Once well beyond the refugee camp and quite relieved to be on the homestretch, cruising in his Scout that now had nearly a full tank of gas, Max felt a strange mix of emotions coursing through him, along with a heavy dose of adrenaline. It was a mix of guilt, anger, frustration, and extreme anxiety at the prospect of informing Oscar that his beloved Elizabeth was on the verge of marrying his archenemy. And it was all because of David, that deceitful, lying priest! Max couldn't believe he had played along. But in spite of this selfish inclination to blame it all on David, he badly needed David's counsel. And one thing was for damned sure. He was not about to face Oscar all on his own.

David was stooped over in his garden when the sound of a vehicle in the distance caught his attention. He gathered his salad makings and headed back to his living quarters. As soon as the Scout came into view, he breathed a great sigh of relief. Arms wide, he walked out to greet Max as the dust settled.

"So good to see you," he said as he and Max embraced for an instant.

"It's good to see you, too," said Max. "But we need to go see Oscar as soon as possible."

"What's wrong?" David asked.

Max didn't know where to begin. "That's kind of complicated. What have you got to drink?"

All David had was tea but it was local and very good. Max recounted the situation, highlighting how Oscar Newman had become a pawn that figured strangely into the plight of the refugees. It was the basic diamonds for weapons deal, with a slight twist. Oscar Newman was somehow caught in the middle.

"It's a trap," said David. "This marriage to Elizabeth. All he wants is to lure Oscar out into the open, out of hiding. Why the Melanie Woo interview on CNN? He wanted worldwide coverage, Internet-in-your-face coverage, of this wedding."

Max raised his brow. "Interesting theory," he said.

"This is terrible," said David. "But I agree with you. Oscar has no choice but to come clean."

"I thought at first I could just rig up some phony picture of Oscar looking dead."

"In a coffin?"

"I guess. Like I said, I was just saying what needed to be said so I could get out of there. It didn't occur to me that Jocko would send an eyewitness. But we need to get to Oscar as soon as possible."

"We'll leave first thing in the morning. It's too late today, and besides, we both need some food and some rest, not to mention a plan for getting him out of here, assuming he even agrees to leave."

They rose before dawn and set out to meet the day, David with a knapsack full of food and Max with a knapsack full of medical supplies. They were very careful to keep to a path that concealed them from view as much as possible, staying in the shadows as best they could until they found the base of the escarpment and began their ascent up the now-familiar trail.

It was still quite cool within the forest, and the early-morning sounds of vervet monkeys pierced the air as they cried out all sorts of alarms. Many colorful birds flitted all about. They barely spoke, in part to save their breath and in part because neither of them knew precisely how to proceed with this delicate mission.

They found Oscar still asleep on his crude bed within the semi-confines of his dugout shelter. Not far away, muffled snoring emanated from an odd pile of animal skins, signifying the presence of Jack McGraw. Olitunu was nowhere in sight.

"Great security," said Max, as he set down his pack full of supplies and knelt down next to Oscar. The latter awoke with a start, panicked at first, but as his eyes adjusted he not only looked awake but seemed genuinely pleased to see his visitors.

"Bless you," he said. "How nice of you two to finally come pay me a visit."

"Good morning, Oscar," said Max. "Sorry, I've been way too busy dealing with the refugees. Every day's a crisis. People much worse off than you. But tell me, how are you feeling?"

"That depends," he replied, "on what news you bring me."

"We'll get to that after I have a look at you," Max replied.

"And after you've had some breakfast," David interjected. "I have some fresh bread and cheese and some melon from my garden."

David reached into his knapsack and pulled out a small tablecloth that he laid out on the barren dirt floor. He then set out a few plates and a small breadboard while Max applied his stethoscope to Oscar's chest. David sliced the bread and cut up a few generous portions of cheese. Then he cut the melon open. Oscar could smell its ripeness as he took a few deep breaths for Max. He was beginning to salivate at the notion of eating real food again, instead of the foul curdled milk and sometimes bloody concoctions Sarna supplied a couple of times a day.

"Your heart sounds good," said Max. "How are your chest wounds healing?"

"Getting better all the time," he responded as he sat up and went straight for the food David had arranged so neatly. "Bon appétit," he said as he grabbed a piece of bread and folded it around a wedge of cheese. He did not wait for a reply before stuffing it in his mouth. He chewed in blissful peace, closing his eyes and savoring every morsel. David said a quick blessing under his breath before helping himself to the melon. Max put his stethoscope away, realizing that any furthering of the medical exam would have to wait. Then came a groggy yet familiar voice as Crazy Jack poked his head up from layers of assorted goatskins.

"What in the hell is goin' on here?" he said.

"Good morning," said David as Jack McGraw pulled up beside him. "And thank you for being such a trustworthy companion to our friend during his unfortunate incarceration. But please tell me, where is your guardian?"

"Ollie Tuna?" Jack replied. "He took up with that young girl, Sarna, who brings us them nasty Maasai smoothies. They got a little stick-and-mud place up top, with a few cattle to tend to. And they're kinda tight with the Loliondo Maasai who live up that way."

Jack then picked up some bread and some cheese and threw a piece of melon in the middle. Oscar wiped his mouth with his forearm.

"So," he began, "to what do I owe this particular visit? Surely you didn't come all this way to bring me breakfast in bed."

David and Max looked at each other. Where to begin?

"Oscar," said Max, "we came to get you out of here. I think you're well enough to travel."

"Excellent suggestion," Oscar responded. "I am so completely bored here I could scream. But if you've come to take me away, I presume you've made contact with Elizabeth. Where is she?"

Max put his lips together as if to reply, but all he could do was release a gasp of air that signaled his exasperation at having to bring Oscar up to date. David cut in.

"It is all my fault," he said. "I was only trying to protect you. That's why I told them you were dead. It was an impulsive thing to do, I realize—an impulsive thing with rather unfortunate consequences, I'm afraid."

Oscar looked confused and quite alarmed. "What has happened? Is Elizabeth all right?"

Max took over. "She's all right, as far as her health and personal safety."

"Then you've spoken with her?"

"Uh no, Oscar, I haven't. While I was working in the camp, I tried e-mailing her several times. Without a phone number, I just tried the Internet. I heard back from a couple of Elizabeth Le Clercs but none were her."

"But if you haven't communicated with her, how do you know she's all right?" Oscar was now standing, looking down at the two of them with an expression of fear and apprehension.

"I saw a video clip of her while I was online. Melanie Woo was interviewing her."

"Really? What about? How did she look? What did she say?"

Neither Max nor David responded, not immediately, at least.

"Tell me. Something is very wrong isn't it?"

Max bit the bullet. "Yes, Oscar. Something's very wrong. Melanie Woo wasn't just interviewing Elizabeth. She was interviewing Peter Dermenjian as well."

"You'd better have a seat," said David. Oscar grew more apprehensive as he sat back down on his bed, his eyes stretched wide open and his face frozen as he awaited the news, news that could not possibly be good.

"Oscar," said Max, not mincing any words. "She's going to marry him."

It took a few minutes for the meaning to sink in. Oscar tilted his head to one side, clearly not believing what he just heard. "You can't be serious," he responded dryly. "When?"

"Tomorrow, according to Melanie Woo."

"Tomorrow?" said Oscar, completely and utterly incredulous and clearly shaken to the core.

He stood up and walked calmly out toward the middle of the campground. The news was sinking in slowly, like a depth charge. David and Max remained seated, awaiting the inevitable eruption. Oscar lowered his head. Here it comes, Max thought. But instead Oscar looked back at the two of them, bewildered and hurt beyond comprehension. He opened his mouth as if to speak but words failed him. He just turned away and kept on walking. David and Max jumped up and ran after him. Crazy Jack threw on some pants and hobbled along as he tried to zip up his fly.

"Listen," said Max, "the Scout has a full tank of gas. It's parked down by the schoolhouse. You look fit enough. We could be there in a couple of hours. Then we'll hop in and we'd be in Nairobi this afternoon, in time to contact the media and let everyone, including Elizabeth, know you really are still alive."

Oscar remained silent and continued walking, opting for the path out toward the overlook.

"Oscar," said Max, "where do you think you're going? Let's head on down and get you out of here. To hell with Joseph and this jail sentence. It was just a way to keep you safe from Dermenjian's search parties. Joseph won't care."

But still Oscar said nothing. He just kept walking.

"I'm certain I can convince Joseph to let you go," David chimed in. "In fact, with all the trouble posed by this refugee camp, I'm sure the elders have all but forgotten about you."

"So it appears," Oscar replied.

"Tell you what," said Crazy Jack, "just give me a couple more weeks to get my rock samples all together, and we'll head for Mombasa. Then we'll rig up *Esmerelda* and head out for the island. What do you say?"

Oscar looked at him as if he were indeed crazy but kept on walking. When they reached the precipice, Max quickly ran ahead. He wasn't about to let his number-one patient throw himself off a cliff just because the love of his life was about to wed the one man who had become, of late, his bitterest enemy. Oscar brushed Max aside with a swipe of his huge arm and walked up to the edge.

"Oscar," David pleaded, "don't do anything rash now. There is still hope if we act quickly."

Oscar turned suddenly and stared David down with a look so full of scorn and anger that David took a step backward in alarm. "Hope, you say? Hope? Hope is all I had, until now. Now I have nothing. Nothing except for some memories that will torture me for the rest of my life, memories of the woman I have loved for so many years and who was to have been *my* wife. That is all I have left, except for the certainty that Peter Dermenjian will track me down, and if he can't find means to excise from me the whereabouts of those diamonds, he will most certainly kill me to keep me from testifying against him for his brother's murder. And to keep me from his wife!"

"That's exactly why you need to burst on the scene right now!" Max pleaded. "It will be sensational. 'Missing Nobel Laureate Found Alive in East Africa!' And what's more, he's prepared to testify that it was Francis Dermenjian's own brother who pulled the trigger. The media will have a field day with that, especially if we can pull this off in time to stop the wedding."

Oscar raised his bushy eyebrows. "And what makes you so sure that, or anything, would stop the wedding? Peter Dermenjian is a very handsome and very wealthy man, a bachelor of some repute, however ill. He, too, has lost a loved one. Evidently, they've been commiserating."

Max looked at David, who took over from there.

"You're right about that. One reason we haven't been able to get ahold of Elizabeth is that, well, it appears she's been staying with Peter since you disappeared. What better way to keep a close eye on her than to take her in, consoling her while he continues the search for you?"

"Naturally," said Oscar, "knowing full well that if I were to resurface, I would do anything possible to get through to her."

"Exactly," said Max. "David thinks this whole wedding might be a setup, too. A trap to lure you out of hiding in case you're not dead. But even if it is, we have the element of surprise on our side. And Oscar, I mean it. She can still be your wife. We just need to get moving."

"Moving? Moving where? To a jailhouse until I stand trial for the murder of Francis Dermenjian? To some absurd newscast of my return, of my survival after my personal doctor and my personal priest have pronounced me dead to the world? How would you explain all that?"

"I don't know," Max responded, "unless you simply explain that you were an eyewitness to Peter Dermenjian killing his brother and we all feared for your life. Besides, you were very sick, recovering from malaria and some serious wounds."

"Yes," David added, "I will happily confess that I lied about you being dead because we believed your life was in danger."

"Gentlemen," said Oscar, "if this is indeed a trap, then my life is very much in danger. Not that it's of much use to me. But the roads will be heavily guarded, and I don't have a shred of identification."

"If Dermenjian's people are out looking for you, you won't need any identification," said Max. "And speaking of Dermenjian's people, there's a whole other side to this situation."

Oscar peered out over the immense valley below, looking over the sprawling mass of refugees on the other side of the Ewaso Ngiro. Then he looked down at the

436

cascade of gray rocks and dull-green shrubs and stunted trees that protruded here and there from the side of the cliff.

"Yes. There are indeed many sides to this situation," Oscar observed. "Which one did you care to discuss?"

"It's like this," Max began. "If you don't take a chance and come clean right now, you'll have to really convince the world, or at least Peter Dermenjian, that you are truly dead."

Oscar, looking even more stunned, cocked his head to one side again. "And why is that?" he inquired.

Max looked down at the ground. "Because he wants clear evidence, photographic evidence, that you are truly and irreversibly dead."

"Does he, now?" Oscar replied. He sat down, much to Max's and David's relief, on a rocky outcrop several feet from the edge.

"Yes," Max responded, "he does. So much so that tomorrow Jocko's sending one of his valiant crew to witness your exhumation. He wants that kind of evidence, photographic, with a credible eyewitness. It's pretty obvious that Jocko and his boys, the ones who ransacked the clinic and made off with your medical records, are working for Peter Dermenjian."

Oscar straightened up. A shudder ran through his body. "Dermenjian's people are coming to exhume my body?" he exclaimed.

"That's the general idea. Actually, it was my idea, to be honest. Jocko was indicating he would come dig you up if that's what it took to get evidence that you were dead, so he could get beyond the business of finding you and get on to talking seriously about arming his paltry militia. I offered to provide some photographic evidence. I didn't know exactly how but I knew I needed to buy us all some time, which is all that we have right now. But the clock is ticking. We have less than twenty-four hours to get you out of here."

"Twenty-four hours?" Oscar repeated.

"That's right," said Max. "Twenty-four hours to either get the hell out of Dodge or somehow convince Jocko you're really dead, once we dig you up."

"Dig me up?"

"That's right. By tomorrow morning. So what's it going to be? Spring back to life or wallow in the grave somehow?"

"Hell of a choice," Oscar replied. "Sounds like checkmate to me. Dead either way. I just cannot believe she would marry the bastard."

He stood back up and looked out over the precipice once again. Max rose to his feet.

"Look, Oscar," he pleaded. "I can understand how you must feel. I never realized Elizabeth was such a beauty. Quite a woman, really."

Oscar wheeled around, his jaw set tight and his eyes on fire. "What did you say?" he asked as he moved closer.

Max fumbled for a response. "I just said she's beautiful. I had never seen her until the interview with Melanie Woo."

"And what did you mean by 'quite a woman'?"

"Uh, look, I'm a guy. I couldn't help noticing she's got, well, nice breasts. I'm sorry. I didn't mean to offend."

Oscar turned away and stepped to the edge once more. "The wretched bastard. Of course. Now I understand. She's pregnant, damn it. Time was running out, and with me dead, I suppose she let things get a bit out of hand. That has to be it. She always had an adequate bosom but it didn't really attract that much attention. How large were they?"

"Her breasts?"

"Yes, her breasts, damn it."

"Well," Max stammered, "they were, uh…"

"Just show me," Oscar replied as he lifted his hands to his chest, indicating to Max that he should simulate their current dimensions with his cupped hands.

Max felt ridiculous but did his manual best to convey the proper proportions, which were certainly beyond adequate.

"Indeed," Oscar replied. "Are you sure?"

"Yes," said Max, "I'd say they were about this big."

"Tell you what," said Oscar, "I may be wrong but I'm willing to bet she's carrying his child. Are you going back to the refugee camp?"

Max looked more confused than ever. "That depends," he said, "on what we do with you. I'm all for making a run to Nairobi. We'll get you to the British embassy, then I'll find Captain Olengi and get my damned passport back. After all, what I came here for is over. And I'm really ready to get the hell out of this country."

Oscar looked him up and down. "Are you, now?"

"Yes, I am. Your foundation appears to have dissolved, or at the very least it has no interest in my welfare. And I certainly didn't come here to spend all my days stitching up horribly maimed and disfigured refugees. I think I need a break. And maybe a few stiff drinks. But first we have to get you on your way."

"And if I refuse?" Oscar responded.

"Then you are a coward and a fool."

"Perhaps the former. And most certainly the latter, if as I suspect she is indeed pregnant. Imagine my embarrassment. Sorry, dear, thought you were dead. So I went ahead and found another man to father my child."

"She's not that desperate," David added.

"What do you know about all this?" Oscar responded. "Oh, but I forgot. You're not as celibate as most priests. Perhaps you do have a legitimate point of view, but no matter. I am not going to thrust myself on the scene when there is so much at risk. Dermenjian's people will most certainly be watching the roads. The police will no doubt be on high alert. As far as we know, there is still a warrant out for my arrest. Dermenjian likely has plenty of connections with the local judiciary such that they would certainly find a means and a basis for incarcerating me."

"Wait a minute," Max objected. "You're a goddamn Nobel Peace Prize winner. You're an idol and a British citizen. You would have all the rights any British citizen could possibly have in such a situation."

"And in the end, it's his word versus mine, a man who was quite delirious at the time."

"Even then you would get off."

"And if I did, what then? Go pay Elizabeth a visit and bring little gifts for her newborn child? No, I won't surrender on their terms. I have to do this on my terms. And that may take some time. Max, you must return to the refugee camp."

"What? Why?"

"Because I need you. I need you to keep tabs on Elizabeth. I need you to come and report to me every so often what news you find on the Internet. Certainly, the news that Peter Dermenjian's wife is pregnant would make some headlines."

"Melanie Woo would see to that," David chimed in.

"Right," Oscar continued. "You can tell me if my hypothesis is correct. Only then can I know how to proceed."

"But what about preempting the wedding?" David asked.

"Don't be preposterous. If she's indeed marrying Peter Dermenjian tomorrow, given where we are now and all the obstacles in between, the odds of us pulling off a media blitz prior to the ceremony are extremely bad. And if she's indeed pregnant, there's no stopping it anyway."

Max looked over at David. They both gave minute shrugs of their shoulders, admitting that the chances of making a break for it as they had planned were growing fainter by the minute.

"Well, if you've made up your mind not to attempt an escape, what do you propose we do about exhuming your body tomorrow?"

Oscar rubbed his hairy chin. He looked back out over the Rift Valley. "What is it geologists call these places?" he asked.

"What places? Rift valleys?" said Max.

"Yes, rift valleys. There's some German word."

"Graben," David replied. "It means 'grave.'"

"Yes, that's it. The world's biggest grave. Excellent. I believe I'm about to become one with it."

Chapter 54

Quite resolute in his determination to remain at large, Oscar set out on the long trek down the steep, winding trail that would eventually lead to David's schoolhouse and to the small cemetery just beyond it. With Olitunu still missing in action, his escape was quite unremarkable. David and Max led the way, while Jack McGraw trailed behind, toting a duffel bag filled with his latest rock samples. For Jack McGraw had not been wasting time up on top of the escarpment. Far from it. Apart from cleaning the rifles that had been seriously charred, and keeping an eye on Oscar, which he did less and less as Oscar healed and gained strength, he had made several excursions to the site of his latest gold strike. And he was more content than ever before with his findings, chuckling to himself from time to time and thankfully keeping to himself.

Once well into their descent, Oscar queried Max about his half-baked plan to prove him dead once and for all.

"Well," said Max, ducking under an overhanging branch, "when Jocko said he wanted to come exhume your supposedly dead body, I just pictured you lying in a wooden box, looking two months gone. And I'd just take a picture of you."

"And you know what two months gone looks like for a pasty Brit like me?" Oscar replied.

"More or less," said Max. "I spent two summers working in the LA county morgue. You wouldn't believe what the coroners bring in."

"What about recently exhumed corpses?"

"Yeah, there were those, too. Although most came from pretty shallow graves. Killers are usually in a hurry to dispose of the bodies, you know."

"Yes, of course," said Oscar as he plodded forward a bit unsteadily.

"Perhaps we should rest for a moment," David suggested.

"Very kind of you, Father," said Oscar as he found a convenient tree to lean upon. It was far more exercise than he'd had in many months. He knees were trembling and he was sweating profusely. And his various wounds were telling him in no uncertain terms that they were still not completely healed. The raw scars upon his chest were the most painful testament to his new found passion for darts, played with Maasai spears. It had been another way to pass the time, testing his skill and strength against Ollie Tuna's in between rounds of *bao*.

441

"You boys sure are settin' a mighty brisk pace," Jack commented as he caught up to the pack.

"There's no time to lose," David replied.

"Yes," Oscar agreed. "It seems I have a little date with destiny. How does the song go? Get me to the crypt on time?"

"Very funny," said Max. "Only this particular crypt happens to be occupied. And I don't relish the idea of disturbing its occupant."

"Nonsense," Oscar replied. "There's no need for that. David, you do have more of the boards that you used to build Senento's coffin?"

"Just a few. They were left over from the siding I put up around my house."

"Good. Then you actually have plenty of it."

"But it's on the side of my house…"

"Yes. But we only need to borrow it for a while. How about an auger and drill?"

David rubbed his hairy chin, pondering. "I believe I have one down below somewhere. Why?"

"A dead man's got to breathe, you know," he replied.

They arrived at the schoolhouse just before noon, drenched in sweat. Max made straight for the well. They each quenched their thirst and mopped their brows with a damp cloth.

"Now that you have squandered quite a bit of my water," David remarked, "I suggest we all sit down and discuss just how in God's name we are going to pull this off. I have more bread and a few more melons. I'll fetch another cheese from the cellar."

"Capital idea," Oscar replied, "but I do have a plan."

And he soon revealed it as they finished off the remains of the bread and melon and nearly devoured the entire round of cheese David had brought up from his ever-diminishing supply. He augmented the simple repast with a few leftover biscuits and filled a large pitcher with water from the well.

"Max," Oscar began, "you're unfortunately the strongest man among us. So I'd suggest you start digging, along with Jack the prospector here. The soil should still be soft enough from the original excavation."

"Right," said Max. "How come I always get to dig all the graves around here?"

"David, you and I will build another coffin. We'll drill a few holes in the back so I can breathe. Then we'll set it down on top of Senento's coffin. I trust his is not one of those shallow graves you were describing earlier?"

He was peering at Max, who had just ripped off one of the last chunks of bread.

"It's plenty deep," he replied. "Don't know that it's wide enough for the likes of you, though, especially inside a box. You're a little broader in the beam than Senento."

"We'll need to take a measurement," David interjected.

"Nonsense. Can't you see how trim I am?" Oscar replied as he stood up from the table and wiggled his still large, though slightly shrunken, belly for all to see. He was quite a sight. His khaki shorts and old denim shirt were quite dirty, bleached out, and threadbare. His walking shoes were in tatters.

"Seeing you like this reminds me," said David, "what attire would you like to be buried in? I have a few nice robes if you like."

"Really? In what colors?"

"I'm afraid they are all black. The church insists on it."

"No problem. Black suits my mood perfectly. And how about the morbid makeup department?" Oscar continued as he gnawed on a stale crust of bread.

Max cleared his throat after taking a long drink of water. "Depends on how morbid you want," he said. "A little charcoal or wood ash mixed with flour and water would go a long way. If you had a touch of blue indigo, that would be perfect. Or maybe we can find some ripe berries. The blue tones are critical."

Oscar raised a curious eyebrow.

"Certainly," David replied. "I have berries in my garden that are nearly ready to eat."

"Excellent," said Oscar, who seemed to be relishing the prospect of playing dead. After all, his life as he had known it was completely over.

"One more question," said Oscar. "Would you have any spare wine corks?"

"Wine corks?" said David. "What on earth for?"

"You'll see," Oscar replied. "But gentlemen, I suggest we get to it. We'll need to be done by nightfall so I can get a good night's sleep. After all, who knows at what hour Jocko's party will appear?"

"You ain't gonna sleep in that grave all night, are ya?" Jack inquired.

"Whatever it takes," said Oscar, deadly serious, for this was indeed the cover of darkness he had desperately needed ever since he had learned of the tragic news

443

about Elizabeth and Peter, news that not only had pierced his heart but was still busily tearing it to shreds.

It was a busy afternoon. David located several boards, more than he had anticipated but still not quite enough to enclose the rather bulky would-be corpse that now lay prostrate upon his living room floor.

"You need to relax," said David. "You're trying too hard. Rigor mortis doesn't last forever."

"And what do you know about corpses?"

"You think I haven't seen my share of death? Comforting the dying is where a priest really gets to earn his keep."

"Yes. While his church gets half the inheritance."

"Very funny. Now just lie still again while I measure you one more time."

And so they spent the afternoon, exchanging barbs while assembling what amounted to nothing more than a large wooden prop in this dark theater of the absurd. It unfortunately required unfastening several of the boards clinging to the side of the schoolhouse. David chose an aspect of his modest quarters and teaching institution that was rather inconspicuous, the side farthest removed from the cemetery. It was also hidden from the parking area.

"Excellent," said Oscar as they pulled the last board loose from its rusty nails. "These should go on top. They're much more weathered than the others."

"If you wish," said David, "but we will need to make them look as though they, too, have been buried for some time."

That was not a problem. For Max, having considered the matter further as he and Jack McGraw redug Senento's grave, realized that in order to be more convincing, the coffin should remain partially buried. They just needed to leave the upper torso and head uncovered, with holes drilled in the rear panel away from the viewing platform on the opposite end.

When the oversized, rectangular coffin was finished, David and Max carried it down to the renovated grave site. Max, with considerable help from Crazy Jack, had already reached Senento's coffin. The dirt was still fairly loose and they carved out a good foot of space all around it to accommodate the overhanging upper story of this now-duplex grave. Using the same old rope that had been used to set Senento down, David and Max carefully lowered Oscar's coffin until it rested on and completely covered, poor Senento.

444

"Excellent," Oscar remarked. "Now for the corks. Jack, did you bring the auger?"

Jack nodded, looking quite uncomfortable. He handed it to Max.

"You sure about this?" Max inquired.

"Absolutely," said Oscar. "A little olfactory authenticity should go a long way toward convincing any doubting Thomas that I am merrily rotting away in this particular graben within a much larger graben."

David shook his head in dismay as he handed Max a small bag of corks, corks that he had saved simply because they had all come from various highly memorable and precious *grand crus*. "This is most disrespectful," he protested, but in vain.

For Oscar had already convinced them that tapping into the wretched odor emanating from Senento's rotting corpse, just as the inspection party approached, would be an excellent insurance policy. All he needed to do was to pull the corks at the appointed time from the holes drilled through the bottom of his coffin clear through the top of Senento's, and the effect, he was certain, would be quite dramatic, assuming the stench didn't cause him to retch. It was already quite potent and Max could not keep from gagging as he turned the auger. Once he'd penetrated Senento's inner sanctum, the smell nearly knocked him over as he worked quickly to insert a cork into each hole that he drilled. Once the task was completed, David lent him a hand and pulled him up out of the hole. Max looked at Oscar.

"I can't believe I just did that. This whole charade is really getting out of control."

They all retired once again to David's quarters, where they shared more bread and cheese. The melon was all gone. David scraped together a small salad from his garden and pumped more water.

"Now for the pièce de résistance," Oscar proclaimed. "Are you ready to make me look as ghoulish as can be? I want to make sure Peter Dermenjian is convinced beyond any shadow of a doubt that I am utterly and completely dead."

"All the better for the eventual haunting?" Max wondered out loud.

"Not a haunting," Oscar replied, deadly serious. "More a reckoning, perhaps, but on my terms. So let's get on with it."

The anger and the pain in Oscar's voice said it all. They were now totally committed to completing the scene of this horrendous act of deception.

"I'll start mixing some flour and water," said Max. "David, can you fetch some of those berries? And Jack, how about sifting some ashes from the fire pit?"

They all did as requested and returned to find Oscar lying on his back upon the kitchen table. Max was busy lathering some thick creamy matter and carefully applying it to Oscar's face.

"Great timing," said Max.

He grabbed some of the ash Jack had collected and rubbed it into the flour-and-water mixture that he had just rubbed onto Oscar's hairy cheeks. Then he grabbed a few of the berries and squeezed a bit of the juice and rubbed it in, too. He massaged Oscar's cheekbones and then lifted and sorted and replaced bits of the mixture until it all resembled what Max thought a man in his mid-forties should look like if he happened to be several weeks dead. Oscar obliged by keeping his eyes closed and staying very still while Max carved various furrows in his sallow-looking cheeks.

"Not bad," said David. "You could fool me."

So Max carried on, working over the forehead and even the ears.

"Now we need to whiten the beard and the hair," said Max.

This was easily accomplished with more flour and some ash, just to keep a touch of gray in the otherwise well-aged pseudocorpse.

"What about the hands?" said Jack McGraw.

"Let's save some of that mixture for bedtime," said Oscar. "I need to get the robe on first and get situated."

It was another call to action. But by the time the sun was low enough to touch the lip of the Nguruman Escarpment, Oscar was covered with a flour, ash, and berry death mask and lay limp in the bottom of the fake coffin, which completely covered Senento's. His blue hands, with blue-stained fingernails, were folded across the black robe that had been treated with flour and bleached to look seriously weathered. His wild hair and beard were gray and white, and even his eyebrows were blanched.

"Pretty convincing, if I don't say so myself," said Max, standing up top and looking down at the dug-up grave and the alleged corpse of Oscar Newman.

"Yes," said David, "the light may be fading but it's certainly authentic looking."

"Damn straight," said Jack as he turned and headed back to the schoolhouse, shaking his head in disbelief. He was more than a little spooked by it all.

Max and David turned to say good night.

"Oscar," said David, "I am truly sorry for concocting this stupid lie. I honestly never thought it would play out like this."

"Pas de problème," Oscar mumbled. His mouth barely moved, for he certainly did not want to risk undoing any of the extreme makeup that was still drying all over his face. What if it cracked and peeled off in the morning? But there was no recourse now. As they say in Monte Carlo, *les jeux sont faits.*

He lay motionless as Max covered him over with the weathered top boards they had removed from the sides of David's schoolhouse. Then he heard the few short rusty nails David had recovered being hammered into the boards that were now just inches in front of his face.

The darkness was suffocating, despite the air holes drilled in the rear panel. For very few of the late evening's rays penetrated even the upper inches of the rectangular shaft of red-brown dirt that now formed the walls of the grave, a grave that was to have been Senento's own private and eternal resting place. Oscar's remorse at having violated this sacred space was second only to the strangling concept that Elizabeth Le Clerc, his beloved Elizabeth, was about to marry Peter Dermenjian. And no doubt she was carrying his child.

He closed his eyes, listening to the clumps of dirt being shoveled onto the rickety casket. Each load landed with a thud just above his feet and shins. The sensation of being buried alive, of being left for dead in the middle of the alleged cradle of humankind, sent such chills through his body that he briefly considered bolting. He had never before experienced claustrophobia. But if ever there was occasion for such a feeling, this was it. What worried him most was whether the tears seeping uncontrollably out of the corners of his eyes would cut gullies into the near-perfect death mask and reveal this deception for what it was—a disrespectful high-stakes gamble, a bluff so irreverent and cowardly that he felt himself trembling. It would be a very long night indeed.

He heard Max bid him good night and state that they would give him plenty of warning as the photo brigade approached in the morning, assuming they arrived as scheduled. Oscar grunted a crude good night, then all went silent. And the silence was suffocating, along with the absolute darkness.

He lay still for quite some time, daring not to move. Yet his legs were aching, and though there was very little room for maneuvering, he managed to turn slightly onto his side and curl up a bit, craning his neck toward the air holes. The scent of his gravely bunk mate rotting below was still strong, but his olfactory senses were gradually getting used to it.

The initial panic wore off slowly. With an ample supply of air, a touch of wiggle room, he clung to a fairly delusional sense that this one night lying deep within a grave deep within the Great Rift Valley of East Africa would buy him his freedom, freedom from pursuit by a man who would most certainly threaten him with torture, if not death, to obtain the coordinates of the long-lost Dermenjian diamonds. Yes, the cursed Dermenjian diamonds which, as Francis had explained, issued from the very depths of the earth, deep within the mantle, eons ago. He remembered the eerie feeling of staring down at the remnant hot spring that may have served as a vent for the diamond-rich kimberlite pipe, wishing he could somehow follow the gushing hot spring to its very source.

But six feet down in this grave, far from said hot spring, was as deep as he was going to get. And it was plenty deep. He thought about the walls of his grave and wondered what volcanic outbursts had created them. No doubt it was Lengai, with help from all the others along the Avenue of the Volcanoes, as Francis had called it, spewing ash all about. They were the ones that had exploded so long ago and buried that poor father and his son at Laetoli. And buried all those skulls in Olduvai. He again pictured that father and son scampering across the ancient savannah as the ashfall began. But soon it was him, Oscar Newman, holding out an arm, sheltering his progeny as they ran through a dust cloud filled with tiny fragments of hard rock that stung like a million bees. Breathing was very difficult. Wild animals were stampeding all around them, lions growling and wildebeest grunting loudly. Yet the rock dust kept on pouring down. And then running became harder. They tried to keep up. But the boy could run no more, so Oscar just hunkered down on top of him, sheltering him, as the dust and rock grew deeper, and deeper, until they both fell asleep.

Oscar tossed and turned within the confines of his meager casket the remainder of the night, dreaming bizarre dreams of life on the savannah as it may have been way back prior to the emergence of *Homo sapiens*. He even dreamed that he found his own fossilized skull down in an Olduvai-like gorge. It looked like all the other dusty and broken fossilized skulls but somehow he knew it was his, especially when it began speaking to him, saying, "Hello, Oscar, how are you?" It was all most disturbing. Yet it was far less disturbing than the events of the next morning.

Much as expected, a Jeep drove up to David's schoolhouse at the crack of dawn. Quite unexpected, however, was the sight of Captain Olengi himself at the wheel and the man known as Banyon beside him. David threw on his black robe and stepped outside to greet them. Max reached for the shovel he'd left by the door.

"Good morning," David shouted, retracing what were becoming some all-too-familiar steps toward this Captain Olengi.

"Good morning," said the captain as he stepped forward to shake David's hand. "And thank you for your cooperation in this delicate matter."

David simply shook his head. "This is most irreverent," he replied rather solemnly. "But if there are any questions regarding the fate of Oscar Newman, I want them to be settled once and for all. I have enough to deal with, given this refugee crisis, and I don't want any more skeptics or CNN reporters popping in to inquire any further about poor Dr. Newman."

"Then may we assume that the corpse is available for viewing?" said the captain.

"Not quite," said Max, walking toward them with shovel in hand. "We ran out of daylight last night, but we're real close to having the coffin exposed. Give me about fifteen minutes."

Captain Olengi looked over at Banyon.

"I'll help you," said Banyon, Jocko's so-called witness, who was carrying an expensive-looking camera.

"Sure thing," said Max, not smiling in the least.

And so they strode off toward the cemetery, leaving David alone with Captain Olengi. These two looked at one another and, realizing there was nothing further to discuss, hastened after Max and Banyon the mercenary.

"Max," shouted David, much louder than necessary, "wait for us!"

It wasn't quite loud enough, however, to awaken Oscar, who continued not only to sleep but to snore quite profoundly. Max heard a burst of loud snorts emanating from the exposed grave when they were but twenty yards or so away.

"I suggest you all wait here," he said. "I just want to make sure there weren't any visitors during the night, if you know what I mean."

They understood. A few boards standing between hunger and an aging human corpse would be nothing to so many carnivores of the savannah. Captain Olengi nodded his approval. As Max advanced he made some loud noises, the kind designed to scare animals away. The only animal he managed to scare, however, was Oscar, who awoke with such a start he hit his head on the casket board above him. But in an instant he knew the game was afoot. He reached down beneath his black robe and felt for the corks Max had installed. He grasped them one by one and yanked them free, careful to keep them concealed beneath his billowing robe.

The stench was overpowering. Oscar tried to hold his breath but it was not possible. He still needed to breathe. Yet the horrid odor he thought he'd grown accustomed to came on with such force and such foulness it was all he could do to keep from retching. But he knew he must hold steady. It would not be long until the whole charade would be over. Max was already shoveling away the last bits of dirt that had covered the lower part of the casket.

But then came a sensation, something crawling up his ankle, and on up his leg. Then a similar sensation on his other leg. Whatever kind of creepy crawly they were, a host of them were soon busy exploring underneath his black robe, crawling across his stomach and up his chest. With every breath he experienced a new wave of them, and with every new wave the foul stench grew stronger. Oscar, trying not to panic, realized what had happened. Some kind of beetle or scarab that had been feasting on the remains of his bunk mate had discovered fresher game up top. Completely to Oscar's horror, they came bustling up from beneath the robe onto his neck. Once they climbed onto his face, however, he felt nothing. Of course! Whatever they were, the flour-water-berry-ash mixture that made up the death mask seemed to attract them. But there was nothing he could do. Max was already starting to pry the top boards off.

"This should do it," said Max as he pried the last nail loose. "You had better stand back. The odor could be pretty overwhelming."

Banyon readied his camera. Max lifted the lid of the coffin and let out a loud shriek as he propped it open for all to see. And what they saw was not at all what Max or David had expected to see. The grotesquely beautiful death mask Max had created was now nearly covered with large black beetles who appeared to be busily devouring the pseudoflesh on Oscar's face. As the lid came off, the beetles quickly scattered, revealing a face that appeared even more ghoulish than before. It was still an eerie bluish-gray, and the small bits the beetles had removed did not detract at all from the deathly tableau. Banyon clicked away with his camera while David and Captain Olengi covered their noses. Max climbed out of the hole and gazed back down at Oscar. It seemed his countenance was even stiffer than the night before, no doubt due to the terror of the sudden beetle invasion.

"Do you believe it now?" said Max, looking squarely at Banyon. The latter raised his head.

"It was never a matter of believing," he replied. "It was simply a matter of documentation."

"Then are you both now satisfied?" David demanded to know. "Can we now rebury this poor man before the stench attracts all the vultures and hyenas?"

Captain Olengi gave a nod of approval, looking a bit downcast, perhaps a tad ashamed he had been party to this early-morning intrusion. But these photos would certainly bring closure to all the demands by others, particularly the British government, to keep searching.

"Just one more thing," said Banyon. With that he set aside the camera and drew a pistol from his jacket, which he aimed right at Oscar. As he began to squeeze the trigger, David nearly tackled him. The bullet slammed into the side of the grave.

"What in God's name do you think you are doing?" he screamed. "Hasn't this man been through enough? How dare you attempt to inflict more damage on this poor man, a Nobel Peace Prize Laureate at that. Get out, both of you. This is my cemetery and you will leave now that you have your documentation."

Captain Olengi grabbed Banyon by the arm. "Come," he said. "Father Sebastian is right. There is no question in my mind that that is indeed Dr. Newman in this grave. Thank you for arranging the viewing."

All the while he held a handkerchief near his nose. The cork trick, aided by the flesh-eating beetles, had helped win the day. Captain Olengi had to nearly drag a rather distraught Mr. Banyon back to the Jeep. They came, they saw, and they concurred. Oscar Newman was long gone.

451

Chapter 55

As Peter and Elizabeth turned to face the congregation seated before the altar, beneath the tall Gothic arches of Sainte-Marie, they were nearly blinded by the flashes from dozens of cameras seeking to capture the moment, one many had thought would never arrive. There were so many skeptics who doubted that Peter Dermenjian, the wealthy and much renowned playboy of the Riviera and beyond, would ever succumb to any single woman, much less marry her. There was of course speculation concerning a possible festering fetus, but so far the story that had captured the headlines was how their respective losses had brought them together. There were cries of bravo, *félicitations*, and such as they made their way down the aisle while the bells of Sainte-Marie rang loud and clear, announcing to the entire countryside that they both had said "I do." And though she despised being so much the center of everyone's attention, Elizabeth knew that it was all a part of this grand charade, this awful act of deception that she still considered somehow essential to the well-being of the child within her.

Madame Le Clerc was so moved she could barely contain herself, daubing at her teary eyes with her handkerchief while rejoicing with all her friends and the other guests who approached her in droves. Limousine after limousine conducted the wedding guests to Peter's villa, where dozens of tables were set about on the large terrace that surrounded the pool. White linen and fresh roses adorned every table, and all featured elaborate place settings with enough dishes, glasses, and silverware to accommodate a four-course dinner.

And the dinner was excellent, thanks to André and his crew, lasting for hours and culminating with the arrival of an immense multitiered wedding cake shooting Roman candles high into the darkened sky. Most of the guests were by then highly inebriated. There were many toasts to the bride and groom, including one by Edouard, who praised his sister for having the sense to return to her homeland, despite the inconveniences. Dr. Meinz, well aware of Elizabeth's delicate condition, made a point of keeping Elizabeth's champagne glass full but only with nonalcoholic bubbly. No one suspected a thing. She even pretended to be slightly abuzz, often clinging to Peter for support.

But the next morning, as the distant bells of Sainte-Marie were calling the congregation to assemble for Sunday Mass, she wondered where he might be.

Certainly, she had not expected him to actually consummate the marriage. That was out of the question. For ever since she had shared with him the news of her pregnancy, he had treated her like a princess, doting on her, assuring her every comfort, including her own magnificent bedroom in the west wing, overlooking the Mediterranean. But he would no sooner shed his seed upon their developing fetus than set his villa on fire. Her uterus had become hallowed ground, the incubation chamber for what he hoped would be his son, his heir, someone who shared his blood and to whom he could entrust his fortune, as well as his never-dying quest for the mother lode of diamonds he knew lay somewhere out in the Great Rift Valley of East Africa.

She had slept poorly and now felt rather anxious. The wedding party had lasted nearly until dawn. Though she had turned in just past midnight, after most of the guests had departed, several of Peter's friends had carried on rather raucously well into the night. She had heard them splashing in the pool, singing quite drunkenly, and having a gay old time. Unable to sleep, she had peeked out her window and saw that a few of them were naked, including two young women she did not recognize. The others she knew from the embarrassing night on Peter's yacht. At least Peter hadn't been among them. But where had he been all night?

Tired of sifting through all the events that had occurred, or not occurred, over the last twenty-four hours, she put on a light robe and went in search of her new husband. She searched the main floor, the pool, and surrounding terrace. A few stragglers were still asleep on various lawn chairs. But Peter was nowhere in sight. None of the staff had seen him all morning. That could mean only one thing. Thankfully, she remembered the code for the elevator that led to his private quarters, his elaborate office suite up above. No doubt he had received an urgent call from one of his retail outlets or perhaps one of his diamond producers.

As the door opened she saw him seated at his desk, speaking to someone on the phone. Whatever was the matter, he was highly engaged in conversation and didn't even appear to notice she had entered the room. He was wearing a plaid robe and looked more than a tad hung over. Though unshaven and with his hair in disarray, he still looked quite handsome. She approached him quietly from the rear, intent on simply giving him a good-morning kiss on the cheek. After all, she was now his wife, for better or worse, till death did them part. But before she could get within a few feet of him, she saw emblazoned on the large computer screen that sat before him a most hideous and vile picture. She let out a scream that startled Peter

453

completely. Quite stunned to find his newly acquired spouse standing behind him, he hung up the phone immediately and turned off his monitor.

"What are you doing here?" he asked in a rather rough tone of voice. "You don't ever come in here without some warning."

Elizabeth was trembling and sobbing uncontrollably. For what she had just seen had indeed confirmed her worst nightmare.

"Listen," he said, taking hold of her hand. She snatched it away. "It needed to be done. Everyone, including you, needed confirmation that Oscar was indeed buried in that grave. The Kenyan government arranged for him to be exhumed so there would be no shadow of a doubt."

"How dare you!" she exclaimed. "How dare you do such a thing without consulting me!"

Elizabeth was so enraged and so distraught that she fled from the room, and before Peter could utter another word, she was descending in the elevator to return to her room to try to erase from her mind the horrible image of Oscar lying in his uncovered grave, looking oh so dead, with large insects gnawing at his face. She felt sick to her stomach as she found her bed once again and began to sob hysterically. When Peter knocked on her door, she screamed at him to go away.

"Please," he shouted, unable to force open the door she had locked behind her. "You must understand. I had nothing to do with this. And I also hope you will understand that it is only logical that such information, shocking and abhorrent as it is, would be shared with you and me. I was going to tell you once the wedding festivities were over and all our guests were gone."

It worked. For Elizabeth slowly rose from her bed and walked over to the door to let her husband in. She threw her arms around his neck, sobbing.

"I'm sorry," she said. "It's just so horrible. I wish I had never seen the photo."

"I was quite shocked as well," said Peter. "It arrived early this morning, the last thing I expected to find in my e-mail. But what is done is done. I suggest you rest some more. I'll have some breakfast sent to your room. I don't believe we're expected at your mother's until four o'clock, so just relax and try to come to terms with what we know for certain about Oscar's fate."

He stroked her long hair and kissed her on the cheek.

"I will try," she replied as she briefly rested her head on his shoulder. Then he stood up and left her to try to regain some sense of composure.

Once he was well clear of her, he began shouting orders to his staff. Then he returned to his study and dialed his number-one man, Banyon. Their conversation had been so rudely interrupted.

"Tell me again about the smell," Peter demanded. "Are you certain there wasn't some dead animal stuffed in that box along with him?"

Banyon assured him it was authentic, complete with flesh-eating bugs and a stench that could emanate only from one huge rotting carcass, that being Oscar's.

"Damn it to hell," said Peter as he rose and began pacing the room. Banyon was back on the speakerphone. "He was the link, the link to the diamonds. I wish that American had been a better doctor."

"He's working with the refugees now, in case we need him," said Banyon.

"What good could he be to us now?" Peter replied.

"Who knows? Perhaps Oscar confided in him. You know, in his dying moments."

"Doubtful," said Peter. "But nevertheless, it would be good to keep tabs on him. In case he makes a break."

"Got it covered, boss," he responded.

"And what about that prospector?" Peter continued. "Why haven't you located him yet? Surely he was a party to all this. And that French missionary might know something, too."

"Perhaps," said Banyon. "The old prospector's disappeared."

"Well, find him, damn it. He could be off filing a claim with the Ministry of Mining for all we know."

"In which country, Kenya or Tanzania?" Bandon replied. "Could be either one."

"Well, at least we know the route they took on their way to Natron, more or less. Only, the reconnaissance work so far hasn't turned up anything other than old fossil beds. It's time to do some seismic work."

"It could be tough to get the permits. Lots of wildlife sanctuaries."

"Don't make me laugh. Every bureaucrat has his price, especially in the Rift Valley. And besides, that's why I pay you so handsomely. To change people's minds."

"Right. But we're talking about world class. The Mara, the Serengeti, Ngorongoro. No way you could get away with blowing shot lines out there."

"My geophysical team thought they saw some anomalies in the vicinity of Lengai from the magnetic surveys. It's geologically impossible, if you ask me. But it's worth checking out. Besides, nobody ever goes there."

"That's right," said Banyon, "just the millions of flamingos that breed out on Lake Natron."

Peter laughed. "Right," he responded. "And I doubt very much they'll be signing any petitions."

Safe within her room, Elizabeth found herself once again drawn down into that deep, dark cavern in her heart where all her feelings about Oscar swirled about in one great, ugly tangle of pain and disbelief. It was a place she had frequented less and less as her wedding day approached, comforted by the belief that she carried Oscar's child within her. But then she saw the horrid photo and all the wretched certainty it conveyed. For throughout the entire ordeal, ever since he had gone missing, she had clung to a modicum of hope, small as it might have been, but hope that somehow Oscar might still be alive. But now she had seen *the* photograph. There could be no doubt it was Oscar, albeit a slightly decomposed shadow of his former self, lying in an uncovered casket deep within his grave, being eaten by large insects!

Try as she might, she could not erase the revolting image from her mind. She cried and cried into her pillow until it was drenched with tears. How cruel to have this confirmation of her worst fears arrive the day after the wedding, at a time when she should be feeling joy and elation and, in theory, a sense of love and belonging. Yet in some ways, this shocking news helped to reaffirm the course she had chosen. With all hope of ever seeing Oscar alive again completely crushed, the knowledge that their child would have a legitimate, if not genetically correct, father gave her some sense of well-being. And so what if she had agreed to a prenuptial arrangement that allowed her rights to but a very small portion of Peter's assets in the not-so-unlikely event of an eventual divorce? At least the child would be well situated, conceivably a billionaire! And if it meant tolerating Peter's sexual exploits while she took her place as the mother in residence, so be it. She had all she needed and then some, including a well-equipped room and part-time nurse for Oscar's stroke-impaired mother down the hall. In fact, she thought to herself, she needed to pay Eleanor a visit and tell her the sad news.

She slipped on her bathrobe and tiptoed down the hall. She found Eleanor seated in her wheelchair. A pretty young nurse had just washed her thin, graying mess of hair and was busy drying and brushing it.

"Bonjour, Madame," she said as she plucked a few withered strands of hair from her brush.

"Bonjour," replied Elizabeth. The nurse gave a slight curtsy before gathering up the combs and brushes and abandoning the two of them.

"Hello, Eleanor," she began as she pulled up a chair and grabbed hold of her withered left hand.

"How are you feeling?" she asked, not expecting in the least any sort of reply or sign of comprehension. Eleanor sat there as always, slightly hunched over and listing to her right, the side most heavily affected by the paralyzing series of strokes she had suffered years ago. Her face was nearly rigid, and the bits of saliva she let dribble from the corner of her mouth from time to time always landed safely in a plastic bowl that was cleaned and replaced regularly.

"I have more sad news about Oscar," she began. And then she proceeded to explain that photographic evidence had been found. "He is indeed buried in that grave down in Kenya, in Father Sebastian's cemetery. I am so sorry I ever agreed to let him go on that 'pilgrimage,' as he called it, to the cradle of humanity. I can only hope that he has found his peace."

She paused there to look into Mrs. Newman's eyes, searching for some glimmer of consciousness, of comprehension. Finding none, she continued on.

"Eleanor," she said, "I have some other news as well. News that you may find comforting."

Again, and as always, there was not the slightest trace of interest in what Elizabeth was saying to her.

"I am pregnant," she continued. "I am pregnant with Oscar's child."

If ever there was news that should have brought her rocketing to attention, this was it. But still no reaction whatsoever.

"But it is a secret. Peter thinks it's his child. That's the only reason he married me. And it's the only reason I married him! I know it's a wicked thing to do, but I did it for Oscar and for our child. I just could not bear the thought of having his baby out of wedlock and of bringing another fatherless baby into this world. I hope you will understand and that you will forgive me."

More tears were now rolling down Elizabeth's cheeks while Eleanor Newman sat stone-like. Elizabeth stood up and wheeled her over near the window, where she could gaze out at the Mediterranean and watch the yachts and other pleasure boats cut foamy wakes in the azure sea. She kissed her on her head and then left her there, knowing her secret would be safe.

They left for Balgères at half past three. Peter held her hand firmly during the entire ride. Sitting in the back of the sleek limousine, Elizabeth tried to compose herself sufficiently in preparation for the onslaught of embraces, congratulations, and kisses on her cheeks that simply had to be repeated at every new encounter with the shrinking wedding party.

They arrived at Madame Le Clerc's home after nearly all the guests had arrived. But before they could even get inside, Edouard emerged, looking quite agitated.

"Elizabeth," he said as he embraced her quickly and nodded toward Peter. "I must speak with you alone."

"What is it?"

"Meet me out in the rose garden as soon as you can get away from this seriously over liquored mob. And watch out for Father Brodard. He's already half soused."

She gave her brother a painful smile before retreating to find Peter navigating through a long line of guests consisting of Elizabeth's closest family members and, as Peter had none, his closest business associates and Riviera cronies. Several were clearly Middle Easterners, wearing diamond-studded turbans.

Madame Le Clerc stood by the hearth, Father Brodard by her side. Peter struggled to get through the welcoming line so he could pay his respects to his new mother-in-law.

"Madame Le Clerc," he said as he took her right hand and bowed down to kiss it. "How nice to see you again."

Madame lowered her head and smiled politely. Then came Elizabeth.

"Bonjour, Maman," she said as they exchanged bisous, cheek for cheek.

Father Brodard then proceeded to do the same, though it seemed he leaned in a bit heavily, possibly attracted by Elizabeth's new runaway breasts that she had tried to conceal beneath her billowing white pants suit.

She left them to converse with Peter and, sensing the coast was clear, headed for the garden. Dr. Meinz intercepted her on the way and handed her a fresh flute of her own special bubbly.

Once clear of the crowd, she located Edouard at the far edge of the garden. He was pacing nervously.

"All right," she said. "What news do you have that I don't already know about? I have seen the photograph. Nothing can top that."

Edouard turned to face her. He was clearly distressed. "Take a look at this," he said as he handed her a Marseille tabloid with the all-too-familiar photo of Oscar in his grave juxtaposed with a photo of the two newlyweds traipsing down the aisle.

"It's utterly tasteless," he said, "but I thought I should show it to you before you see it for yourself."

Elizabeth looked at him and then at the full-color spread on the front page of this rag, which clearly showed Peter and her walking arm in arm down the aisle. They were both smiling for the cameras, making a most fetching couple. But immediately adjacent, and at the same large scale, was the repulsive photo of Oscar she was trying so hard to forget, until the dinner was over at least. But there he was again, all deathly blue-gray and withered and crawling with flesh-eating bugs, beneath a large headline that read *"Elle a bien choisi!"*

"Bien choisi?" she said, quite furious as she teared up once again. "As if I had any choice in what happened to Oscar! How can they be so cruel! Whatever you do, don't let Mother see it."

"It's too late," he replied. "Aunt Rose called her this morning as soon as she spotted it. You know how they are, these sisters. You may as well assume everyone here has seen it or heard about it."

He paused, awaiting a reaction. Seeing no change in her expression, he charged ahead.

"And speaking of Mother," he resumed, "when are you going to tell her the big news?"

She did not reply. Her gaze was fixed on the photo, on the image of Oscar, her one-time true love—while he was alive, at least, and while he was not traveling all over the world without her, often putting his life in danger. To wit.

"Elizabeth," he repeated, "when are you going to tell her the news?"

459

She looked up, tears again sliding down her pretty cheeks. "In a month or so, once I know the fetus is truly viable. So far the signs are good. But right now, I just need to get through today. Can you help me?"

Edouard stepped forward and embraced her. "Here," he said, handing her a delicately scented handkerchief. "Dry your eyes and then follow me into the house. You can duck into the powder room off the kitchen and try to recompose yourself. I'll make sure you're not bothered. Do you need any mascara?"

She smiled and hugged him; then they headed off to face the diminished collection of wedding guests, knowing it would all be over soon. No more embracing, no more sloppy kisses, and no more pretending. Just getting down to leading a new life, one that would be Oscar-free, except for one thing. Deep inside she believed was a goodly piece of him, slowly growing, slowly developing, a mass of cells busily dividing and dividing, differentiating into little arms and legs and organs. Yes, the miracle of life stirred within, governed by a presumed mélange of her genes and Oscar's. And armed with that knowledge, she knew she could withstand just about anything, even Father Brodard's lingering bisous.

Chapter 56

Never in her wildest dreams could Elizabeth have imagined that at that very moment Oscar was not only very much alive but preparing to plead his case before Joseph. It had taken several hours to recover from the shock of the horrid night he'd just spent in the tight-fitting casket, straining for sufficient air that reeked of death. The flesh-eating beetles crawling up his legs and over his large torso and onto his face had nearly undone him. Never before had he been forced to repress such a powerful urge to simply scream out loud. It had taken all his willpower to just lie there while those foul little creatures nibbled at his face. David's explanation that the beetles weren't really interested in eating him, that they were simply females rushing to lay their eggs in the high-protein death mask, did nothing to comfort him. He was still shaking even after the mask had been scraped off and washed away in David's solar-powered shower. And the gunshot! Had no one seen him tense up like a suddenly petrified corpse? Thankfully, all eyes had turned toward Banyon as David pushed him away from the grave, causing the bullet to lodge in the earthen sidewall instead of inside Oscar's body.

And while he had been able to sleep some, he could not erase from his mind the dreamed-up images of being buried alive under so much falling ash, like the Laetoli father and son, and seeing his own fossilized skull back at Olduvai Gorge. Perhaps it was all because his entire life was now imploding on him, all his dreams falling apart and raining down on him in waves of misery and disbelief.

But the deception had worked better than any of them could have imagined. And somehow, by the following day, he had come up with a new plan. Though a bit short term, it was nonetheless a way to remain well out of sight while trying to be of some service, of some use to the Maasai, as long as he was still their prisoner. And most of all, it was a way to repay poor Senento, who, despite being dead, had just saved his life.

"I doubt very much Joseph and the elders will agree," said David as they traced their way eastward through the savannah.

"I believe it's worth a try," said Oscar. "What do I have to lose, anyway? I've already lost everything I ever cared about, and I'm impotent to boot. Hell of a journey, this."

"Correction," said David, "you're not impotent. You're simply sterile. Certainly, you should know the difference."

"Of course," said Oscar. "But there really is no difference. For I've lost the only woman I ever loved."

They found Joseph conferring with the elders beneath their primary council tree, a large acacia whose branches all grew up and outward in graceful arches and terminated for some strange reason at precisely the same height. The leafy, flat-roofed canopy commanded a good deal of shade.

David approached with caution, telling Oscar to stay behind and out of sight.

The sun was setting over the escarpment and shadows were long as Joseph, standing before a small wood fire, pounded a large stick covered with beads against the palm of his hand to emphasize his points. He and a few others had just returned from an excursion east of the Ewaso Ngiro. They had concluded it would be best to move the bulk of the cattle from here in their general vicinity, south of the Kalema Road and west of the Ewaso Ngiro, across the river. They would join the rest of the herds to the east where there was better grass, despite the closer proximity to the refugees. But they would leave the women and children behind here on the right bank, with proper protection. It would require a lot of preparation, building more manyattas and cattle kraals before such a redistribution of Maasai resources could take place. And crossing the Ewaso Ngiro via the bridge on the Kalema Road would be tricky. It would be necessary, though, to avoid losing cattle in the muddy riverbed, either from becoming too stuck or from being attacked by the odd crocodile.

David approached the congregation, bowing very humbly toward Joseph while apologizing for this interruption. To his amazement he saw that Ntanda was seated among the elders, next to Nilenga, the *laibon*. This was a first. But the moran would be essential for security as everyone crossed the bridge.

"A-itoomon," said Joseph. Welcome.

"I am so sorry to disturb you," David began. But before he could proceed, Nilenga objected. The elders conferred very briefly before Joseph turned to David and handed him the stick, the "talking stick." David now had the floor.

He bowed again as he accepted the smooth, club-like piece of wood adorned with beads on one end.

"I wish to confer with you regarding Oscar Newman," said David, in Maa of course. "He is extremely grateful for the kind treatment the Maasai have provided.

Were it not for the Maasai, both here in Kenya and nearby in Tanzania, he would surely be dead. He is nearly cured now and would like to be of service to the Maasai people."

David could tell by the grunting and facial expressions that he was hardly winning them over.

"There have been reports that this man, Oscar Newman," he continued, "killed our good friend Francis Dermenjian. I have told you and he has told you that he did not commit this crime. However, you wanted more proof before releasing him, as the government of Kenya had posted a warrant and a reward for his arrest. I am here to tell you that Captain Olengi of the Kenya National Police has informed me in no uncertain terms that Oscar Newman is no longer being sought for this heinous crime."

He paused and looked at everyone in turn, making eye contact to ensure each person had understood. Of course he neglected to tell them why Oscar Newman was no longer wanted for the crime, that Captain Olengi believed Oscar was dead. Ntanda began to speak but Joseph cut him off. David had the talking stick.

"Dr. Newman is therefore a free man," said David, resuming his discourse. "Free to return to his former life. However, he does not wish to do so. He wishes to remain here and to be of service to the Maasai in any way he can, to express and repay his gratitude for all you have done to save his life and return him to good health. He would especially like to help poor Senento's family, if there is anything he can do."

There he paused and waited for a reaction before passing the talking stick back to Joseph. The appropriate translation for "reciprocal altruism" eluded him, but he hoped he'd gotten the point across.

"He is still our prisoner up there," said Joseph, pointing toward the Nguruman Escarpment.

"I'm afraid not," said David. "He was abandoned and I brought him down to my schoolhouse for his own safety. And I have brought him with me."

Joseph glanced at Ntanda, chief of security, whose expression signaled it was news to him. "Where is he? And what does this mzungu have to offer? He knows nothing about the ways of the Maasai," said Joseph.

"Why, he is a doctor of medicine," David replied. Then, turning toward the shrubs behind which Oscar had been hiding while listening and wondering what in hell was going on, he shouted, "Oscar, please join us."

463

"We already have a white doctor," said Joseph.

"Yes, but he is helping the refugees."

"He has promised to come visit us when he can. What else can this man do?"

"He is a strong man. He can help you with your move. And he can help to tend to your herds."

That elicited a round of laughter, the idea of this *sapuk*, this fat man, trying to herd Maasai cattle! As Oscar approached the laughter got louder.

"At least any hungry lion would surely eat him before attacking the cattle!" said one of the elders, speaking out of turn.

Joseph scowled at him for breaking protocol, but David responded.

"Did you not know he has already survived a lion attack? He is a very brave man."

Had they forgotten? After all, they had insisted on seeing the scars. More muttering ensued until Joseph took charge once again.

"He knows nothing about life on the savannah. How would he protect himself, much less our cattle? There are many predators, and one must be quick and accurate with the spear."

This brought a rise out of Ntanda. He stood up and reached for the talking stick. Joseph eyed him suspiciously but ceded the floor. Ntanda looked around him, at the elders, at his father, and lastly at Oscar.

"He is very good with the spear," he said. This was clearly news, judging by the reaction of the elders. They began muttering again to one another, expressing their disbelief. He walked over to Oscar and handed him his spear.

"You will hit the tree," he said in English. He was pointing at the trunk of the council tree. Judging from the many scars on the trunk, Oscar was not the first to be put to such a test. He accepted the spear and the challenge. This was too easy! The tree trunk, a good three feet in diameter, was no more than twenty feet away. It was obvious the elders felt he could survive in Maasailand no better than they could survive the streets of London, but if this was all it took to prove otherwise, then so be it. But then Ntanda began walking away from the circle. He motioned to Oscar to follow. He didn't stop until they were at least fifty feet from the trunk. Now this truly was a challenge!

Oscar looked pleadingly toward David. David simply smiled back, as if to say, "Be careful what you wish for." The elders all scrambled to get clear of the tree, obviously not trusting in the least Oscar's ability to throw the spear anywhere near the target. David, too, stepped back, well out of harm's way. Oscar rubbed his hands together and looked around. All eyes were on him. He hefted the spear, trying to find its center of gravity. It was easy to find, as that part of the shaft exhibited a patina of sorts created by the sweat and oils from the palm of Ntanda's hand. Oscar felt the point with his left hand and slowly let it slide down the blade.

"A-pi!" he shouted, looking all about just to remind everyone that it was he who had sharpened all the spears.

Hearing this mzungu utter a word in Maa caused a few eyebrows to rise. But Ntanda was growing impatient.

"A-nang'," he shouted. Throw it, for God's sake!

Oscar hefted the spear again and rolled his shoulders up and down in a circular motion, trying to loosen up.

"A-nang'!" shouted Ntanda once again.

Oscar smiled back and took a deep breath. He looked at the trunk of the council tree. It was much farther away than the tree he and Olitunu used as a target in their little game of Maasai darts. But he had no choice. He bent his knees and took more deep breaths, repeating the motions he learned at the University of Glasgow that had enabled him to set the school record for tossing the javelin. He even closed his eyes, remembering just how it felt back then, in the heat of competition. After a few deep knee bends, bouncing up and down as he took more breaths, he twisted his body to the right, opened his eyes, and stared briefly at the large tree trunk now shimmering in firelight. Then his body uncoiled as his massive right arm came forward very rapidly over his head in a sudden, powerful whoosh of energy and let the spear fly away. It flew straight, with only a trace of an arc, and buried itself about chest high in the tree trunk with a loud thud. The shaft of the spear made a twanging noise as it vibrated like a tuning fork. The elders all gasped and began to chatter, clearly impressed. One of them shouted out to Ntanda to give it a go. He wisely abstained.

They all returned to the circle by the fire, everyone still marveling at what they had just witnessed. But Ntanda still held the talking stick.

"These are difficult times," he began, as if that were news. "As you have seen, this mzungu, as fat as he is, can throw the spear very well. And he wishes to be of service, especially to Senento's family. Senento's cattle are many. And they are being tended to by Senento's youngest son, Matthew, who recently became a moran. I believe I can speak for him. Matthew does not wish to tend to cattle. He wishes to join the rest of us, guarding the Kalema Road. We can use him, especially if we are to move our people and their belongings, particularly their cattle, along the Kalema Road."

At this point Joseph stood up and asked for the talking stick. Ntanda handed it over to his father. David looked on, quite stunned. Ntanda was the last person he had expected to serve as Oscar's champion, not after the way he had treated him as a prisoner. Oscar tugged at David's sleeve, clearly wanting to know just what the hell was going on. David again signaled to him to just sit tight and keep quiet.

"Yes, this man can throw a spear," said Joseph. "But what does he know about cattle?"

David quickly jumped up and requested the talking stick. "In his homeland he raises many sheep," he began. "He also tended to cattle in his youth. Let him work with Matthew for a while. At least give it a try. What have you got to lose?"

"Just all of Senento's cattle," Nilenga observed. He had thus far remained quiet.

"Let Matthew decide," Ntanda proposed.

Joseph, who still held on to the talking stick, mulled this over. It was getting late and there were far more important matters at hand. He looked at the others, awaiting any objections.

"So be it," he declared, hearing none. Then he declared the meeting adjourned.

The elders all gathered their blankets and pipes and tobacco pouches and began to shuffle off toward their respective manyattas. Oscar, the object of these latest deliberations, watched as they all departed. He sensed that it had gone well, especially since he had miraculously hit the target.

"Well," he said to David, "are you going to tell me what in hell just went on or keep me in suspense all night?"

"Come," said David, "I will explain. Let us return to my quarters and see what we can find to eat."

"Excellent idea," said Oscar, who was rubbing his chest wounds and wondering if he might not have ripped them open again with all that exertion. And as they departed, Ntanda was still struggling to remove his spear from the massive, knotty trunk of the council tree.

Chapter 57

As expected, Matthew was overjoyed when Ntanda approached him the following morning with the proposal. He was so pleased, in fact, that he immediately set off toward David's schoolhouse to meet the oversized mzungu who had offered to guard his father's cattle. At least he knew how to throw a spear, according to Ntanda. It was an opportunity he could not let pass. After all, the life of a moran was all about confronting danger. And while there was always the threat of lions, he had seen none in all the weeks he had been looking after his father's herd. Meantime, nearly all the other members of his age class, those circumcised before him, were busily employed protecting the Kalema Road. He had now been called up to the front lines, where he belonged, where all would see that he, too, was a true moran, a true Maasai warrior.

He knocked on the door of David's schoolhouse before either David or Oscar were awake. David stumbled to his feet and threw on his bathrobe.

"Eng'asak il murani," he said as he opened the door. He was very pleased to see Matthew standing tall in his orange shuka, clutching spear and shield. His ochre-plastered locks were relatively short for a moran, but his earlobes were newly adorned with beads and he displayed such an aura of newborn arrogance that David almost started laughing. *"A-jing',"* he said. Please enter.

Matthew held his ground. *"Kaji ol-o-ibori?"* he asked, wanting to know where the big white man was.

Before David could muster a reply Oscar was behind him, wrapped in an old blanket and rubbing the sleep out of his eyes.

"What's happening?" he said.

"Looks like it's time for you to be off to work," said David.

Oscar then recognized the young moran as Matthew, the Maasai boy suddenly turned young man thanks to the circumcision Max had performed on him months before, when Oscar had first arrived in Maasailand. It seemed he was taller and a bit more filled out around the shoulders. And he now possessed a certain swagger, an impatience.

"Come," he said, switching to English, "it is time for the cattle to graze. I must show you where. But first you must show me your scars so I know that you are a brave man."

Quite caught off guard, Oscar glanced at David, shrugged his shoulders, and lowered the blanket. His huge barrel chest bore the unmistakable scars, still scabbed over in a few places, that could have been inflicted only by a lion's claw.

"Does it still hurt?" he asked.

"It is nothing," Oscar replied.

"Then where is your spear? We must go."

David intercepted here and explained in Maa that Oscar did not own a spear.

"But Ntanda says he is very good with the spear. How can that be if he does not own one?"

"I'm sure Ntanda can lend him one. After all, he did sharpen them all."

"I will be there in a moment," said Oscar. He disappeared but returned fully clothed, which is to say wearing his tattered shorts and denim shirt that constituted all the clothing that he possessed.

"Non!" said David. "You cannot guard cattle dressed like that. You need to cover your entire body or you will be as red as a baboon's ass by noon. Wait here. I have another robe you can wear."

He disappeared briefly before returning with another of his priestly black robes. It was clean, unlike the last robe he had loaned Oscar, which he had ended up burning, covered as it was with ash, dirt, and dead beetles. Oscar threw the fresh robe over his head and let it settle all around his large body. David gave him a packet of biscuits, a wedge of cheese, a large bottle of water for the road, and a broad-brimmed black hat to keep the sun from frying his brain, again. Then he grasped Oscar by the shoulders.

"You're in for a real education, my friend."

"Yes," said Oscar, "I suppose you are right. But thank you, thank you for all you have done for me. I know I have been quite a bother."

"Think nothing of it. You are always welcome here."

And so Dr. Oscar T. Newman, inventor of the famous Newman Insert and long-lost recipient of the Nobel Peace Prize, embarked on his new career as a cowboy in priest's clothing deep in the wilds of the Great Rift Valley of East Africa. As he and Matthew strolled off into the sunrise, David simply shook his head.

"Incroyable," he said to himself. *"Incroyable!"* Then he headed back inside his humble quarters to brew some much-needed coffee.

By the time Matthew and Oscar reached the sprawling manyatta where Matthew lived, the only cattle that remained penned inside were Senento's. And they appeared none too happy to be the last ones out of the gate. A few of the women stared at Oscar with bewildered expressions. For this huge bearded man was draped all in black and was preparing to help herd over one hundred cattle, Senento's prized herd! Even the cattle appeared slightly spooked as they bounded for the open spaces, each one maintaining a wide berth around Oscar, while Matthew shouted out to the surging mass of bovine energy in his native tongue.

Soon they were walking briskly side by side through dry, open savannah that had been heavily grazed. Some of the cattle were beginning to trot, loping along at a pace Matthew considered excessive. They were clearly interested in reaching the grazing area as soon as possible.

"Akiti!" he shouted, and slow down they did. Then he turned toward Oscar. *"Akiti,"* he repeated, *"akiti."*

Oscar repeated the sounds a couple of times until Matthew nodded, signaling that was close enough. Oscar broke into a broad grin and Matthew smiled back. Maybe this would work out after all.

Then Matthew pointed to each of the cattle, calling out each one's name. He started with his favorites and indicated which calves belonged to which cows. Oscar listened and repeated the names and relations as best he could. Clearly, this would take a fair bit of repetition. So many of them looked exactly alike!

The sun was now well above Mount Kilimanjaro and it was growing hotter by the minute. Oscar felt the sweat rolling down his legs, beneath his black robe, and wondered if he had enough water to get through the day. Before them Lengai hovered in the distance. The air at the base of the great mountain shimmered, testament to the heat already rising steadily from Lake Natron, whose caustic surface lay somewhere beyond the huge swamp fed by a dying Ewaso Ngiro.

The terrain was dipping ever so slightly to the south, with fewer and fewer clusters of thorn trees. As they marched on they also saw fewer and fewer of their Maasai comrades tending their herds. Occasionally, they would spot a few Maasai woman carrying large bundles of firewood on their heads. Matthew would shout hello to them and they would raise a hand in greeting. Finally, they reached a spot where a small tributary to Natron gave rise to riparian woodland. The shady area beckoned and Oscar was quite happy to see the cattle heading in that direction.

The cattle quickly dispersed and settled down to grazing on the odd stems and grassy leaves left over from the previous day's ruminations. Matthew paused under the shade of a thorn tree, leaned upon his spear, and raised one leg, flamingo style. Oscar stared at his companion, his young teacher in the art of Maasai animal husbandry, and sought to achieve a similar state of repose. He failed miserably, of course, barely able to raise one foot off the ground let alone cock it against the opposite meaty thigh. He settled, after several attempts, for simply leaning on the spear Ntanda had indeed provided. Matthew, on the other hand, stood as still as a reed in calm waters. His lithe frame was delicately balanced over his left leg, which was locked at the knee, while his right foot sat cradled in the lean mass of muscle along his inner thigh, just beneath the bottom of his short orange shuka. His right hand held his spear while his left hand clutched his ornate shield, close by the small sword sheathed within his Roman-like scabbard. Oscar thought he recalled reading somewhere, or perhaps Francis had told him, that the moran actually resembled quite closely, in terms of attire and hairstyle, the Roman legions of old. He wondered if there might somehow be a connection. Regardless, there was no doubt whatsoever in his mind that he had walked not only several miles in distance but far back in time, to a realm that was, in fact, timeless. For the tending of cattle on the open range was as timeless as human civilization itself. And what struck Oscar most was how easily and how adeptly Matthew slipped into the role of eternal protector, content to stand and observe with a nurturing eye and weapons at the ready, while these large yet scrawny purveyors of meat, milk, and of course roofing material settled into their grazing routine, nibbling away and occasionally mooing at their neighbors.

Though shaded by overhanging branches, Oscar's view of Lengai was not obscured in the least. He could not stop staring at it as he gazed past Matthew.

"Sidai," he said, pointing at Lengai. It was one of the first words Sarna had taught him.

"Yes, it is beautiful. It is the Mountain of God, Engai," Matthew replied in English. Fortunately, and largely thanks to David, Matthew's command of the English language was surprisingly good, which explained why the elders had never made an issue out of the fact that Oscar's command of the Maa language was next to nil.

470

"Do you know the legend?"

"No," said Oscar, "please tell me."

Matthew explained, using simple words, how long ago Engai had had three children. He gave them each a gift. The first child received an arrow to hunt animals. He gave the second a hoe to help grow food. And to the third child he gave a stick to help herd cattle. He was the father of the Maasai.

"What was his name?"

"Natero Kop," said Matthew, smiling.

"Natero Kop," said Oscar. "He must have been something else."

Matthew gave a quizzical look. Something else?

"How did it happen?" Matthew inquired, quickly changing subjects. He was pointing to Oscar's chest. Oscar understood that his only real credibility as a potential Maasai herdsman stemmed from his having survived a lion attack. Big medicine. Oscar pointed toward Gelai.

"Over there," he said, "I was trapped. A moran killed the lion as he was attacking me. With his spear, right through the heart."

Matthew's eyes grew wide as Oscar pretended to launch his spear. "What moran did this?"

"His name was Olabon. He lives over there, in Tanzania."

Or so he assumed. He was again pointing at Gelai, whose volcanic shoulders rose high above the swampland to the south and east of them.

"Maybe I will meet him one day," said Matthew with a hopeful smile. "But please, tell me. Why do you stay here in Maasailand? Why do you not return to your country? This is no place for a white man like you."

Oscar continued to lean on his spear while taking in the incredibly wild and beautiful scenery. He admired the rolling savannah dotted with thorn trees and the odd ungulate; the volcanoes to the south that were perhaps the original source of all human flesh and bones; and the scrawny cattle, who, thanks to the Maasai, managed to eke out an existence in this inhospitable country, sharing its resources in a strained harmony with all the wild creatures. Finally, he let his gaze come to rest on this magnificently appointed young Maasai warrior, who was teaching him how to guard cattle.

"A good question," he replied, "one that is difficult to answer. I think the best I can say is, I came here to complete my education."

It was a rather strange answer to a fairly simple question. Matthew chose not to pursue it. These mzungus are bizarre creatures, he thought. But he also knew that, whatever his motivation, Oscar was now his ticket out of the manyatta and hopefully into some real danger, where he could prove himself a warrior.

It was a long day, but it passed quickly as Matthew continued to point out the names of the cattle, the Maasai names for the plants they would eat, and all the animals they saw. Oscar tried and tried to repeat it all properly, often causing Matthew to break into laughter. They saw giraffes, *il-meuti*, and zebra, *il-osirat*, and many Thomson's gazelles, *ink-oiliin*. Fortunately, they saw no lions, *il-ng'atunyo*. It was difficult enough to simply pronounce the Maasai name for the king of beasts let alone even imagine dealing with him face to face. The very thought of such an encounter, especially all on his own, sent shivers down his spine as Oscar recalled the horror of the attack he had suffered months ago. Had he really thought this all through? Reciprocal altruism, such a concept!

They returned to the manyatta at the end of the day, all the cattle sufficiently fed and, most importantly, safe and accounted for. The western sky was glazed in orange as they entered through an opening in the thorny brush that otherwise surrounded this tiny village that Senento and his three wives had shared with three Maasai junior elders and their respective wives and children, many of whom were still quite young. As the youngest of Senento's brood, which numbered well over a dozen, Matthew was embarrassed to still be living here. He should be long gone, guarding the Kalema Road.

Once the cattle were all securely penned in, he showed Oscar to his new temporary home, explaining that this was where his father, Senento, and his mother, Meko, had lived. It looked like a standard-issue Maasai home, although it sorely needed a roof job. Matthew explained that Meko, who was Senento's second wife, had been living ever since Senento's passing a few doors down in a new and smaller stick, mud, and dung dwelling built especially for the senior widow. It was customary, he explained.

They stooped inside and he showed Oscar a newly cured cowhide lying on a fresh pile of straw that would be his new bed. There was even a clean leather-bound pillow. It was dark but not as rank as Oscar had feared. He lay down on the bed and discovered much to his delight that it was as comfortable as any bed he had known since venturing into Maasailand. Matthew told him to rest, that he would call him when dinner was ready. It was all Oscar needed to hear. He had consumed the meager rations of bread and cheese from David well before noon. Now he was starving, but not so starving that he couldn't sleep. It had been a very long day indeed, and rarely in his life had he walked so much and certainly never before in such a challenging and deteriorated state of health, both in body and in mind.

As he exited the home of his deceased father, Matthew was surprised to find his mother, Meko, waiting for him. He greeted her with head bowed, a manner unbecoming a proud young moran. But she was, after all, still his mother. And he could tell immediately that she was quite pissed.

"Ime en-kirurare enk-aji minyi!" she shouted.

She was telling him that Oscar could not sleep in his father's home. Matthew smiled at her, took her by the arm, and led her back toward her own new house. He knew she would come around in time.

But not in time for supper, which consisted of a soup made from animal fat mixed with water and featured chunks of cow kidney floating on top. There was also some day-old cornmeal soaked in a mixture of cow's blood and sour milk. And there was more sour milk to be had as the gourd was passed around. Oscar, accustomed to eating strange foods with people from all sorts of strange cultures, smiled at Meko as he inhaled the rations set before him.

"Supat!" he declared as he finished off his bowl of watered-down fat. *"Ashe naleng!"*

No, it really wasn't good, at least not to him, but that didn't matter. Telling her it was and thanking her profusely did matter. Oscar could see she was not comfortable with his suddenly usurping her deceased husband's home and his newly restored bed. But he needed a place to lie low as much as Matthew needed a way to be sprung from this boyhood trap, a trap created when his father had stepped forward hoping to promote peace but instead received a bullet in his gut. He smiled at her again but she returned nothing but scowls. As soon as his wooden bowl was empty, she snatched it away. A second helping was definitely not an option. Though his taste buds were relieved, his stomach cried for more.

Meko began talking to no one in particular as she scraped what little was left in the bowls into the fire. Matthew translated.

"She does not understand why you are here," said Matthew, "nor do I. So I cannot explain. She says if you want more education, you should go see the teacher, David."

473

Oscar laughed. It was time to come clean. "Tell her the Maasai saved my life and I wish to repay them. Tell her," he continued after a moment of reflection, "that Senento saved my life."

Matthew jumped up. "What are you saying? You told me a Tanzanian warrior saved you. What has my father to do with this?"

Oscar stared at the ground. "I believe he saved my life as well. He helped to hide me. There are very bad people looking for me."

"When? My father has been dead for many days now."

Oscar looked up at Matthew, who was now standing over him looking more confused than ever. Oscar stood up as well and began to pace before the fire.

"What does it matter? I believe he saved my life and I wish to be of service to his family to repay my gratitude. Is that so confusing?"

"Then who is looking for you?"

"The man who killed Francis Dermenjian."

"Why does he look for you?"

Oscar looked Matthew straight in the eye. "Because I saw him do it."

Oscar learned a great deal over the course of the next several days. Matthew proved to be a good teacher and Oscar was the best of students. He listened carefully and repeated commands to the cattle not only with credible pronunciation but also with the proper gusto. And he railed at himself whenever he mistook one cow or calf for another.

They traveled in a slow, elliptical orbit through this small, secluded valley, advancing a bit every day. As Matthew explained, they would return to the same piece of ground about every two weeks. That way the grass would be recovered and a second helping, and presumably a third and perhaps a fourth, would be possible before the land turned brown again, well after the long rains had subsided. Oscar marveled at how the wild birds would follow the cattle's progress, working over the cow pies and getting fat on the grubs and fly larvae that thrived in the rich organic droppings. Matthew explained that grazing in this way is actually good for the grasses as well as the wildlife. At least that's what he had learned in David's school, and it seemed to work much better than the old practice of letting the cattle graze on one area until it was nothing but barren earth. It made sense, for the wildlife were plentiful and they did not seem particularly bothered by the cattle. It was as if they'd made their peace long ago. There were twisty-horned eland and white-striped zebra, ungainly wildebeest and graceful gazelles, prancing giraffes and—much to Oscar's delight—defiant baboons. They generally appeared in packs and put on quite a show, with their fiercely whiskered heads and their colorful bottoms alternately popping up and down amid the remaining tall grasses.

Back in his new home Oscar continued to try to win Meko over, but to no avail. She fed him begrudgingly, along with Matthew, but his portions always seemed smaller. Thankfully, the bed was still comfortable, and so far she hadn't tried to kick him out of the house she once shared with Senento.

As he lay sleeping after a long day of herding cattle, all the while enduring a crash course in Maa, Oscar was awakened by the sound and, unfortunately, the wetness of a downpour, perhaps the last gasp of the long rains. It was a very rude awakening. He tried in vain to move his bed out of the way of the dripping purée of rainwater mixed with freshly hydrated mud and dung. He spent the night huddled in the one small dry spot he could find.

The rain finally paused early in the morning. The center of the manyatta was a sea of mud and the cattle were not happy. Oscar stepped out to survey the scene and soon found Matthew standing beside him. Matthew took one look at Oscar, who was covered with roofing sludge, and burst out laughing. But he offered to take the cattle out on his own that day, allowing Oscar to see to the leaky roof and perhaps clean himself up a bit.

Left all alone, Oscar looked about, sizing up the situation. Apparently, his was not the only Maasai dwelling to have sprung a leak. Women were busy scooping up handfuls of mud and mixing it with the cow dung that was abundantly available and applying it to their respective rooftops. He noticed that the men were nowhere to be seen, and he knew they would certainly not be caught dead slinging the mud-dung concoction. That was woman's work. Yet Oscar saw that as far as his leaky roof was concerned, that was his problem. He tried to catch Meko's attention, pointing to the rooftop of her former abode. As he was covered in filth, there was no need for further explanation. Meko looked at him and merely shook her head as she continued to scrape away at a fresh hide in need of curing. Evidently, her newly constructed quarters had withstood the downpour. It was clearly up to Oscar to fend for himself.

It all seemed simple enough. Just grab a handful of mud and a handful of fresh manure, rub them together as if making a mud pie like he did as a child, and apply as needed to the affected area. Easier said than done. For the hole in the roof was on top and getting to it would require a ladder or some form of support. And heavy as he was, the idea of climbing on top of the roof, as the women did, and risking caving in the entire structure was not a chance worth taking. It was bad enough to have usurped Meko's former home. To completely destroy it would be disastrous.

He reached as high as he could with his right hand full of mud dung, only to have it slide down his arm. His black robe was already covered with the stuff, but now it had found a way inside, via the billowing sleeve, and it was sticking to his ribs. Turning around, he watched to see how the women were faring. Almost all of those who were in the roof-patching mode were on top of their houses, slathering away. How did they get up there? He thought he saw them looking at him from time to time. And they were all laughing.

Smiling back at them, he tried to heave a generous portion of mud doo up near the suspect hole in the roof. It splattered all over. Perhaps a bit more clay, he thought, to give it more cohesion. But the soil here was quite sandy. What to do? There were a few crude stools about but nothing substantial and tall enough to stand on.

After a few moments of contemplation, he sat down on a ragged hide near the entrance to his new domicile. How could such a simple life suddenly become so complicated? Try as he might to resist the temptation, his thoughts turned to Elizabeth. And the thought of her pregnant with Peter Dermenjian's child, in lieu of his, ripped through his heart once again.

How long he sat there staring at the ground he could not say. But luckily, a few of the women came to his rescue, perhaps out of pity. Without uttering a word, three of the local wives who had completed their respective home repairs wandered over and attended to Oscar's roof problem. It wasn't until Oscar heard them chattering as they helped one another position themselves that he realized what was happening. They were fixing his roof! *His* roof, in *his* new home! He stood up and marveled at how easily and how adroitly they dealt with the problem at hand. They helped one another get in the right position and sent up handfuls of doo mud like a bucket brigade. In ten minutes the job was done. And luckily the sun shone bright once again, promising that the new patching compound might be cured and sealed before the next set of downpours.

Once back on the ground they approached Oscar, who had been saying "ashe naleng" over and over, thanking them profusely for their kindness. They were middle aged but seemed quite fit, despite being snaggle-toothed with droopy breasts. And they were certainly in good spirits, laughing and pointing at Oscar like he was the most ridiculous sight they had ever laid eyes on. Meko had of course refrained from the merriment, still occupied along with a couple of young girls with her hide curing. Oscar noticed her occasional disdainful glances in the direction of her former home, where her neighbors were engaged in helping the large, dark-haired stranger who had wandered into their camp.

Now they were all pointing at Oscar's filthy frock and his unkempt curly locks and scraggly beard that hadn't been trimmed in many weeks. The once jet-black robe David had loaned him was now covered in dirt from the savannah and the dung and mud from on high. It was even in his hair. The tallest of the women approached him, sizing him up.

"Ol-ojuju," she said, *"a-iture in-kishu."* The two other women reeled with laughter at this, calling him the "hairy one" and suggesting he might scare the cattle looking like that.

Oscar smiled and then repeated "ashe naleng" a couple of more times, which evoked even more laughter. He looked deep into the tall woman's eyes, squinting in the bright morning sunlight. What the hell was she saying?

Then she grabbed Oscar by the beard and made like she wanted to cut it off with her hand. And then the penny dropped. She was telling him he was long overdue for a shave!

"Iyie?" he asked, pointing at her with one hand while pretending to trim his beard with the other. Do you want to do it? This brought on more laughter and evidently encouragement from her two friends. The woman, whose face was long and deeply furrowed like Joseph's, smiled at Oscar, displaying the traditional large gap in her front lower teeth.

"I-lotu," she said. Oscar smiled, comprehending at long last one single word. Come!

He followed the threesome across the expanse of the cattle barren inner sanctum of the manyatta to another Maasai dwelling that looked like all the others. Oscar had counted thirteen dwellings, with some hidden behind remnant brush. Most of the others were more in evidence. There was a crude stool outside this one. With a wave of the hand the tall woman directed Oscar to take a seat, which he promptly did. She left him to duck inside her home while the other two women examined his black-and-brown robe, shaking their heads and speaking rapidly to each other. The taller woman emerged with a gourd and a knife of sorts. It reminded Oscar of the blade Max had used during the circumcision but he dared not ask, as if he knew how. Words were spoken and the other two women turned to leave, still laughing softly to themselves. What were they up to?

The taller woman grabbed the calabash and splashed some milk all over Oscar's beard. She smiled at him and then aimed the crude knife at his whiskers.

"Ai enk-arna Lassoi," she said. More words he could understand! Her name was Lassoi.

Oscar smiled back. "Oscar," he said, patting himself on the chest. At last he was getting to know someone! He had been living among these Maasai for over a week now, and finally he was interacting with someone besides Matthew.

She grabbed his beard and made a deft slice, cutting it to within a bloody hair of his chinny-chin-chin. This was more than he'd bargained for. But it quickly occurred to him that shaving his beard entirely was perhaps the single most important physical transformation he could make if he wanted to be, while not actually dead, at least less recognizable alive. And it was quite apparent that these women were very adept at the shaving technique, in spite of the crude-looking cutting implement and the soured milk that was now running down all over him. Their hair was so short it looked more like a shadow than actual hair. And the heads of nearly all the men, apart from the moran, were cleanly shaved on a regular basis. And so he submitted to the slashing of the knife through his various chin hairs, right down to the very nubbins. He watched as large chunks of black, white, and gray hair fell to the ground. It was so liberating and, other than the odd tug on some stubborn whisker, quite painless.

It was going well when he saw the other two return, one carrying an armload of cloth or hides. It was hard to tell. The other carried a yoke-like apparatus across her shoulders with a bucket of sorts on each end. He soon discovered that one was filled with water, the other with an ochre-like concoction. They watched while Lassoi finished shaving off Oscar's beard. After another application of sour milk, he was ready for the final strokes that took care of the remaining stubbles, leaving his face and chin as clean and soft as a baby's bottom. And so white! Oscar rubbed his large hand across his face, amazed and quite impressed with Lassoi's delicate skills. But then the other two pounced. One grabbed his long, straggly hair on one side and began untangling and straightening it. The other woman attacked the other side. They pulled and, with crude wooden combs, they gradually worked out the kinks. Then they began to pour water through it while continuing to comb out the crud he'd accumulated since leaving David's schoolhouse. Once his hair was fairly clean and fairly straight, they all began making tiny braids. Oscar found this rather amusing, content to be putty in their hands. And when the braiding was done, they began to weave tiny beads into them, like counterweights to make his hair hang straight like a moran's hair! And then came the ochre. They plastered it in and slathered it all over. How he wished he had a mirror! But the ochre application didn't stop at the hairline; it continued over most of his face, at least the newly shaved portion.

When the ochre had been properly allocated along moran lines, they all began tugging at his priestly frock. It, too, was as much an aberration as Oscar. Lassoi made a motion to just take it off. A stunned Oscar quickly mulled this over. It was a good idea, in general, to comply with the simple wishes of the locals wherever he traveled. What the hell? He pulled the dirty black cloth over his head and stood there with nothing but his boxers. This set the women into a serious fit of laughter. Once they finally recovered, however, the shorter one began wrapping a piece of orange cloth around his waist. She was sizing him up for his very own shuka. It was no doubt tantamount to a Scotsman's getting his first kilt! And the other woman wrapped a large piece of orange-plaid cloth around his shoulder. She was sizing him up for a Maasai cloak, one that would keep the sun off him as well as give the cattle a more familiar sight to rest their eyes on.

When Matthew returned late in the day, he looked all about for his portly protégé. The cattle were lowing as he left them to fend for themselves now that they were again safe within the confines of the kraal. Oscar was not in his humble home but Matthew could see that the roof had been repaired. He sought out his mother, who pointed across the way, shaking her head but not uttering a word. Yet he thought he caught her smiling as he turned away. As he crossed over to the other side of the kraal, working his way through the cattle with gentle prodding of various bony hindquarters, he saw a moran, standing tall, whom he did not recognize. His back was to him but no moran he knew had such broad shoulders. The hair looked freshly braided, with lustrous beads contrasting with the burnt sienna hues of the newly applied ochre. When this "moran" turned around, however, just as Matthew cleared the cattle field, he suddenly froze.

For there stood Oscar, all six feet four of him, his hair braided and coated with ochre, his face slathered with not only ochre but dark ointments that concealed every inch of his otherwise lily-white face and torso. Apart from his girth, he looked every bit the part, proudly showing off his new outfit consisting of an orange-and-black-plaid blanket over his shoulders and an orange shuka around his waist along with his leather scabbard and sword. His legs, too, had been finger-painted with ochre, and on his large feet were new Maasai-style sandals. In one hand he held a Maasai shield and in the other a spear. Matthew began to howl with laughter. The three women stood nearby, laughing as well but looking quite proud of their handiwork. Oscar posed for his new Maasai friend, turning this way and that, obviously quite pleased with his magnificent new look. Then he, too, began to laugh, so loud and so hard that Matthew finally stopped and simply stared at him in awe—and perhaps a bit in fear.

Chapter 58

The streambed glistened. Jack could see a few quartz crystals shining back at him as he adjusted the angle of his gaze to take maximum advantage of the rays of sunlight filtering through the forest canopy. He reached his hand down into the cool water. Just as he seized a good-sized pebble, almost clear in complexion, he felt the tip of a rifle barrel pressing against the back of his neck.

At first he thought they were claim jumpers. But he soon realized they weren't miners by any stretch. It was two of the refugees, Jocko's goons, and they were armed to the teeth. They ordered him to start walking, lugging all his rock samples, which were quite heavy. He had been meaning to sort through them and jettison any duplicates just to bring the weight down, then add them to the growing number of samples in David's priest hole. They bushwhacked through steep and very dense brush, Jack leading the way. The barrel of the rifle jabbed him time and again, pushing him onward, while branches whipped him in the face. Footing was bad in places, and whenever he would fall a strong hand would grab him by the arm and pick him back up, then prod him with the rifle again. His ribs hurt from all the jabs, and walking was made even more uncomfortable by virtue of the mess he had made in his pants when they first apprehended him and he felt the cold metal against the back of his head.

They arrived at the refugee camp after walking for several hours. Once they had passed through the slit cut in the now-completed chain-link and barbed-wire fence that marked the southern border of the sprawling compound, Jack began to fear the worst. Not only was he being taken prisoner, they now knew where his gold strike was.

Once inside the compound they handed him over to Banyon. He'd been waiting rather impatiently. He took one look at the bedraggled old prospector, his khaki shirt covered in grime and sweat, his ragged jeans covered in mud. The man was a mess, and as the full ripeness of Jack's body odor reached him, Banyon called to a couple of lackeys nearby.

"Clean him up," he ordered, "then bring him to the general's tent."

The general, right. Jocko was no more a general than any of the hundreds of rebels who had followed his migration to these premises. But he was the boss. A couple of young girls being kept in one of the tents were ordered to strip Crazy Jack down and wash him from head to toe.

Jocko was seated at his computer when he heard Banyon calling to him from outside.

"We got him," said Banyon.

Jocko's wide face lit up, and he was smiling from jowl to jowl as Banyon dragged a somewhat sanitized Jack McGraw, dressed in clean boxers and a drab army shirt that was far too big for him, into the inner sanctum of Jocko's tent. Jocko extended his stubby hand in greeting. Lean as he was, Crazy Jack had a miner's grip. Jocko winced slightly and invited Jack to have a seat.

"Sorry to have taken you out of your way," he began, "but we would like to ask you a few questions. Care for a drink?"

In spite of his overall misery, those were magic words.

"You betcha," said Jack, who watched with great anticipation as Jocko reached for the bottle of Scotch on the table and proceeded to pour Crazy Jack a double shot.

"I would like to welcome you to our humble camp. It is not exactly where we would like to be, but for now, it must suffice. I understand you are a prospector, is that correct? You are here in Kenya in search of, shall we say, riches?"

Jack took a healthy swig of whisky. Ooh baby, it was good. He polished off the glass before bothering to answer the question. Jocko refilled it, patiently awaiting an answer.

"You got that right," he said, "but I ain't had no luck here so far."

"Really?" said Banyon, hoisting the heavy sack of rock samples up onto the table. "Then what's all this? Looks to me like you've got some nice, clear-looking gemstones here."

Jack looked perplexed as he took another sip. "Them's just quartz crystals. They ain't worth nothin'."

There were, in fact, a number of large quartz crystals, the kind that can be infused with gold when conditions are just right and a little seam in the earth's crust opens up and hot, mineralized fluids from deep within rise up to fill the void. But neither Jocko nor Banyon could tell the difference between quartz and diamond, or between gold and fool's gold, for that matter.

"Fine," said Banyon, "just quartz crystals. Then pray tell, where are the diamonds?"

Crazy Jack took a big gulp. Then he began to laugh. He couldn't help himself. He realized the pressure was off. They weren't interested in his gold mine; they were after Oscar's alleged diamonds!

"Why, you got to be kiddin'," he replied, still laughing as he finished off his second double shot. "There ain't no diamonds around these parts!"

Banyon looked over at Jocko and then reached for the glass. Jack was still smiling, awaiting the next refill.

"Maybe you should try a little harder to remember," he said, "especially if you want any more whisky."

Suddenly, he stopped laughing. The party was just getting going!

"How did you meet Oscar Newman and what was your relationship with him?"

Jack looked up at Banyon, who was leaning right over him. His breath was hot and reeked of tobacco. "We was just friends," said Jack, cowering as he glanced over at the beautiful bottle on the table. "That American doctor was takin' care of the both of us."

Banyon shot a look over at Jocko, who shrugged his shoulders as if to say "big deal."

"It was you who was lying on that cot, pretending you'd been mauled by a lion. Let's see your scars."

He grabbed the tattered army shirt and ripped it open. Jack's skinny chest was covered with white, curly hairs but there were certainly no scars.

"Why were you protecting him?" Banyon shouted.

"Please," said Jocko, "no need to raise your voice. We have sufficient ways to make him talk."

Jack began to tremble. This was getting serious. "I, uh, was just doin' what the doctor ordered. He jes' told me to lie down on the cot and keep still. Then he put all them bandages on me."

"And where was Oscar Newman?" He was shouting again.

"The priest hid him down in his cellar. They musta thought you was the police coming to arrest him. Everybody said he killed that nice professor, Francis somethin' or other. Only Oscar said his own brother did it. Can I have that drink now?"

Jocko refilled the glass but left it on the table. Jack started to tremble a little harder. That sure was good whisky.

"Why don't you tell us more about the diamonds. And your business arrangement with Dr. Newman. Was Francis Dermenjian in on it, too? After all, you're a prospector, a geologist, I presume, and we all know what Francis Dermenjian was looking for. There was a piece of kimberlite on the roof of the Land Rover. Do you know what kimberlite is?"

Jack swallowed hard. Maybe Oscar wasn't as crazy as he'd thought.

"Course I do," he answered, "but there ain't no way in hell there's any diamonds in this here Rift Valley. It's all way too young, geologically speakin'. Diamonds is some of the oldest minerals ever to see the light of day. Now, could you hand me that glass?"

"Not just yet," said Banyon. "It was definitely kimberlite and it definitely came from somewhere in the Rift Valley. So why don't you just tell us where they found it and you can have the whole damn bottle. And there's more where that came from."

Jack looked up at Banyon, who was standing over him again, angry as hell. "I'd like to help you," he stammered, "but like I told you I only met Oscar after them young Maasai brung him to see that American doctor. Why, I even helped save his life."

"Really?" said Banyon. "And just how did you do that?"

"I gave him some blood. We both got the same kind. Ain't that a hoot? I mean, he'd been nearly killed by that goddamn lion! And he was crazy with malaria, fevers had jes' about fried his brain. Now, how 'bout that drink?"

Banyon looked over at Jocko and smiled. Jocko once again just shrugged his shoulders. Banyon reached for the glass and handed it to Jack McGraw, who grabbed it with both hands and quickly brought it to his lips.

"Thanks," said Jack as he wiped his mouth with the back of his sleeve. "Damn, that's good."

"You're welcome," said Banyon as he turned to walk away. "So you helped save Newman's life. Then what happened?"

"Well," Jack continued, "like I said, they hid him down in the priest's cellar. Me and Oscar, we got drunk on the priest's wine and he told me 'bout the diamonds, but I didn't believe him. Still don't believe there's any diamonds in this here valley. I wish to God I knew where they were. Then I'd be rich for sure. But Oscar said he couldn't tell anybody where they found 'em, him and that Francis fellow. Poor bastard. Anyways, I still got my island and that's all that matters."

"Your island?"

"Yep!" And then Jack began to whoop and holler until he finally stood up and went into his hula dance again. Banyon grabbed him by the shoulder and pushed him back down on the couch.

"I don't want to hear about your fucking island!" Banyon shouted. "Where the hell is Oscar Newman right now?"

Jack swallowed hard, as both Banyon and Jocko were now standing over him. They sure as hell meant business.

"Oscar?" he replied. He was beginning to slur his words. "Why, that rascal's, uh, lessee, oh yeah. I remember now. He's dead and buried back behind the priest's schoolhouse."

Banyon closed his eyes, wincing. "He's truly dead, is he?"

"Why, sure. You seen him. You and that army captain. I even helped the doctor dig him up for ya."

"Really? I don't recall seeing you at the grave site."

"That's cuz I didn't want nothin' to do with lookin' at no corpse. It was bad enough just diggin'. Man, did it stink down in that hole. Matter of fact, you could thank me for helpin' out by pourin' me jes' another couple of fingers worth in that glass."

"I think you've had enough for today. Why don't you sleep on it and see if your memory improves. You're not leaving here until we get the truth out of you."

"I done tol' you the truth," said Jack.

While Jack McGraw was escorted back to a well-guarded tent, Banyon placed a call to Peter Dermenjian on his satellite phone, as instructed. Banyon conveyed what they had squeezed out of the prospector thus far, all of little value in the quest for the source of the diamonds.

"Surely you can find more persuasive means to make him talk," said Peter. "Certainly he was instrumental in locating the kimberlite. And he must be very good underneath that old Texan prospector façade. I have no doubt he's a coconspirator, along with Newman and my deceiving brother. What are the odds? They discover the source of the diamonds and, oh, there just happens to be a geologist in camp. Right. Get whatever you can out of him, using whatever means. Just don't kill him."

"Yes, sir," Banyon replied. "We'll make sure to keep him alive. I think we have enough blood on our hands already."

"Don't you be insolent with me," Peter shot back. "My brother's death was an accident and you know it. But let's move on. Have you obtained permission for running those shot lines yet? I want to start in Mto wa Mbu and work our way north. We know they traveled down the Avenue of the Volcanoes. And that young Maasai they gave a ride to said they had shovels and large rocks with them."

"I've tried several times but I haven't been able to get through to the right officials in Dar es Salaam."

"Perhaps you should go see them in person. And bring along the right incentives."

"It's a bit out of the way. And I have my hands full at the moment with this crazy prospector."

Peter let out a long sigh of frustration. "Look, I haven't much time. My new mother-in-law is coming for dinner. We're breaking the news to her."

"About the baby?"

"Yes. About the baby. We got the test results back. It's a boy!"

"Congratulations. When is it due?"

"Not until November. We're hoping to make a trip down before then. Elizabeth wants to visit the grave site to pay her respects as soon as she can muster the courage."

"I assume this is not yet public information."

"Not yet. But I suspect it won't be long. She's showing quite a bit already. I must be going. Let me know what you can wring out of the prospector. And if you don't have those damn permits by next month, we'll simply proceed without them."

"Right," said Banyon. He set the phone back on its charger and went to find that bottle of whisky. Only now it was his turn.

Jack was escorted the following afternoon back to Jocko's tent, terribly frightened but looking forward to more of that good whisky. Upon entering the tent, however, he noticed a different arrangement. There was a metal chair in the middle of the room, and he could hear the rumble of a generator that must have been parked just outside the tent. There were wires on the floor, and a large metal box with various dials sat on Jocko's desk. He tried to make a run for it, but Banyon had a hold on his arm and forced him into the chair. Before he knew what had happened, he was strapped down and his shirt was all unbuttoned down the front. Then Banyon wrapped a metal strap around his skinny right ankle.

"Well, Mr. McGraw," said Banyon once Jack was secured in the chair. "We're going to go over the same questions one more time. Only there will be no whisky, just a different sort of enticement."

He walked over to Jocko's desk and picked up something that looked like a microphone. Then he approached Jack and waved the instrument over him. He was wearing thick rubber gloves. This did not bode well. With a flick of the wrist, he lightly touched Jack on the arm. A jolt of electricity poured through his body. He screamed and shook as the shock dissipated.

"Please," Jack begged, "I done told you everything. Jes' let me go."

"Not until you tell us where the diamonds are. You're a prospector. That's what you do. You look for precious metals and precious gems. So tell us. Where are they?"

He waved the electric wand in front of Jack's face. Jack just trembled, and before he realized what was happening he had wet his pants.

"I jes' don't know," he stammered. "All I do know is Oscar was stranded down by Lake Natron. That's where he come down with an attack of malaria. And that's where that Francis fella was killed. I swear I never seen Oscar Newman before them Maasai brung him to see Max Taylor, that young doctor."

"Then let's start from the beginning. When did you arrive in Africa?"

"Back in January."

"And who sent you?"

"I got a contract with a Texas mining outfit. They sent me here to look at gold prospects. They paid my expenses, and if I find anything I'll get a good commission."

"And what have you found so far?"

Jack hesitated. He looked over at his sack of rock samples. They were sitting next to a number of spare AK-47s piled on top of some metal boxes. Banyon brought the wand up next to his right temple.

"All right," he said, "I found somethin'. But it ain't no diamonds."

"Then what is it?" Banyon's face tightened.

"A gold strike. That's where them rocks come from."

Banyon smiled. "Well, well," he said. "I recall you telling us you hadn't found anything."

And he lightly touched the wand to the middle of Jack's bare chest. He screamed in agony and began shaking so hard the chair nearly fell over. His jaw clenched shut as he went into convulsions. Banyon waited for his subject to recover before continuing the interrogation.

"So, if you lied to us about your presumed gold find, why should we believe your story about the diamonds, or the lack of them?" Again he waved the wand in front of Jack's face. Tears were streaming down his cheeks and his breathing was rapid.

"I ain't lyin'. I don't know about no diamonds."

Banyon looked over at Jocko, who simply shook his head. "Okay," said Banyon. "We'll try this again in a little bit. Think hard on this, Mr. McGraw. This is your last chance."

Banyon and Jocko exited the tent, leaving Jack alone, still trembling from the shock therapy he'd just experienced. But to his horror, they returned shortly, carrying a large box covered by a dark cloth which they set on the table a few feet in front of Jack.

"I'll bet you're wondering what's underneath that cloth," said Jocko. "If you just tell us the information we need, we won't even take a peek. So, one more time. Where are they?"

The now-familiar panic attack began to well up, starting at his ankles. And seconds later Jack's heart was pounding. There really was just one way out and he knew it. All he needed to do was tell them that Oscar Newman really was alive and they'd let him be. Yet he could not bring himself to betray his new friend. Surely they would kill Oscar if they found him, after putting him through this same kind of torture until he told them where he and Francis had discovered the diamonds.

Banyon stared at him, waiting for an answer. Hearing none, and growing quite impatient, he pressed the wand hard against Jack's chest. The electricity shot through him like a bolt of lightning, causing all his muscles to tighten so hard that his jaw finally locked up. Even if he wanted to, he could not begin to speak. His heart was pounding even harder and rather irregularly. He looked at Banyon with pure hatred. Banyon simply shook his head from side to side and walked over to the table. He grabbed the covering on the large box and lifted it up. Only then did Jack realize his worst fears had yet to peak. For the box was really a metal cage and within the metal cage was the most terrifying of creatures.

"I hope you're not too afraid of snakes," Banyon teased. "Ever come across one of these in your travels? A black mamba? I'm afraid they're quite deadly."

And he lifted the latch and opened a small door. The silvery-brown serpent began to slither, its forked tongue darting in and out as it eased its way out of the cage. It was at least six feet in length.

"No!" Jack shouted. Now this was pure panic. "Get him away!" he screamed, even louder than before.

He might as well have said "here, snakey, snakey," for the deadly serpent found its way down the table leg and onto the beat-up rug below. It lifted its large head well off the ground and looked straight at Jack McGraw as its tongue darted in and out faster than before, revealing its sinister fangs set against the inner blackness of its mouth, from which its name is derived. It was true that he had run across black mambas before, and he knew how quickly they could strike and how quickly paralysis would set in, followed by suffocation. He needed to speak up, now! But it was as if the paralysis had already set in. He was too terrified to speak.

"Os-Os-Oscar…is…," he began, but before he could get any further, the tent flap opened and there was Max.

"Oscar is dead," said Max. He was accompanied by a Kenya National Police officer. In one fluid motion Max grabbed the pistol from the officer's holster and took aim at the deadly viper. With one loud blast the head of the snake was blown away and the body began to twist and writhe on its own. Max handed the pistol back to the soldier.

"Thanks," he said, smiling sheepishly. The officer, clearly impressed with such marksmanship, turned the pistol toward Banyon.

"You two," he commanded, with a nod toward Jocko, "outside."

Jocko began to laugh but did not put up a fight. Nor did Banyon.

"Are you all right?" said Max as he untied Jack. Then he removed the metal band from his ankle. Jack was evidently too shaken up to respond. He just kept staring at the body of the now-headless snake. It was still twisting slowly on the rug, which was now stained with its blood.

"Look," Max continued, "gather up your things and meet me out by the Scout. I'm taking you back to David."

Chapter 59

"What the hell is so damn funny?" said Max once they reached the Kalema Road. "You haven't stopped laughing since we left the refugee camp."

"It ain't nothin'," said Jack between giggles. "It's just good to be alive. Thanks again for savin' me from that damn snake. Yer one helluva good shot. Jeez, I hate snakes."

If only Max had peeked inside the heavy sack of alleged rock samples he'd loaded into the back of the Scout, he would have understood. He would have seen that there were no rocks at all, but in their place were a couple dozen AK-47 ammunition clips. Only then would Max have understood why Jack was laughing, imagining Jocko opening one of the heavy boxes of ammunition back in his tent only to find a bunch of rocks. But Jack wasn't about to tell Max about the ammo. He was looking forward to breaking the news to Ntanda. For not only were the previously burned-out rifles back in working order, they were now ready for use, to help right the balance between the well-armed refugees and the spear-wielding moran. He would show them how to shoot and then, just like in cowboys and Indians, the Indians would have more of a fighting chance.

"And you're just damned lucky I went looking for Jocko when I did," said Max. "When his goons told me I'd have to wait to see him, I knew something was up. All the young girls were accounted for and then I heard you screaming."

The news Max had wanted to convey to Jocko in hopes it might earn him another break from the mayhem, news garnered after days of making rounds to examine all the pitiable warriors who looked to Jocko for leadership, was that all his loyal men were fit for duty. But in the end that didn't matter. The Kenyan police officer agreed it made sense for Max to return Jack McGraw back to wherever he'd been before Jocko and company abducted him for some "routine" questioning. Jocko was in no position to argue.

Max was only too happy to return Jack McGraw back into David's care. It was where he belonged. After all, David's priest hole had become the core shack for all of Jack's rock samples, his proof in the mineral pudding that he had himself one damn fine gold prospect, even without the samples he'd forfeited for the ammunition. They arrived at the schoolhouse in the late afternoon, long after the last student had departed.

David greeted them warmly as always, relieved by Jack's return but very alarmed by the stories he told of how he'd been treated by Jocko and company.

"Why, that's pure torture," he observed, "and all over this crazy story about a cache of diamonds."

"I told 'em I didn't know nothin' about no diamonds but they wouldn't believe me," Jack replied. He had already helped himself to David's sofa and looked to be settling in quite comfortably.

"Sorry," said Max, "I'm supposed to head straight back but I need to check on Oscar. I don't suppose you could help me locate him?"

"Certainly," said David, "but we must leave at once if we're to be back before darkness falls. I should warn you, though, Oscar has taken on a new look. Try not to laugh too hard."

They crossed over the newly swollen creek bed and headed south through fairly open savannah that would eventually transition into the marshlands along Natron's north shore. The manyatta was about halfway.

Oscar was fast asleep when they arrived, sprawled out on the leather hide that covered his straw bed. It had been another hard day alone on the range with all the cattle. Matthew was nowhere in sight, having long since abandoned Oscar to take up his position on the Kalema Road.

"Oscar," said David, "Max is here. Time for your exam."

As he rolled over, Max shined a light in his face and saw for the first time what David had meant by his "new look." Apart from his shaggy, ochre-laden braids, the black-and-red markings all over his face reminded Max of a Mardi Gras character. But he managed to stifle the impulse to laugh out loud.

"Hello, Oscar," he said. "You look fabulous. But I need to check you over before these batteries run out."

It was already getting dark outside. He handed the flashlight to David and proceeded with the exam, relating as he did Crazy Jack's close encounter with Banyon and Jocko.

"I'm happy to hear he's all right," said Oscar, "and relieved to know he did not divulge any sensitive information, such as the fact that I'm not dead. Not yet, anyway."

"I think you're safe here. With that disguise, no one will recognize you."

"Any word on Elizabeth?"

"No, but I'm sure there will be media coverage if you're right about her being pregnant." The scar tissue was still quite red and a bit puffy, but the healing process was proceeding on schedule. "I'll be sure to let you know whenever I learn anything. Now roll over and let me check your soda burns."

And that's how they left it. Max was pleased to see that Oscar's health was steadily improving. Spending his days herding Maasai cattle seemed like good therapy, as long as no lions tried to reopen his wounds.

His rounds completed, Max returned to the refugee camp the following morning while Jack McGraw returned to his prospecting, David settled back into his teaching, and Oscar resumed his duties as the new moran on the block, a tenderfoot with an imposing presence, one that Max felt was sure to keep predators at bay. Hopefully, that included human predators.

Max welcomed the news from the guards at the gate to the compound. His orders were to return to Red Cross central. Apparently, he had been relieved of Jocko duty. No doubt his sentence had been reduced for bad behavior.

Life back with Dr. Bichette and company gradually became slightly more tolerable as the steady stream of maimed and badly wounded refugees slowed to a trickle. Evidently, the upheaval that had caused the surge of Ugandans to flee their homeland had subsided. So Max spent his days checking on infections, administering pain medication, and doling out the precious antibiotics on a priority basis that required him to choose among those he thought had the likeliest chance of surviving. Beds were placed side by side with only narrow aisleways allowing access to the hundreds of victims too sick or too maimed to join the general mass of refugees sprawled out over the hundreds of acres of what had been prime Maasai grazing territory just several months before. Given the heat and the high humidity, it seemed like just a matter of time before some sort of pestilence overtook the whole place.

And the clock was ticking. The so-called deadline for the withdrawal of the refugees was just two days away and Max was understandably quite eager to know how much progress Christine and Dr. Brecht and their colleagues were making toward relocating the thousands and thousands of Ugandans with nowhere to go. From his perspective, there'd been no progress at all. And since Peter Dermenjian's associates had already attempted to wring the truth out of Crazy Jack, he worried that Christine might be next in line. He approached Dr. Bichette

492

in the late afternoon as she was pouring over medical reports and requested permission to check in on his friends over on the west end of the compound.

Dr. Bichette lowered her head, all the better to make eye contact. Her thin reading glasses rested precariously on the tip of her skinny nose.

"You mean that German woman and her young assistant? I, too, have been wondering about them and what progress is being made on the relocation efforts with the deadline so close at hand. Our server is down so there hasn't been an update on that front in quite some time. But you must be quick about it, assuming you can arrange for the other physicians to look after your patients. Bring me a detailed report regarding the relocation effort as soon as you can."

No problem. In fact, serendipity had never smelled sweeter. Fortunately, Max was able to talk a few of the other doctors into keeping an eye on his patients for the night. Payback time would come soon enough.

Though he was still confined to the crowded spaces of the refugee camp, driving through the masses of displaced Ugandans almost felt like a release. At least they were spaced somewhat apart, unlike those inside his medical tent. Here the people were relatively busy, laying thatch on the roofs of temporary shelters, fetching water in their multi-stained jerrycans, carrying firewood, and cooking down the maize and powdered milk the UN provided. They were a sorry lot but far less so than the patients he'd been tending to for months now.

The days had flown by so quickly since he'd first entered the refugee camp, when he had been confronted with sometimes dozens of new victims on a daily basis. His fingers had even begun to cramp up at times from laying in too many sutures. But he now managed to keep a firm grip on the wheel as he steered his way slowly but carefully through the densely populated compound.

Keeping a firm grip on the wheel was one thing. But keeping a firm grip on himself was another matter altogether. The thought of seeing Christine conjured up memories of their night together in Nairobi, vivid memories of how lovely and how downright sexy she had not only looked but behaved when they were dancing. And then they were in his room. He felt the dreaded but inevitable rush come over him. It had been far too long.

He found her seated outside the row of tents where the "processing" supposedly took place. It was late in the day and Christine was alone. And she was sobbing. Max pulled to an abrupt halt, cut the engine, and jumped out.

"Hello!" he shouted. "Everything okay?"

493

Christine froze. She recognized that voice! She jumped to her feet and ran toward Max, arms outstretched, smiling as her tears ran down her cheeks. Max had never imagined such a warm welcome but it was certainly okay with him. They hugged for quite some time. Christine's embrace was very firm, very sincere, and very invigorating.

"What's wrong?" said Max, finally breaking free.

"What isn't? Just listen."

She pointed toward a large tent from which two raised voices, both of them female, carried through the thin canvas walls and beyond. Only they were speaking in Dutch.

"What's going on?"

"It's Gertie and Inga, the alleged woman in charge, having another argument. Dr. Brecht keeps trying to tell her how to do her job."

"Really," said Max. "I can just imagine."

"You don't have to imagine because you can hear it. She's telling her how she needs to put pressure on the various members of the various committees in the various countries who are even considering taking in some of these refugees. They're all bickering over quotas. Meanwhile, we're trying to piece together families and so many of the boys are missing, and it's just awful to think they've been brainwashed by now and turned into zombielike child soldiers, little killing machines."

"It's all really horrible," said Max. "I've never seen bodies all cut up like this. And I thought LA street gangs were brutal."

They hugged another moment in silence as Christine collected herself.

"So," she began, wiping her eyes with her sleeve, "what brings you here?"

"I wanted to see how you and Dr. Brecht are getting along. And how the relocation is going."

"That will take a while. Let's go back to my tent and I'll brew up some tea."

"Sounds wonderful," Max responded. In fact, it was just what the doctor ordered.

But whatever illusions the doctor may have had regarding Christine and about what might or might not lie in store for them all evaporated rather quickly as Christine began recounting the dismal progress, as if such a word was even applicable to the relocation effort. So many had been brutally murdered, yet so many more were missing and presumed dead. She recounted days spent moving from battered tent to battered tent with Dr. Brecht, interviewing hundreds and hundreds of refugees, and all their stories were similar and all their stories were so sad. Missing fathers, missing brothers, sisters who had been abducted to be turned into sex slaves. That's where she really lost it. Max moved closer and put his arm around her shoulder.

"I know," he said. "It's tough. And speaking of displaced people, I need to tell you about Oscar."

And so he brought her up to date, complete with details about the surprise attack by the flesh-eating beetles.

"That's horrible!"

"Yes," he replied, "but the whole world bought it."

"Even Peter Dermenjian?"

"Let's hope so. But he may come looking for you. His people already worked Crazy Jack over. If his goons come by, just remember Oscar's dead and buried."

"Right," said Christine. "That's all I need right now."

They were alone in her tent. A single candle flickered on the small table next to the bed on which they were seated side by side. Max massaged her neck, which was understandably quite tense.

"Max," she said, "can you do me a favor?"

"Sure," said Max, adrenaline pumping. "You name it."

"Can you take me with you next time you go see Oscar? I need a break. And I really miss David."

Like an act of mercy, Dr. Brecht came barreling into the tent. She was quite angry and proceeded to relay all the important things that idiot Inga van Hoven had failed to do. Then she noticed Max.

"Dr. Taylor," she shouted, "what are you doing on these premises?"

"Not much," he responded. "Not much at all. But if she's free, then I guess I'd like a word with Inga. I'm on a mission to bring Dr. Bichette an update on the relocation effort. Her server's down."

"Doesn't matter. There have been no updates," said Dr. Brecht, "and barely any progress."

After a meager dinner with Christine and a lonely night in a spare tent, Max made the trek back to the field hospital and relayed the news to Dr. Bichette. Inga had printed out a summary of the relocations to date. The news was disconcerting but, judging from the expression on Dr. Bichette's face, not too surprising. She was a true veteran of refugee camps.

"So how long before your server is up and running?" he inquired. Surely he had earned some log-in time.

"There is some progress. At least I can access the Internet, if not our own local system."

Finally, a bit of good news. It meant he should be able to perform a search on Peter Dermenjian to see if there were any stories about the supposedly expectant couple.

"Any chance I could check my e-mail later on?"

"Go complete your rounds. With a little luck we'll still be connected when you're done."

So he donned a surgical mask and headed back into the sea of sickness and despair that had become his new home. Two of his patients had died in the past week and a third was well on his way. It was just a matter of time. No point in administering antibiotics but the pain medication was a must. Hopefully, a delivery of morphine was on the way. They were going through it fast.

His daily rounds completed, he checked back with Dr. Bichette. "You are in luck," she said. "The Internet is working and I have a meeting with the nursing staff. You can use the computer if you like."

"Great, thank you!"

He ignored his e-mail and went straight to searching for any news regarding Peter Dermenjian and his new bride. It had been a month since their wedding, so surely the word would be out if Oscar was correct about Peter having knocked her up. He found quite a few articles on Peter Dermenjian and his business interests, but finally he clicked on a featured article in a Marseille tabloid. There was a colorful photo showing the happy couple arriving at the doctor's office arm in arm. Peter was smiling and Elizabeth was waving, with her body slightly turned. Her swollen waistline was not only expertly captured by the photographer but circled and highlighted with an arrow as well. The story was all in French but he understood the headline well enough: "Diamond King's New Prospect."

"Damn," said Max. "Oscar was right."

He printed off a copy and went looking for Dr. Bichette. He needed another hall pass, a couple of days furlough, and he wanted it now. He ambushed her as she was leaving her meeting with the nurses.

"What can possibly be so urgent?" she wanted to know. "You've already lost your primary patient, Dr. Newman."

"He wasn't my only patient over there," he replied, thinking about Crazy Jack. "And I have an obligation to Joseph and his people. Besides, he too deserves an update on the status of the refugees, especially since the deadline is tomorrow and there's been very little movement. I'd like to take Christine Olson along. She's been working with Inga and Dr. Brecht since she stopped her research project with the Maasai. She can bring him up to date."

Dr. Bichette rubbed her chin. "Very well," she said. "But we really need you around here. You're a very good doctor, in spite of your recent losses. So be as quick as you can."

She handed him the temporary release that he needed to get past the guards, good for three days. He raced off to again plead with his colleagues to please look after his patients, just one more time.

True to his word, he swung by tent thirteen the following morning to pick up Christine. She was startled to see him again so soon but was even more startled that Dr. Brecht agreed it made sense for Christine to brief Joseph. The deadline had arrived and so far very few refugees had been repatriated.

Once beyond the gatehouse, Christine erupted with details of life in close quarters with Dr. Brecht and the enormous pressure to do an impossible job for people living in deplorable conditions. And that included her conditions sharing a tent with Gertie, who had strict policies regarding lights on and lights off, and who snored so loud she sometimes sounded just like stampeding horses. At least she had managed to arrange a couple of days off on such very short notice. There were still hundreds more families yet to be interviewed, much less relocated.

They found David behind his house busy making cheese. He looked very out of character dressed in baggy white pants and a sleeveless white shirt as he lifted a large strainer filled with curdled whey out of a steaming pot. The best he could do was nod toward them and shout hello.

"How was the crossing?"

"Pleasantly uneventful," said Max. "The moran troops are well positioned. But I swear just a few of Jocko's men could take them all out in no time at all."

"Then they would really have the Kenyan government on their ass," replied Father Sebastian. "But it's good they are well in charge. The big cattle drive is about to happen, down the Kalema Road. But before we get to all that, you must come inside. I have brewed some very good beer."

He left the strainer full of whey to settle out and drip-dry in the shade of a tarp he'd strung up just for the cheese making. He placed some cheesecloth over the top, wiped his hands clean, and proceeded to give them each a hug.

"So nice to see you, Christine; what a nice surprise."

"It's so good to see you, too," she replied, squeezing his hand. "I've really been needing a break like this."

"So the Maasai are on the move again?" said Max as David handed him a glass of brown, foamy liquid.

"Yes," said David. "The Maasai are about to move the bulk of their cattle across the Ewaso Ngiro. They have spent the last month building new manyattas and cattle kraals to prepare for their arrival. With the threat of the poachers so much closer, security for the cattle is top priority. And herding them all over the bridge will be a logistical challenge, to say the least. Many of the newly relocated Maasai will be moving their household goods as well. It worries me very much. The Maasai are all extremely angry right now, as the refugees should already be gone and this move should not be necessary. But they have had no word from Captain Olengi and Joseph is nearly apoplectic. In any event, cheers, and to your good health."

"I'll drink to that," said Max.

"I'll drink to anything," said Christine. But the weight of David's summation gave them pause. "Well, how the heck is Oscar doing?" she continued. "Max says he's dead and buried and back alive again."

"You mustn't tell a soul," said David. "It's all most despicable. I can't believe I allowed it to happen in my own cemetery."

"Don't forget," said Max, "Oscar being dead was all your idea in the first place."

David didn't bother to respond. He simply reached for the bottle and topped off their glasses.

"Well," Max continued, "speaking of Oscar, I have some news."

He reached into his shirt pocket and pulled out the copy of the article and handed it to David. As he unfolded it his eyes grew wide.

"Nom de Dieu," he exclaimed. "So it's true."

"What's true?" said Christine. "Let me see that." She grabbed the article from David and stared at the photo. "I don't get it. What's the big deal?"

"That's Elizabeth," said David. "She was supposed to marry Oscar. But believing he is dead, she has married Peter Dermenjian, brother of Francis, and as Oscar guessed correctly, she is carrying his child. We must break this news to him, but very carefully."

"Holy shit," said Christine. "She sure didn't waste any time finding somebody new!"

"Hell, he's a frickin' billionaire," said Max.

"Nice looking, too," she added. "Lots more hair than his brother."

"Why don't you two come help me press this cheese into molds," said David as he stood up. "Then we can set off to pay Oscar a visit. I'd better bring him some of that beer. He's going to need it. And Christine, I should warn you. Oscar has a new look."

"That's for damn sure," said Max.

They were waiting for him back at the corral when Oscar returned from another long day out on the range. The herd came loping in ahead of him but Oscar's booming voice, shouting orders to the cattle as they navigated their way through the portal and back to their quarters inside the fortification, clearly signaled his arrival. It was quite a spectacle. Still beardless and swathed in his shuka and Maasai blanket, and holding his spear in one hand and a long stick in the other, which he used to prod the bovine masses along, he entered entirely unaware that he had guests in waiting. And they were all staring at him, quite in awe of the transformation. His broad, painted face and ochred hair made him look almost barbaric.

"Yikes," said Christine. "Is that really you, Oscar?"

He broke into a huge grin. "Christine, Max, David, what a pleasant surprise. Come, sit. What news?"

They all hugged somewhat awkwardly, as no one wanted to come away with or smudge Oscar's makeup or his red clay–plastered hair, which had grown to shoulder length.

"I brought you some beer," said David, reaching into his knapsack. "And some biscuits."

"Excellent," said Oscar, "and what else? What news?"

David looked at Max as if to say, "Why don't you do the honors?"

499

"Oscar," said Max. "There's no way to break this to you gently, even with a slug of David's beer. You were right. She's pregnant."

The dark-brown bottle David had just given to him slipped out of Oscar's hand. Fortunately, it hadn't yet been opened and landed softly on the leather hide upon which they were all seated.

"How do you know?" he whispered back, his eyes wide and his mouth hanging open.

"I read about it online," Max replied. "One of those cheap Marseille tabloids showed a picture of them."

"May I see it?"

Max looked to David for help. David shrugged his shoulders, as if to say *"pourquoi pas?"* He reached into his knapsack again and pulled out the folded piece of paper. Then he slowly handed it to Oscar, who studied it for some time, not saying a word. Daylight was fading but there was enough light for Oscar to see his beloved Elizabeth standing beside the most horrible of men, a man who had killed his own brother and then tried to pin the blame squarely on Oscar. And there she was, smiling and waving and showing off her swollen belly.

After a few moments he let it drop.

"I knew it," said Oscar.

"How in hell could you have known that?" chirped Christine.

"It's my fault," said Max. "I saw an interview with the two of them. I told Oscar they were getting married and made a dumb comment about her figure. Something about C cups instead of B cups."

Christine looked at Max like he was insane. Meanwhile, Oscar stood up and walked away without a word.

"Oscar," David shouted, "please come back."

He stopped and turned around. "Thank you very much for your visit. And the beer. I'm sorry, but I need to be alone right now."

They watched as he continued on toward his primitive new home, stooped to get through the low entry, and disappeared inside, no doubt to lie down after a long day's trek and to try to come to grips, somehow, with the awful but not unexpected news.

"Oh dear," said Christine, "I'll bet he's in there crying his eyes out."

"Yeah," said Max. "I hope it doesn't ruin his makeup. But look, as long as we're here, I want to go see Joseph. Christine can give him an update about the relocation effort. It's not good." He was looking at David.

"Yes," he said. "Let's go pay him a visit. I'd love to see his reaction."

It was a bit of a trek to a neighboring manyatta but they found Joseph outside his home, eating his dinner. He set his bowl aside as soon as he saw them approaching. He stood up and walked forward to greet this trio of foreigners, wearing a grim expression. Surely they were bringing him some news of the refugees, unlike Captain Olengi, who had broken his promise, a key condition of the agreement, to keep him informed on a regular basis. He greeted David first and then Max and Christine. He invited them to sit. David translated while Max summarized the situation, deferring to Christine for details.

"How much longer, then?" Joseph asked, his eyes turning red with anger.

"Il-apaitin'," she replied. Months. Joseph stood up and brandished his fly brush several times. He began pacing.

"The captain brings me no news," he said. "He has broken his promises." Then he looked straight at Max. "You will take me to see him. Tomorrow morning."

"I'm sorry, I can't do that," said Max, looking toward David. "I wish I could, but Dr. Bichette would have my head."

"Would she now?" David responded, a bit more animated. "Clearly, Joseph needs some answers and Captain Olengi has been avoiding him. This crisis can't go on indefinitely. And it's in everyone's best interest, including Dr. Bichette's, for Joseph, who represents all the Maasai in southern Kenya, to speak directly with the Kenyan government and make them live up to their agreement!"

David was right. Joseph needed to see Captain Olengi and Max had the only means to deliver him. It would mean a few more days off but surely Dr. Bichette would understand. All he needed was for Christine to deliver the message.

"Christine," he said, "it looks like I've got another pressing engagement. We need to leave first thing in the morning."

"But we just got here!" she protested. "I haven't even said hello to my friends."

"Well then, I suggest you get to it."

Another lucky break. Checking in with Captain Olengi, even as Joseph's chauffeur, had plenty of appeal. After all, the man still had his passport, an essential item if he was ever to escape this misguided and totally off-course African diversion and get back to reassembling his life.

Chapter 60

The crossing was once again slow but uneventful. The moran stationed at precise intervals all recognized Joseph in the passenger seat. Each one saluted as they passed by, raising his spear high in allegiance. Joseph nodded at each of them in turn, like an army general on inspection day. They passed through the checkpoint at Lake Magadi without incident. When they reached the gates to the refugee camp, Max hopped out and explained the situation to the guards. He would be back in a couple of days. The guards didn't care. They were much more interested in Christine. She was actually trying to get back inside.

The road to Nairobi was rougher than he remembered, but compared to the Kalema Road it was like floating on air. Joseph hadn't said a word the entire trip, other than uttering a few terse comments in Maa to the guards at the Magadi checkpoint. Whatever he said it made them cower. As they approached downtown Nairobi, he began to mumble under his breath. This was clearly not where he wished to be.

By the time they arrived at the Kenya National Police headquarters, it was already lunchtime. Captain Olengi's secretary said he'd be back at one o'clock but his afternoon was completely full.

"You may have a seat over there," she said, pointing to a hard wooden bench. "And fill out these forms, stating your business."

She handed Max a clipboard and a questionnaire that looked like a college entrance exam. It included many questions neither he nor Joseph cared to answer. And Joseph was looking more and more pissed by the minute.

It was just past two o'clock when Captain Olengi finally walked through the door, his necktie loosened and a toothpick dangling from the corner of his mouth. But his uniform was spotless. He pulled up short and looked over at his secretary. The muscles in his cheeks tightened up like tennis balls. But he quickly turned toward Joseph and Max and broke into a broad smile.

"Joseph, Dr. Taylor," he began, "how nice to see you. I don't recall having an appointment with you. Is there some sort of emergency?"

Joseph stood up very slowly and stared at Captain Olengi. His fierce look, brows simmering with anger, eyes nearly squinting, conveyed nothing but contempt.

"Please," said the captain, "come into my office."

Joseph followed the captain down the hall to a large office, more expansive than the one he had occupied the last time Max had dropped by, the day after that dreadful night on the town with Christine. Joseph entered, but as Max was about to cross the threshold, Captain Olengi turned to address him.

"Dr. Taylor, I believe whatever Joseph wishes to discuss is between him and me. You may wait in the reception area."

"Hang on," said Max, "what Joseph wants to discuss is the same thing I want to discuss. What are you doing to resolve the little housing crisis out there in Maasailand? You've got my passport, and depending on how long this is going to last, I might just want it back now so I can get the hell out of here."

"Very well," he said. "Come in, then."

Stunned that his little tantrum had worked, Max lowered his head and muttered a polite thank you.

"Have a seat," said the captain. There were two wooden chairs and Joseph was already occupying one of them, ready for the talks to begin. Unfortunately for Max, Joseph launched into a tirade of sorts, speaking rapidly in Maa with many a point driven home with a wave of his fly brush. Max could barely understand. Captain Olengi replied just as briskly, throwing in some Swahili now and then, leaving Max in the conversational dust. But it ultimately became clear that Captain Olengi was trying to convince Joseph that good progress was being made. It wouldn't be too much longer, have patience, et cetera. This did not sit well with Joseph, who turned toward Max.

"Dr. Taylor," said the captain, "Joseph says you have information regarding the relocation effort."

"That's correct," he replied. "I spoke directly with Inga van Hoven. She's in charge of the relocation effort inside the camp. She says there's been little progress to date and it doesn't look very promising. She showed me the numbers and, well, I'd have to agree with her."

Too bad he'd given the table showing the data to Dr. Bichette. Clenching his teeth, Captain Olengi looked around the room before responding.

"I have the official numbers. It will not be that much longer." He then stood up, indicating this meeting was over. Joseph stood up as well, flushed with anger. He uttered a few more unintelligible sentences before turning with a huff to leave. Captain Olengi called after them as Joseph and Max walked out the door. He first shouted to Joseph in Maa then to Max in English.

"Dr. Taylor, tell Joseph he can sue the fucking United Nations as well. As if we all don't have enough shit to deal with."

Next stop, McDonald, Schlepp, and Greevey, the law firm handling Maasai legal affairs. They were located in a modest, older building in downtown Nairobi. The more affluent clientele sought out the more prestigious law firms paying higher rents in much taller buildings. These were the haunts of do-good lawyers making modest livings supporting environmental causes and the rights of native peoples. Most of their financial support came via philanthropic contributions funneled through various NGOs. Max dropped Joseph off at the curb.

"See you at the hotel," said Max. "Good luck."

"Ashe naleng," said Joseph before turning and walking off toward the squat brown building wherein some poor unsuspecting receptionist would have to somehow steer this fiercely determined native son toward some kind of legal mind that hopefully had some answers. And those answers would concern the additional concessions the Kenyan government would have to agree to now that the eviction deadline had arrived and the refugees had hardly budged. It would also include penalties for failing to provide regular updates, as originally agreed to—agreed to but thoroughly ignored by Captain Olengi, the designated contact.

Max wondered why he'd neglected to inquire about the prospects of actually retrieving his passport. It all happened so fast. Whatever. He knew he couldn't just pick up and skip town, not with the patient load he had. But when would it end?

He took advantage of the free time by heading over to Nairobi General in search of meds. Maybe a little extra morphine or some antibiotics would help assuage Dr. Bichette's anger at his being gone so long. Luckily the woman at the pharmacy was sufficiently impressed with Max's credentials, especially the green card signed by Captain Olengi. His platinum Visa card didn't hurt his chances, either. An hour later he walked out into the bright afternoon sun with a small duffel bag filled with several kinds of antibiotics and a goodly supply of morphine. It was more than he'd hoped for. And who knew, maybe someday he'd actually be reimbursed for the expenses.

That night he dined at the Carnivore, a restaurant dedicated to serving cuts of wildebeest, ostrich, and other wild game skewered on Maasai swords and beautifully roasted over open fires. Well fed and sleepy from a few glasses of wine, he went back to the Hilton, took a hot shower and went to bed. And when he descended to the lobby the next morning after the best night's sleep he'd had in months, he found Joseph waiting impatiently.

His legal affairs in order, or at least in less disarray, Joseph was ready to get back to his people. It was definitely time to move the cattle and the Maasai families who own them, especially since the traditional pastures were still occupied by the Ugandan invaders and apparently would be for some time.

Max tried to engage Joseph in a little conversation on the way back home, but he was in no mood for more talk. Max let it go and focused on just playing chauffeur, getting back quite literally into the groove of traveling once again down the all-too-familiar and all-too-bumpy Kalema Road.

Joseph summoned the elders to another council that evening. Planning for the move—a move that meant organizing and relocating over a hundred extended Maasai families, all their belongings, and all their cattle—was well underway. It was more like a strategic reallocation between the two portions of Maasailand still under Joseph's control—south of the Kalema Road, that is. The Ewaso Ngiro sliced through it such that a third of the land, the part where Joseph and most of the elders currently resided, not far from David's schoolhouse, lay to the west. It was now largely overgrazed. The other two-thirds lay to the east, eventually bumping up against the alkaline wasteland bordering Lake Magadi. More importantly, this land was literally just across the road from the refugee camp, the source of the poachers, who had not slacked off in the least.

What concerned Joseph most of all were the guns. Jocko's goons had begun to blatantly brandish them as the moran threatened with their spears. No shots had been fired or spears launched, but Jocko's boys were clever. They would operate in packs, creating diversions while the other half ventured in for the kill and quickly made off with the meat. Captain Olengi had promised to step up the border patrols, but he had promised many other things before, things that never happened. Things the attorneys were supposed to fix. All the more reason to get a move on, to strengthen their resistance and provide greater protection not only for their cattle but for their women and children. Joseph was, of course, completely unaware of the recent arrival of ammunition for the AK-47s, weapons he thought had long since been destroyed. Not so. Ntanda was ecstatic.

Left alone with his herd of cattle and his newly broken heart, Oscar wandered through the days leading up to the move, barely cognizant of where the cattle were roaming or what they were eating. The elliptical path through the small valley Matthew had led him to was now well worn down, the grasses quite thin. The long rains were long since over.

And so was his wedding day, stolen from him by cruel twists of fate, all linked to the man now married to his precious Elizabeth. Knowing she was heavy with child, Peter Dermenjian's child, he could think of nowhere on earth he wanted to be. So he spent his days walking, watching the animals come and go, feeling the good earth beneath his feet and hoping for more rainfall, perhaps a few drops that might help wash away his tears.

When word came down that the move was afoot, Oscar turned himself into a human ox, assembling supplies and lashing them together with vines before hefting them onto his back. Loaded down like a one-man pack train, he plodded on down the Kalema Road along with all the others. Some of the men who were better off had a mule or a real ox to carry their belongings, while each woman carried a large pile of goods stacked precariously atop her head. Oscar had simply grabbed what he could from his own surrounds, as well as Meko's—stools and bedding and pots and pans and calabashes and all the other nonperishable items the Maasai relied on—and headed off toward the new encampment. He left the cattle behind as the others had done, hungry but presumably safe within the manyatta's inner sanctum.

What Oscar failed to understand was that while Meko and some of the other women from his particular manyatta were moving east, he was not. As soon as he arrived at their destination, a familiar-looking circle of recently constructed Maasai homes, he was told by one of the elders to set down his load. The elder pointed to another pile of goods, more of the same, really, that needed to be moved back to where he'd started out. Why, this was nothing more than a housing exchange! There were many more young mothers and young children in this manyatta, and it was they who were moving back to the other side, farther from harm's way.

Oscar began to catch on. The women of childbearing age, as well as all their young, were moving west, simply exchanging addresses with the incoming elders and their various wives. Since the elders generally possessed far more cattle than the younger men, a few new manyattas were needed. It was more work but it would lessen grazing pressure out west. Oscar could see that many of the men were cutting brush and finishing the assembling of the thorny walls of the new outer enclosures, walls that would hopefully be impenetrable to their feline enemies, as well as all others. He offered to help, but the elder, obviously the man in charge of

506

this sector, directed him to hoist his new load and head on back along with the women and their children. Oscar was apparently not considered essential to the fortification effort, despite his reputation as a man who knew how to throw a spear. His job was to not only continue to watch over Senento's cattle, far from the Kalema Road, but help watch over the young mothers and their children while their husbands remained behind to help fend off any potential offensive Jocko might put into play. So Oscar lifted another sizable load onto his aching back and headed back homeward, listening to the women singing as they marched and herded their young ones along the dusty track.

While Oscar, along with several of the older moran, was left to care for the new arrivals, Ntanda made sure his younger, more agile moran were all well positioned, including his most trusted mates armed with AK-47s. The latter kept out of sight, hidden in the brush near the small bridge over the Ewaso Ngiro, while the others were divided into two ranks, one to protect the cattle on the move, the other to keep watch over the remaining herds. The bridge was the critical piece, a constriction in the otherwise open savannah where the cattle would be herded along in very tight quarters.

Joseph himself stood sentry on the east side of the bridge, watching the flow of cows, calves, steer, and the occasional bull—tremendous masses of beef, horns, blood, and bones all clattering their bells and bellowing loudly while their respective herders and all their helpers, surely every boy between ten and fifteen, poked them along and tried their best to keep them in line. Joseph kept a lookout for poachers, as did the many moran stationed at the crossing. It was midafternoon when he spied some suspicious movement in the brush to the north. A lion attack was another possibility, but such a bold move against so many armed warriors would be as foolish for a lion as it would be for Jocko's goons. But much to his amazement and disgust, three armed refugees approached, holding their hands in the air, apparently signaling they merely wished to talk. How brazen! Their weapons were shouldered and the manner in which they walked, waving their arms up high, was not at all menacing. They seemed to be shouting but nothing could be heard above the very loud din of the cattle and their bells. Joseph, accompanied by several moran, spears at the ready, walked toward them.

"Entasho!" Joseph shouted. And they did stop. But they were laughing, which enraged Joseph even more. *"Kainyoo a-yieu?"*

He asked them what they wanted and they all laughed again.

"Liny en-kiteng!" replied the tall one in the middle, whose AK-47 dangled off to one side. We want your cattle. What else? Joseph lit into them while the moran gripped their spears tighter and lowered them just a trace. The tall man continued to laugh. He was telling Joseph how kind it was of his people to bring in a fresh batch of cattle, the others having been fairly well picked over. Such cheek! He went even further, suggesting that it was pointless, and very dangerous, for the Maasai to keep trying to prevent him and his comrades from gathering a little sustenance. Wouldn't it be better, he suggested, if the Maasai would simply agree to "donate" several animals a week to the refugee relief effort? It would be much simpler. His friends thought this hilarious. Joseph did not. He ordered them back to their compound, with threats of violence if they did not leave immediately. The three all got a good laugh out of that. But they turned and said good-bye, wishing them luck with the cattle drive and saying that, naturally, they would be back.

Infuriated, humiliated, and damn sick and tired of this refugee crisis, Joseph nonetheless returned to the mission at hand, moving cattle.

The three would-be poachers headed back, unaware they were being followed. Ntanda and two of his colleagues had watched and even overheard much of the exchange. Ntanda gripped his new rifle as they marched along, silently pursuing these arrogant pigs who had invaded Maasailand, his land, and now talked of their simply handing over Maasai cattle to them. He was well beyond outraged. He waited until they stopped for a rest. The tall one, the one who had spoken so callously, lit up a cigarette.

"Entasho!" shouted Ntanda. The three turned to see three fierce-looking moran threatening severe bodily harm not with their traditional spears but with shiny, well-oiled AK-47s, complete with magazine cartridges.

Ntanda told them to drop their weapons. They each obliged, clearly stunned that these quaint, spear-toting Maasai warriors were now aiming very lethal weapons at their guts. Even if they didn't know how to shoot well, there was no question that a quick burst of bullets from each magazine at this close range would cut them in half.

"Entapal!" he shouted, and clear out they did, as fast as they could. Ntanda picked up one of the rifles left behind and smiled at his comrades. It was a good day.

News that the Maasai had real weapons reached Jocko within minutes of the return to camp of his three newly disarmed soldiers. Never one to be rattled, Jocko calmly relayed the news to Banyon that evening. By all accounts, the rifles were all shiny and appeared to be brand new.

"Brand new?" said Banyon. "Then someone else has joined the party. I'll have to take that up with Peter Dermenjian."

Actually, that was good news. For one thing, if Jocko ever found out he and Peter Dermenjian had tried to play both sides of the street weapons-wise, he knew Jocko would not hesitate to slit his throat. Banyon left promptly, off to retrieve his satellite phone. Who else could be arming the Maasai? And why?

"Guns?" said Peter Dermenjian, incredulous. "The Maasai have guns? Now where on earth did they get them, after refusing the ones we offered them? Surely not from the Kenyan government."

"Surely not, but they apparently looked fairly new. Who else could be weighing in?"

Peter took another puff on his cigar. "Who cares," he said. "The Maasai, at least the ones in Kenya, matter little now that we know Newman is dead. Let's just focus on running those shot lines down the Avenue of the Volcanoes. Do you have the permits yet?"

"No, and it will be very difficult. The flamingos are getting ready to nest out on Lake Natron."

"Oh, come now. Don't tell me a bunch of frisky flamingos are going to stand in the way of tracking down the diamonds. Let's get on with it. I'm feeling more and more certain they're in that valley. They certainly didn't find them in the Mara or the Serengeti or Ngorongoro Crater. And Natron is just one vast sea of soda. The diamonds have to be back in that valley somewhere. Remember, the young Maasai out that way said they had shovels. It's simply a matter of honing in, getting a better perspective on what's going on down below the surface. With all those volcanic vents, who knows, maybe one gathered up some kimberlite along the way."

"Well," said Banyon, "if you're so certain now, maybe you should come down and show me just where the hell to run those shot lines. And then maybe you can bail me out of jail."

It was a moment before Peter responded. "Not a bad idea. But I'm afraid there are some complications on this end at the moment."

"Really. Like what?"

"It's Elizabeth. She's in her second trimester now, and I've promised her a trip to visit Oscar's grave before the baby arrives. But the doctor has ordered bed rest for the next few weeks. The fetus may not be well attached, if you know what I mean."

"I see. Then send your consultants. Just don't leave it up to me where to run those shot lines."

"Yes, I will do that. And I'll be down to visit as soon as the situation improves. Just see what you can do about those permits."

"All right. But I'm running low on funds. If I have to make a trip to Dar es Salaam, it's going to put me in the hole quite a bit. And if I have to bribe some lowly official, then—"

"Okay, I've heard enough. I'll see that your bank account gets a little padding. But not by much, mind you."

Chapter 61

Dr. Meinz tapped gently on her bedroom door. It was late afternoon and Elizabeth hadn't slept all day. In fact, she had barely rested, worried sick that she could be on her way to having a miscarriage. The spotting might be nothing, or it could be signaling the end of her—unbeknownst to Dr. Meinz—self-inflicted pregnancy via highly suspect seed.

"It's me, Dr. Meinz," he said. "Your brother Edouard has come to see you."

"Do come in," she replied.

"I won't be long," said Edouard as Dr. Meinz opened the door for him.

"Yes," he said, "she needs her rest."

He entered with a slight bow and approached her bedside. Then he leaned over and, smelling faintly of gardenias, kissed her gently on each cheek.

"Hello, dear sister," he began. "I'm sorry to bother, but when Mother told me the news I had to come see you. Are you all right?" He pulled a chair up near the bed, pausing to admire the lovely view of the Mediterranean afforded by large south-facing windows before sitting down.

"I'm scared," she said, "but all I can do is wait, wait to see what happens next."

"I'm sure all will be fine. You are still young and healthy."

"I'm not that young," she responded. "Menopause could be right around the corner."

"Nonsense," said Edouard, "and even if you do miscarry, you and Peter can always try again. There's time enough for that, certainly."

Time enough, yes, but not for this one-time-only, give-it-your-best-shot attempt with what she believed were the last living vestiges of Oscar Newman. Surely it had been Oscar in that stainless-steel container she had found deep in the cryogenic freezer several months ago. For not only did it bear an inscription to Oscar from his mentor in medical school, but it was dated and, most importantly, bore Oscar's initials. But it was all gone now, out to pasture in a sense. No, there would be no second chances, not with Oscar anyway, if she were to lose this child.

"I doubt we'd have any better luck," she said. "You know and I know he never would have married me if I weren't carrying his child, his heir. It's all he cares about, aside from his diamonds."

"Pas du tout!" Edouard exclaimed. "I do believe he has great affection for you."

"Only as the prospective mother of his child. Without that, I have no meaning and very little value in his life. He would send me and Eleanor packing the moment he learned that I'm no longer pregnant."

"Seriously? Then why on earth would you stay with such a man?"

"Please," she responded, "I'm as guilty as he is."

Edouard raised his neatly plucked eyebrows, quite taken aback. "What do you mean, you're as guilty as he is?"

"It's very simple. The only man I ever loved was Oscar, and now he's gone. So please don't judge me too harshly if I choose a man who may love me only as a mother and never as a wife."

"I see," he replied. "And where is he now?"

"He had a meeting in Toulon. We were supposed to take a trip to Africa, to his homeland in Kenya where we would, among other destinations, visit Oscar's grave. I was finally ready to face reality. We even ordered a headstone. But not now. Not since I've been ordered to remain in bed until the bleeding stops."

"So sorry. But assuming that's not such a long time, will you then be off to pay your respects?"

"That's the plan. As soon as I get the all clear from my obstetrician. And Dr. Meinz concurs."

"Naturally," said Edouard, well aware of how much time the curious Dr. Meinz spent administering to her welfare.

But like many plans, plans that are really nothing more than rays of hope, her plan for a short bed rest followed by a bit of limbering up before venturing off to visit Oscar's grave failed miserably. Instead she found herself playing endless rounds of canasta with her brother and catching fleeting glances of Peter between his many trips, which were about the only thing he had in common with Oscar. Days turned to weeks and soon nearly two months had passed by before she had cleared another hurdle. She was now free to move about. But travel abroad was still out of the question.

Meanwhile, Oscar, the presumed father of her wayward fetus, continued to guide Senento's cattle every day, looking for greener pastures beyond the small valley he and the cattle had come to know all too well. At night he tried to converse with the other herdsmen, still struggling but slowly picking up the

512

language, especially the local dialect, so as to understand as best he could how those confined to the west of the Ewaso Ngiro could hopefully share the land, at least until the refugees were gone and they could once again move north to their traditional grazing areas, trampled down as they would be. So far he'd understood very little, other than that everyone was very angry that the refugees were still there, even though the deadline for their withdrawal had long since passed.

He had expanded the range of his herd, which was now quite comfortable under his guiding hand. But it required a lot more walking. He knew all the cattle by name and called out his commands loudly and with great authority, holding his spear in one hand while prodding them along with a stick in the other, just as Matthew had done.

On rare occasions he would spot a few pink-and-white flamingos flying overhead, usually very early in the morning. He remembered Francis telling him they generally migrated at night. On one particular day, however, around midmorning, he saw a huge flock of them flying north. What was going on? It was only after they had passed overhead—hundreds of them, if not thousands—that he heard the explosions coming up from the south. It was a series of loud bangs, like a long string of very powerful firecrackers going off. Then another string, and another. Only these were no firecrackers. And certainly not gunshots. He had seen a movie once about uranium exploration in remote Australia, among the aborigines who opposed it. And like those uranium miners in the film, Peter Dermenjian was no doubt running seismic shot lines. He's closing in, thought Oscar, wondering how much longer before Peter located the anomaly on the western flanks of Gelai, a kimberlite pipe that had no business being there among all the soda springs feeding Natron.

Once the cattle were secured in the manyatta at night, he would sometimes leave the smoke and chatter, as well as all the confusion about how to apportion the range land, and just simply walk off into the night beyond the manyatta's thorny confines. Dark as it was, nothing could come close to the darkness he felt within, a bitterly cold and vast emptiness swirling with regrets and self-directed admonishments. Not that everything was his fault. Fate had certainly lent a hand. But why?

It may have been that last question that helped vault him out into the night. He would roam not quite unafraid but indifferent. Death would overcome one day and, what the hell, he was as ready as he'd ever be.

His favorite destination, especially on clear nights following the long rains, was a small clearing with a large, flat rock in the middle, a half mile or so west of the manyatta. He would lie down on this slab of stone, as if he were the main course at some wild African buffet. Then he would let go of his spear and simply focus on the phenomenally huge sky above and its millions upon millions of stars, its billions of suns shining bright. And there were so many more he knew he couldn't even see. His situation, and all his problems, seemed much less significant as the infinite sea of stars twinkled and shone and bled white light across an otherwise dark and endless sky. Shooting stars, tiny flecks of stardust sucked into the earth's atmosphere, would crisscross the firmament, as if it were some kind of celestial shooting gallery. It was good therapy. And sometimes he would spend the entire night so reclined, wrapped in his Maasai blankets, tempting fate.

It was early one morning after such a night that Oscar returned to find Father David Sebastian waiting for him just outside his humble home.

"David!" he bellowed. "Sorry to keep you waiting. If only you had phoned ahead!"

"Good morning, Oscar," said David. "I was hoping to catch you before you head off with the cattle. Where have you been?"

"No need to worry," Oscar countered. "I've simply been out communing with the heavens."

"Really?" said David. "Then what news from above?"

"Hard to say. But I have learned one thing."

"Which is…"

"Which is that I now understand why the universe is so infinitely large."

"Have you? And why is that?"

"It just has to be in order for all this incredible life to exist here, something so miraculous, so improbable as you and I even having this conversation."

"You sound rather *Homo sapien*–centric, Oscar, as if the universe simply revolves all around us and our little blue-green planet just for our benefit."

"No. It's all about probability or, more precisely, the improbability of all *this*." He pointed all around him, to the earth in general and all the life upon it.

"I see," said David, laughing as he embraced his friend, this Cornish moran of such huge proportions compared to the locals that he'd become known as *ol Tatuani,* a legendary giant in Maasai oral tradition who lived in a cave. It wasn't far from the truth and he certainly looked the part. The "mask of the lion"—half ochre and half black oils, painted on Oscar's face by the three women responsible for his overall Maasai makeover—was quite impressive, perhaps even frightening to the uninitiated. If the manyatta were ever attacked, Oscar could be the first line of defense.

"How are you, my friend?" said David as Oscar took a seat by the fire pit, which still smoldered from the prior evening's cookout.

"Alive, as you can see. Beyond that, it's hard to say."

"You have lost weight. You look good."

"Thank you. Did you bring me anything to eat? Or drink? I'm starving and would love another bottle of your excellent beer. Sorry to be so pushy, I just don't get out much anymore."

David smiled his warm, familiar priestly smile. "You are in luck," he replied. "I brought you some bread, a round of cheese, and a thermos of freshly brewed coffee to start your day off right. And a bottle of berry wine to sip after a long day's cattle drive."

"Why, thank you, David. This is very kind of you."

"It's the least I can do. I have been wanting to visit with you for some time now. The situation, I fear, is very bad. And I have worried about you. I simply pray to God that somehow the refugees will soon be gone and life can return to normal."

"Yes, wouldn't that be nice. Wouldn't it be nice if God fixed up everything just right for you and me, and for everyone? And it all fit nicely together somehow, no strife anywhere? It might take a miracle or two, but if anyone could pull it off, it would be God, right? God Almighty."

"Even if he could," said David smiling, "it would be much too boring. What good is life if we're not all out here trying to keep ourselves, as well as each other, from drowning in our own soup, which is rather thick these days, especially around here?"

"Right," said Oscar. "No fair expecting divine intervention to bail you out after divine intervention got you into a pickle in the first place."

David laughed, accustomed to Oscar's digs about religion, Catholicism in particular. "Divine intervention," said David, pouring them each a bit more coffee. "Such a concept. But it's what keeps most religions alive."

Oscar found that admission quite amusing as he took another sip of the delicious brew. "Alive?" he responded. "Then surely you must believe in it and, more importantly, trust in it, in order to keep doing what you do. But here's some

515

religion for you, especially if we're talking about staying alive. Reciprocal altruism. Isn't that pretty much 'I'll take care of you today, and maybe you'll take care of me tomorrow'? That kind of thing? It sounds like the crux of Christianity to me. And if Richard Leakey is right, that reciprocal altruism enabled our species to eventually dominate the earth by helping each other through various hardships—hardships that all other species had not the intelligence, the will, the ability, or the compassion to overcome—then perhaps all this 'religion' is merely a reflection, a manifestation of this most basic evolutionary tenet? It's not a matter of religion at all. It's how we evolve."

David laughed again. "So," he began, "you think we're still evolving?"

"I certainly hope so. Lord knows we can't go on living like this."

"And reciprocal altruism is what's been pushing us along, independent of any acts of God?"

"Or perhaps in spite of your so-called 'acts of God,'" said Oscar.

David considered this a moment and shook his head. "I'm afraid there's a very fundamental flaw in your logic," he protested. "In Christianity, there's no expectation of reciprocity. Altruism simply is. It's not like you do something nice for someone and then you have some kind of credit in someone else's reciprocity account."

"Really?" said Oscar. "No expectation of reciprocity? Then what in God's name are you doing here? You're a missionary out to convert the souls of these nomadic heathens, to make them behave more like Christians, to be kind, to be altruistic, n'est-ce pas? Don't you expect a little reciprocity after all your teachings? Not to mention a bit of peace and harmony?"

"Reciprocity is always appreciated," said David. "Peace and harmony, those are ideals that seem to have gone astray lately."

"Yes, they have," said Oscar. "We can certainly agree on that point. But enough of this philosophizing. What news do you bring?"

"There's not much to report. The refugee camp is stable. At least there are hardly any more of them streaming in. But the relocation will take more time."

"I'm not surprised," said Oscar. For he had spent far too much time in and around refugee camps throughout his career. They seemed to go hand in bloody hand with parts of the world where human reproduction far outpaced the ability of local natural resources to keep up with demand. In the global game of musical chairs, there simply weren't enough chairs to go around. And it was getting worse as the band played on.

"How are the Maasai faring, in your opinion?" David inquired as he sliced into a new round of his famous cheese. "That's what I wanted to discuss with you. After all, you live with them now."

"What do I know?" said Oscar. "The elders are all on the other side now. I'm simply a cattle guide by day and an alleged protector of women and young children by night. But rest assured, they're all pissed as hell."

"I've no doubt," said David. "And who can blame them? Their country has been invaded."

"But with their elder leaders' blessings," Oscar reminded him.

"They had no choice but to negotiate decent terms. Speaking of which, I had a message from Joseph and he asked when the American doctor would be back. He wants to pay Captain Olengi another visit with his attorneys. Perhaps you could get a lift into Nairobi with them. Everyone believes you're dead, so no one will be looking for you. That is, if you're looking to get back to Great Britain somehow."

"Right. But, you see, I have no papers whatsoever. I must have lost them back on Gelai when I was quite out of my mind. And I don't want to leave. Not yet. I'm still working for the Maasai. And I intend to stay on, at least until this refugee crisis blows over."

"That could be quite some time."

"So it seems," said Oscar, "so it seems. But until then, I will look after Senento's cattle. Then we shall see what lies ahead."

They both knew that what lay ahead was entirely commensurate with the movement of Ugandan refugees out of Maasailand proper. And much of that was in the hands of Inga van Hoven and her valiant crew of "volunteers," including Dr. Gertrude Brecht and her star pupil, Christine Olson, who were by now barely on speaking terms. Day after day they would visit with dozens of fragmented families, gathering threads of information about missing family members as well as extended family. At night all the data had to be transcribed and entered into a huge database that tried to tie all the loose threads together. Naturally, Christine inherited the job of data entry. Yet Dr. Brecht never stopped looking over her shoulder. It was driving her crazy.

But at least there had been some progress. Most of the country-by-country quotas had been established and paperwork was underway for relocating quite a few families—barely a hundred but a good start. Maybe the human logjam was starting to move a bit downstream as the waters of compassion rose ever so slightly among those countries who had signed off on their respective quotas.

Back at Red Cross central, Max continued his daily rounds. They were far less macabre but still painful, as quite a few of his badly hacked-up patients had failed to recover. Thank goodness he had stocked up on morphine. And with far fewer newcomers, he had time to help out in the children's ward. Here the main challenges were hunger, which was quite manageable provided UN food donations kept up; dysentery and other gastric disorders, which were just plain messy but usually controllable; and HIV. Max had certainly seen a fair share of Maasai children stricken with AIDS, but it was much less prevalent among the Maasai compared to the refugees. Lethargic and seemingly without hope, each child was still somehow able to smile at him as Max joked and made faces while preparing to administer another shot of antiretroviral solution. Watching their progress, or lack thereof, was painful. It made him miss his daughter, or the little girl who should have been his daughter, even more. And that made him miss Christine—a pretty face, a soft shoulder, and then some.

With his patients relatively stable, he was able to wrangle another leave slip out of Dr. Bichette. He arrived at tent thirteen unannounced, parking the Scout well beyond the double row of tents where the volunteers and professional aid workers resided, adjacent to the large administration tent. It was after hours and normally everyone would have been back inside their quarters, relaxing after another hard day or perhaps preparing a custom-made meal instead of partaking in the daily gruel served up at the communal dining hall. But on this particular evening no one seemed to be at home. They were all sequestered inside tent thirteen. Max approached the imposing canvas structure and, seeing an unguarded tent flap, peered inside. He half expected to see Dr. Gertrude Brecht lecturing them all about how to run a proper refugee camp. Instead he was stunned to see a table draped with the sky-blue United Nations flag and, behind the table, three UN officials in their Sunday best. One of them, a tall blond fellow in a highly decorated UN peacekeeper uniform and a baby-blue beret, was speaking to those assembled.

"…and I extend to you not only my gratitude on behalf of the United Nations and all its affiliates, but also warm thanks and congratulations from the UN secretary general, who has sent appeals to all member countries urging them to contribute more and, most importantly, to open their doors."

Around thirty people, all presumably working on the relocation, were seated in several rows of folding chairs. Max spotted Dr. Brecht in the front row, furiously taking notes. As he scanned the small crowd, he finally located Christine, third row back, leaning forward with her hand on her chin, looking quite skeptical. But the tall blond UN official resumed.

"There are intensive efforts underway to bring more human resources here to help move these refugees on toward new lives. The UN is working closely with the International Rescue Committee, who has issued an advocacy alert specific to this campaign in the hope and the expectation of raising substantial sums for this particular relief effort. We are also working with many other international organizations…"

And he went on to rattle them off by name and to try his best to assure those assembled that help was on its way. But they all knew better. Many were veterans of these campaigns and knew how the song and dance progressed. Dr. Brecht was one of them. When it came to the Q and A session, she pounced and Max felt he'd had enough. He wandered back toward Christine's tent and waited inside. It was dark and almost cool. He lay down upon her cot and tried to take stock of everything. Help was on the way! Oh boy. Provided someone somewhere put up the money. But at least this crew was getting some kind of pep talk. Back at Red Cross central it was all about taking it one day at a time. Some would live, others would die. But Max didn't expect any more help any time soon. The wave of cruelty had already crested.

Sometime later Max awoke with quite a start. He had no idea how long he'd been asleep, but when Christine grabbed him by the shoulder and shook him rather firmly, he came to in a hurry.

"Max," she said, "what are you doing here? What's going on?"

Max looked around, stunned and embarrassed that he had actually fallen asleep. "Sorry," he said as he sat up and rubbed his hands through his hair. "I didn't realize you were having a visit from the UN. That's pretty cool."

He tucked up his knees and she took a seat at the foot of the bed, stretching her long legs out in front and dangling a flip-flop with one toe.

"Pretty cool. Right," she countered. "'Help is on the way.' Even if he's right, there won't be any more help here for months. Meanwhile, it's ask them all the entire list of questions, carefully record the information, and don't forget to footnote which answers are more reliable than others based on observed states of emotional or even physical distress, et cetera."

"Lots of drudgery," he said. "We all get a big dose of that around here. And frankly, I'm getting a little worried. This place could blow any time. Joseph and his attorneys filed a lawsuit against the Kenyan government. And there's a rumor that even the Maasai have guns now. Can you believe that?"

"Nothing shocks me anymore."

"Me neither," said Max. He wanted to tell her about the boy with no lips but he thought better of it. He was far too focused on and mesmerized by *her* lips. Such a lovely profile.

"To be perfectly honest, I'm ready to get the hell out of here," she said. "We've done our time."

"What about your dissertation? I mean, aren't you getting some kind of academic credit for all this?"

"Good question. Gertie wants to write a book about this whole mess. And she says she wants me to help edit, maybe even be a coauthor."

"Sounds like exploitation to me."

"Right. What else are graduate students for?"

"What would you do if you left?" he asked.

"Go back to UCLA, I suppose, and try to sort out where I stand in terms of getting my damned PhD. My whole research project went to hell, and if all I've done is waste three years of my life out here, then I don't know what." She finally turned to look at him. "I just have to get away from her, Max. She's okay in small doses but I cannot live like this."

She was nearly in tears again. Max turned sideways and moved closer so they were thigh to thigh. He put his arm around her and she leaned toward him.

"Maybe we should both try to get out together," he suggested.

She looked at him with those lovely green eyes, eyes that had opened wide at the mention of leaving together. His heart racing, he leaned over and kissed her, very lightly and very briefly, until she pulled back and quickly stood up.

"Sorry," she said, "this is just getting a little too complicated. Let's go get something to eat. I'm starving. Besides, she could walk in here any minute."

All things considered, it was a very good visit. And the memory of that brief kiss helped Max get through the next couple of weeks with his spirits in better-than-average form. The notion of getting out, of getting home, sounded better all the time. Even better if he and Christine could make their way out together, maybe do a little traveling before heading back to California. Such were the notions running through his mind early one morning in mid-October when he caught a whiff of smoke. And then another. Looking south, he saw a long line of smoke and in an instant he was panic stricken. The Maasai had started the annual burning of their traditional grazing lands, refugees be damned.

Chapter 62

A slight breeze blew from the south, fanning the flames that Ntanda and his comrades had set all along the edge of the Kalema Road. It was that time of year, time for cleansing the land of all invasive species. They had separated hours earlier, bearing unlit torches and fully loaded automatic rifles. Although they had never really been tested, Crazy Jack swore up and down they'd work if they needed them. But when it came to cleansing the land, and returning stored-up nutrition back to the soil, fire was always the best tool available. All that was required was some combustible material and a bit of oxygen. Both were in plentiful supply. Add a little spark or, better yet, a long torch drenched in oil, and voilà, a sea of fire stretching for miles from the banks of the Ewaso Ngiro all the way to Lake Magadi, all of it steadily marching northward, directly toward the refugee camp.

They had painted the southern fringe of the compound with flame and stood back to watch. Conditions were perfect, exactly the kind of day Ntanda had been awaiting ever since he'd learned that the Maasai had filed a lawsuit against the government of Kenya. Did his father seriously believe that all this insult, this invasion, would be turned around by some exceedingly slow and no doubt corrupt legal process? No, it was time for action.

There were twelve of them, one for each AK-47 that Banyon had left behind, his great gift to the Maasai. Jocko's boys had continued to help themselves to Maasai cattle, despite the knowledge that the Maasai had guns. Only Ntanda knew better. Once the Maasai fired, then Jocko's troops would waste no time cutting them all down. No, they needed to wait, to wait until conditions were just right. And now they were. All his most trusted and loyal mates were with him, including his latest recruit, Matthew, the youngest moran, who was perhaps lacking in experience but who possessed one very important quality—a lust for vengeance, a burning desire to avenge his father's murder.

They ran along behind the flames, through charred scrub and grassland, looking for anyone who might try to penetrate the wall of fire. But a half mile or so of dry brush lay between the Kalema Road and the southern fence, porous as it was, of the refugee compound. It would take a bit of time to reach Jocko and his friends, but by that time the fire would be raging, unstoppable.

News of the fire traveled quickly. When it reached Joseph, who was seated before his home brewing some tea, he erupted in an anger unlike any his neighbors and friends had ever seen. He was beyond livid. He knew all too well that Ntanda was very angry about the lawsuit. But this was catastrophic. Even if no one was killed, the Kenyan government would surely use this maneuver as grounds for abdicating all agreements, all the detailed amenity improvements for the Maasai. But he also knew it was too late. The wind was blowing from the south. And it would continue to do so. He summoned his elders and they assembled for a trek north to witness the inevitable damage and no doubt a fair bit of carnage.

About two miles or so downwind, Dr. Maxwell Taylor was running as fast he could. He'd first reported the fire to Dr. Bichette. She'd stood frozen, contemplating the impossible. There was no way the hospital or any of its patients could be moved, not in the short time left before the fire arrived. Where would they even go? Max had told her he was heading down to the main administration tent. Their only hope was constructing a serious firebreak.

From his travels to see Jocko and the gang weeks before, he knew that the biggest physical break was where the main perimeter road separated Jocko and his troops from the rest of the refugees. That's where they needed to get busy. Moving refugees back from the roadway, gathering blankets to smother flames, grabbing shovels, all would be necessary right away if the whole camp was to be saved, or at least the refugees north of the perimeter road. He didn't give a damn about Jocko and company.

The scene at camp headquarters was utter chaos. It wasn't really clear who, if anyone, was in charge. In fact, Max had never entered the main office area before, accustomed to simply following orders from Dr. Bichette. The camp administrators seemed far more concerned with safeguarding their files and computers than saving all the refugees who now stood in harm's way. A water truck pulled up alongside the main administration tent, ready to pump water at the flames, while quite a few employees loaded up their vehicles, looking to make a break for it before flames engulfed the entire camp. Max screamed at them all to come to their senses and help construct a firebreak. Having grown up in Southern California, where fires threatened neighborhoods every summer, he knew enough about fighting fires to know that a sizable firebreak was their only hope. They acted like they couldn't hear him, ignoring his pleas.

He raced back to his own tent, hoping his seldom-seen roommate, Ivan, might be there. As the man in charge of camp maintenance, surely he would know where they kept all the shovels. But he was once again nowhere to be found. Looking southward, Max saw the smoke rising high into the sky, much closer than before. And there was the Scout. All he had to do was climb in and head for the border. But what about Christine and Dr. Brecht? He couldn't leave them, nor could he abandon his patients. No, leaving was out of the question. This required an orderly approach and some fast thinking.

Looking all around, he spotted the main equipment yard. The gate was locked. Inside were a few pieces of heavy equipment, including a large front loader with a huge bucket used for hauling garbage and such. He vaulted the fence and ran toward the large yellow machine, his heart pumping blood and adrenaline in almost equal proportions. The smell of smoke was getting stronger. He jumped up into the cab and, much to his delight, found that the key was in the ignition. He hadn't a clue how to drive such a machine but he was usually a quick learner. There were a dozen or so levers, various pedals, and a dashboard covered with knobs and dials that meant nothing to him. Letters that in days gone by had identified what was what had long since faded away. He turned the key and the machine lunged forward slightly. It was in gear, but which was the clutch pedal and which was the gear shift? He tried all combinations until he felt something move. Was he in neutral? He turned the key again and the engine turned over. But it still would not start. Where was the choke? After a few more attempts and trial by elimination, he found the choke as well as the throttle lever. Precious minutes flashed by, but finally, he found the correct combination. Now if he could only figure out how to put it in reverse and then turn it around!

After more trial and error, and a fair bit of cursing, he succeeded in moving the big brute of a machine. As it began to back up, he realized there was no steering wheel! Looking down, he figured out what those two big pedals were for—they controlled the speed of the large and rather rusty metal tracks that provided the locomotion. He pressed down on the left pedal and the machine backed around to the right, a good start. But where was first gear, or any gear that would launch him toward the locked gate? He noticed a large black man yelling at him from the other side of the fence. No doubt he was telling him to cease and desist, but Max could hear only the loud roar of the engine. Ignoring the man's protests, Max finally located a forward gear and released the clutch. He turned the throttle up as far as it could go and pressed his feet all the way down on the two large pedals. The big yellow machine lurched forward. Within seconds it was bearing down on the gate at top speed. The black man jumped out of the way as Max covered his face, hoping no bits of the crumbling gate would come back to bite him. In a matter of seconds, the gate was no longer obstructing his way. It was now firmly attached to the bucket as he swung right and headed out toward the main set of roads, dragging a fence post or two after him.

Not far to the south, Jocko was rudely awakened by the strong smell of smoke and the panicked screaming of his troops as they scrambled to deal with the wall of fire that was bearing down on them. He told the young girl who had shared his bed to get the hell out while he threw on his old army fatigues and ran outside, still buckling his belt around his pronounced waistline. Everyone was running, grabbing a few precious items, such as their rifles, and fleeing to the north. Jocko yelled at the top of his lungs for everyone to stop immediately. They all ignored him. He ran back inside his tent and came out carrying his own rifle and fired a few rounds into the air. Some stopped but most of them kept running, deserting their general, deserting him until Jocko lowered the tip of his rifle and shot one of them in the back. The would-be deserter crumpled to the ground.

The wind had picked up and the wall of smoke now towered over the southernmost reaches of the camp. They had already retreated once from the vicious warlords up north. That was bad enough. To face another retreat—a retreat from a foe as renowned for brutality as the Maasai, but who were by comparison to those up north merely quaint, spear-wielding pastoralists—was out of the question. They were simply burning their fields, an annual event. Okay, the fire would take out the tents, all their personal belongings, and those too timid to pierce the wall of fire, a relatively thin swath of flame. Wrapped in blankets, heads covered, wetted down if possible, they should all be able to run right through it. And then they would be free to start over. It would mean a few weeks of minor suffering, but relief would arrive. Captain Olengi would see to that.

"Gentle soldiers," he shouted out to his men, all of whom were frozen in place. "Run from me at your peril. We will not be defeated by a little fire." And he proceeded to tell them to scour their quarters for any blankets, towels, even shards of tents or old tarps, and wrap themselves up tight, but be ready to run. Then he told them to douse themselves with whatever water they could find and to, above all, keep their rifles well protected from the flames. They might well need to use them against the Maasai once on the other side.

His men, a few hundred hardened troops who had seen their fair share of atrocities, could barely hear him above the roar of the approaching firestorm. Those in front understood. Half of them ran for their tents; the others ran for their lives. No way Jocko could shoot them all. And why waste the bullets? The fire would likely catch up with them if they chose to flee. The best chance for survival was to simply run in the opposite direction, straight through the fire, as fast as possible and with ample, readily shed-able, and preferably damp protection.

By this time Max had reached the perimeter road. He knew what he had to do but it wasn't going to be easy. With more trial and error he had learned how to raise and lower the bucket. He just needed to cut a swath twelve feet wide, just north of the perimeter road, through a sea of terrified, screaming refugees who were all beginning to flee as fast as they could. Not only did he have to cut a wide swath, he had to do it in such a way as to convince everyone not to worry, to just stay put. All would be well. Just don't mind me while I bulldoze all your meager possessions into oblivion. And by the way, no human stampedes; you'll only end up trampling each other to death.

The first hundred yards were the hardest. He was pelted with all manner of debris but he kept shouting to them in his best Swahili, "This will stop the fire, do not run." Most of them were running anyway and couldn't hear him. But slowly, as the width of the road doubled and a much wider inflammable corridor separated them from the other side, they seemed to understand. More and more of them merely backed off and fewer and fewer ran away. And those that tried to run away made slow progress, given what little space was available amid the great sprawl of blue UN tarps and assorted temporary shelters and, more significantly, the others in their way trying to effect their own escape.

About every hundred yards he would make an abrupt turn to the right, taking out more rickety tents and obliterating what little civilization had formerly resided there. It slowed him down but he had to push all the dirt and debris caught by his bucket off to one side every now and then. As he pulled back out and began to wipe clean another couple hundred yards of the firebreak, he heard a roar beside him. Looking over, he could not believe his eyes. An army Jeep driven by Inga van Hoven was passing him on the left. Dr. Brecht sat in the passenger seat holding a bullhorn and Christine sat in the back. Dr. Brecht was broadcasting a message in several dialects of Swahili and at a volume the refugees might actually hear, telling them to stay put, do not run, you will all be safe. Christine looked up at Max as he gripped the levers on the big yellow machine and continued ripping the place up, pushing as much flammable material as the blade would handle off to the side. She gave him a huge smile and blew him a kiss. He smiled back at her, but blowing back a kiss was out of the question. This beast required both hands on the controls at all times.

Farther south, the wall of flame was fast approaching. It had already burned through the perimeter fence, reducing to cinders the wooden posts that used to hold the chain-link fencing upright. It was all now a mass of twisted metal and burning wood lying a mere hundred yards beyond the area occupied by Jocko and his loyal men.

They were aligned just inside the first row of tents, all wrapped up in whatever spare blankets and hastily shredded bits of tent canvas they could find. Their rifles were neatly strapped across their backs, leaving their hands free to pull the protective layers tight around them and their weapons.

On Jocko's command they all charged forward, though running was difficult with their feet and legs so heavily insulated. Nonetheless they charged into the wall of fire. All of them but Jocko. He held back like a good general looking after his troops, waiting to see if the others would get through and if they would simply be mowed down on the other side.

It was a fair question. For Ntanda had given clear instruction to all his lieutenants, who were dispersed across a wide expanse of newly blackened savannah, to fire over their heads. Just a few rounds to chase them back, back into the fire. Like herding cattle, only using a gun instead of a stick. But if they didn't retreat, they were to disarm them. And if they didn't drop their weapons, they were then fair game. But they had to mind their ammunition, for they had but one magazine clip apiece.

Matthew had understood the instructions. He crouched as low as possible while still creeping forward, holding his rifle high in the air and well away from the hot, smoldering ground. Looking left, and then to the right, he spotted two of his comrades between the shifting shrouds of smoke rising from the freshly incinerated savannah. It was like guarding the Kalema Road, where the moran always kept in eye contact with one another, only they were now much farther apart. Ntanda was on his left flank keeping an eye on the rookie. They were all moving forward together, following the linear course of the fire at a distance that didn't singe the bottoms of their feet too much, always on the lookout for Jocko and his boys. The smoke rose in front of them in swirling layers infused here and there with rays of amber as the sun climbed above the eastern horizon.

They each had a red flag they would wave to help them spot one another, when they were not breathing through it. Ntanda had thought of everything. Plodding onward, Matthew peered through the layers of smoke, stifling the urge to cough, pretending to be invisible, waiting for an enemy sighting. So far there had been none. For if there had been, he would have heard the shots.

There was little cover left besides the smoke. But his dark skin, covered only by a dark loincloth, and his newly darkened braids, covered expressly with the ash, all made for good camouflage. He marched on through the charred savannah, looking and waiting for the enemy to appear.

It began all at once, a full-on charge of screaming, go-for-broke refugee soldiers emitting a uniform war cry that simply translated to "ready or not, here we come." They burst through the wall of flames like upright cocoons of fire, some running, some stumbling, many just plain falling to the ground. Some were screaming in agony, grabbing at their eyes that had been blinded by sudden flame-ups as they tried to maneuver through the burning face of the wind-driven inferno.

While there was certainly no shortage of oxygen—for the fire, at least—breathing was a challenge. And the air was much too hot. Those who had held their breath too early ended up taking their final breath of fire. Some tripped and fell and literally went up in flames. Worst of all, many of those who had tripped or collapsed, for whatever reason, and fallen into the flames were ripped apart by the exploding bullets lodged in their ammo clips.

Yet there were others, the lucky ones, or perhaps the smart ones, who managed to break through, to shed their prophylactic shells on schedule, afire but safely behind them, and then march onward, unhitching their well-protected rifles, wary and fire tempered. These were the men who appeared before Ntanda and his mates as the sun rose over Maasailand.

Dozens of these survivors burst through the last of the smoky clouds that billowed from the heels of the fire, blackened all over and running as fast as they possibly could. Clutching their rifles, they were ready for the next challenge, which would be Ntanda and friends, who were clearly outnumbered and far too dispersed, for the eruption of smoldering refugee soldiers emanated from a relatively small section of the wall of flames. They were headed straight for Matthew.

Even though the fire had whittled Jocko's loyal troops down to less than half of their original strength, those who remained were the strongest by far. And they were now all highly enraged not only by the discomfort they'd just been put through but by the loss of their comrades. The time had come. Ntanda fired the first volley over their heads. It did nothing to stop or remotely slow them down. They responded by firing back, a round that fortunately went over Ntanda's head as he flattened himself out on the charred ground.

Matthew heard the shots and, holding his rifle just the way Crazy Jack had taught him, fired off a round, too, as did his moran comrade to the east. It gave the impression, intentional or not, that there was more to Ntanda's war party than the twelve moran each situated about a quarter mile apart. Jocko's men spread out, keeping low but clearly not interested in putting down their weapons. One of them fired a volley back at Matthew, who was flat on the ground, looking for better cover.

The rifle had worked, giving quite a kick, just as the crazy American had promised. Bullets were flying overhead but he was ready. They were still too far off to shoot with any confidence and he clung to a hope that they would simply give up, throw down their arms, and surrender. No matter how they responded, it was not a time for rash behavior. He checked to see that his rifle was ready for action. Fair game, he thought. Weren't they all?

Then he looked up. There were four of them charging straight at him as he crouched in the smoldering ashes. He could now clearly see the faces of the men, still screaming at the tops of their lungs as they charged. And he clearly recognized one of them. It was the beady-eyed, broad-faced goon who had shot his father. Matthew stood straight up and took aim.

"*Entasho!*" he shouted. Much to his surprise they did stop; they all but froze as Matthew aimed his rifle alternately from one to the next. While they did not drop their guns, they did not raise them, either, keenly aware that Matthew had the upper hand for the moment.

"You," he shouted in Swahili, "you killed my father."

The broad-faced one with the narrow-set eyes stared at Matthew and began to laugh. "I am so sorry," he replied. "I did not mean to kill him. I meant to kill the other one, the one who slit my brother's throat. But now I am going to have to kill you as well."

He looked over at his friends and laughed. Then he whipped back around and raised the tip of his rife. The sounds of exploding bullets filled the air as Matthew realized he was too late. For much to his amazement the four refugees all fell forward, their stomachs ripped open by the blasts from Ntanda's rifle before Matthew had even begun to squeeze the trigger on his own weapon.

"You missed me again," said Ntanda as the would-be assailant lay dying.

The view from above was stunning and simply unbelievable. Hovering just south of the flames, Melanie Woo watched closely out the helicopter's window as Jocko's men came surging out of the wall of fire. Quite a few were falling, then writhing on the ground like cocooned moths unable to shed their burning chrysalises.

"My God," she shouted to the pilot, "can you get a little closer?"

"Yes, but let's not stay here too long," said the pilot, a Yemeni fellow who worked for a local news station, normally just doing traffic reports. If only they'd had more notice, she would have brought Edward along, a real photographer with a very state-of-the-art video camera as well as CNN's own helicopter. Only he was off on another assignment in Tanzania. So Melanie had contacted her Yemeni friend and begged him to take her to the scene once reports came in that the Maasai were attempting to set the refugee camp on fire.

He tilted the ship forward and slowly descended as they headed west, following the line of flames. Armed only with her cell phone, she recorded the scene below as Jocko's loyal soldiers spilled out of the thin wall of fire, crossing over from the inflamed tent city to the north to the newly charred landscape to the south, toward a confrontation with a dispersed group of Maasai, presumably the moran warriors who had set the place on fire to begin with. And they were clearly carrying guns and firing at the charging refugees.

"I can't believe the Maasai are shooting at them!" she shouted as the chopper zoomed in for a better view.

"Just a little closer and then we go," said the pilot, clearly less thrilled than Melanie to be part of this adventure.

Jocko witnessed the killings from a distance, having negotiated the wall of fire and shed his outer garments before they burned through. His troops were out in

530

front, seeking out the miscreants who had set his little world on fire. Such a rude awakening! Looking up, he saw the helicopter and recognized right away that this was not the law, not the government. This was the news media. That just would not do. He was not about to let the whole world witness what he and his troops were about to do to these damn Maasai. He raised his rifle and took careful aim. Just one shot should do the trick.

He was right. The bullet pierced the glass bubble and hit the Yemeni pilot in the shoulder. He fell onto the stick and his machine began to lose altitude.

"I'm hit," he shouted above Melanie's frantic screams. "Sit tight and I'll try to get us down safely."

The helicopter quickly picked up speed and altitude as the slumping pilot sought to regain control. Another shot glanced off one of the runners before they were up and away.

Jocko had to laugh. That was too easy. But now down to business. His men were arrayed in a long line, steadily marching forward. As soon as he'd heard the bullets start to fly, he'd known they were in trouble. The reports were on target— the Maasai did have weapons. And apparently, they knew how to use them. But where were they? He pulled out his binoculars, another perk for being general, and scanned the theater in which he and his men were now engaged.

Ntanda rolled over and called to Matthew.

"*Abori,*" he whispered. Get down. The young man was still a bit in shock, watching the insides of the man who had killed his father, and who had nearly killed him, spilling out onto the ground. But he understood and obeyed, lying down on the ground that was still quite warm.

"*Tusujuaki!*" he ordered. Follow me.

Easier said than done. Ntanda began to slither on his elbows, crawling through the burned-out brush, beating a fast track to the east. It was time to close ranks but who knew? Certainly not the rest of the team, unless they, too, had sensed that the action was in the middle and decided to all get together. Strategically, it cut both ways. The more dispersed they were, the harder they would be to find. Good news for those on the edges but bad news for Matthew and Ntanda.

Jocko sat on top of a slight rise, safely situated in between the front line to the south and the receding flames, which were now ripping through Jocko's depopulated tent city. Rounds of leftover ammo were exploding in all directions in the old neighborhood. But there had also been some ammo exploding down below, to the south. And that ammo had killed four of his men.

Upon seeing their comrades cut down before their eyes, Jocko's men also dove for cover. They were all crawling forward, waiting for a signal or perhaps some direction. In truth, they had had no direction other than to get to the other side of the fire. Mission accomplished, but now what?

Jocko watched it all unfolding, all his men moving like so many worms through the blackened landscape, while the moran did the same. It was easy to trace, as all the ashes and dust they stirred up rose above them, betraying their respective positions. Like ghostly traces, they were easily followed by those who had a stake in all this—and a good pair of binoculars. Jocko kept an eye on close encounters but, more importantly, he kept track of the two who had started all the trouble. They would be the first to die.

Back in Nairobi, Captain Olengi was apoplectic. His phone ringing off the hook, he had just received word that not only had the Maasai set the world on fire, they had apparently tried to shoot down a local news station's helicopter. What the hell could he do about it now? He'd just gotten off the phone with his fire command. Tanker planes were loading up with water but it would be at least half an hour before they would be airborne. His secretary interrupted him.

"Your helicopter will be ready in ten minutes," she told him. "And Peter Dermenjian is on hold. He wishes to speak with you right away."

The tennis balls in his cheeks were ready to explode, he was grinding his teeth so hard.

"Hello, Peter," he said, picking up line two. "Yes, it's true. The whole place is ablaze. I've ordered up some tanker planes to douse the fire. But the latest reports are that the southern sections of the compound have already been destroyed. It looks like some of Jocko's boys made it through the fire and are about to take on the Maasai who started all this… Yes… I agree, they should make short work of them and… Yes, all right… See you tomorrow. Have a good flight."

He slammed the phone down so hard it nearly cracked the receiver. Then he headed up to the helipad, where he and two advisers to the prime minister were to meet for their unscheduled overflight to witness the ongoing destruction firsthand. So much for having a nice lunch with his wife on this, his fiftieth birthday.

The fire roared through the southern portion of the camp, each tent going up with a whoosh of fire and a crackle of exploding bullets. Max was thankfully out of range, having reached the western edge of camp, just beyond the massive sprawl of refugee tents and tarps and pots and pans and all the other household items he'd been steadily destroying. But it was no time to slow down. He had to make it all the way to the Ewaso Ngiro, the other major piece of the firebreak.

Sweating profusely, he kept both pedals to the metal as he raced to complete the firebreak on time. The smoke was so bad that breathing was difficult and it was getting harder to see. He had already come very close to running over a number of the refugees, mostly small children whose mothers had lost track of them. But so far no casualties.

Though his eyes were focused straight ahead and the roar of the machine blocked out most other sounds, the beat of the helicopter's blades was unmistakable. Looking up, he saw through various wisps of smoke that it was a local news helicopter, spinning as it hurtled through the air, losing altitude, clearly in danger. Adrenaline raced through his body as he watched someone—a woman with long dark hair—jump out of the helicopter mere seconds before it crashed in a great ball of smoke and flames just on the other side of the Ewaso Ngiro.

"Oh my God," he said to himself, realizing that the person could very well be ace reporter Melanie Woo. No doubt the pilot had tried to find her a soft landing spot in the marshes bordering the Ewaso Ngiro, marshes that could well be teeming with crocodiles. First things first, he thought, trying to calm down. Finish up the firebreak and then see if you can find her, and maybe the pilot, too. What a day from hell if ever there was one.

To the south, Matthew crawled along on his belly, following Ntanda as he searched for his moran colleagues. Peeking up from time to time, he saw no sign of them, nor could he see any of the refugees. Had they fled? Or was everyone simply hunkered down, waiting for the other guy to make the first move? Everybody had guns, automatic rifles that, as Matthew had clearly witnessed, could just saw you right in half. Ntanda stopped, frustrated that he couldn't locate his men. But he dared not wave his red flag, not now.

Jocko was losing patience. Leaning against a rock that provided ample protection, not that he was in range, he lit up a slim cigar. It wasn't the quality he was used to, but it was a nice break from the ambient smoke he'd been breathing for the last half hour. But it was getting late. Surely someone other than the media had noticed by now that central Maasailand had just been torched and that the entire refugee compound full of over fifty thousand Ugandans fleeing brutal

533

persecution in their homeland was on fire. In other words, there wasn't much time before the cops arrived. He stood up and shouted out to all within shouting distance. And that, he figured, would be a fairly large area, given that all the brush, scrubland, and grassland had just been reduced to just inches of ash and smoldering bits of wood. In other words, no cover and no sound barriers.

"Gentle soldiers," he shouted, "gentle soldiers one and all, Ugandan and Maasai as well."

It was like speaking into a vast and empty blackened space. The newly charred land sloped gradually to the south with minor undulations, but all was quite out in the open, with no place to hide. Jocko shook his head, ashamed.

"You are all warriors! Why do you crawl on your bellies like so many snakes? Get up, get up and let go of your weapons. It is no time to fight. As warriors you know when to fight and when to make peace. My people and I, we thank the Maasai for your kindness. It is not our wish to stay, to deprive you of your homeland simply because we have been deprived of ours. We have been waiting, powerless, waiting for new homes for many months. We do not wish to stay. So please, let us simply pass through."

These words, spoken in Swahili, reached Ntanda as he lay on his side, looking for his troops, pondering his next move. Ideally, he would caucus with his boys. But the only boy around was Matthew, lying beside him, frightened, clutching his rifle.

"What should we do?" said Matthew.

Ntanda sat up to take a look around. These were the swine who had been stealing their cattle for months. Passing through? Where to? There was no place for them to go. Yet there was Jocko, striding toward them. Ntanda gave a stern look toward Matthew and then toward his gun. Without his uttering a word, his meaning was clear. It said "cover me." And then he stood up, holding his rifle to one side.

"Tell your men to stand and drop their rifles," he shouted. It was a bold move. Any one of Jocko's boys, or even Jocko himself, could have taken him out. Matthew kept his targeting right eye trained on Jocko, looking through the rifle sight as the American had taught him.

"That I will," said Jocko, and he shouted to his men to stand up and then lay down their rifles.

Ntanda watched in awe as his troops did as ordered by their commander. One by one they all stood, emerging from their highly dispersed and decidedly prostrate positions, covered in soot and ash. Perhaps they welcomed the notion of a cease-fire, as dozens of them stood and let their rifles fall to the ground. They held their hands up as well, signifying they were no longer a threat.

"And now it's your turn," said Jocko, puffing away on his skinny cigar as he approached Ntanda. The latter called out to his troops, all of whom had been moving closer, at a slow, crawling pace, to the center of the confrontation. He told them all to stand, which they did. Once Jocko saw there were only twelve of them, he started to laugh. This tiny army had just roasted them out of their new digs?

Once all twelve were standing, including Matthew, who still kept Jocko firmly in his sights, Ntanda told them to drop their weapons as well. Many of them looked at him like he was crazy. But they followed his instructions, even Matthew, however reluctantly. This left only Jocko and Ntanda in possession of rifles. They were no more than twenty yards apart. Jocko threw his rifle down on the ground.

"You see," he began, "we come in peace."

Ntanda threw his rifle down as well while he gripped the handle of his knife, which was embedded in its sheath tied to his loincloth. Perhaps not as lethal, it was a weapon he knew much better. And it always flew straight. Jocko walked up and extended a hand, as if in peace.

It was quite easy for him, a lefty, to reach behind, grab his pistol, and fire two shots, one each into Ntanda's and Matthew's heads. As they slumped to the ground, Jocko turned toward his troops, laughing, with a nod that said, "It's okay, you can pick up your rifles now." The Maasai were disarmed and he still had several shots left in his pistol. Then, out of nowhere, a shot rang out and Jocko's face exploded, a hideous sight indeed. The refugees started to reach for their rifles when a burst of bullets ripped over their heads. They all ducked then stood straight again, looking to see who had fired these shots, who had just killed their leader.

A lanky, soot-covered figure stood up fifty yards west of where Jocko lay bleeding, killed instantly by a single bullet. It was none other than Crazy Jack McGraw, former Texas Ranger. No way was he just going to lie back and miss all the action. Besides, he had to make sure those guns worked okay.

Jack McGraw walked up to stare down at Jocko to make sure he was gone. "You son of a bitch," he cried, kicking his limp body. "You and your damn snake didn't know who you were dealin' with, did ya?"

He looked at Ntanda and Matthew, lying just a few feet away.

"Sorry, Ntanda, I was too late. Too damn late."

Also too damned late were Joseph, his crew of elders, and the hundred-odd moran to whom Ntanda had given strict orders—no matter what happens, no matter what you see or hear, stay at your posts. They arrived in one long line of orange-clad, spear-toting Maasai men and warriors, all keeping apace of Joseph as details of the horrid scene before them became more and more clear. The ten who remained from Ntanda's loyal contingent had their rifles aimed at the refugees, who were frozen in place, hands behind their heads. Jack McGraw stood beside the ten rifle-bearing moran, making sure they held their fire.

Joseph stopped to take it all in, the four refugees lying dead, and not far to their right, three more bodies. These he recognized. Jocko's cigar was still smoldering by his side, his fat belly pointing skyward. He took a few steps forward and peered down at his son. He knelt down on one knee and kissed him on top of his lifeless head. Then he did the same to Matthew, poor Senento's son, who deserved much better than this.

He heard a gasp from the refugees and watched as they all fell to their knees. Turning around, he saw that Oscar had arrived, ol Tatuani, the giant. Beside him stood Father David Sebastian, dressed in his dark priestly robe and looking like Judgment Day had finally come, which it unfortunately had for Matthew and Ntanda.

Chapter 63

He had to find Melanie as soon as possible. There was no telling what her situation was, assuming that had been her jumping from the helicopter. Who else could it be? He had definitely seen her dark hair trailing behind as she plummeted to earth. Even if she had survived the jump, the denizens of the marsh might have already— well, he really didn't want to think about it. He just needed to get to her. Max watched the gas gauge as he motored on, hoping he had enough fuel to make it clear to the river and maybe a bit beyond.

He cut across the roadway, keeping the bucket just deep enough and adjusted to the proper angle to scrape away the grass and shrubs. Somewhere out here was another fence line, the western edge of the compound. But out here he had no guide, no road to follow. It was all wild, with signs indicating it was off limits to the refugees for some reason.

He soon found out why. For straight in front of him was a massive mound of debris, foul enough to smell even through the thick smoke. It was the local landfill, a favorite haunt of his roommate, Ivan. Piled high with all the refuse from an instant city of some fifty thousand, it stretched both north and south. It wasn't too difficult a decision—escape to the north or head south into the jaws of the raging fire. Besides, he would likely be doing Ivan a favor by letting the fire lend a hand with the decomposition process.

As he rounded the foul pile of latrine waste and food waste and discarded trash from not just the refugees but all the staff, he could barely make out the green ribbon of vegetation that bordered the river about a quarter mile in the distance. If nothing else, Max had beaten the fire, beaten it to the western edge before it caught up to him and his new best friend, the mighty track-mounted front-end loader. The beast of a machine had performed marvelously, more so as Max figured out what each of the controls was for and how to not just raise and lower the bucket but how to adjust its angle of attack. He came upon the western fence and ran through it without even slowing down. Now, however, he faced another daunting challenge, crossing the Ewaso Ngiro.

The riverbank was gentle enough, and on the other side the marshes stretched off to the west, where the smoldering wreckage of the helicopter near the far edge sent plumes of black smoke skyward. He cut the engine in order to study the situation and to listen for any distress signals from Melanie. He surveyed the river

537

from where he sat in the cockpit. No sign of a body, thank goodness. Then again, if she had landed in the river, well, he really didn't want to think about that, either. Although he didn't see any, he figured there must be at least a few crocodiles around. It looked like their kind of place.

He shouted out for her as loud as he could. No response. She could be anywhere. It was time to start searching, but how? He climbed down and walked to the banks of the river. The footing was good so far, and no sign of predators. Maybe the fire had driven them off? He walked out into the shallow, flowing river laden with brown silt. The bottom, too, was firm but the other side looked like trouble. Reeds lined the far bank and beyond the reeds were more reeds and sedges and tall marsh grasses. He waded across and looked out over the expansive marshland. Was she out there somewhere? He shouted for her again. And he listened for a long time. There were so many birds it was hard to tell if any of those calls might be an Asian Melanie bird stuck in the mud somewhere. He shouted her name again. And he listened once more.

Perhaps it was his imagination, but he thought he heard a cry, faint but more human than birdlike. "Melanie!" he shouted. And then he listened, cupping his ears to block out the sounds of the fire behind him and the rippling of the water in the river. Focused on the marshland, he closed his eyes, trying to discern if any possibly human sound might be present within the cacophony of buzzing insects and birdcalls that dominated the sound waves. The sound he thought might possibly be her voice was straight out in the middle of the marsh. He called to her again and he waited for a reply, just like all the birds who were calling out to one another in all manner of voices and rhythms.

There it was. Maybe it was just some marsh bird telling her mate to get lost, or maybe it was Melanie emitting a very faint call for help. He took a couple of steps in that direction and was quickly ankle deep in swamp water. Pursuing her on foot, if it was her at all, would be very slow, very wet, and very dangerous, especially if the local reptile population included crocodiles. And why wouldn't it?

Max ran back across the Ewaso Ngiro and jumped into the cab. He turned the key and she fired right back up. Almost as trusty as his old Scout.

Easing her across the river, keeping the bucket high, Max felt like he was riding some huge mechanical elephant. He climbed up the opposite bank, which was much lower, and gazed at the marshland ahead. He cut the engine and listened.

In addition to the local inhabitants' buzzing, singing, and croaking, he heard the dull rumbling of an airplane. Turning around, he was quite surprised to see a large tanker plane flying low. From its trajectory he surmised it was about to dump its load over the smoke and ashes that once were Jockoland. The wall of smoke from the fire remained to the south and was much smaller than when he'd been chugging along the perimeter road. Maybe the firebreak had worked!

"Son of a gun," he said to himself. He watched and waited for the plane to drop down lower and then open its bottom and let fly what had to be thousands and thousands of gallons of water in a linear, airborne stream that, if nothing else, would perhaps show the world that the government of Kenya had the situation under control. Then he turned his attention back to the mission at hand.

"Melanie! Can you hear me?" he shouted, wondering when a search party with proper rescue equipment might pounce on the scene. But until then, it was all up to him.

He thought his ears might be playing tricks on him again but a very faint cry, the slightest of whispers, floated across the expanse of marsh grass, reeds, and sedges. It came from the same direction as what he thought he'd heard before, a female voice crying, "Help me." He had no choice but to investigate, realizing full well that this heavy metal machine might just ooze on down into the organic muddy soils of the marsh and sink out of sight.

Focusing on a large fever tree in the distance, he started the engine and shifted into first gear. He inched forward, trying to gauge the firmness of the new medium he was entering before it swallowed him and the loader in one gulp. As the reeds and sedges bent over, crushed by tons of metal, Max thought about how many laws he'd be breaking if he were to drive such a machine into a swamp of this magnitude and beauty back in the States. No doubt Kenya had laws against this, too, but no matter. He was going in, and hopefully over, to the other side.

The front end dipped down a couple of feet, giving him a fright, but leveled off once the rear end was immersed in the same muddy medium. But Max could feel that the entire machine was slowly sinking. He hit the throttle, hoping to overcome gravity and that sinking feeling by moving faster before the ground beneath just gave way. Or maybe there was a solid substrate below. How far below was a question he dared not explore. Besides, bugs were all over him and more speed meant fewer bites in the long run.

539

Birds flew up by the dozens out of the reeds and the grasses that grew nearly at eye level. He certainly could not afford to sink below their level and lose sight of the fever tree. But he also could not afford to go too fast and possibly run right over her, if Melanie was indeed stuck in the mud somewhere beyond. Much to his dismay, he knew he would have to stop and shut off the engine in order to locate her. When he was about a third of the way across, he did as much then quickly called out to her.

"Melanie!" he shouted again.

This time there was no mistaking it.

"Help me! Help me, please!"

The voice was shrill and filled with terror. And it came from a spot straight ahead. Max quickly fired up the engine, having sunk a good six inches. But he regained some ground as he moved forward, standing up in the cab, searching for a sign, a hand, a flag, anything. The fear of crushing her made his heart race almost as much as the thought of rescuing her from what would be a horrible death. He could not erase the image of her falling from the sky, jumping feet first into the softest landing spot around. She could be up to her neck in mud with who knows what marsh creatures making a meal out of her.

Halfway across he cut the engine again. Before he could even call out to her, he saw something scrambling through the tall grass and reeds, then another. His first thought was of crocodiles. But no, couldn't be. Crocodiles would have made short work of her. But the shape was similar. He stood up again, feeling the machine settling in, and then he saw it, a Nile monitor lizard.

"Over here," she shouted, though it was still a muffled cry.

Max started the engine and crept along slowly, sinking slightly, until he saw an arm waving a large pink cell phone.

He pressed harder on the right pedal and came abreast of her. She was sunk in the mud up to her armpits, covered with mud and dirt and insects. No wonder her cries had been so faint. She was surrounded by thick marsh vegetation. And she was very stuck.

"Melanie," said Max as he shut the engine and hopped down into the muck. "Are you all right?"

"I don't know," she said, nearly hysterical and all in tears. "Just please get me out of here."

"I'll try," he said as he reached for her arm.

"Take this first," she said as she handed him her cell phone. "And don't drop it. I got it all on there."

"The fire?"

"And the fighting between the Maasai and the refugees. It was horrible."

"Damn, you are good," said Max as he put the device in his pants pocket and grabbed both her arms. She really was stuck, and he feared that if he kept pulling like this, he would be, too.

"I've got an idea," he said. "I'll swing around and lower the bucket. Just grab on with both hands and I'll try to lift you up out of there. But you're going to have to hang on tight."

"Okay," she said, trembling while tears streamed down her face, cutting rivulets in her muddy complexion.

He jumped back into the cab and started the engine, wondering how far he could afford to sink before he'd be hopelessly stuck. So far he was winning the battle of gravity versus speed. He backed up a few feet and maneuvered to a spot where it was safe to lower the bucket. It came down slowly while he adjusted the angle to give Melanie a cleaner edge for gripping. She grabbed on.

"Got it?" Max shouted, easing back on the throttle.

"Yes," she shouted. And he began to slowly raise the bucket. It was hard for him to see if she was able to maintain her grip. The only way was to keep on raising it high enough to see if she was still there. Up and up, slow and easy, until at last he saw her come into view, hanging on for dear life with both hands as the bucket finally lifted her clear of the foul marsh mud. Her white blouse was completely ripped open in front and her breasts looked like they were about to burst out of the harness that was holding them in, along with bits of marsh vegetation wedged into her cleavage. Her jeans were covered in grime but at last her feet were free, shoes or sandals long gone. He cut the engine.

"Can you climb into the bucket?" he shouted.

"I'll try," she shouted back. Fortunately, Melanie had always been very fit and very strong. She chinned herself up and swung a leg over the edge of the bucket. Then she climbed in, clearly not concerned in the rush for salvation about her torn-up blouse.

Max shifted into low gear and the tracks turned but went nowhere. He tried reverse but that led only to ground he'd already covered. He managed to go a few feet before the big metal tracks just spun in place again.

"Damn it!" he shouted. But then he took his left foot off the pedal and slammed the right one all the way down. To his great relief, the machine spun to the left, where fresh marsh grasses waited to be crushed. He circled around until he spotted the fever tree and what looked like the shortest route to dry land. Then it was full speed ahead, with hopes that he was not simply headed for some open water that might be obscured by the tall marsh vegetation.

Fortunately for both of them, that was not the case. In fact, the bottom became even firmer as they approached the far shore, where upland vegetation—acacias and savannah grasses, as opposed to the marsh variety—predominated. In fifteen minutes Max pulled ashore and, after lowering the bucket, cut the engine. He jumped down and ran around to the front to help Melanie out onto terra firma. He was too late. As he came around she was standing, holding on to the side of the bucket, and trembling all over. Before he could open his mouth to speak, she began hugging him and thanking him over and over and over. He held her close, stroking her dark hair that was wet and slimy and laced with bits of vegetation. She smelled to high heaven. The decaying organic matter in the anaerobic muck in which she had been marinating reeked of the rotten-egg smell of hydrogen sulfide. But somehow it didn't bother him.

"Thank you," she sobbed again. "I was sure I was going to die out there. It was awful, just awful. These huge lizards were going to eat me, I just don't know what they were waiting for. They kept licking at me, flicking their big tongues out at me. I don't know what stopped them."

"Those were Nile monitors. They weren't going to eat you. They were probably just eating all the bugs you attracted. But you really should thank them."

"Why? For breathing on me with the most hideous breath you can imagine while they were licking my face? I tried to beat them away with my arms but they kept coming back."

"I'm sure it was terrible," said Max. "But you should thank them. They like to eat crocodile eggs."

"They do?"

"Yes, they do. You're really lucky to be alive. Are you hurt?"

"My hips are very sore from the impact. And my legs are like jelly. But I don't think anything is broken. That poor pilot! Someone shot him!"

"It looks like he crashed by the edge of the marsh," said Max. "At least *that* fire didn't spread."

"I was just trying to get some footage of the Maasai shooting at the refugees who fought their way through the flames. We got too close and one of them, a refugee I think, managed to shoot the pilot."

"This whole world has gone insane," said Max, "but look, let's try to get back to the river and you can wash up. Then we'll try to figure out our next move."

Chapter 64

He circumnavigated the marsh until he came to a spot near the Ewaso Ngiro with a more pronounced riverbank and not a whit of marshland. Nor did he see any crocodiles. The water was flowing more swiftly, though it was no more than a foot deep.

"I doubt we'd find a better spot," said Max. "I'll keep an eye out for Mr. Crocodile if you want to go down there and wash up."

She turned and looked at Max. "I guess I'll have to strip down."

"That's okay," said Max. "After all, I'm a doctor. I've seen naked women before."

That was true. But this was no doctor's office and Melanie Woo was by no means the average patient. So he sat down on the riverbank, several feet above the level of the rippling waters, keeping an eye out for intruders while Melanie tiptoed in, removed her buttonless blouse, and unhooked her bra. All the mud and grass and slime that had been caught therein fell into the water and floated away. Her back was to him as she then removed her jeans, or tried to. Wet and caked with mud, they clung to her as if they'd been sprayed on.

"Let me know if you need any help with that," Max shouted. He was serious. She ignored his offer and finally, after a fair bit of struggling, managed to pull them down past her perfect hips and, bending over, lowered them below her knees. As she stepped out of them, Max felt his pulse quickening. Then she removed her little red thong. He diverted his eyes to again look around, knowing how well crocodiles could conceal themselves and attack without warning. But the water was pretty clear and the shoreline on the other side had been burned clean of vegetation, affording no shelter for any lurking reptiles. Melanie tossed her blouse, jeans, red thong, and bra onto the river's edge and turned toward Max, holding her hands over her breasts.

"I guess all I can do is lie down in it," she said a bit meekly.

"Go for it," said Max. "It'll feel great."

She walked out into the middle where the water was the deepest.

"Here goes," she said. And she lay down in the water, head upstream, and rolled on the sandy bottom, her firm body half immersed and half exposed while she rubbed her fingers through her hair. A plume of mud and other bits of debris sailed downstream. By now Max had forgotten about any crocodiles.

After soaking in the river, rolling, and cleansing herself with her bare hands, she stood up, resigned to the fact that there was no hiding from the good doctor and seeming not to care.

"That feels much better," she said as she walked over toward her garments, hands at her sides. "Now if I can only get the muck and the smell out of these jeans."

Then she proceeded to kneel by the river and do her wash like a native African while Max looked on, smiling for the first time in quite a while.

Once her clothes were sufficiently cleansed of the mud and the muck, she set them out to dry on a branch overhanging the river. She turned around and looked at Max, naked as the day she was born. He looked back and smiled. Then she began to tremble once again. Max took one step toward her and she ran into his arms, sobbing. He held her close as she hugged him with all her might.

"Thank you," she whispered in his ear, "thank you for saving me."

He pulled back to look at her lovely face, as beautiful without any makeup as when she was all prettied up for the camera. "You're welcome. I'm just glad I found you in time."

"So am I," she answered. Though still trembling on weakened legs, she lifted her head and kissed him firmly on the lips, a kiss unlike the one he'd shared with Christine. Now his knees were beginning to buckle.

"You know what?" said Max, as he caught a whiff of his own body odor. "I think I could use a bath, too. Your turn to stand guard."

Not only had he been sweating profusely all day long but his clothes reeked of smoke. The combination, especially now that he was next to Melanie's freshly bathed body, was too much. Before she could respond he stripped down to his boxer shorts and waded out into the middle of the river. He lay down and began rolling around on the river bottom just as Melanie had done, clearly not worried or at least not thinking about any potential predators.

"God, this feels good," he said, smiling at her as lay on his back while the cool water flowed past him. She picked up his clothes and knelt down to do his wash, soaking them in the water and wringing them out.

"You don't need to do that," he said.

"It's the least I can do. Hand me your boxer shorts as long as I'm at it."

Was she serious? Now it was his turn to be uncomfortable, to lie naked before the world. True, he was still in reasonably good shape, his once-trim athletic body only slightly the worse for wear. He handed over his boxers, wondering why it was that whether he was limp or rigid as a gun barrel, he always felt embarrassed to be seen naked by a beautiful woman.

After he finished bathing and Melanie had finished his laundry, they lay down side by side on a small sandy beach while the sun dried out their clothes.

"Don't you think we're maybe a little too exposed here?" she said.

Max thought it over for a minute. Every time he looked over at Melanie basking stark naked in the late-afternoon sun, he felt the blood rushing to his loins.

"You're right. I've got an idea."

He jumped up and hiked back to the machine. He started it up and drove it closer to the river, where the bank wasn't as abrupt. He lowered the big wide bucket and scooped up half a yard of sand.

"Why don't you climb in?" he shouted to her as she strolled along the riverbank.

"Not bad," she responded. "A beach in a bucket."

Max laughed as she climbed in and lay down. He raised it higher, above the river, then he cut the engine, jumped down, and, grabbing the lip of the bucket, raised himself up and climbed in. Not only did the bucket afford protection and privacy, it was shady in there. Melanie was lying down, smoothing out the sand beside her. She smiled at him as he lay down, noticing that his gun barrel was straightening out. She rolled over and they kissed again. He felt her firm body against his and the rush of blood to all points north and south. Her breasts pressing hard against him were very firm. In fact, they were too firm. She had implants! And he, a doctor, hadn't even noticed. No matter. Their moment had arrived. They made love on the beach in a bucket, safe from any wandering predators, as the sun went down over the Nguruman Escarpment towering above them to the west. And if Melanie's legs and hips were sore from the rude crash landing in the muddy marsh, it certainly wasn't evident as their bodies moved in unison, joined together in the most primitive, essential, and pleasing of pastimes.

They spent the night wrapped in each other's arms or nested together front to back like spoons. Max gave Melanie his shirt as the temperature began to drop. She returned the favor by keeping close to him and sharing her body heat.

They were awakened by a rapidly approaching helicopter. It hovered above before slowly descending and landed not far from the massive front loader, revealing the large red letters "CNN" painted on its side. Max and Melanie sat up and watched as Edward, Melanie's ace photographer and standard pilot, opened the chopper's door and hopped down to the ground.

"Edward!" screamed Melanie. And in an instant she, too, was down on the ground and running toward him, wearing nothing but Max's oversized shirt. Max just sat in the bucket and watched.

"I heard the news last night and came as soon as it was light enough to see," said Edward. "I can't believe you survived that crash. No one thought you had. They said getting the fire under control was their top priority and that all resources would be devoted to that end. They said the chances of finding you alive were next to nil. But here you are, alive, thank God!"

"No, not thank God, but thank Max," she responded, pointing back toward the big yellow machine and its raised front-loading bucket, inside of which Dr. Maxwell Taylor sat waving and smiling a bit sheepishly.

"Hello," he said as he finally stood and discreetly tried to fasten his belt buckle. He jumped down from the raised bucket and walked over to shake hands with Edward.

"Thanks for coming," he said, "but please, what the hell happened with the fire?"

"It could have been much, much worse," said Edward. "Most of the damage was confined to the southern portions."

"Again, thanks to Max," said Melanie. "He used that big machine there to create a better firebreak. He most likely saved the refugee camp from a horrible end. In fact, this is a huge story and we need to get busy. Do you have all your equipment?"

"Of course," said Edward. "And a full tank of petrol. But I'm not about to film an interview with you in this sad condition! We should head back to Nairobi and clean you up."

Max listened in horror. Surely he was not about to just whisk her away and leave him to somehow return the mass of metal behind him to its rightful owners, assuming they were all still alive.

"Here's an idea," said Max. "Father David Sebastian runs a school for the Maasai not too far to the south. You've been there, Melanie."

"Yes, I remember. We did a piece on the death of Dr. Oscar Newman at his grave behind the schoolhouse."

"Right," said Max. "You could wash up at David's and we could all find out how the Maasai fared through this whole crazy ordeal."

"I love it," said Melanie. Then she turned toward Edward. "But first, can you transmit the video I took yesterday back to CNN Nairobi? We're way out of cell-phone range. It's not up to your standards, but it's a pretty good look at the fighting between the Maasai and the refugees not long after the fire was started."

"No problem," said Edward as she handed him her pink cell phone. "I'll send it now while you two gather your things, if you happen to have any things."

Melanie excused herself momentarily, grabbed her clothes, and, hiding behind the front loader, squeezed herself back into her jeans and wrapped her tattered blouse around her. Once they were airborne, Edward steered his craft eastward, so Max could see firsthand that the fire had stopped quite abruptly at the firebreak he had constructed single-handedly. But south of there smoke still oozed from the charred savannah. It was a sad sight but one that occurred every year about now. And it did have benefits, at least for fire-tolerant species. Looking down from on high as they headed south along the west side of the Ewaso Ngiro, they saw game big and small running in all directions. Max had never seen so many animals, the majority no doubt lucky to have escaped the fire and crossed the river.

When the schoolhouse came into view, Max pointed out a clearing where Edward could land. But they all could see that a sizable group of Maasai had gathered within the small cemetery beyond the schoolhouse. Once they had landed, Max pleaded with Melanie and Edward to stay near the schoolhouse, to wait in Father David's quarters while he checked out what was going on out back.

"Look," he said, "this is most likely a Maasai funeral service and I don't think CNN was invited. Okay?"

Melanie smiled at him. "No problem," she said. "I understand." Edward just shrugged his shoulders.

Max circled around the back and hurried past David's garden, not stopping until he saw Father David standing at the head of a new grave site adjacent to Senento's—or Oscar's, depending on your point of view. But it clearly was not Oscar's, for he was standing there, too, along with Crazy Jack and a sizable crowd of Maasai, everyone sobbing while David finished his eulogy. A crude wooden casket sat poised above the grave.

David spotted him as he approached and nodded discreetly in his direction. Oscar, still dressed up in his Maasai best, had his back to him. He recognized a few of the others, mostly elders, but where was Joseph? Surely he would have attended if he could. Max sidled up next to Oscar as David was finishing his eulogy. Oscar was whimpering like a baby.

"Hello," Max whispered. Oscar looked to his right.

"Max!" he whispered back, clearly stunned to see his personal physician at his side.

"We need to talk, soon. Who are they burying?"

"Matthew, I'm afraid, right next to his father," said Oscar, wiping his tears away with the back of his hairy hand.

The ceremony ended with the lowering of the casket and the passing of the shovel. Oscar made his contributions and paid his respects, as did Max.

"Poor kid," said Max once the crowd began to disperse. "Listen, I'd really like to know exactly what in the hell happened down here but first I need to tell you that Melanie Woo is sitting up there in David's schoolhouse."

"What? She's alive? I was so afraid she was inside the helicopter that was shot down!"

"She was," said Max, "but trust me, she is most definitely alive."

Was she ever.

"That's wonderful news!" said Oscar. "It doesn't make up for Matthew but that's one less casualty."

"And who were the others?"

"Ntanda and quite a few of the refugees, I'm afraid, including Jocko."

"Jocko?" said Max. "Holy shit. Melanie is going to have quite a story. And Ntanda?"

"I'm tempted to say he had it coming. He organized the setting of the fire."

"So does that explain Joseph's absence? He's off burying his son?"

"I'm afraid not. Captain Olengi popped by yesterday after the confrontation. He arrested Joseph and hauled him off to jail."

"To jail? Unbelievable!" said Max. "That's terrible. But at least the refugee camp survived intact, more or less."

"Yes, so we've heard. That is most fortunate, miraculous perhaps considering the path of that fire."

Max declined to comment, at least on that note. "But what about you?" he said. "What's your next move?"

Oscar looked around and sighed. "It's time for me to go. Matthew was almost like a son to me. He taught me all about grazing and he introduced me to the cattle, all the cattle he loved so well, and he taught me much about Maasai ways. But I just can't stay here anymore, after all the tragic events of yesterday."

"Really?" said Max. "Then I'll be back for you as soon as I can get away. Maybe we can both get the hell out of here. But right now I'd better get back to Melanie before she comes looking for me and finds you instead."

Chapter 65

Getting back to Oscar meant first getting back to the refugee camp and his trusty Scout. Melanie Woo and her sidekick, Edward, certainly had the means, but once Melanie had showered and mended her blouse as best she could, she insisted on interviewing Max before the camera, to explain how he had helped to keep the fires the Maasai had set from devouring the entire refugee camp. She went on to describe how he had rescued her personally from the jaws of the dreaded swamp. It was not far from the wreckage of the helicopter in which she should have perished if not for the heroic efforts of the poor Yemeni pilot who had been shot but somehow managed to maneuver the doomed craft over the marsh, the safest place for her to jump and perhaps survive, before it crashed and killed him.

Once she and Edward had finished with Max, and the funeral party had completely dispersed, she insisted on interviewing Father David in front of the freshly dug grave.

"In addition to nearly setting fire to the entire refugee camp, the Maasai, quite uncharacteristically, took up arms against the refugees, engaging them in a bloody confrontation that CNN, and only CNN, has captured on video," she began once Edward had the camera rolling again. "And one of the victims of the confrontation, a young Maasai warrior named Matthew, is buried right here, alongside the grave of Nobel Peace Prize Laureate Oscar Newman. Apparently, Matthew's father was killed by the refugees as well.

"I am here with Father David Sebastian, a missionary who runs a school for the Maasai. Father Sebastian, you are very close to the Maasai. Do you have any idea how the Maasai came by the automatic weapons they used to kill several of the refugees?"

David looked to Max for help. He simply nodded.

"Peter Dermenjian helped to arm them," he replied. "I suppose he was concerned the Maasai would be overrun by the well-armed refugees."

"And who armed the refugees?"

Again David looked to Max for help. He just shrugged his shoulders.

"That I don't know," he replied.

Melanie signaled to Edward to cut the camera. This would require much more investigation off the record. She hammered away with question after question until the overall picture began to clear up.

"But if the rifles fell into the fire and all the bullets exploded, even if the rifles could be salvaged, where did the moran find more ammunition?"

David and Max looked at each other once again.

"I don't know that either. I suggest we head back to the schoolhouse," said David. "I'll brew more coffee and see if I can locate our prospector friend. Maybe he can shed light on that since he was part of the gunfight."

True, but Crazy Jack McGraw had taken refuge with Oscar as soon as Matthew's casket had been lowered into the grave. Having witnessed the Kenya National Police arresting Joseph the day before, he had good reason to keep a low profile. After all, not only had he helped to arm the Maasai, he had killed Jocko. No way he was about to face any cameras, even if he was damn proud of what he had done.

The coffee was quite strong and the stale cookies David offered up were soon gone, but there was no sign of Crazy Jack. "He's probably gone back to prospecting," said Max. "And I need to get back to the refugee camp. So if we're done here, maybe we could…"

"Okay," said Melanie, "but just one more thing. What else can you tell me about Peter Dermenjian? Why does he have such a stake in all this?"

David and Max again looked to one another. Whose turn now?

"It's not entirely clear," said Max. "It may have something to do with his brother's murder."

"How so?"

"Because Peter Dermenjian killed him," said Max, "and tried to blame it on Oscar Newman, an eyewitness to the murder. I think he was giving guns to the refugees in exchange for their help in locating Oscar."

Melanie stared wide eyed for a moment, stunned by this latest development. She took notes furiously. "This is incredible! But why did he kill his own brother?"

"I'm afraid that's still a mystery," said David.

"Did he kill Oscar, too? After all, he did marry his fiancée. You could say there was plenty of motive."

"No," said Max, "he didn't kill Oscar. I'm—I mean, I was Oscar's doctor. And I can assure you Peter Dermenjian did not kill Oscar."

Melanie thanked David profusely for his hospitality and all the information, on and off the record. Once back in the air, flying north toward the refugee camp, they spotted a couple of Red Cross vehicles combing the area, retrieving the bodies of Jocko's soldiers who hadn't survived the curtain of fire. Farther on they could see the charred remnants of the southern portion of the camp. But the northern portions, beyond the newly widened perimeter road, were more or less intact.

Edward put down not far from the main administration tent. A crowd gathered as the spinning blades began to slow down. Max hopped out first, then waited for Melanie. He caught her as she landed, while Edward attended to the task of securing the craft. The crowd erupted in cheers as the two of them walked forward. There was Dr. Bichette, Dr. Brecht, and Inga van Hoven walking toward them, and not far behind them, Christine. Her smile faded quickly, however, as Melanie Woo began hugging Max after explaining how he had saved her life.

But Max was not done with his heroics. He had one more mission: finally springing Oscar Newman. Once convinced his patients were stable, he approached Dr. Bichette. She didn't hesitate to write him a three-day pass. After all, he had single-handedly saved nearly the entire camp! He took off in the Scout, wondering what in the hell he was going to do with Oscar. Rescuing Melanie and Crazy Jack were minor accomplishments by comparison.

He found Oscar waiting for him at David's schoolhouse. He had already made the break from his Maasai friends and neighbors, yet he was still in full-fledged Maasai attire. And his war paint was as fresh as could be.

"Hello, Oscar," said Max, jumping down onto the dusty parking lot. "You're looking fantastic, as always. May I assume you're ready to get moving?"

"Max!" exclaimed Oscar. "At last! I thought you would never come. But yes, I am ready. I just have to gather a few things."

"Okay, take your time. But pray tell, what exactly is your destination?"

"The British embassy," he responded, before entering David's quarters to retrieve his Maasai blankets, spear, and a calabash full of ox blood.

"What's that for?" said Max.

"You'll see. Let's go."

He had already said his good-byes to David, promising to return as himself, Professor Oscar T. Newman, Nobel Laureate. For now, he was still ol Tatuani, the overweight, overaged moran looking to get free. But David took a quick time-out from his class to embrace him one last time before Oscar jumped into the passenger seat.

"Be very careful," said David.

"Don't worry, my good friend," Oscar replied. "I'm in good hands."

Right. Max then embraced David.

"Keep us in your prayers," said Max. Then he took his place in the driver seat and they were away down the Kalema Road.

"How the heck are we going to get you past security?" said Max.

"Don't worry," said Oscar, "I have a plan."

And it was fairly simple.

"How many Maasai do you know who carry ID cards? As soon as we get near the officials, I'm going to smear myself with this ox blood I saved in this calabash. You're a doctor, you can tell them you're taking me to hospital, another victim of the shoot-out between the Maasai and the Ugandans. Then you just drive me to the embassy. I'm sure they have my fingerprints on file, if they have any doubts about who I really am."

Max thought this over as he again, but possibly for the last time, steered his way through the ruts and ridges that made up the Kalema Road. "Good as any plan, I guess," said Max, wondering how he would make his own escape. Or would he? After all, Melanie had an office in Nairobi.

They made the crossing in good time, marveling at the newly blackened surface of what had once been a beautiful expanse of African savannah, full of wildlife, with excellent grazing potential. Until the refugees arrived. About a hundred yards before they reached the guardhouse at Lake Magadi, Oscar smeared his chest with ox blood. He had already covered himself in dark pigments, the ol Tatuani look, hoping to conceal the fact that he was indeed quite Caucasian in origin. His other garments—cape, blanket, orange shuka—covered the rest of him. Then he assumed the position of a wounded Maasai warrior slumped over in the seat.

"I sure as hell hope this works," said Max as he pulled to a halt.

Max handed over his green card signed by Captain Olengi. Then he explained that he was a doctor, and he was taking this wounded Maasai to the hospital in Nairobi. The two guards on duty both acted like they had never seen a Maasai of such proportions. They asked what was wrong with him and Max told them he'd been shot and time was of the essence. They looked down at the blood covering

554

Oscar's chest and waved them through, well aware there had been some shooting going on out west.

"Excellent," said Oscar once they were in the clear. "What have you got to wipe off all this blood?"

There were some rags under the backseat, as well as sterile gauze in the medical bag Max always carried with him. In this case, the rags would suffice. By the time Oscar had cleaned up the blood, they had arrived at the turnoff north to Nairobi.

"Take a right," said Oscar.

Max took his hands off the wheel and turned to face his passenger, incredulous. "What are you talking about? Nairobi's that way." He pointed to the left.

"I know," said Oscar, "but I need to make a little detour. It won't take too long."

"What on earth for?" said Max.

"You'll see," said Oscar, "you'll see. And if you don't, then I really was completely out of my mind."

The track south, heading straight toward Gelai, was in even worse shape than the Kalema Road. Shombole, another much smaller volcano, was off to the right, just north of Lake Natron. Max drove for a good half hour without saying a word. It was already past noon. Where the hell were they going?

Eventually, the track, which had been continually deteriorating, became absolutely impassable.

"End of the road," said Max, throwing up his hands.

"We can walk the rest of the way," said Oscar.

"How far?" said Max.

"I'm not sure," Oscar replied. "I was quite delirious at the time. But I have to know if it was real or if I dreamed it all. I suggest you bring a firearm, if you still have one, and make sure it's loaded. I can assure you there are lions about."

"Great," said Max, reaching through to the back of the Scout, where he kept his rifle. "So we could be just chasing some of your delusions, like this whole diamond thing."

"Precisely. Let's get going."

Having traveled this far, Max had to admit his curiosity was beyond piqued. What in the world was Oscar looking for? They began walking, finding their way across a few deeply incised stream channels that contained no water. Gradually they worked their way downhill, to the soda-caked surface of Lake Natron. Only it was now very hot, midafternoon—not a time to be flirting with Natron's notorious heat waves.

"Are we getting close?" said Max.

"I don't believe it's too much farther. You see that hole in the soda crust out there? That's where the Land Rover fell through. Someone must have picked it up with a big helicopter and hauled it away."

"Probably a big Sikorsky," said Max, wiping his brow. "I hope this won't take too much longer. It's really getting hot."

"Up there," said Oscar, pointing up the hill, "that's where the lava tube is, where Francis and I took refuge."

"Is that where we're headed?" Max inquired, stopping to look uphill to see if he could spot an opening in the side of this huge volcano.

"No," said Oscar emphatically, "definitely not. I never want to see that hellhole again."

They trudged on through brush and grassland, skirting the edge of Lake Natron, though from their perspective it hardly looked like a lake at all. To Max it was more like the Bonneville Salt Flats.

"Listen," said Oscar, peering out to the west. "You can hear them."

Max stopped and cupped his hand to his ear. Yes, there was a noise, a low guttural warbling sound, clearly avian chatter coming from the middle of the lake. They were too far off to see, and the wavering air above Natron's caustic surface obscured any form that might otherwise have been visible.

"They're nesting now, probably nearly fledged, I imagine. Flamingos, perhaps a million or more out there, extracting new life from this seemingly dead lake."

"That's great," said Max. "We came all the way out here to do a little bird-watching? I would have brought my binoculars instead of this rifle if I'd known."

"No," said Oscar, "that's not why I've brought you here."

They kept walking, sometimes right across the soda-caked surface of Natron wherever the roughly hewn flanks of Gelai proved too steep and difficult to negotiate. Yet that surface was far too hot for sustained travel. Finally, Oscar spotted some sand dunes, or more precisely dunes made of volcanic ash.

"We're almost there," said Oscar. "Keep your rifle at the ready. We're close to where that lion attacked me."

556

"Great," said Max, looking around in all directions as they trudged on through the ash swales.

"There it is!" said Oscar, who was growing increasingly excited with every step. He was pointing to a solitary tree, to the spot where he had buried the socks filled with diamonds. Unless, of course, he had merely dreamed it all up.

Ten minutes later they were sitting beneath the tree, taking sips of water from the canteen Max had brought along.

"Okay," said Max, "instead of bird-watching we're on a botanical mission. What's going on, Oscar?"

Oscar said nothing. He put down his spear and, kneeling down, began to dig with his hands. Max looked on, stunned but beginning to sense that the moment of truth had arrived. Oscar was digging frantically, expanding the hole, searching.

"What are you looking for?" said Max, who got down on his hands and knees and began digging beside a speechless Oscar. His breathing was heavier as the anticipation grew. So far nothing. Then Oscar dug a little to his right.

"There it is!" he shouted, digging more frantically than before. A minute later he grabbed on to something and, with one free hand, loosened the ash around it. Then he carefully, using both hands, lifted his old socks, still tied together, up out of the hole.

"Okay," said Max, "you found your old socks. Now what?"

Oscar kept silent as he untied them. Max could see they were filled with something, rocks of some kind. And before Oscar could pull a handful of raw diamonds out to show him, the penny dropped.

"My God!" said Max. "You didn't dream all this, did you?"

"No, sir," said Oscar. His face lit up as he showed the handful of diamonds to his friend. "I most certainly did not."

Max picked one of them out to study, a large, amber-colored stone that must have weighed a few carats at least. "Amazing," he said.

"Yes, truly amazing. Now you know why I dragged you down here. Now we can get going back to Nairobi. I'll need you to keep these safe for me while I deal with the embassy officials."

"No problem," said Max.

Oscar placed the diamonds back in the socks, which were none the worse for wear after sitting for months in the dry ash. Then he tied them together again and slung them around his neck, as he had done when he'd escaped from the lava tube and from Peter Dermenjian. They filled in the hole they had dug and headed north. But they had taken only a few steps when they heard a familiar noise, the air-slapping sounds of an approaching helicopter.

There had been a fair amount of traffic over Maasailand ever since the fire. News helicopters, Kenya National Police and Kenya Army helicopters, and such. So it was not unusual to hear such sounds, but this one was getting closer, though it remained out of sight. But not for long. Looking up, they both saw the blue helicopter with the yellow diamond icon on the side flying up and over the top of Gelai.

"It can't be," said Oscar. "It can't be."

But it was. Peter Dermenjian had found him, along with the long-sought-after and extremely precious sunset diamonds. There was no place to run, nowhere to hide. Max made sure his rifle was fully loaded and the safety was off. They watched helplessly as the helicopter descended with Dr. Meinz at the controls. He set it down on one of the more expansive dunes, sending sharp-edged grains of glass-like ash flying in all directions. Max covered his face as best he could with one arm, keeping the rifle aimed at the big glass bubble. Oscar simply began to back away, horrified.

Peter Dermenjian was the first to disembark, followed by Banyon, who was holding a shotgun. Max held his ground, his rifle now trained on the big black man with the big bad gun. Oscar just kept backing away onto the soda crust of Natron.

"Well, well," said Peter as the rotors slowed to an inaudible spin. "What have we here? Oscar Newman, if I'm not mistaken. I knew you were alive, you bastard!"

He shouted out the last line while Oscar remained silent, just backing away, the diamond-filled socks still hanging around his neck. Dr. Meinz, wearing his old blue suit, climbed down from his pilot seat and stood between Banyon and Peter Dermenjian.

"What do you want?" said Max, his finger on the trigger. These were not good odds, especially with Oscar backpedaling, receding farther and farther onto the crusty lake.

"Him!" shouted Peter. "I want Oscar Newman, dead or alive."

"Really," said Max, "what good is he to you dead? He's the only one who knows where your goddamned diamonds are."

558

"Is that so? The fact that I find you here with him leads me to believe otherwise. Newman," he shouted, "come on in or your friend here's a dead man."

Banyon had his shotgun aimed right at Max and Max had his rifle trained on Banyon. Then he turned it on Peter.

"Even if he fires, I'll get a shot off," said Max, "and you'll be dead, you son of a bitch."

"Keep it up, Dr. Taylor, and you'll find your way to a much more painful, excruciating death than a quick and simple blast from a 12-gauge shotgun."

Great. They stared one another down for a moment or two. Then Max saw something moving in the background. Two lion cubs were scrambling down a scree slope, no doubt curious to see who had wandered into their backyard. Oscar was right, this was lion country. And Oscar was still backing away, saying nothing. But he, too, saw the lion cubs, and he realized the lion that had attacked him months before had no doubt been protecting his pregnant partner. One of the cubs stumbled and let out a yip. Banyon turned around for an instant.

"Little bastards," he said. "I hate lions."

He fired at the little cub, who took the shot in its hindquarters, which were nearly blown off. The other cub quickly ran back up the hill and disappeared. Banyon wheeled back around. Max had hesitated. Surely he could have gotten off a clean shot, if only to wound him.

"How did you find us?" he shouted.

"Simple," said Banyon, "I put a bug on your car months ago. We've been tracking you for some time."

"That's right," said Peter, "and when you took that right turn instead of heading to Nairobi, we knew something was afoot. And we were right, weren't we, Conrad?"

Dr. Meinz had not moved, and he looked more than a bit anxious. He smiled nervously but kept silent. The only sounds were the lion cub's whimpering as he lay dying near the bottom of the scree slope, and the suddenly louder sounds of the flamingos across the lake.

"What are you doing here, anyway?" said Max, trying to buy some time. "Why aren't you back in France with your wife? Shouldn't you be having a baby instead of picking on defenseless lion cubs?"

"So you've been checking up on me as well. I'm flattered. Elizabeth is back at the hotel. She wanted to visit Oscar's grave, of all things, before the baby arrives.

We were planning to make that trip tomorrow, but now I see it's all been a hoax, just as I'd always believed. But I have to admit that photo was rather convincing, beetles and all."

"Yeah," said Max, scanning the background. Maybe some Tanzanian moran would come to the rescue again. "It was a pretty good makeup job. Almost as good as his current disguise."

He wanted to look behind him, not knowing where Oscar was. He wouldn't last long out there on the griddle-like surface of Natron.

"Newman!" Peter shouted again. "This is your last chance. Come on in or say good-bye to your doctor friend here."

Tough talk but it was still one on one, Banyon's shotgun versus Max and his Winchester. That is, until Peter walked over to the helicopter and pulled out a pistol. Whoops, time for some more fast thinking.

"Look," said Max, "maybe we can work something out. I mean, I don't know exactly where the diamonds are; only Oscar knows for sure. But I have a pretty good idea. If we work together, I'll bet we could figure it out."

"And just where do you think they are?" said Peter, smiling, knowing he had the upper hand, two guns to one. It was just the way he liked it. Max knew he needed to keep talking as he took a few steps to his left. Banyon turned, keeping him in his sights no more than thirty feet away, standing on top of the broad ash dune with the scree slope behind him. The lion cub had stopped whimpering and the flamingos had settled down.

"My guess is they're farther south, east of Lengai somewhere. Oscar said you were running some shot lines down there, so maybe you saw something. I know he was very concerned that you were getting close to them. Maybe if…"

He kept talking while keeping an eye on the mother lion, who was coming to check on her cub; he made sure Peter and Banyon never took their eyes off his rifle.

"So if we organize a crew and take a few core samples, I'll bet we could find them and…"

And the stealthy cat disappeared but he kept on talking, rambling, pretending he knew something of the local geology, talking about fault lines and weak spots in the crust.

"Are you done yet?" said Banyon. "I'm tired of listening to your bullshit."

"I'm sorry about that," said Max, his eyes suddenly wide as could be. For there she was, creeping up the back of the ash swale. "You know what, I think we have some company."

He motioned with his eyes and Banyon turned around just in time to see the lioness springing, coming at him with fangs bared and her huge claws extended. He raised his shotgun but he was too late. A giant front paw knocked it away. Peter Dermenjian raised his pistol but it flew out of his hand as a blast from Max's rifle nearly took his hand off with it. He and Dr. Meinz scrambled to get back into the safety of the helicopter, horror stricken as they watched Banyon being mauled.

Max backed away slowly, keeping his rifle trained on the helicopter, hoping the lioness would be working over her latest prey for a while. Banyon screamed as he tried to fight off the beast, but soon he stopped screaming and stopped flailing. The lioness looked around, then called to her remaining cub. It came scrambling down the scree slope again to join her for a late lunch.

Chapter 66

Dr. Meinz flew the helicopter out over Lake Natron, buzzing Oscar as he headed north, walking on the rough soda crust through the sweltering, suffocating heat above the lake. Normally a fairly confident pilot, Dr. Meinz struggled to maintain control of his ship. The rising heat waves and fluctuating air density were challenging as the helicopter bounced up and down, but more worrisome were the reflections of the sky in the shallow water beyond the nearshore soda crust. It was terribly disorienting and Dr. Meinz was well aware that too many pilots had crash-landed on Natron because they could not tell up from down.

"This is getting us nowhere," said Peter. Dr. Meinz completely agreed. Oscar Newman, dressed in his Maasai garb, just kept plodding along, seemingly oblivious to the threat from above as Peter Dermenjian called out to him using a bullhorn.

"Give it up, Newman," he shouted. "You and I know you can't survive out there for much longer."

It was true. The temperature on the lake's surface was nearly 120 degrees. Oscar was roasting, but so what? He had spent the last few months tending to Senento's cattle in extreme heat. So what if it was now ten to fifteen degrees hotter than he'd grown accustomed to? He just kept walking, heading north, feeling the sweat pour out of his body beneath his Maasai accessories, not knowing or really caring where he ended up.

"Tell you what, Conrad," said Peter. "You can set me down and I'll keep an eye on him. You head back to the hotel. Bring her here. She's the only thing that will lure him in."

"Elizabeth?" said Dr. Meinz. "Don't you think it's a bit hot and—"

"I said set me down and get her, do you understand?"

He reached into a small compartment and pulled out another pistol and checked to make sure it was loaded. He also grabbed his binoculars and the bullhorn. Dr. Meinz, as always, did as he was told. He landed the craft not too far from where the Land Rover had been stranded.

"Be as quick as you can," Peter ordered as he stepped down onto the soda crust.

"Yes, sir," said Dr. Meinz. And he headed off back to Nairobi.

Meanwhile, Max made his way north along the shore, retracing the route he and Oscar had taken, keeping an eye on anything that moved. The stories Oscar had told about the lion attack he had survived were like nothing compared to the mauling he had just witnessed. But he had to admit Banyon had it coming. There had been no need to shoot that cub.

Oscar, no longer threatened by the hovering helicopter that had charged at him, plodded on, searing under the equatorial sun that reflected off the white crust in harsh rays that burned his eyes. He was near the edge of the crust now, far from the shore, and the sounds of the flamingos, hundreds of thousands of them slurping red algae with their inverted beaks, busy feeding their young, filtered through the wavering air. The crust was thinning and, looking west, he could now see the faint pink outline, wavy in the intense heat, of the masses of lesser flamingos hard at work trying to survive, as he was, in their most inhospitable breeding grounds. Looking ahead to wherever it was he was going, he saw a solitary flamingo, perhaps a subadult too young for the party, standing erect right in his path. He stopped short and marveled at this long, lanky pink bird, who stared back at him with glaring red eyes.

"This is all your fault, you know," he said to the bird, who picked up one pencil-thin leg and moved closer. Its top feathers were all ruffled up, like it was about to pick a fight. "Please," said Oscar, "I have enough problems. I'm just passing through."

After two more steps the bird spread its huge wings and took off west back to the pink masses. Oscar shuffled onward, his feet burning not just from the heat but from the caustic soda that was eating away at his sandals. His toes were on fire, but what did it matter. Peter Dermenjian was now calling to him from the shoreline, telling him to surrender, telling him to just give it up.

It was tempting. No doubt someone would find the diamonds someday, and they would build a diamond mine, and the flamingos, well, there just wouldn't be as many. Big deal. So many other species were disappearing it was probably just a matter of time.

"Newman!"

There he was again. Walking was getting more and more difficult, and he was certainly feeling more and more light-headed by the minute. Dehydration would soon win out and he would collapse before he reached, well, before he reached wherever he was trying to get to, which was really nowhere. He just knew that

Peter Dermenjian could never survive out here on the lake under the intense sun that was heading westward as the day stretched on. The heat was his only defense, his asylum.

"Newman! Quit pretending. You know you can't stay out there forever!"

The sound of Peter Dermenjian's voice crackling through his tinny bullhorn did nothing but fill Oscar with even more contempt. He had accused him of murder, of a murder *he* had committed, then seduced his wife-to-be. Now she would bear *him* a child, while Oscar had nothing but lifeless, powerless, rudderless gametes that had neither the idea how nor the will to swim upstream to spawn. Just a drone, that's all he was and would ever be.

He had seen the helicopter fly away. Now he could see it was returning. What was going on? Off to refuel? Or to get more weapons or reinforcements now that Banyon was dead? Whatever. He knew he wouldn't last too much longer. His mouth was as dry as the windblown ash he'd buried the diamonds in, the diamonds that now hung about his neck and felt like they weighed a ton. He was weakening, his feet were on fire. And his world was as dark and bleak as this day was bright and warm.

Dr. Meinz returned the helicopter to the precise spot where he'd previously landed. Evidently, Peter's coaxing and threatening had not worked, for he saw Peter standing, binoculars in one hand, bullhorn in the other. Elizabeth saw him, too.

"For the last time, Dr. Meinz, what is going on? Why did you bring me here?"

She was as furious as she was large around the middle. Getting down from the helicopter presented many challenges in terms of maintaining equilibrium, given her new weight distribution. Dr. Meinz lent a hand as carefully and as gently as he could. Peter made straight for her.

"What on earth is going on?" she demanded. "Dr. Meinz won't tell me anything other than there's something you want to show me."

"That's right, my dear. Not something—someone."

"Excuse me! Out here? Who could there possibly be who is so important you have to drag me away from the hotel so urgently, in this condition, to meet him or her way the hell out here? You have to be out of your mind."

Peter let out a huge sigh, wiping his brow with a handkerchief already soaked in sweat. "You're not going to believe this," he said, "but Oscar Newman's out there in the middle of Lake Natron."

564

Elizabeth froze momentarily, then began to swoon. Fortunately, Dr. Meinz had anticipated such a reaction and was right behind to steady her.

"What did you say?"

"I said Oscar Newman is out there, and he refuses to come in. Still delirious, I suppose. I thought perhaps you could convince him to just come ashore."

Again she looked like she might just fall right over. Her advanced state of pregnancy notwithstanding, this news, if it could possibly be true, and this heat, which was truly unbearable, hit her like two tons of large, warm bricks.

"Just give a shout," said Peter. "Maybe he'll talk to you."

Elizabeth looked at Peter. He looked haggard, worn out. She had never seen him look haggard, nothing even close. "All right," she said, wondering if perhaps he was suffering from heatstroke and attendant delusions. "I'll give it a try. Oscar!" she shouted. "Are you out there?"

She waited a moment. No reply.

"Just as I thought. You've been out in the heat too long."

But before Peter could reply, a sad, terribly sad retort reached her ears. All it said was yes. And then the familiar voice repeated itself, "Yes, I'm out here."

"Oh my God!" said Elizabeth, turning toward Peter. "Oscar!" she shouted again. "Is that really you?"

The words, spoken by his beloved Elizabeth, floated through the air and kissed him on his eardrums. Is that really you? Good question. For whom had he become? Ol Tatuani? Or Oscar the Coward, who refused to stand up to his enemy? Once upon a time he had been a college professor, an overindulging geek who loved working in a laboratory alongside this beautiful woman who was again speaking to him, or to whomever he was now.

"It's me, I suppose," he cried out.

"Then come on in," Peter added, throwing away the bullhorn. They were close enough now. "Come on in and she's yours again."

Elizabeth turned and looked at Peter, aghast. "What?"

He shrugged it off. "I'm just trying to get him to come to his senses, if he has any left, or he's going to die of heat exhaustion. It could be 130 degrees out there."

Come on in and she's yours? Did Oscar really hear that? Sorry, just can't trust this one, he thought. Besides, she was carrying his baby. But it was something to work with.

"That's a good start," yelled Oscar, leaning on his spear. He wasn't too far from the hot spring Francis had been monitoring. The steam was rising up and he could smell the sulfur fumes. He began walking toward her, toward the voice he had longed to hear for so many months.

"Here's one for you. Why don't you show Elizabeth where you killed your brother? Then I'll consider your offer."

There was a shot across the bow. And an even bigger ton of bricks.

"What's he talking about?" said Elizabeth. This was far too much information all at once. Again Dr. Meinz helped to steady her. Her breathing was becoming quite labored, and she was trembling like a very frightened child. Oscar? Out there? Alive? She had long since given up hope, resigning herself to a life with this kind, if unloving, man who had taken her in while searching far and wide for her beloved Oscar. Why wasn't he dead, like in the photograph? And speaking of dead, what was this about killing Francis?

Peter looked over at Elizabeth. Her penetrating stare, her piercing look that was waiting for an answer, for the truth, leveled him. "And if I do show her where he died, not that I meant to kill him, will you come in? Will you show me where the diamonds are?"

"Perfect," Oscar muttered to himself. "Absolutely!" he yelled back.

"Deal," said Peter. "Come, my darling."

He grabbed her by the hand and began to drag her farther out onto the crusty, caustic surface of Lake Natron. Her head was swimming.

"Where are you taking me?" she begged. "And what happened to Francis?"

"All in good time," he said. "Just keep moving."

Walking with a fully extended belly was hard enough on a level sidewalk, but this jaunt over the lips and edges of hard soda crust required paying far more attention, more attention than Peter had patience for. It looked like a good deal, Elizabeth and child for the coordinates of the diamonds, the kimberlite that had eluded generations of Dermenjians. He could always make another child, but he would likely never have a chance like this to find the diamonds, not in his lifetime.

"Here we are," said Peter, standing before the gaping rectangular hole in the crust where Francis's new Land Rover had gone in. Elizabeth's mouth hung open and tears streamed down her face as she began to more than suspect, but believe that Peter had killed his brother, Francis, on this very spot.

"Satisfied, Newman?" shouted Peter. "Here we are! Now get the hell over here before we all die from this heat."

Oscar kept walking in Peter and Elizabeth's direction. "Just one more thing," he shouted. "Why did you blame it on me?"

This was too much.

"Enough!" screamed Peter. "Enough! Get in here, get in here if you ever want to see her alive!"

Now it was Elizabeth's turn to scream as Peter pulled a pistol from deep within one of his pockets. "Oh my God," she cried, "he's got a gun!"

That he did, and he leveled it at her head.

"Get in here, Newman, right now."

Oscar was coming in. He was already right by the new hot spring, the one that had caused all the trouble in the first place, throwing Francis off course and dissolving the otherwise robust soda crust that should have allowed Francis to simply drive across Natron's surface, grab his samples, and be gone by sunup. But all that might have been, and all that was, came down to this moment. Peter was holding a gun to Elizabeth's head.

"All right, Dermenjian," he shouted, "you win. I'm coming in. And I'll show you where your bloody diamonds are!"

Finally! Peter lowered the gun and covered his eyes, trying to shield out the intense sun that sat much lower in the sky now, so low it was hard to make out just where Oscar was. If he was coming in, he was hard to spot, but then the sun made seeing anything in that direction quite difficult. He kept looking, hoping to see a large silhouette emerge from all that sunlight.

He wasn't about to. Not that Oscar wasn't coming in like he'd promised. He was just taking a different route, one he had traveled before. Only this time his spear provided just the right amount of ballast as he glided through the hot, soapy water, his soda-burned feet churning as fast as they could. His chest was burning, too, as his lung tissue absorbed one deep breath's worth of oxygen, not nearly enough fuel for this crossing. But the light from the Land Rover's hole in the crust clearly marked the spot. Not much longer. He may have been weakened, and he had certainly been despondent, but life now had new meaning.

Peter Dermenjian never knew what hit him. Looking out for Oscar, calling his name did no good. Then the water within the hole in the crust erupted, and before he even realized this was Oscar coming in, the spear had passed clear through him.

567

Doubling over, he fell forward, staring wide eyed at the dark, fast-approaching water, oblivious to the fact that Oscar had kept up his end of the bargain.

Elizabeth screamed so loud a pink cloud of flamingos rose instantly off to the west, beyond the spectacle of Oscar, bare chested, standing in hot water up to his substantially slimmer waist, his hair in tiny, slightly reddish, shoulder-length braids, and his face clean shaven. The hot water had washed away all his scary makeup and most of the ochre-clay mix. Beside him the body of Peter Dermenjian floated face down, the tip of a Maasai spear rising from the middle of his back, all covered in blood.

Dr. Meinz ran to steady her as her legs turned to jelly. She was shaking like a leaf.

"Did he hurt you?" It was Oscar's voice. "You said he had a gun."

"He did, but you—you—where did you…come from? You're supposed to be dead."

Oscar climbed out onto the crust and stood tall, his soggy orange shuka the only vestige of clothing on his body apart from his sandals. "I'm sorry to disappoint."

Elizabeth opened her mouth to speak but no sound emerged. Instead she doubled over as the first wave in a long set of contractions brought her to her knees. Oscar rushed in but Dr. Meinz, with his arm around her for support, turned her away and began leading her toward the helicopter.

"Can I lend a hand?" Oscar shouted. "I'm a doctor of medicine, you know."

"I believe your hand has done enough already," Dr. Meinz yelled back at him.

"Oscar," Elizabeth gasped, looking back over her shoulder as Dr. Meinz led her away from him.

"Elizabeth!" he cried to her. "Please forgive me, I didn't want to kill him. Please let me go with you."

Dr. Meinz turned around very slowly. "I can assure you there's no room for you."

He helped Elizabeth up and into the helicopter, pushing her delicately from behind. Then he jumped into the pilot seat and put on his headset. Oscar kept walking closer, his hand outstretched, staring at Elizabeth through the big bubble of a windshield. She was doubled over in pain, yet she never took her eyes off him. The engine roared and the blades began to turn, slowly at first, then with greater speed, pelting Oscar with clouds of soda fragments that sprayed in all directions.

Yet he kept walking closer, oblivious to the stinging all over his body, until the helicopter rose up off the crust and flew away. Moments passed as he watched it finally disappear over the shrub-covered flanks of Gelai.

"What the hell just happened?"

It was Max.

"And where have you been all this time?" said Oscar.

Max turned and pointed to a spot just to the south, along the shoreline. "Over there, hanging back, ready to rush in and save the day. Thank God you beat me to it."

Max walked over to the opening in the crust and looked down at Peter Dermenjian floating in a sea of blood.

"Nice work."

"I didn't want to kill him," Oscar repeated, "but he was holding a gun to her head. Quick, let's get moving."

"Where to?"

"To the hospital, where else?"

"The hospital? Are you kidding? You just killed her husband, the baby's father. I really don't think you'd be welcomed at her bedside right now."

"But we must, I must—"

"Tell you what. I'll take you to Nairobi, to the British consulate. I think the faster you get out of this country the better. How are your feet? And what happened to your diamond necklace?"

Oscar hadn't even noticed the socks were missing. "It must have fallen off while I was swimming. It's okay, the diamonds are back where they belong."

Chapter 67

By the time they reached downtown Nairobi, it was well past dark. Max pulled up to a small hotel with a dimly lit sign indicating rooms were available.

"Wait right here," said Max.

Oscar was content to wait in the passenger seat of the Scout, for his feet were still on fire. The walk from the scene of the crime to the Scout, well over a mile, had been excruciating. Regardless, he was once again Dr. Oscar T. Newman, MD, professor of medicine at the University of Glasgow School of Medicine, chief of gynecological research, and a recent recipient of the Nobel Peace Prize. It didn't matter that all he was wearing was the ragged orange shuka. He no longer carried a spear, which was otherwise encumbered. He no longer wore the lion mask, having lost the ol Tatuani look in the steam-cleaning waters of Lake Natron. There were no more Maasai cloaks or blankets, no more sheathed swords, no herding sticks, and no more calabashes filled with ox blood. And more importantly, there was no more Banyon and no more Peter Dermenjian. Just Oscar and his fingerprints.

Inside the barren hotel room, Max looked over the soda burns covering the soles of Oscar's feet. Fortunately, all the time Oscar had spent as a pseudo-Maasai herdsman, walking and walking day after day, had toughen his feet up considerably.

"Lucky you had all those calluses," said Max, applying some salve he carried in his emergency medical bag. "This could have been much worse. Tomorrow morning we'll get you some comfortable shoes and some clothes. I don't recommend walking into the British embassy dressed like that."

Oscar was not about to argue. He took a long hot shower while Max went out to find some take-out food, for they hadn't eaten since breakfast. When he returned with some steaming rice and little boxes filled with a variety of Asian specialties, Oscar was sound asleep, snoring loudly.

"Guess I'm eating alone again," said Max.

In the morning he unbraided Oscar's hair and gave him a trim. Then he took Oscar's measurements and went looking for a suitable set of clothes befitting a man of Oscar's notoriety who would soon be back in the public eye.

"Try this on," he said when he returned. He was holding up a light-tan linen suit. "I got you a couple of shirts, too, some underwear, socks, and a belt. Oh, and I bought you this pair of sandals. Your feet need to breathe."

"Thank you, Max. I'll repay you as soon as I get back to Scotland."

"Right," said Max. "Why don't you get dressed and we'll head down to the consulate."

"No," said Oscar. "I must go see her."

Max threw up his hands. "All right, but you'd better be quick about it. I'm sure Dr. Meinz has called the police by now. They'll be looking for you."

"I don't care. I have to go see her."

Max knew there was no arguing. Oscar's mind was made up.

It was a short drive but traffic was heavy. Dressed in his new suit and sandals, Oscar walked into the hospital quite gingerly, wincing with every step. Max was ahead of him, running interference. He had given Oscar a dark pair of sunglasses that he wore as they navigated through the hallways and elevators until they stood outside room 322.

"Let me see if the coast is clear," said Max. He tapped lightly on the door.

"Who is it?"

It was definitely her voice.

"My name's Dr. Taylor. May I come in?"

"Of course."

Max peeked inside. She was lying in her bed looking extremely tired. Her stomach was deflated, though, a good sign.

"How are you feeling?" he asked.

"A bit worn out," she said. "Are you my new doctor? I don't recall seeing you before."

"No. I'm not your new doctor. I'm Oscar's."

She shuddered at the mention of his name. "Oscar? Where is he?"

"Right here," came a voice near the door.

As Oscar entered the dimly lit room, Elizabeth's face turned ashen. "My God, it is you. I thought I must have dreamed it."

"Excuse me," said Max. "I think I'll leave you two alone. But Oscar, we don't have much time."

"I know," he said, "I know."

Oscar stood just inside the doorway, wearing his new linen suit, a light-blue shirt, and brown Italian sandals over dark argyle socks. His hair, trim and neatly combed, framed a broad, clean-shaven face that was very tan, much darker than his new suit. All in all, a vast improvement over their previous encounter.

"Oscar," said Elizabeth, the color returning to her cheeks, "where have you been? Why didn't you come back to me if you were alive?"

"Believe me, I tried. But there was no way to get word to you. Then I learned that you were married and expecting a child."

"I see. So you purposefully stayed away."

"I was very ill and wanted for murder. Peter was after me, hunting me down."

"Peter? But why would he…"

"Because I saw him kill Francis, his own brother."

Elizabeth covered her mouth in disbelief.

"I'm terribly sorry about Peter. I didn't want to kill him, but I thought he was about to harm you and—"

"Yes," she interrupted. "I know."

He stood awkwardly, holding his hands together in front of himself, looking her over. "It appears you had your baby."

"Yes, a little boy. He's in the NICU, the preemie ward. I wasn't due for a few more weeks. But they say he should be fine, just a precaution. It was the shock of it all, of seeing Peter like that…and then you."

"Yes, I understand. But I feel terrible depriving the child of his father. I hope that one day you'll be able to forgive me."

"Oscar," she said, "please sit down."

There was a chair in the corner. He pulled it over next to the bed. Elizabeth took a deep breath, her eyes welling up with tears again.

"It's all right," she whispered. "You didn't kill his father."

Oscar's eyes grew wide and his jaw dropped. "You're not serious. You mean he survived? The spear went clear through him."

"No. Peter Dermenjian is dead."

"Then what are you saying? You had an affair?"

"Hand me my purse," she interrupted. "It's on top of the dresser."

He did as she asked. "What's going on?"

She dug around inside her purse before pulling out an object that looked like an oversized compact, a purpose it now served, made of stainless steel, with an inscription on the side. She handed it to Oscar, who raised it up and examined it.

"'Congratulations, Oscar! You've now arrived!'" he read out loud. "Where on earth did you find this?"

"Back in the laboratory, in the deep freeze. It was you, wasn't it?"

Oscar stared at her, completely immobile, his facial expression so devoid of movement, so locked into place one might have thought he was about to have a seizure. In a manner of speaking he was, as he tried very hard to seize, to grasp, to begin to process this unbelievable bit of news.

"Oscar, please," said Elizabeth, "please tell me it was you."

He continued to stare, though his mouth began to quiver as he struggled for words. "Yes," he said, "yes, I believe it was. Just a bit of a joke between my department head and me. I was still in my twenties, always looking to save a bob or two on fresh semen for my experiments. But you don't mean that…"

"Yes, I do mean. When would you like to meet your son?"

Again he stared, motionless, all his energy devoted to deciphering these last spoken words. "My what?" he stammered. "My son?"

"Yes, your son."

"But Peter Dermenjian…he was your husband. Did he know?"

"Of course not. Let's save that for later. Why did you fake that photograph? You were all over the news."

"It's a bit of a long, strange story. Let's save that for later, too. Much later."

He stood up and then sat down beside her on the bed, looking deep into her eyes. He leaned over her very slowly, put his massive arms around her, and lifted her up and kissed her, and she kissed him back for a long, long time, until there came another knock upon the door.

"Who is it?"

A nurse poked her head inside. "There's someone to see you," she said, "and he's very hungry."

The tiny infant was wrapped head to toe as the young black nurse set the child in Elizabeth's arms. Oscar marveled at the sight of Elizabeth lowering her gown and setting the child on her engorged breast.

"He weighs almost five pounds," said the nurse. "That's pretty big for being so premature. He needs to eat."

"Like father, like son," said Elizabeth.

"I'll be back for him soon," said the nurse. "He'll need to go back on the monitor."

Upon her leaving, the only sound to be heard was that of a newborn suckling on his mother's breast, gurgling and slurping and having quite a feast. His little head, covered with wet black hair, peeked out from his white blanket wrappings, fresh from the womb. Oscar watched in awe. It was the miracle of life, of his and Elizabeth's merged into one—one highly unlikely, highly improbable baby boy who was showing not only signs of life but signs of vigor as he sucked away, more vigor than one might expect from most preemies.

"Would you like to hold him?" she asked as the sucking sounds subsided.

Such a question. This was the moment he'd been hoping for ever since he'd come to realize that his utmost desire in life, however ironic, was to raise a child. And not just any child. It had to be hers, Elizabeth's, the fruit of the loin of this beautiful woman before him who was now handing him their son.

As he reached forward, the thought of holding this tiny, fragile being in his huge, sunburned hands terrified him. Then he remembered. He remembered Laetoli, the father and the son plodding through the ashfall 3.6 million years ago. He reached out and lifted the lad, so light and so alive, out of her hands. And then it happened. The squinty-eyed baby, fully sated with mother's milk, was ready for a siesta. But when Oscar held him up before himself, the eyes opened, brown like his, and suddenly, contact. Their eyes locked onto each other, briefly, but long enough for Oscar to feel not just a connection with his new son. It went far beyond, deep into his soul, like looking into a hall of mirrors and seeing the reflections of every generation that had preceded them. All the way back to Laetoli.

"He's got your dimple," said Elizabeth.

It was true—in the middle of his chin, beneath little bulging cheeks. He was as red as a poached pear, smacking his tiny gums and savoring mama's milk.

"Hello there," said Oscar, examining him up close. "He's beautiful."

"Better be careful, that's the most he's ever eaten." She handed him a diaper to throw over his shoulder, and just in time. Oscar put him against his shoulder and patted his little back. He spit up right on cue.

"Lucky me," said Oscar, "it's about the same color as my suit."

Someone tapped on her door again.

"Come in," said Elizabeth, assuming it was the nurse. But it wasn't.

"Hello again," said Max, stepping inside and closing the door behind him. "Congratulations, Elizabeth. I'm glad you made it to the hospital in time. But speaking of time Oscar, I hate to say it, but once the police catch up to you, you'll be arrested and then the press will be all over you. The quicker you get back to Scotland, the easier all this will be to deal with. You've got some serious legal battles ahead."

Oscar smiled serenely. "Sorry," he replied, "I simply can't leave. Not now, not unless we can all go together."

"But that's impossible," said Max.

"He's right," said Elizabeth, "my doctor says we'll be here for a few days, until our little boy is cleared to leave."

"*Our* little boy?" said Max.

"That's right," said Oscar, gently bouncing him up and down. "It's unbelievable, isn't it?"

Before Max could respond there came another knock upon the door.

"Come in," said Elizabeth, again expecting the nurse. Wrong again, as Dr. Meinz peeked inside.

"Dr. Meinz," she said, "please come in."

And he did but came up short, contemplating the vision of Oscar Newman standing tall on the other side of the bed, holding a sleeping infant over his shoulder, while Elizabeth sat up in bed, smiling like he had never seen her smile, radiantly, contentedly.

"Elizabeth, really. This man murdered your husband."

"Is that so? I thought he was trying to save my life. In fact, you should be ashamed, letting Peter threaten me with a gun like that."

Dr. Meinz lowered his head. He was holding a bouquet of flowers in one hand, his hat in the other, dressed as always in his trademark blue suit. "I was as surprised as you were. I'm certain he would never have used it. It was just a ploy, a way of luring Oscar out of harm's way."

"And it worked," said Oscar. "This is the woman I love. I would kill any man who threatened her life. Any man or woman, for that matter."

There was some commotion in the hallway and soon another tapping on the door.

"*Bonjour! Devine qui c'est?*"

It was Edouard, of course, who opened the door next, ushering in Madame Le Clerc before him. She took one look at her daughter, then looked at Oscar holding the child, and fainted straightaway. Luckily, Dr. Meinz caught her as she swooned and helped her to a chair.

It was getting very crowded and very awkward. Finally, the nurse rushed back in.

"I see you are suddenly very popular. It is time for the baby to go back to the NICU."

Oscar handed the boy over.

"I don't mean to be rude," she continued, "but this woman needs to rest."

"But we've just arrived," said Edouard. "We caught the first plane to Nairobi after Elizabeth phoned."

"What's wrong with her?" said the nurse, referring to Madame Le Clerc.

"She fainted," said Dr. Meinz. "Bit of a shock, all this. I'm sure she'll come around, but if you have any smelling salts…"

"I'll see what I can find," she replied, glancing about the room at this strange assortment of characters before taking the baby away and shutting the door behind her.

Edouard stepped forward to give his sister a hug, a peck on the cheek, and some hearty congratulations on the baby, as well as sincere condolences regarding Peter. But he could not take his eyes off of Oscar, still standing on the opposite side of the bed with a milk-stained diaper over his shoulder. He had never seen Oscar without a beard, but there was no mistaking him. The stature, the broad face, the irritating smile.

"Hello, Edouard," he said, "nice to see you again."

"Yes," said Edouard, awestruck. "Nice to see you. They said you were dead. But now you're alive and Peter Dermenjian is dead. Will someone please explain what in hell is going on?"

He looked down at his sister and then all around the room. Nothing but blank stares everywhere, except *chez Maman*. She was still out cold.

The door opened again but rather than a nurse bearing smelling salts, a much different personage appeared dressed in a much different uniform. It was Captain Olengi. He entered the room with barely a knock, a single tap on the door, and then he just walked right in. By his expression, it was obvious to all that he had not come to congratulate Elizabeth. He looked around the room as everyone save

576

Madame Le Clerc stepped back. His eyes floated from one individual to the next, pausing a moment on Max, whom he no doubt recognized, until they rested on Oscar.

"Mrs. Dermenjian," he stated, walking closer to the bed. "I am sorry, but I have received some very bad news. Your husband has been killed. We found him floating in Lake Natron, a Maasai spear through his chest."

Elizabeth looked up at the dark, round face, the jaws taut, the eyes close set. "Yes," she said, "I know. He and his friend Mr. Banyon were hiking near Lake Natron. They had been missing for some time. Dr. Meinz and I went searching for them in his helicopter. We found Peter like you said, and the shock was too much for me. That's when I went into labor."

Oscar looked on, astounded. Didn't Olengi know?

"I see," replied the captain, looking around the room quite suspiciously. Again his eyes rested on Oscar. "Excuse me, I don't believe we've met."

Max held his breath.

"That's not quite true," said Oscar. "You were kind enough to come visit me in my rather grave condition." He even dared to laugh at his little joke.

"Don't tell me," said the good captain.

"Yes, I'm afraid it's true. Oscar Newman here, at your service."

The captain stared at Oscar, his eyes like two lasers that wanted to slice him to bits. "Once again, when I can least afford it, you reappear. Where the hell have you been?"

Oscar hesitated, smiling, looking around the room, for that was a topic that was on everyone's mind, except Max's. He stood in the back near the door, running one hand through his mess of red hair. "It's a long story," said Oscar.

"I have no doubt," said the captain. "And I intend to hear it all. I'm placing you under arrest for the murder of Francis Dermenjian. You will come with me."

"Please," Elizabeth begged, "let him stay a while. He's a Nobel Laureate. Can't this wait until tomorrow?"

"No," said the captain. "I'm not letting this man out of my sight, not until he's under guarded surveillance. I've had quite enough of his disappearing acts."

"Well, my dear," said Oscar, handing Elizabeth the sullied diaper. "It looks like I must be off. Wonderful to see you again." He leaned over and kissed her on the cheek. She reached for his hand but he pulled it away, smiling. "I'll be back," he whispered, then turned toward Captain Olengi. "Ready when you are, sir."

"Just a minute. I'm not through yet. Dr. Meinz, it was you who radioed the report about Peter Dermenjian. I'll need a statement from you."

"And don't forget him," said Oscar, pointing to Max. "He's another witness."

Captain Olengi turned and glared at Oscar. "If you don't mind, I'll conduct my own investigation. Dr. Taylor, is this true?"

Max sighed and nodded. "Yeah," he said, "I was there, too."

"Very well. I'll see you both in my office this afternoon at two. Don't be late."

Max, shaking his head in dismay, caught Oscar's eye as he was leaving.

"C'est la vie, mon ami," said Oscar, still smiling, "c'est la vie."

The nurse reentered once Captain Olengi and Oscar were gone. "Is everything all right?" she asked. "I brought some smelling salts."

"Yes," said Elizabeth, "everything is all right, except for my mother. I'm worried about her."

One whiff of ammonia and Madame Le Clerc shot upright, disoriented but awake.

"Mon Dieu," she said, looking around the room. "J'ai vu un fantôme. Mais il est parti."

Edouard laughed. "Mother says she thought she saw a ghost!"

It was a short ride to police headquarters. Oscar sat in the back of the police car, thankful that Captain Olengi had at least refrained from putting him in handcuffs. More importantly, he had agreed not to mention anything about Oscar's sudden reappearance to anyone, especially the press.

"Don't worry," the captain said, "I don't want anyone to know who you are. I already have more questions before me than I can possibly answer. And you are nothing but one big question."

They arrived at the jailhouse shortly before noon. Captain Olengi, never one to miss lunch, checked Oscar into a dingy gray cell, one that was already occupied.

"There. You can visit with Joseph. Just be glad you're not him."

Joseph sat on the edge of a small cot covered with stains. He looked up at Oscar, his long face hanging off his heavily furrowed brow. He showed the faintest signs of recognition before looking down at the floor again.

"Hello, Joseph," said Oscar. How strange to be incarcerated with a great man like Joseph, a leader Oscar had grown to respect very highly, who had just lost a son, while Oscar, a coward in hiding all these months, had unwittingly gained one. "I'm sorry about Ntanda."

Joseph looked up. "Thank you," he replied, then hung his head again, waiting to appear before the tribunal that would decide his fate, as well as that of his people. Oscar was hailed by the good captain shortly before two o'clock.

"If you have anything to say to me before the others arrive," he began, "I suggest you say it now."

"I have only one thing to say to you, Captain Olengi. I did not kill Francis Dermenjian."

"I see. So you're claiming you are innocent. Let me assure you, I will get to the bottom of this."

He rang for his secretary to lead the others in. So here we go again, thought Oscar, remembering the last time he had been tried for killing Francis. He wished he were somehow facing Joseph and the elders again instead of this Captain Olengi.

Dr. Meinz was the first to enter, still holding his hat, which by now was even more crumpled than usual. Max came in behind him and they all sat down before Captain Olengi, who was seated behind his desk.

"Gentlemen," he began, "thank you for coming today. Let us start with Peter Dermenjian before we get to his brother. I must say it's very sad to see the Dermenjian line extinguished so tragically. The Dermenjian family has lived in Kenya for several generations. Life will be much different without them.

"Dr. Meinz, let's begin with you. You reported yesterday that Peter Dermenjian was dead and you gave very precise GPS coordinates regarding the location of his body. What do you know about *how* he died?"

Dr. Meinz gripped the edge of his hat while his nervous eyes drifted from Max to Oscar. "We spotted the body from the helicopter. And like you said, Captain Olengi, he was killed by a Maasai spear."

The captain leaned back in his chair. "Yes, a Maasai spear. Why would the Maasai want to kill Peter Dermenjian?"

"I don't know, sir. Perhaps they believed the rumors that it was Peter who killed his brother, Francis, a good friend of the Maasai."

"A rumor that no doubt originated with this individual," said the captain, gesturing toward Oscar. "Can you think of anyone in particular who might have had it in for Peter, among the Maasai, that is?"

Dr. Meinz fidgeted with the edge of his hat before responding. "Yes," he said, "yes, I can."

"And that would be?"

"A young moran named Olabon. He found Oscar and should have collected the reward money. But Oscar slipped away."

"I see," said the captain. "And Peter never paid him."

"That's correct."

"So there was a motive. Do you have any idea where we might find him?"

"Not really. But I believe he lives in Tanzania, near Ol Doinyo Lengai."

Oscar and Max listened attentively, very attentively. Dr. Meinz wasn't turning him in. Not yet, anyway.

"About your other theory, that some of the Maasai believe Peter killed his own brother. Any truth to that rumor, as far as you know?"

Dr. Meinz gripped the hat with both hands. Beads of sweat covered his wide forehead as he looked down at the floor. "Yes, yes," he said, "it's true. I saw it. And so did he. That's why Peter wanted him dead."

"But not you, his loyal servant."

"Correct, sir."

Captain Olengi spun around in his chair. "Dr. Meinz, are you prepared to make a statement on the record that you were a witness to Peter Dermenjian killing his brother?"

"Yes, sir."

Captain Olengi immediately picked up the phone and ordered in a court reporter. "Dr. Taylor, do you have anything to add?"

"Uh, well, just one thing. Can I have my passport back?"

"Very well, as soon as Dr. Meinz provides his official testimony. At that time I will release Dr. Newman. Then I will inform the Tanzanian police that they should question a moran named Olabon regarding the murder of Peter Dermenjian. Thank you, gentlemen."

Captain Olengi acted like the meeting was over, reading through more files while waiting for the court reporter.

"Just a moment," said Oscar. "What Dr. Meinz just related is very nice conjecture regarding a fine young man named Olabon, who saved my life, among other good deeds. But I can assure you that, just as I did not kill Francis

Dermenjian, Olabon did not kill Peter. I did. He had a gun to his wife's head, threatening to kill her, the woman who should have been married to me."

The tennis balls returned instantly and Captain Olengi was once again enraged. He leaned back in his chair and let it swivel, turning away to collect his thoughts. Max looked at Oscar as if to say, "Are you crazy? You were in the clear!"

Captain Olengi spun back around to enter his final decree. "Dr. Newman, you are free to go. And I beg you to go. Please, I have more than enough problems right now without dealing with you and the deaths of Peter and Francis Dermenjian. If Peter's personal physician is willing to testify that he killed his brother, Francis, that's good enough for me. And if this Olabon had a motive for killing Peter, that, too, is good enough for me. The thought of going through a very public trial when the refugee situation is so critical is too much. Besides, apparently, one way or another, Peter Dermenjian got what he deserved."

Oscar continued to protest, but once the court reporter had taken Dr. Meinz's statement not only were they were free to go, it was mandatory. Captain Olengi rifled through his desk, finally coming up with the passport belonging to Dr. Maxwell Taylor.

"Here you are," he said. "Thank you for all your help with the refugees. And before you go, please take that box on the floor over there. I believe it contains the files belonging to that American girl."

Max couldn't believe it—freedom at last! And Christine's long-lost files to boot! Once outside, Dr. Meinz turned to Oscar.

"There's no need to worry about Olabon. They'll never find him. He's another one of Peter's victims."

Oscar looked over at Max, plodding along with the box filled with Christine's files, including her hard drive. "Unbelievable," he said. "Poor Olabon, such a fine young lad. But nonetheless, it appears that once again I've been saved by a dead man."

EPILOGUE

An old Maasai proverb says the whole world may burn but a little patch can survive. Joseph's world had certainly been burned, in many respects. And more than a little patch had survived, the part containing the vast majority of their uninvited guests. It weighed heavily in Joseph's favor as the tribunal decided his fate, not that he could take any credit for the limited damage to the refugee camp. Nonetheless, all the provisions in the Maasai's contract with the government were upheld, pending adequate funding. Joseph, however, was permanently stripped of his official powers, in the eyes of the Kenyan government at least.

As for the refugee camp, a sudden surge of new doctors and relocators slowly began to turn the tide, curing and repatriating hundreds more every day—all thanks to very generous support from the new CEO of Dermenjian Diamonds, Ltd. For Madame Le Clerc's attorneys had made legal mincemeat of the prenuptial agreement Peter had forced Elizabeth to sign, citing the medical reports that clearly showed Elizabeth had been on a steady diet of barbiturates at the time. A supporting statement from Dr. Meinz, who administered said barbiturates, sealed the deal. So now she owned everything. Well, almost.

For despite a delay of one year to the day, Oscar and Elizabeth were finally married by Father David Sebastian at the church of Sainte-Marie in Balgères. Guests included Elizabeth's closest family members, plus Max, Christine, Melanie Woo, Captain Jack McGraw, and of course little Francis Newman, asleep in Uncle Edouard's arms. And off to one side of the nave, Mrs. Eleanor Newman looked on from her wheelchair, a nurse by her side.

The reception was held at *le mairie,* the local town hall. There was plenty of champagne, a string quartet, and tables full of the finest Provençal delicacies. Max had just stuffed a *gougère* in his mouth when Melanie Woo tapped him on the shoulder.

"My ride is here," she said, "so I need to say good-bye, and to say thank you once again." She threw her arms around him and hugged him tightly, lingering long enough for Max to chew and swallow the cheesy little cream puff.

582

"Good luck in Paris," he said, knowing she had a flight to catch from Marseille to Paris, where she would begin her new assignment. Her eyewitness account and video of the confrontation between the Ugandans and the Maasai, along with her exposé on "the real" Peter Dermenjian and the story of her own rescue by Dr. Max Taylor were highly acclaimed, enough to earn her a promotion, as well as a relocation. To Paris!

"I wouldn't be going if not for you," she replied. "You saved my life."

Max simply blushed as she hugged him once again.

"Don't be a stranger," she added as she ducked into the taxi that had been idling nearby, leaving Max quite speechless.

"Reckon we should be headin' out, too," said Captain Jack, who had watched the whole scene. Christine stood beside him, glaring at Max once again.

"Right," said Max. Oscar and Elizabeth, along with little Francis, were just leaving the reception in horse and carriage. "Time to head back home."

And it was. For Max and Christine had volunteered to crew for Captain Jack McGraw aboard his sailboat, *Esmerelda*. They would make their way from Mombasa across the Indian Ocean and eventually find their way back home to Southern California. But not before stopping at Captain Jack's island. For he really did have his very own island, a tropical paradise. But that's another story altogether.

ACKNOWLEDGMENTS

I am deeply indebted to many people who shared their critiques of early and later drafts of a story that evolved over the course of some thirty years. Thankfully, they all encouraged me to persevere. My sister Mary Hillman in particular provided so much support and lent her professional editing services as I struggled to undangle modifiers and recognize who were point of view characters and who were not. Years later, as the story finally came into focus and neared completion, I hired Kirsten Colton (TheFriendlyRedPen.com) to copyedit the manuscript. She did so much more than that and I cannot thank her enough. Her insight, professionalism, and sensitivity, along with basic editing techniques, helped transform the manuscript into the story I always hoped it would be.

I am also deeply indebted to my wife, Jan Riley, an English major and librarian who has read more books than anyone I know or will ever know. Her on-point critiques and especially her patience while I snuck off to pen a few more paragraphs are much appreciated. And so many friends and neighbors, especially Sue Nebeker, gave me great feedback and urged me onward. Finally, Jessica Chandler (SeattleBookDesign.com) did a truly superb job on the cover.

But this book never would have been conceived to begin with were it not for the extraordinary efforts by the Leakey family and all the paleoanthropologists, archaeologists, lab technicians and their kin who work so hard to uncover, quite literally, who we are and where we came from—and how we became the climax species.

Made in the USA
Coppell, TX
16 May 2020